THE DETECTIVE **JACK CALLUM** TRILOGY

Three gripping mystery books set in the 1950s

MAYNARD SIMS

JOFFE BOOKS

Published 2016 by Joffe Books, London.

www.joffebooks.com

This book is a work of fiction. Names, characters, businesses, organizations, places and events are either the product of the author's imagination or are used fictitiously. Any resemblance to actual persons, living or dead, events or locales is entirely coincidental. The spelling is British English.

ISBN- 978-1-911021-75-9

NO EVIL

(Jack Callum Book 1)

MAYNARD SIMS

First published 2016
Joffe Books, London
www.joffebooks.com

THERE IS A GLOSSARY OF ENGLISH SLANG IN THE BACK OF THIS BOOK FOR US READERS.

AUTHOR'S NOTE

Certain liberties have been taken in this novel with the geography of Hertfordshire. I hope that the residents of that beautiful county, which has been my home for many years, will understand. MS

Dedication

For Hugh Maynard and Norman Sims

See no evil,
Hear no evil,
Speak no evil.

Three wise monkeys

CHAPTER 1

SUNDAY AUGUST 10th 1958

Frances Anderton planned to be home before breakfast. She let herself out of the Blainey house and took a deep lungful of the warm, summer air. She stepped down the crazy-paving, through the gate and out into the tree-lined street.

She walked briskly along the street, then continued under the trees into Glendale Road. A milkman trundled by, bottles rattling. Nobody else was about. She crossed the road and took the small lane that led to Riverdale Avenue, a few streets away from her parents' house.

The previous evening her mother had sent her to stay with family friends, and now she was regretting the argument she'd had with her father. He'd never hit her, but last night he had come very close to it. All because of that stupid dress.

She was fourteen, for heaven's sake! She should be allowed to dress how she liked. She was too old for the gymslips and ankle socks her father insisted she wear. She wouldn't — couldn't — remain his precious little girl forever. He should let her grow up. Fiona hadn't had these problems, she was sure. Her older sister wore what she chose, *and* she went to parties, mixed with boys. Father didn't make *her* life miserable.

She passed a young man, crouching down beside a gleaming motor scooter, in two-tone blue. He appeared to be tinkering with the engine.

"Hello," he said. "It's Frances, isn't it?"

She was taken aback. "Yes. How do you know who I am?" He was smartly dressed in a fawn jacket and cream slacks. His fair hair was short, neatly parted and combed, and he was very good-looking. He was smiling, looking straight at her. Suddenly she was aware of her freckles, the wire braces on her teeth, and her unruly shock of ginger hair.

"You're Fiona Anderton's sister, aren't you?"

"Are you a friend of Fiona's?"

"Oh yes, Fiona and I go back a long way. Derek Webster." He held out his hand.

"Very pleased to meet you."

"Likewise. What do you think of the scooter?" he said. "I've only had it a few weeks."

"It's very . . . smart."

"It's more than smart," he said. "It's a Phoenix, designed by the great Ernie Barratt; it's got an all-steel body and a 150cc engine. There're not many of these around."

She wasn't really sure what she was supposed to be looking at, but pretended she did.

"Would you like a go?"

"I . . . I don't know how."

He laughed. "Not drive it," he said. "I'll take you for a spin, if you like, on the pillion."

"I'd better not."

"Don't you trust me?" he said. "Don't you think I can ride it properly?"

"No, it's not that. I'm sure you ride very well."

"Then where's the harm?"

She glanced down at her Timex *Alice in Wonderland* wristwatch. Embarrassed by it, she covered it with the sleeve of her blouse. "I don't want to be late for breakfast," she said.

"You worry too much," he said. "Your sister doesn't."

"All right then," she said, nettled. "Take me for a ride on your wonderful Phoenix."

"Well done. Just hop on and hold onto my waist. I'll have you home in time for breakfast." He straddled the machine and steadied it as she climbed aboard.

She settled behind him, and he eased it forward off its stand. Moments later they were heading down the street.

"Not too fast!" she called above the engine's noise.

"Just relax," he called back, "and when I lean into a bend, follow my lead and lean the same way."

Within minutes they had left the leafy streets behind and were heading into a part of town she didn't recognise. The neat houses with their tidy gardens were replaced by warehouses and factories surrounded by chain-link fencing.

"Where are we going?" she asked.

"Away from the traffic," he replied. "I want to show you what this beauty can do." His hand jerked up, twisting the accelerator. The engine rose in pitch and, thrust backwards, she held tighter onto his waist.

The scent of his hair oil was almost overpowering, and she turned her face aside to take a lungful of fresh air.

"I think I've had enough now."

He didn't answer. They had entered a long, straight stretch of road and he increased their speed still further.

"I'd like to go home," she said, but the air buffeting her face whipped away her words.

Moments later they had left the chain-link fences behind. Now there were streets with houses.

"I want to go back now!"

Finally he acknowledged her. "Yes, of course." They were slowing down. "I just have to make a stop and then I'll take you straight home."

"Thank you," she said with relief.

The avenue was lined with trees. He made a left turn, into a drive leading to a large Victorian house surrounded by high privet hedges, that stood apart from its neighbours. He drew up outside and switched off the engine.

"I just have a call to make," he said as he dismounted.

"Should I come with you?"

"No, you wait here. I'll only be a moment."

She watched him as he trotted up the steps, unlocked the front door and disappeared inside.

She sat on the pillion and looked at her watch again. It had only been twenty minutes since he had offered her a ride, but it seemed much longer, and she was starting to wish she had never accepted. She wished she was back home, enjoying breakfast with her family, making peace with her father. She wasn't cut out to be a rebel.

* * *

She had one foot on the ground and was about to go and see how much longer he was going to be when someone grabbed her roughly from behind. A cloth — a rag or a pad that smelled sweet and sickly — came down tightly over her nose and mouth. She had no time to cry out; whoever had grabbed her was strong, and she was hauled backwards off the scooter. She flailed her arms and kicked out with her sandaled feet. One foot connected with the rear fender, gashing her toe.

She was dragged back over the ground, her feet kicking out weakly. Then her eyes closed, and she sank into blackness.

* * *

Webster walked from the house, unfolded the wad of crisp one-pound notes, and slipped them into his wallet. He kick-started the scooter, and seconds later was steering out of the drive and into the street. At the gateway he paused and looked back at the house. The front door was closed and the place looked empty, almost abandoned. A slight pang of guilt caused him to shiver, until he felt the reassuring weight of the calfskin wallet in his pocket, and the thought of the money, so easily made, banished it from his mind.

"Until next time," he said, and twisted the accelerator, off to begin his Sunday. He was hungry; looking forward to his eggs and bacon breakfast. All this activity had given him an appetite.

* * *

Derek Webster walked into the ABC café. As he approached between the Formica-topped tables, the smaller of the two youths waiting for him rose and went across to the counter. A fat, balding, middle-aged man wearing a creased white shirt and scruffy grey trousers was dispensing tea from a large stainless-steel pot into white enamel mugs. "Three teas," said David Neville.

"Wait your turn," the man behind the counter said and nodded towards the two people standing there.

"Yes," Neville said. "Of course."

Webster went over to the table where the larger youth was sitting, and pulled out a chair. "All right, Pete?"

Peter Lamb folded his face into something resembling a smile and nodded. "Davy's just getting the tea," he said.

"I want more than just tea. I've had a busy morning." Webster looked at the blackboard behind the counter, where the day's menu was written in neat, precise capital letters. "I think I'll have a full English breakfast."

Neville returned, slopping tea as he set the mugs down.

"So?" Lamb said. "How did it go?"

"Like clockwork," Webster said. "Piece of cake." He poured a stream of white sugar into his mug from the glass dispenser.

"Was Gavin happy?"

"He seemed to be," Webster said. "But you'd know better than I would on that score."

"What do you mean?" The smile slid off Lamb's face.

Neville watched the exchange with interest, "Well, you two are—"

Lamb's hand shot out from beneath the table and gripped him around the throat, hauling him from his chair.

"We're what?" said Lamb, tightening his grip.

"Friends," Webster said quickly, as Neville's face began to turn crimson. "He meant friends; good mates, that's all. That's right, isn't it, Davy?"

Neville managed to nod his head. Lamb drew in a breath and released his grip. Neville collapsed into his seat, clawing at the top button of his shirt.

"When does he want us to get rid of her?" Lamb said, calm now.

"He said he'd telephone."

"It's your job," said Lamb.

Webster smiled. "I know," he said. "I know just the place to dump her."

Neville picked up his mug and took a noisy gulp. It hurt to swallow.

Lamb glared at him. "You get rid of the next one," he said to Neville. "So put your mind to it."

"I know, Pete. I know." Neville wiped tea from his mouth with the back of his hand.

"Good." Lamb turned towards Webster. "Did he pay you?"

Webster smiled, took out his wallet and set it down on the grey Formica.

When Peter Lamb had first approached him and asked if he wanted to make some easy money, he had jumped at the chance. He'd had his eye on the Phoenix 150 for some time, but the scooter cost too much. These little jobs he was doing for his old school friend Lamb and, by extension, Gavin Southland, had enabled him to put a down payment on the Phoenix and meet the weekly instalments. He'd been reluctant to bring in David Neville but Lamb had suggested it, probably because Neville had access to his father's car. When he and Lamb had introduced them, Gavin Southland had seemed to warm to Neville. Webster guessed Neville's "pretty boy" looks had impressed the older man.

Lamb was staring at the wallet. "Well?"

Webster picked up the wallet and flipped it open. "Same split as usual?"

"Why shouldn't it be?" Lamb said.

Webster took out the wad of one-pound notes and started counting them into three equal piles. "Money for old rope, this."

"I told you it would be," Lamb said, scooping up his cut and jamming the notes into his pocket.

Webster picked up his mug and raised it. "Here's to the next one. May they keep coming."

Lamb and Neville touched mugs.

CHAPTER 2

SUNDAY

He could hear *Last Train to San Fernando* coming down the stairs. Jack Callum sighed, laid down his newspaper and went out into the hall. Tennessee Ernie Ford had been bad enough last year, but at least his rich baritone had been easier on the ear than this skiffle nonsense.

"Eric!" he called. "Turn that racket down!"

"Oh, leave him alone, Jack." Jack's wife, Annie, came out from the kitchen, wiping her hands on a tea towel. "Weren't you ever fourteen?" She was an attractive woman in her forties, with light brown, shoulder-length hair.

"Yes, Annie, I was, and I remember having better taste in music."

"So *you* say." She dabbed the end of his nose with a floury finger.

"Hey!"

"Dinner in ten minutes."

"Something nice?"

"Roast pork with crackling and apple sauce."

"It smells delicious."

For the past hour the aromas floating out from the kitchen had been making his mouth water. Upstairs the volume was lowered slightly.

Jack went back to his armchair in the sitting room and picked up the newspaper. Spurs had lost again. It was only a pre-season friendly against the Portuguese side, Benfica, and Terry Medwin had scored the Spurs' only goal — a real belter — but, nevertheless . . . It didn't bode well for their season opener against Blackpool in a couple of weeks' time. Jack had followed Tottenham Hotspur football club since childhood. Growing up in Edmonton, North London, he hadn't really had a choice. A few of his friends supported Arsenal but he had always considered that treachery on an epic scale. Even when he moved from London and came up here to live and work in rural Hertfordshire, his footballing heart and soul still resided at White Hart Lane. If he were a stick of rock he'd have 'Tottenham Hotspur' written all the way through him.

The telephone in the hall started to ring and he glanced up at the clock on the mantelpiece. Ten to one. Who could be phoning at this time on a Sunday afternoon?

"I've got it, Jack!" called Annie. A few moments later she stuck her head round the sitting-room door. "It's for you. Sergeant Brewer."

"Andy? On a Sunday? What on earth does he want?"

"Well, you'll never find out sitting there with your head buried in the sports pages."

With a sigh, he heaved himself out of the armchair, blew a kiss at his wife's departing back, and went to take the call.

"Andy," he said. "To what do I owe this dubious pleasure?"

"I'm sorry to disturb your Sunday, sir," said Desk Sergeant Andy Brewer. "But you're going to have to come in. The balloon's gone up."

Jack raised his eyebrows. Brewer was a past master at exaggeration. "What colour?"

"Sorry, sir?"

"The balloon, Andy. What colour is it?"

"Oh, red, sir, definitely red. The Chief Super's on his way in as we speak, and *he* was in the middle of a golf tournament. Wasn't best pleased to be called in, I can tell you."

"Don't worry about it, Andy. You've probably saved him from another humiliation. He'll thank you for it one day."

"I doubt that, sir. So, shall I send a car?"

"Don't trouble. I'll drive myself. It will give me time to brood about the Sunday dinner I'm missing."

"So, I'll tell them you're on your way?"

"Yes," Jack said. "You tell them that."

"Was it something nice, your dinner that is?"

"Pork — roast pork."

"Ah, I can't touch pork. Gives me the bellyache."

"Philistine," Jack said, and rang off.

He grabbed his raincoat from the rack and went into the kitchen.

"Oh, no, Jack. Not today. Not now."

"Sorry, Annie, they need me."

"Well, they certainly need something, but that something isn't you. How long are you going to be?"

"I can't say. I'll be back later."

"What's going on?" she said.

"I don't know. As my sergeant so eloquently put it, *the balloon's gone up*."

"Andy Brewer always did have a way with words."

Jack looked longingly at the shoulder of pork resting on the kitchen counter.

"Save me some," he said.

"Of course I will," Annie said. "But it won't be the same. The crackling will be leathery."

Jack winced. The crackling was his favourite part.

"I'm shedding hot tears of pain at this gastronomic treat so badly thwarted," he said.

Annie threw the tea towel at him, "Get along with you. We have two children who will happily devour your share if you don't want it."

"Speaking of which, where *is* Rosie?"

"In her room. Mooning over a boy. She thinks she's in love," Annie said.

"Again? We've been down that road before."

"I'm afraid so."

"It'll pass. It always does."

"Always?"

He wrapped her in his arms and kissed her cheek. "There are exceptions to any rule."

"Stay safe."

"Cross my heart."

He sat behind the wheel of the Morris Oxford. He'd had it for over a month now and kept telling himself he would take Annie and the kids out for a spin. A picnic perhaps — sandwiches, sausage rolls and hard-boiled eggs, all washed down with hot sweet tea from his Thermos. So far he hadn't managed it. Something always came up. He'd left London and taken this posting in the hope it would give him more time to spend with his family. Fat chance. The crimes here were not so violent, but there were just as many of them.

* * *

It took him ten minutes to drive to the station, where he parked next to Chief Superintendent Lane's gleaming, ivory Rover. There was another, unfamiliar, car parked next to the Rover — a Bentley Continental. "Now, there's a car I'd like," he mused. "Probably wouldn't get the chance to enjoy it, though," he added to himself.

"Sorry about this, sir," said Andy Brewer, as Jack pushed in through the station door.

"Not your fault, Andy. Where's the party?"

"In your office, sir," said Brewer. "Chief Superintendent Lane stormed in and took it over."

"Bloody cheek. What's wrong with his own office?"

"The decorators arrived yesterday. It's all dustsheets and emulsion paint in there. *Taupe*, I ask you."

"What the hell's taupe?"

"It's the colour he's having — a sort of brownish grey, or is it greyish brown? I'm not sure."

"Why can't he just have sludge green like the rest of us?"

"Because he's the chief super."

Jack shook his head in mock despair and made his way up the stairs to his office. It wasn't much — a desk, a couple of chairs, a filing cabinet and a hat stand — but it was his, and he'd worked long hours for it.

"Ah, Callum, good of you to come in at such short notice." Lane was a large, balding man with a ruddy complexion and a paunch that his neatly pressed uniform failed to conceal.

Jack thought the middle-aged man beside Lane looked vaguely familiar. Lane turned to him. "Warren, this is the officer I was telling you about. Detective Chief Inspector Jack Callum, one of my finest. Jack, Warren is a close, personal friend of mine."

Warren, was a tall, athletic-looking man with sallow skin and a dyspeptic air. He took a step forward and stuck out his hand. "Warren Anderton."

"Warren's the managing director of Anderton Plastics," Lane said. "But you knew that, of course."

"Of course," lied Jack.

Anderton sat down at the desk next to Lane. "So you'll help me?" he said.

Jack remained standing. "Yes, of course, if you tell me what it is you need help with."

Anderton's face crumpled and he dabbed at his eyes with a handkerchief. "Fourteen! She's only fourteen."

Jack shot a questioning look at Lane.

"Mr Anderton's daughter seems to have gone missing," Lane said. "She went to stay with some friends last night and didn't come home this morning."

"Is it usual for your daughter to stay overnight with friends?" Jack said. He certainly wouldn't let Rosie stay out all night, Saturday or not, and Rosie was two years older.

"They're very good friends of both my wife and myself." Anderton bridled. "What are you implying, Chief Inspector? That I let my daughter run wild?"

"No, nothing of the sort, sir."

Lane laid a hand on Anderton's arm. "Calm yourself, Warren. Inspector Callum didn't mean anything by it."

"She's a good girl, my Frances. She doesn't misbehave."

Jack doubted that. Frances Anderton was a fourteen-year-old girl. All fourteen-year-old girls misbehaved to some degree. They were genetically predisposed to cause their fathers as much anxiety and heartache as possible. He was sure he'd seen that written somewhere.

"Do you have a photograph of her, sir?" he said.

On the desk Anderton smoothed out a colour photograph, an 'en-print.'

"That's her. That's my Frances."

Jack picked it up and studied it. Frances Anderton was a fairly plain, freckled-faced girl with a shock of curly ginger hair and wire braces on her teeth. She wore a smile of youthful innocence. Perhaps Anderton was right. He could not imagine a girl who looked like that causing grief to any father.

"When did you last see her, sir?"

"When I dropped her off at Pam and Richard's last night."

"Pam and Richard?"

"Pam and Richard Blainey. Richard's my finance director and Jessica, my wife, has known Pam for years. They went to school together. St Theresa's convent school."

"And you say she didn't return home this morning. What do Mr and Mrs Blainey have to say about it?"

"Frances told them she'd walk home by herself. It's only half a mile."

"Is that something she normally does?" Jack said.

Anderton's stare was blank.

Jack tried again. "Does she usually walk home, by herself, when she visits the Blaineys?"

Anderton shook his head. "I can't really say. You'd have to ask my wife. She'd know."

"I'll do that. Is your wife at home at the moment?"

"Where else would she be?" Anderton snapped. "She stayed behind in case Frances shows up."

"Yes, of course. Very wise."

"So what are you going to do to find her?" Anderton said.

Jack took a breath. "Does your daughter have any friends she might have gone to see on the way home?"

Another blank look.

"Yes, I see. I'll ask your wife," Jack said. "Perhaps I should go and see Mrs Anderton now."

"If you think that's appropriate, Chief Inspector," Lane said.

"Well, sir, it seems Mrs Anderton has most of the answers to my questions."

Anderton bridled again at Jack's implied criticism.

Before he could speak, Jack continued, "I'd like to interview the Blaineys as well. Perhaps I can do that once I've spoken to your wife?"

"Very well," Anderton said. "I'll telephone them and tell them to expect you."

"If you would, sir. That would be very helpful."

* * *

Jack was relieved to get away. "Give Eddie Fuller a ring, Andy, and tell him I'll pick him up outside his house in twenty minutes."

Brewer winced. "He won't thank you for that, sir," he said. "He was on a promise last night — Judy, the barmaid from the Dog and Duck. He's been trying to ring her bell for weeks."

"My heart bleeds," Jack said. "And tell him to shave. We're interviewing a managing director's wife. We can't turn up there with him looking like he's been up all night — even if he has."

* * *

Detective Sergeant Eddie Fuller climbed into Jack's car, trailing a cloud of heavy scent. "Ye gods, Eddie, you smell like a tart's boudoir."

"I was told to shave before meeting you, sir," Fuller said. "It's my aftershave."

"Have you got shares in the company, or do you buy it by the gallon? Open a window, quick."

"What's the SP?" Fuller turned the window winder.

"A child's gone missing, and the chief super wants us on the case."

"What makes this one so special? I thought you had the weekend off."

"I did," Jack said. "I'm giving up a perfectly good shoulder of pork to be here, and Chief Superintendent Lane gave up his golf tournament. It's not just any ordinary missing child. This is the fourteen-year-old daughter of Warren Anderton, managing director of Anderton Plastics, and a personal friend of the chief super."

Fuller lit a cigarette and flicked the match out through the open window. "I guessed it was something a bit unusual when Andy told me he'd had to call Lane in from the links. What do we know about her?"

"Not a lot, but then neither does her father, which is why we're paying Mrs Anderton a visit. We'll see if she knows her daughter any better than he does."

They began to pick up speed. "Nice car. Is it new?"

"New to me," Jack said. "Bought it from a friend of a friend with twenty thousand miles on the clock."

"I won't ask you what you paid for it."

"I wouldn't tell you if you did." Jack took a scrap of paper from his pocket and handed it to Fuller. "That's the address."

Fuller spread the street map across his knees. After a couple of wrong turns they found themselves in a wide street, lined with trees and large houses.

"Plastics you say? Christ, I'm in the wrong game. There it is. Number seventeen. The one with the gates."

CHAPTER 3

SUNDAY

The young woman stood in the doorway and stared at the two men with ill-concealed contempt. She was dressed in a conservative grey suit, her blonde hair neatly secured in a French pleat. She was very attractive.

Jack showed her his warrant card. "Chief Inspector Callum. This is Sergeant Fuller. I think Mrs Anderton is expecting us."

The young woman stood aside. "Come in and wait here."

She left them standing in a large hallway, while she disappeared into one of the adjoining rooms. A few moments later she re-emerged. "Mother will see you in the morning room. This way." Her tone was peremptory.

"Why do I get the feeling I should be tugging my forelock?" Fuller said quietly. "I bet you're glad I wore the aftershave now. Bound to impress the ladies."

"If you say so."

Mrs Anderton was an older, bejewelled version of the young woman who had answered the door. The hand she extended dripped with expensive-looking rings. "Jessica Anderton. You've met my eldest daughter, Fiona?"

Jack nodded. "Callum," he said. "Chief Inspector. I have a few questions, if you don't mind."

"If it means the safe return of Frances, then I don't mind at all." She seated herself in an elegant burgundy chesterfield and waited.

"Has anyone been in touch with you regarding your daughter?"

She shook her head, gasped and put her hand to her mouth. "You don't think someone might have taken her?"

Jack raised his hands. "No, no. We mustn't get ahead of ourselves here. These are just the routine questions we always ask."

Jessica took a deep breath, evidently trying to calm herself.

Jack paused, then spoke again. "I'd be interested to know if Frances has ever done anything like this before."

Jessica shook her head again. "No. This is utterly out of character."

"Frances is a swot." Fiona Anderton sat down beside her mother.

"Fiona! She's not a swot. She appreciates the value of a good education, that's all."

"Meaning that I didn't?" Fiona said.

"Meaning that she won't be able to rely on her looks to get on."

The air between the two women crackled. Fuller stared down at the floor. Jack pressed on.

"Are there any friends Frances might have visited on her way home from the Blaineys?"

Again Fiona interjected. "She doesn't have any friends."

"Mrs Anderton?"

Jessica shook her head. "We only moved here a year ago, when Warren was made managing director. Frances hasn't yet been able to form any meaningful friendships."

"It hasn't stopped *me*," Fiona said.

"Frances isn't like you, Fiona. You're five years older than her. She's still a child. She doesn't find it easy . . ." Jessica let the sentence die. "Frances is a shy girl, Inspector. It's why I was so happy when she was invited to stay with the Blaineys. They have a daughter of a similar age. She and Frances go to the same school."

"Sarah Blainey's a little swot too," Fiona said. "They're like two peas in a pod."

"Have *you* any idea what might have happened to your sister, Miss Anderton?" Jack said.

"Have you tried the library?"

"It's Sunday," Jack said. "Libraries don't open on Sundays."

"Really?" Fiona said in a bored voice.

"If you don't mind me saying, Miss Anderton, you don't appear to be very concerned by your sister's disappearance."

Fiona looked at him steadily. "I just don't think it's a big deal." She turned to her mother, "I mean, involving the police. I really don't know what Daddy was thinking."

"Your father's worried about her, Fiona."

"He's never worried about me like that," Fiona said. "But his precious Frances, his baby, goes missing for a few hours and he's calling in the cavalry."

Jessica threw up her hands. "Oh, Fiona, you're impossible. Your father cares for you both equally. He doesn't favour—"

The doorbell rang.

"That will be Pam and Richard," Jessica said. "They knew you wanted to see them so they said they'd come over."

While her mother answered the door. Fiona began screwing a cigarette into a long, ivory holder. "Do either of you have a light?"

Fuller produced a silver lighter. Fiona took his hand and guided the lighter, inhaling and blowing out smoke in a thin stream.

"I take it you don't get on with your sister," Jack said.

"We get on. I just don't like a fuss, that's all. Frances lives in her own little world. She's probably gone to the park or something and lost track of the time. You'll find her somewhere, I'm sure, her nose buried in a book."

"Your parents seem very worried . . ."

"Fiona! I told you before about smoking in the house. If you're going to use those filthy things at least have the good grace to do so in the garden." Jessica Anderton returned, flanked by the Blaineys.

As Jack shook hands with the couple, Fiona walked to the French doors and stepped out into the garden.

Jack turned to Fuller. "Smoke if you've got them, Sergeant."

"What? Oh yes. Miss Anderton, do you mind if I join you?" Fuller followed her outside.

"These young people," Jack said to the others. "Money to burn, literally."

"So, Chief Inspector," Richard Blainey said. "Have you had any news yet?"

Jack ignored the question. "You have a daughter, I understand."

"Sarah, yes."

"And Frances didn't happen to mention to her where she was going when she left your house?"

"No. As far as we were all concerned, Frances was going straight home."

"Did she seem bothered about anything at all?"

"Not to me," he said. "Pam? Do you think Frances had anything on her mind?"

Pamela Blainey was a small, mousy woman in her mid-forties, with tightly permed hair and a pale complexion. "She didn't seem to have a care in the world. Besides, if Frances had something on her mind, I'm sure Jessica would have told me. That's right, Jessica, isn't it?"

"Of course, Pam." She turned to Jack. "Chief Inspector Callum, I'm not sure where you are going with this line of questioning, but I feel you're on the wrong track. You seem to be implying that my daughter may have run away because she was worried, troubled about something. I can assure you, that simply isn't the case. Frances is a happy child. She works hard for the marks she gets at school, but that's *her* choice. My husband and I don't put her under any pressure. We feel our children should be free to enjoy their childhood."

"Commendable," Jack said. Having met Fiona, he doubted there was much in the way of parental control of any kind in the Anderton household.

"Is there anywhere she likes to go, perhaps to spend some time alone?"

"Apart from the library, and the church, no."

"What church would that be?"

"St Stephen's. It's on the Helton road. My husband and I attend whenever we can."

"You go there as a family?"

"As I say, whenever we can, though sometimes it isn't easy to find the time."

"Mr Anderton is a very busy man," Blainey said, "as I'm sure you can imagine, what with his business duties. It's not easy to run a company. There's not a great deal of free time available to him."

"So Frances sometimes goes there alone?"

"Sometimes, but I phoned Reverend Fuller, and he hasn't seen her since last Sunday."

"Well," Jack said. "I don't think I have any more questions for the moment. Unless you can think of anything else that may be relevant?"

Jessica shook her head and Blainey shrugged.

"Well, there is this," Pamela said. "But I'm not sure it has anything to do with Frances." She produced a small, blue envelope from her handbag.

"What's that?" Blainey said to his wife.

"I found it, propped up against the door when I brought the milk in this morning."

"And you didn't think to mention it?" Blainey said.

Pamela shook her head. "I was busy getting breakfast so I just popped it into my handbag. I thought it was probably a note from the milkman. Then we got the call to say Frances hadn't made it home and it just went out of my mind."

"May I see?" Jack said.

He took a corner and used a pen to slit it open. Inside was a folded sheet of paper, in the same blue colour as the envelope. Careful not to smudge any latent fingerprints, he unfolded the paper.

It looked as though a child had made it. Three small figures, in the middle of the page, drawn in what looked like green ink.

"What are they? The three bears?" Blainey was peering at the picture over Jack's shoulder.

"I don't think they're bears," Jack said.

"What then?"

"I think they look more like monkeys. I'm afraid I'll need to take this back to the station with me. I'll get my people to take a closer look at it."

"Do you think it has something to do with Frances going missing?" Jessica said.

"Too early to say," Jack said, folding the letter away. "Of course, if it leads us anywhere, you'll be the first to know. I'll send an officer round to take your fingerprints, if that's okay. For elimination purposes."

* * *

"Did you enjoy your cigarette?" They were back in the car.

"Now there's a girl with a huge chip on her shoulder."

"Yeah, I thought as much. That's why I wanted you out in the garden with her. I thought she'd be more likely to open up to you, you being more her age."

"Closer in age but not in social standing," Fuller said. "At first it was as much as I could do to get her to even look at me."

"What did you learn?"

"That she has no respect for her parents, and thinks it's a huge joke that her father was made managing director. She says that if he runs the company the way he runs his household, they'll be bankrupt within a year. She refers to her mother as a doormat, and doesn't like her sister very much."

"A productive chat then."

"Oh, once she started talking she wouldn't stop," Fuller said. "She spewed out vitriol, all directed at her nearest and dearest, and I'm not really sure what they've done to deserve it.

"Spoilt little rich girl."

"I was about to say rich cow."

"Steady, Fuller."

"I'm sorry, sir, but girls like that make my blood boil. They have everything dished up to them on a plate and all they can do is complain about how hard their spoilt little lives are. Oh, she has a boyfriend by the way."

"Is that significant?"

"Only insofar as Mummy and Daddy don't know, and wouldn't approve of him if they did."

"Sounds like rebellion to me. Does he have a name, this boyfriend?"

"Adam, but that's all. No last name."

"Not very helpful. Does she have any idea what might have happened to her sister?"

"She thinks she might have run away. It would appear her visit to the Blaineys wasn't all it seems. There were major ructions yesterday between Frances and her father. Jessica Anderton sent her to stay with the Blaineys until things calmed down. Apparently this isn't the first time it's happened."

"Any idea what the row was about?"

Fuller shrugged. "Your guess is as good as mine, sir. But if Fiona is to be believed, not everything in the Anderton household is as perfect as Warren Anderton and his wife like to pretend."

"Well, food for thought. Good work, Sergeant. I'll even forgive you the aftershave . . . just this once."

He drove back to the station, dropping off Fuller on the way. He left the envelope and drawing with one of the boffins in forensics, and went home. There was little more he could do until the following day, when his full squad would be assembled.

* * *

It was just after six by the time he walked into the kitchen. A large saucepan of water was gently simmering on the cooker, bearing his Sunday dinner.

"Go and wash your hands, Jack," Annie said. "I'll serve up. I've kept it warm as best I can."

He pecked her on the cheek. "I'm sure it will be delicious."

"It won't be."

She was right. The crackling was like old cowhide.

* * *

Later that evening, when the kids had gone to bed, he told her about his day.

"Do you think she'll turn up?"

"I think she might. Everything I've learned so far leads me to think that Frances Anderton has run away from an unhappy home life."

"Poor Mrs Anderton. She must be going through hell, her daughter disappearing like that."

Jack nodded as he sipped his cocoa. He knew from bitter experience what Jessica Anderton was going through, and it was something he wouldn't wish on his worst enemy.

"Early night?" he said.

"How can I refuse an offer like that?" said Annie.

CHAPTER 4

MONDAY AUGUST 11th 1958

Police Constable Alistair Kirby examined himself in the mirror. His uniform had just been cleaned and pressed. The trousers were creased sharp as a knife, and their cuffs hung the requisite half an inch above boots that were polished and buffed to perfection. Satisfied with his reflection, he brushed a small piece of lint from the sleeve of his tunic, adjusted the black fabric belt around his waist and took the leather dog lead from a hook on the back of the door.

From out in the hallway came a low bark and Satan emerged from the shadows.

Kirby dropped his hand and let the large, black Alsatian nuzzle it. "Good boy," Kirby murmured, and clipped on the lead.

At his command the dog fell into step beside him and they left the house.

The morning air was fresh, with a slight hint of autumn, even though it was still early August, and Kirby breathed in deeply. It was a new day and a new adventure.

With his military gait and impeccable uniform, Alistair Kirby was a well-known — and formidable — figure in the town. Ordinary people rarely approached him and his dog, and the local tearaways and ne'er-do-wells actively avoided him. "Copper" Kirby was as feared on the streets as Regimental

Sergeant Major Kirby had been on the parade grounds. Twenty-five years of military service with the Royal Fusiliers had left him ill-equipped to deal with civilian life. Now, the police force gave him order and purpose. Life as a "beat bobby" suited him, and he had never sought higher rank. A hand on the collar of some local villain, the occasional arrest of a drunk, afforded him all the job satisfaction he needed.

His beat took him across the park, around a small circular lake, and past the pavilion. At the other side of the cricket pitch there was a small woodland area where he could pause to let Satan do his business, and then it was back up to the play area where, during the summer months, children rode the see-saws, the roundabout, or the wooden swings hanging from stout steel chains.

He liked the hush that fell over the playground as he passed. Respect. He lived by it, always had, and he couldn't exist without it.

He took the leaf-strewn path leading into the small wood and unclipped the lead from the dog's collar. The Alsatian remained at his side until he gave the order, and then he bounded off into the trees. Kirby removed his peaked cap and ran a hand over his severe crew cut, counting down the seconds. The police dog training school had taught Satan to respond to basic commands, but Kirby had moulded the dog. It had taken countless hours, building a rapport with the animal and forming a bond that was unbreakable. Satan was now more than just a police dog; he had become an extension of Kirby himself.

The time he'd allotted for the dog to do his business was up, but the dog hadn't responded to his call. He struck out in search of the animal. Calling to Satan, he stomped through the bracken and crushed the brambles beneath his boots. A bark sounded in the distance. "Come, boy!" he called, but there was only another distant bark.

Kirby pushed through a large stand of dense rhododendron and heard the dog bark again, closer. He was coming to the point where woodland thinned out into scrubland at the edge of the park. Then he saw the Alsatian. The dog was standing over what looked like a pile of rags, as if on guard, turning his head as he heard his master approaching.

"What is it, boy?" Kirby said as he drew close. "What have you got there?" Then he saw orange hair caked with mud, the half-naked body of a girl. "Oh, good grief," he said quietly. He ordered the dog to stay, and turned and ran back to the park gates and the emergency police box that stood just beyond.

* * *

Detective Sergeant Eddie Fuller rang the doorbell of the large, semi-detached house on Rupert Street and checked his watch. He was running early this morning and there was every chance the guv'nor would not be ready.

Annie Callum greeted him with a bright, "Good morning, Eddie. Jack's not come down yet. Come through. We're in the kitchen."

He greeted the Callum children as he entered the sunlit room. The kitchen overlooked Jack Callum's beautifully kept garden, filled with dahlias, chrysanthemums, and the tall spikes of hollyhocks, all a rainbow of colour.

"The garden's looking lovely, Mrs C."

"Jack's work, not mine," she said. "I just look after the weeding and deadheading. Take a seat, Eddie. Toast?"

"Don't mind if I do." Fuller took his place at the table between Eric and Rosie. "Have you been on your paper round yet, Eric?"

"Long since," Eric said, through a mouthful of cornflakes. "Two rounds today."

"Are you saving up for something?"

Eric nodded and swallowed. "Dad said I can have a guitar if I buy it myself."

"Do you play?"

"I want to learn."

"What kind of music do you like?"

"Lonnie Donegan. Skiffle."

"I like him," Fuller said.

"Have you heard his new record?"

"I've got it."

"Really?

"I play it all the time. I think it probably drives my landlady crazy," Fuller said. He lived in one room above the greengrocer's in town. With the shared bathroom and kitchen it wasn't much, but adequate for now.

"What kind of guitar do you want?" he said.

"A cheap one. I've saved just over a pound."

"If you save another ten shillings, you can buy my one from me," said Fuller. "It may not be like the one Lonnie plays, but it's nice. It's a Hofner. Twin F-holes, single cutaway, low action. It plays like a dream."

"And you'd let me buy it from you?"

"I don't see why not. But I want thirty shillings for it, not a penny less."

"Eddie," Annie said. "That really isn't necessary. Eric can buy one down the market when he has enough money."

"It would be my pleasure, Mrs C. I've been meaning to sell it for some time now. I'm afraid my skiffle days are behind me now. If I sell it to Eric here, at least I'll know it's going to a good home. Besides, it'd be nice to know I'm fostering new talent."

"Some hope," added Rosie. "He doesn't know how to play."

"Well, I can show him the three basic chords. After that I'm sure he'll pick it up as he goes along."

"Did you ever play in a group?" Eric said.

"For a while. There used to be a skiffle club in a room above the Dog and Duck in town. I used to play there once a week." Fuller smiled at the memory.

"And you'd teach me?" Eric's eyes were wide.

"Yes. Why not?"

Annie took the toast rack across to the table. "There's honey, jam or golden syrup. Or Marmite or Bovril if you'd prefer something savoury."

"Just butter is fine for me," Fuller said.

* * *

Jack was using his new safety razor, a birthday present from Annie. He scraped away at shaving soap and stubble, persevering, though unconvinced that it was any improvement on his usual straight blade. He heard the telephone ring downstairs, and then footsteps clattering up the stairs.

"Dad!" Rosie called through the bathroom door. "It's for you. Work."

He wiped the remaining foam from his face with a towel and a silent curse. His morning routine was sacrosanct.

He listened carefully, scribbling notes on a pad by the phone. In the kitchen, Eric and Rosie were both eating their cereal, Annie was at the cooker and Fuller was pushing a last corner of toast into his mouth.

"Dad! Eddie said I can buy his guitar for thirty shillings," Eric called out. "And he's going to show me how to play some chords."

"That's nice," Jack said. "And is he going to put you up at his place while you do it? We could have some peace and quiet then. Good morning, Sergeant, I didn't hear you arrive. That was the station on the phone. They've found a body."

Annie gasped. "Oh no, Jack. Not that poor girl."

"It looks like it might be." Jack pulled the last slice of toast from the rack, and spread it thickly with butter.

"We'd better head in, then," Fuller said.

"If the girl's dead, then it won't hurt her if I take a minute to eat a slice of toast and drink a cup of tea."

"Fair point, I suppose."

Annie picked up the teapot. "Top up, Eddie?"

"Don't mind if I do," Fuller said. "That's if you have no objections, sir."

"No, you go ahead." Jack bit into his slice of toast.

"Did they say how the poor girl was killed?" Annie said.

Jack shook his head. "No. They just said the circumstances were unusual."

"What does that mean?" Fuller said.

"You know as much as I do, Sergeant."

* * *

From the back seat of Fuller's car, Jack said, "I got it wrong, Eddie. Yesterday I believed it was just a child running away from a dysfunctional family, and now this."

Fuller glanced around at his boss. Jack Callum's face seemed full of despair and his hands were shaking slightly. Fuller had never seen his DCI this upset before.

"What they told me does not make for good conversation over the breakfast table." He shook his head. "So wrong."

"You mustn't blame yourself, sir. I thought the same as you." Fuller started the car and pulled away from the kerb. "Was it bad, then?"

"They found her half-naked body in the park," Jack said. "Her mouth was sewn shut, so were her eyes, and something that appears to be candle wax had been poured into her ears."

"Bloody hell," Fuller said. "I can see why you didn't want to say anything in front of your wife and kids."

"Indeed."

"There are some sick people out there," Fuller said.

"Yes, there are, and it falls to the likes of you and me to see that they're caught and put away for a very long time. If they don't hang, of course."

"A policeman's lot . . ."

"Not a happy one at all. We'd better head straight to the park. They won't move the body until the doctor's signed it off."

* * *

They pulled in through the park gates. An ambulance was there already; they were preparing a stretcher. PC Alistair Kirby stood just inside the gates, and he saluted as they climbed out.

"I found the body, sir," he said to Jack. "Or rather Satan here did." He cast a fond look at the ferocious-looking Alsatian sitting obediently beside him. "I'll take you down there."

Kirby set off at a march, the two detectives trotting behind him.

CHAPTER 5

MONDAY

Jack stared down at the mutilated body of Frances Anderton. "Help me out here, Sergeant. What kind of person can do this to a child?"

Fuller didn't answer.

"A monster, sir. Pure and simple." Alistair Kirby was standing a respectful distance from the crime scene, watching four CID officers scour the area for clues, but he was listening to everything.

Jack turned to him. "Have you experienced anything like this before, Constable?"

Kirby shook his head. "I was on the Western Front during the war, and saw many atrocities, but no, sir, nothing like this."

Doctor Barry Fenwick was crouched over the body. "If it's any consolation, judging from the lack of blood, I'd say that her eyes and mouth were sewn shut after she was killed. As for the paraffin wax poured into the ears I can't say whether that was done post or ante-mortem."

"Any idea how she was killed?" Jack said.

"Strangulation. There's a ligature mark on her throat. Thin twine or cord, I'd say. We'll know more when we get her back to the mortuary."

"Any idea who's performing the post-mortem?"

"I would guess Hepton," Fenwick said.

"Maurice Hepton?"

"*Sir* Maurice Hepton. He was knighted in the Birthday Honours."

"Really? I had no idea."

"Well, if you do cross his path, make sure you remember to call him *Sir Maurice*. One of my colleagues forgot and received a tongue-lashing."

"Should I bow as well?"

"Wouldn't do any harm." Fenwick smiled. "But seriously, Hepton's a damned fine pathologist, up there with Sir Bernard Spilsbury and Keith Simpson."

"Simpson hasn't been knighted," Jack said.

"It's not what you know . . . I hear Hepton's wife plays bridge with various minor Royals, and by all accounts Violet Hepton is a force to be reckoned with."

"Barry, your knowledge never ceases to astound me. Any idea on the time of death?"

Fenwick returned his attention to Frances Anderton's body. "From the temperature of the body, I would estimate time of death to be somewhere between nine a.m. and one p.m. yesterday. Can't be more precise, I'm afraid. Establishing time of death can be awfully tricky."

"Then if you're right, Barry, Frances Anderton was killed before we even started looking for her." He turned to Kirby. "And this is how you found her, Constable?"

"Yes, sir."

"I'm surprised no one found her before you did, out in the open like this."

"This part of the park was closed off yesterday, sir," Kirby said.

"And why was that?"

"Routine maintenance of the playground rides, sir. Can't have the kiddies around when that's going on."

Jack thought for a moment. "So, you have a group of workers performing maintenance on the slides and see-saws, someone dumps a girl's body a hundred yards away, and no one sees anything." He turned to Fuller. "Get onto the council. I want a list of names and addresses of all those who were working here yesterday."

"Very good, sir."

* * *

Back at the station, Chief Superintendent Lane remained camped in his office.

"Have you given Anderton the news?"

Lane nodded grimly.

"How did he take it?"

"Not well. Not well at all. They've taken her body to the County Hospital. Sir Maurice Hepton will perform the post-mortem. Anderton will have to make a formal identification once Hepton's finished his work. Eyes sewn shut." He shuddered.

"And lips, with candle wax poured into her ears," Jack said.

"But why?"

"See no evil, hear no evil, speak no evil," Jack said. "It ties in with the sketch left on the Blaineys' doorstep this morning."

"Sketch?"

"The lab boys have it now," Jack said. "I think it's a picture of three monkeys. See no evil, hear no evil, speak no evil. The sketch didn't make any kind of sense until I saw Frances Anderton's body. Now it does."

"So you think whoever committed this awful crime is sending a message of some kind?"

"It would appear so, sir."

Lane shuddered again. "Sometimes, Jack, I wonder what kind of sick and twisted world we're living in."

"I'm afraid the Japanese tore the blinkers from my eyes when I was stationed in Burma. I hadn't seen real cruelty until then."

Lane tapped a pen against his teeth. "Do you think this could be somehow connected to Warren's firm? I hear he's a tough man to do business with. A disgruntled customer or supplier?"

"It's something I'll be considering," Jack said. "All we can hope is that this was a one-off crime, and not something more sinister."

"What are you suggesting?" Lane said.

"This has all the hallmarks of a ritual killing."

"But you have no evidence to support that."

"The mutilation of the body and the sketch of the three monkeys left at the house. That's your evidence," Jack said.

"But all we have is one murdered girl."

"So far," Jack said. "Let's just hope it stays that way."

"Why do you think the sketch was left on the Blaineys' doorstep and not at the Andertons'?" Lane said.

"Yes, that's been bothering me too, and I don't have an answer for you. It could be simple expediency. There's no easy access to the Andertons' house. It has a high wall and iron gates. Not easy for a killer to sneak in and leave a letter on the doorstep. From what I understand, the Blaineys' home is open to the street."

"And you think Frances Anderton was the intended target and not the Blainey girl?"

"I'm not deciding anything yet, sir. It's too soon to tell. Once the investigation is properly underway, we might get a clearer picture."

"We have to find this monster, Jack, and find him soon."

"I couldn't agree more, sir. Couldn't agree more."

He excused himself and went to find Fuller. "How's that list coming along?"

Fuller looked up. "Six names, six addresses. The council were most forthcoming."

"Good. Take DC Grant and go and check them out. See if any of them saw anything yesterday morning."

Fuller called across to Detective Constable Harry Grant, who was carrying a cup of tea back to his desk. "Harry, get your skates on, you're coming with me."

Grant took a mouthful and set down the cup. "I was enjoying that."

* * *

"Where are we going?"

Fuller handed Grant the sheet of paper. Grant scanned the names and addresses as they walked across the car park to a black Wolseley. He slid behind the wheel and passed the sheet back to Fuller. "I know where most of these streets are," he said.

"We'll probably find most of them are out at work," Fuller said, "but the council also gave me their work schedules, so finding them should be easy enough."

"Is this about Warren Anderton's daughter?"

"Yes."

Harry Grant shook his head. "If we find the bastard who did it, I'll rip his arms off."

"Join the queue," Fuller said. "The guv'nor gets first shot, with me running a close second."

Grant eased the Wolseley out onto the High Street. "It always gets to you when kids are involved."

"It certainly does, Harry."

* * *

Jack picked up the phone and dialled through to the switchboard. "Hello, Helen. Can you get me the number of Tottenham Grammar School?"

Helen found the number and called him back to read it out to him.

"I'm trying to get in touch with Doctor Poole, Alan Poole. He used to be head of your history department," he said to the woman who answered the phone.

"I'm afraid Dr Poole retired three years ago."

"I see," Jack said, and introduced himself. "Do you have any idea where I might find him now?"

"He moved away from the area."

"Do you have a number for him?"

He recognised the prefix. Poole was living nearby, in Hatfield, and was quick to answer.

"This is Detective Chief Inspector Callum of the Welwyn and Hatfield police. I was wondering if I could come and see you?"

* * *

Poole lived on a leafy street, in the older part of town, away from the New Town development programme.

His house was large and detached, with a front garden given over mostly to shrubs and conifers.

Poole emerged from around the side of the house. "I'm working in the back garden," he said. "Come through."

Jack followed him along a path that led to nearly half an acre of sweeping lawns and mature trees, with three large island flowerbeds and an ornamental fishpond.

"It's an impressive garden," he said. Alan Poole was much as he remembered him from his school days; older, greyer, and slightly shorter, but that was probably because he walked with a pronounced stoop. The man must be in his seventies by now.

"Glad you like it," Poole said. "It's a bit of a passion of mine."

"Mine too. But my garden's not a patch on this."

"I consider myself to be very fortunate. I bought the house for the garden. After living in London all my life, it seemed like paradise."

"Yes, I can imagine," Jack said. He felt the same about his own house.

"What do you grow?" Poole asked him.

"Vegetables mostly, but dahlias and chrysanthemums for colour."

"Fuchsias are my weakness," Poole said. "I have over thirty different varieties."

They halted at a small circular paved area, furnished with a round wooden table and four chairs, and surrounded by flowerpots of various sizes, all containing fuchsias.

"You sit there," Poole said. "Would you care for a cup of tea? I was just in the middle of making one when you arrived."

"That would be grand."

"Right, I won't be long." He walked back to the house and reappeared five minutes later with a tray. He poured the tea from a brown earthenware teapot.

"Biscuits?"

"Thanks."

"Well," Poole said. "This is very nice, very sociable. I don't get many visitors. What can I do for you, Chief Inspector?"

Jack sipped his tea.

"I want to pick your brains, if I may," Jack said. "I remember, years ago, during one of your lessons, you spoke of the legend of the three wise monkeys."

"One of my lessons?"

Jack nodded.

"Were you a pupil of mine then?"

"Back in '24 and '25."

"Good heavens. You *are* turning the clock back." Poole took a long look at Jack. "Yes, I think your face is vaguely familiar. Callum, you say? John Callum?"

"Most people call me Jack these days."

"Very good on the Industrial Revolution, I seem to recall. Had a bit of a passion for early machinery."

Jack was a good thirty years younger than Poole but his memory wasn't half as sharp. "The three monkeys?"

"You remember that? It's gratifying to know that some of my lessons stuck in the mind. Sometimes, teaching a class of teenage boys, you felt that your words were just being sucked away into the ether with no effect at all. Anyway, the three wise monkeys. What do you want to know?"

"I remember you telling us that the legend could be interpreted in different ways."

"Yes, yes, indeed it can." The old man sipped his tea, sat back in his chair and closed his eyes. "The three monkeys embody the proverbial principle of *see no evil, hear no evil, and speak no evil.* Their names are *Mizaru,* who covers his eyes and sees no evil; *Kikazaru,* who covers his ears and hears no evil; and finally *Iwazaru* who covers his mouth — speak no evil, you see? The legend is Japanese in origin, and, as I say, open to a few interpretations.

"In the Buddhist tradition, the proverb is about not dwelling on evil thoughts, but here in the West, both the proverb and the image of the three monkeys are often used to imply a lack of moral responsibility for wrongdoing — looking the other way or feigning ignorance. I've also read of it signifying a code of silence in criminal gangs, but I think you'd be better placed than me to speculate on that. Is that any use to you? I take it this has something to do with one of your investigations."

"Yes, it's helpful and yes, it does have some bearing on a case I'm investigating."

"Would you care to enlighten me?"

Jack told him what he knew.

"Oh, how very distressing," Poole said. "That poor child. So, do you think she was killed because she witnessed something she shouldn't have?"

"That's one of the avenues I'm going down," Jack said.

"Well, it's not really faithful to the legend, but I can see your reasoning. More tea?"

Jack spent another thirty minutes with the old man, which included a tour of his greenhouse.

"Stay in contact, Jack," Poole said. He shook Jack's hand vigorously. "Feel free to drop in any time. I've got all this knowledge up here . . ." He tapped the side of his head, ". . . and nothing to do with it. It just rattles around in there, and I'm sure the facts fall out of my ears and vanish if they're not used."

Jack said he would stay in touch and took his leave.

CHAPTER 6

MONDAY

Jack closed his book and glanced up at the clock on the mantelpiece. "Rosie, turn on the wireless. It's nearly seven. Give it a chance to warm up."

"*Journey into Space*?" Eric said hopefully from a dining table that was partially covered by his homework.

"Not tonight. Mantovani and his orchestra, from the Savoy ballroom. I need some music to relax by; it's been a long day."

Eric pulled a face and went back to his algebra.

"Mother!" Jack called. "It's nearly seven."

"Coming!" Annie called back. "Just drying the saucepans."

Rosie turned on the radiogram. She was ironing the tabard she wore in her job at the local baker's. "I think I'll go upstairs when I've finished this, and play some records."

"No, you won't, young lady. It's Monday night, and Monday night is?"

"Family night," Eric and Rosie chorused, without enthusiasm.

"All done." Annie entered the room untying her apron. "Rosie, must you do that in here? It's what the kitchen is for."

"*You* were in the kitchen, Mum. I didn't want to get in your way."

"You could have done the drying-up. That wouldn't have been in my way."

"I'm doing the ironing!"

"Yes," Annie said. "In the *living room.*"

Mantovani's orchestra filled the room, strings cascading.

"May we listen now?" Family nights were important to Jack; they provided an escape from the world of crime. "Mother," he said to Annie. "Sit yourself down and enjoy the music."

Annie draped her apron across the back of a dining chair and sat down opposite him. "This is nice," she said. "Eric, how are you getting on with your homework? Do you want your dad to help you?"

"Nearly finished, Mum. Only three questions to go."

"Shhh!" Jack closed his eyes and hummed along to *Charmaine.*

The doorbell chimed just as the music approached its coda.

"Ye gods! What now?"

"I'll get it," Annie said.

"No, Mother. You've just cooked dinner *and* washed up. You sit and relax. I'll go and see who it is."

He opened the front door and stared at the young woman confronting him, unable to speak. She had bleached 'Marilyn Monroe' hair and wore a gabardine mackintosh.

"Joanie?" he finally managed.

"Hello, Dad," said the young woman.

Without another word, Jack turned on his heel and walked back into the living room, leaving his eldest daughter standing on the doorstep.

"Who was it, Dad?" Annie said.

Jack sat down heavily in his chair, shook his head and said nothing.

"Jack . . . ?" Eventually Annie gave up waiting for him to reply.

"Good God!" she said, as she reached the front door. "Joanie. Three years without a word and now you turn up, out of the blue. Why now?"

"It's Monday night, Mum," Joan said with an uncertain smile. "Family night."

* * *

Jack sat in his armchair and stared into the empty hearth. Mantovani was still serenading but he wasn't listening. He was thinking about Joan, his first child, born three months prematurely, and just inside wedlock.

1939 had been a momentous year. Thirty thousand souls were lost in a Chilean earthquake. Britain went to war with Germany, and he enlisted in the army, going off to fight just as Joan took her first breath. Her early weeks were fraught. The doctors had been dubious about her chances of survival, but he'd never had any doubts. He knew his daughter was a survivor, a fighter. And so her name was never an issue — it had to be Joan: Joan of Arc, the Maid of Orleans. For years he'd called her his little *Jeanne d'Arc.*

He'd always encouraged her independent streak, admiring her passion for life and her ability to meet it head on. It should not have been a surprise to him, then, when she met and fell in love with a much older man. Ivan, a Czech émigré, had come to England during the war to fly with the RAF, and stayed on. The difference in age worried both him and Annie, and they had tried hard to discourage the romance. Their home began to resemble a war zone, ringing with constant battles until, the day after her sixteenth birthday, Joan crept out of the house when everyone was sleeping, and eloped with Ivan.

Jack had not seen or heard from her since.

He listened to the voices as they moved from the front door to the kitchen.

"Who was at the door, Dad?" Rosie paused in her ironing.

"Eh? Sorry?"

"Who was at the door?" Eric echoed from the dining table.

"Your sister."

"Don't be silly, Dad. Rosie's right here."

The skin around Jack's eyes tightened. "Your other sister."

"Joanie?" Rosie squealed incredulously and rushed out to the kitchen.

Eric was more circumspect. He ambled across to where Jack was sitting and rested a hand on his shoulder. "Don't worry, Dad."

* * *

Mantovani finished playing. Only then did he push himself from his armchair and walk to the kitchen, where he paused in the doorway. They stood in the centre of the room, the four of them, locked in a tearful embrace. They didn't look up.

He turned away, grabbed his coat from the hall and left the house.

The light was fading as he entered the park. He took the path down to the woodland area, passing the park-keeper's hut. A grey-haired old man in a threadbare, blue serge uniform emerged, clutching a large bunch of keys. He looked up as Jack went past. "I'm closing up!" he called. "You've got half an hour before I lock the front gates."

Jack ignored him and continued to the spot where Frances Anderton's body had been discovered the previous day. He stood, staring down at the flattened bracken.

He had never expected to see Joan again. After the initial pain, he'd convinced himself that his precious *Jeanne d'Arc* was gone forever. He'd told himself he could live with that; and that if she ever showed her face again he would have nothing to do with her. He wasn't ready for this pain.

A flashlight shone into his face, blinding him. "Okay, and what do you think you're up to?"

Jack put a hand up to shield his eyes. "It's all right. Police."

The light went out. "Sorry, sir. I didn't recognise you." The voice belonged to PC Kirby.

Jack lowered his hand. "Don't you ever rest, man?"

"The villains don't, so why should I? Are you feeling all right, sir? You look pale."

"Had a bit of a shock, that's all," Jack said.

"I'm still feeling it too. That poor child. Her poor father."

"Do you have children, Constable?"

"Just the one daughter, sir. My Gillian. You?"

"Two . . . er, three," Jack said. "Come on, let's walk. The park-keeper is about to lock the gates."

They walked away from the woodland and back through the park.

"How old is your daughter, Constable?"

"Twenty-four, sir."

"And she still lives with you?"

Kirby nodded and tugged the lead, bringing Satan to heel. "I dare say she'll meet a fine man one day, get married and settle down with him, but for the moment there's just the two of us. It's been that way since Mrs Kirby passed, five years ago."

"Does she work?"

Kirby nodded. "Yes. When I left the army, my wife and I pooled our savings and bought a small livery stable out on the Weston Road. Caroline, my wife, ran it for a time, while Gillian was growing up. We didn't make a great deal but, supplemented by my police salary, we rubbed along pretty well. But then the cancer got her and I had to make other arrangements. I didn't really want to sell up. The stables had been our home for nearly ten years by then, but Gillian had the bright idea of starting a riding school. She'd been brought up with horses and was comfortable around them, and was, still is, a pretty fine horsewoman. So over the last few years she's built the school into the best in the area. We've still got the livery side of the business, so what she makes with the school is her own money. One day, as I said, I'm sure she'll meet someone and settle down, but for now, I treasure every moment I have with her."

"You're a very lucky man."

"I know I am. It's why I feel so much for Warren Anderton. He has wealth, a fine house and the final say in how his company's run, but I'm sure he'd give it all up tomorrow to have his daughter back, even for one day."

They reached the park gates.

"Thank you, Constable. You've helped me see the wood for the trees."

Slightly perplexed, Kirby gave a small salute. "Happy to oblige, sir. Happy to oblige."

* * *

Jack entered the house through the back door. The kitchen was empty, the clock above the door reading ten past ten. Probably everyone was in bed. Rosie had an early shift at the baker's and Eric had to catch the bus to school at eight. Jack made himself a cup of cocoa and took it through to the living room.

"Did you make me one?" Annie said from the armchair. The room was lit only by a standard lamp in the corner, which cast a shadow across most of her face. He couldn't read her eyes.

"Have this one," he said. "I'll make myself another." He set the cup down beside her.

"Thanks. Where have you been?"

"Walking. I needed to get some things straight in my mind. Walking helped."

He sat down in the armchair facing her. Cocoa could wait. They needed to talk. "Joanie?" he said.

"Sharing with Rosie tonight. I'll clear out the box room in the morning, so she can have a bedroom of her own. We still have the put-you-up. It will do until we can buy a bed at the weekend."

"I didn't think we'd ever have to," Jack said.

"She's come home, Jack. Our girl's come home." She reached out her hand.

He took it and squeezed, lightly. "Why?"

Annie sighed. "Ivan's left her. Gone back to Czechoslovakia."

"Why?"

Annie shook her head. "I don't know all the details. You'd be better asking her yourself."

"So we're having her back? After what she did?"

"We can't turn her away, Jack. She knows she's been a very foolish girl, but we can't punish her. She's been through enough."

"When did Ivan leave her?"

"Six months ago. They were renting a flat over a shop in Palmers Green. She kept up the rent for as long as she could by working as a barmaid at a pub, but when the landlord there got too friendly she left. Eventually her savings ran out and she couldn't afford to keep the flat on. She was scared, coming back here. She didn't know how you'd react."

Jack stared blankly at the tiles in the fireplace. "I didn't do very well, did I?"

"Who could blame you? You were shocked."

"You could say that. I'll speak with her in the morning."

"Be gentle with her, Jack."

"When she left, *the way she left*; it broke my heart, Annie. I thought I'd never forgive her."

"There was blame on all sides, Jack. We could have tried to be more understanding. I mean, she was in love. I remember when we first met; you were the only thing I could think about for months. I used to drive Mum and Dad up the wall, mooning over you. I should have remembered that feeling when Joanie first told us about Ivan."

"Yes," Jack said. "Being in love is like a sickness. It addles your brain. I'll be gentle with her."

Annie picked up her cocoa. "I'm all in; I'm taking this up." She came over and bent to kiss the top of his head. "You're a good man, Jack Callum."

"I'll be up shortly. Warm my side of the bed."

"I'll make it as warm as toast for you."

"As a dutiful wife should." It was one of their private jokes.

He sat for another few minutes before following his wife upstairs. At the door to Rosie's room he paused, and then quietly looked inside.

The two girls were lying head to toe in Rosie's single bed. They breathed in a soft whisper. Moonlight poured in through the window, touching their faces. He took a step into the room and stared down at Joanie. He swallowed, and tears pricked at his eyes. "Welcome home, my little *Jeanne d'Arc,"* he said softly, and brushed a blonde curl from her eyes. "Sleep tight."

"Ssstight," she mumbled without waking.

CHAPTER 7

TUESDAY AUGUST 12th 1958

When Jack came downstairs, Annie was standing at the cooker, making scrambled eggs

"Are the girls up yet?"

"Rosie was up early; she's gone to work," Annie said. "I'm letting Joanie sleep in. The eggs are for Eric. He's just finishing off the last of his homework in the living room."

"He should have done that last night. When you asked him about it, he said he only had three questions to go."

"Yes, well, things didn't exactly go according to plan last night, did they?"

"I suppose not."

"Are you going to speak to Joanie before you go to the station?"

He buttered a slice of toast and checked his watch. "Not unless she gets up in the next ten minutes. Eddie will be here in—" The doorbell rang. "In fact he's here now." He swallowed a bite of toast and a mouthful of tea. "Got to dash."

Annie frowned at him. "Jack, you *will* speak to her, won't you?"

"Yes, of course I will . . . later." He grabbed his coat from the hall and opened the front door. "A bit prompt today, aren't we, Sergeant?"

"I'm chasing up Douglas Madison. He was on the council's list but I couldn't get hold of him yesterday. He was working over Hitchin way but nobody knew quite where. If you don't mind stopping off on our way in, I thought we could go to his house and try to catch him before he leaves for work."

"Good idea. Where does he live?"

"Just off of Birchwood. It will only take us a couple of miles out of our way."

As they drove, Jack told Fuller about his meeting with Dr Poole. "So now you know as much about this case as I do," he concluded. Fuller parked in front of a row of terraced cottages. They had cream stuccoed walls, and windows flanked by green, louvred shutters.

The woman who answered the door wore a pink nylon overall and dark blue carpet slippers. She looked about forty, with stringy, mud-coloured hair hanging around a doughy face. Her watery blue eyes screwed up as she read Jack's warrant card. She sighed. "What's Dougie done now?"

"Nothing, as far as we know," Jack said. "We just need to ask him some questions."

"You'd better come in, then," she said, and yelled up the stairs, "Douglas Madison! Get your lazy arse down here. People to see you." She led the detectives into a small, cramped kitchen.

Something noxious was bubbling away in an aluminium pot on the decrepit gas cooker.

"Excuse the stink," she said. "Just boiling some fish heads for the cat. Sit yourselves down."

Jack and Fuller sat down at the kitchen table, attempting to keep clear of the smears of tomato ketchup and drying spilt milk.

"Dougie!" she yelled again, and listened. There was a thump above them. "'S'all right. He's up." She buried her arms in a pile of dishes filling the sink.

Jack glanced around the room, with its yellowing wallpaper and sticky strips of flypaper hanging from a cobwebbed ceiling. "Can I get you a brew?" she said.

He looked at the grey, grimy cloth she was using to clean her plates and said, "No thanks. I've not long had my breakfast."

Fuller, too, was staring at the dishcloth. "I'm fine."

A small man came into the kitchen. He was dressed smartly in a sports jacket and fawn slacks and his thinning hair was pomaded to a brilliant shine. He walked across to the table, extending a pink, freshly scrubbed hand.

"Douglas Madison," he said. "And who would be the gentlemen here to see me?"

"Detective Chief Inspector Callum," Jack said. "This is Detective Sergeant Fuller."

"Delighted to make your acquaintance." Madison shook Jack's hand vigorously. "Always pleased to meet members of the local constabulary."

"Pour yourself a cuppa, Dougie, though it's probably stewed by now. I made it ages ago."

"Thank you, dear. You've met my wife," Madison said to Jack. "Susan, did you think to offer the gentlemen a cup of tea?"

"Yes, she did, and we're fine," Jack said

"Well, that's splendid." Madison squeezed into a seat at the table. Jack noticed that Fuller had suddenly taken a deep interest in the fly-specked strip hanging from a corner of the ceiling.

"So what can I do for you, officers?"

"You were at work on Sunday, at Norton Park. Maintenance of the playground rides, as I understand it."

"Yes, that's right."

"Well, I don't know if you've heard, but a young girl has been murdered and her body was dumped in the woodland area of the park, sometime during the day on Sunday."

The colour drained from Madison's face. "Murdered you say? That's dreadful."

"Yes," Jack said.

"So we were wondering . . ." Fuller had his pencil poised above an open notebook. ". . . if you saw anything untoward that day?"

"What? Like someone dumping a dead body, you mean?" The precise vowels and clipped diction had deserted Madison, and his voice rang with a Middlesex accent. "I think I would have noticed something like that, don't you?"

"Which of the rides were you working on?" Jack asked him.

"The witch's hat. I was greasing the bearings."

"And the witch's hat is?"

"It's that upside-down cone that spins like a roundabout and goes up and down," Fuller explained helpfully. "A friend of mine broke his leg on one of those, years ago. Caught his leg between the seat and the ground. Nasty."

"Yes, thank you, Sergeant, for that insight." Jack turned his attention back to Madison. "The witch's hat is in the far eastern corner of the playground, am I right?" he said. "That's no more than fifty yards away from the wood, isn't it?"

Madison nodded.

"You're not suggesting that my Dougie had anything to do with a murder, are you?" Susan Madison moved away from the sink and stood over her husband protectively, while she dried her hands on a tea towel as grubby as the dishcloth she'd been using.

"We're suggesting nothing of the kind, Mrs Madison. It's just that we're very short of witnesses and your husband was in the area nearest to where the girl's body was left."

Madison was shaking his head. "I don't know what to say. I didn't see anything, apart from . . ."

"Apart from what?"

Madison looked flustered. "I thought he'd gone into the trees to relieve himself."

"Who, Dougie?" Jack said.

"A man. Just a man."

"Can you describe this man?" Fuller said, pencil hovering.

Madison sat back in his seat. "I really didn't get a close look at him. I was at the top of the pole, greasing the bearings. Tricky things, witch's hats. You have to get the lubrication just right or the bearings grind against each other, and that can lead to—"

"The man you saw?" Jack prompted.

"Yes, right. I didn't get a good look at his face because he was wearing a hat, a trilby, and he had the brim pulled down over his eyes. Didn't want to be seen, I expect. I mean, taking a Jimmy Riddle in a public place, with the gentleman's lavatory not a hundred yards away."

"What time was this?

"About four. We'd just had our afternoon tea break."

"Height?" Fuller said.

"Medium."

"Weight?"

"Er, medium, I'd say."

"Hair colour?"

"He had the hat."

"Young? Old?"

Madison shrugged. "I'm not being a lot of help here, am I?"

"So far you've described someone of medium height, medium build, who could be young or old, and wears a trilby, so no, Dougie, you're not. In fact I'd say you're about as much use as a witness as a bread roll," Jack said.

"Well, there's no need to be insulting. He's trying to help," Susan Madison said.

"Did you see anyone else while you were up the pole?" Fuller said.

"Apart from the park-keeper, no."

"And was the park-keeper near the wood? Could he have seen the man you failed to describe?" Jack said.

"No. He was at the wood a while before I saw the man in the trilby. While I was drinking my tea. He was pushing a wheelbarrow into the wood."

"What was in the wheelbarrow?"

"How would I know?" Madison said. "It was covered by a tarpaulin."

Jack thought for a moment. "How long after you saw the park-keeper did you see the man in the trilby?"

"I can't really say. I suppose about half an hour or so. I remember thinking that he was lucky the park-keeper didn't catch him taking a wee."

"Describe the park-keeper," Jack said.

"About thirty or so, I'd guess. Medium height, medium build, hair . . . covered by a park-keeper's hat . . . You're thinking it might have been the same man?"

"I saw the park-keeper last night when I went to the park," Jack said. "He's seventy if he's a day."

"Oh. I see."

"Is there anything further you can tell us about the park-keeper?" Fuller said.

"Sorry," Madison said. "I'd help if I could."

Jack got to his feet and handed Madison a card printed with the station's number. "Well, thank you for your help, Dougie. If you think of anything that may be of use to us, you can reach me on that number. We'll see ourselves out."

Back in the car Fuller said, "Strange couple. An odd match."

"It takes all sorts, Sergeant. So what have we learned?"

Fuller gave a snort. "Well, it would appear we're looking for a man in his thirties, who wears a trilby and impersonates park-keepers. That narrows the field somewhat."

Jack shook his head. "You and Grant go back and speak to the others who were working at the park that day. See if any of them can describe the park-keeper." He paused for a moment and then said. "What happened to the wheelbarrow?"

"What?"

"Madison said he saw the park-keeper pushing a wheelbarrow into the wood. Let's assume he had Frances Anderton's body there, covered by the tarpaulin."

"But when he saw the man in the trilby who'd been taking the supposed leak, he didn't mention the wheelbarrow," Fuller said.

"So what did he do with the barrow? And the tarpaulin for that matter. Let's go back to the park."

* * *

They stood near the spot where the body had been discovered and looked about them.

"Four of our boys gave this area a pretty good going-over yesterday," Fuller said.

"Agreed. But they weren't looking for a wheelbarrow, were they?"

"Very true."

"What's that through there?" Jack pointed through the trees.

"It looks like a shed of some kind."

A small shed, built from creosoted timber, stood fifty or so yards outside the radius of yesterday's search. It had a pitched roof covered with grey roofing felt. A single small window was caked in grime so thick the glass was opaque. The door was secured by a simple butterfly catch. Jack spun the catch and prodded the door open with the toe of his shoe.

"I'm sure they searched this yesterday," Fuller said.

The interior of the shed was as dirty as the window. Dust and dead leaves covered the floor, and thick cobwebs covered the walls. Jack hated spiders.

"And what would they have found, Sergeant?" Jack took a breath and stepped inside. "A spider-infested toolshed with a couple of rusting spades, a broken rake and very little else. Apart from a wheelbarrow and an old tarpaulin. Not enough, really, to register on anybody's radar."

Fuller stared at the old wheelbarrow propped up against the shed wall. "Well, I'll be blowed." He ran his fingers through his hair.

"You'd better call this in and get a couple of officers back here." With one eye on the spiders, he crouched down and lifted a corner of the tarpaulin. "Let's see what else they missed."

CHAPTER 8

TUESDAY

"You have your office all to yourself!" called Andy Brewer, as Jack entered the station some hours later.

"Has the chief super got his own office back?"

"The decorators are moving their stuff out now," Brewer said. He nodded at a man in paint-splattered overalls, carrying a stepladder down the stairs.

"Good."

"Did you want to add a *riddance* to that, sir?"

"You know me better than that, Andy. I would never be so rude. I'll be in *his* office if you need me."

* * *

"Ah, Jack," Lane said. "What do you have to tell me?"

"We have a witness who saw a man wheeling a barrow into the woods Sunday afternoon, dressed as a park-keeper, but *not* the park-keeper. We've found the wheelbarrow and have two men down there now, dusting for fingerprints and checking for any other evidence."

"Do we have a description of the man?"

"Only a very vague one. I have Fuller on it now, sir. He's having another go at the men who were doing the maintenance work on Sunday. He can ask more useful questions this time around."

"Good. I'm sure I don't need to emphasise that we need a positive outcome on this one, Jack. And fast."

"We're doing what we can, sir."

"Yes, I'm sure you are. Do you realise how many people in this town rely on Warren Anderton for their jobs? He's a very important figure in this area. The chief constable was on the phone to me this morning asking how the investigation is going. He belongs to Anderton's Lodge, and of course he's very upset that such a thing could happen to a fellow Mason. I stalled him, but he's ringing back this afternoon. I'd like to have something positive to tell him."

"When *I* have something positive, you'll be the first to know."

"And *I* know you won't let me down, Jack."

Jack went back to his office. He and his men could only do so much, especially if all the witnesses turned out to be as useless as Douglas Madison.

He took a briar pipe from the drawer of his desk, filled it from a round tin of Bondman tobacco and tamped it down. He rarely smoked, but sometimes it helped him to concentrate. After all, it worked for Sherlock Holmes.

* * *

"We have three people who saw the park-keeper on Sunday." Fuller had been gone for most of the morning.

"Descriptions?"

"We have a few more details to go on," Fuller said. "All three put his age at nearer twenty than thirty. All agree he was fairly handsome. One of them saw him without his cap and said his hair is fair to mousy."

"Fair to mousy?"

"That was the best he could do."

"And he's in his twenties." Jack said. "Closer to Frances's age, I suppose."

"Do you think the age is significant?"

"It might be. It could be someone she knew."

"Unlikely, sir. At that age the gap between fourteen and twenty is huge."

"But not when you're nineteen," Jack said. "What do we know about Fiona Anderton's secret boyfriend?"

"Apart from his name — Adam — nothing at all. She's playing her cards very close to her chest."

"Then I'm going to see her," Jack said. "Find out what she can tell me about him. There must be a reason why she's keeping him a secret from her parents."

"Do you want me to come, sir?"

"No, you stay here and wait for the boys to get back from the park. I'll handle this alone."

* * *

"My parents are out," Fiona Anderton said at the door. "They've gone to arrange the funeral."

Jack stood on the doorstep, his hat in his hands. "First, let me offer my sincerest condolences."

She shrugged. She looked different from when he last saw her. Her face was free of make-up, her hair was down, curling about the shoulders of a black roll-neck sweater, and her legs were sheathed in tight, neatly pressed, black slacks that ended in black satin pumps. She looked younger, more vulnerable.

"Actually, it was you I came to see, Miss Anderton," Jack said. "May I come in?"

She stared at him for a moment and then stood aside to let him enter. "Come through to the morning room."

She went across to the fireplace and took a cigarette from a box on the mantelpiece. "Well, what can I do for you, Inspector?"

"Do you mind if we sit down?"

"It's a free country."

Wondering what had happened to Jessica Anderton's no-smoking rule, Jack sat in an armchair facing Fiona.

"Forgive this intrusion," he said.

She shrugged again. "I have the time," she said. "It's not as if I can go anywhere until they get back." She blew smoke, almost defiantly, up at the ceiling.

"Oh? Why is that?"

"Well, you know how it is, Inspector, all hands to the pumps in times of crisis. I have to guard the telephone to make sure my father doesn't miss some important message from an underling." She curled her lip. Her relationship with her father was evidently fractious. "So, what can I do for you?" she said.

"Your sister must have come as a terrible shock."

She sucked in smoke again. "Do you mean her death, or her birth?"

He wasn't sure how to answer.

Fiona gave a brittle laugh. "I'm sorry, Inspector. I didn't mean to put you on the spot like that. I don't suppose you're used to the petty rivalries of teenage girls."

"I have two daughters myself, Miss Anderton, of similar ages to you and Frances. I don't think there's much you can say that would shock me."

"*Touché*," she said. "I suppose I deserved that. Please, carry on with your questions."

"Apart from the petty rivalries, did you and your sister get on?"

"As well as most sisters, I expect," Fiona said. "She was five years younger than me so there were never any issues about borrowing my clothes or records."

"Or boyfriends, for that matter."

Her eyes narrowed. "What do you mean by that?"

Jack smiled. "Well, I know with my girls that Rosie, my youngest, regularly had crushes on the boys her elder sister brought home. I wondered if the same thing applied to you and Frances."

"It might have. I never asked her."

"So you wouldn't describe your relationship with your sister as close?"

"It was as close as I chose it to be. She was a child, Inspector. There were certain things I had no desire to share with her."

"Like the boyfriend you keep secret from your parents."

She crushed the half-finished cigarette into an ashtray and stood up. "I think you should leave now."

Jack remained in his seat. "But you do have an on-going secret relationship?"

"That's none of your damned business."

"It *is* my business if it could have some bearing on your sister's murder."

She reached for another cigarette and sat down again.

"My friendship with Adam had nothing to do with Frances. She only met him once and that was by sheer chance."

"Adam who?" Jack spoke gently.

"Adam . . . Channing."

"And how long have you known Mr Channing?"

"*Professor* Channing. He's a lecturer at the London School of Economics. I studied under him for a year after leaving school."

"And now he's your boyfriend?"

"He's my *lover.*" She tilted her chin defiantly, as if determined to shock him.

Jack was unmoved. He knew how to play that game. "I can see why your parents wouldn't approve," he said. "A man like that, in a position of trust, taking advantage of a young woman."

"Oh, don't kid yourself, Inspector; it was I who took advantage of him. He tried to resist, but when I've made up my mind that I want something, I generally get it."

"I'm sure you do." Jack thought that what she really wanted was a good shake. "Is he married?"

"Unhappily, yes he is."

"Unhappily for him, or for you?"

"Both of us, really. His wife's an invalid. It's not a proper marriage but he can't leave her."

"Can't or won't?"

She shrugged. *She's enjoying this*, Jack thought. *She's probably pleased to finally be able to tell someone about it.*

"So when did Frances meet Professor Channing?"

"At an end-of-term party," she said. "I understood he wouldn't be attending because of his wife, so I invited Frances along. You can imagine my surprise when Adam showed up. His wife was staying overnight in hospital having some tests, so he was up there with her and staying at a hotel."

"Doesn't he live in London?"

"No. He has a house near Stevenage, hence the hotel."

"Let's get this straight," Jack said. "His sick wife was in hospital undergoing tests, and so he decides to go to a party."

"He was at a loose end," Fiona said. "He was bored, at the hotel by himself, so he thought he'd come along and show his face. It was a surprise, I can tell you, albeit a lovely one."

"Charming. And you introduced him to your sister?"

"No, of course not. Do you think I'm totally irresponsible?" The nostrils were flaring again. "No, Adam just sat at our table. She met him then."

"How old is Professor Channing, Fiona?"

"Forty-five, or is it six? I can never remember."

"And the age gap doesn't bother you?"

She shook her head. "Not a jot. Adam's a man, Inspector, not like the boys my own age. They're so immature. He's a brilliant, kind, compassionate man."

"Try telling that to his wife," Jack said, getting to his feet. "I'll see myself out."

Fiona walked to the door with him anyway. "You won't tell them," she said. "My parents. You won't say anything to them about Adam."

"It's not my place to do so, miss. But I would advise you to tell them. Sooner rather than later."

"They'd never understand."

"Sometimes parents can surprise you."

As he drove away, he saw her watching him from the doorway, biting her lip. "Silly girl," he muttered.

* * *

Back at the station he went up to see Superintendent Lane, not that there was much Lane could pass on to the chief constable, but internecine politics were his boss's concern. Then he went in search of Fuller.

"Take me home, Sergeant. I've had enough for one day."

"How did it go with Fiona Anderton?" Fuller asked as they walked to the car.

"The boyfriend's not our man, but we'll check him out anyway." Jack said. "His name's Professor Adam Channing and he's a lecturer at the London School of Economics. He and his wife live in Stevenage. But he's too old to be our park-keeper, and we're looking for someone who lives locally, or at least has local knowledge and has somewhere he can keep the girls he abducts while he does what he does to them, prior to dumping their bodies."

"Girls?"

"I have a bad feeling about this one, Eddie. I think Frances Anderton was just the first. Call it a hunch."

"I hope you're wrong, Jack."

"So do I, Eddie. So do I."

CHAPTER 9

TUESDAY

Jack arrived home to find everyone sitting in the back garden. Annie had got the deckchairs out from the shed and they were all enjoying the late afternoon sun, even Eric, who was usually bored by anything that didn't involve climbing trees or kicking a football around. Jack's three girls were wearing flowery sundresses. Annie had her chestnut hair tied up in a ponytail, which gave her a girlish look, and took him back to their courting days.

"Sit yourself down, Dad," Annie said. "Rosie has made some lemonade. I'll fetch you a glass."

Jack settled himself into a striped canvas chair and slipped off his shoes. Despite the setting, the atmosphere in the garden was tense. His two youngest kept looking from him to Joan, anticipating an emotional explosion. Annie came back with a glass of lemonade and handed it to Jack.

"Eric," she said to her son. "You have your homework to do. Get yourself inside and get on with it. I don't want a repeat of yesterday. And Rosie, I want you to give me a hand with dinner. You can peel some potatoes."

Their grumbles of protest were met with a curt, "Now!" Both children got obediently to their feet and followed her into the house.

It was Joan who finally broke the ensuing silence. "Mum isn't very subtle, is she?"

"She tries her best. This hasn't been easy for any of us."

"I suppose not," Joan said. "Where did you get to last night? I was expecting a tongue-lashing — or a dressing down at least."

"You were right to expect it," Jack said. "Which is why I went for a walk: to clear my head."

"And calm down?"

"If you like."

"Would an apology make any difference?"

Jack took a sip of lemonade. It was very sweet and he grimaced. "It might. If I thought you meant it."

Joan sat forward in her seat. "But I do apologise, Dad. I really do." Her voice caught in her throat. "You can't imagine how hard it was to come back here yesterday, not knowing if you could bear to even look at me, let alone talk to me. When you took off last night, I feared the worst, even though Mum told me things would be all right."

"Your mum knows me pretty well," Jack said, with a fond smile. "Better than I know myself sometimes." He lapsed into silence again.

"Mum said she told you what had happened with Ivan," Joan said.

"I should knock his block off."

"It's not really his fault."

"Whose fault is it, then — Harold MacMillan's?"

"I don't think Ivan realised what he was taking on, Dad. I was a brat, a sixteen-year-old who thought she knew it all."

"How long before you realised you didn't?"

"When we moved into the flat above the shop and I had to behave like a wife." She tugged at her platinum hair. "Mum made it look, *makes* it look, so easy; juggling the home finances, the cooking and the cleaning, looking after a husband and catering to his needs. I soon found out that it isn't so easy. I was only sixteen and I wanted to be out, going to parties, dancing till dawn, down at the Palais."

"And he didn't?"

"Ivan had a job as a labourer, working on a building site in Holborn. By the time he got home in the evening, all he wanted to do was have his tea and listen to the wireless. I couldn't really blame him but, as I said, I was young and a brat, so we argued. We argued a lot — violently."

"Did he ever strike you?"

She lowered her eyes. "Only if I really deserved it."

Jack reached out and took her hand. "No woman deserves to be hit by the man she loves, no matter how much she thinks she might; and any man who raises his hand to a woman is a coward, nothing more, nothing less. I'm glad it ended before he could do any permanent damage."

"One day he just upped and left," she said. "He packed his bags, went down to the docks and boarded a tramp steamer to Marseilles. At least that's what Radek told me."

"Who's Radek?"

"Another Czech, a friend of his. They used to work together on the building site. It was Radek who got me the job at the Queen of Diamonds. It was his local and he knew the landlord."

"Mum told me how that worked out."

"I've made some bad choices, Dad."

"Yes, you have. But you're lucky to have come out of it relatively unscathed. You could have got yourself into trouble. At least you didn't have an unwanted child to . . ."

Joan started to cry, the tears rolling down her cheeks.

"Oh, Joanie!" Jack got out of his chair, squatted down at her side and wrapped his arms around her. "What happened to the child?"

"There was a woman," she said through her sobs. "In Hackney. She provides *special services* for unmarried mothers."

"People like that are parasites," Jack said bitterly. "Taking advantage of young girls; trading on their misery and desperation."

"I didn't have a choice, Dad. We could barely afford to feed ourselves, let alone a baby." She gripped his sleeve. "Please don't tell Mum what I did," she whispered. "She doesn't know."

He handed her a handkerchief. "I think we'll keep that between ourselves," he said. "Your mum longs to be a grandmother. If she ever finds out that you . . . well, it would just about finish her off. I don't want her to suffer any more than she has. She's a good woman, your mum, one of the best. You could learn a lot from her."

"Will you give me the chance to try?"

"Take as long as you need. This will always be your home."

She wrapped her arms around his neck "I love you so much, Dad."

They stayed like that for a long moment.

Unconditional love. He'd had no idea what the term meant till Joanie was born. As he'd stared down at the pink, wrinkled infant, so vulnerable and defenceless in her hospital crib, he'd understood. He felt it now — acutely.

"I don't like it, by the way," he said into her ear.

"What?"

"The hair. It makes you look like a tuppenny tart."

"Not one of my smartest decisions. I had it done when I was working at the pub. I thought it was in keeping with my new job. Don't worry though; Mum's friend Avril is coming tomorrow to put it right."

"I don't know. You come back here and disrupt our lives, and now you're turning my home into a hairdressing salon."

"Sorry."

He hugged her tight. "Apology accepted."

CHAPTER 10

TUESDAY

Sandra Duncan packed her books in her haversack while Miss Havelock dismissed the evening class.

"Before you all disappear for the night, remember that next week we'll be looking at nutrition, and how we can provide a balanced diet for the children in our care. If you can all read chapter eleven of your text book in preparation."

As the class filed out of the room a few of the girls were making arrangements to rendezvous at the local pub.

"Are you coming, Sandra?"

"Not tonight, Diane. I have to catch my bus." Sandra was pleased she'd been asked to join them. Despite all her school friends' promises to keep in touch, friendship had ended when the school gates closed behind them for the last time. The girls she worked with at the bank were a fairly closed bunch, and so far she hadn't been welcomed into the club. She'd told herself it was because she hadn't been there long, but it was months now and she doubted things would ever change. It was why she liked the children. They didn't look down on her.

It was why this evening class in childcare was so important to her. Her dream was to leave the bank and go abroad to work with children, maybe as a governess or a nanny. She'd chosen France, partly because she'd learnt the language, and partly because she could no longer see a happy future for herself in

England. She hoped that in a different country, where nobody knew her, she would have the chance to build a better life, start afresh, with a clean slate.

Her bus was already at the stop as she came down the steps out of the school. "Blast!"

She started to run, but she knew she wasn't going to make it. As she ran out onto the street the bus was pulling away. The next one would not be along for another thirty minutes.

There was a bench a few yards away. She sat down and opened her haversack, took out her textbook and found chapter eleven. She could just about read the words in the orange light of the sodium lamp behind her. At least it would pass the time until the next bus came along.

"Can I give you a lift?"

The young man standing in front of her was casually dressed, but his clothes looked clean and pressed. His hair was short and neatly cut, fair, almost blond, with a side parting.

"I'm waiting for the bus," she said.

He smiled at her. "I thought you might be . . . as you're sitting at a bus stop."

"I just missed one."

"My sympathies. You're in for a long wait. The buses are all up the spout tonight. Something to do with an accident in town."

"I didn't realise."

"So, would you care for a lift?"

She looked beyond him, for a car. She hadn't heard one pull up.

"I don't see your car."

"Ah."

"So how do you intend giving me a lift?"

"Look over there." He sat down next to her and pointed at a motor scooter parked at the side of the road.

"You're offering me a ride home on that?"

"Yes, why not?"

"Because I value my life?"

He laughed. "It's perfectly safe. *I'm* perfectly safe. Scooters aren't like motorbikes. They haven't got the speed for one thing, and I never take risks, especially if I have a passenger."

"Thanks," she said. "But I don't think so."

"Have you just come from the school?"

"Night school."

"I thought so, from the book. What are you reading?"

"It's a book on childcare."

"Really? You don't look old enough to have a child."

She felt herself blushing. "No. I mean, I don't have children of my own. I want to look after them though, as a job. Perhaps abroad."

"Derek," he said, sticking out his hand.

"Sandra. Sandra Duncan."

"Very pleased to meet you." He looked along the street. "Are you sure you wouldn't like a lift? You could be stuck here for hours, you know."

"No, really I . . ."

"Come and have a look at my scooter. You can see for yourself how safe it is." He got to his feet and stood, waiting. When he showed no sign of moving on she sighed, slipped her book into her haversack, and stood up. "All right then. Just a look."

He smiled at her. He had kind eyes, she decided.

They crossed the street and walked to where the scooter was parked. As they reached it, he said, "It's a Phoenix 150. Only three months old. You can't really see in this light but it's blue, two-tone."

"It looks very nice."

"Sit on it. Try it for size."

"I don't think—"

"Where's the harm?"

She shrugged and climbed on.

"Now, hold the handlebars and put your feet up on the footrest."

She did so.

"See how comfortable it is?"

"Yes, it is," she said. "Very comfortable." She glanced back along the road. There was still no sign of an approaching bus. "Hours, you say, for the bus?"

"One at least, possibly two. It's very snarled up in town."

"And you really don't mind giving me a lift?"

"It would be my pleasure, Sandra. Where do you live?"

"Gleave Road. Do you know it?"

"Know it? I was born and raised two streets away. North Avenue."

"I don't recall ever seeing you around."

"No, my family moved when I was six. Not far away though. We're still in the area."

"So it wouldn't be taking you out of your way."

"Not at all."

She thought for a moment. "All right then. I accept your offer."

It was not as if he could do anything to her while she was sitting behind him on the scooter, and she really did want to get home tonight.

"Splendid! I can be your knight in shining armour on his gallant steed — well, on his shiny blue motor scooter anyway."

"Two-tone blue motor scooter."

"Exactly. Move back onto the pillion, and off we go."

She shuffled back and he climbed aboard and kick-started the machine. "I just have to make a stop on the way. It will only take a few seconds."

CHAPTER 11

WEDNESDAY AUGUST 13th 1958

"There are people here to see you."

Andy Brewer pointed his pen at a middle-aged couple sitting on the bench beneath the noticeboard. "The name's Duncan: Mr and Mrs Duncan."

Jack went across and introduced himself. "So, Mr and Mrs Duncan; how may I help you?"

Mr Duncan got to his feet. He was a thin, balding man wearing horn-rimmed glasses and a sports jacket with leather patches on the elbows. "It's our daughter, Sandra, Chief Inspector. She's missing."

Jack's voice sounded hollow to himself. "When you say *missing*, what do you mean exactly?"

"She didn't come home last night. She went out to her evening class at half past seven. My wife and I aren't what you would call late birds, so by nine o'clock we were in bed. Then this morning, when Allison went to take Sandra a cup of tea, her room was empty."

"Her bed hadn't been slept in," Allison Duncan said. She was a petite woman whose auburn hair was rigid in a lacquered shampoo and set. Her tweed outfit wouldn't have looked out of place at a local gymkhana. She stared up at Jack, and her face was strained as she bit her lip to stop herself from crying.

"Have you called her friends to check that she didn't stay with one of them?"

"We tried that," Duncan said. "But no one's seen her since she left the school at nine thirty last night."

"Which school would that be?"

"St Clements. She's taking a course there in childcare. She has some misguided idea about becoming a nanny — with a French family of all things. She speaks the language, you see."

"How old is Sandra, Mr Duncan?"

"Eighteen."

"And is there anywhere she might have gone, after finishing her evening class?"

"She always gets the bus straight home," Allison said. "Sandra's a good girl. She takes her studies very seriously and never stays up any later than half past ten. Staying out all night — well, it's just unthinkable."

"Come up to my office," Jack said. "I'll have to go over some things with you. A cup of tea?"

Both of them nodded. Jack went back to the desk.

"Andy, could you see that a tray of tea is sent up to my office? And alert Superintendent Lane. Tell him that we might have another missing girl."

"Will do, sir."

* * *

"Another missing girl, Jack?" Lane said.

"It certainly looks that way. Sandra Duncan, eighteen years old, didn't return home from evening class yesterday."

He laid out a colour snapshot showing a plain girl whose brown hair had been severely cut into a blunt pageboy style that did nothing to enhance her looks.

"It won't do, Jack. It simply won't do. We're stretched enough as it is, searching for Frances Anderton's killer, without this to contend with. We've even got the national press asking questions. The *national press*. What am I supposed to tell them?"

"Tell them our investigations are proceeding."

"But they're not *proceeding*, are they? We're no closer to finding the killer than we were twenty-four hours ago."

"I think you're being slightly unreasonable, sir."

Lane slammed his palm down on the desk, causing pencils to rattle. "Damn it, Chief Inspector, I don't think it's unreasonable to expect you to do your job."

Lane was under pressure from all sides and needed a whipping boy. He was evidently struggling to bring his temper under control.

"I'm sorry, Jack. I realise you're doing your best. I just feel we should be doing more."

"I'll go back over the evidence. We might have missed something."

Lane took off his glasses and polished them with his handkerchief. "Yes, do that. And keep me apprised of your progress with the missing Duncan girl."

* * *

The noticeboard now held two photographs. Jack called the detectives to gather round.

"We have another missing girl." He pointed. "Sandra Duncan, eighteen, works at Lloyds Bank in town. Before that, she was a pupil at the County School. She was last seen leaving her evening class at St Clements at about nine thirty p.m. last night. She never arrived home."

"Perhaps she went out with friends after her class," said Harry Grant.

"That has been suggested to her parents, but they assure me she would have gone straight home. They say she is a *good girl*."

"All parents say that about their children," Grant said. "It doesn't mean that she is."

"Fair point, Harry, and I agree. Parents always see their kids through rose-tinted lenses. So, we'll assume nothing about the girl's character. Frank and Trevor, I want you to check out St Clements, get a list of the other students and interview them all."

Detective Sergeant Frank Lesser and Detective Constable Trevor Walsh exchanged glances. "That could take all day, sir," said Lesser.

"Is there somewhere else you have to be, Sergeant?"

"No, sir."

"Good. St Clements it is then. It will save you hanging around here and cluttering the place up. Myra?"

WPC Myra Banks got to her feet.

"Myra, I want you to cut along to the bank. Have a chat with the manager and see what you can find out about our missing girl. Speak to the staff, especially the female ones, and see if they can give us a broader picture of her than the one provided by her parents. Some people show a completely different side to their personality at work."

"Yes, sir," Myra Banks said. She was young, just out of uniform and on secondment to CID, and so far Jack had been impressed by her. He didn't think it would be long before she was ready for a probation period, and after that she might very well become an important cog in the machine.

"Eddie, take Constable Grant and go down to the County School. Talk to her old teachers and any of her classmates who are still there."

The officers filed out of the room and went off to their assignments. Jack sat down at a desk and stared at the clock on the wall. Five to ten. He couldn't shake the feeling that all their efforts were going to be too late, that Sandra Duncan was already dead.

* * *

"I'd like to see the manager."

Myra looked through the brass grille at a cashier with a bad case of acne who was busy counting a pile of pound notes.

"Of course. Who shall I say wants to see him?"

"WPC Banks, Hertfordshire Constabulary."

"And can I say what it is concerning?"

Myra looked at him.

"Yes. Yes, of course. I'll go and call him." He walked past the other cashiers and rapped on a door at the rear. The barked, "come in," was clearly audible where Myra stood, waiting. The middle-aged man who finally emerged was tall, dressed in an immaculate, navy blue pin-striped suit over a crisp white shirt, set off by a red and blue striped tie.

"WPC Banks? Cecil Marsh. I'm the manager. What can I do for you?"

"Good morning, sir. I'm making enquiries about a girl who works here — Sandra Duncan?"

"Yes, Miss Duncan. She's not been with us long. Joined the bank about six months ago. Is she in any kind of trouble?"

Their conversation was attracting the attention of the four cashiers behind the counter as well as a little old lady with a bulldog on a lead.

"Do you think we could go somewhere and speak in private? Your office perhaps?"

"Of course," said Marsh. "This way." He turned to look at the cashiers, who immediately bent their heads over their work.

"Take a seat, officer." Marsh indicated a small straight-backed seat across the desk from his own brown leather office chair.

"Right, officer. You were saying?"

"Sandra Duncan. I was wondering what you could tell me about her."

Marsh went across to a wooden filing cabinet and pulled open a drawer. He thumbed through the files and took out a manila folder, from which he proceeded to read.

"Sandra Duncan, born the fifth of June, 1940. She joined us in January this year." He read on in silence for a moment. "Quite an impressive list of exam results. Hobbies include languages, reading and knitting. Lives with her parents at 21 Gleave Road, Hatfield. Her parents' names are Arthur and Allison. He is an insurance actuary, she is a prominent member of the parish council. Regular churchgoers. I actually know them quite well, from the Rotary club. A very pleasant couple."

"And Sandra? How would you describe her?"

Marsh closed the file and frowned. "A 'wallflower' is the term I would use."

"A wallflower in what way?"

"Well, she doesn't mix much with the other members of staff. Takes lunch by herself in the staff dining room, and generally has her nose buried in some book. I'm not speaking out of school, but I have heard some of the other girls pass catty remarks about her."

"What kind of remarks?"

"About her clothes and choice of hairstyle — or lack of one — and . . . well, I'm not sure this is relevant . . ."

Despite his formal demeanour, Cecil Marsh seemed to enjoy a bit of gossip.

He leaned across the desk in a conspiratorial manner. "A rumour went around the bank a little while ago that Sandra was involved with a man. A man who was a number of years older than herself."

"Does he have a name, this man?"

Marsh shook his head. "Not that I've heard." He sat back in his leather chair. "Would you mind telling me why you have such an interest in Miss Duncan?"

"She's missing. She didn't come home after her evening class last night."

"Oh, good gracious. Arthur and Allison dote on her. They're probably beside themselves."

"They're very concerned, yes. We all are."

"I'll give Arthur a call to see if there's anything I can do."

"I'd like to talk to the rest of your staff. Perhaps we can use this office to carry out the interviews?"

"And perhaps not. I appreciate you have your job to do, Miss Banks, but I am a very busy man and my appointment book is full for today. I need my office. There's a room upstairs you can use. It's the staff restroom but I'm sure no one will complain if you set up in there."

CHAPTER 12

WEDNESDAY

DS Frank Lesser came out of the school secretary's office and trotted down the stone steps, clutching a folded sheet of foolscap paper. He climbed into the Wolseley, beside DC Trevor Walsh.

"Did you have any luck?"

"I have this," he said, holding up the piece of paper. "There's no one here from the evening classes during the day, but the secretary's given me a list of everyone who was in Sandra Duncan's class last night. There's only eight in the class plus the tutor, so it shouldn't take us all day to track them down."

"If you don't mind me saying, Sarge, you seem to be in a bit of a rush today. Is something wrong?" Walsh said.

"There's a show on tonight at the Granada in Edmonton."

"Are you fighting?"

"Keep it under your hat but, yes, I am. Third on the bill, so if I get my skates on today, I can still make it."

"What would the guv'nor say if he found out you were moonlighting as a wrestler?"

"He'd probably throw a fit, so we keep mum about it, alright?" Lesser reached behind him, took a brown leather Gladstone bag from the back seat and unzipped it. The bag contained a pair of wrestling boots, a black sequinned cape and something that looked like a balaclava.

"So the Black Phantom fights again. I'll have to come and see a match some time."

Lesser pulled the balaclava over his head. Only his eyes and mouth were exposed. "What do you think?"

"I think that if I saw you out in the street wearing that thing I'd probably arrest you."

Lesser pulled off the mask, stowed it back in his bag and threw it onto the rear seat. He unfolded the piece of paper the secretary had given him and ran his finger down the list of names. "Eunice Havelock, the teacher. She's the closest. We'll go and speak with her first. Park Drive. You know it?"

"Yes, I know it. We'll be there in five minutes. It is all fake, isn't it, the wrestling?"

"Try telling that to the old grannies who sit ringside. They would terrify some of the villains I've nicked in my time. Hatpins, pointed combs . . . one old girl clobbered me with her handbag once. The problem was she had half a house brick in it."

"Ouch."

"Indeed. Nearly laid me out, I can tell you."

"But the matches themselves . . ."

"Don't strain your brain over it, Trev. Just look at it this way. There are six matches plus an intermission, and the show ends at ten thirty on the dot. The results are pre-determined but a lot can go wrong if someone doesn't do their job properly. It's why I train so bloody hard. One wrong or badly timed move and I could break an arm or a leg, and then my cover would be blown, mask or no mask."

They pulled into Park Drive.

* * *

Eunice Havelock lived in a bungalow with a pink, Montana Rubens clematis almost hiding the bottle-green door. The rest of the front garden was similarly overgrown, and was a riot of summer colour.

Walsh twisted a small key and a bell sounded loudly within.

Eunice Havelock was dressed for the garden in baggy khaki trousers and a plaid shirt, with rubber galoshes over her shoes.

"Yes?"

"Mrs Havelock . . ." Lesser began.

"It's Miss. Miss Havelock."

"Sorry." Lesser showed her his warrant card. "I understand you take evening classes at St Clements School."

"Indeed, I do, young man. How does that concern the police?"

"It concerns one of the students you were teaching last night, a Miss Sandra Duncan."

"Oh yes, Sandra. Lovely girl. She shows great promise, that one. I understand that she wants to work with children, possibly abroad."

"So we're led to believe," Lesser said. "May we come in and ask you a few questions?"

"Yes, of course. Nothing's happened to Sandra has it? I worried all night, seeing her going off like that — on a motor scooter of all things."

* * *

The restroom looked as though it hadn't been decorated since the nineteen thirties. It was furnished with a very plain wooden table surrounded by four chairs, and a threadbare sofa that looked like it might have been fashionable at the time Stanley Baldwin was prime minister.

Myra sat at the table, took out her notebook and waited for the first member of staff to arrive. A tap on the door, and a porcine woman wearing a peach-coloured knitted twinset entered.

"Please take a seat."

"Battle," said the woman.

"Sorry?"

"Battle. Phyllis Battle. Mrs."

"Thank you for sparing the time, Mrs Battle," said Myra.

"Only too pleased to help." Phyllis wore a pair of wire-framed spectacles, and each time she spoke her head nodded and the glasses slipped down her pudgy nose. She pushed them back with a jab of her index finger.

"I want to talk to you about Sandra Duncan."

"All right," Phyllis said.

"How well do you know her?"

"Not well at all. She hasn't been here that long, just after Christmas last year." The nodding, slipping and pushing was beginning to mesmerise Myra.

"Would you describe her as a friendly girl?"

"Not especially. In fact I found her quite sullen, morose even."

"So there's not much you can tell me about her personal life?"

"Nothing at all. As I say, I barely knew her. You'd be better off talking to Charlie."

"Charlie?"

"Third cashier, Charlie Simpson. I think he was quite sweet on her, but then Charlie's sweet on anything in a skirt. Quite the ladies' man is our Charlie."

"Well, perhaps you can ask him to come in on your way out."

"Is that it?" Again, the nod — and the spectacles.

"For the time being. I'm only really interested in talking to people who know Sandra."

Phyllis frowned suddenly. "Sorry, I'm sure. If I knew I was wasting your time I wouldn't have bothered to come in to see you."

"No, really. I want to speak with everyone who works here. The slightest piece of information, however minor you consider it, could be a great help to our investigation."

Slightly mollified, the woman got to her feet. "I'll send Charlie in next."

As she bustled out, Myra had a feeling that this was going be a very long morning.

* * *

"Tell us about the motor scooter," Lesser asked.

They were drinking tea at Eunice's kitchen table.

"What do you want to know?"

"Did Sandra make a habit of going home on a motor scooter?"

"Good heavens, no. She was a bus girl, like me. Sometimes we'd travel home together."

"But last night she rode her motor scooter?" Walsh said.

"Perhaps I didn't make myself clear. She took off on the scooter, but she wasn't driving it — is that the correct term? Do you drive a scooter? Anyway she was a passenger, sitting on the back, the pillion I think they call it."

"I see," said Lesser. "Did you see who was driving it?"

"Not really. I'd just come out of the school and was standing in the doorway when I heard the scooter start up. I looked across the road and I saw it pull away with Sandra sitting on the back. I knew it was her because of her rather unusual haircut, but I couldn't really see who was on the front seat, though I got the impression it was a man, and that surprised me because she's never mentioned a boyfriend."

"I'm pretty sure she didn't have one," Lesser said.

"Can you describe the scooter?" Walsh said. "Colour? Make?"

"Make? I really have no idea," Eunice said. "I can't even recognise the makes of cars. As for the colour, that's difficult because of the street lights, but I would guess green or blue."

Walsh made a note on his pad.

"You say you worried all night about her," Lesser said. "Why was that?"

"Because it was *Sandra*. Like I say, we used to travel home on the bus sometimes and we'd chat. She seemed, how shall I put it, a little naïve. Not very worldly-wise for an eighteen-year-old. In many ways she was just a little girl. I sometimes wondered if her desire to look after children, especially babies, was just a childish desire to play with dolls. It's strange, this class I take. It attracts all sorts, from young mums just starting out, to experienced mothers looking for ways to make their lives easier, to girls like Sandra, who treat the care of children as a calling, a vocation if you like."

"Is there anything else that you can tell us about her?" Lesser said.

"Only that I think her desire to go and work abroad was more an idea of escape than anything else."

"An escape from what, exactly?"

Eunice stared at the two policemen over the rim of her cup. "Have you met her parents?"

"Not personally," Lesser said. "But I understand that they are very protective of their daughter."

"Perhaps a little too much," Eunice said. "I haven't met them myself, but from the way Sandra spoke about them, I got the impression that they are very controlling, and hardly allow the girl any life of her own. I know they are very churchy. Good Christian stock."

"And that's a bad thing?" Walsh was a regular churchgoer and a devout Catholic. He was sensitive to any criticism of his faith.

"Not in itself," Eunice said. "Although I've never found the need for faith. Spending time in my garden, tending my plants, I find that Mother Nature is all the sustenance my soul needs. But for a young woman, forced by her parents to live constrained by the Christian belief system . . . I think it would be very suffocating. Thus her desire to go abroad, and get away." Eunice set down her cup with an air of finality.

"And there's nothing more you can add?"

"No, I don't think so. Is Sandra all right?"

"We don't know," said Lesser. "She didn't make it home last night."

"There wasn't an accident, with the scooter?"

"Well, now you've told us about it, it's one of the avenues we'll be pursuing."

Eunice wrung her hands. "Oh, I do hope nothing bad has happened. Sandra is a dear girl, with all her life to live. It would be a tragedy if she were involved in some terrible accident. You hear such awful stories these days."

"Well, let's not get ahead of ourselves," Lesser said. "I'm sure there's some fairly mundane explanation for her not going home last night, and I'm also sure we'll find out what it is."

"I do hope so. If there's anything more I can do, please let me know."

"It's a shame you haven't got an 'imaginary friend' you can pray to," said Walsh, and his sergeant glowered at him.

"Good day, Miss Havelock," said Lesser.

"Keep it buttoned in future, Constable," Lesser said, as they climbed back into the Wolseley.

"What do you mean?"

"You know very well what I mean," Lesser said. "Just because someone doesn't share your beliefs, it doesn't mean you can tell them they're wrong and you're right."

"My faith is very important to me."

"Yes, and I respect that, but just remember for next time we're interviewing a witness to keep it to yourself. It takes all sorts, Trevor."

Walsh started the car in silence. They didn't speak again until they reached the next address on the list.

CHAPTER 13

WEDNESDAY

Charlie Simpson was in his early twenties. He was a sharp dresser; his charcoal-grey suit was immaculately tailored, looking like it must have cost a week's wages. His hair was dark brown and blow-dried into an elaborate quiff. He strolled casually into the room and sat down at the table, tugging at the knees of his trousers. He was evidently a young man who cared about his appearance. Myra hoped he would have more to impart than Phyllis Battle.

"Hello," she said. "WPC Banks."

"Very apt."

"Sorry?"

"Banks — in a bank. Sorry. Charlie Simpson, third cashier."

"What can you tell me about Sandra Duncan?"

"Mouse?"

"I beg your pardon?"

"*Mouse* — Sandra, it's what I call her."

"Doesn't she mind?"

"I think she's just pleased I notice her."

"And she'd be pleased about that, would she?" Myra shuffled the papers in Sandra Duncan's file, trying not to come out with something rude. "How well do you know Sandra?"

"Not very well, but better than most. The other people here, well, they're a close-knit bunch. They don't accept newcomers easily."

"But she's been working here for six months," Myra said.

"And Mouse isn't the easiest person in the world to get along with."

"But you do?"

"I took her for a drink when she first arrived, but it wasn't a great success. She wanted me to take her home at nine. She said her parents would worry if she were out any later." He shrugged his shoulders. "After that I wasn't bothered. I know a lot of girls, and I like to go out with the ones who know how to enjoy themselves."

"Yes, I'm sure you do."

"Hey, I'm always a gentleman."

"You're a real charmer, Charlie, aren't you? Now, getting back to Sandra, do you know if she's got anyone special in her life — a man?"

Simpson laughed. "Mouse? A man? You have to be kidding."

"I understand that a rumour went around the office a little while ago, that Sandra was seeing a man a lot older than herself."

"Rubbish," Simpson said. "I know where that came from — Linda Kramer, one of the typists. She's always making stuff up about people. She likes to stir it, does Linda. She's married to a real bore, and makes up gossip to brighten up her day. She's a sad case, really. Someone should buy her a wooden spoon."

"So there's no truth in it?"

"Mouse, with an older man?" he said scornfully. "No. The only older man in her life is her father. Why do you want to know about her anyway?"

"She's missing. I'm trying to build up a picture of her. What she's like, the people in her life, that sort of thing."

Simpson leaned back in his seat. "Well, you're asking the right person," he said. "As I said, I know her better than most, and believe me, outside of the bank, Sandra doesn't have a life, social or otherwise. She lives like a nun."

"Did you happen to see her last night?"

"What was last night? Oh, Tuesday. Sorry, Tuesday is singles night at the *Palais*. I never miss singles night."

"No. I'm sure you don't." Myra snapped shut her notebook. "Thank you, Mr Simpson. It's been most illuminating. Perhaps you could send the next person in?"

Simpson didn't get up. "Do you go out much? I wouldn't think it's easy for a policewoman to find a date . . . Wednesday nights at the *Palais* are usually good."

"Thank you, Mr Simpson. That will be all."

He stood up and shrugged. "You really don't know what you're missing."

"You know, Mr Simpson, I actually think I do."

* * *

Linda Kramer wore her blonde hair in a short poodle cut. Her horn-rimmed glasses swept up at the sides. She seemed to be going for glamour in her spectacles if nowhere else.

"I've been told that you started the rumour that Sandra was seeing a much older man."

"It was the truth. No word of a lie." Linda appeared to be on edge; she sat perched forward on her chair, hands tightly clenched. "It was Charlie Simpson that told you, wasn't it?"

Myra said nothing.

"He's a fine one to talk. He's always gossiping about people."

"What made you so sure about Sandra?"

"I saw them, in the park, sitting on a bench together. They seemed to know each other very well."

"Did you recognise the man?"

"I know his face — he might have been in the bank a few times — but not his name."

"Can you describe him?"

"About forty something, dark hair, swept back. Very good-looking, a bit like that actor, Ray Milland."

"And what were they doing on the park bench?"

"Arguing."

"How can you be sure?"

"Because he was holding onto the sleeve of her blouse very tightly and he had a face like thunder."

Myra made a note on her pad.

"I don't suppose you happened to hear what they were arguing about?"

Linda shook her poodle cut. "I was too far away," she said. "I'd just bought myself a cup of tea at the pavilion and had taken it to one of the tables. They were over by the tennis courts."

"How long did you watch them for?"

"I wasn't spying on them, you know."

"I'm sure you weren't," she said. "Just one colleague looking out for another."

Linda moved further forward.

"Exactly. That was it exactly. I could see the man was very angry with her, and I didn't know what he was likely to do."

"And how did Sandra seem during this argument?"

"She looked scared."

"Scared?"

"Like he might attack her at any moment. In the end she pulled away from him and stormed off towards the gates. She passed by me but didn't seem to notice me. She was crying."

"And what about the man?"

The poodle cut shook again "I don't know. When I looked back, he'd gone."

"So when you got back to work did you ask Sandra about it, check to see if she was all right?"

"It was none of my business. Besides, Sandra and I aren't friends; we don't talk."

"I see. How long ago did this take place?"

"A week ago last Thursday."

"You're sure about that?"

"Definitely. I always take my lunch to the park on Thursdays, and it wasn't last week, so it must have been the week before."

"Thank you, Linda. You've been very helpful."

For the first time, Linda Kramer seemed to relax. She smiled and sat back in her seat.

"That will be all," Myra said.

"Oh, right."

When Linda had left the room, Myra read through her notes. If Linda was to be believed, Sandra Duncan was not as shy and timid as people had suggested. Arguing with an older man, in a public place, was not the behaviour of a shy, retiring wallflower. Chief Inspector Callum would find this interesting.

* * *

"It's the desk, sir," Brewer said. "Arthur Duncan's here to see you."

"I'll come down." Hopefully this meant Sandra had turned up. Jack could do with some good news.

It wasn't.

He knew it as soon as he saw the fretful face of Arthur Duncan — and the pale blue envelope clutched in his hand.

"How can I help, Mr Duncan?"

"I found this on the front doormat a little while ago." Arthur Duncan held out the envelope.

Jack flattened it out on the desk. The sheet of paper inside was almost identical to the one left at the Blaineys' — a fairly childish drawing of three monkeys.

He kept his face neutral as he said, "Did you see who delivered this?" The envelope bore no address or stamp.

"No," Duncan said. "I heard the letterbox go and thought it might be Sandra coming in. We keep a spare door key hanging from a piece of string by the letterbox, just in case one of us forgets our keys."

Just make it easy for the burglars, thought Jack. People's stupidity astonished him sometimes.

Arthur Duncan was still talking. ". . . but it wasn't. It was just that, lying on the mat." He stared down at the drawing. "What does it mean, Chief Inspector? What are those things? They look like monkeys."

"Three monkeys. We've yet to ascertain their significance, Mr Duncan."

"So you've seen something like them before?"

"Yes." Jack mentally kicked himself for saying too much.

"When?"

"We saw them in relation to another case we're working on."

"This case?"

Duncan took from his pocket a folded copy of the local newspaper, and slammed it down on the desk. The headline screamed up at them: WARREN ANDERTON'S DAUGHTER FOUND DEAD.

Damn!

CHAPTER 14

WEDNESDAY

It had not been easy to calm Arthur Duncan, but eventually Jack convinced him he should go home and be with his wife in case Sandra came back. All he could do now was wait for the reports to come in from his team. That sketch confirmed his worst fear.

Fuller and Grant returned from the County School with little to add to the puzzle. The headmistress remembered Sandra Duncan, but only vaguely, and none of the teachers were able to add much more. Of the girls who had shared classes with her, only one of them offered any concrete information about her, in the form of a few bitchy remarks about Sandra's plainness and lack of personality. "When Sandra entered the room it was like someone had just left it," was Barbara Dawson's only contribution of note.

"She just didn't make an impression on anybody," Fuller said.

"The invisible girl," Harry Grant added. "Sad, really."

"Even more so when you consider that this was left on the Duncan's doormat this morning." Jack showed them the drawing.

"You're thinking we're too late," said Fuller. "Like Frances."

"That was my first thought when I saw it," Jack said.

A gloomy silence settled over the room. It lifted only slightly when Myra came back from the bank.

"We need some good news, Myra," Jack said, chewing the end of a pencil.

"Well, I don't know about *good* news, but I've found out a bit more about her."

"And that would be?"

"A couple of weeks ago Sandra was spotted in the park, having an altercation with a man."

"A man? That contradicts everything we've learned so far. Tell me more."

Myra gave a precise account of the Linda Kramer interview.

"That's the best description she can give? Dark-haired? Good-looking?"

"She says he looked like Ray Milland."

"Oh, that's all right then. We'll go and arrest *him*. I'm not sure his Hollywood career is going too well at the moment, anyway." Jack threw his pencil at the wall. "Why can't people be more bloody observant?"

"I'm sorry, sir."

"No, Myra. It's not your fault. I apologise for my outburst. You did good work. At least it's moved the investigation forward. Could any other members of staff corroborate Miss Kramer's story?"

"*Mrs* Kramer. And no. Most of them thought she was making the whole thing up. She has a reputation as a gossip-monger."

"So this could just be tittle-tattle?"

"I don't think so. I think I'm pretty good at reading people, and I didn't get the feeling she was lying."

Jack leaned back in his chair and thought for a moment. He trusted Myra. He had learned from experience that a good copper's instincts were often more valuable than some evidence. "Okay," he said. "We'll start trying to track down *Ray Milland*."

"I asked the people at the bank if they recognised the description but no one was forthcoming," Myra said.

"Then go to the park and check with the owner of the pavilion. Take Sandra's picture with you, and see if he saw her and this dark-haired man together. If he has, he might have some idea who he is, or at least provide us with a better description of him."

"Bit of a long shot, don't you think, sir?" Fuller said.

"Yes, Eddie, I do, but long shots are all we have right now, and sometimes they pay off."

* * *

It was after four when Lesser and Walsh returned from their interviews with the evening-class students.

"A motor scooter?" It seemed the more they discovered about Sandra Duncan, the less Jack and everyone else knew about her. "They say it's always the quiet ones," he mused. "How reliable a witness is Miss Havelock?"

"She's very level-headed," Lesser said.

"Can she describe the driver?"

"She was too far away to see clearly."

"But she's sure it was Sandra she saw on the back of it."

"Oh yes, she's certain about that, and she thinks the scooter was either blue or green."

"Well, that's something, I suppose, but without a description of the driver, it doesn't exactly move us forward. No, our best lead is the man Sandra was arguing with in the park. We need a name for him, and what Sandra's relationship to him was. Let's see if Myra has any luck."

* * *

"I'm just closing up," said the man behind the counter.

"Brian Porter?" asked Myra.

"That's right."

"And you own the pavilion?"

"For my sins." Porter was a reed of a man with angular cheekbones and a protruding Adam's apple.

"Do you recognise this girl?" Myra held out Sandra's photo.

Porter took the picture from her and held it at arm's length. "I've seen her in here once or twice," he said. "Why? What's she done?"

Myra ignored the question. "Was she in here a week ago last Thursday?"

He closed his eyes and was silent for a moment. "That was the day I took my dog to the vet. We had to close early."

"But she did come in that day?"

"Oh yes. I thought it odd because she usually came in on Tuesdays. I suppose it was because she was meeting Tim, so she changed her usual day."

"Tim?"

"Tim Fellowes, captain of our bowls team."

"I see."

"They shared a pot of tea out there on the veranda." He pointed to a covered terrace that ran across the front of the pavilion. "It didn't look like it was a happy meeting."

"In what way?"

"They appeared to be arguing."

"Have you any idea what they were arguing about?"

Porter snorted. "Are you suggesting I eavesdrop on my patron's conversations?"

"No, not at all. But arguments? Raised voices? Sound travels."

"Well, it didn't travel to these ears," he said. "But it went on for a while. They finished their tea and took the argument down to the bench by the tennis courts."

"Do you know how long it went on?"

"I couldn't say. It was lunchtime. It gets a bit frantic in August. A lot of people from the offices and shops come in on their lunch breaks."

"Do you know Tim Fellowes well?"

"I was a member of the bowls team for a short while in fifty-five, but I wasn't really good enough, so I stood aside to let a more competent player take my place. Know your strengths, but be aware of your weaknesses, and I was very aware of mine."

"Can you describe him?"

"An excellent bowls player and a superb captain. A master tactician."

"Physically?"

Porter smiled. "I can do better than that." He went across to a framed photograph hanging on the wall and took it down.

"Here you are."

A small brass plaque affixed to the frame bore the legend, *Winner of the All Herts Lawn Bowls Cup. 1957.*

"We won that last year, mind. I wasn't playing then so I'm not in the photograph."

"But Tim Fellowes is?"

Porter leaned over and pointed to a tall, good-looking man standing in the centre of a motley group of what looked like pensioners, all in white flannels. "That's Tim. Our leading light."

Myra studied the photograph. Tim Fellowes did bear a striking resemblance to Ray Milland.

"Do you know where I can contact him?"

"I don't know where he lives, if that's what you mean, but he has an office in town. *Povey and Fellowes.* They're solicitors."

"I've heard of them. They're in the High Street, aren't they?"

"That's right, although you won't catch him there now." Porter looked up at the clock on the wall. It said five past five.

"May I take this photograph?"

Porter looked doubtful.

"We'll let you have it back."

"I'll need a receipt."

"Of course."

* * *

"We have a name and a photograph for our friend in the park," said Myra on her return.

"Really?" Jack said. "Good work, Myra."

"His name is Tim Fellowes. He's—"

"The solicitor?" Eddie Fuller said.

"Yes. Do you know him?"

"Only by reputation. A real slippery one is our Tim."

"Yes, I know him, and you're right, Sergeant. He is a bit of a smooth customer. What on earth would he be doing, arguing in public with Sandra Duncan? I would have put them in totally different worlds."

"Excuse me, sir." Andy Brewer appeared at Jack's elbow.

"What is it, Andy?"

"A body's been discovered, sir. A young woman. Down on the golf course, in one of the bunkers."

"Bloody hell!" Jack muttered. "Come on, let's get down there."

"All of us, sir?" said Lesser.

"Yes, Frank. Unless you think that wrestling "Judo" Al Hayes at the Edmonton Granada is more important than the murder of a young girl?"

Frank Lesser looked somewhat pale. He turned to Walsh. "How the hell did he know that?" he whispered.

"Who knows?" Walsh whispered back. "But he didn't get it from me. Come on."

* * *

Two gleaming black Wolseleys, bells ringing, tore through the gates of the golf club and pulled up outside the clubhouse, drawing curious stares from the half dozen or so golfers milling around their vehicles in the gravelled car park.

A grey-haired man in corduroy work trousers and a tatty tweed jacket emerged from the clubhouse. He seemed to have been waiting for them.

"Arnold Masson, Head Greenkeeper," he said, as Jack approached.

"Were you the one who found the body?"

"Nah, that was Wilf, one of my lads."

"And where is Wilf now?"

"He was taken poorly. Shock, probably. So I sent him home."

"I'll need to speak to him. Please give my sergeant here his address before we leave. Now, can you take me to see the body?"

"This has properly shaken me up," said Masson, as he led them across the links. "I've worked here for over forty years and I've never had anything like this happen."

They reached the second tee and Masson came to a halt. "It's in that bunker. I'll stay here if you don't mind. I've seen enough for one day."

Barry Fenwick, doctor's bag in hand, trotted across the grass towards them.

"Another one, Jack?"

"Looks like it." Jack stopped Fenwick before he climbed down into the bunker. "Wait a second, Barry. Tell me what you see."

"I see a dead girl, lying in a sand trap. What—?"

"Look at the sand."

"There's nothing to see."

"Exactly. Where are the footprints?"

"I don't see any."

"There aren't any. Whoever dumped her here was careful not to leave any."

"Well, I'm afraid I can't be so careful. I have a job to do." Fenwick dropped down into the bunker.

"He could have stood on the grass and rolled her down the slope," Lesser said.

Jack shook his head. "Look at the way she's lying. On her back, arms crossed on her chest. She's been arranged like that. Almost posed. We need to talk to the boy who made the discovery, and see if he interfered with the scene at all."

"He lives in Wilshaw Road, just the other side of the course," Fuller said. "I can go and see him now."

"Yes. Do that. I'll meet you back at the station." Jack climbed down into the bunker and crouched beside Fenwick. "Initial thoughts, Barry?"

There was a flash as Walsh photographed the scene.

"Get one showing how the body was arranged," Jack said. He and Fenwick stood back.

"My initial thoughts are that whoever killed Frances Anderton was also responsible for the murder of this girl. Ligature marks on the wrists and on the throat. Eyes and mouth crudely sewn shut and wax poured into the ears."

"That's what I was afraid of."

CHAPTER 15

WEDNESDAY

"Adam, it's me."

"Fiona? Why are you phoning me at work? We had an agreement," said Adam Channing.

"Yes, well, things have changed. Frances has been killed. Murdered."

"Good God! Are *you* all right?"

"Yes, no . . . I don't know. The thing is, the police have been here and they know about you, about us."

Silence.

"Adam? Adam?"

"When did it happen?" he said at last.

"They think it was some time on Sunday. The thing is, Adam, I think they're going to want to question you."

"They have me down as a suspect?"

"They're going to want to question everyone who knew her."

"But I didn't know her."

"But you *did* meet her, at the end-of-term party."

"That was months ago and — sorry to say this about your sister, Fiona, but she hardly registered."

"Yes, I can understand that. Nevertheless . . ."

"Did you give them my address?"

"No, but they know you're a lecturer at the LSE."

"Well, that's something. At least I won't have PC Plod turning up at the house, upsetting Gwen."

"Is that your only concern? Adam?"

Silence again.

"What other concern would I have?"

"Well, being a suspect in a murder case for one thing."

"You say she was killed on Sunday?"

"That's right."

"Well, on Saturday, Sunday and Monday I was up at Falkirk in Scotland at a conference. Gwen's sister came down to stay with her while I was away. So as long as they come to the college to interview me, I can't see it presenting much of a problem, can you?"

Fiona let out her breath in a thin stream, unaware until then that she'd been holding it. She lit a cigarette and noticed that her hand was shaking.

"I need to see you."

"Of course," he said easily. "I want to see you too."

"No, Adam, I *need* to see you." Tears ran down her cheeks. It was such a relief to hear that Adam had an alibi. She hadn't really believed he had anything to do with her sister's murder, but Chief Inspector Callum had set the wheels of doubt whirring in her mind.

"Can we meet?"

"I have a lecture to prepare tonight."

"Please, Adam." She knew she sounded desperate, and she hated herself for it.

"Okay, but not until the weekend. Saturday evening. Our usual place. Eight o'clock?"

"Thank you. Adam, I'm sorry, but I feel so useless. It's the shock I expect."

"Yes, of course. There's no need to apologise. I understand. It must be awful for you and your parents. Your poor sister."

The line went dead. She hung up the phone and went into the morning room.

Her mother was lying stretched out on the chesterfield, a damp cloth across her eyes. "Who were you on the phone to?"

"No one . . . er, just a friend."

"Why isn't your father in yet? How he could just go to work, as if nothing has happened."

"It's probably for the best, keeping occupied. I'm sure he'll be home soon."

Jessica removed the cloth. Her eyes were red and sore from constant crying. She sat up, wringing the cloth in her hands, ignoring the water dripping onto the shagpile. "Frances has gone, Fiona."

Fiona sat down next to her mother and put an arm round her shoulders.

"Someone's taken our baby from us." Jessica began to sob.

Fiona pulled her close. *Yes*, she thought. *But at least that someone wasn't my Adam.*

* * *

The house on Wilshaw Road was a neat two-up two-down in the middle of a terrace of identical houses. It nestled in the centre of an estate of new-builds. These characterless estates were slowly killing any charm this part of Hatfield may once have had.

Eddie Fuller rang the doorbell and waited. Finally the door was opened by a grey-haired man in his late sixties or early seventies. He was wearing a beige cardigan and baggy jeans, patched at the knees.

"Hello. I was looking for your son."

"I haven't got a son."

"Wilf?"

"Yeah, that's me."

"Sorry," Fuller said. "Arnold Masson said you were one of his lads."

"That's right. He calls all of us his *lads*."

"I was expecting someone younger."

"Obviously. Are you here about the body?"

Fuller nodded.

"Then you'd better come in."

* * *

Adam Channing leaned back in his office chair and tapped a pencil against his teeth. Fiona's call was not unexpected; he was merely surprised she had waited until Wednesday. He picked up the telephone receiver and dialled.

"Hello?"

"I've been told to expect a visit from the police concerning the Anderton girl."

"Are you surprised, Adam? You sound surprised. Surely, this is what we were expecting."

"No, I'm not surprised."

"Then you know what to say. Your trip to Scotland will prove very fortuitous."

"Yes, I know."

"Then stay calm. It should play out just as we planned."

"I *am* being calm. I'm just bringing you up to date."

"Have you called Tim yet?"

"No. He's still in Zurich."

"Ah yes, until tomorrow. Well, there's no point wasting a long-distance call to tell him something we were expecting anyway. I'll telephone him when he gets back to his office tomorrow and let him know. No doubt he'll be getting a visit from them too — about the Duncan girl. He made sure he was seen talking to her."

"Do you think it's going well?"

"Like clockwork." The line went dead.

Channing put the phone down.

Like clockwork . . . The bastard.

* * *

Rosie Callum piled the last of the loaves onto a wooden tray, and picked up another to load the cakes. There was a tap at the window and she looked into the smiling face of a young man with short, curly hair. "Are you closed?" he mouthed at her.

Rosie shook her head and pointed to the door. A few seconds later the bell jangled and he pushed his way inside.

"I thought I was too late. Do you have any sausage rolls?"

"I have a couple left. Are they for your tea?" She mentally kicked herself for asking such an inane question. He would think she was a bit dim, and that was the last thing she wanted. The young man was one of her regular customers. She knew his name was David and that he worked at the insurance offices along the street, but that was all she knew about him. Except that he had kind brown eyes and a slightly lopsided smile that made her knees go weak.

"I'll take them, then." He watched her as she put the sausage rolls into a paper bag, flipped it over and deftly twisted the corners.

"You did that like an expert."

"Years of practice."

"You don't look old enough to have years of practice."

"You'd be surprised. I'm sixteen, you know. That will be a shilling."

He pulled a handful of change from his pocket and sorted through it, finding two sixpenny bits. He handed them to her and she gave him the bag. "Anything else I can do for you?"

"Do you like films?"

"What kind of films?"

"The kind you watch at the cinema."

"Yes. I do like films, and I like the cinema, though I don't go that often."

"Would you like to go — with me? *High Society* is playing at the Metropole. Frank Sinatra and Grace Kelly. It's a musical."

"I like musicals."

"So, will you come? Please say yes, because I really want to see it, and I hate going to the pictures by myself."

She knew she was blushing. "When did you think of going?" "How about tonight? There's a show at eight thirty. I could pick you up and we could drive into town."

"You have a car?" It was unusual for someone his age to own a car.

"It's my dad's, but he lets me use it on special occasions."

"And taking me to the pictures is a special occasion?"

"Oh yes, very special."

The blush deepened. She thought she probably looked as red as the cherries on the iced buns.

"Well, as it's a special occasion, I'd better say yes."

"I was hoping you would. My name's David by the way. David Neville. My friends call me Davy."

"Rose Callum. Rosie."

"Well then, Rosie, I'll pick you up at seven thirty. Where do you live?"

She told him.

"I know where it is. Until tonight then."

"Until tonight."

She waited until he had left the shop and then went to the door and locked it, flipping the sign from OPEN to CLOSED.

"Have you locked up?" called a voice from the back of the shop.

"I've just done it." Rosie stuck her head around the door of the back room. Mrs Painter, the owner of the bakery, was sitting at the staff table, intent on the *Daily Mirror* crossword, a cup of coffee at her elbow.

She looked up at Rosie. "You'd best be off, then. Make yourself look beautiful for tonight."

"You heard?"

"He seems like a nice enough lad."

"I'm sorry. I didn't mean to . . ."

Mrs Painter looked at her over her half-rimmed reading glasses and adjusted her ample bosom, which strained against the white nylon of her overall. "We were all young once, Rosie. Even me."

* * *

"Can you drop me off at home?" Jack said to Walsh, who was driving. The mood in the car was sombre. No one felt much like talking.

The last thing Fenwick had said hung over the car like a dark cloud: "It looks like she's been interfered with."

At his house Jack climbed wearily out of the Wolseley. "We'll pick this up tomorrow. I've had enough for today."

As he trudged up the path, Rosie breezed in through the gate. She ran up to him and kissed his cheek. "Hello, Dad!"

"Hello, yourself. You look cheerful. Had a good day?"

"The best."

As soon as they entered the house a harsh chemical smell assailed them. Then Jack saw Annie's friend, Avril, and understood. Hairdressers used all manner of concoctions these days. Avril was in the hallway, shrugging herself into a tangerine duster coat.

"Are you off?"

"Mission completed, Mr Callum. My work here is finished." Avril gave a mock salute.

"They're in the kitchen. Go and take a look."

Jack squeezed past her and walked into the kitchen. Annie was sitting at the kitchen table, sharing a pot of tea with a young woman with dark cropped hair. Jack stared at her for a full thirty seconds before he realised he was looking at his eldest daughter.

"Joanie?"

"Yes, Dad, it's me. Do you like it?"

"Very Audrey Hepburn. Did you mean to go that short?"

"According to Avril all the peroxide had damaged her hair permanently . . ." Annie said.

"So I decided to go for broke and got her to chop it all off and colour it," Joan finished for her. "Do you approve?"

"Is there any more tea in that pot?"

"I'll get you a mug," Annie said.

"Well? I'm waiting."

Jack smiled. "It looks lovely. Very . . . fetching."

"Fetching?"

"Very attractive. It suits you. More than the blonde did, anyway."

"When did Dad become such an old fuddy-duddy, Mum?"

"He's your father, Joanie. He's always been that way."

"Well, I think it looks gorgeous," Rosie said, as she entered the kitchen. "I've been thinking about getting mine cut."

"Ooh, Rosie, you should. It would really suit you with those cheekbones of yours."

"Steady, Joanie," Jack said. "I haven't got used to your haircut yet, without you organising a mass shearing in my house."

"Tell him, Mum; it's nineteen fifty-eight. Lots of girls are wearing their hair like this these days."

"Leave me out of this," said Annie.

"Very wise," said her husband.

"But then," Annie said to her eldest, "seeing yours might persuade me to do something different with mine."

Jack raised his eyes. "You see, Joanie. Back no more than forty eight hours and already you're starting a revolution."

"Liver for dinner," Annie said. "Why don't you go and clean up, Jack, and we can all sit down to a civilised meal?"

"Amen to that," Jack said.

"Can I use the bathroom first, Dad? Only I'm going to the cinema tonight and I need to get myself ready. I'm being picked up at half past seven."

"Picked up?" Joan said. "You've got a date?"

Rosie said nothing and blushed furiously.

"You *have* got a date!" Joan ran and grabbed Rosie's arm, propelling her out through the door. "Come with me, little sis. I'll help you with your make-up."

They clattered up the stairs to the bathroom.

"I think I'll take my tea and go and listen to the radio in the living room."

"Sorry," said Annie. "Eric's in there doing his homework. Stay here with me and tell me about your day."

Jack looked at her and gave a brief shake of his head.

"Was it that bad?"

"Worse."

Annie moved away from the sink and came up behind him, wrapping her arms around his waist. "I'm sorry you've come back to a madhouse. I didn't think Avril would take as long as she did."

"It doesn't matter. She did a fine job. And I don't mind."

"You don't mind what?"

"If you want to cut your hair. I won't mind."

"You're being serious."

"It's not important. It's only hair. It will grow back."

Annie sat down beside him and took his hand.

"You *have* had a bad day haven't you?"

"It was pretty grim. We found another dead girl. Dumped on the golf course this time."

Annie's grip tightened. "Oh no, Jack."

CHAPTER 16

WEDNESDAY

A while later Joan came downstairs. She found Jack and Annie in the living room.

"What do you think of your youngest daughter now?" She pulled Rosie into the room behind her, as if presenting her at court.

Rosie was wearing make-up — too much, Jack thought — and her hair had been styled into a sophisticated side sweep.

"You're not going out like that," Jack said flatly.

"Jack?" Annie said.

"Dad!" chorused the girls.

"Go back upstairs, Rosie, wipe that stuff of your face and put on something more suitable. You're sixteen, not twenty-six."

Annie got to her feet. "Jack, I really don't think it's necessary—"

"Annie," Jack said severely. "There's a monster out there killing girls of Rosie's age, and you're prepared to let her go out of this house dressed like a tart."

Rosie burst into tears and ran from the room. Annie looked at her husband incredulously. "Jack, how could you?"

"I could because I care about our daughter's safety."

"You're overreacting."

"Maybe I am. But I'm still not allowing Rosie to go out."

"But she's so excited, Jack. I think it's the boy she's been mooning over for weeks."

"I don't care. She stays in tonight, and every night until we catch him."

Annie glared at him and then stormed out of the room, up the stairs after her daughter.

Jack sat, arms folded, staring into the empty grate.

"My running away taught you nothing, did it?" said Joan.

"It taught me that I have to keep my family safe."

"So what do you want to do? Wrap us all in cotton wool until you've slain all the monsters? Well, for your information, Dad, there will always be monsters out there — believe me, I know. I've met plenty. But you can't protect us from them all, no matter how much you want to. Rosie's growing up, and treating her like a precious piece of Dresden china is not going to help her grow into a proper woman."

"Like you, you mean?"

Joan came across and sat at his feet. "I made mistakes, Dad, and I admit it. But you can't keep Rosie locked up and then be surprised if she does the same as me."

"But this boy who's taking her to the pictures, we know nothing about him. For all I know he could be Jack the Ripper."

"And he could be a perfectly respectable young man who sees your daughter for the beautiful and intelligent young woman she is. If you carry on like this, you'll end up driving her away. The time I went away was the worst of my whole life."

"Mine too."

"Well, I don't want that for you, or for Rosie. Meet this boy — Rosie tells me his name's David, and he works for an insurance company in town — meet him and find out what he's like. You assess people all the time — it's your job. If you think he's not on the level, then keep her home and I'll back you up, but if not, let her go out tonight. Give her the chance to be the young lady she so wants to be."

Jack sat back in his chair and closed his eyes. "Daughters. Who'd have them? Eric never gives me these problems."

"Give him time, Dad."

Jack reached out and stroked her hair. "And when did you acquire such great wisdom?"

"It's the way you and Mum brought me up," Joan said.

"I suppose I should go and apologise."

"It wouldn't do any harm."

"Sometimes I can be a bloody fool," he said.

"It's why we love you."

* * *

Jack knocked on Rosie's door. Annie opened it and glared at him. "May I speak with her?"

"Not if you're still being pig-headed and rude."

"It's all right, Mum!" called out Joan. "Let him talk to her."

Annie looked at her eldest daughter uncertainly. Joan gave a small nod and Annie stepped out onto the landing, leaving the doorway clear. Jack walked into the room and closed the door behind him.

On the bed, Rosie sat with her knees drawn up to her chin, mascara streaking her cheeks.

"May I sit down?"

Rosie sniffed tearfully and gave a slight shrug of her shoulders. Jack sat down on the bed.

"Your mum was right," he said. "I was overreacting."

Rosie remained silent and waited for him to continue.

"In my job I see all manner of terrible things. I did today, and the day before yesterday, and these things terrify me. For all my experience dealing with this kind of thing, handling the tragedy and loss, nothing prepares you or makes you immune from the fear that one day these things could happen to your own family. Does that make sense?"

Rosie nodded and sniffed again.

"I'd like to meet this boy before he takes you out."

A small spark of hope glimmered in Rosie's eyes. "I can invite him in tonight before we go, so you and Mum can meet him."

"Do you think we'll pass muster?"

"Mum will. You, I'm not so sure of," she said, with a wan smile.

"Am I that much of a dragon?"

"You're pretty scary. But I think David will like you."

"So that's his name? David?"

"David Neville. He sells insurance."

"Well, that's a respectable occupation."

"And he's taking me to the cinema in his dad's car."

"So his father obviously trusts him."

"Oh, Dad, you'll really like him. He has the kindest eyes."

Jack stood up and walked to the door. "Am I forgiven?"

Rosie gave a rueful smile and nodded.

"Then you'd better repair your make-up before he arrives. You look like a panda. I'll send Joanie in. She can help you fix it."

Joan was standing outside the door. "I think she needs help with her make-up," he said, holding the door open for her.

Joan pecked him on the cheek. "As fathers go, you're not so bad really."

"As daughters go, you're not so bad yourself," he said, and watched as she went across to the bed and hugged her sister. Then he turned and walked slowly down the stairs, ready to fix things with Annie.

* * *

Jack watched through the window as David Neville parked a Ford Anglia outside the Callums' house and walked up the path to the front door. He rang the doorbell and waited.

It was his wife who answered the door, but only because she moved more swiftly from her own vantage point behind the net curtains.

"Hello," she said. "You must be David. I'm Rose's mother. She'll be down in a minute. Please come in."

She opened the door wide, and stood aside for the young man to enter.

"We're in here," she said.

Neville followed her into the living room where Jack was waiting, with Joanie and Eric in attendance. Jack was in civvies, wearing a dark red sweater over a shirt and tie. He was deliberately standing by the fireplace, leaning casually against a wooden mantelpiece adorned with framed photographs, showing this was a family, and he was the head of it.

He stepped forward and stuck out his hand. "Jack Callum," he said. "I'm Rose's father."

"David Neville." Jack could tell that Neville was rather pleased with his own firm handshake. Jack's father had always insisted on the importance of first impressions. 'You can tell a lot about a man from the way he shakes your hand.' Thanks, Dad. It seemed quite a few father's passed on that piece of sound advice.

"So, David, how did you meet my daughter?"

Jack wanted this young man to know that Rosie's father was no fool. He was obviously weighing him up and making no pretence otherwise.

"We met at the baker's," David Neville said. "I buy my lunch there."

"And what film are you taking my daughter to see?"

"High Society, sir."

"Ah, Bing Crosby — a real singer."

"And Louis Armstrong."

"Indeed. Have you seen it before?"

Neville shook his head. "It's the first time they've shown it at the Metropole."

"Well, I'm sure you'll enjoy it. When did you pass your driving test?"

"Two years ago, sir."

"Two years? How old are you?"

"Nineteen."

"Jack," Annie said. "Stop interrogating the poor boy." She turned to Neville. "You'll have to forgive my husband, David. Sometimes he forgets he's not at work."

"At work?"

"My husband's a policeman."

Jack watched the boy swallow. He could see his Adam's apple bob. "Is that a problem for you, David?"

"No, not at all, sir. My dad was in the police too, when he was in the army. Military police, of course."

"He was a Red Cap, then."

"And never lets me forget it."

"The Red Caps do a difficult job. I know; I'm ex-army myself."

There was a silence as the living-room door opened and Rosie stood in the doorway. "I'm ready," she said.

Like a fish escaping the hook, Neville hurried to the door. "Rosie! You look . . . radiant," he said. Jack almost smiled.

Rosie flushed. "Thank you," she said diffidently. "You look very nice too."

"Well, go on, get along with you!" Annie clapped her hands and shooed them to the door. "You don't want to miss the start of the film."

"We'll be all right, Mum. There's Pathé News and Pearl and Dean first."

"And what's coming next week," Neville added.

"Then you won't have to break any speed limits to get there, will you?"

"No, sir."

"Back no later than eleven. Rosie has work tomorrow," Jack said.

The front door closed and a car engine coughed into life. "You probably scared the life out of the poor boy," said Annie.

"I was waiting for the questions on the Highway Code," Eric said. "That would have been fun."

"Was I really that bad?" Jack said.

"As inquisitions go, I think he got off pretty lightly," Joan said.

Jack smiled darkly, went across to the radiogram and switched it on.

"And you won't come to bed until Rosie is safely tucked up in hers, will you?" Annie said.

"Not a chance," Jack said, and settled himself to listen to the news.

* * *

The harsh ringing of the doorbell broke into Alberto Semprini's piano. Jack looked up at the clock: 10.55. Jack went to let his daughter in.

Rosie was standing on the doorstep, facing the street. She waved as the Ford Anglia pulled away.

"Did you have a nice evening?" Jack said.

Rosie turned and came inside. "Wonderful! It was so romantic. And Grace Kelly is *so* beautiful."

"Are you seeing him again?"

"I think so. He's going to come into the baker's tomorrow." At the bottom of the stairs Rosie paused. "Did you like him, Dad?"

"Your mum does, and Joan. Eric is still deciding."

"But did *you* like him?"

"I think he seems like a nice lad."

"But you don't think he's good enough for me."

"I didn't say that."

"You didn't have to. It's in your voice."

Jack wrapped his arms around his daughter and pulled her close. "Listen, princess. No boy you bring home will ever be good enough for you, but all fathers think that. It's my role in life to disapprove."

"But that's so unfair!"

"That doesn't mean I'm always going to be right, though. I said I think David is a nice enough lad. Okay? Be satisfied with that for now."

Rosie looked at him sternly. "For now. But once you get to know him better, you'll approve of him."

"I wait to be convinced. Now, off to bed with you. It's late. You have work tomorrow."

"Night, Dad!" And Rosie trotted up the stairs, humming to herself.

Jack recognised the tune. He'd taken Annie up to London to see *High Society* when it first opened in the West End, and on the train back home, both of them had been humming the same tune. He could still picture the scene. There was Bing Crosby reclining in an open boat, pretending to play the concertina while Grace Kelly lay with her head in his lap. Their duet was called *True Love.*

CHAPTER 17

THURSDAY AUGUST 14th 1958

The hog-bristle brush inscribed a long gash of vermillion down the canvas. Gavin Southland stepped back to admire his work.

"It's probably one of your best yet," said a voice behind him.

Southland slowly turned away from the easel. Tim Fellowes stood in the doorway of the studio, staring at the painting, a look of mild distaste on his face.

"I'm reasonably satisfied, though I'm not sure I got the hair colour right. I think the girl's hair was more ginger, difficult to capture. Have you just got back?"

"My flight landed two hours ago. I came straight here."

"Have you eaten? I can make breakfast for you."

"I ate at the airport. I thought the airport wouldn't do much to damage a cup of tea and toast, though they tried. Did you have any problems with Sandra?"

"I've already started the preliminary sketches."

"I wasn't talking about your painting. I was referring to the disposal."

"Ah, that. I'm assured it went well. She was found on the golf course yesterday." Southland smiled. "In a sand trap."

"Risky. He might have been seen."

"You worry too much, Tim. He was very careful. He stole one of the golf carts from the clubhouse to carry her across the course and set her down just so, as per my instructions, and returned the cart before it was missed."

Fellowes stared at his old university friend. He was becoming increasingly disturbed by something reckless he saw in Southland. "You took a chance," he said.

"Art cannot progress unless you're willing to take chances," Southland said. He turned back to the canvas and picked up his brush. "I'm really not happy with this colour."

Fellowes went across to a cabinet in the corner of the studio and poured a small measure of whisky into a cut-glass tumbler from a crystal decanter. "The golf course? Really?"

"Picture it, Tim. The young virgin lying there, serene, on a background of pure golden sand. Quite Pre-Raphaelite, don't you think? I told him to be careful not to leave any marks in the sand. It had to be perfect."

Fellowes walked back to the door. "I'd better get on," he said. "I just wanted to make sure there were no hitches."

Southland limped to the door and rested his hand on Fellowes' shoulder. "It's all going exactly as I expected, Tim. All we have to do is to keep our nerve and stick to our plan. The police will be chasing their tails for weeks."

"Well, that's the idea, isn't it?" Fellowes said. "If you need me I'll be in the office for the rest of the day."

He drove into town, his mind turning over the possibilities. He needed a way out of this, but how? He'd have to talk to Adam Channing. He knew Channing felt as he did, but Gavin Southland had made it clear that they would have to abide by the rules of this game he was playing. If not, the consequences for the two men would be devastating. He wished he had never met Gavin Southland. But it was too late.

* * *

"How did you get on yesterday?" Jack and Fuller were seated in Jack's office.

Fuller smiled. "Masson's idea of a 'lad' needs redefining."

"Not a youngster then?"

"Wilfred Ellis is older than Masson himself."

"Did he see anything?"

"Apart from a golf cart trundling across the links, sometime yesterday afternoon, not a lot."

"I was wondering how they would have transported a body across the course without being seen carrying it."

"But he'd be taking a hell of a risk of being seen."

"Who would take notice of a golf cart on the links? Most golfers are too wrapped up in their own game to worry about what other players are doing."

"He's getting bold," Fuller said.

"Bold — or reckless. I don't suppose Ellis saw who was driving it?"

"He didn't notice."

"No, of course not. We couldn't be *that* lucky. We'll have to check out the course and see who was scheduled to play that day. They might have seen something."

"Do you want me to go?"

"Yes, and take Myra with you. She did good work yesterday."

"You like her, don't you?"

"I think she has the makings of a damned fine detective. She's tenacious, and has the ability to think on her feet. We could do with more like her on the team."

There was a tap on the door and Brewer walked into the office. He handed Jack a manila envelope. "This just came in from the lab. It's the forensic report on Frances Anderton."

"Thanks, Andy." Jack tore open the flap, took out a sheaf of paper and started reading. "Her eyes and lips were sewn with black silk embroidery thread."

"Significant?" Fuller got to his feet.

"It might be. Why use silk thread when polyester or cotton would do the job just as well?"

Fuller shrugged. "Search me."

"I'll go into town and have a chat with Tim Fellowes after I've broken the news to the Duncans. His secretary said she was expecting him to be in the office by about ten."

* * *

Tim Fellowes walked into the office and hung his fedora on the hat stand. His secretary, Doris Worthington, came out from behind her desk. "Hello, Tim. The old man's been asking for you."

Fellowes frowned. Cyril Povey was fast turning into the bane of his life. When Povey had offered him a junior partnership, Fellowes had been somewhat reluctant to accept. He'd enjoyed working for himself — he liked the freedom and autonomy — but rising taxes and the increasing cost of renting an office in the centre of town, had made it impossible to continue. Povey's offer had bailed him out of an increasingly sticky financial situation.

But the old man wasn't being charitable. He knew that taking on a junior partner enabled him to offload the bread-and-butter work: conveyancing, petty lawsuits and minor criminal cases, leaving him free to pick up the high-end, more lucrative side of the business. It also gave him more time to spend on the golf course.

"Come in!"

Fellowes pushed open the door to Povey's office.

"Ah, Tim, you're back. Did you have a good trip?"

The antique walnut-veneered desk almost hid Cyril Povey's wizened frame. Peering over rimless, half-moon spectacles, the old man looked like some kind of grey burrowing creature unaccustomed to sunlight.

"Not too bad. I got all the contracts signed as agreed," Fellowes said.

"I still don't know why you had to fly off to Switzerland just to get a couple of signatures, when the whole transaction could have been handled just as well by post."

"Lassiter was delighted to be able to talk through some of the clauses. Besides, I paid for the trip out of my own pocket, so it cost the firm no more than the price of two days' work. I can soon make that up."

Povey looked at him steadily for some time and then shrugged. "I suppose so. In my day it wasn't so easy to hop on a plane and fly off to exotic places."

"I would hardly describe Switzerland as exotic. In fact Lassiter's chalet is quite modest. Its most ostentatious aspect is the view over the lake, and you can get that up in Cumbria."

"It makes you wonder why he chooses to live out there."

"Alfred Lassiter likes the tax laws more than the view. A man in his position . . ."

Povey snorted. "Position! I knew Freddie Lassiter when he was running around the streets with the backside hanging out of his trousers and his brother's cast-off shoes on his feet. He made his fortune when he married Virginia Allsop, and only then because her father died and his entire estate went to her. Grant Allsop was a very shrewd businessman, and as rich as Croesus."

"You sound bitter."

"Probably because I am. Ginny Allsop was the love of my life. We were engaged until Lassiter made his move on her. She was dazzled by his good looks and easy way with the ladies. He made this provincial solicitor look very ordinary indeed."

"At least you kept him as a client. His business brought in two thousand pounds last year alone."

Povey looked bleak. "What price a broken heart, eh, Tim?"

"She's not exactly girlishly slim now, if that's any consolation to you; she's fat with varicose veins."

Povey looked past Fellowes over to the mantelpiece above a small fireplace in the corner of the room. In the centre sat a silver-framed photograph of a young woman with a porcelain-smooth face and vibrant eyes beneath a mop of unruly curls.

The intercom buzzed.

"What is it, Doris?"

Doris's voice crackled through the speaker. "Is Tim in there with you?"

"Yes, he is."

"Then can you tell him he has a visitor?"

"Does his visitor have a name, Doris?"

"It's Detective Chief Inspector Callum from Welwyn and Hatfield police station."

Povey released the button on the intercom. "DCI Callum to see you, Tim. Is it concerning a case?"

"Not that I'm aware of. Callum . . . I don't think I've ever dealt with him before."

"Oh, you'd remember if you had. Like a dog with a bone, that one. I've seen a number of sure-fire acquittals end up in the cells of Dartmoor and Pentonville thanks to Callum. Once he has his teeth into someone, he rarely lets go. And though I'm loath to say it, he's hardly ever wrong. He has a copper's nose; can sniff out wrongdoers at a dozen paces."

"I'd better watch my step, then." Fellowes gave an easy smile.

In the outer office stood a tall, well-built man of about forty-five, wearing a dark suit, and leaning casually against Doris's desk.

"DCI Callum?" Fellowes took the proffered hand. "What can I do for you?"

"May we speak privately?"

"Of course. Come through to my office. Hold my calls, Doris."

Fellowes made himself comfortable in a luxuriously upholstered leather office chair behind a mahogany desk. Jack sat down opposite in the chair's poor relation.

"Now, how can I help?" Fellowes said as Jack tried to settle in a seat that was too small for him.

"Sandra Duncan. Is that name familiar to you?"

"It is indeed. Miss Duncan is a client of mine. I trust she's done nothing to warrant a police investigation."

"I'm afraid Miss Duncan is dead, Mr Fellowes."

CHAPTER 18

THURSDAY

"Dead? Good God! I was only speaking with her the other week. Was it some kind of accident?"

"Miss Duncan has been murdered, Mr Fellowes."

"Murdered? Good God!" Fellowes said again. "By whom?"

"That is what we are attempting to find out." Jack was watching Fellowes closely, particularly his eyes. So far the shock they registered looked pretty genuine.

"The poor girl," Fellowes said. "Who in their right mind would want to kill such an inoffensive creature as Sandra Duncan? I didn't know her well, Chief Inspector, but I'd have thought she wouldn't say boo to a goose, let alone upset anyone enough for them to want to murder her. Her poor parents. Do they know yet?"

"I've just come from seeing them. They haven't taken the news well."

"Who can blame them? I understand they were devoted to their daughter."

"Indeed. As for your previous point, about who Miss Duncan might have upset, I have a number of witnesses who saw you arguing with her in the park, three weeks ago today. That would be the twenty-fourth of July. Could you tell me what that argument was about?"

Fellowes looked troubled. "I'd like to, Chief Inspector, but I'm afraid that comes under the rules of client privilege, and I'm ethically bound by that to hold my tongue."

"Yes, I understand that, but in these circumstances . . ."

"I would need a written waiver from Miss Duncan's next of kin before I could possibly make any disclosure regarding the matter Miss Duncan and I were discussing."

Jack leaned back in the chair. He had a brief image of himself becoming wedged in it. He sat forward. "But you don't deny you were arguing."

"I think arguing is too strong a term for it. A heated debate, perhaps?"

"And is it customary to hold onto somebody's sleeve to restrain them during a *heated debate*?"

"I resent the implication that I was restraining Miss Duncan in any way."

"Really. How would you describe the action then, sir?"

"I laid my hand on her arm, certainly, but it was to calm her. The debate, as I said, had become rather heated."

"And you're not prepared to tell me what this *heated* debate was about?"

"If I receive written permission from—"

"Yes, her next of kin. I understand that. What I don't understand though, sir, is why you should be conducting what sounds like a very serious business meeting in a very public park, especially when you have a perfectly good office here."

"Happenstance."

"I'm not sure I follow. Happenstance? Is that a legal term I'm not familiar with?"

"It means coincidence, Chief Inspector."

"I know what it means, Mr Fellowes. You're saying that meeting Sandra Duncan in the park and engaging her in a heated debate was just a coincidence. Am I right?"

"Yes — and no. I mean, I met her in the park by chance, and she engaged *me* in a debate."

"I understand that you started your discussion in the pavilion over a cup of tea, and then took it down to the bench by the tennis courts. Is this a correct summation of how the meeting went?"

"More or less."

"Well, is it more, or is it less?"

Fellowes leaned back in his chair. It was quite wide enough for the man's athletic physique. *No chance of him getting stuck*, Jack thought.

"Let me take you through the sequence of events, as they happened."

"I'd be grateful if you would."

"I had a light morning — only a couple of appointments — and when I'd dealt with them I took a stroll down to the park, to the bowling green to be precise, to get in an hour's practice. The club has a tournament coming up at the beginning of September and I wanted to be match fit. Anyway, I finished my practice and went along to the pavilion for a drink, a cup of tea, and there was Miss Duncan. She appeared to be taking her lunch out on the veranda. She invited me to join her, saying that she had a few questions she wanted to ask me. I didn't mind. I thought it would save her the inconvenience of making an appointment and trekking into town to visit me here."

"Very magnanimous of you, I'm sure. How would you best describe your relationship with Miss Duncan?"

"I wouldn't describe it as a *relationship*. Well, not in that way."

"What way would that be, sir?"

"You're making it sound as if we were a couple caught in a lovers' spat."

"I don't think I am, sir, but if you've drawn that inference then I'm sorry. I'm just a simple copper trying to make sense of two people meeting in the park, having a blazing row, resulting in the young lady rushing away in tears, and you're telling me that it was strictly business. Forgive me if I sound a little sceptical."

Fellowes frowned. "All right. Going against my principles, I'll give you the gist of what our conversation was about. Perhaps that will put your mind at rest."

"It would be a great help to hear what actually happened that day."

"If you've done any kind of digging into Sandra's life, you will have realised that she was not the most personable of young women — no boyfriends, didn't mix well with others."

"That's the impression I've been given so far."

"Well, all of that is absolutely true. So much so that she had decided to leave the country and start again somewhere else — France, I believe."

Jack nodded.

"She had encountered opposition from her parents, who were of the opinion that if their daughter were to proceed with her plan, she would be on a downward slope to depravity and debauchery."

"What, *by going to France*?"

"The Duncans lead what can only be described as a very sheltered life, heavily influenced by their Christian beliefs and the teachings of their church. Arthur Duncan threatened that if Sandra made good her promise to go abroad, he would cut her off without a brass farthing, and she asked me if he was able to do that. When I said he was perfectly within his rights to do so, she got very upset, railing against her parents, saying they had no right to interfere with her life, and that they were determined to ensure she was miserable for the rest of her days."

"A slight overreaction, I would have said."

"I agree with you. But Sandra was adamant that the world, myself included, was conspiring against her to stop her pursuing her dream. She was very upset, hence the tears and my attempt to calm her."

"Did you have any contact with her after the incident in the park?"

"No, nothing. I haven't heard a word from Mr and Mrs Duncan either, thank heavens. I'm afraid their type of evangelical bigotry leaves me a little cold."

"They were only trying to protect their daughter's virtue."

"And look where that got them — their precious daughter lying dead on a mortuary slab. Well, I suppose they can give her a good Christian burial, if nothing else."

"A bit harsh, sir. Not a believer yourself, then?"

"If I can't see, smell or touch it, then I find it hard to believe in it. And to ruin a young woman's life over what is basically a superstition, I find nothing short of criminal. Sandra was a sweet girl and had a lot to offer the world. Her death is a tragedy."

Jack was watching Fellowes closely. He was very aware that 'Miss Duncan' had become 'Sandra' as the solicitor became more impassioned. He wasn't convinced that their relationship was *strictly business*, no matter what Fellowes said.

"Well, I think I've taken up enough of your time, Mr Fellowes." He managed to extricate himself from the chair and got to his feet.

"I'm glad I could be of some help."

Jack walked towards the door. "Just out of interest, sir, can you account for your whereabouts over the last seventy-two hours?"

"Zurich," Fellowes said. "That's in Switzerland. I flew out Monday evening and got the first flight back this morning. You can see my passport if you like." He began to reach into his pocket.

"Would you mind?"

Fellowes handed him the dark blue booklet.

"Stamped at both ends of the journey," Fellowes said. "As you can see."

"I wasn't aware Immigration was always so thorough."

"I always insist on getting it stamped. It's an *aide-memoire*. Helps me remember my whereabouts at any given time."

"Well, it certainly does that."

CHAPTER 19

THURSDAY

"I'm sorry to trouble you again so soon. May I come in for a moment?"

Arthur Duncan stared blankly at Jack.

"This won't take long."

Duncan continued to stare. The man looked shattered. His eyes were red from crying and his face was pale. He seemed to have aged ten years in the hour since Jack had informed him of his daughter's death.

"Mr Duncan?" Jack laid a hand on the man's arm.

Duncan started. "Yes, yes, come in, but please keep your voice down. Allison is resting upstairs."

Jack followed him into the living room.

"Please, sit down," Duncan said, indicating a chair by the fireplace. He flopped down onto the sofa, leaned forward and rubbed his hands over his face. "It feels like this day will never end. Do you have children, Chief Inspector?"

"Yes, three."

"Then you must understand what I'm feeling."

"I can barely imagine."

"How do Allison and I get past this? Parents should never outlive their children. It isn't natural. It's not God's way." Duncan dabbed at fresh tears with a sodden handkerchief.

Jack cleared his throat. "This is probably not the time to mention this, Mr Duncan, but it's important for the investigation into your daughter's death. Was there any conflict between yourself and your daughter in the past few months?"

Duncan took a breath and slowly nodded his head.

"About her moving abroad?"

Duncan buried his face in his hands. "I didn't want her to leave us. I would never have gone through with it. I loved Sandra more than life itself. I — I just couldn't bear the thought of her going away, that I might never see my little girl again . . ."

"You threatened to cut her out of your will?" Jack spoke as gently as he could.

Duncan nodded. "But it was just to make her think about what she was intending to do. I never meant to actually carry it through."

"Get out." Allison Duncan stood in the doorway. She'd thrown a housecoat over her clothes and her hair was awry. "Haven't you spread enough misery for one day, without coming back here and accusing my husband?"

Jack got to his feet. "I wasn't accusing your husband of anything, Mrs Duncan. I was simply asking—"

"Shut up! I heard what you were asking him. And he was right. He needed to show that little hussy what would happen if she chose to go down that sinful path."

"Mrs Duncan—"

"Shut up and get out of this house!"

"Allison," said Duncan from the sofa.

"And you can be quiet as well! If you had been more of a man and taken a more active role in your daughter's upbringing; shown her God's way, the true path, none of this would have happened. She wouldn't have grown up thinking she was above His teachings; that she could make her way through life without His love."

"I'd better go," said Jack.

"Yes, and don't come back. We have nothing more to say to you and your kind."

Jack felt the woman's gaze boring into his back as he walked down the hallway and out through the front door. He pulled the door closed behind him. Sometimes he hated his job.

* * *

"There's room on top!"

Simon Nelson stepped onto the bus and glanced into the crowded interior. Every seat seemed to be taken, and there were even a couple of passengers standing in the aisle. Shrugging his school satchel from his shoulder, he started to climb the stairs as the bus moved away.

It was nearly empty on the top deck. The rear seats were occupied, but apart from a lone passenger sitting at the front, all the other seats were vacant. It was his lucky day.

He dropped his satchel onto a double seat halfway along and slid in next to it. He took out an exercise book and, using the back of the satchel as a makeshift desk, attempted again to solve a maths problem that had been giving him problems at school.

Simon was fifteen and a conscientious pupil. He wasn't a swot, but he did want to get good exam results. He knew he would need them if he was to fulfil his ambition of getting a job at the de Havilland Aircraft Company, just half a mile from home. He'd inherited his love of airplanes from his father, who had been a Mosquito pilot during the war, and had then gone on to work in the Research Department at the factory until his death seven years ago. Spurred on by his father's memory, Simon concentrated all his efforts on achieving his goal, and he was determined that a stupid mathematics problem would not defeat him.

He didn't look up when somebody sat down in the seat next to him.

"You like all that school stuff, do you?"

Simon glanced around. It was a boy a few years older than him, who had black hair styled in an elaborate Brylcreemed quiff, along with tight black drainpipe trousers and a purple Edwardian-looking drape jacket. He had black suede shoes with thick crepe soles. The boy had a bad case of acne and smelled of cigarettes.

He leaned across and snatched the book from under Simon's nose. He handed it to one of his two friends standing in the aisle, who were similarly dressed and looked every bit as menacing as acne boy himself.

Teddy boys. Stories about them circulated in the playground at school — lurid tales about clashes with the police, fights with bicycle chains and flick knives, of innocent people set upon for no reason. Simon looked about him frantically, for some means of escape.

"What's your name?" the boy said.

Simon mumbled.

"Didn't catch that."

"Simon. Simon Nelson."

The boy smiled at him. "Well, Simon Nelson, today's your lucky day."

"Is it?"

"It's his lucky day, isn't it, lads?"

The two Teddy boys in the aisle smiled evilly. "If you say so, Billy," said the taller one. His jacket was bright red; his blond hair was greased and styled like acne boy's. His smile displayed a set of uneven, tobacco-stained teeth.

The boy draped an arm across Simon's shoulder, leaned towards him and lowered his voice. "The reason it's your lucky day, Simon, is that I've decided that I'm going to let you get off our bus."

"Really?"

"Yep. I'll even let you get off under your own steam, just walk off like any other passenger."

"Thank you." Simon clutched his satchel to his chest and tried to stand up.

The boy clamped a bony hand across his leg. "But . . . for granting you this huge favour, I think I deserve a reward. I deserve a reward, right, lads?"

The two other boys nodded.

"Definitely."

"Right."

"What do you want?" Rivers of sweat were pouring down Simon's back but his mouth was parched.

"Well, that watch will do for a start. Gold is it?"

Simon nodded. The wristwatch had been a gift from his mother last Christmas.

"And whatever money you have in your pocket."

"But I don't have any." Simon fumbled to unbuckle his watchstrap.

The boy next to him shifted slightly. There was a small click and something sharp pressed into the side of Simon's neck.

"You're not going to disappoint me, Simon, are you?"

"But it's true. I've only got my bus fare, nothing more." Simon was close to tears, hoping desperately to hear the sound of the bus conductor's feet coming up the stairs.

The boy reached for the watch. "Well, I'll take that, for starters— Ow! Get off!"

The person who'd been sitting at the front of the bus had moved quickly. He grabbed the boy's wrist and twisted it back on itself, forcing him to open his fingers and drop the flick knife.

Simon looked up at his saviour. He was a young man, possibly in his late teens or early twenties, well-built and tall enough to have to duck his head slightly to avoid hitting the roof of the bus.

Simon looked at the Teddy boys in the aisle. Both of them were watching the scene, looking pale and frightened. The blond one hesitantly reached into his pocket

"If that hand comes out with a knife, I'll use it to gut you."

The Teddy boy withdrew his hand.

The young man dragged Billy to his feet and pushed him down the aisle, where he ended up in a heap on the floor.

"Now, get off the bus, all of you, before I lose my temper."

The two Teddy boys hauled their friend to his feet and hurried down the stairs as the bus pulled up at the next stop.

The young man sat down in the seat next to Simon. "Are you okay?"

"Yes. Thank you."

"I can't abide cowards, and that's what they are. Peter Lamb," he said, and stuck out his hand. With the other he scooped up Simon's maths book from the floor and handed it back to him.

Now he was next to him Simon realised that Peter Lamb wasn't as old as he'd first thought. He looked down and saw Billy's flick knife resting in his lap, where the boy had dropped it. Using his thumb and forefinger he picked it up and handed it to Lamb

Lamb took it, muttered, "Nasty," and put it in his pocket.

Simon stared out through the window and gave a small groan as he realised he didn't recognise where he was. "I've missed my stop."

"We'll get off at the next one and I'll walk you back."

"You don't have to do that. I'll be all right, really."

"Nonsense. Besides, I didn't see where those yobs went. Can't have you running into them again. You might not be so lucky next time."

As the bus pulled into the next stop, Lamb stepped from the bus and put his hand out to help Simon alight. Rather self-consciously Simon took the proffered hand, and stepped down onto the pavement. He looked about him, with no idea where he was.

"Where do you live?" asked Lamb.

"Myrtle Grove. Do you know it?"

Lamb nodded and smiled. "Myrtle Grove? Off of Campion Way? I know it. This way."

They walked along a tree-lined avenue to a junction, and turned right. There were more turns and more anonymous streets and eventually Simon said, "Are you sure this is the way? Only I don't recognise anything yet."

"This is *my* way," Lamb said. "I know all the shortcuts around here."

After another turn Simon found himself walking down another unfamiliar street, beside a high privet hedge. The hedge finally ended at a set of iron gates, and Lamb surprised him by turning in and pushing one of them open. "I have to make a call. An old friend of mine."

CHAPTER 20

THURSDAY

Simon glanced at his watch. If he hadn't missed his stop he'd be home by now.

"It will only take five minutes."

Simon hesitated.

"Come on."

Simon gave an uncertain smile and followed Lamb through the gates onto a gravel drive belonging to a very large detached red-brick house, with cast-iron gutters and drainpipes painted black, and high sash windows, cloaked with thick grubby-looking curtains. Simon hung back as they approached the green front door.

Lamb glanced back at him. "Come on. He doesn't bite." He pressed his thumb on a ceramic bell push. Deep within the house, a bell shrilled.

The man who answered the door was shorter than Lamb and a lot older. He had on a paint-streaked cotton smock over a pair of baggy woollen trousers, and brown leather sandals. He was in his late thirties. There was grey in the black hair at his temples, and silver streaks ran through his neatly trimmed goatee beard.

He looked Simon up and down. "What a pleasant surprise. Do come in."

"Hello, Gavin. I've brought a friend. I hope that's all right."

"It's absolutely fine, dear boy. What's his name?" The man continued to stare at Simon.

"This is Simon. He had a nasty run-in with a gang of Teddy boys on the bus on his way home from school."

"And now you're escorting him home?"

Lamb nodded.

"Lucky for you that Peter was on hand," said Gavin Southland.

Simon recalled the smell of Brylcreem and cigarettes, and the prick of the knife at his throat. He shuddered. "Yes, it was very lucky."

"Come through." Southland led them into the house, down a long hall. Simon noticed that he walked with a pronounced limp.

Paintings lined the walls. Simon didn't think they looked very good. They were all portraits, and all the subjects were young. At the end of the hall Southland pushed open a door and stood to one side.

They entered a large, densely furnished room with more paintings on the walls. The room was lit by sunlight seeping in through a set of French doors that gave onto a wild, unkempt garden. It was the only light in the room; all the windows were draped with heavy brocade curtains. The room felt enclosed, claustrophobic.

"Take a seat," said Southland. "I'll fetch some drinks. "Beer for you, Peter?"

"Fine."

"Can I tempt you with a peppermint cordial, Simon?"

"That would be very kind, sir." Simon didn't really want a drink. He wanted to go home, but didn't want to appear rude or ungrateful.

"He likes you," said Lamb when Southland had gone to fetch the drinks.

"Does he?"

"He doesn't break out the peppermint cordial for just anybody."

"Are you two related?"

"Me and Gavin? Good heavens, no. Gavin's an artist and I model for him sometimes. Oils and acrylics mostly, but sometimes he'll just sketch me in charcoal."

Simon didn't know what to say to this. Lamb had a fleshy face, and was far from good-looking.

Lamb laughed. "I know what you're thinking. I'm not exactly Dirk Bogarde, am I?"

"I'm sorry, I didn't . . ."

"No, you're right. Gavin's not interested in my face. I'm a life model. Do you know what that means?"

Simon shook his head.

"He's interested in the human body." He pointed at a large painting hanging above the fireplace. "That's me." In the picture Lamb was sitting on a high-backed chair, legs discreetly crossed, face turned away from the artist. He was naked. If Lamb hadn't said so, Simon would never have guessed it was him. It really wasn't very good.

"Don't you find it embarrassing, posing in the nude?"

Lamb shook his head. "I did at first, but not now. Besides, it's worth it for the money I can make by just sitting for a few hours with my clothes off. You should consider doing it yourself, if he asks you. I think he might; I saw how he looked at you when we got here."

"And how was that?" Southland limped back into the room carrying a tray of drinks.

"I was telling Simon here that you can always spot a possible life model."

"That I can," Southland said. "That I can. Would you be interested in doing a spot of modelling, Simon?"

Simon blushed furiously. "No . . . I mean, I couldn't possibly . . ."

"That's a shame." Southland handed him a tumbler of clear liquid. As he raised the glass to his lips Simon smelled the peppermint. It was very strong. He took a tentative sip, wincing slightly as the sweet liquid caught his throat. He coughed.

"I haven't made it too strong for you, have I?"

"No," lied Simon. "It's fine. Very nice."

"That's good. Now, Peter, to what do I owe the honour of this visit?"

"We were passing by, and I thought I'd just call in and pick up the money you owe me."

Southland sipped from his own glass. "Great heavens, you're right. I still owe you for that last sitting. Peter, forgive me; I forgot I hadn't paid you. I'm mortified."

"It's just I'm going out tonight and could use the cash."

"Of course, of course. Wait here and I'll just fetch my wallet." He turned to Simon. "Don't be shy. Drink up. There's plenty more where that came from."

Simon smiled and gulped at the sickly drink.

* * *

Jack glanced up as Myra walked into the office. "Is Sergeant Fuller not with you?"

"He went straight to the canteen. We missed lunch."

"Didn't *you* want something?"

Myra shook her head. "Got to watch my waistline."

"How did you get on at the golf course?"

"It was pretty much a waste of time. No one had a round booked that day. We checked out the golf cart but there was nothing in the way of fingerprints. He must have wiped it down or worn gloves. Either way, he left us no clues."

"And no one saw him take it and drive halfway across the links?"

"He was bloody lucky, excuse my French."

"Either that, or he knows the golf course well enough to know he wouldn't be observed."

Myra sat down at the desk. "Do you think we're looking for a golfer, then, someone who uses the course a lot?"

"We could be. What I *do* think is that we're not having an awful lot of luck with this case. Our killer seems to be invisible."

"We'll catch him, sir. He has to make a mistake sooner or later."

"Let's just hope it's sooner, before he gets the chance to kill again." He went to the noticeboard and stared at the photos of Frances Anderton and Sandra Duncan. Myra came and stood beside him.

"Why these two girls, Myra? Where's the link?"

Myra stared at the photographs. "They're different ages, from different backgrounds, and totally different in looks. It beats me."

"Then forget about the differences. What did the girls have in common?"

Myra pondered this for a moment. "Well, neither of the girls was very worldly-wise. Frances was very young and, by all accounts, quite naïve, and Sandra came from a very sheltered background; someone described her as a wallflower."

"As you say, neither of them were worldly-wise, and so both of them could be taken in by, say, an older, smooth-talking man. Tim Fellowes is a bit of a smooth talker. I wouldn't have thought he'd find it difficult to charm Sandra Duncan. Frances Anderton came into contact with her sister's boyfriend, Adam Channing, a college lecturer who, again, is quite a bit older. Channing is obviously a smooth enough operator to ensnare Fiona Anderton who, believe you me, is nobody's fool. Both men seem to have a penchant for much younger girls."

"But you said that Channing didn't fit the description of our park-keeper."

"Yes, and Fellowes claims that his relationship with Sandra was strictly business, even though I still find it unlikely that a solicitor would have an argument with a client on a bench in a public park. But he was out of the country when Sandra Duncan went missing."

"So that rules him out," Myra said. She wasn't sure where her boss was going with this train of thought. She'd learned a lot about him today from talking to Eddie Fuller. She had found out for the first time that Callum's eldest daughter, Joan, had eloped with a much older man a few years ago, and had recently returned to the family home when her marriage ended. She wondered how much that event was influencing his thinking.

"Have you spoken to Professor Channing?" Myra asked.

"I called the LSE a little while ago. Apparently he's off today, looking after his sick wife, but he's expected back tomorrow. I'm going up to London to speak with him."

* * *

Simon sipped his cordial. He tried to listen to the conversation between Lamb and Southland but their words kept blurring into each other and he couldn't follow.

In the back of his mind, a small voice was whispering to him that he should be getting home but somehow the urgency seemed to have disappeared. The armchair he was sitting in was wonderfully comfortable and he found his eyelids fluttering. It was taking all his willpower to keep them open. The inside of his mouth was coated thickly with peppermint, but he could taste something else now — sharper, slightly medicinal. He didn't like it.

Finally he struggled out of the armchair, got to his feet and stood there, swaying slightly. "I should be . . ." The furniture in the room seemed to sway. "I shou . . ." His knees buckled and he sank to the floor.

As he lay on the rug he was briefly aware of Peter Lamb standing over him, looking down.

"Take him upstairs and put him in one of the bedrooms." Southland's voice came from somewhere far away, and then Lamb was reaching down and scooping him up in his arms. Simon closed his heavy eyes.

CHAPTER 21

THURSDAY

"Goodnight, Rosie. See you in the morning," Mrs Painter shut the door and locked it behind them.

"See you! Bright and early." Rosie set off briskly along the High Street. She wanted to call in at the newsagents before they closed, to pick up a fashion magazine. She needed some fresh ideas about what she ought to be wearing. On her way to the baker's that morning, she had caught sight of herself in the window of the chemist next door and been horrified at how frightful she looked in her blue pinafore-style dress and her awful *little girl* plaits. *"You look like an overgrown schoolgirl,"* she said to herself. How could any boy, least of all David, take her seriously when she looked like this?

Joanie's return had made Rosie take stock of her own appearance. Her sister dressed more elegantly than she did. The clothes Joanie wore were not expensive, but they fitted perfectly, enhancing her figure, and her chic new haircut made Rosie feel even more inadequate. She wasn't brave enough to get her own hair cut short, but at least she could get rid of the plaits and start wearing clothes that were more suitable for a young woman her age.

Mr Shadbolt was already pulling down the dark blue window blinds but the door of the newsagent's was still open and she slipped inside.

The magazines were displayed on a rack by the wall.

"I'm just closing up!"

"I'll only be a moment," said Rosie.

"Oh, it's you, Rosie. Sorry, I thought it was a customer. Take your time."

She pulled out a magazine, took it over to the counter and handed it to Shadbolt. He was a small, barrel of a man with a crinkled face and woolly grey hair. He settled his round, wire-framed glasses on the bridge of his nose and looked at the magazine. "*Vanity Fair*? My, it seems like only yesterday that you were coming in here for your copy of *School Friend*."

"Time flies, Mr Shadbolt."

The old man chuckled. "It certainly does. That will be one and six, please."

"Thank you." Rosie handed him half a crown.

"And tell your dad that this month's copy of *Practical Householder* has a feature on landscape gardening that he'll find interesting."

"I'll be sure to mention it. Thanks."

"Hello! Fancy bumping into you."

Rosie looked up into the smiling face of David Neville. She was terribly conscious of her ridiculous pinafore dress and her stupid plaited hair. She felt herself blushing.

"I wasn't expecting to see you. I was just on my way home."

"Would you like some company? I could use a walk."

"That would be nice."

"I really enjoyed the film last night," he said as they walked.

"Me too. Grace Kelly's so beautiful, so elegant. That wonderful dress she was wearing in the car with Frank Sinatra . . . it made mine look like a potato sack."

"I thought you looked very nice."

"Get away with you!"

"I mean it. You looked very pretty. Beautiful, in fact."

"Now I know you're lying. Either that or you need glasses."

He tugged at the magazine she was carrying.

"Very posh. If you start wearing clothes like that I'll have to get another job, to earn enough to keep up with you."

"I could never afford clothes like that."

"Then it seems a bit pointless buying the magazine."

She looked at him sharply. No, he wasn't mocking her; he was smiling and there was no malice in his eyes. "You wouldn't understand. You're just a boy."

"Sure I understand. I buy magazines full of cars I could never hope to afford, not as an insurance clerk anyway. But there's nothing wrong with dreaming that one day, I just might."

"Me too. One day I could be wearing clothes direct from the Paris catwalks!"

"And I'm sure that one day you will, if you set your mind to it."

"What makes you say that?"

"Because, from what I know of you, once you set your mind to something you'll achieve it."

"And you know that based on one trip to the cinema?"

"I'm a quick learner. But you'll have to come out with me again, just so I can be sure."

"I'd like that."

"Tonight?"

"I'm washing my hair. What about Saturday?"

"That sounds good to me. Do you like dancing?"

"I love it."

"Well, I'll pick you up at seven. There's a jazz band playing at a club I know in Stevenage. They've got a dance floor."

"That sounds great!"

"But don't expect too much from me. I've just about mastered the quickstep and waltz, but my foxtrot . . ."

"I can foxtrot. I'll teach you. If you're such a quick learner, you should pick it up in no time."

"Well, here we are."

"So, I'll be seeing you Saturday. Goodbye!" Before she realised what was happening he had leaned in and pecked her on the lips.

She took a step back, amazed. "Right . . . er, Saturday . . . yes. See you then."

She watched him walk away.

"Well, you look like the cat that got all the cream," said Annie as Rosie walked into the kitchen.

"Yes. I think I just did."

* * *

"Shepherd's pie." Annie set down a deep Pyrex dish on the table. "Give me your plates. You first, Dad."

Jack handed her his plate and watched as she ladled out the lamb mince and creamy mashed potato. He hadn't eaten all day and the aroma rising from the Pyrex dish was mouth-watering. "There's broccoli and carrots from the garden, but the peas are frozen — we've used all the fresh ones."

"Frozen is fine." Jack helped himself to a spoonful of each. "You girls would know; where's the best place around here to buy embroidery thread?"

"Jennings, in town," Annie and Rosie said together.

"Is Archers in Hitchin still there?" Joan said. "That's the haberdasher's I used when I was making my own clothes. They had more variety than Jennings."

"You're right," Annie said. "I always use Jennings because it's closer, but Archers is still there. Why do you want to know, Dad?"

"I'm thinking of taking up a new hobby."

"No you're not," said Eric.

"Can't you see me sitting here in the evening, making cushion covers and samplers?"

"Frankly, no," Annie said. "If you're that keen on working with a needle and thread I have a pile of darning I can give you."

"It's for a case I'm working on."

"Dad," said Eric. "Can you lend me ten bob?"

"Is this about that guitar?"

"Well, I've saved a pound already, and Eddie wants thirty shillings for the guitar."

"So what's wrong with waiting until you've saved the rest?"

"But that will take ages, and I want to learn to play now."

"Let me think on it. You do realise it will mean no pocket money until you've paid me back?"

"I've thought of that."

"I'm sure you have."

"Dad," said Rosie. "David wants to take me to a dance on Saturday night. Can I go?"

Annie intervened. "Oh, for heaven's sake, you two. Let your father eat his dinner in peace."

Jack smiled at her. "All answers will be given once I've eaten this delicious meal your mother has made for us. Joanie, do you have anything you want to add to the list?"

"Only the bed."

"Oh yes. Your mother and I are going to Bennets at the weekend to see if we can pick one up."

"You see, he answered *her*," Eric said, disgruntled.

"Eric! Eat your dinner. I don't want to hear another word from you until you've cleared your plate."

"Thank you, Mother," Jack said. "This really is quite delicious, you know? Of course, it's the home-grown vegetables that make it."

"Cheek!" Annie gave him a playful tap on the ankle with the toe of her shoe.

"Ouch! Careful, woman — you'll cripple me."

"You big baby. I hardly touched you."

* * *

"What's this dance David wants to take you to?" They sat in the living room waiting for the radiogram to warm up. Annie and Joan were in the kitchen washing up, and Eric was lying on his stomach on the rug, reading a comic.

"I think it's a jazz club in Stevenage."

"So it's not a dance?"

"They have a dance floor. Really, Dad, I don't know any more than that, but it's a chance to go out, on a *Saturday night*. Chances like that don't come along every day."

"Then of course you should go."

"You mean it?"

"I said it, didn't I?"

Rosie launched herself out of her chair and wrapped her arms around his neck. "Thank you!"

"But you must be back by eleven."

Her hold on his neck loosened.

"But, Dad, it's Saturday night!"

"Okay. We'll make it twelve, but it's straight in when you get home. No spending half an hour on the door step saying goodnight to him."

"What kind of girl do you take me for?" She was smiling.

"A very pretty, sixteen-year-old girl just starting out on a romantic relationship. I remember what your mother and I were like — so it's home and straight in, okay?"

"What about the ten bob?" Eric called from the rug.

"I'm still thinking about it."

"That's not fair!"

"Press me on it again and I'll say no."

Eric glowered at him.

"Another look like that and I'll say no as well. Now go and see if your mother needs any help in the kitchen."

Rosie waited until her brother had left the room. "Thanks, Dad. I won't disappoint you."

CHAPTER 22

FRIDAY AUGUST 15th 1958

"What's this?" Jack got into the car and handed Fuller two notes: one green and one brown.

"Thirty shillings. That's right isn't it? For the guitar?"

"Yes. But I thought Eric was buying it."

"He is, but he's still saving up, and if he doesn't get the damned thing soon he'll drive me round the bend. Last night he asked me to lend him the ten shillings he was short. I didn't say yes or no. This morning I came down to breakfast to find a letter propped up against the teapot, asking the same thing, but this time going into some detail about his desire to learn to play and make a name for himself in the music business."

"So you're indulging him."

"No. I'm giving him the chance to prove himself."

Fuller's look was sceptical.

"You'll understand when you have children, Sergeant."

"If you say so, guv."

"Can you bring it round tonight? I'd like him to get started as soon as possible."

"Sure thing. When do you want me to begin the lessons?"

"As soon as you like. I'll pay you for your time. How does five bob an hour sound?"

"It's too much. Much too much. I'll happily teach him, gratis."

"That's good of you. Drop me off at the train station, will you? I'm going up to the LSE to interview Adam Channing."

"Is there anything you want me to do while you're gone?"

"I want you to go to Jennings in town and Archers in Hitchin — the haberdashers. See if anyone has bought a quantity of black silk embroidery thread and needles recently. The needles will be curved. He couldn't have sewn the eyes and mouth shut any other way without doing more damage to the surrounding tissue."

"You've been giving this some thought."

"Morning, noon and night. I'm even dreaming about it."

* * *

Jack walked through the high, grey-stone arch of the London School of Economics and presented himself at the reception desk.

The woman behind the desk was wearing a green knitted twinset, and had a pair of spectacles perched on her protuberant nose. She was in her fifties. "May I help you?"

"Professor Adam Channing. I understand he's a lecturer here."

"He is, but I'm not sure if he's in today."

Jack pulled his warrant card from his pocket. "Can you check?"

"Yes, of course." She squinted at the card. "Detective Chief Inspector."

After negotiating a seemingly endless maze of grey corridors, he reached a door bearing Channing's brass nameplate. He knocked and entered.

Adam Channing was sitting at a desk covered with textbooks and untidy piles of paper.

Channing did not look up. "Marking," he said, indicating the bundles of paper. Jack watched him. Channing certainly didn't look like a Lothario. His hair was too long, curly and grey. He was quite thin; his cheeks were sunken, and there was a day's growth of stubble on his chin. Jack wondered what a pretty girl like Fiona, who could have had her pick of eligible bachelors, would see in a man like this — but then he'd thought the same about Joanie when she first brought Ivan to the house. Ivan was certainly no oil painting, with his dark, sunken eyes and flat, Eastern European features. Joanie said he had charisma. Perhaps the same was true of Channing. Jack had given up trying to understand the workings of teenage girls' minds.

He waited a few more minutes and then coughed loudly.

Finally Channing looked up, and his eyes widened when he saw Jack. "I'm terribly sorry. I thought you were a student."

Jack introduced himself.

"How do you think I can help you, Chief Inspector?"

"I'm looking into the abduction and murder of Frances Anderton."

Channing seemed troubled. "Yes. Fiona told me. A dreadful business, truly dreadful. I'd been expecting a visit from the police."

"Really? Why would that be?"

"I was given to understand that you were talking to everyone who had any contact with Frances."

"We are. I would have come yesterday but you were at home — caring for your sick wife."

Channing sighed, and pulled a briar pipe from his jacket pocket. He took his time, filling and lighting it and taking long pulls to get it burning.

"I'm sorry if you find this tiresome, sir."

"I'm willing to help in any way I can, Chief Inspector. It's your provincial attitude I find tiresome."

Jack hadn't hidden his disapproval. If Channing found it tiresome, well, so be it. "Tell me about the evening you met Frances Anderton."

"It was the end-of-term party. I was surprised to see her there. She was underage, and there was a bar. Fiona must have found a way to smuggle her in."

"And, while she was at the party, did you engage her in conversation?"

"Only to pass the time of day. To be quite honest with you, Chief Inspector, she barely registered. Frances was a timid little creature. She sat at our table drinking Tizer through a straw, watching what was going on around her, but not really engaging. I wondered why Fiona had brought her along."

"When did you last have contact with Fiona Anderton?"

"I spoke to her on the phone on Wednesday. That's when she told me about Frances."

"It must have come as quite a shock."

"I was upset for Fiona and her parents but, as I said, I barely knew the girl."

"And can you account for your whereabouts last weekend?"

"Surely you don't consider me a suspect, Chief Inspector?" Channing smiled.

Jack didn't like that smile. There was a trace of mockery in it.

"I'm not ruling anyone out at present."

"Commendable. Leave no stone unturned. But I'm afraid you'll have to cross me off your list of suspects. From Saturday until Monday I was up in Scotland, at a seminar in Falkirk to be precise."

"And someone can corroborate that?"

"I should think the staff at the Prince Edward Hotel can confirm my presence there, as well as the twenty or so other attendees."

"What was it about, this seminar?"

"Comparative politics."

"Interesting?"

"Oh, very. One of the items on the agenda was a discussion of the book Robert Dahl published a couple of years ago: *A Preface to Democratic Theory*. Professor Alan Probert came over from Yale to present a paper on it. Fascinating stuff."

"Riveting, I should imagine. But then I'm just a provincial copper, so what would I know?"

"Quite." Channing's face still bore a slight smirk.

"Well, thank you for your time, Professor Channing. If I think of anything else, can I find you here? No more trips to Scotland?"

"I have a clear diary as far as I know. So I should be here."

* * *

Jack left the London School of Economics with the uneasy feeling that Channing was playing a game with him. The professor had said nothing specific to lead him to such a conclusion, but his air of condescension had annoyed Jack. His lover's sister had been murdered, yet the good professor didn't appear to give two hoots about it. He hadn't even asked about the circumstances of Frances's death. He wasn't going to cross Channing off his list of suspects, despite the alibi that had him four hundred miles away at the time she was killed. There was something about the professor that called for further investigation.

* * *

"Nothing from Jennings," said Fuller, when Jack got back to the station. "But someone bought a quantity of embroidery thread from Archers several weeks ago."

"Black?"

"All the colours of the rainbow, apparently."

"Black isn't in the rainbow."

"Oh, they bought black as well."

"Curved needles?"

Fuller shook his head. "Just the thread."

"Do Archers have a record of the sale? Who was it that bought it? A name and address?"

"I'm afraid not. The shop assistant at Archers remembers the sale, though. It was bought by a man and he paid cash."

"Of course he did. And I take it the shop assistant failed to get a description."

"A man in his forties, with dark brown, thinning hair starting to go grey at the temples. He had a thin goatee beard and walked with a limp."

"Who is this assistant, Sergeant? Does she want a job? That's the best description I've heard all week."

"Susan Clark. She's worked at Archers for fifteen years, so it's unlikely she's looking to change her employment."

"Oh, well. Never mind. Good work."

"And the Chief Superintendent wants to see you in his office."

"Terrific."

* * *

"What did Channing say? Is he a viable suspect?"

"He has an alibi for last weekend. Apparently he was up in Scotland. I've got Frank Lesser checking it out."

"So was it really necessary to go all the way up to London to interview him? Couldn't you have obtained the same information over the telephone?"

"I'm sure I could. But you can't get the measure of a man from a telephone conversation."

"Well, now you've met him face to face, what do you think?"

"I didn't like him."

"I don't like a lot of people, Jack. It doesn't mean they're all killers."

"Granted, but there was something off about Channing."

"Off?"

Jack shrugged. "Nothing I can really put my finger on. But it was enough for me not to dismiss him from our enquiries just yet."

"I hear that Joan, your eldest, has come back home."

This caught Jack off balance. "Sorry?"

"Joan's come home."

"Yes. Yes, she has." He stared at his superior, wondering what the man was implying.

"Try to keep objective, Jack. With Channing, I mean. I know we want to solve this case, but we mustn't allow our personal feelings to influence our judgement."

Jack barely managed to stifle a retort. "No, sir. I won't."

"Splendid. That's all right then. Let me have the chit for your travel expenses before you leave tonight."

CHAPTER 23

FRIDAY

"Myra? Take yourself off to the library and get me everything you can find on Professor Adam Channing. He's currently a lecturer at the LSE."

"Employment record? Stuff like that?"

"Everything," Jack said. "I want to know what makes him tick. And while you're there, compile a dossier on Tim Fellowes."

"You're looking into both of them?" said Fuller.

"I am."

"Why?"

"Similar types."

"You mean they're both middle-aged men with alibis for the days of the murders."

"There's that, and the fact that they both seem to enjoy the company of younger women."

"There's no crime against that," said Lesser.

"No, Frank, you're right. There's no crime against it. Did Channing's alibi check out, by the way?"

"Cast iron," said Lesser.

"I thought it might be."

"Dead ends then," said Fuller.

"So it would seem."

"Then why are you wasting Myra's time checking them out?"

Jack went across to the noticeboard and stood staring at it. "I don't know. There's just something about both of them that isn't right. Call it a copper's intuition if you like."

"Or a bloody waste of time," said Lesser under his breath. Jack heard him, but let it go. He couldn't blame his officers, or even Lane, for their scepticism, and maybe they were right to doubt his instincts. Maybe Joanie's return had exposed feelings he thought he had long buried. He stared at the photographs of Frances and Sandra and saw Rosie and Joanie looking back at him. He shook his head. "I'll be in my office," he said, and left the room.

As he was walking through the door he nearly collided with Andy Brewer. "There's a lady downstairs in reception. She claims her son didn't come home from school yesterday."

"Her *son*?"

Brewer nodded.

* * *

"When did you last see your son, Mrs Nelson?" Jack showed the tearful woman into his office. "Please take a seat."

Sonia Nelson dabbed at her eyes with a handkerchief. "I suppose it was at breakfast yesterday morning."

"When did you realise he hadn't come home?"

"This morning, when I took him his cup of tea. He wasn't in his bed."

"Not yesterday afternoon, after school?"

"I have to work in the evenings, since my husband died."

"I'm sorry. Have you been on your own for long?"

"Seven years this November. He died the day after bonfire night, 1951."

Sonia Nelson was an attractive thirty-something woman who had honey-blonde hair and wore too much make-up. Her tears had made her mascara run, leaving two black streaks down her rouged cheeks.

"Has this ever happened before? Simon not coming home."

Sonia shook her head vehemently. "No, never. That's why I thought I should come straight to you."

"Well, you did the right thing."

Sonia made a frantic lunge across the desktop and grabbed Jack's sleeve. "You have to find him, Mr Callum. He's all I've got left!"

Jack gave her a reassuring smile and disengaged her fingers from his shirtsleeve. "We'll certainly make every effort to locate your son, Mrs Nelson."

After another tearful thirty minutes he had learned everything he needed to know about Simon Nelson, and had a seven-by-five-inch school photograph of him taken in the March of that year.

"I thought he might have gone to the factory after school. He does that sometimes."

"Sorry? Factory?"

"The de Havilland Aircraft Company. He'll go there and stand outside the fence, watching the planes take off and land. Obsessed, he is. Just like his father. Fred was a fighter pilot during the war, and when it ended he went to work there. His obsession with planes rubbed off on Simon."

"But he wasn't there, not this time."

"No. He's obsessed by them but not so he'd stay out all night."

"We'll start looking for him straight away. Thank you for coming in." Jack walked her to the door. "And try not to worry. I'm sure he'll turn up. He's probably off on some adventure somewhere. I know what teenage boys are like."

"Do you have a son, Mr Callum?"

"Yes. My Eric's about your boy's age. His latest nine-day-wonder is guitars and skiffle music."

"Then you know what it's like."

"I do indeed." Jack walked with her into the reception area.

"Hello, Sonia. Starting a bit early today, aren't we?" said DC Harry Grant. He was leaning against the reception desk.

Sonia Nelson's looked startled, but she recovered herself when she saw who was speaking.

"Oh, it's you, Harry. It's Simon. He didn't come home last night."

"Don't you worry, Sonia. I'm sure he'll turn up. If not, you're talking to the right man." Jack saw her out.

When he returned Grant was still leaning against the desk.

"So how do you know Sonia Nelson?"

"Who? Sexy Sonia? I've pulled her in more times than I can remember."

"Pulled her in? Arrested, you mean?"

"Sonia's one of our regulars, sir. She's on the game. Has been since her husband died a few years back."

"I've never seen her before." Brewer spoke from behind the desk.

"No, Sarge. She works nights, when you're at home, tucked up in bed and drinking your Ovaltine."

"Haven't you got any work to do, Constable?" Jack said. "Instead of standing here gossiping like an old woman."

"Yes, sir." Grant headed off to the squad room.

Jack followed him and pinned Simon Nelson's photograph to the noticeboard. "Right. Gather round. We have another missing child — a boy this time. His name is Simon Nelson, fifteen, and a pupil at Birchwood Secondary. His mother hasn't seen him since yesterday morning, and she's worried sick."

"His mother's Sonia Nelson," added Grant.

"Sexy Sonia?" called Fuller from his seat.

"The same," said Grant.

"That's enough, Constable," said Jack. "*Mrs Nelson* is *very* worried about her missing boy, so let's pull out all the stops and try to find him. In the light of recent events, I don't have to impress upon you that speed is of the essence."

"You don't think it's the same person who took the two girls, do you, sir?" said Fuller.

"I'm not ruling anything out just yet."

Jack spoke to Fuller when they were out of earshot of the others. "How do you know Sonia Nelson? No, don't answer that. I'm not sure I want to know. Anyway, I'm going home shortly. We'll start again in the morning. Is Myra back from the library yet?"

"She's on her way. I'll send her to your office when she gets here."

"Good. And don't forget about the guitar."

"I'll pop round at about half past seven."

"That will be fine. It will give Eric a chance to finish his homework before you start distracting him."

* * *

"An undervalued resource," said Myra Banks.

"Pardon?"

"The public library. It's an undervalued resource. It's amazing what you can discover once you start scrolling through those microfiche files."

"Take a seat, Myra, and tell me what you found out."

"Would it surprise you to know that Adam Channing and Timothy Fellowes went to the same university?"

"At the same time?"

"Channing was a year ahead of Fellowes but they shared two years."

"Which university was this?"

"Cambridge."

"What courses?"

"Channing was studying for a degree in psychology and Fellowes was reading law."

"What are the chances of them crossing paths while they were there?"

"Highly likely, they were both at Corpus Christi College. Everyone studying at Cambridge is a member of a college, where they live and socialise, and each college is quite small, they'd have been sure to have bumped into each other from time to time."

Jack leaned back in his seat. "Was there much else?"

Myra held up her notebook. "I nearly filled this. I'll type it up before I go tonight and let you have it in the morning. Sergeant Fuller said there's another missing child. A boy this time."

Jack nodded.

"Do you think this disappearance is linked to Frances and Sandra?"

"Time will tell."

"If he turns up dead, you mean?"

"Yes."

Myra shook her head and got to her feet. "I'd better go and type up my notes." She paused at the door and looked back at him. "I haven't been with the force that long, sir, but this kind of case . . . it's not normal, is it?"

He held her gaze. "No, Myra, thankfully not."

"But we *will* catch him, sir, won't we?"

"Yes. We'll catch him — eventually."

Myra Banks gathered herself, twisted the doorknob and let herself out of the office.

Jack stood up and slipped on his coat, ready for home and some sanity.

* * *

Lane stopped him on the stairs.

"Before you go, Jack, can you just pop into my office?"

The office still smelled of fresh paint. Sitting at the desk was a man he didn't recognise, of about his own age.

"Jack, this is Detective Chief Superintendent Fisher from Scotland Yard. I want you to hand over to him all our files on the Anderton and Duncan cases, and I hear we have another one."

"Simon Nelson, yes. He went missing yesterday."

"Then perhaps I can have those as well," Fisher said, addressing Jack directly.

Jack turned to Lane. "Would you mind telling me what all this is about?"

"It's about our lack of progress in solving these cases, Jack."

"But it's only been—"

"I know, Jack, you feel aggrieved, but this hasn't come from me."

"Then where *has* it come from?"

"Orders from on high, Jack. The chief constable feels we're not making sufficient progress in apprehending this killer and has asked Scotland Yard, specifically DCS Fisher and his team, to step in and assist us."

Fisher cleared his throat. "If I may interrupt you there, Chief Superintendent, our brief is not to assist, but to take over the investigation." He looked at Jack, a slight sneer on his lips. "From you, Chief Inspector, I'll expect nothing less than one hundred per cent cooperation. The sooner we can catch this bugger, the better."

"In the meantime, Jack," said Lane, "you've got a bundle of open cases sitting on your desk. Get results on some of those and the chief constable might start looking on you favourably once more."

Jack stared at the pair of them: Fisher with his expensive-looking suit, highly polished brogues and condescending manner, and Lane, who gave in to the chief constable's every demand. Jack had not been neglecting his other cases, but a robbery at a local off-licence hardly merited the same attention as murder.

"Will that be all? Sir?"

"For now, Jack."

"If you can organise those files for me, post haste," said Fisher.

Jack nodded sharply and strode from the office.

Still seething, he went to the squad room, told his officers what was happening and ordered them to get the files ready. He silenced their protests with a wave of his hand.

"Any problems you have then I invite you to take them up with Chief Superintendent Lane. It's now out of my hands. Frank, how are we doing with the off-licence case?"

"It's in hand, sir."

"Move it from the back burner and turn up the heat. Let's see if we can crack it. And Eddie, where are we with the post office robberies?"

"I have a few leads."

"Good. Firm them up."

Jack went across to Myra Banks who was busy typing up her notes. "When you've finished transposing your notebook, Myra, perhaps you'll see to it that I get my copy first."

"Will do, sir. I take it you're not just going to roll over and accept this," she said quietly.

"The hell I will," Jack growled.

"That's what I thought, sir. Could I drop your copy off at your house tonight, sir?"

Jack smiled at her. "If it's not putting you out, Myra."

"No problem, sir. No problem at all."

CHAPTER 24

FRIDAY

"Well, you've got a face like thunder," Annie said. "Bad day?"

"They've taken the case away from me. Apparently I'm not making speedy enough progress on it."

"Oh no, Jack. Who're *they*?"

"Lane and the chief constable. They've assigned some bod and a task force from Scotland Yard to handle it instead."

"Can they do that?"

"They just have." Jack went across to the sideboard and poured himself a large Glenfiddich single malt whisky, knocking it back in a single gulp.

"I'm sorry, Jack. This case has been giving you sleepless nights. They can't fault your dedication. It just seems so unfair."

"Whether it's fair or not doesn't really come into it, nor does my insomnia. The chief constable wouldn't have taken such a decision lightly. I suspect pressure has been brought to bear."

"Pressure? From whom?"

"Warren Anderton is the first name that springs to mind. He's an important man in the area and a brother Freemason to the chief constable."

"Really?"

"That's my best guess."

"You men and your silly secret societies."

"Hey, don't lump me in with them. I never joined the Masons."

"Only because they've never invited you."

"No. It's because I'm not really their type. I don't go in for funny handshakes and rituals."

"Thank heavens. Dinner won't be long. Go and get cleaned up before we sit down."

"Oh, Myra Banks is dropping by later, to bring me some files. And Eddie's going to pop in at about half past seven with . . ." He glanced around and lowered his voice. ". . . with what we were discussing this morning."

"Then I'd better make sure Eric has his homework finished." She smiled at him. "And Bennets in town is having a sale all this week, so we can go in tomorrow afternoon and look for a bed for Joanie's room."

* * *

Jack had just taken a bite of his lamb chop when the doorbell rang. "That'll be Myra."

Myra Banks saw the napkin tucked into his collar and her smile faltered. "I'm sorry, sir. I didn't mean to disturb your dinner."

He waved away the apology and took the folder from her. "That's not a problem, Myra. This is much more important."

"Well, you've got the first copy. The boys from Scotland Yard won't get it until tomorrow."

"I didn't mean to put you in a compromising position, Myra."

"Well, I mean, sir, it's a bloody cheek. We do all the legwork and then they step in and claim all the glory. Everyone on the team feels the same."

"The least we can hope for is that there *is* some glory to claim. Was there any news on the Nelson boy before you left?"

"I haven't heard if Scotland Yard's got any further with it."

"Ah well, I'll check tomorrow when I get in. Thanks for popping this round, Myra. I want to have a chat with you on Monday about the possibility of you working for the CID permanently."

"I'd like that, sir."

"I think you'd be a good fit."

"Thank you! Well, I won't keep you from your meal any longer." She started to walk down the path. Then she paused and turned back. "Just one more thing, sir. Superintendent Fisher and his men have moved into your office."

Jack raised his eyes. "Yes, Myra. Of course they have."

* * *

"Of all the bloody cheek!"

"Language, Dad," said Annie.

"Sorry. But Scotland Yard have moved into my office. *My office!* Is nothing sacred?"

Annie gave a small shake of her head. "More potatoes?"

Jack marvelled once more at the way his wife could defuse a tense situation. "Yes, why not?"

They were washing up when there was a tap at the back door.

"Hello, Eddie!"

His sergeant was standing on the back doorstep, a black canvas guitar case in hand. "I came around the back because I wasn't sure if Eric knew I was bringing this round.

"You did the right thing. I haven't told him yet."

"We want it to be a surprise," Annie said from the sink. "Do come in, Eddie. Cuppa?"

"Please, Mrs C."

"Sit yourself down."

Jack dried the last plate and joined Fuller at the table.

"What do you think about Scotland Yard getting involved?" said Fuller.

"No shop talk," said Annie.

"Sorry, Annie." Jack said. "Actually, I'm spitting nails," he said quietly to Fuller.

"I thought you might be," Fuller muttered.

Annie sat down with them, ending their murmured conversation.

"Do you want to go and call him, Jack?"

"Eric! Have you finished your homework?"

"Just done, Dad!"

"Then come into the kitchen."

"What do you want?" said Eric.

"There's someone here to see you."

"Hello, Eddie. What are you doing . . . ?"

The words died on his lips as he spotted the guitar case leaning against a kitchen chair. His eyes widened, and he turned to his father.

"Really?"

"You can go without your pocket money until you've paid me back, and you can thank Eddie for bringing it round."

"Thanks, Eddie. Can I see it?"

Fuller grinned, and lifted the guitar case.

"It's a little dusty and could probably use a new set of strings, but it plays fine." He handed the guitar to Eric, smiling at the stunned expression on the boy's face.

"It's the most beautiful thing I've ever seen! Are you sure, Eddie?"

"It's nearly in tune. Here, let me." He took the guitar from Eric, made a slight adjustment and strummed. "That's better. How would Sunday morning suit you, for your first lesson?"

Eric nodded his head vigorously.

"It's a date, then. Sunday at eleven."

"Thanks, Eddie," said Annie.

"My pleasure, Mrs C. You'll be listening to him on the wireless one day."

"Dream on," said Rosie, from the doorway.

"I'm serious. You've heard that Tommy Steele. He's hardly *Segovia,* but with three chords and a wiggle of his hips, he has the girls going crazy."

"Yes, but he's *Tommy Steele,*" said Rosie.

"Hey!" said Eric.

"Take no notice of her, Eric," said Joan.

"You see, Eddie," Jack said, "The guitar's not been in the house five minutes and already World War Three's broken out."

"My cue to leave, I think." Fuller rose from the table and went to the door. "Thanks for the tea, Mrs C. I'll pick you up in the morning, guv."

"When we get to the station, we'll probably find we've been moved out into the car park."

* * *

Jack lay in bed with Myra's file propped against his knees. Annie lay beside him, buried in a Catherine Cookson novel. She yawned and closed the book. "Are you going to be much longer?"

"I'm nearly done. You can put your light out if you're tired."

"You know that never works. I can't sleep unless it's completely dark. What's so fascinating, anyway?"

He told her what Myra had found at the library.

"Interesting. But what does it mean?"

Jack closed the file and reached over to turn off his bedside lamp. "I'm not sure. Do you remember that Hitchcock film we went to see a couple of years back? *Strangers on a Train*?"

"I remember. Farley Granger and Robert Walker."

"Do you remember how each of them killed the other's victim, to give themselves a perfect alibi?"

"Surely you don't think that's what happened with those two girls?"

"It's an idea."

"An idea out of a book. Patricia Highsmith, wasn't it?"

"I only know the film. You're the one for detective stories."

"Yes, but it's *fiction.* People don't go around committing murders using plots from crime novels."

"But what if they did? You have two men and two murders. Adam Channing was up in Scotland on the day Frances Anderton was murdered, and the day Sandra Duncan was killed, the man seen arguing with her in the park was in Switzerland. What if they killed the other's intended victim, giving themselves perfect alibis in the process?"

Annie yawned again and sank beneath the sheets. "It's an intriguing theory, Jack. But you're forgetting one thing."

"Oh?"

"Motive. As I remember it, Farley Granger and Robert Taylor had strong reasons for wanting their victims dead. In your case you have a fourteen-year-old girl whose main interests seem to be reading books and going to church, and a young woman who wouldn't say boo to a goose, whose sole ambition in life, apparently, was to be a children's nanny. Hardly the types to drive middle-aged men to commit murder."

"Unless there was more to it than that."

"Such as? You said that Sandra had been interfered with, but Frances wasn't touched in that way, so that's a major difference. Frances's father is a fairly prominent public figure and controls a wealthy company, but Sandra's dad is what — a minor civil servant? So that's another difference between the two cases. I think you're trying to make the facts suit the crimes. Both girls had their eyes and lips sewn shut, which suggests to me that you're looking for one man, a very sick man, but a sole operator."

It was Jack's turn to yawn. "You're probably right. Goodnight."

"Goodnight. And try to get some sleep tonight. You're getting bags under your eyes."

"I saw them when I was shaving. Bags under the bags." He closed his eyes.

CHAPTER 25

SATURDAY AUGUST 16th 1958

"Are you sure it's him?" Jack said into the telephone.

"The body fits the description," Andy Brewer said.

"Have you told Superintendent Fisher?"

"He's not in yet, sir, and I'd thought you'd rather be the first to know."

"Good man. But make sure you tell him as soon as he gets here. I don't want anyone accused of obstructing the Yard. I'll be there shortly."

He went back to the kitchen and picked up his slice of toast. It was cold.

"Shall I make you another?" said Annie.

"Don't trouble. I've got to get to work. Simon Nelson's turned up."

"Alive?" There was silence. "Oh."

"That makes it three deaths in one week. We've never had anything like this before."

"Are you sure it's the same killer?"

"You were telling me last night that it was. This one has most of the hallmarks of the other two, so I suspect it is."

"Except that this time it was a boy."

"Yes," Jack said. "That's what so bloody odd about it. Normally a killer such as this goes for a certain type. This latest one breaks all the rules." The doorbell rang. "That'll be Eddie," he said, and went to get his coat.

* * *

"They've found the Nelson boy," Jack said as they got in the car.

"Dead?"

"As before. This time he was left on the railway embankment, just along from the Digswell viaduct."

"An easier place to dump a body, I suppose," Fuller said.

"Certainly less public. The spot where he was found backs onto the allotments."

"Then perhaps he's learning something. Not taking any unnecessary risks."

"I don't know if that's a good thing or not."

"Why's that?"

"Because it means he's learning, getting better at it."

"Are there any other differences?"

"The eyes and lips are sewn up, and wax has been poured into his ears, so no difference there."

"Has he been . . . touched?"

"Sexually molested like Sandra Duncan, you mean?"

"I suppose I do, yes." Fuller was evidently uncomfortable talking about it.

"I don't know, Eddie. It's too early to tell. I dare say Hepton will be able to tell us that, once he's done the post-mortem. The body's been taken to the hospital. I'll give them a call when we get in and find out what time it's been scheduled for, and then I'll go along and observe."

"Will Superintendent Fisher let you?" said Fuller.

"Just let him try and stop me. He may have taken over the investigation, but it's still my case, and I'm not having it hijacked without a fight."

* * *

Jack burst into Lane's office without knocking. "Thanks for the support yesterday, Henry. It's good to know you were looking out for me."

Lane shrank back. "My hands were tied, Jack. What else could I have done?"

"You could have thrown your weight behind your own men, for starters. We have a loyal team here with some excellent officers, senior and junior. At the first word from on high, you pull the rug out from under their feet — and mine."

"I'm sorry, Jack; I was under pressure."

"Pressure from Warren Anderton, no doubt."

"I can't really say, but it *was* his daughter who was killed."

"Then it's a pity he didn't behave more like a father on Saturday night, instead of driving his daughter out of the house, so she had to go and stay overnight with friends. What's made him put pressure on the chief constable is nothing more than guilt."

Lane stood up and walked to the window, looking out at the car park. He watched a gleaming, black Wolseley pull in. "Fisher and his men have arrived," he said.

Lane was well aware of Jack Callum's passion for the job, and he respected his abilities. He knew that Callum was angry and frustrated. He had felt the same way yesterday. Jack was correct in his assumption that it was Warren Anderton who had put pressure on the chief constable. The two men attended the same Freemasons' lodge, and Lane was well aware of the power of the brotherhood in his town.

"Try to work with him, Jack. I know Brian Fisher — I was at Hendon with him. He's got a reputation for being something of a martinet, but he's a pretty good copper for all that: he's had some good collars down in London. You never know; he might bring a fresh perspective and get things moving forward."

"I wish I shared your confidence. But I just don't see how a London man can have a better perspective on local killings. The officers here know the area like the backs of their hands."

"Jack — as a favour to me . . ."

"As a favour to you, Henry, I'll continue to work on the case, and I won't get in Fisher's way."

"Thank you, Jack."

"But God help him if he gets in mine."

* * *

"It's good of you to see me, Sir Maurice," said Jack.

"It's not my usual *modus operandi*," said Hepton. "But, in the circumstances, I think we need to apprehend this creature before he takes any more victims." Hepton had a shock of unruly grey hair and a slim goatee beard. He regarded the world from intelligent blue eyes that seemed ready to take on the entire world in a fight. Jack guessed he was somewhere in his fifties.

"You think we're looking for a single killer, then?"

"I'd be very surprised if we weren't."

They were sitting in a small office leading off from the mortuary.

"Your reasons?"

Hepton flipped open a thin file and began to scan the pages of handwritten notes.

"All the bodies that have come to me in the past week show marked similarities. The eyes and lips in all three cases were sewn shut with the same type of silk thread."

"Embroidery thread, yes. I read the reports on Frances Anderton and Sandra Duncan."

"Ah, good. It's gratifying to know that someone reads my reports. I like to think I'm an important resource for the investigation team, not just some old, dried up, 'expert' witness, hauled out when the case comes to court."

"Well, I think forensic pathology is an important factor in any murder investigation."

"Thank you for that. It's nice to hear it from the horse's mouth, so to speak. Anyway, to continue, the paraffin wax used to fill the ears all came from the same source. Household candles of the most common variety — the type you can buy in any ironmonger's store, even Woolworths sells them. All three victims were strangled using a waxed rope, a washing line or something of a similar gauge. Frances Anderton seems to have been subdued a short time before death with something like trichloromethane — you probably know it better as chloroform. I make that assumption because of the slight redness around the girl's mouth. It was a bit difficult to see at first because of the damage caused to the lips by the sewing, but in her case, the assailant must have used a significant quantity of the stuff because there's a slight trace of redness around her nostrils as well.

"Awkward stuff, chloroform, if you don't know what you're doing with it. The old trick that writers of detective fiction are so fond of — holding a pad of chloroform over a victim's nose and mouth to knock them out — doesn't actually work very well; you'd have to hold it there for about five minutes. I think he did just that to the Anderton girl. She wouldn't have given in without a struggle, and that would explain the gash to her foot — she kicked out and her foot caught on something."

"But what about Sandra Duncan?"

"Ah, there I think he realised the mistake he made with the first abduction, and moved on to injecting the girl with a narcotic. I'm still waiting for the blood analysis to come through, but I found a small puncture mark in the side of the girl's neck."

"And the boy, Simon Nelson?"

"Different again. I checked the stomach contents and there was a significant amount of peppermint cordial in there. Peppermint has a very strong flavour and could mask the taste of all manner of narcotics; again I'm waiting for the results of the chemical analysis."

"And yet you still see it being the same man, despite the different methods of subduing the victims."

"Oh yes. The use of embroidery thread and paraffin wax, you see, and the fact that they were all strangled using the same type of rope. I've no doubt that we're dealing with a single perpetrator, but one who is evolving, learning from his past mistakes and refining his method. The fact that he has done all this in barely a week is worrying, very worrying indeed."

"Was there any evidence of sexual interference?"

"Nothing that I could see. No bruising to the genitals or anus, which you would expect to see if the boy had been sodomised."

"Thank you, Sir Maurice, much appreciated. And thank you for your time."

Jack walked from the office, in time to see Fisher push his way through the double doors at the end of the corridor.

Fisher stormed along the corridor towards him.

"Callum! What the hell are you doing here?"

"He was here to see me," said Hepton, emerging from the office. "What business is it of yours?"

Fisher introduced himself, still glaring at Jack. "I'm here to get the results of the Nelson boy's post-mortem, Professor Hepton."

Jack watched Hepton bridle. "Then you're going to have to wait for my report like everybody else — and it's *Sir Maurice* to you."

"I really must insist, *Sir* Maurice . . ."

"You can insist all you like, Superintendent, but it won't make me change my mind. Wait for my report." He turned abruptly, walked back into the office and closed the door behind him.

"I think you've offended him, sir," Jack said, trying not to smile.

Fisher's glare deepened. "I'll see you back at the station, Chief Inspector, and you'll damned well tell me what you two were talking about."

Jack's salute was almost mocking. "Yes, sir."

* * *

"What the hell do you think you're playing at, Callum?"

It was strange, almost surreal, to be sitting on the wrong side of his own desk.

"I wanted an early start, sir."

"So you go behind my back and interview an important witness without the say so from me."

"With respect, sir, you weren't here, and I didn't think we had the time to waste waiting for you to arrive from London."

Fisher's eyes narrowed. "Be very careful, Chief Inspector. I can very easily have you back pounding the beat."

"I'm sure you can, sir.'

"You're a cocky sod, aren't you, Callum?"

Jack said nothing.

"But Chief Superintendent Lane speaks very highly of you, and I've checked your arrest and conviction record. Quite impressive. So, just this once, I'm willing to overlook your indiscretion. But I emphasise, *just this once.* You pull a stunt like that again and I'll have you back—"

"Pounding the beat, sir. Yes, I got that."

Fisher's glare intensified. "The chief superintendent said you have other cases pending, so you'd better go and attend to them."

"Yes, sir," said Jack, and got to his feet.

"Hold hard! Before you get on, you can tell me *exactly* what Sir-Maurice-bloody-Hepton told you. And leave nothing out."

CHAPTER 26

SATURDAY

The hall was large. It heaved with people. Rosie had imagined a small intimate nightspot with tables and chairs, subdued lighting, and perhaps a small jazz band playing subtle melodies as couples slowly smooched. Instead she felt as if they had gate-crashed a giant wedding reception.

The room was brightly lit and cigarette smoke hung heavy in the stale air, making her eyes smart. A long bar took up most of the end wall, and several young men were working behind it, dispensing drinks to a stream of other young men, all dressed for an evening out in sharp, mohair suits, and shiny shoes and hair. Their girlfriends sat in small groups at the tables pushed back along two adjacent walls. Against the other wall was a low stage where a seven-piece band blasted out the current hits, together with some jazz standards. In front of them was the dance floor where several more adventurous couples were practising steps they had learned from *Victor Sylvester's Dancing Club* on TV.

"Archie Trott and his band!" David Neville shouted above the din, guiding Rosie across the dance floor to a vacant table in the corner. "They're one of my favourites. They're really good. Sit yourself down and I'll go and fetch the drinks. What would you like?"

"Do they sell Coca Cola?"

"*Coca Cola*? On a Saturday night?"

He'll think I'm just a kid, Rosie thought. "Er — Babycham." *I'll just have the one. Dad will never find out.*

"Babycham it is. I'll be back in a minute."

Rosie sat alone at the table, feeling self-conscious. She took a powder compact from her patent leather handbag and flipped it open, checking her hair in the small mirror. She'd let Joanie loose on it, and her sister had managed to make her look sophisticated with just thirty minutes of teasing and a liberal spray of hair lacquer. She closed the compact and watched Neville as he stood at the bar, a ten-shilling note gripped between his finger and thumb, waving it occasionally at a barman.

* * *

"Half of bitter and a Babycham," Neville said to the barman, and glanced back at the table to see that Rosie was all right.

"Who's your girlfriend, Davy boy?"

Neville turned and found himself face to face with Derek Webster. Towering behind him stood Peter Lamb, his straight black hair brushed back from his face and pomaded flat, giving him a look reminiscent of Bela Lugosi. Both of them wore suits, which made them look more menacing.

"I haven't got a girlfriend," Neville said.

"So who's the Babycham for, your mother?" Lamb growled.

"I—"

"Come on, Davy," said Webster. "The little tart you came in with? Who is she?"

"Rosie. But she's not my girlfriend. Not properly anyway."

"Well, take her drink back to the table and then meet us in the gents toilet." Webster wheeled round, Lamb following close behind him.

Feeling suddenly sick, Neville paid for the drinks and carried them back to the table. He put them down. "I have to go to the lav. I'll only be a minute."

Rosie looked up at him, concern in her eyes. "Who were they?"

"Just some chaps I know."

"Friends?"

"Just some chaps."

"Are you all right? Only you look a bit green."

He managed a smile. "I'm fine. Something I ate, probably." He scurried off before she could respond. She watched him go, and then picked up her glass, sipping the drink cautiously, screwing up her nose as the bubbles tickled her nostrils. She checked her watch and turned her attention back to the dancers.

* * *

The gents smelled of disinfectant, stale urine and the ubiquitous cigarette smoke. Webster and Lamb were waiting for him. Derek Webster had a comb in his hand and was standing in front of the mirror making some minor adjustments to his neat hair. Peter Lamb was leaning against the sinks that lined one wall, using the toe of his winkle-picker shoe to score lines and circles in the puddle of water at his feet.

"Ah, Davy," said Webster, staring at him from the mirror. "Good of you to join us."

"What do you want, Del?"

"Have you told Gavin about the tart?" Lamb said.

Neville shook his head.

"Do you think that's wise?" said Webster, turning away from the mirror to face him.

"He doesn't need to know."

Webster and Lamb exchanged looks.

"Oh, I think he does," Lamb said. "You know how the game works, Davy. We fetch them and turn them over to Gavin, and, when he's finished with them, we get rid of them and Gavin pays us. *That's* how it works."

"A perfect financial arrangement," said Webster.

"And we don't want you messing it up." Lamb moved away from the sinks towards him.

Neville took a step backwards. "I'm not messing anything up. I've played my part. I did the golf course."

"Yes, and you did it well," Lamb said. "A golf cart. Inspired. But you still need to tell Gavin about the tart."

"Her name's Rosie."

"Yes, Rosie," Webster said. "He needs to know."

Neville shook his head. "Not this one. She's special."

"They're all *special* . . . to Gavin," said Lamb.

The door to the toilet opened and a young man walked in, unbuttoning his fly. He glanced at the three young men, saw the look on Peter Lamb's face, hurriedly buttoned up, turned tail and walked out again.

Lamb went across to the door and leaned against it, holding it closed. "So are you going to tell him? Or do you want us to do it for you?"

"Please, Pete. Don't tell him."

"So *you* will?" said Lamb.

Neville nodded. "Yes, I'll tell him. Just give me a few days."

Lamb crossed to him and laid his arm across Neville's shoulder. "I'll tell you what, Davy. Del and I are your mates. We'll let you have the weekend with her. That's the rest of today, and all day tomorrow. You can take her for a picnic in the park, or over the common, something nice, just for the two of you. And then on Monday, before you go to work, you can go round to Gavin's and tell him all about Rosie. If you don't, I'll tell him myself. You never know, he might let you keep her."

"But he might not," said Webster, grinning sardonically.

Neville opened his mouth to protest but then closed it again. He knew it was futile.

Lamb pulled open the door. "Run along. Have a nice evening. Enjoy the dancing."

Still feeling sick, Neville hurried from the toilet and went back to the table where Rosie sat sipping at her Babycham.

"Feeling better?" Rosie said.

He stuck out his hand. "Let's dance."

He pulled her onto the dance floor, put his hand on her waist and led her in a lively quickstep to the strains of *This Can't Be Love.*

The quickstep finished and without a pause Archie Trott and his men launched into a slow waltz.

David Neville was a fluid dancer and Rosie had worked hard to keep up with him in the quickstep, but now she was able to relax. She leaned into him.

"I'd like to see you tomorrow," he said, putting his lips close to her ear.

"This evening's got a long way to go yet."

"I know. But tomorrow I thought it would be nice to do something, just the two of us. A picnic, maybe?"

She felt like she was dancing on air. "Yes," she said, as the music carried her away. "I think I'd like that."

* * *

"Nice evening, love?"

"Wonderful, Mum!" Rosie walked into the living room. "We're going for a picnic tomorrow. Is everyone in bed?"

"Your dad's not long gone up. Joanie went up early to try out her new bed — your dad and I spent most of the evening sorting out the box room. I know it's only a single but it's still more comfortable than the put-you-up. And we sent Eric up to his room at about eight. We couldn't stand the tuneless strumming. I'll be glad when Eddie gets here tomorrow to show him how to play the damned thing properly. Now, what's all this about a picnic?"

Rosie sat down on the settee and crossed her legs underneath her. "He came out with it just like that. We were dancing and he suddenly blurts out that he wants to spend the day with me tomorrow, and would I like to go on a picnic."

"That's very nice. It sounds as if he's quite sweet on you."

"Oh, Mum, do you really think so?"

"Spending the day with you? Taking you on a picnic? Yes, it sounds to me as if he's smitten. Is he supplying the food?"

"Heavens! We didn't even discuss it. What am I going to do?"

"For one thing, you don't panic. There's stuff in the larder you can use. There's a fresh loaf, some ham off the bone, a pound of cheddar, and there's those sausage rolls you brought home for your dad's tea tomorrow."

"Won't he mind?"

"I'm sure he'll be most put out, but if you take them you'll be doing his waistline a favour, so it's for the greater good." Annie got to her feet. "Look, you turn in. You look tired — too much dancing I expect. I'll put on some eggs to boil. You can have a couple of those each."

Rosie got to her feet and hugged her mother. "Thanks, Mum."

"You just make sure you have a lovely day tomorrow."

Rosie grinned. "Oh, I think I will."

Annie went out to the kitchen and put some eggs on the stove to boil.

"Making tea?"

"Jack Callum! You gave me a start. I thought you were in bed."

"I couldn't sleep."

"You're not still thinking about that case?"

"Afraid so."

"Sit down at the table, then, and I'll put the kettle on."

"I thought that's what you were doing."

She shook her head. "I'm boiling some eggs for Rosie. David is taking her on a picnic tomorrow."

Jack sat at the table. "Is he indeed? He sounds keen."

"As mustard."

Jack raised his eyebrows.

"Don't look surprised. In case you haven't noticed, your little girl is growing into an extremely beautiful young woman. I'm just surprised that would-be suitors aren't queuing along the road for the chance to take her out."

"It will happen one day," Jack said glumly.

"Is it making you feel old?" Annie sat down next to him, taking his hand in hers and squeezing it.

"*Life* is making me feel old, pet."

"Get away with you, you old grouch. When I look at you I still see the handsome, virile young man I married."

Jack pulled her onto his lap and kissed her.

The kettle began to whistle.

She broke off the kiss. "Saved by the whistle. Is that an expression?"

Jack smiled at her fondly. "Make the tea, woman."

"Perhaps we can take it up with us?"

"What a deliciously decadent idea," he said. "Shall I bring the biscuits?"

She shook her head. "I have something just as sweet in mind, and my way, we won't get crumbs in the bed."

As she poured water into the teapot he went across and nuzzled the back of her neck. "You're a temptress, Annie Callum."

"I know."

CHAPTER 27

SUNDAY 17th August 1958

"So that's A, D and G," said Eddie Fuller. "With those three chords you can play all manner of songs."

Eric perched on the edge of the armchair, the guitar resting on his knee, his fingers contorted to make the chord shapes. His tongue stuck out between his teeth as he concentrated. He looked across at Fuller. "What songs?"

Fuller smiled. "What about a song by one of your heroes. Lonnie Donegan? *The Rock Island Line*?"

"Yeah! I love that one. Will you show me how it goes?"

"You know, Lonnie was the same age as you are now when he got his first guitar."

"Really?"

Fuller nodded and smiled. "And he's done all right for himself, hasn't he? Now, hand me the guitar."

* * *

"He's improving." Annie stood at the sink peeling potatoes, and listening to the sounds coming from the other room.

"He hasn't got that good that quickly," Jack said. "That's Eddie playing."

"You mean we haven't got a child prodigy on our hands?"

"I think the hit parade's safe for another couple of years yet," Joan said, her hands buried in a mixing bowl, rubbing butter and sugar into flour to make a crumble topping for their pudding. "Do you know where Rosie's gone for her picnic?"

"She was muttering something about the common," Annie said.

"On a warm Sunday afternoon? She'll be mad if she does. The place will be packed."

Jack looked up from his newspaper. "Did Mum tell you that Rosie took the sausage rolls that I had earmarked for my tea?" he said bleakly.

"Then she did your arteries a favour," Joan said.

"But not my stomach. I was looking forward to them."

The telephone in the hall started to ring.

"If that's work, you're not going in," Annie said.

"Don't worry. I'm not having another roast ruined," Jack said as he went to answer it.

* * *

"Andy, what can I do for you?"

"I just thought I'd let you know, sir, another envelope has arrived. Light blue like the last one, no stamp."

"Who is it addressed to?"

"The Chief Investigating Officer."

"Not Sonia Nelson? And when you say it's arrived, when was this?"

"I found it here on the desk when I got in."

"So whoever delivered it simply walked into the station without being seen and left the envelope there."

"It certainly looks that way," said Brewer.

"He's a cheeky sod. Open it, Andy, and carefully take out what's inside. Try not to smudge any latent fingerprints."

There was silence on the other end of the line as Brewer did as he was requested.

"It's the same as before, sir — three monkeys, drawn in green ink. Are you coming to check it out?"

"Is Superintendent Fisher there?"

"It's his day off, sir."

"Not any more. Give him a call and get him there to investigate." *See how he likes a stone-cold Sunday dinner*, Jack thought as he hung up. *Petty and childish, Jack — you won't go to heaven.* Smiling to himself, he went back to the kitchen and picked up the newspaper.

* * *

Fuller walked into the kitchen. Annie was still at the sink, now scrubbing carrots.

"You're making progress, Eddie. It's a vast improvement on yesterday."

Fuller smiled. "What he lacks in talent, he makes up for in persistence and determination."

"He takes after his father. Can I get you anything?"

"A glass of water would be grand. Where's your husband?"

"Outside. You'll probably find him in the greenhouse." She ran some water into a glass and handed it to him. He gulped it down and opened the back door.

The heat struck him as soon as he stepped outside. He walked down the path to the large greenhouse. Jack was inside, watering the tomato plants. They were heavy with green fruit. Some of them were starting to ripen, a pale orange flush creeping over the skins.

"You have a good crop this year, sir."

"Jack, please, Eddie. It's the weekend." Jack sent a steady stream into the earth from the watering can. "You don't garden, do you Eddie?"

"My landlady wouldn't be very pleased if I did. It would probably help if my flat had a garden."

"Shame. It's very restful, as well as being productive, and it's therapeutic. I can lose myself out here. I find it focuses the mind."

"I can see that it would." Fuller was leaning against the doorframe.

"Another letter arrived," Jack said. "Three monkeys again. This time left at the station."

"At the station? Not at Sonia's?"

Jack shook his head.

"Perhaps he doesn't know where she lives."

"That was my initial thought, but then Andy Brewer told me that it was addressed to *The Investigating Officer*. Strange, don't you think?"

"You're thinking that he's trying to send us a message?"

"That's exactly what I'm thinking," Jack said, moving to another plant.

"What do you think it means?"

"I think he's taunting us, Eddie, the same way that Jack the Ripper used to taunt Fred Abberline and his men, only more obliquely."

"From what I've read, a killer does that because, deep down, he wants to get caught."

"Yes, I've read that too, but I'm not sure that's the case here. As I say, the message is oblique, so bloody oblique as to be obscure. No, I think he's challenging us: 'Look at me, you dim coppers, do you think you can catch me?'"

"I wouldn't take it personally, Jack."

"I'm not. No, damn it, *I am*! This chap thinks he's smarter than me, thinks he's fireproof. Why? What makes him so sure I won't be able to catch him? He's killed three times in a week. That's a very short time frame for your average multiple killer. He's barely giving himself enough time to draw breath. It doesn't make sense. What's his motive? It doesn't fit with anything I've come across, or read about before. A sexual motive only applies to one of the victims. There's evidence that Sandra Duncan was molested, but no sign of anything like that with Frances Anderton or Simon Nelson."

"So can we write off sexual deviance as the motive?"

"We can certainly discard it as the primary motive. No, there's something else at work here — something I just can't put my finger on."

"Well, I suppose it's Scotland Yard's problem now."

Jack set down the watering can. "Yes, I suppose it is."

Fuller was watching his boss closely. He'd seen that same look of steely determination on the face of Eric Callum just minutes before, as he struggled with the guitar chords. "But you're not going to let it go, are you, Jack?"

"Am I hell. Are you staying for a bite to eat, Eddie? Annie's cooking a leg of lamb. Apple crumble to follow."

"It's tempting, Jack, but I'm meeting Judy after her shift at the Dog and Duck. I thought we'd go for a walk this afternoon. She likes walking."

"She sounds like the healthy type."

"She likes to keep her body in shape."

"As I'm sure you do."

Fuller smiled. "I'm sure I don't know what you mean, Chief Inspector."

Jack dug in the pocket of his corduroy trousers and pulled out a handful of coins. "Five shillings," he said, and handed Fuller two half crowns.

"I told you, Eric can have the lessons for free," Fuller said, refusing the coins.

"Buy Judy an ice cream when you're out for your walk. I insist." He pressed the money into Fuller's hand. "And thanks. From what I heard, Eric's sounding a lot better than he did last night."

"Oh, he'll master it in the end. He likes a challenge — just like his father."

* * *

Dusk was beginning to settle over Hertfordshire when David Neville eased the car into the kerb, outside the Callum house.

"Thank you for a lovely day," Rosie said to him.

"You're very welcome," said Neville. "Thanks for bringing the food, though I feel bad, inviting you for a picnic and expecting you to bring your own."

"It wasn't a problem." She reached for the door handle but didn't open the door. "Well," she said. "I suppose I should go inside."

"I suppose you should." David Neville slid his arm around her shoulders.

"I've got work tomorrow."

"Yeah, me too," he said, leaning across and kissing her.

She had been waiting all day for him to kiss her, but it still took her by surprise, and she was breathless.

She glanced around at the house, imagining her entire family standing at the windows, but there was no sign of anyone looking out at her.

"I suppose—" she started, and he kissed her again, more intensely this time, covering her mouth with his, his tongue darting into her mouth and dancing with her own. She closed her eyes and let herself relax, enjoying the sensations aroused by her first, real, adult kiss. She kissed back passionately, with a delicious thrill as his hand crept up inside the front of her blouse and cupped her breast.

"We shouldn't . . ." she said, but hadn't the will to stop him.

It was only when the hand moved down to her thigh and crept under her skirt that the alarm bells started ringing in her mind. As his fingers skimmed the lace of her underwear, she brought her own hand down and clamped her fingers over his wrist.

She tore her lips away from his. "No!" she said. "Not that. Not yet."

But he wrenched her arm away and moved his hand further up her skirt.

Suddenly she was fighting him, twisting her face away to stop him kissing her, and smacking his arm. "I said no!"

When he refused to stop, she brought her hand back and delivered a stinging blow across his cheek. "I'm not that type of girl, David Neville!"

He reacted with shock, falling back into his seat and sitting there, wide eyed, his breath coming in short gasps. Finally he found his voice. "I'm . . . I'm sorry," he stammered.

She was glaring at him. "You ruined it," she said, and reached for the door handle again, this time opening the door.

She stepped out of the car.

"Rosie, wait. I'm sorry I . . ."

She was standing outside the car, looking in at him, shaking her head. "Everything. You ruined everything." She slammed the car door and ran up the path, fumbling in her purse for her front door key. As she slid the key into the lock, she heard the car's engine roar, and the squeal of rubber on tarmac as he sped off down the road.

Annie was standing in the hallway as Rosie burst in through the door.

"I thought I heard a car. Have you had a nice time?"

Without looking up, Rosie barrelled past her and ran up the stairs. Her bedroom door slammed shut and then there was silence.

Joan came out into the hall and stared at the shocked expression on her mother's face. "Was that Rosie?"

Annie nodded.

"Where is she?"

Without a word Annie pointed up the stairs.

Joan frowned. "I'll go up and see if she's all right."

"She's very upset," Annie said, shaking her head. "I don't know what—"

"Leave it to me," said Joan, and trotted up the stairs.

Annie walked into the living room and, ignoring Jack and Eric's questioning looks, went across to the sideboard and poured herself a sherry.

"Problems?" Jack said.

"The course of true love . . ." Annie said, and knocked it back.

CHAPTER 28

SUNDAY

Joan tapped at the bedroom door. "Rosie? Are you all right in there? Can I come in?"

"Go away and leave me alone!"

Joan turned the doorknob and stepped into the room. Her sister was lying on the bed, her face buried in the pillow.

Joan went across and perched on the edge of the bed. She reached out and stroked Rosie's hair. "Do you want to talk about it?"

Rosie shook her head.

"Well if you do, I'm right here," said Joan. Rosie reached behind her and found Joan's hand. She intertwined her fingers with her sister's and squeezed hard.

"Men, eh?" said Joan. "What would you do with them?"

Her face still buried in the pillow, Rosie nodded her head. "He ruined everything," she said, her voice muffled.

"Yes," Joan said, still stroking her sister's hair. "They make a habit of doing that. Do you want to tell me what he did?" She spoke gently.

Rosie shook her head.

"Just between you and me. Mum and Dad don't have to know."

Rosie turned around on the bed and faced her sister. "Promise you won't tell?"

"Cross my heart."

Rosie looked into her sister's face. She shut her eyes. "He tried to touch me," she said softly.

"Where? Your breasts?"

Rosie shook her head. "The other place."

"You didn't let him touch you there, did you?"

Rosie shook her head.

Joan let out a sigh. "Well, that's all right then."

"It's not all right. It will never be all right," wailed Rosie.

"You didn't let him touch you, so no harm done."

"You don't understand. I made him stop . . . but I didn't want to. I wanted him to touch me."

Joan stared at her, and then leaned forward and took her in her arms. "Oh, you poor lamb."

* * *

"So why all the histrionics?" Jack said as he climbed into bed beside Annie.

"Search me," said Annie, and picked up her book.

"Doesn't Joanie know?"

"I'm sure she does, but she's staying tight-lipped."

"If that boy's done anything to upset my Rosie I'll take his bloody head off."

"You're such a typical man sometimes, Jack. You can't solve everything with a left hook."

Jack expelled a breath. He hadn't even been aware he was holding it. "Yes. You're right, as usual. Are you going to talk to her?"

"I looked in on her before I came up. She's sleeping like a baby. It will keep, but I do intend to find out why she was so upset. I made a mistake with Joanie all those years ago, trying not to pry, and look where that led. Now, let me read my book. I'm just about to find out who done it."

"Which is more than I am." Jack switched off his bedside light.

* * *

The Old Sergeant public house was on PC Alistair Kirby's regular beat, and every Sunday evening it was usual for him to stop by to have a chat with the landlord and owner, Ted Fairly, to make sure everything was as it should be. In return for the consideration, Fairly would provide a bowl of mild ale for Satan and a tomato juice for Kirby.

As Kirby pushed open the partly glazed double doors, he wrinkled his nose at the smell of beer that assailed him. Someone in the corner was pounding out *Daisy, Daisy* on the piano, and the regulars were united in song.

"Everything in order tonight, Ted?"

"It is now, Al." Fairly slid an earthenware bowl half-filled with mild ale across the bar to Kirby. "Mind, I thought we were going to have some trouble in here earlier. We had some of those Teddy boys in, behaving like the scum they are, but Ray and his friends soon sorted them out and sent them packing." He nodded towards three very well-built men, propping up the other end of the bar and singing lustily.

"With a security detail like that you hardly need my visits," Kirby said, and set the bowl down on the floor for Satan to lap.

"It does no harm for the punters to see a uniform in here every now and then. It makes them feel safe. Your usual?"

"Please, Ted. I'm a little parched. It's still warm out there."

"And close too," Fairly said. "I wouldn't be surprised if we have a storm later."

"After I've finished my beat, hopefully. I left my waterproofs back at the station."

"I can always lend you an umbrella."

"I think not," Kirby said with a smile. "But thanks all the same."

Kirby took his drink and made a circuit of the pub, nodding at familiar faces, pausing to watch a couple of the regulars playing dominos, and stopping at the throw line to watch the darts team as they practised for a forthcoming match with a rival pub.

By the time he got back to the bar he had finished his drink. Satan's bowl was empty, and the dog was lying on the floor, eying the earthenware dish expectantly, as if hoping for a refill.

Further along, Ray, one of the pub's unofficial protectors, was saying his goodbyes. "I'm off then, Ted!" he called out across the bar.

Fairly threw him a salute. "See you tomorrow, Ray. And thanks for earlier."

Kirby set his empty glass down on the bar and watched Ray lurch unsteadily across the pub and elbow his way out through the doors.

"He's drunk."

"After ten pints you would be too," Fairly said.

Kirby reached down and picked up Satan's lead. "I'd better be off myself. Come on, boy. You've had enough for one night." He tugged on the lead and the dog got to its feet, still eyeing the empty bowl. "I'll pop in sometime in the week," he said to Fairly.

"See you, Al."

As he went out into the street, a low rumble of thunder greeted him. He adjusted his cap and looked up at the sky. There was no moon, but he got the impression of thick cloud above him. "Just what I need," he muttered as a fat raindrop splashed against his cheek.

He saw Ray weaving his way along, pausing at each lamppost and holding on to it as if he might topple over at any minute.

Kirby turned to follow him. It was on his beat anyway and he was concerned that the man might step out into the road and under a car or bus. Not there was much chance of that happening. There wouldn't be a bus along for at least another hour, and there were few cars around at this time of night. In fact there was no one on the street except for Ray, and Kirby with his dog. Which was why the shout took him by surprise and made Ray stop in his tracks.

"Hey, big man! Not so tough now, are you? Without your mates to back you up!"

Three Teddy boys appeared in the road and started moving towards Ray. "Now, look, fellas, I don't want any trouble, right."

"Wrong." The Teddy boy, who had a Brylcreemed quiff and was wearing the regulation tight drainpipe trousers and thick-soled shoes, moved away from the group and stood directly in front of Ray, pressing him back into the lighted doorway of a shop. The Teddy boy reached into his pocket. Kirby heard a click and saw something metallic glint in the shop lights.

He reached down and unclipped the dog's lead. "Sic him, Satan."

Like a greyhound out of the trap, the dog tore across to the Teddy boys. The dog's sudden appearance, growling and then barking loudly, made two of the Teddy boys turn tail and run. It was too late for the Teddy boy holding the flick knife. Before he realised what was happening, the dog had launched itself at him and clamped its jaws on the wrist of the hand holding the flick knife.

Kirby ran three steps behind the dog as it did just what it had been trained to do. By the time he reached the scene, the Teddy boy was on the ground, struggling pathetically to fend off the dog, and Ray was leaning against the door of the shop, vomiting.

Kirby took out his torch and shone it into the tear-streaked face of the fallen Teddy boy. "Hello, Billy. Now what have I told you about playing with knives?"

Billy was writhing on the ground, trying to free his arm.

"I didn't mean anything, Mr Kirby. Honest," he said. "Get him off me — please!"

"Satan, leave!" Kirby barked, and the dog released its grip on Billy's wrist. Kirby leaned down and snapped a handcuff over it, attached the other cuff to his own wrist, and hauled Billy to his feet.

Ray had partly recovered and was leaning against the door, wiping his mouth with a khaki handkerchief. "Do you know this clown, Officer Kirby?"

"Let's just say that Billy and I are acquainted," Kirby said. "Now, I suggest you get off home. You'll have no more trouble tonight."

"But what about him? He attacked me," Ray said belligerently.

"Don't you worry yourself about him. Billy here is going to spend the night in a police cell. If you wish to press charges then be at the station first thing tomorrow and the CID will take your statement."

"But I've got to go to work tomorrow."

"You're welcome to come back with us to the station now, if you like. I'm sure the duty officer will oblige."

Ray seemed to consider this for a moment, and then closed his eyes and started to sway again.

Kirby stepped back sharply to avoid the spray of vomit that emerged. Finally it stopped and Ray groaned as he dabbed at his lips again. "Best get home," he mumbled.

"You're probably right," Kirby said, picking up the flick knife and closing it. He clipped the lead back onto Satan's collar and tugged on the handcuff, stepping out of the doorway at a sharp pace and pulling Billy along behind him. Every few paces the Alsatian looked up at the handcuffed Teddy boy and growled.

"Don't let him go for me again," Billy pleaded as they walked back to the police station. Rain was now falling steadily from the sky, accompanied by rolls of thunder and the occasional flash of lightning.

"Don't worry, Billy. He had his dinner earlier. You were merely a snack."

"Bastard dog," Billy muttered.

"Billy Flynn," Kirby said to the desk sergeant when they arrived at the station. "Attempted assault with a deadly weapon. He needs to spend the night in the cells until the Chief Super decides what to do with him."

"Bread and water for him, Constable Kirby?" Desk Sergeant Alan Turner said with a slightly evil smile.

"We don't want to spoil him, Sergeant."

CHAPTER 29

MONDAY AUGUST 18th 1958

"Chief Inspector!" called Fisher. "My office, please."

Jack followed him upstairs and into the room that until a few days ago had been his. An extra table had been brought in and two of Fisher's men were seated at either end of it, both with files open in front of them as they read through witness statements.

"Inspector Lymon and Sergeant Greyling," Fisher said. "Two of my best men. Gentlemen, may we have the room?"

They closed their files and trooped out.

"Take a seat, Callum."

Jack pulled up a chair and sat down at the desk.

Fisher shrugged off his raincoat and hung it on the hat stand, moved around the desk and sat down in Jack's office chair. "Since I arrived here I've been reviewing your investigation," he said, glancing down at a sheet of paper lying on the blotter in front of him. "And I'm afraid I have to say that I'm not impressed."

Jack said nothing.

"Perhaps you can help me try to make some sense of your thinking," Fisher said. "These characters, Fellowes and Channing, why haven't you eliminated them from your enquiries? Both men have cast-iron alibis. Damn it, man, one of them was in Switzerland for Christ's sake, the other up in

Scotland. So why are you wasting precious resources investigating men who weren't even in the country when the crimes were committed, and there's nothing to link them to the Nelson boy."

"But they know each other."

"*Possibly knew* each other, at university, what, twenty-odd years ago? Chief Inspector, you're reaching. You have no concrete evidence connecting them to these murders."

"They each knew one of the victims."

"Circumstantial. As I said, you're reaching, trying to turn coincidence into evidence."

"I don't think so."

"Well, that's your opinion," Fisher said. "My opinion is that you've been sending your men down blind alleys, investigating improbable, if not impossible, suspects." Fisher picked up the piece of paper, screwed it into a ball and dropped it into the wastepaper basket. "Needless to say, I've eliminated them from *our* enquiries. Have you looked at the sexual motive?"

"Yes."

"But you haven't taken it anywhere."

"There isn't anywhere to take it yet."

Fisher took a file from the small pile on his desk and flipped it open. "The pathologist's report on Sandra Duncan," he said. "Hepton thinks that sexual congress took place, post-mortem."

"Yes, I read that, sir."

"Then we're looking for a sexual deviant. Have you checked in the files for similar cases of necrophilia?"

Jack shook his head.

"No, I didn't think so. But no matter. I have my men working on that angle now. Which brings us to your rather far-fetched theory about the three monkeys."

"I think it's valid. You saw the letter that was left at the desk yesterday."

"Yes, and I did not appreciate your man Brewer contacting me at home on a Sunday to drag me down from London to look at a child's scribble."

"They're significant, sir."

"So *you* say. *I* think it's another blind alley — another avenue to send your team down that will eventually prove fruitless. You can't even be sure they're monkeys. They look more like the three bears to me. In other words, Chief Inspector, a bloody fairy story."

Jack stared down at the desk in front of him. Fisher was rubbishing his work, and nothing Jack could say was going to convince him otherwise.

"So I'm tearing up your investigation, Chief Inspector, metaphorically at least, and starting my team on other avenues. You've wasted a whole week on this and essentially got nowhere with it. And that is what I'll be telling the chief constable when I see him later on today."

Jack stared at Fisher steadily. "As is your prerogative, sir. Was there anything else?"

"Not at the moment. But I will be calling on your team to do most of the legwork on our investigation. You will make them available to us."

"Of course."

"I must admit that I'm very disappointed, Chief Inspector. I'd heard some good things about you before I came up here, but from what I've seen of your methods so far, I haven't been impressed, not impressed at all."

"I'm sorry I've been such a disappointment, sir."

"Disappointing me is the least of your worries, Chief Inspector. My report on this shambles will go on your record, and then officers more senior than me will look at it and take the appropriate action. If you're fortunate you'll receive a rap on the knuckles and nothing more. Your past record stands in your favour, so demotion, while it remains a possibility, seems unlikely, but nothing is certain in this life. That will be all."

"Very good, sir." Jack turned and left the office.

In the corridor, Lymon and Greyling were sharing a whispered conversation. Jack walked past without acknowledging them and went down to the squad room, where a small desk had been cleared for him. He felt the eyes of his team on him as he sat, taking slow and steady breaths, trying to quell his anger, which was threatening to erupt.

At the adjacent desk Fuller was speaking with a scruffy-looking young man with unkempt hair who wore a crumpled, mud-spattered, purple drape jacket, and drainpipe trousers, scuffed at the knees.

"Name?" Fuller said.

"You know my name."

"For the record."

"Flynn, Billy Flynn."

"And you realise you're being charged with possession of a deadly weapon, and intent to use said weapon?"

"I wasn't going to use it. I just wanted to shake him up a bit, that's all."

"And is that your defence?"

"It's as good as any. You lot will be stitching me up anyway."

"Do you deny being in possession of the weapon — a flick knife to be exact?"

Billy shrugged. Fuller made a note on his pad.

"You haven't asked to see a solicitor?"

"I don't know one, and, as I said, what's the point?"

"A duty solicitor can be appointed to you."

Billy said nothing. He was staring intently over Fuller's shoulder at the photos of the murder victims pinned on the noticeboard.

"Have you anything to say? Any mitigating circumstances that might help your case?' Fuller's patience was slowly eroding.

"I need my comb back. That prick down the cells took it off me. Said I might harm myself with it."

"A comb?"

"Yeah, the bastard. What did he think I was going to do, comb myself to death? I mean, look at the state of me. Bloody trousers are ruined. Mud and dog spit all over my jacket. I'll have to buy new ones — a week's wages right there. The least you can do is give me a comb so I can make myself look presentable."

A smile twitched at the corners of Fuller's mouth. "Okay, Billy, I'll get you a comb . . . but you need to give me something in return."

"What?"

"A full account of the events of last night, and an admission that you intended to use the knife to carve up Raymond Willows. What do you call it? Striping him?"

Billy leaned forward in his seat and shook his head. "Do you think I've just come off a bleeding banana boat? You let me have a comb and I'll tell you about the boy."

"What boy?"

"The one in the photo there." Billy pointed at the noticeboard.

Fuller stared at him for a moment and then turned and looked at Jack, who was listening intently. Something was making the hairs prickle at the back of his neck. He went across to Fuller's desk and pulled up a chair. "Chief Inspector Callum," he said. "Billy, is it? What can you tell us about the boy in the photograph?"

"Comb?"

"Let him have your comb, Sergeant."

"What?"

"Your comb. Mr Flynn here wants to tidy himself up."

Fuller stared at Jack incredulously. He shook his head, produced his comb and handed it to Billy.

"Mirror?"

"Don't push—"

"Fetch him a mirror, Sergeant."

Swearing under his breath, Fuller pushed himself to his feet and went off in search of a mirror.

"Right," Jack said. "What can you tell me about Simon Nelson?"

"Was that his name? Only we were never introduced."

"That was his name, Billy. Simon Nelson, fifteen years old, strangled and dumped on the railway embankment between here and Welwyn."

Billy glanced round, apparently looking for Fuller and the mirror. Then he turned back to Jack. "Okay, I'll tell you what I know," he said.

* * *

"So this young man on the bus who interrupted your chat with Simon — do you have a description of him?"

"I can do better than that. I'll tell you his name." Billy was almost triumphant. He had given the copper an edited account of what had happened on the bus on Thursday. It looked like the fool was buying it. He had learned from experience that the rozzers were gullible; they'd swallow any old toffee if you dressed it up in a language they understood, and gave them some facts they were eager to hear. That was why Billy had never had any use for solicitors. He relied upon his guile to get him out of trouble.

"So what is his name?"

"Peter Lamb. He's a big bugger — really big."

"How do you know this Lamb?"

"He went to my school. Couple of years above me."

"So did he recognise you on the bus?"

"Nah, I doubt it. I wasn't a Ted then, just a spotty kid in a school uniform, and Lamb was the school bully, so I kept my head down and stayed out of his way. Anyway he was thick as shit, like the rest of his mates."

"And the last time you saw him on Thursday he was talking to Simon on the bus?"

"Yeah, chatting with him and acting all brotherly."

"Why are you smiling?"

"Well, everyone at school knew Lamb was a bender — queer as a coot. I'm sure that Simon there saw him as his knight in shining armour, his bloody saviour. Little did he know. I'll bet Lamb had other ideas in mind."

"Do you know where he lives?"

"Nah. But I know where he works: Hennessey's in town — the chemist's. He delivers for them, on his push bike; takes pills round to all the old bids that are too lazy to go and get them themselves."

Fuller returned with a shaving mirror from the officer's restroom and handed it over. Billy set the mirror down on the desk, adjusted it so he had a clear view of himself, and then began to comb his hair into its former elaborate quiff.

"So is that it, then? Can I go now?"

Jack looked at Fuller who was regarding Billy Flynn with ill-concealed contempt. "I take it Mr Flynn's been read his rights?"

"Yes, Chief Inspector," Fuller said, now understanding where this was leading.

"Then charge him and take him back to the cells. While you're at it, get on the telephone to the duty solicitor and tell him we have a client for him."

"Hey! You can't do this. We had a deal."

"Indeed we did, Billy, and we're very grateful for the information. You got your comb and a mirror, and I hope you and your quiff will be very happy together. Get him out of my sight, Sergeant."

"With pleasure." Fuller hauled Billy to his feet.

Jack sat down at his desk and called across to WPC Banks. "Myra, do you know Hennessey's in town — the chemist's?"

"Yes, sir!"

"Then get your coat. You're coming with me."

CHAPTER 30

MONDAY

Doris Worthington looked up from her typewriter at the young man who had just walked into the office of Povey and Fellowes. "May I help you?"

"I'd like to see Mr Fellowes," said David Neville.

"Do you have an appointment with Mr Fellowes?"

"No, but I'm sure he'll see me."

"Really? Take a seat over there and I'll check for you."

Neville went across to the seats lining the wall and sat down, watching as the secretary pressed a button on the intercom and spoke quietly into it.

Neville heard Tim Fellowes' disembodied voice float from the speaker. "Send him in."

Fellowes met him at the door. "David! Good to see you. Do come in."

Neville walked into the office and Fellowes closed the door behind him. Inside, he suddenly turned and brought his face to within inches of Neville's. "What the hell do you think you're doing, coming here?" he hissed.

Neville backed away. "I needed to see you." He was close to tears.

"What on earth for? Haven't you been paid?"

"Yes, I have . . . it's not that."

"What then?" Fellowes sat down at his desk, his eyes on Neville's face.

"I've met someone — a girl."

"So?"

"I took her to a dance on Saturday and bumped into Peter and Derek. They said I should tell Gavin."

"And so you should," Fellowes said. "You boys entered into an agreement with us, David. We tell you about suitable candidates and you bring them to us, and when Gavin has finished with them, you dispose of them as he instructs you. In return you are all paid handsomely. Are you telling me you wish to renege on that agreement?"

Neville shook his head. "No, Mr Fellowes. I don't want to back out of the agreement, but this girl — she's different. I think she's special. She could be *the one.*"

Fellowes leaned back in his chair and yawned. "Oh, David, please. How old are you? Twenty-one, twenty-two? And you're talking about this girl being *the one*? You sound pathetic, do you know that?"

"But Rosie's special."

"Is that her name? Rosie? What make her so special?"

"She's sweet and kind, and very pretty."

"An ideal subject for Gavin, then."

"Tim, please. Have a word with Gavin for me. Persuade him that Rosie's not suitable for what you want."

"Why should I?"

"Look, I've more than played my part in all this. I dumped the girl on the golf course for you. I took a huge risk following Gavin's instructions. It was all right for you. You were up in Scotland, away from it all. It would have been my neck in the noose if I'd been caught."

"Yes, and I'm very grateful. But what you're asking . . . Look, I don't like this thing any more than you do. I had no idea you were friends with Peter Lamb, or that he'd ask you to get involved, but you came into it of your own free will."

"So did you."

Fellowes looked at him steadily. "You really think that, don't you?"

"Well, didn't you?"

"You don't know the half of it," said Fellowes quietly.

Neville stared at him. There seemed to be genuine regret in Tim Fellowes' voice.

Fellowes suddenly got to his feet. "Look, here's what I'll do. I'll have a word with Gavin on your behalf. I'll make no promises. He knows what he wants; he has a clear goal in mind, so the chances are that he won't let you keep her. But I'll do my best to persuade him. Is that good enough for you? We still need you on the bowls team, and we don't want anything to get in the way of that."

"Okay."

"Right then, cut along. I have work to do. Call me tonight and I'll let you have Gavin's decision."

"Thank you." Neville did not look at Fellowes. He was afraid to see the lie in his eyes. "I'll wait to hear from you."

"And, David?"

"Yes?"

"Don't you ever dare come here again. Understood?"

Neville nodded and hurried from the office.

Fellowes sat down at the desk, rubbed his eyes and picked up the phone.

"Adam. We need to talk."

* * *

Hennessey's was like an old apothecary's shop, with large mahogany multi-drawer cabinets and rows of shelves holding jars and bottles of every shape, size and colour. They were mostly used for display purposes now, but some of the slightly worn handwritten labels told of a shop with a rich history, and reflected a time when ingredients such as camphor, arsenic and alum were their stock in trade.

"Shop!" Jack called. The bell above the door also announced them, but there was no sign of movement from behind the old glass-topped counter.

"Won't keep you a moment!" came a querulous voice.

Myra was walking slowly around the shop, stopping to look in the glass-fronted display cabinets and peering at the white bottles of Old Spice aftershave, the grey oval tins of talcum powder.

"Christmas presents for your boyfriend?" Jack said

"My dad, more like. I can't imagine ever going out with a man who wears that. Much too old-fashioned."

"I wear it myself sometimes."

"I know. No offence meant."

"None taken."

"Can I help you? Do you have a prescription?"

They turned and saw a tall, cadaverous man standing behind the counter. He was smiling at them, which made him look rather ghoulish.

Jack produced his warrant card. "And this is WPC Banks. We'd like to ask you some questions, if we may."

"Ernest Hennessey. Ask away, Chief Inspector. My time is yours."

"That's very good of you. Actually we'd like to ask you about one of your employees."

Hennessey seemed to be taken aback. "Freda? You want to ask me about Freda? She's been with me for years. Not in any trouble I hope. It's her day off, otherwise she would have been here to help you when you first came in."

"A young man?" Myra said. "Peter Lamb?"

"Peter?"

"He works for you?"

"Well, yes, I suppose he does — now and then. He helps with the deliveries mostly, and he's an absolute boon when it comes to stocktaking. Strangely enough, I've never thought of him as an employee, but I suppose, now you come to mention it, I do pay him for what he does, so that would make him an employee, wouldn't it?"

"Is he around?"

"What's today? Monday? Yes, Monday. So he won't be in until after lunch, and then he'll be taking out the deliveries."

"Do you have an address for him?"

Hennessey scratched his balding head. "Well, I suppose I must have, somewhere. You'd be better off talking to Freda about that sort of thing. She looks after all the paperwork — has a system — a complete mystery to me. But it's her—"

"Day off? Yes, I gathered that. Is there any way you'd know where to find it?"

"I suppose I could try." At that moment a stout woman in tweeds, dragging a yapping terrier on a lead, entered the shop, a prescription clutched in her hand.

"Mrs Davenport. Is that your usual?"

"It's my sciatica, Ernest. Doctor Frost thinks he might have a handle on it, but I'm not convinced." She handed Hennessey the prescription.

He glanced at it. "Would you like to wait for it? It will be about fifteen minutes."

"Yes, I can wait."

"Mr Hennessey?" said Jack. "Peter Lamb's address?"

Hennessey looked flustered. He glanced at the prescription in his hand, at Jack and then back to the prescription. "Just give me fifteen minutes," he said. "And I'll be with you."

"Give me strength," Jack mumbled darkly.

* * *

Thirty minutes later Hennessey emerged with a slip of paper clutched in his hand. "Peter's address! I knew it had to be here somewhere."

"Mill Road," said Jack to Myra. "Do you know it?"

She nodded. "Yes, I know it. It's one of the roads leading onto the council estate."

"You can drive, then. I don't know it at all." He turned to Hennessey. "Do you have much call for chloroform? Only I noticed you have a bottle of it on your shelves." He pointed to the top shelf of the cabinet where a number of bottles were slowly gathering a c of dust.

"Ah, trichloromethane, no, not these days," said Hennessey. "I used to use it in some of the processes, years ago, but it's largely been superseded now by less volatile compounds. In those days I had to use a fume cabinet every time I used it in case I put myself to sleep. It will do that, you know, if you inhale it for long enough — but I don't suppose I've used the fume cabinet in over fifteen years."

"But you still keep the bottle on your shelves?"

"For display only these days. If you look closely, there are a number of bottles up there that would have many a modern day pharmacist running for the hills, but I like to keep them to remind myself of how things have changed since I first started in this business."

Jack smiled. "I still have my first set of handcuffs at home. Clunky things compared to today's stainless-steel jobs. I suppose I keep them for the same reason."

"Peter's not in any kind of trouble, is he?" Hennessey said suddenly.

"Nothing for you to worry about. We just need to eliminate him from our enquiries."

"That's a relief. He's very useful to have around. He knows all the addresses, and my customers know and like him."

Myra took his arm and squeezed it. "I'm sure there's nothing to get alarmed about. We just want to ask him a few questions, that's all."

"Good. That's very good to hear. It's so hard to find people you can rely on these days."

* * *

Outside in the car, Myra spoke. "Did you mean what you said in there, about him having nothing to worry about?"

"No."

"That's what I thought."

"Consider this, Myra. Peter Lamb, as far as we know, was one of the last people to be seen with Simon Nelson, and we know from the forensic report that chloroform was used in the abduction of Frances Anderton. Not an easy thing to get your hands on, I would have thought, and yet Lamb works in a place that has a bottle of the stuff just sitting on the shelf. Remember what Hennessey said about Lamb being useful at stocktaking time? He must have known the bottle was there. It would be easy to decant the stuff into another container and spirit it away. It's not as if Hennessey was going to check. You heard him yourself. He hasn't used it for years. And the other drugs used in the abductions — Hennessey's is a convenient source."

"You have a point."

"And another thing . . . You saw the bottles on that top shelf. Years of dust on them, except for the bottle of chloroform. There was very little dust on that one, which suggests to me that someone has used that bottle quite recently."

Myra smiled. "The art of detection is not dead!"

"I hope not. Or all the time I spent as a kid reading Sherlock Holmes stories was totally wasted. Drive on."

CHAPTER 31

MONDAY

The house on Mill Road was in a state of disrepair, with peeling paintwork and brickwork that badly needed re-pointing. There was no doorbell, so Jack rapped on the door with his fist. After what seemed like an age the door was opened by an elderly man wearing sunglasses, impeccably dressed in a white shirt, navy blue tie and grey slacks. His white hair was neatly cut and swept away from his face, but on his feet were an incongruous pair of maroon carpet slippers.

"Hello. Can I help you?" He appeared to stare somewhere to the left of Jack.

Jack introduced himself and Myra. "Mr Lamb, I'd like to speak with your son, if I may."

The man turned his head towards the voice and Jack realised that he was blind. "My son's dead."

"Peter Lamb?"

The man smiled. "You mean my *grandson.*"

"Right. May we see him? We have a few questions we'd like to ask him."

The man continued to smile. "I'd like to help you. But I'm afraid he's not here at the moment."

"I see. Will he be back any time soon?"

The old man shook his head. "I really couldn't say. It's Monday. He always goes out on a Monday. He could be back at any time. I'd ask you in to wait for him, but it could be a long one. Then again, he could be back in the next ten minutes."

"Perhaps we could do that, then — maybe for ten minutes or so? It would save us calling back."

"Of course." The old man stood aside. "Go on through. The living room is at the end of the passage, on the right."

Jack and Myra walked into the house, wrinkling their noses at the smell of burnt toast.

"Forgive the smell. I made a bit of a balls-up with the grill."

"Is it just you and your grandson that live here?" Myra said.

"It is now. My wife passed five years ago. We've been alone since then."

"I'm sorry," said Myra.

Jack was looking around the room, noting the old, comfortable-looking armchair placed at one side of a tiled fireplace. Every flat surface was covered with photographs in all manner of frames, from tarnished silver to cheap plastic Woolworth's specials.

An oval mirror hung above the fireplace and pictures were pinned to the walls, copies of old paintings taken from magazines and books.

"Please take a seat." The old man waved airily in the direction of a couple of dining chairs pushed up against the wall.

An ancient Bakelite wireless stood on an oak sideboard. It was broadcasting music, but the volume was set so low that Jack had to strain to hear what was being played. "Glenn Miller," he said, finally identifying the tune.

"The Joe Loss Orchestra, actually," the old man said. "But an easy mistake to make. *In the Mood.* It's Joe Loss's signature tune."

"Wasn't it Glenn Miller's as well?"

The old man laughed as he settled into his armchair. "You fell into the trap that so many people do. You assume that as Miller recorded the original, it was his signature tune, but it wasn't. That honour went to *Moonlight Serenade.* Is the wireless loud enough for you? Can you hear it?"

"It's a little quiet, but it's fine."

The old man ran his fingers over his wristwatch. "A quarter to eleven," he said.

Jack looked at him in surprise and then it dawned on him that the watch had no glass and he was tracing the hands with the tips of his fingers.

"So you'll give him ten minutes. Is that enough time for a cup of tea?"

"Oh, I think so."

"I'll make it," said Myra, standing up.

"Would you, my dear? That would be very kind." The old man turned in Jack's direction. "Is she pretty?" he said. "She sounds pretty."

"Very pretty," said Jack.

Myra smiled, mouthed "Liar," and went out to the kitchen.

"Yes, I thought so."

"Do you take sugar?" Myra called from the kitchen.

"Two please! It's in a bowl in the cupboard above the sink."

"Do you know where everything is?" Jack asked him.

"Of course," the old man said. "I have to." He pointed to his dark glasses. "I know the contents of every cupboard, what's on every shelf, and the position of every piece of furniture. It would be a disaster if I didn't. I'd be falling arse over tip every five minutes."

"When did you lose your sight?"

"1944, at El Alamein. Bloody hand grenade. Shrapnel."

"You seem to cope very well."

"I get by. Having Peter here helps. He's my eyes more often than not."

"It must be a great comfort."

"When my son and daughter-in-law were killed in forty-seven, the authorities wanted to take him away from me, put him in some damned orphanage. They didn't think I was capable of looking after him. But I fought them like I fought the bloody Nazis, and won. The irony is, now he looks after me."

"You're very close?"

The old man nodded. "He's a good boy. Hasn't got much up top — never much of a scholar, but his heart's in the right place."

"The pictures on the walls. Are they for his benefit?"

"Well, they wouldn't be for mine, would they?"

"No, I suppose not."

"Peter loves art. Sometimes he will sit and describe the pictures to me, and he describes them so well it's almost as if I can see them . . . Come to think of it, that's where he could be right now."

"Where's that?" Jack said.

"He could be at Gavin's."

"Gavin's?"

"Gavin Southland. He's a local artist. Lives about ten minutes away. Has a big house on Ridge Road — a bloody mansion according to Peter. Fancies himself as a bit of a bohemian, so Peter tells me."

"And you think your grandson may be there?"

"More than likely, I would have thought. Peter sits for him now and then, for pin money. It supplements the pittance they pay him at Hennessey's. Bloody old miser, Ernest Hennessey is. Tight as a nun's . . . Suffice it to say, Ernest is frugal, always has been. So Peter's lucky to have a friend like Gavin who's willing to pay him just to sit there while he makes sketches of him. Supposedly they're very good, but I have to take Peter at his word on that one."

They stayed for another thirty minutes, drinking tea with the old man and listening to his wartime anecdotes and stories of his grandson's childhood.

* * *

"To listen to him you'd think Peter Lamb can walk on water," Myra said as they got back to the car.

"For all we know, he can," Jack said.

"Well, he certainly likes to look at himself. The walls of his bedroom are covered with sketches of him. Charcoal, pencil — he certainly has some artistic talent."

"It's not him who has the talent. He sits for a local artist. Lamb's just the model."

"Anyone I would know?"

"You might. Does the name Gavin Southland mean anything to you?"

Myra looked thoughtful. "Gavin Southland . . . It's ringing a bell somewhere. I've definitely heard or seen . . . No. I can't place it. Back to the station?"

"Might as well. The old man thinks that his grandson may be at Southland's now. He has a place on Ridge Road, but that's a very long road and I don't fancy spending the rest of the day knocking on doors."

"We could stop at the library, and check the electoral roll."

"Good thinking."

* * *

"There it is! Gavin Southland, 41 Ridge Road."

"Sssssh!" They weren't the only occupants of the dimly lit library.

"Come on, let's go and pay him a visit."

"Can we go back to the station first, sir? I just want to check something out. I think I remember where I've seen Southland's name before."

* * *

"I knew I'd seen it!" Myra ran her fingers down a list of names. "This is the list I printed out from the microfiche the other day. Gavin Southland was a student at Corpus Christi College, Cambridge, at the same time as Adam Channing and Tim Fellowes."

Jack took the list from her and perused it, scratching his head.

"A coincidence, sir?"

"I don't believe in them, Myra. I think we're onto something here. This could be the breakthrough we've been waiting for."

"Are you going to tell Superintendent Fisher about this?"

"Yes, of course — once we've checked it out."

"So are we off to Ridge Road?"

"Presently. But first we're going to go and have another chat with Mr Fellowes. Let's find out what else he's omitted to tell us."

* * *

"I don't wish to be speaking out of turn, sir," Myra said as they reached the car park. "But shouldn't Sergeant Fuller be accompanying you on this?"

"By rights, Myra, he should, but Chief Superintendent Lane has most of the squad tied up on the post office robberies, and the rest of them are investigating the off-licence break in, which leaves you as my number two. Unless you have a burning desire to go back to uniform and spend your days dealing with traffic offences and giving crime-prevention talks to the WI."

"I'd rather stick with you, sir,"

"I thought you might say that, and it's good experience for you. As I said to you before, you have a nose for this kind of work. There are a lot of good coppers out there, Myra. Good detectives are harder to find."

"Thank you, sir. I'm very grateful."

"I'll remind you of that when you're pulling triple shifts and sitting in a freezing cold car surveilling suspects around the clock. It's not all glamour, you know."

"I'll bear that in mind, sir."

* * *

"Detective Chief Inspector Callum," said Fellowes. "Two visits in the space of a week. To what do I owe the pleasure?" He looked at Myra. "And this would be?"

"Detective Constable Banks," said Jack. Myra raised her eyebrows.

"Won't you both take a seat?"

Jack sat at the desk. Myra pulled up a hard chair and sat down next to him. Jack pulled out his notebook and pretended to read from it. "Does the name Adam Channing mean anything to you, sir?"

"Not at all, Chief Inspector. Should it?"

"You were at Corpus Christi College, Cambridge at the same time," said Myra.

"Was I indeed? I suppose it's possible. I can't be expected to keep track of everyone who was there."

"What about Gavin Southland? Does that name ring any bells?"

"Was he at the university as well?"

"Yes," said Jack. "He was."

"Look, Chief Inspector, what is all this about? Only I'm a bit pushed for time at the moment," He made a show of looking at his watch. "My next appointment will be here in a little under five minutes."

"I'll be as quick as I can, sir. If, as you say. you don't remember him, you won't be aware that Gavin Southland lives just fifteen minutes away from where we're sitting."

"Here, in Hatfield?"

"Ridge Road, to be precise."

"Well, they say it's a small world. I guess that proves it. You'll have to give me his address before you leave. I'll look him up. It's never a bad thing to reconnect with people from the past."

"*Reconnect*, sir?" said Myra. "An odd choice of word if, as you say, you didn't know him at university."

"A figure of speech, Constable, nothing more," Fellowes said easily.

"Were you aware that Sandra Duncan was sexually assaulted, probably after she was killed," Jack said suddenly.

The smile dropped from Fellowes' lips and he blinked three times, rapidly. He recovered himself quickly. "No, I wasn't aware of that. How ghastly."

"Quite."

"Then you have to find this person quickly, before he can take another life," said Fellowes.

"I'm afraid it's too late for that, sir. Only this time the victim was a teenage boy."

Fellowes closed his eyes for a moment. "What was his name?"

"Simon Nelson. He was fifteen."

"Dreadful," Fellowes said. The intercom buzzed. "What is it, Doris?"

"The Penhaligons are here, Tim."

"I'll only be a few more seconds. Was there anything else, Chief Inspector? As you can see . . ."

"You're a very busy man," Jack said. "No, I think that will be all for now. If you could rack your brains, sir, and see if you can recall either Adam Channing or Gavin Southland and give me a call if you do?"

"Certainly." Fellowes reached across the desk to shake Jack's hand.

"We'll see ourselves out," said Jack.

* * *

Myra and Jack walked to the car. "If you don't mind me asking, sir, what was the point of that? He could be lying about not knowing Channing and Southland."

"Oh, I'm sure he was, Myra. The visit was meant to drop the names in his lap and see how he reacted."

"And he denied knowing them."

"Yes, he did," Jack smiled. "Tell me, Myra, have you ever heard the phrase, *As the tongue speaketh to the ear so the gesture speaketh to the eye*?"

"Can't say that I have, sir."

"Francis Bacon said that about King James in the early sixteen hundreds. He was referring to the king's ability to read people, their body language. So, while Fellowes was denying knowing Channing and Southland, his body language was telling me something entirely different."

"I didn't see it, sir."

"You would have done if you had known what to look for. Do you ever get an odd feeling where you suspect someone's lying to you?"

"Oh yes, I've had that."

"Well, you're not imagining it, and there's nothing supernatural about it either. Consciously or subconsciously you're picking up signals from them, little things, the way they move their eyes, their posture, all sorts of little *tells* that alert you to the fact that they're not speaking the truth. It's something you really need to read up on. It will help you enormously when you transfer to CID permanently."

"About that, sir. In there you introduced me as Detective Constable."

"I'm aware of that, Myra. Well, it's only a matter of time isn't it?"

Myra smiled.

"When you next go to the library, see if you can get hold of a book called *The Language of Gestures* by William Wundt. You'll find it invaluable. I know I have over the years."

Jack climbed into the car beside her. "Ridge Road. Let's go and see if we can track down Peter Lamb."

CHAPTER 32

MONDAY

Peter Lamb froze as the doorbell sounded from downstairs. "Who's that?" he said, his voice rising in panic.

"Stay calm," said Gavin Southland, as he slid from the sumptuous four-poster bed he was sharing with Lamb. He covered his nakedness with an elaborately embroidered silk kimono. "It's probably the police."

"The police?" Lamb's voice rose higher.

"Relax. I've been expecting them. Tim telephoned me a little while ago. They'd just been to see him." Southland limped to the door. "Just stay here and don't make a sound."

"Hello," Southland said, opening the door to Jack and Myra. "Can I help you?"

Jack showed his warrant card and made the introductions. Southland noticed Myra staring at his attire.

"I'm afraid you interrupted my siesta. I'm something of an early riser and about midday I usually take myself off to bed for a couple of hours, to revitalise."

"I'm sorry to have disturbed you, sir. But we're looking for Peter Lamb. I understood from his grandfather that he might be here with you."

"Well, he's not," Southland said calmly. "But you are very welcome to come in and see for yourself."

"Not that I'm doubting your word, sir, but if we could just pop in for a moment or two. I have a few things that you may be able to clear up for us yourself."

"Please." Southland ushered them inside.

They followed him down a wide passageway, through the house, and into a large glass conservatory. A third of the floor space was taken up by large ceramic flowerpots containing exotic ferns and palms. At the far end of the conservatory was a freestanding auricula theatre, with ranks of spectacularly coloured and patterned primulas: a florist's dream. Shelves covering the wall held some of the most unusual orchids that Jack had ever seen, their pots interspersed with small curios. Jack wandered over and picked up a small gold coin sitting on its own stand. He turned it over and over, noting the hole at its centre and the writing around the edge.

Southland limped across to him and plucked it from his fingers, replacing it in the stand. "Excuse me," he said. "Acid from the sweat on fingers can damage the metal."

"Yes, of course," Jack said. "I'm sorry."

"Not a problem," Southland said with an easy smile.

It was stiflingly hot in the conservatory; the humid air was moved listlessly around the room by an underpowered ceiling fan, whose flat wooden blades rotated lazily.

Jack pulled a handkerchief from his pocket and mopped his already perspiring brow. He felt as if he had just walked into the middle of a Tennessee Williams play.

Southland noticed his discomfort. "Please excuse the heat, Chief Inspector, but I find it helps this." He slapped his leg. "Polio, as a child," he said in answer to Jack's unspoken question. "Summer is my friend. The winter, not so much." He pointed to an easel standing in the middle of the floor, the work-in-progress hidden by a white sheet. On a small table standing next to it, were jars containing brushes, knives and a couple of well-used artist's palettes.

"I tend to work in here during the summer months. During the winter I have to retreat to my studio inside the house."

"When did you last see Peter Lamb?" Jack asked.

"Earlier today as it happens. He came in to sit for me first thing this morning." He limped across to the easel and pulled back the sheet. Jack and Myra were treated to a large painting of a naked young man holding a decorously placed rugby ball.

"That's Peter," Southland said. "One of my better pieces, though I say so myself."

Jack stood in front of the painting. "Would you say that it's an accurate likeness?"

Southland smiled. "I'd like to think so. I'm certainly no Rembrandt, but I think I do as well as I can with the tools God gave me."

"Do you have any idea where Mr Lamb might be now?" Myra said, her eyes averted from the painting.

"Not really. He left here just before I went up to have my siesta. I understand he had some errands to run in town."

"That would be what, an hour ago?"

"Approximately."

"Does the name Tim Fellowes mean anything to you?"

"Indeed it does."

"Really?"

"We went to the same university. I heard he'd become a solicitor. Has a practice in town, I believe."

"Do you have regular contact with him?"

Southland laughed. "I don't have any contact with him at all, Chief Inspector. We moved in different social circles at Cambridge. We were never friends. When I heard he was a solicitor working out of Hatfield, I was at pains *not* to have any contact with him. I'm not a great believer in raising ghosts from the past. It always seems such a futile endeavour to me. Life is to be lived in the here and now, not in some imagined nostalgic idyll."

"What about Adam Channing, another college pal of yours?"

"Ah, there you have me. The name means nothing, I'm afraid."

Jack mopped his brow again. "That's a shame. I thought there might be a connection."

"I'm afraid not. What's he done, this Channing character?"

"Nothing, as far as we know. We just need to eliminate him from our enquiries."

"Well, I'm sorry I can't help you."

"No matter," Jack said lightly. "If you see Peter Lamb before we can track him down, perhaps you can tell him that we'd like to speak with him?"

"Am I able to tell him what your interest is?"

"That won't be necessary, sir. Just tell him to call me at his earliest convenience." He handed Southland one of his cards.

Southland took it, read it, and stowed it away in the pocket of his kimono.

"Thank you for your help, sir."

"I'm afraid I haven't been of much assistance."

"I wouldn't say that, sir. A police investigation is rather like one of your paintings. You add to it stroke by stroke, detail by detail, until you build up a complete picture."

"An interesting analogy. But the two things are quite different, I'm sure. I would think a police investigation is compiled of random facts coming together to make a credible whole. It doesn't allow for wild flights of imagination or the elements of self-expression, which is what art is all about."

"I think the actual truth would surprise you, sir. We'll see ourselves out."

* * *

"Was it the police?"

"Yes," said Southland, pulling back the sheets and sliding into the four-poster beside Lamb.

"What did they want?"

"You."

"Why me?"

"I have no idea, but I think it might be wise to keep a low profile for a while, until we know."

* * *

"It was hotter than Hades in there," Myra said as they stepped outside and walked to the car. "I thought I was going to pass out at one stage."

"I was stationed in Burma during the war," Jack said, "and I thought I could take the heat, but that glasshouse wasn't pleasant. How he can work in there, I'll never know."

"But was it a useful visit, sir?"

Jack was miles away. "Eh?"

"Seeing Southland, sir. Was it useful?"

"Well it brought us no nearer to finding Lamb, and it failed to establish a connection between Southland and the others, but there *was* something."

"What, sir?"

"I don't know, Myra." He shook his head as if to dislodge the cobwebs shrouding his thoughts. "But something I either I saw or heard is niggling away at the back of my mind, and just as I feel I'm bringing it to the front to be identified, the damned thing slips away again. It's like trying to grab a handful of smoke."

"I'm sure it will come back to you, sir."

"I wish I had your faith in my thought processes, Myra."

* * *

Tim Fellowes sat in his car in Hatfield train station car park. As Adam Channing emerged from the entrance Fellowes reached across and opened the car door.

"It's good of you to drop everything and come up," he said, as Channing slid into the seat beside him."

"I only had marking to do," Channing said. "No, you were right to call me. Is Gavin at home?"

"Where else would he be? He rarely goes out," Fellowes said. "And we need to see him right away. He's out of control, Adam, and now we're in this as deeply as he is. We've got to rein him in, slow him down somehow. The mad bastard is going to get us hanged."

Fellowes started the car and drove out of the car park.

"Do you really think he messed with the girl like the police say?" Channing said.

"No, I don't," Fellowes said. "We know Gavin's tastes don't run in that direction, neither do Lamb's. But the police must know something. Why else would they say such a thing?" He changed gear and pulled off the main road. Minutes later they were turning into Ridge Road.

Southland took a long time coming to the door. He stood there, looking at the two men. "Tim, Adam, what an unexpected pleasure. Come through."

He led them through to a large, comfortably furnished lounge. "Take a seat. Drinks. Whisky for you, Adam? And Tim, are you still taking that God awful Russian firewater?"

"Vodka, on ice," said Fellowes.

Southland limped across to a small cabinet in the corner of the room. "Would you mind telling me what the hell you're doing here?" Channing waited while Southland added two cubes of ice to Fellowes' vodka, and then spoke.

"The police told Tim that Sandra Duncan had been sexually assaulted, post-mortem. Is this some great artistic statement?"

Southland blinked furiously, his brandy glass an inch from his lips. He turned to Fellowes. "You didn't mention that when you called. I was half expecting their visit, but this . . ."

"I wanted to speak with Adam first, before I said anything to you."

"You don't think I'd touch her like that, do you?" Southland drained his brandy in a single swallow.

"We wanted to ask you directly, face to face," said Channing.

Southland hurled the empty glass at the wall. "What do you take me for?" he yelled at them.

"We were hoping you'd enlighten us."

"Jesus Christ, isn't it enough that my vision has been ruined, that my artistic statement has been defiled, without you two fools coming here to my house and accusing me of something so obscene?"

"That's what we thought," said Fellowes. "But we had to hear it from you."

"Sex was never the objective. You know that, and now the police will think we're just the same as all those perverts who rape and kill."

"Worse," Channing said. "They'll think we're necrophiliacs."

Southland poured himself another brandy and looked down at his hand. It was shaking badly. "It was David-bloody-Neville. It has to be him. He was tasked with getting rid of the body."

"He came to see me today," said Fellowes.

"Why?" asked Channing.

"It seems he's fallen in love. He was all bleeding hearts and flowers. He wants me to have a word with you, Gavin, to ask you not to use her in your plan."

"Can I have another vodka?" said Fellowes.

Still standing at the bar, Southland picked up the bottle and poured another measure. "Adam?"

"I'm good," Channing said. He'd never been much of a drinker and the one scotch was already making his head spin slightly. He knew that he needed to be thinking clearly.

Using their intellects to outsmart the police had been Southland's idea, the perfect crime, conceived one boozy evening in the college bar. It was one of those idiotic youthful challenges that should have been forgotten when they'd graduated and gone on to their different careers.

But they couldn't let it go. At Cambridge, they would meet up once or twice a month, and the idea would re-emerge. After perhaps ten such meetings, it had metamorphosed from a student folly, a fantasy, into a definite plan, a real challenge. For reasons best known to himself, Southland pushed the hardest to make it happen, and Fellowes and Channing, always slightly in awe of the older man, paid lip-service.

And so it had remained until the past April when, orchestrated by Southland, events took a darker turn.

CHAPTER 33

APRIL 1958 (BEFORE THE CRIMES TOOK PLACE)

See no evil, hear no evil, speak no evil

Tim Fellowes had stayed in touch with Adam Channing since their student days and considered him a firm friend, even if they met infrequently.

"I don't know how Gavin Southland tracked us down," said Fellowes during the drive down the A1 to Hatfield. "I haven't heard from him for ages Not sure I really liked him all that much at university."

"Why on earth do you think he's invited us?" Channing said, not for the first time during the journey.

"I don't know, maybe to show off the big house he inherited from his great aunt," Fellowes replied, but he had an unpleasant feeling that there was another reason for their dinner invite.

* * *

Southland met them at the door of a sprawling Victorian house, tucked away behind a high privet hedge on a tree-lined avenue. He greeted them effusively and ushered them inside. They went into a large dining room where a table was set for dinner with a white, bone-china service and gold-plated cutlery.

The opulence made Fellowes wonder about the size of the estate his aunt had bequeathed to Southland.

Fellowes had always found Southland a little too exotic for his tastes. An artist, so naturally outside the parameters of what Fellowes considered proper.

Their fellow dinner guests were a rather motley assortment of arty types.

There was Luther, a thin-faced man with a curling waxed moustache and arched eyebrows, painted in. His companion Veronica was a big-breasted woman who hid her ample frame beneath a voluminous purple paisley dress. Her hair was in a matching turban with a peacock feather, and she wore impenetrable dark glasses. She was introduced as a sculptor, as talented as Barbara Hepworth.

Sitting next to Southland at the far end of the table was a youth, around eighteen or nineteen, with a fleshy, pasty face, and black, swept-back hair. His dark hooded eyes regarded them incuriously. Southland introduced him simply as Peter. From the way Southland fawned over him, Fellowes was in little doubt about the nature of their relationship.

Despite his initial reservations, Fellowes found the conversation stimulating. It ranged from high art to the philosophy of bohemianism; from the work and life of artist Eric Gill, to more light-hearted subjects such as West End revues and risqué Soho cabaret acts. Everyone joined in, except the enigmatic Peter who sat silently throughout, looking on with contempt.

The food was plentiful and superbly cooked — apparently Peter was as useful in the kitchen as he no doubt was in the bedroom — and the wine flowed. It was just after midnight when Veronica — "I used to be a dancer on the stage, my dears, before I put on the pounds and decided to do something with my hands instead of my feet," — announced that she was going to take Luther home — "before I have to carry him out of here."

Luther got unsteadily his feet and let himself be led out on the motherly arm of Veronica.

"They're a lovely couple," Southland said after he had seen them to the door and waved them off. "Been married to each other for nearly twenty years. Screw whoever they like, of course. True bohemians."

"I suppose we should be getting off as well," said Fellowes. The sooner the better, he thought.

"Nonsense! We still have lots to catch up on." Southland turned to his companion. "Peter, fetch the absinthe from the cabinet in my studio."

"Do you two remember the conversations we used to have at university?" Southland said.

"About what?" said Channing.

"Whether it would be possible, using our combined intellects, to outwit the police and commit the perfect crime."

"Not that old chestnut again, Gavin," Fellowes said. "You really ought to put that one to bed. We're not students anymore, mooning over Dostoevsky. That kind of stuff is fine when you're that age, but then you join the real world . . ."

". . . and become bourgeois bores," said Southland.

"Steady on, Gavin," said Channing.

But Southland would not be dissuaded. "Well, look at you now, with your safe, respectable jobs. Pillars of the community, both of you."

"We can't all be bohemians, Gavin," said Fellowes. He couldn't contain his irritation any longer.

"I'm an artist! I don't recognise convention. My only judge will be posterity." Southland said with his familiar dramatics.

Lamb came back into the room holding a silver tray on which sat a bottle of green liquid, a bowl of sugar cubes, a jug of iced water and a silver absinthe spoon, pierced and fluted with a point at one end. "Perhaps this will jog your memories and send them floating back to when we were all free spirits, with the world at our feet."

"I don't know. I think we've drunk enough. We should be going." Channing made to get to his feet, but Southland clamped a hand over his wrist.

Fellowes was watching Southland's eyes, which had a slightly mad gleam. He realised that the evening could very easily turn ugly. "Perhaps just the one, eh? How about it, Adam? For old times' sake?" One drink, and they could get off. This had all been a mistake.

Channing relaxed into his seat. "Okay, just one, and then we head home."

"Peter, you do the honours." Southland turned to the others. "Peter works in a pharmacy. He knows all about mixing things. Don't you, Peter?"

Lamb said nothing, but a smile spread across his face, for the first time that evening.

Fellowes watched the drinks being prepared and calculated the number of minutes before they could escape.

* * *

The next thing Tim Fellowes was aware of was sunlight pouring through the window and the sound of birdsong.

"What the hell?" Instead of lying in his bed at home, he was sprawled backwards on an overstuffed leather couch. He looked across the room to where Adam Channing was folded into an armchair, dead to the world and snoring loudly.

His whole body ached, particularly his head. Fellowes pushed himself off the couch and staggered across to where Channing was sleeping. "Come on, Adam. Wake up. It's morning."

"Eh? What?" Channing said thickly. "I only had the one drink."

Fellowes felt as if he'd grown an extra tongue. "I know. Me too. The absinthe must have been drugged. I think Gavin slipped us a Mickey Finn."

Fellowes shook his head, which made him feel as if his brain was slopping about in his skull. Gingerly, he sat down on the edge of the armchair and tried to make some sense of what had happened to

"I thought I heard you getting up," came Southland's booming voice as he entered the room. He was wearing a beautiful silk kimono.

Peter Lamb was a pace behind Southland, his eyes watchful, almost as if he was ready to spring.

Southland was holding a camera. He put it to his eye and said, "Say cheese."

The flash made them blink. Southland let the camera drop from his fingers and hang from a small strap. "Now," he said. "Time to come with me, if you'd be so kind."

They didn't have far to go.

"This is my dark room," Southland said, and Fellowes stood still inside the room while his eyes adjusted to the lack of light.

"Impressed?" Southland said, beaming at them.

"So you have a dark room," Fellowes said. "Hardly that remarkable."

"I thought you would be sceptical, Tim, you always were."

"And you were always rather too full of yourself."

"We had some fun in the night. Show them, Peter."

Lamb pulled the end of what looked like a length of string and Fellowes saw that there were images hanging up on the developing line. Photographs, lots of them, black-and-white, and as accusing as a pointing finger.

Fellowes looked at them, and was aware of Channing giving short gasps of shock as he realised what he was seeing.

"Give me a closer look," said Channing, pushing past him.

Without a word, Fellowes stood back. He had seen enough. He knew what Southland had done, and he suspected he knew why.

"I am a true artist," said Southland. "Anyone looking at them would have no idea that you were both unconscious when these were taken."

Fellowes glared up at Southland. "Why?"

"You were going to renege on our agreement," Southland said simply.

"We had no agreement."

"That's not the way I see it. These photographs are my guarantee that you will keep your word."

Channing came to a photograph in which he lay naked on a bed, entwined in the arms of an equally nude Peter Lamb. With a sound of disgust he launched himself at Southland, ready to strike.

Lamb stepped quickly between them and pushed Channing back. "Bastard!" Channing shouted.

Fellowes took the photographs down one at a time and ripped them in half. Southland made no move to stop him. Instead he watched with an indulgent smile on his lips. "Tear away, Tim," he said. "They're just the tip of the iceberg. As I said, we had a busy night. There are many more where those came from. You're a solicitor. What is the prison sentence for homosexual acts these days?"

Fellowes looked at him bleakly. "What do you want?"

"Ah, you're beginning to realise the extent of the jam you're in. The newspapers would crucify you if they got their hands on these. Heaven knows how your personal reputations would suffer, even if you weren't prosecuted."

"So what do you want from us?"

"I'm planning my masterpiece, a triptych based on my long-held Buddhist beliefs. For that I need models, preferably female, but male will suffice, ideally young and beautiful. Neither I nor Peter mix with that type of girl. You two must come into contact with suitable models every day. All I want you to do is get hold of their names and addresses. You can leave us to take care of the rest."

"And you'd hire them as you would any other model?" Fellowes said.

Lamb snorted with laughter. It sounded like a donkey braying.

"No, Tim. I won't be paying them anything, nothing at all. You see, what I am planning satisfies my artistic needs, but also addresses our old plan. Can I defeat the police, using only my intellect? I believe I can."

"You're insane."

"Were you ever in any doubt about that?" said Southland.

The look in Southland's eyes changed and Fellowes knew that his old friend was deadly serious.

"I am going to paint three young people and produce my masterpiece. You are going to provide the models. I am going to keep faith with our student pledge to outwit the police, and indeed the whole so-called establishment, using my intellect and erudition."

"What happens to the three youths?"

"You will dispose of them — following my strict instructions," Southland replied.

Channing and Fellowes exchanged a glance.

Fellowes had to admit, to himself at least, that there was a perverse side to his nature that Southland had undoubtedly recognised. He got a vicarious thrill from Southland's plans. He might himself be unable to harm a girl or young man, but the thought of being involved was exciting. Even the photos, regardless of their blackmail potential, had given him a strange tingle.

"I think this is all going to turn out rather well," Southland said, as he poured out drinks.

Fellowes couldn't wait to leave. He'd known no good would come of this.

CHAPTER 34

MONDAY August 18th 1958

So now they were accomplices to two murders — three, if DCI Callum was to be believed, and Channing was starting to feel extremely apprehensive.

"Simon Nelson," Fellowes said suddenly to Southland.

"Eh?"

"The policeman, Callum, who came to see me today. He said there had been another killing. A teenage boy called Simon Nelson. Was he another one of your bloody models?"

"Such a pretty boy. That was Peter, acting on his own initiative. He rescued this boy from a gang of Teddy boys and brought him here. Why he didn't take him home I'll never know, but he didn't, and once the boy was here . . . well, it was too good an opportunity to pass up. Think of it, what better way to throw the police off our scent than to give them a victim of a different gender?"

"Jesus! Does this never end?" said Channing.

"Why didn't you consult with us first?" Fellowes added. "Supposedly we're all in this together. We have as much to lose as you do. We've come a long way from gross indecency. We're looking at capital punishment if we're caught."

Southland looked aggrieved. "I know, but there simply wasn't time to do anything about it. The boy was here. The odds of him keeping his mouth shut were minimal. I had to act, and fast. Though I do find it gratifying to see that you're now as invested in the game as I am."

"You haven't given us much choice," Fellowes said bitterly.

Southland sipped his brandy. "No I didn't, did I?"

"And you can say, hand on heart, that there was no sexual motive for this one?"

"Well, he was an extraordinarily pretty boy, Adam, but no. Sex didn't enter into it. It was purely an artistic decision."

"I'm beginning to doubt your wisdom in using Peter and his friends to help you," said Fellowes.

"And I'm beginning to tire of your hypocrisy. You knew David from the bowls club, Tim, and you were more than ready to vouch for him when Peter suggested him for the job."

"And look where that led," said Channing, earning a sharp look from Fellowes.

"The fact is, the boys have been important. It was a masterstroke on Derek's part to dump the first girl's body in the park and then disguise himself as a park-keeper. Think how many man-hours the police wasted running down that particular blind alley. Peter disposed of the boy on the railway embankment efficiently and discreetly. Even my idea of dumping Sandra in a bunker on the golf course was fairly inspired, and not without artistic merit — if David had followed my instructions to the letter."

"Instead he decided to have some fun with her, the sick bastard," said Channing. "You didn't see that coming did you, Gavin?"

"No, I did not. David needs to be suitably punished, and you can leave that to me. I think it's wise if we don't see each other — for the foreseeable future anyway. We can communicate by telephone, but don't come here again — unless you're invited."

"Agreed." Fellowes and Channing were both relieved to bring this meeting to a close.

"Right. Now get out. I'll contact you if anything else urgent or unexpected crops up."

Southland accompanied them to the door, returned to the lounge and poured himself another brandy. He was furious at having his decisions questioned. "How dare they?" he said to the empty room. If they only knew what all this was taking out of him, and what was driving him on.

That policeman today — Callum — had an air of authority that reminded him of his father. He too had been a policeman. He was a bully, with not a single shred of empathy, whose response to finding that his son had polio was to run away. He'd taken up with some little whore almost young enough to be his own daughter, and had left his wife to care for a desperately sick child. As the years went by, the crippled boy swore that one day he would have his revenge on his father and all the men like him who put order and discipline before care and nurture; matters of the law before matters of the heart.

His thoughts turned to David Neville. He had entrusted him with disposing of Sandra Duncan's body and doing it in such a way that it would become art. This one would not be dumped unceremoniously like the first girl; she would be presented as a tableau, a still life. But David's perverted lust had sullied that image, so he must pay.

Southland picked up the telephone and dialled.

"Derek, I need you to do something for me."

CHAPTER 35

TUESDAY August 19th 1958

The summer rain had stopped, making the whole world smell cleaner, fresher.

Rosie Callum was feeling fresher as well. The incident with David Neville on Sunday had disturbed her, more so than she had admitted to her sister. Yesterday she had struggled to reconcile what she had felt when he'd kissed her and touched her breasts, with the morals that had always guided her. Today, with the sun shining again, and the heat of passion washed away, she was feeling more capable of facing the day and dealing with the bakery customers without that guilt hanging over her.

"Hey! Rosie? It is Rosie, isn't it?"

Rosie stopped in her tracks and looked around at the young man sitting on the motor scooter parked at the kerb.

"Do I know you?"

"It's Derek Webster — from Saturday night at the dance. Davy's friend."

She smiled as she recognised him. "Yes, of course. You look different in casual clothes."

"I was hoping I might see you. Davy told me you worked along here."

"At Painters, yes. Why did you want to see me?"

"It's Davy who wants to see you," said Webster.

"Why doesn't he ask me himself then?"

"You know Davy."

"What does that mean exactly?"

Webster smiled darkly.

"Is it about what happened on Sunday?" said Rosie.

"It could be. He didn't say. All he told me was it was important he sees you."

"Then he should be here himself."

"He would if he could, but he can't. That's why he asked me to pick you up and bring you along."

"Where is he, then?"

"Working. He's at a house on the other side of town, talking insurance with the owners; otherwise he would definitely have come to see you himself."

"Well, it will have to wait until later. I have to get to work." She turned and made to resume her journey.

"Wait! He's really upset about Sunday. He's desperate to talk to you. I've never seen him so cut up about something."

Rosie hesitated. "Was he *really* upset?"

"He seemed devastated. Look, I don't know what went on between you two, and I don't want to, but I'm just trying to help a mate out here."

"How long will it take?" Rosie's resolve was starting to crumble.

"We can be there in ten minutes. After that, I suppose it's up to you two."

Rosie glanced at her watch. She still had twenty minutes until the baker's opened. Mrs Painter wouldn't mind if she were a few minutes late.

"Okay. Take me to see him."

"Hop on," said Webster.

* * *

Jack's report to Fisher had met with the usual apathy. He was getting used to having his ideas dismissed out of hand by the Scotland Yard man, and he was considering keeping them to himself in future.

"We've got someone in the frame for the post office jobs," Fuller said as he returned to the squad room.

"Anyone I know?" Jack feigned interest.

"Reggie Bull."

"Christ, that's a name from the past," Jack said. "I thought he was doing a five stretch in Wandsworth."

"He was. Got out after three for good behaviour."

"They don't know him very well then, do they? A nasty piece of work that one. The owner of the Co-op still walks with a limp after Reggie's firm turned them over and went off with their Christmas takings."

"Yes, but the prosecution failed to make a case against him on that one."

"But not the job he got sent down for. We got him in the end. That's why I'm surprised he's out so soon. And you like him for the post office jobs?"

"They've got his mucky little signature all over them."

"Well, good luck with that one. A slippery customer is our Mr Bull."

"What about you? What are the gods from Scotland Yard letting you do, now you're effectively off the Three Monkeys case?"

"Frankly, Eddie, I may as well take up knitting for all the good I'm doing here."

"That's not so bad. They've forecast a harsh winter this year. You could knit yourself a Spurs scarf."

"With matching gloves and bobble hat. I'd be the envy of the terraces."

"That you would."

"And for your information, it's not the Three Monkeys anymore. Fisher thinks the pictures we've been getting are of the three bears, as in the fairy story."

"Fisher's off his chump," said Fuller. "According to Frank, who's been working with them, they're getting nowhere."

"The clues are out there, Eddie, you just have to know how to interpret them."

"And I suppose you do?"

Jack winked and tapped the side of his nose.

Fuller smiled. "You old . . . I knew you wouldn't let it alone. Knitting, indeed."

"It's still my case, Eddie, whether Fisher likes it or not. If I turn anything up that I feel he needs to know, I'll tell him, but until I do . . ."

"You're the boss."

"Whisper it quietly, Eddie. At least until we're rid of them."

* * *

"Where are we going?" Rosie shouted over the noise of the scooter engine.

"We'll be there soon!" Webster steered them onto Ridge Road.

They were on a street that Rosie didn't recognise. There were large detached houses on either side, hidden behind brick walls and barred gates. They were passing one now, tucked in behind a high privet hedge. Webster pulled in through wrought iron gates, steered the scooter across a gravel forecourt, and brought it to a stop outside a large Victorian house. He pulled the scooter up onto its rest and stepped off, smoothing the creases out of his grey slacks.

Rosie climbed from the bike and made a half-hearted attempt to tidy her windswept hair. "Are we here? Is David inside?"

Webster ignored her and walked towards the front door, fishing in his pocket and producing a key ring.

"The owners let you have a key?"

Webster stuck the key in the lock and Rosie grabbed his arm. "I don't think we should," she said.

Webster shook her off. "I really don't get what Davy sees in you, you silly little bitch," he said, and pulled back his fist.

Before she could react, the fist connected with her cheek. For a moment the world spun and lights danced before her eyes, and then she pitched forward, unconscious, into his arms.

* * *

"Mrs Callum? It's Barbara Painter. I wondered if Rosie is going to come in today."

"But she left here over an hour ago. She should be with you by now."

"Yes, that's what I thought, but one of my regular breakfast customers has just come in and told me she saw Rosie take off down the street on the back of a motorbike."

Annie felt a small hole open up in the pit of her stomach. "Was it a motorbike or a motor scooter?"

"Does it matter?"

"It's very important, Mrs Painter. A bike or a scooter?"

Annie heard the woman cover the mouthpiece with her hand, and the muted question.

"Phoebe, was it a bike or a scooter?"

The answer was indistinct.

"It was a scooter," said Mrs Painter.

The hole became a chasm.

"So will she be in?"

"I . . . I . . . I'm not sure. I'll call you as soon as I know."

She disconnected and rang Jack at the station.

"Annie — it's not like you to call me at work."

"It's Rosie, Jack. I think she's been taken."

"Rosie? What?"

"She's been taken. Mrs Painter just called me. Rosie hasn't turned up for work, and one of the customers saw her being driven away on the back of a motor scooter. Jack, what shall I do?"

"Annie, calm down. You could be jumping to all the wrong conclusions here. For all we know, David might ride a motor scooter. They're very popular with the kids these days."

"But David drives a car."

"It was his dad's car he took Rosie out in. He might well use a scooter to get to work."

Annie tried to remember if Rosie had ever mentioned a scooter. Nothing.

"You're probably right. I'm overreacting I expect. I just heard the word 'scooter' and immediately thought of what you told me about Sandra Duncan. I shouldn't have called. I'm just being stupid."

"No you're not. Did Mrs Painter say what colour the scooter was?"

"No. I'll call her back."

"No, *I'll* call her. You can go and make yourself a cup of hot sweet tea, and calm down. When I hear anything at all I'll ring you. And don't worry; Rosie's not stupid. She knows better than to go off with strangers."

"I'm sorry, Jack. Just call me when you hear anything."

"I will. Promise."

"Problems?" asked Joan.

"Just your mother being overprotective. Sometimes I forget you're all growing up so fast."

* * *

"Mrs Painter, it's Jack Callum, Rosie's dad. I'm sorry that Rosie has let you down today."

"It's most unlike her, Rosie's usually so reliable."

"You didn't see her get on the motor scooter yourself?"

"Not personally. That was Phoebe Russell, one of my regulars."

"Did Mrs Russell happen to notice the colour of the scooter?"

"If she did, she didn't say."

"Is there any way we can find out? Does she have an address or a telephone number?"

"I don't know them, but it doesn't matter. She only works two doors along in the dressmaker's. I can pop along and ask her."

"If it's no trouble."

"Well, I have a couple of people to attend to, and then I'll go and find out. Can I phone you back?"

"If you would. It's a direct line, so it will put you straight through to me."

"I'll call you back as quickly as I can."

Jack sat looking at the telephone and tried to control his breathing. Despite what he had told Annie, he was terrified.

"Something wrong, sir?" asked Fuller. He was sitting at the next desk and had seen Jack making the telephone calls — and his face as he did so.

"It's Rosie. She hasn't turned up for work this morning."

"Perhaps she's taking a sick day."

"She's not at home either. That first call was from Annie. She thinks something bad has happened. Rosie set off for work first thing this morning as usual, but she never got there. The last time she was spotted was on the back of a motor scooter riding away from the baker's where she works."

"Was it a two-tone blue scooter?"

"That's what I'm waiting to find out. Her boss at the baker's is going to call me back."

"So it's too early to reach any conclusions."

"That's what I told Annie."

"There you go then."

The telephone rang beside him and he snatched it up.

"Hello?"
"Hello, Mr Callum. It's Barbara Painter."

CHAPTER 36

TUESDAY

Jack's hand came down hard on the desk and he swore loudly, drawing startled looks from the others in the room.

"Chief Inspector?" said Fuller, but Jack was already at the door.

"Jack!" Fuller called after him.

Fisher looked up from his desk as Jack barged into the office. "Where are you with your search for the motor scooter?" Jack yelled at him.

Greyling and Lymon rose from their table. "Chief Inspector, I really don't—"

"Get out, both of you!"

Fisher looked at them. "It's all right. Leave us."

They glared at Jack and left the office.

"Right. Do you mind explaining why you burst into my office like a Friday night drunk and start ordering my men around?"

"My daughter's been abducted, driven away on a two-tone blue motor scooter, probably by the same bastard who took Sandra Duncan. So I'll ask again, where are you with your search for it?"

"The scooter is just one of many leads we are following. I'm sorry about your daughter, but it still doesn't give you the right to come bursting into my office like a madman."

"It seems the only way to breathe some life into this Mickey Mouse investigation of yours. I don't know how you do things down in London, but up here we value good police work, and my team and I know how to get things done."

"And you think we don't?"

"I don't think you and your men could find your dicks in a blackout."

"Just remember who you're talking to."

"I'm talking to the man who took a perfectly fine investigation and flushed it down the toilet. The man with his head so far up his own backside he wouldn't know a clue if it came up and bit him on the arse."

"How dare—"

"That's enough! Both of you!" Chief Superintendent Lane stood in the doorway, his face white, the veins in his neck prominent. "Would one of you mind explaining what on earth's going on in here? I can hear your racket in my office, so can most of the station."

"Callum's daughter's been snatched, sir, and he barged in here accusing me and my men of not making sufficient progress on the Three Bears investigation."

Lane's face softened. "Is this right, Jack? Has Rosie been abducted?"

"It certainly looks that way, Henry." Jack was breathing hard, and he was trying to control the urge to smash something.

"I'm sorry, Jack. I'm sure Superintendent Fisher is doing his best."

"Well, his best isn't bloody good enough."

"I was trying to tell him, sir, that our investigation is progressing slowly. The way he burst in here and started shouting at me and my men is nothing but insubordination."

"Oh, do shut up, Brian. Jack's daughter has been taken. How do you expect him to react?"

Fisher shut his mouth and glared at them.

"If I can lead the investigation again, sir, I'm sure—"

"You'll do no such thing," said Lane. "Go home, Jack. Your wife is going to need you there."

"But, sir . . ."

"Home, Chief Inspector. That's an order."

Jack held his eyes for a moment and then something went out of him. His shoulders drooped and he walked out of the office and down the stairs to get his coat.

"Where are you going?" asked Fuller.

"I'll be at home if anything comes up, Eddie."

"Do you need a ride?"

"I'll take a pool car. I need some time on my own to think."

* * *

"Oh, Jack!" Annie threw her arms around him as he walked through the back door.

From the kitchen table Joan looked up at him. "Will she be all right, Dad?"

"I'll get her back, Joanie, one way or another."

"Is that a promise, Jack?" said Annie. "Do you promise me that my little Rosie will be all right?"

"You have my word. Be a pet, Joanie, and make your mum and me a cup of tea."

* * *

Sunlight streamed in through tall windows. Rosie blinked hard to clear her vision, and tried to work out where she was. She was tied to a wooden chair, her wrists strapped to the arms, and her ankles tethered to the legs.

She attempted to turn her head, but the pain in her cheek made her cry out. She would have screamed but no sound came. Her mouth had been stuffed with fabric and a gag wound around her head, covering her face.

In the centre of the room, facing Rosie, stood an empty artist's easel. Brightly-coloured paintings leaned against the walls, life studies, and Rosie recognised David's other friend from the dance on Saturday night.

But he wasn't the only subject. Leaning against the far wall were three paintings; two of them were of girls, naked, their small-breasted bodies lovingly rendered. The third was a full-length study of a young boy, also naked.

But it was their faces that shocked her. The dead, expressionless eyes and mouths sewn shut, dribbles of blood snaking down from the sealed eyelids and perforated lips.

She struggled against her bonds, but it was no use, and she soon gave up. Then she saw a small table standing a few feet away. Upon it were arranged a large church candle, a box of matches and a small stainless-steel, kidney-shaped dish. Its contents were horrifying.

When she saw the wickedly sharp, curved needles and the small skein of black silk thread, she knew that the paintings of the three young people had not come from the artist's imagination. They had been taken from life. Or rather, death. She fainted.

* * *

They sat at the kitchen table drinking tea. "Did you get to the bottom of why Rosie was so upset on Sunday night?" asked Jack. Annie was torturing a handkerchief, endlessly twisting and knotting. "She wouldn't tell me. I did try a couple of times. I'm sorry."

"I suppose it doesn't really matter now," Jack said.

"David tried it on with her," Joan said flatly.

"What?"

"He tried to get into her knickers."

"Joan!" said Annie.

"I'm just telling you what Rosie told me."

"You did right to tell us," said Jack. "My first instinct about him was spot on. I should have knocked his block off, the dirty little . . ."

Joan laid her hand on her father's arm. "She wasn't crying because he tried, Dad. She was crying because she wanted him to."

"Oh, dear Lord," said Annie.

"Don't take on, Mum. She stopped him touching her because, no matter how much she wanted it, you and Dad have brought her up to respect herself. She's a credit to both of you. I wish I'd had her strength when I was her age."

"You came good in the end," said Jack.

"But not before putting myself through the wringer first."

Jack got abruptly to his feet. "I can't just sit here and do nothing. I'm going to telephone Eddie and see how they're getting on."

Annie spoke wearily. "If there was any news they would have called you. Please, Jack, sit down and wait with us."

Jack saw the fear in her eyes. He sat back at the table. "Well, I suppose no news is good news."

* * *

"Where did you and the guv get to yesterday?" Fuller asked Myra as they passed each other outside the squad room.

"We were trying to track down Peter Lamb. We went to Hennessey's, and then we went to Lamb's house and spoke with his grandfather."

"No joy?"

Myra shook her head. "The grandfather gave us the name and address of a local artist Lamb poses for to make some pin money, but no luck there either. Apparently he was running some errands in town."

"Do you fancy another trip to the chemist then?"

"There's nothing to lose. I'll get my coat."

They parked outside Hennessey's and looked in through the shop window. "I can't see him in there," said Myra.

"You know what he looks like, then?"

She couldn't forget the painting of a naked Peter Lamb at Southland's yesterday. She shuddered. "Intimately. He makes deliveries for the chemist on a push bike. He could be around the back of the shop."

Fuller opened the car door. "Come on. There's an alley that runs down the back of this row. Let's check."

"Really?"

"It's just a long shot. Indulge me."

Myra followed Fuller to the end of the street and down a narrow passageway between two shops. "I could have gone in and asked to see him."

"The element of surprise. It can't be overestimated."

They emerged from the passageway and found themselves in the alley, bordered on each side by high fences with wooden gates set in at regular intervals. Beside each gate were large metal dustbins, each about four feet high, and boxes of rubbish discarded by the shops on each side.

"Which one's Hennessey's gate?"

"Probably the one with the bicycle parked outside."

As they approached, a shadow fell across the alley, and the sound of an engine. A motor scooter.

They ducked behind one of the dustbins as the scooter drew up and the gate to Hennessey's backyard opened. Peter

Lamb stepped out into the alley and looked along at the scooter, raising a hand in greeting.

"Do you think they saw us?" Myra whispered.

"Quiet. Watch and listen. Let's see what they're up to."

CHAPTER 37

TUESDAY

Barbara Painter finished serving a customer and looked at him, her eyebrows raised. "Any chance I can have a word with Rosie?" asked David Neville.

"Sorry. She hasn't come in today."

"She told me she was working all week. She didn't mention taking a day off."

Mrs Painter narrowed her eyes. "I know you, don't I? You've been in here before."

"I'm Rosie's fellow."

"Are you indeed? I thought you'd only been out with her the once."

"We've been courting nearly a week. Do you know if she's at home?" Neville glanced round as an elderly man entered the shop.

"Good morning, Barbara."

"Your usual, Ted?"

"Yes, and one of those iced coconut buns, please."

"Well, is she?" said Neville.

"Is she what, dear?" Mrs Painter reached into the window display and took out two Chelsea buns.

"At home."

"Not according to her mother." She put the buns in a bag and twisted the top. "Just one coconut bun?"

"You'd better make it two, Barb. They're very tasty."

David Neville tapped his foot.

"So you're obviously not the one with the motor scooter," she said.

"The what?"

"The scooter, dear. Rosie took off on the back of one, shortly before I opened up this morning."

The blood drained from Neville's face. He seemed to sway slightly.

"Are you all right, dear? Only you've gone very pale."

"I'm fine . . . thank you." He rushed to the door, making the bell jangle as he ran out into the street.

"Youngsters today," said Mrs Painter to the old man. "Always in such a rush."

"It'll be a shame when they do away with National Service. They're phasing it out, you know. What young people in this country need is a good dose of army discipline," he replied.

"The country will go to the dogs."

The old man smiled ruefully. "Some would say that it has already, my dear."

"Two shillings." Mrs Painter passed the bag over the counter and held out her hand for the money.

* * *

Neville ran across the garage forecourt to a workshop at the back of the building. The large double doors were pushed open, and the space inside was occupied by three cars with their bonnets up. Grease-stained mechanics in overalls toiled in the warm, oily air, sweating profusely, occasionally mopping the perspiration from their faces with blackened rags.

"Derek! Webster?"

A large man with an oil-streaked face and a halo of dirty grey curls looked up from beneath an old Ford Prefect and wiped his forehead on his sleeve. "Wrong day, mate. He's not here."

"Where is he?"

"Dentist, I think. That's right, isn't it, Bert?"

"I think so, man." Bert was a tall, rangy black man whose cheeks bore tribal scars from his Nigerian childhood.

"Is he coming back?"

Bert shrugged. "Search me, man. I'm not his mother, am I?"

"Okay. Thanks."

Neville ran from the workshop, onto the street that would take him to Ridge Road and Gavin Southland's house. Webster and Lamb had warned him they would take matters into their own hands if he didn't speak to Southland. He just hoped he could get there before it was too late.

* * *

Jack paced the kitchen, pausing at the window every few steps.

He was missing something. He had seen or heard something in the last few days that would throw this case wide open, but the thought kept escaping. He needed to clear his mind, busy himself with some mundane, undemanding task.

He stopped pacing. "I'm going out to the greenhouse." Annie and Joan sat at the kitchen table; Annie sipping yet another cup of tea, Joan chain-smoking, stubbing the cigarettes out after a couple of draws.

"Good idea," said Joan.

Annie looked at him bleakly. Her face appeared to have aged in the few hours since she had heard the news about Rosie. Her eyes were red from crying and deep lines were etched into the corners of her mouth and around her eyes. Jack wanted to take her in his arms, to smooth those lines away, to stroke her hair and tell her that everything was going to be all right. But he couldn't even look her in the eye in case she saw his fear.

In the greenhouse an old battered chest of drawers sat opposite the row of tomatoes, scarred from years of cutting, re-potting, and all the other horticultural tasks with which he filled his free time.

He picked up a seed tray and filled it with potting compost, tamping it down until he had an even seedbed. He took one of his begonias from the shelf above the chest of drawers and selected a plump, sturdy leaf. Laying it flat on the top of the chest, he took out his penknife and started to cut the leaf into small squares, lining them up on the surface of the compost and pinning them flat with thin, wire hair pins. This repetitive, mindless work helped relieve the tension in his neck and shoulders that was starting to give him a headache, and it allowed his mind to roam freely.

When he had cut up the first leaf and covered half the compost, he plucked another one and began to trim again. He only noticed that he'd cut the top of his finger when he saw the blood pooling on the wood.

"Damn!" He stuck the cut finger in his mouth, and with his uninjured hand pulled open one of the drawers. He rummaged through seed packets, plant labels, boxes of rooting powder, searching for a sticking plaster.

He taped his finger and had just started putting everything back in the drawer when he noticed a small leatherette box, stuck down the side of the drawer, half-hidden by pages from a seed catalogue. He took out the box, laid it down on the chest and opened it up.

Inside, pinned to a cushion of black velvet was a black, red-and-yellow striped ribbon attached to a gold six-pointed star: his Burma Star campaign medal.

It had been lost years ago. He had searched the house for it, turning out every cupboard and drawer, and it had been here in the greenhouse all the time, in the chest of drawers he had taken from the bedroom.

It sent memories flooding into his mind: friendships made in the heat of battle, fallen comrades and hard-fought campaigns to capture and recapture positions; treks through the jungle in searing heat and drenching monsoon rains. He took the medal from the box and held it in his fist. Finding the medal awakened not just wartime memories, but something else. He closed his eyes.

He was back in Burma, picking over the wreckage of a temple in Mandalay that the Japanese had laid to waste, killing all the monks and leaving their dead bodies scattered amongst the ruins. He was a young man again, weeping at the carnage, the loss of innocent souls at the hands of a ruthless enemy, and then something came into his mind that made him drop the medal back in the box, shove it in his pocket, and run back to the house.

* * *

Myra stepped out from behind the dustbin and walked towards the young men. Peter Lamb was leaning against the fence. His friend straddled the scooter, a cigarette dangling from his lips.

"Hello, boys. I wonder if you can help me."

Derek Webster leered at Myra. Lamb ignored her.

"Nice scooter. I like that colour."

"Custom job. It's a Phoenix 150. You can get them in plain blue, but mine's two-tone."

"I can see."

"A mate of mine did it for me specially. Fancy a spin?"

"I bet you say that to all the girls."

"And they usually say yes."

"Is that right? Did Sandra Duncan say yes? And Rosie Callum? Did you take *her* for a spin?"

Webster's eyes showed panic. He kick-started the scooter, twisted the throttle and tore away past her.

"Hey!" She moved to run after him and Lamb elbowed her in the face, splitting her lip and making her head spin. She staggered against the fence as Lamb mounted his pushbike and took off in the opposite direction.

Fuller watched the encounter with interest, it had all happened too quickly for him to step in. But Myra certainly had some guts.

As Webster's scooter took off along the alley, Fuller grabbed the dustbin and threw it into his path. The scooter's front wheel hit the side of the bin and it stopped dead. Webster flew out of the saddle and landed in a heap in front of it. Fuller handcuffed Webster, took out his police whistle and gave it three short blasts. Leaving Webster curled up on the ground, groaning, he went to see if Myra was alright.

She was dabbing blood from her mouth with a handkerchief. "Lamb got away. I'm sorry."

"Not to worry. We'll get him soon enough, and we've got the other one."

"He took a bit of a flier. Is he badly hurt?"

"If he's the one who took Rosie and the others, then he isn't hurt badly enough. It's a pity he didn't break his bleedin' neck."

In the distance a dog barked and Alistair Kirby came running towards them from the end of the alley with Satan beside him.

"Keep your eye on this one," said Fuller. "I'll go into the shop and call for a Black Maria."

Webster lay on the ground whimpering. "You've broken my bloody back."

Kirby looked down at him. "It's not your day is it, son? One wrong move and Satan here will rip your throat out." He turned to Myra. "What's he done anyway?"

"We think he and his friend snatched DCI Callum's daughter and are keeping her somewhere."

Kirby said something to Satan and the dog began to bark, inches from Webster's face. Derek Webster started to cry.

* * *

Jack burst in through the back door, ran down the hall and took the stairs two at a time.

In the bedroom, he yanked a small leather suitcase from the top of the wardrobe, opened it on the bed and rifled through the contents. He found a small pile of dog-eared photographs and looked at each one before dropping it onto the bed.

"What are you doing?" said Annie from the doorway.

He was studying an old black-and-white snapshot.

"I know where Rosie is," he said.

CHAPTER 38

TUESDAY

Jack reached up to the top of the wardrobe and took down a black metal security box. He took a small key from his key ring and opened it. The Browning revolver was freshly oiled and in immaculate condition. He took it out and dropped it on the bed. Then he took out the small box of ammunition, dropped it beside the gun and sat down.

"Jack? What are you doing?" Annie watched as he fed bullets into the chamber.

"I'm going to get her back."

"With that?"

"I'll make Southland pay for what he's done."

"Call the station, please! Let them deal with it."

He didn't speak. He stood up and stuck the revolver in the waistband of his trousers.

Annie grabbed his arm. "No, Jack. Not like this. Let them deal with it, please!"

"She's my daughter." He ran out of the room.

"She's *my* daughter too!"

Out of the house, he threw himself in behind the wheel of the pool car. He pulled out into the street, narrowly missing a milk float that was making lazy progress along the road.

"'Ere, watch it!" the milkman shouted after him.

* * *

David Neville ran in through the iron gates and sprinted across the forecourt to the house, hammering on the front door with his fist. "Come on, Gavin, open up!"

He stood on the front step, his heart pounding in his chest, his breath coming in ragged gasps. Finally the door opened a fraction and he threw his weight behind it, bursting it open.

"Where is she? Where's Rosie?"

"Hello, David," said Southland. "How good of you to drop by."

Neville stepped forward and grabbed the front of Southland's kimono. "Where is she?" Then Neville made a small surprised sound and stepped back, releasing his hold on the silk robe. He looked down at the front of his shirt and watched the blood spreading out from a small hole in his stomach. His eyes went down to the thin, bloody knife in Southland's hand.

His legs buckled and he sank to his knees. "You've stabbed me."

"An A for observation, you perverted little shit." Southland nudged him with his knee, and David Neville toppled backwards onto the carpet.

"Why?"

"For defiling my artistic statement. For being unable to control your base instincts, your pathetic animal lust."

Neville clutched at his belly. "Help me!"

"It's not worth my time." Southland leaned forward and drew the knife across Neville's neck, slicing his throat through to the windpipe and severing the carotid artery.

"What are you doing?"

Southland span around on his good leg. Lamb was standing in the doorway, his pale face had gone green.

"Solving a problem, Peter. If you're going to be sick, please do so outside. This carpet has had enough spilled on it."

* * *

Annie listened to Jack's car scream out of the drive and then ran downstairs and picked up the telephone.

"Sergeant Brewer? It's Annie Callum here. Is Eddie Fuller available?"

"Hold on a moment. May I say, we're all very sorry about Rosie."

Annie held onto the phone, biting her lip to stop herself screaming at Brewer to hurry up.

He came back on the line. "Eddie's out on a case at the moment, but Superintendent Lane would like a word."

There was a pause. "Annie, Henry Lane here. How are you holding up?"

"Hanging on, Henry, but it's not me I'm worried about, it's Jack. He stormed out of here a few minutes ago. He suddenly announced that he knew where Rosie was and was going to get her back."

"Did he say where she was?"

"No. He just said something about making Southland pay for what he's done, but I didn't know who he was talking about."

"Okay then, Annie. We'll take it from here."

"No, Henry, you don't understand. He loaded his old army service revolver and took it with him."

"Dear God," said Lane under his breath. "Okay, Annie. I'm ringing off now, and you're not to worry. We'll handle it."

* * *

"Where's Fuller?" Lane said.

"Making an arrest." Brewer glanced through the station doors as a Black Maria pulled up outside.

"In fact, here he is now."

The driver got out, went around and opened the back of the van.

Fuller and Myra stepped out, followed by a battered-looking Derek Webster. Bringing up the rear were Alistair Kirby and his dog.

Lane rushed out of the station to meet them. "Who is Southland and where does he live?"

"I know, sir," said Myra.

"Right, you two. Come with me. We'll take my car. I'll bring you up to date on the way."

* * *

Jack screeched to a halt outside Gavin Southland's house. In his rage he hadn't really thought what his approach was going to be. All he knew was that he had to get Rosie back. He got out of the car and, ducking low, ran in through the gates.

He was surprised to find the front door wide open. He looked into the house and saw the body of David Neville lying on the hall carpet in a pool of blood, a savage gash at his throat. Jack could hear voices coming from further inside.

Taking the revolver from his waistband, he cocked it and moved forward cautiously. The voices seemed to be coming from the direction of the conservatory. Jack crept along the passageway until he was standing just outside the door.

"Don't panic, Peter. We can get rid of his body the same way we disposed of the others."

"But the police . . ."

"Are no further forward in their investigations than they were yesterday."

Jack stepped forward into the conservatory. "I wouldn't be too sure of that."

Southland spun round and hurled the knife at him, but it sailed past Jack's ear and stuck in the doorframe.

"You bastard!" Peter Lamb hurled himself towards him, arms outstretched.

Jack shot him in the leg, sending him crashing to the ground, shouting and writhing in pain.

"Where is she?"

"Who?"

"Rosie. I know she's here."

"Oh, the little tart."

In three strides Jack crossed the floor and pinned Southland against the window. He rammed the barrel of the gun under his chin.

"That 'little tart' happens to be my daughter."

He watched the blood drain from Southland's face. "Oh dear. There seems to have been a bit of a balls-up."

"Take me to her." Jack pressed the barrel of the gun hard into Southland's throat.

"All right, all right, just don't kill me."

"Just give me an excuse." Jack eased the pressure, turned him around and moved behind him, grinding the gun barrel into the small of Southland's back.

"She's in my studio. I haven't hurt her." Southland started to move forward, past the shelves of orchids. "What gave me away? If you don't mind me asking."

"Your choice of interior décor." Jack pointed to the small brass discs with holes in their centres and embossed oriental writing that separated each pot. "Coins. Buddhist temple coins, as I'm sure you are well aware. The last time I saw anything like them was in a ruined temple in Mandalay during the war. Your penchant for eastern mysticism betrayed you in the end."

"Ah, how one's plans are so easily undone."

Jack pressed the barrel harder into Southland's back.

"Okay, okay. This way."

* * *

Rosie's eyes opened wide as Jack and Southland came into the studio. She gave a muffled sob, straining against her bonds.

Jack pushed Southland forward, keeping him covered with the gun. "Untie her and step away."

From behind him he heard a bellow of rage and glanced round in time to see Peter Lamb hurtling towards him. Before he could get off a shot Lamb crashed into him, bringing him to the ground. The gun flew from his hand and went clattering across the floor of the studio.

Lamb was strong. The boy's hands closed around Jack's throat, his thumbs pressing into the windpipe. A rushing sound filled Jack's ears and the room started to spin. Out of the corner of his eye he saw Southland limp across the room and take another knife from the pot on the table beside Rosie. He moved towards her.

It was enough to galvanise Jack. He brought his knee up to Lamb's bloodied thigh and smashed it into the muscle. Lamb cried out and his grip on Jack's throat loosened. Jack rolled onto Lamb, straddled him and punched him twice in the face. With a groan Lamb collapsed back on the carpet and Jack scrabbled across the floor for his revolver.

His fingers closed around the butt and then he heard Rosie squeal. He turned around and froze when he saw Southland crouching behind Rosie's chair, with his knife at her neck. Rosie's eyes were wide and she was making small noises through the gag.

“Is this how it’s going to end, Chief Inspector? No, I don’t think so. You don’t strike me as a man who would let his daughter die for the sake of an arrest. Am I right?” He moved the point of the knife, and a small bead of blood oozed from Rosie’s neck.

Rosie’s eyes grew wider and tears started to trickle down her cheeks.

“It’s all right, Rosie. Don‘t move,” said Jack.

“Do you hear that, Rosie? I’d listen to what he says if I were you.”

“If you hurt her—”

“You’ll do what, precisely? Shoot me? Hardly the actions of a law-abiding citizen.”

“How do you know what I’m capable of?”

“I know your type, Callum. My father was a policeman — another bloody gutless wonder — and he ran out on us when he was faced with something he couldn’t control. Coppers, you’re all the same. If you can’t put cuffs on it and throw it in a cell, then you fall apart.”

“You think?” Jack levelled the gun at him and fired. The bullet took Southland in the shoulder, sending him spinning away. At the same time, Rosie rocked the chair, sending it toppling backwards, and the back of her head struck the linoleum floor. As Southland, clutching his shoulder with one hand, the knife in the other, moved towards her, Jack fired again. He missed. The bullet bored a hole in the lino.

“Drop the knife.” For a moment Jack thought Southland might not, but then his fingers opened, and the knife clattered to the floor.

Still covering Southland with the revolver, Jack went across to Rosie and with his free hand he unbuckled the straps tethering her wrists and ankles.

Rosie tore the gag from her face and spat out the rag. She staggered over to Jack and clutched him. “I’m sorry, Daddy.”

“It’s okay, poppet. Everything’s all right now.” Jack gestured to Southland with the revolver. “Sit.”

As Southland limped across the room, Jack glanced around at the three pictures propped against the wall. Then his gaze alighted on the table that held the needles, silk thread and the half-used candle. His anger mounted again. He took a step forward and aimed the gun at Southland’s face.

Southland glared up at him defiantly. "Go on then. Shoot me. End it now."

Jack cocked the revolver and steadied his aim.

"Do you think death frightens me?"

Jack's finger tightened on the trigger.

"Put the gun down, Chief Inspector."

Lane stood in the doorway. Fuller and Myra were behind him. Lane held his own police-issue revolver, pointing at Jack. His hand was perfectly steady.

"I *will* shoot you, Jack."

"Please. Dad. Put it down."

Jack looked down into his daughter's face and he lowered the gun.

Lane signalled to Fuller, who handcuffed Southland and hauled him from the room.

"The gun, please, Jack." Lane held out his hand.

Jack handed it to him, and put his arm round Rosie's shoulder. "Let's go home, pet."

CHAPTER 39

WEDNESDAY August 20th 1958

"Just give me five minutes with him."

"I don't think that's necessary," said Fisher. "You've closed the case. Webster and Lamb are talking to us, singing actually, and they've told us everything. My men are picking up Tim Fellowes and Adam Channing. They'll be charged as accessories to murder and will most likely go away for a very long time."

"But I need to speak with Southland. I need to know why he sewed the mouths and eyes shut."

"Well, he hasn't told *us*, so why should he tell you?"

"Please."

Finally Fisher relented. He hadn't yet admitted that he'd miscalculated the investigation or, in the words of the chief constable, made a complete and utter cock-up.

Callum had been right all along.

"Okay," said Fisher. "But you're not going in there alone. Detective Sergeant Fuller will accompany you to make sure things don't get out of hand."

* * *

Jack opened the door and stepped into the interview room. Fuller followed him in and took a seat beside him at the small wooden table.

Southland appeared calm. "You're wasting your time. I've made my statement and I've nothing more to add."

"You know you're going to hang?" said Jack.

"Then I'll hang. I achieved what I wanted to achieve and led you lot a merry dance in the process."

Jack looked at him steadily. "Is that it? You were trying to make a point of some kind?"

Southland smiled and said nothing.

"Why the three monkeys, Gavin?"

Southland stared at him, and for a moment Jack thought he was going to remain silent, and then Gavin Southland began to speak. "You recognised the temple coins."

"I did. Eastern mythology is not widely known about. The fact that you were au fait with it made alarm bells sound in my mind."

"Would you call yourself a religious man, Chief Inspector?"

"Not especially."

"But you believe in the immortal soul?"

Jack shrugged, wondering where Southland was going with this.

Southland leaned forward, clasping his cuffed hands together. "I used to be like you. I was taught at Sunday school to believe in God; stories and parables that meant nothing very much. When I was struck down with polio I lost all the little faith I'd once possessed. How could there be a God if he let a boy, an innocent boy, suffer in that manner, reducing him to a cripple to be pitied and ridiculed? I was bitter, but I was determined to succeed in life, to win despite the unfair hand I'd been dealt."

"Is this story going anywhere, Gavin? Only I have criminals to catch."

"I thought you wanted to know why I sewed them up."

"I do. Please continue."

"After I left university I was eager to travel. University had whetted my appetite for learning, and I was anxious to continue. I took myself off to the Far East — China, Japan, Tibet. Finally my journey ended in Burma, where I found the coins in a ruined temple, much like you did. I was searching, you see. I was looking for the most important thing my illness had taken away from me: my faith, my belief in a higher power, something greater than myself."

"And did you find it?"

"Oh yes. Oh yes, I found it."

"I'm very pleased for you. It still doesn't explain—"

"Please let me continue. In the religions of the East, I found a belief that, at long last, made some sense to me."

"I wish it did to me . . ." Fuller said. Jack hushed him.

"I don't expect you to understand, so I'll try and simplify it for you. The meaning of the three monkeys has been debated for centuries. Different religions have their own interpretations, but I'll tell you what I believe. The three monkeys represent the *Sanshi;* the three spirits residing in every human being. These spirits report good and bad deeds to a God, a higher authority, which can then reward or punish as it sees fit. I was merely making sure they would have nothing to report."

"And is that it?"

"It's what I believe. Who are you, Chief Inspector, to question those beliefs?"

Jack stared at Southland for a full minute before he rose to his feet and left the room.

Fuller caught up with him outside. "Sir? If you don't mind me asking, what the hell was all that about?"

"It was exactly that, Eddie: *Hell.*"

"Well, it went over my head."

"He just told us why he sewed their eyes and mouths shut and poured wax into their ears."

"Did he?"

"I read the interview he gave Fisher, and now I think I understand. After years of living a godless life, without faith, he knew his thirst for revenge against his father — a man who had deserted him when he needed him most — would conflict with his recently discovered faith. The three monkeys, Eddie: see no evil, speak no evil, hear no evil. In his own twisted way, he was trying to prevent the *Sanshi* taking messages back to his god. He painted them, making a triptych — some kind of religious, artistic statement. *He was trying to save his soul.*"

"By killing people?"

"Murderers find all sorts of reasons to justify what they do."

* * *

Lane was waiting for Jack outside the interview room.

"Chief Inspector; a moment if you please."

Jack nodded. He knew what was coming.

Lane sat behind his desk. His hands were clasped together rather formally, on the surface.

Jack stood, not quite to attention, hoping to convey some respect for the man seated before him.

"Regulations dictate that I have to report the discharge of a pistol by a serving officer. You understand that, don't you, Chief Inspector?"

"Yes, sir. I fully understand your position."

"Do you? Do you really?"

Suddenly Lane slammed a palm down hard on the desk. "An unauthorised pistol! How long have you had it?"

Jack shrugged. "Brought it back at the end of the war and didn't give it another thought, to be honest."

"Yet you knew where it was, had it in excellent working order, and had sufficient ammunition to make it a viable weapon!"

"I can see your point, sir." It was true. He had lovingly attended to the cleaning and oiling of the revolver, keeping it along with his discharge uniform. He knew the perils that could befall a copper and his family. At the back of his mind had been the thought that a working gun might come in handy one day. And he had been right.

"By rights, I should be reporting this to the chief constable. I should have done so already."

"I'm sorry for the embarrassment I've caused you, sir. Do you want my warrant card?"

Lane sighed and made a noise in the back of his throat that might have been taken for irritation.

"Did you intend to use it?"

"I shot two men, sir, so I think I—"

"Jack! You shot one young thug in the leg to disable him, and you shot Southland in the shoulder to stop him harming your daughter. That is not what I meant."

"I think I know what you mean, sir."

"Would you have killed Southland, Jack? That's what I'm asking you. For God's sake, the man had taken your daughter, your Rosie, and was threatening her with mutilation and death! It would be wholly understandable if you'd wanted the man dead. He's evil. Would you have killed him if I hadn't stopped you?"

Jack let out a deep breath.

"Henry, I think I should express my gratitude that your fortitude probably prevented me doing something I might later have regretted."

"I thought that might be the case."

"I killed people in the war — I dare say you saw some action yourself. I've shot villains in the line of duty as a serving police officer, but I can't say that I've ever felt easy with it. There are nights, even now, when I wake in a sweat and feel the heat of the jungle suffocating me again. The life of even the lowest criminal cannot be disposed of without a cost."

"Quite so." Lane looked pensive.

"Might I ask you something, sir — man to man, as it were?"

"Yes, Jack, I would have shot you, to stop you doing something you would have lived to regret."

Jack sat down. "I thought that might be it."

Lane's face assembled itself into a grim smile. "I would have aimed to wound though, not to kill."

"Very reassuring."

"Chief Inspector, the matter is closed. It goes no further than this room. There were others present at the scene, but I think we can rely on their discretion. Your . . . war souvenir will be returned to you once forensics has finished with it."

Jack stood and grasped Lane's outstretched hand.

"Bloody good job, Jack. A first rate investigation and a decent result."

"I just wish I could have acted a bit quicker and saved those other poor young lives."

"Don't dwell on it; you know better than that. Did you know Southland's father was one of us?"

"A copper — yes, I read that in the report."

"Bit of a bully, by all accounts."

"Southland killed those poor young people out of some kind of twisted revenge on his father. Fellowes and Channing are both weak men but Southland also had some kind of hold over them. Their statements are going to make for interesting reading."

"You're due some leave — take a couple of days off. Spend time with your family. They need you now. I'll see you on Monday."

"If you're sure, sir. Absolutely. Thank you, Henry — the garden has been a bit neglected of late. Now if you don't mind, I have a certain London copper to evict from my office."

* * *

Jack entered his office without knocking just as Inspector Lymon and Sergeant Greyling shuffled out, clutching cardboard boxes.

"I'll be grateful for the return of my office . . . sir."

"Think you're the bee's knees because your crazy theory worked out, do you?"

"I think the team got a good result. In the end."

"Meaning after I made a monumental foul-up by taking you and your precious officers off the case."

"I think you'll find it was an authority higher than either of us who made that decision."

"Yes, well, I'm off. I'll leave you to your provincial duties."

"Quite so, sir. Get back to the smoke and the real villains. Wouldn't want a triple murder to stand in the way of real crime, now would we?"

"You really are an impudent man. You know that don't you, Callum?"

Jack brought his face close to Fisher's. He could smell whisky and mint on the man's breath. "You are a pompous ass, Fisher. You put people's lives in danger because you had your head so far up your own backside that you couldn't see that we, the provincial coppers you sneered at, might be right and you, with all your Scotland Yard bells and whistles, could be wrong. At least one young person died because your arrogance led you down the wrong track. Worst of all you nearly got my daughter killed. Lucky for you she's unharmed or else you really would see how impudent I can be. Have a nice trip back . . . sir."

Jack pushed past Fisher and sat down behind his desk.

"You know the way out," he said.

CHAPTER 40

SATURDAY August 23rd 1958

Jack walked with his arm around Eric's shoulders. Annie, Joan and Rosie, their arms linked, followed close behind. They sang *When The Spurs Go Marching In* with the rest of the Tottenham supporters. He led the way through the crowd thronging towards the White Hart Lane turnstiles, and up the concrete steps to the terraces, where they assembled with thousands of others, waiting for the match against Blackpool to get underway.

The stadium resounded with the sound of partisan cheers and the clatter of football rattles.

"Do you think we'll win, Dad?" said Joan.

"Judging by the way they've been playing recently, Joanie, I think it's highly unlikely. But I'm a Spurs fan; hope is second nature to us."

He looked at his eldest daughter, whom he'd only just got back. She had seen and experienced too much for a girl her age but she seemed all right, at least on the surface. He was looking forward to getting to know her again.

Rosie was enjoying the festive atmosphere, as they all were. Judging by her look, Jack didn't think the awful events in Southland's house had done any lasting damage. Annie had her arm around her, and he knew Rosie was in safe hands.

As Danny Blanchflower led the Tottenham Hotspur team out of the tunnel and onto the pitch, White Hart Lane erupted in a roar.

Jack shouted to his son above the crowd's noise.

"If you can draw crowds like this with your skiffle music, Eric, I'll be very impressed!"

"Just you watch me, Dad!"

"Don't worry, son. I'll be watching, and cheering for you all the way."

THE END

GLOSSARY OF BRITISH AND PERIOD SLANG

addles your brain: messes with your head
all hands to the pumps: lots of help needed
Babycham: cheap alternative to champagne – made from pears.
balloon's gone up: an emergency situation
balls-up: an error, a mistake
banana boat: derogatory term for immigrants transport to UK
beat bobby: uniformed police officer who patrols the streets
bee's knees: something special
be sick: vomit
knighted: given a British honour
bells ringing: Equivalent of police sirens today
belter: It was a fantastic goal
Biscuits: cookies
Black Maria: a police van
bod: Derogatory term – anonymous person.
boozy: A bit drunk
bread-and-butter work: Routine work
Brylcreem: hair cream/gel to give men's hair shine and smoothness
calling in the cavalry: Asking for reinforcements
Cambridge University: prestigious British university divided up into autonomous colleges such as Corpus Christi or Magdalene. The students live and socialise within their colleges.
car park: parking lot
CID: Criminal investigation division
clobbered: Hit hard
copper: Slang for policeman
council estate: social housing
crazy-paving: Patio, concrete slabs in random pattern
cuppa: A cup of tea
Cuppa: Cup of tea
cut along to: Go along to
dessert: pudding
doormat: meek
dressing down: telling off
emergency police box: telephone box for police use

en-print: an 8 x 10 photograph
excuse my French: sorry I swore
fellow: boyfriend
get you a brew: a cup of tea
get your skates on: Hurry up
glasshouse: greenhouse
go to the dogs: go to rack and ruin, be destroyed
good collars: good arrests
guv'nor: the boss
gymkhana: horse-riding event
gymslips: school uniform of bib and skirt design
half of bitter: beer.
Harold MacMillan: British Prime minister 1957-63
haversack: backpack, rucksack
Hendon: police training school
his beat: the area he patrols
huge chip on her shoulder: resentful
I'm spitting nails: very angry
keep it under your hat: keep it a secret
keep mum about it: keep it a secret
knock his block off: punch him har, block = head
late birds: go to bed at a late hour
lavatory: restroom
loo: toilet
little hussy: girl of loose morals
Lonnnie Donegan : father of British skiffle music
LSE: London School of Economics
mantelpiece: shelf above a fireplace
Marmite or Bovril: meat-based sandwich spreads
Mickey Finn: a drugged drink which makes the drinker unconscious
milkman: person who delivers milk to the house
Mosquito: British Airplane used in Second World War
mooning over a boy: teenage girl infatuated with a boy
off his chump: slang for being mad, crazy
old toffee: lies
off-licence: shop selling alcohol
on the game: prostitute
Ovaltine: malted milk beverage – served hot
Palais: dance hall
Pathé News and Pearl and Dean: adverts before the movie starts

playing cards close to her chest: being coy with the truth
pounding the beat: working as a uniformed officer on the streets
pretty good going-over : a thorough investigation (can also mean beating up)
prick: slang for penis
quite sweet on you: likes you romantically
restroom: place where staff can relax or recover in
rozzers: policemen
ructions: disagreements
S.P.: starting price = the truth about what is being said
School Friend: comic aimed at teenage girls
settee: sofa
sick: vomit
skiffle: 1950s style of popular music
slacks: UK trousers US pants
snapshot: photograph
spewed: vomited
stick of rock: a cylinder of candy often sold at the seaside
sticking plaster: Band-Aid
stitching me up: framing me
swot: a nerd, a geek, someone keen on their studies
tabard: apron worn for some work
tart: woman with loose morals
tart's boudoir: a hooker's bedroom
Teddy boys: Thugs and young tearaways
Ten bob: ten shillings: pre-decimal money — half of £1
tightly permed hair: hair artificially curled
Tizer: fizzy pop/soda
Tommy Steele: 1950s-60s pop star.
tugging my forelock: acting in a subservient manner
tuppenny tart: a cheap hooker
two peas in a pod.: two people similar to one another
very snarled up: gridlocked traffic
Victor Sylvester: popular ballroom dancer and band-leader in the 1950s
whistles and bells: top specifications
winkle-picker shoe: long narrow male shoe
Wolseley: model of saloon car used by the police
yobs: thugs and young tearaways
your lazy arse: ass
your racket: your loud noise

ABOUT THE AUTHOR

Len Maynard & Mick Sims (Maynard Sims) are the authors of several novels with more coming soon. They have written stories, novellas, essays, award winning screenplays, and have worked as editors. www.maynard-sims.com

Jack has his own website too! http://www.jackcallum.co.uk/

Thank you for reading this book. If you enjoyed it please leave feedback on Amazon, and if there is anything we missed or you have a question about then please get in touch. The author and publishing team appreciate your feedback and time reading this book.

Our email is jasper@joffebooks.com

http://joffebooks.com

PRIME EVIL

(Jack Callum Book 2)

MAYNARD SIMS

First published 2016
Joffe Books, London
www.joffebooks.com

This book is a work of fiction. Names, characters, businesses, organizations, places and events are either the product of the author's imagination or are used fictitiously. Any resemblance to actual persons, living or dead, events or locales is entirely coincidental. The spelling used is British English except where fidelity to the author's rendering of accent or dialect supersedes this.

THERE IS A GLOSSARY OF ENGLISH SLANG IN THE BACK OF THIS BOOK FOR US READERS.

Dedication

To the memory of Lonnie Donegan, Wally Whyton,
and Paul Lincoln aka Dr Death.
Pioneers to a man.

AUTHOR'S NOTE

Certain liberties have been taken with the geography of Hertfordshire for the benefit of the story. Hopefully the residents of that beautiful county, our home for many years, will be forgiving. MS

CHAPTER 1

TUESDAY MARCH 17th, 1959

". . . Just remember these three simple rules. One, don't talk to strangers. Two, never go off with a person you do not know, and three, remember that the police are your friends. We are here to listen and help you whenever we can." Jack Callum looked down upon the assembled faces. They stared back at him, their faces a sea of utter boredom.

The headmistress, Cynthia Arnold, sprang to her feet and walked to the front of the stage.

"Very informative," she said. "I'm sure that you would all like to show your appreciation to Chief Inspector Callum for giving up his valuable time to speak to you today." The applause rippled listlessly around the assembly hall and quickly died away. "Now, if you could all make your way out to the playground, slowly please, where . . ." She looked down at the piece of paper in her hand. "Where Sergeant Grant and Constable Cooper will tell you how to stay safe on the roads."

The hall emptied in a rumble of voices and shuffling feet.

"Thank you, Mr Callum. I'm sure they appreciated your words," said the headmistress.

"I suppose the ones who managed to stay awake might have learned something," Jack said. He tucked his speech into his jacket pocket. "I apologise again that Superintendent Lane couldn't be here today."

The headmistress clucked. "Never mind. I'm sure it couldn't be helped. In any case, you proved to be a very successful last minute substitution. Full marks."

"You're very kind."

Henry Lane was more comfortable swinging a golf club than standing in front of a microphone. He had been trying to wheedle his way out of the school talk for weeks. Jack had taken his place following a convenient attack of laryngitis. He enjoyed public speaking even less than Lane.

"I hear your men have brought a police car along with them to help with their demonstration. I have to see this. It's all rather exciting," said the headmistress. She bustled out of the hall.

Jack made his way to the side of the stage and trotted down the short staircase to freedom.

He pulled up short when a voice spoke from out of the shadows. "Did you mean it?"

The speaker was hidden by a fold in the stage curtain.

"Did I mean what?" said Jack. A teenage girl stepped out from behind the heavy brocade. She stood facing him.

"That the police are our friends? We should come and talk to you and you will help."

Jack smiled indulgently. "We'll always listen, and we'll help if we can. Sorry, I didn't catch your name."

"Gerry . . . Geraldine Tanner."

"Well, Geraldine, do you have a problem you want to discuss?"

The girl nodded. A lock of curly blonde hair escaped from beneath her Alice band and fell across her face. "It's my brother," she said.

"And what do you want to tell me about your brother?"

"He's dead," she said, biting her lip pensively. "I killed him."

* * *

"I'm sorry your time has been wasted, Chief Inspector," the headmistress said. "Our Miss Tanner is a great fantasist."

"So she's done this kind of thing before?" Jack said quietly. Geraldine sat in a corner of the office, still biting her lip and staring at her shoes.

"With monotonous regularity," the headmistress said.

Jack continued to stare at the girl. He had broken faith with Geraldine when he told the headmistress. But he'd had no choice. He could not sit alone in a room with a thirteen-year-old girl. People would have seen it as dangerously inappropriate.

"The school secretary has been in touch with her father. Mr Tanner is on his way here now to take her home. He shouldn't be long. They live on the Broadway in Letchworth, you know. A lovely house . . ." The headmistress sounded wistful. In the playground below, Jack's junior officers were using a black Wolseley to demonstrate stopping times to an audience of bored schoolchildren.

Keeping his voice low, Jack said, "And as far as you're aware, Geraldine doesn't, and never did have, a brother?"

The headmistress shook her head. "Our records have her down as an only child. Teenage girls have a great capacity for making up stories, Mr Callum."

"I have two teenage daughters myself," Jack said. He was beginning to find the headmistress's condescending attitude irritating.

"Then I don't need to tell you," she said. "You don't have to stay, you know. I'm sure I'll be able to deal with Mr Tanner when he gets here."

"I'll hang on. I'd like a few words with him. Besides, I have to wait for my men to finish the demonstration. I need a lift back to the station."

"I see." The headmistress stood up, walked to the window and stared out at the car. It was now performing an elaborate skid on the playground's tarmac surface. Jack would have to have a quiet word with Constable Cooper about his tendency to showboat.

"Ooh," she said. "It really is *quite* exciting."

Jack sat down on a hard chair next to Geraldine. After her initial pronouncement about killing her brother, the girl had said nothing more to him.

"Are you all right, Geraldine?"

"I told you, it's Gerry," the girl said. She didn't look at him.

"Sorry. *Gerry*. Are you feeling okay now?"

Finally Geraldine turned to look at him. "You're just like the rest of them," she said. "I trusted you."

Her words cut deep. He had betrayed her.

* * *

Thirty minutes later the school secretary knocked on the door of the office.

"Mr Tanner's here, Headmistress."

"Well, don't keep him waiting, Sandra. Show him in."

Anthony Tanner was a tall man in his mid-thirties. He had lush, wavy brown hair and matinee idol looks. He nodded to Jack and the headmistress, and folded himself into a chair beside the girl. He grasped her hand and held it tightly. "Geraldine, do we have to go through all this again?"

"It's Gerry," the girl said. She wrenched her hand away.

Jack watched Tanner's face turn an angry puce colour. His fingers were clenched.

Jack cleared his throat. "Excuse me, Mr Tanner. Chief Inspector Callum, Welwyn and Hatfield CID."

Ignoring Jack, Tanner turned to Cynthia Arnold. "You called the police? Even though I told you that I would be down here within the hour to sort this out?"

"I . . . I . . ," the headmistress spluttered.

"You mustn't blame Mrs Arnold, sir. I was here anyway, giving a talk to the school. Gerry approached me with her confession."

"And you haven't got enough common sense to realise when you're being led up the garden path?"

"I'm afraid we have to take all such confessions at face value," Jack said evenly. "We'd lose all public sympathy if we didn't."

Tanner opened his mouth to speak again and then, after consideration, closed it and got to his feet. "Come on, Geraldine. I'm taking you home."

"Actually," Jack said to him, "I'd like a quick word with you, if you can spare the time. Mrs Arnold, could you take Gerry outside for a moment and wait with her until we're finished?"

"Of course," the headmistress said. She took the girl's hand. "Come along, dear." She led Geraldine out into the secretary's office and closed the door behind them.

Jack went around the desk and sat down in the headmistress's chair. "Take a seat, Mr Tanner. This won't take long."

Tanner sat down opposite him and glared across the desk.

"A day off from work is it, sir? Only I was wondering why the school called you rather than your wife."

"Not that it's any of your business, Chief Inspector, but I've just come off a long and arduous run at the Lyric. I'll be resting until my next film role starts rehearsing in a fortnight."

"Ah, you're an actor," Jack said.

Tanner nodded curtly. "Furthermore, my wife is not a well woman. She can't leave the house."

"I'm sorry to hear that. Is she bedridden?"

"My wife suffers from a psychological condition. She's an agoraphobic."

"That must be very distressing for you. She can't leave the house at all?"

"Not without a severe panic attack," Tanner said.

"It must be very difficult, with you being away at the theatre all the time. How do you look after Gerry?"

"We have a woman who lives in during the week."

"And she makes sure Gerry gets to school?"

Tanner nodded. "And does the shopping and any other errands that would oblige my wife to leave the house." He glanced at his watch. "Is this going to take much longer?"

Jack leaned forward. "Do you have any idea why Gerry told me she had killed her brother?"

Tanner sighed. "Geraldine is an only child, Mr Callum. We were never blessed with another. I can't say where this latest fantasy has come from. Geraldine is, you might say, highly strung."

"She seemed very . . . convincing."

"She gets that from me. I come from a family of actors. My mother used to be very highly regarded. It's in the genes, you might say."

"Yes," Jack said. "That must be it. The genes."

"Are we finished here?"

"I think so. I won't detain you any longer. You can take your daughter home now."

Tanner nodded abruptly and walked to the door. His fingers closed around the door handle.

"Just one more thing," Jack said.

Tanner turned back to him. "Yes?"

"I take it your daughter has done this type of thing before?"

"What are you implying?"

Jack smiled. "It's just that when you came in you said to her, 'do we have to go through all this again?' Which suggests that what happened today wasn't an isolated occurrence."

"Please understand, Mr Callum. Dealing with my wife's . . . condition, puts a huge strain on us as a family. Geraldine is going through puberty. That on its own is quite enough for her to have to deal with. It's hardly surprising that she seeks refuge in fantasies."

"Oh, I can understand the pressures teenage girls are under. I have two daughters myself. But it's a bit extreme, isn't it? Confessing to the murder of a sibling she doesn't even have?"

"What can I say? Only that I bow to your greater experience in such matters. Good day." Tanner turned on his heel and walked out.

The headmistress bustled back into the office. "What a charming man! And *so* talented. I was lucky enough to catch his 'Hamlet' at the Old Vic a few years ago. In my opinion he was right up there with Gielgud and Olivier."

"Strange," Jack said. "I've never heard of him."

"Well, of course, he's not widely known. But he's just as talented as they are. It was a real coup when Geraldine came here. We are outside her local catchment area, but Mr Tanner insisted. He wanted only the best for his daughter."

"I'm sure he did," said Jack. He smiled indulgently at the woman. "I'm sure he did."

CHAPTER 2

TUESDAY

Jack and his wife, Annie, were washing up after dinner. "So why would a thirteen-year-old girl confess to killing a non-existent brother?" Jack was saying.

"Is she troubled in other ways?" Annie said.

"She might be. Her mum's an agoraphobic. It's an almost pathological fear of open spaces. That can't be easy to live with."

Jack's eldest daughter, Joan, was sitting at the kitchen table, sewing. "It sounds like the daughter's seeking attention. Perhaps her mother gets it all. Does her father take much notice of her?"

"Not enough, probably," Jack said. "I don't think he's there much. He's an actor."

"An actor?" said Annie. "Is he famous?"

"I wouldn't know," Jack said. "I've certainly never heard of him. Joanie, do you still read those trashy gossip magazines? Does the name Anthony Tanner mean anything to you?"

"Anthony Tanner doesn't, but *Tony* Tanner does."

"Really?"

"Yes. He was quite the rising star, once upon a time," Joan said. "He graduated from the Rank Charm School and for a while the magazines were full of him. They had him down as another Dirk Bogarde. They ran features about him, you know the kind of thing: 'At Home With Tony Tanner,' 'Meet Tony Tanner and his Beautiful Family.'"

"Well, he needs to get his money back from Rank, because they certainly failed him in the charm department," Jack said. "You do read a load of tripe, Joanie. So what happened to him? Why is his star no longer rising?"

"Why are you so interested in this tripe?" his daughter said with a smile.

"Call it prurient curiosity."

"The best kind," Joan said. "His wife died a few years ago and he remarried. It caused a heck of a stink."

"I remember him now." Annie put a plate aside and re-joined the conversation. "Didn't he marry Lois Franklin, the 'Cadence Girl'? She was in all the magazines, advertising their beauty products."

"You're right, Mum. A month after his first wife died. Rumours began flying around that they had been carrying on while his wife was dying of cancer. The scandal killed his film career stone dead."

"He's still acting," Jack said.

"Yes, he went back to the theatre. He still pops up here and there in the odd film, but mostly in minor parts. Nothing to set the box office alight. From what I've read, the theatre is his main source of income these days. That and television commercials. He did one for cigarettes a couple of years back."

"Then I shouldn't think Gerry's home life is a barrel of laughs," Jack said. "She loses her real mother to cancer. Her stepmother is unable to leave the house. Her father is out treading the boards night after night, or is away on location."

Annie covered his fingers with her soapy ones. "Why are you so concerned? Surely it's a case for the school board or the family doctor. It's hardly a police matter."

"I feel that I let her down, Annie," Jack said. "I told her and the entire school that the police were their friends and that if they had any problems they should come and speak with us. So she did, and I didn't help. I just batted her back to the school to let them deal with it."

"You did the right thing," Annie said.

"Did I?"

"Of course you did."

"Did mum tell you? I've got a job," Joan said, changing the subject abruptly.

"I haven't had the chance. You tell him," Annie said.

"Avril is taking me on as her apprentice."

"Avril the hairdresser? What do you know about hairdressing?" Jack said.

"Hey, I can shampoo and set with the best of them. I used to do some of the customers at the pub for pin money. Avril said I can help her out on her rounds, and she'll teach me to cut and everything."

"That's good, isn't it, Jack?" Annie said.

"Yes. Splendid." Jack's mind was still on Tony Tanner and his family. "Don't expect me to stop going to the barbers' though. Carlo's been cutting my hair ever since we first moved up here."

"Well, I suppose he'll get it right one day," Joan said.

Jack threw the tea towel at her.

Joan ducked. "Hey, only joking!" she laughed. The mood in the kitchen lightened. Jack didn't like to bring his work home with him but, for some reason, Gerry Tanner had got under his skin. He'd be thankful to get to work tomorrow and go back to chasing some *real* criminals.

* * *

Jack was sitting in his favourite armchair listening to *The Archers*. The radio series, an 'everyday story of country folk,' had prompted his move away from London. So far he'd been happy in the greener, semi-rural setting of Hertfordshire. But he still listened to the saga of the Archer clan whenever he could spare the time.

The doorbell rang. He waited for someone else to answer it, cursing under his breath. Finally, with a "bugger!" he pushed himself out of his armchair.

As he stepped out into the hallway the bell rang again. "Coming!" he called irritably. "Keep your hair on."

Detective Sergeant Eddie Fuller stood on the doorstep.

"Christ, Eddie, haven't you seen enough of me for one day?" Jack said.

"Sorry to disturb, guv. I didn't want to, but Chief Superintendent Lane said I must come and get you."

"Come in and tell me all about it," Jack said.

Fuller shook his head. "I'll bring you up to date while I drive."

"That urgent, eh?"

Fuller nodded.

"I'll get my coat," Jack said.

* * *

"Where are we headed?" Jack said as they pulled out onto the main road.

"Norton Common." Fuller's face was grim. He had said nothing since they got into the car. "The team's already there."

His sergeant's reticence was beginning to annoy Jack. Today's talk at the school had been quite draining. Geraldine Tanner's spurious confession and the uneasy confrontation with her father had made him tense. He'd hoped to have a quiet evening at home listening to the 'Archers' and perhaps some music later. He'd bought the new David Whitfield long player at the weekend and hadn't had a chance to play it yet. Instead he was being driven through the night to Norton Common and its sixty acres of thick woodland. The woods held Muntjac deer, Letchworth's own black squirrel colony, and one of the most unlikely crime scenes he could imagine.

"So are you going to tell me what's waiting for us when we get to the common? Or is this your idea of a mystery tour?"

Fuller glanced around at his boss. "Sorry, guv. My mind's on other things. I was meant to be taking Judy to the pictures tonight. The chief super caught me just as I was heading off. I wouldn't mind but I've had to cancel our last three dates because of work. I don't think she'll put up with it for much longer."

"A messed up social life goes with the job, Eddie. You know that." But Jack sympathised with his sergeant. The job had put a lot of strain on his relationship with Annie during the early years of their marriage. "Try to put your love life out of your mind and just tell me what the case is."

"A particularly nasty murder," said Fuller.

"Anyone we know?"

Fuller shook his head. "No identification so far. A man, mid-forties, found by a dog walker just after six tonight."

"So what makes this murder so nasty?"

"At first the dog walker only saw him from a distance. He thought it was someone taking a leak against a tree. He got closer to him and the man didn't move away. He couldn't. He'd been nailed there and his throat was cut."

Suddenly Ambridge's peaceful idyll was a million miles away. Jack blew through his teeth. "You'd better step on it, and use the bell."

Fuller pressed down on the accelerator, switched on the Winkworth bell and the Wolseley tore noisily along the main road.

* * *

By the time they reached Norton Common the body had been taken down from the tree. It was laid out on the grass. Police doctor Barry Fenwick was crouched over it, conducting the preliminary examination. One of the team had driven his police car onto the common. Its engine was idling and its headlights lit up the scene like a stage set.

A handful of CID officers with torches searched around for clues. Another officer was taking photographs. The gory scene flickered in the blinding light from his flash bulbs.

Jack looked from the blood-spattered tree to the sticky pool of red that sank slowly into the earth at its bole, to the body lying on the grass. "Any idea how long ago this happened, Barry?" he said.

"The body's still relatively warm. Rigor is only just stiffening the jaw and neck. It hasn't reached the other muscles yet, so not long. Two hours. Three at the most."

Jack checked his watch. It was just coming up to eight o'clock. "So, between five and six. Cause of death?"

"Catastrophic blood loss. The carotid artery has been severed. Death would have followed very quickly. Two minutes. Three at the most."

"And what about the stab wounds to the stomach?" Jack pointed to the blood-soaked shirt.

Fenwick shook his head. "Superficial. None of them look deep enough to be fatal. They could be hesitation wounds but I think rather they were designed to cause pain, not to kill."

"It's a shame he was taken down," Jack said. "I would have liked to have seen the body in situ, so to speak."

"Your man took photographs," Fenwick said. "But if it helps you to visualise it, his arms were raised above his head and a six-inch nail had been hammered through the palms of his hands. Judging from the tearing of the flesh on his palms I'd say he was hanging there for several minutes while he was being tortured. His throat was cut before then. The autopsy will yield a more accurate picture of course."

"As will the photographs," Jack said with a shudder.

"Now this is interesting." Fenwick bent closer. He took a pair of tweezers from his bag and started probing the black moustache on the body's top lip. A few moments later he said, "Yes, I thought so." He lifted the tweezers and waved something thin, black and hairy.

"Fake," Jack said, staring at it.

Fenwick nodded. He dropped the false moustache into a polythene bag and returned his attention to the face. "Can I have some more light here!" he called. An officer aimed his torch at the dead man's face. From his swarthy skin the dead man appeared to be a middle-aged man of Latin extraction. Fenwick leaned in closer still and his shadow obscured Jack's view.

"Curiouser and curiouser," Fenwick muttered, as he worked at the face with the tweezers.

Jack moved in to get a closer look. Fenwick appeared to be poking the corpse's nose with the point of his tweezers. Then, with an almost exultant cry of, "Yes, I thought so," Fenwick settled back on his haunches. He looked up at Jack. "Well, what do you make of this?" he said. He brandished a blob of something light brown and fleshy.

"What the hell is that?" said Jack.

"Nose putty," Fenwick said. "Or mortician's wax." He smiled at Jack's bewilderment. "It's a fake nose, Chief Inspector. Judging from the paleness of the skin beneath it, it looks like your man here is wearing make-up — the theatrical kind."

Jack crouched down, took a handkerchief from his pocket and started to wipe the greasepaint away from the face. Suddenly he stood upright.

"Good God!"

"What is it, guv? Do you recognise him?" said Fuller, who'd been watching the whole procedure with a kind of macabre fascination.

Jack stared down at the body. "Yes, Sergeant, I recognise him. In fact I was talking to him just this afternoon. His name is Tony Tanner. He's an actor."

"Well, I suppose that would explain the make-up."

"Yes, but not why he was wearing it tonight. Nor does it explain why he was found nailed to a tree with his throat cut."

CHAPTER 3

TUESDAY

Several yards away from the body, WPC Myra Banks was talking to an elderly man dressed in a windcheater and corduroy trousers. He held an equally elderly golden retriever on a leash.

"I take it that's our dog walker," Jack said. PC Alan Blake was standing nearby looking a little green around the gills. Blake nodded and swallowed loudly. He was only twenty-two, not long out of Hendon, and this was his first murder scene.

"Are you all right, Constable?" Jack said to him.

The young constable shook his head. "I've never seen anything like it."

"You'll see worse. Get off home now. Come in tomorrow morning after a good night's sleep."

"Yes, sir. Thank you, sir," said Blake, and scuttled away.

"Do you remember your first murder, Eddie?"

"It's etched indelibly on my mind, couldn't forget it. It was in Stevenage. An old woman had been robbed for her pension money. Her head was split open like a ripe melon. I threw up for two days solid." Fuller shuddered.

"There's nothing else I can do here," Jack said. "I'm going to break the news to Tanner's wife. Give me the keys and I'll take the Wolseley. Can you get a lift back to the station with one of the others?"

"Don't worry about me. It's a mild night. I'll walk."

"As you like, but talk to the dog walker first. See if he's told us all he knows. Myra!" he called to the WPC. "You're coming with me."

* * *

"Where are we going?" Myra asked.

"Up to the Broadway. A house called 'Elsinore.' We have to break the news to Tony Tanner's wife. It's why I wanted you along . . . to comfort her while I make a cup of tea."

"Great," Myra said grimly. "*I* could always make the tea."

"Your shoulder is more absorbent than mine," Jack said with a smile.

"I doubt it. But I'll do my best."

"Yes, I know you will." He liked Myra Banks. She was on secondment to CID after several years in uniform. Jack wanted to make her position permanent. She had the *nose,* and he knew she would make a good detective.

They turned in through the gates. "Not exactly a Danish castle," Myra said. "But it's still pretty impressive."

The Tanners' yellow brick mansion had been built around the turn of the century. It had a red tiled roof, and four large picture windows took up much of the downstairs frontage. Jack pulled up and switched off the engine. He took a deep breath and glanced at Myra. "Let's get this done."

An elderly plump woman with wavy grey hair and rosy apple cheeks opened the door.

"Chief Inspector Callum and Detective Constable Banks to see Mrs Tanner," Jack said. He showed her his warrant card.

The woman peered at the card and then opened the door. "Please come in and wait in the hall," she said. "I'll tell Lois you're here."

Leaving them standing in the spacious hallway, she disappeared through a doorway off to the left. Jack looked around. There were a number of framed playbills hanging against the stripes of the wallpapered walls. Ahead of them was a wide staircase dominated by an oil painting in an ornate gilt frame.

"The master of the house," Jack said wryly. "Looks a lot different to when we saw him an hour ago."

Myra stared up at the portrait. It showed a handsome man seated on a high-backed chair. He was dressed casually in blue slacks and a cream shirt open at the neck to reveal a dark blue silk cravat. The pose was relaxed. His legs were crossed, his hand on his chin, a cigarette held between his fingers. The artist had painted the blue-grey cigarette smoke eddying up to mingle with Tanner's carefully ruffled hair. He had the look of a rather stylish vagabond.

Myra opened her mouth to say something and then stopped as a tall, elegantly-dressed woman stepped into the hallway. From her elaborately coiffed honey-blonde hair to the tips of her expensive Italian stilettos, Lois Tanner, née Franklin, looked every inch the high-class model she used to be. A smile lit up her carefully painted face and she walked towards them, hand extended.

"Lois Tanner," she said. "Very pleased to meet you."

She spoke with a slight American accent. Jack shook her hand. "Can we go somewhere and sit down," he said. "I'm afraid I have some very distressing news about your husband."

"About Tony?" Lois said. The smile went out like a light. "What is it?"

"If we can just go somewhere and sit down?" Jack said again.

Lois looked flustered. "Yes, yes, of course. Come through."

As Jack followed her out of the hallway he glanced up the stairs. He was just in time to see a young fair-haired girl duck out of sight behind the balustrade.

Lois Tanner led them through the house to a smallish room. Its walls were lined with books and more framed playbills, older than the ones hanging in the entrance hall. Some of the names were familiar to Jack, but he could see from the look on Myra's face that names like Herbert Beerbohm-Tree and Mrs Patrick Campbell meant nothing to her.

"This is Tony's office. Please take a seat," Lois said. She indicated a settee upholstered in deep red velvet. "Now. Would you mind telling me what all this is about?" She pulled a hard chair away from the oak desk and sat down, demurely crossing her legs at the ankle and leaning forward slightly.

"It's your husband, Mrs Tanner," Jack said. "I'm afraid there's been an incident."

"Has he crashed his car again? I keep telling him not to drive so recklessly. Do you know if he'll be home soon?"

"I'm afraid it's something much more serious."

Jack had difficulty finding the words. Eventually he managed to convey that Mrs Tanner's husband would not be coming home that night. Or any other for that matter.

He said what he had to say and a hush settled over the room. Myra got to her feet and announced that she would make a cup of tea.

"That won't be necessary," Lois said. "Hester will make it." Mrs Tanner pressed a black bell push on the desk. A few seconds later the door opened and the plump woman stepped into the room.

"Tea for our guests, Hester, if you please."

"Of course," Hester said. She asked if they wanted milk or lemon and left the room.

"My rock," Lois said. "I don't know how I would cope if it wasn't for Hester. She keeps me organised. She's especially good at helping me with my stepdaughter, Geraldine. I can't leave the house, you see."

"Yes," Jack said quietly. "I spoke to your husband earlier today. He told me about your problem."

"Ah, my *problem*. I suppose that's one way of putting it." There was another silence. "So Tony's dead. That's going to cause problems, especially with Geraldine. She and I have never got on. Tony, dear Tony, has always played the role of peacekeeper between us."

Myra leaned forward. "Forgive me for saying so, Mrs Tanner, but you don't seem exactly heartbroken that your husband has been killed."

Lois winced and Jack glared sharply at the young constable. "What WPC Banks means—"

Lois cut him off. "I am sad. Of course I'm sad, but Tony and I were never going to make old bones together."

"Have you any idea who might have wanted to kill him?" Jack said. "Did your husband have any enemies?"

"Would you like me to compile a list?"

"You're saying that your husband had a lot of enemies?"

Lois crossed her ankles again. "Tony was a . . . how can I put it? Tony was a difficult man. He made enemies as easily as you or I make acquaintances."

"I see," Jack said.

Lois gave a brittle laugh. "I doubt that very much. Go to any West End theatre, or any film set in Hertfordshire for that matter, and ask people what they think of Tony Tanner. Their answers will probably make your hair curl."

"And you?" Myra said. "You don't seem surprised, or even dismayed, that someone's killed him."

"I loved my husband very much — for all his faults," Lois said. She pulled a handkerchief from her sleeve and dabbed at her eyes.

Hester came back into the room carrying a tray. She set it down on a coffee table and squatted stiffly beside Lois, putting an arm around her shoulders.

Lois shrugged her off. "I'm all right, Hester, really. I've just had some very bad news. It's Tony. He's been killed."

"Oh, great heavens! Is there anything I can do?" Hester said.

"You can pour the tea."

Hester poured tea into bone china cups and left the room.

"We'll be needing you to identify the body," said Jack.

Lois looked at him over the rim of her cup. "Well, that's not going to happen." Her voice was steely. "You said that my dear departed husband had informed you about my situation. I won't leave the house."

"But the law requires that . . ."

". . . that a formal identification must be made by the next of kin," Lois said. "Yes, I'm aware of that. Tony's parents are still alive. They're living in Shillington in Bedfordshire. I'm sure they meet your requirements."

"They do but . . ."

"No ifs, no buts," Lois said forcefully. "If necessary I can get my doctor to write a letter excusing me. Mark Francombe understands agoraphobia and has helped me a great deal."

"And Mark Francombe's your doctor?" Myra said, writing in her notebook.

Lois gave her a withering look. "Well, yes. I can give you his address if you like."

"Thank you," Myra said.

"And I would appreciate that list," Jack said.

"List?"

"Of people who might wish your husband harm."

With a sigh Lois got to her feet and went across to the desk. She took a notepad and scribbled the doctor's address and a list of names.

* * *

They walked to the car in silence. After a while Myra said, "The ice maiden cometh."

"I thought she seemed quite emotional."

"She was acting. She didn't show anything until I said she didn't seem upset by her husband's death. Then she turned on the waterworks."

"You're a cynic."

"I'm a woman, sir. It takes more than a few crocodile tears to fool me. She couldn't have had anything to do with it, though, could she?"

"I'm not ruling anything out."

"But you heard her, sir. She can't leave the house."

"She said *won't*, not *can't*," Jack said. "But somehow I can't see her nailing her husband to a tree and cutting his throat in the middle of Norton Common."

Myra shook her head. "And risk chipping her expensive nail varnish? That manicure must have cost her a packet. So no, I don't think so either."

"Check her story with the doctor anyway. Mark Francombe is in East Street. The Millbrook surgery."

"I'll call on him on my way in tomorrow." Myra fell silent, staring out at the darkened streets as Jack drove them back through the town. "I wouldn't put it past her to pay someone to kill him though," she said after a while.

"You've got the mind of a detective," Jack said.

"Well, don't tell him. He might want it back."

Jack smiled. "Can I drop you off at home? It's getting late."

She shook her head. "Thanks, but no thanks. Can you take me back to the station? I have to see Chief Superintendent Lane before I go home."

"Do you think he'll still be there at this time of the evening?" Jack said doubtfully.

"It's at his request, so he'd better be there."

CHAPTER 4

WEDNESDAY MARCH 18th, 1959

"What do you mean, she won't identify the body?" Chief Superintendent Henry Lane paced back and forth in his office.

"Just that," Jack said. "She can't leave the house."

"Well, that just won't do. We need a formal identification."

"If we put any pressure on her she'll get her doctor to write a letter of excuse."

"Excusing her from carrying out her public duty?" Lane said. A vein in his temple bulged. "Never mind her duty as a wife."

"She's agoraphobic, sir," Jack explained patiently. "She suffers from extreme panic attacks if she goes out into the open. Her doctor will confirm that, or so she says. WPC Banks is going to verify it on her way in this morning."

"Never heard such rubbish," Lane muttered. He stopped pacing. "Well, what are you going to do about it, Chief Inspector?"

"His parents live in Shillington. I'm going to pay them a visit and see if they'll oblige."

"Yes, do that. Then we can start to move on with this investigation." Lane sat down at his desk and picked up a pen that was lying on the blotter in front of him. He tapped it against his teeth. "Nailed to a tree and tortured. What a way to go," he mused. "Do you think the wife had anything to do with it?"

"I'm not sure," Jack said. "WPC Banks suggested the same thing."

"Bright girl that one. Anything else?"

"Mrs Tanner gave me a list of people who might wish her husband harm." Jack took the piece of paper from his pocket and laid it on the desk. Lane snatched it up and studied it closely.

"I've heard of some of these names," he said.

"There's a couple I recognise too."

"Looks like our Mr Tanner was about as popular as Mussolini. Are you going to talk to all of these people?"

"I'm going to try," said Jack.

"Well, speak to the parents first. See if they can shed any light."

"I'll get over to Shillington then," Jack said.

* * *

The picturesque village of Shillington is tucked just inside the Bedfordshire border. Jack had been here some years before when he was looking for somewhere to live. He had dismissed it as being too rural after Tottenham, too much of a departure from his urban background.

The Tanners lived in a bungalow at the end of a cul-de-sac. All the houses looked cared for, with neatly cut lawns, tidy flowerbeds and clusters of trimmed conifers.

He walked up a gravel path and rang the doorbell. A thin drizzle had started to fall from the leaden March sky. A tall man with short iron-grey hair and a military bearing opened the door almost immediately. His eyes narrowed as he peered at Jack's warrant card. "You took your time," he said bluntly. "After the harpy called I was expecting you last night."

"The harpy?"

"The Franklin woman."

"Your daughter-in-law?"

"Our daughter-in-law was Polly . . . Dear Polly." His voice caught in his throat. "The harpy took her place, damn her."

"I gather that you two don't get on. So why did she telephone you to say that I wanted to see you?"

"My wife took the call. I rarely have to speak to the Franklin woman, thank God." He extended a hand. "Laurence Tanner," he said. "You'd better come in."

The bungalow was modestly furnished. A three-piece suite dominated the lounge. It was probably new in the First World War, and looked as if it had been through a few battles since then.

"I was hoping to speak to both you and your wife," Jack said.

"Jean won't see you. After she took the phone call from the harpy she took to her bed. She can't believe that her beloved Anthony is dead. Seeing you would bring her face to face with it. She's not strong enough yet."

"Your daughter-in . . . Lois . . . told her why I wanted to see you?"

"You want me to stare at a body on a slab and confirm that it's my son," Tanner said bluntly. "Yes. She told her. No doubt she derived a lot of pleasure from doing so."

"They've taken him to North Herts Hospital. The mortuary there is . . . well, the staff . . . know how to handle these things sensitively."

Tanner flopped down in an armchair and put his hands to his face. Jack had expected to see tears on his cheeks when he took them away. They were dry.

"Don't expect me to grieve, Chief Inspector. I'll shed no tears for that one," Tanner said.

"But he *was* your son, and the manner of his death . . ."

Tanner interrupted. "He was my son, but he was also an unmitigated shit. He broke his mother's heart. He never bothered to visit from one year to the next. And as for poor Polly . . . That girl deserved so much more out of life. When she fell ill and needed her husband at her side she got nothing. While she lay dying my son was off, having it away with that American whore."

There was utter venom in his voice.

"We have a granddaughter, you know. We haven't seen her since her mother passed away. Can you imagine how much that hurts us?" Tanner said, his eyes tearful for the first time.

"I can imagine, sir," Jack said gently.

"Can we go to the hospital now and get this over with?" Tanner said.

"I can drive you there," said Jack.

"Let me go up and see my wife. I'll tell her I'm going to be out for a while. North Herts Hospital you say?"

Jack nodded.

"Bloody inconvenient," Laurence Tanner said sourly.

* * *

They drove in silence for most of the way. Then Jack said, "Lois wrote me a list of names of people who might have wanted to harm your son."

"Did she? May I see it?" Tanner said unemotionally.

Jack handed him the paper. For a short while there was no sound in the car apart from the steady swish of the windscreen wipers, the thrum of the Wolseley's engine and Tanner's slightly stentorian breathing.

"It's a bit short," Tanner said at last. "I can think of at least three more names, not including my own."

"Your son was *that* unpopular?"

"It's hard to credit isn't it? Tony Tanner, star of stage and screen. Loved by the masses, loathed by those who really knew him."

Jack fished in his pocket again, produced a pen and handed it to Tanner. "Just add the names to the bottom of the list, if you wouldn't mind. Don't bother to add your own."

* * *

The mortuary attendant drew back the sheet. Tony Tanner's face was now clear of make-up. "Yes, that's him," Laurence Tanner said. "Cover him up, for God's sake. I don't want to look at him any longer than I have to."

Jack nodded to the attendant and turned to Tanner. "I'll take you back to the station and arrange for a car to take you home."

"Thank you. Jean will start to panic if I'm gone for too long."

"Of the list I showed you, and the names you added, were there any that stood out as being the most likely suspects?"

"I'm not going to do your job for you, Chief Inspector," Tanner said.

"No, sir, I'm not expecting you to do that. I just wondered if any names jumped out at you."

Tanner sighed as he sat down in the passenger seat. "To be quite honest with you, ninety per cent of them mean nothing to me at all. Of the few I recognise, only one of them would have had the guts to do something like this. The last I heard he was in a nursing home after suffering a stroke, so I don't think he's your man."

"I'll take his name anyway, sir."

"Usher. Thomas Usher. My son's old business partner."

"Your son and Mr Usher were in business together?"

"If you can call prostitution a business."

"Prostitution?"

"My son chose to call it an escort agency. He and Usher used to employ whores to cater to the baser needs of his so-called show business friends. He was a pimp, Chief Inspector, nothing more, nothing less. He closed down the business shortly after he met the harpy. I think Usher was very angry about it. Anthony killed the golden goose, so to speak. I knew Usher harboured a grudge over it. He had no show business contacts of his own so he couldn't keep the agency open. From what I heard he lost a packet. And he was a man you wouldn't want to upset."

"Really?"

"Thomas Usher was nothing but a gangster. He owned several drinking dens in Soho and, if my memory serves me correctly, a night club in the West End. The name escapes me now."

"And he's the only one you think would be capable of killing your son?"

"In his heyday he could have killed Tony in the blink of an eye and not given it another thought. But as I say, he's not your man. From what my son told me, the stroke has left him with all the mental acumen of a cauliflower."

Jack nodded. "Well, thank you for that, sir. You've been very helpful." He drove the Wolseley into the station car park. "Now, let's see about getting you a ride home."

* * *

Jack entered the squad room. "Thomas Usher," he said to Fuller. "Have you ever heard of him?"

Fuller shook his head. "Means nothing to me. Should it?"

"Probably not," Jack said. He walked towards the stairs leading up to his office. At the doorway he paused and turned back. "Get on to Division and see what you can dig up on him. He was very active in the South London area a few years ago. Apparently a stroke put paid to his criminal activities."

He looked past Fuller to where Myra Banks was standing with a page from a glossy magazine. She was about to pin it to the incident board.

"Something you want to share with us, Myra?" he called.

"It's a 'Knight's Castile' soap advert from an old copy of *Woman's Own*. I found it at my mother's. She has copies of the magazine going back years." She smiled. "It's the only image of Lois Tanner I've been able to find so far, but I'm still looking."

Jack went across and peered at the advert.

"It was taken before she made her name as the Cadence Girl," Myra said.

The advertisement depicted a young woman smiling into a bathroom mirror and spreading a thick, soapy lather on her porcelain cheek. *"Knight's Castile. My secret for soft, soft skin."*

"Do you women really believe all that guff?" Jack said.

Myra smiled. "I don't, but you live with three others. Try asking them."

"Do you have a photograph of our victim?"

"Tony Tanner?" She shook her head. "The only one I've been able to find so far is a publicity picture from the 1955 *Picturegoer* annual. It's been heavily touched up." She rummaged through a small pile of papers on a desk nearby, pulled out a page and handed it to him.

Jack stared at it. "It makes him look like a waxwork of himself. I suppose we'll have to make do with this until we get a better one."

"I'll get down to the library later," Myra said. "They have copies of *Spotlight*, the actors' directory. I might be able to get a better picture from there."

"Good thinking. See if you can get a better one of his wife as well. One where she's not trying to sell me something."

"That might be easier said than done. She made her name by selling herself."

"In more ways than one, if you believe Tony Tanner's father. I'll be in my office if you need me."

CHAPTER 5

WEDNESDAY

Strange noises were coming from the rear of the Callum household as Jack opened the front door of his house. He could hear the sound of a strumming guitar and a clattering rattle, underpinned by a deep, regular thump, thump, thump.

He stuck his head around the kitchen door. Annie was at the cooker with a wooden spoon, stirring the contents of a large aluminium saucepan.

"What's the racket?" he said.

Annie turned to him, a smile on her lips. "Your son. Eric has some friends round."

"What are they doing back there? Building a tank?"

"They might as well be." Annie lifted a spoonful of steaming brown liquid from the pot and tasted it gingerly. "Hmm. Perfect. Beef stew. I've just got to make the dumplings. Can you go though and tell Eric he only has three quarters of an hour before I'm ready to serve."

"Is it safe back there?"

She smiled. "You might want to take earplugs with you."

Jack shook his head and wandered through to the back room. He raised his eyebrows and looked at the scene. Eric, his fourteen-year-old son, was sitting on a dining chair with his head bowed over a guitar resting on his knee. The fingers of his left hand contorted around the guitar's neck making chord shapes, while his right hand strummed furiously.

A thin boy of a similar age, dressed in jeans and a plaid shirt open at the neck, stood beside him. He had one foot resting on a scruffy tea chest to which a broom handle was attached. Tied to the top of the handle was a thin cord that snaked up from a hole in the tea chest. The boy had his eyes closed and was pulling on the broom handle while plucking at the thin cord with a leather-gloved hand. This contraption was making the thumping sound Jack had heard when he first came in.

In the corner was a boy Jack recognised as Philip Langton, the local butcher's son. He held a glass washboard on his knee. He had metal thimbles on his fingers and he moved them across the corrugated glass of the washboard, making a percussive, rattling sound that jarred the fillings in Jack's teeth.

Jack's daughter, Rosie, got up from an armchair. She was two years older than Eric and already pretty enough to already be turning heads in the street. Eric, still strumming, nodded to her and she started to sing a bouncy skiffle song about a freight train. Her voice was as clear as a bell. She looked across at Jack and stopped singing halfway through the verse.

"Oh, hello, Dad," she said. "What do you think?"

"I didn't know you could sing." Jack had to raise his voice to make himself heard.

Rosie blushed. "I can't, not really. I'm just helping Eric out. This is his skiffle group."

"So I gathered." Jack stared at his son who grinned back at him. The other boys stopped playing and looked at Jack for signs of approval.

Jack smiled indulgently. "Very good," he said. He turned to Eric. "Mother asked me to tell you that dinner will be in forty-five minutes, so you might want to think about packing this in soon."

* * *

Jack sat down at the kitchen table and poured himself a cup of tea from a brown earthenware pot. "Was letting him have a guitar really such a good idea?"

"You should be pleased he's so enthusiastic," Annie said. "It's just a hobby."

"So is stamp collecting . . . and it's quieter."

"Don't be such a grouch." Annie came across and kissed the top of his head.

"Rosie's got a set of pipes on her," he said.

"You would have known that already if you'd ever managed to get to one of her school concerts."

The comment stung.

"It's my job. Crime doesn't stop just to accommodate my social life," said Jack.

"No, but it would be nice if it did, just once in a while." Annie wrapped her arms around his neck. "I'm not nagging, Jack. I just don't want you to miss out on our children growing up because people are beastly to each other. I sometimes wonder what's the matter with them all."

"I ask myself that every day." He changed the subject. "That stew smells marvellous."

"It won't be long." She hugged him briefly and went back to the cooker.

* * *

Eddie Fuller pushed open the swing doors of the 'Dog and Duck' and made his way to the bar. A few of the regulars were there already, though it was still early. His sometimes girlfriend, Judy Taylor, was pulling pints with her usual aplomb. She looked up as Eddie strolled towards her.

"Hello, *stranger*," she said heavily. "What are you doing here tonight? Is it business or pleasure?"

"It's always a pleasure to see you, Judy, but it's business tonight."

She sighed. "Yes, I thought it might be."

"Actually, I'm meeting someone."

"Anyone I know?"

"I doubt it. Charlie Somers, my old guvnor from when I was a DC over at Stevenage. I was his bagman, collected money for him. He went to work for the Met in fifty-three, but we've stayed in touch."

"What will you have while you're waiting?"

"Just a half of bitter. I want to keep a clear head."

Judy took a half-pint glass from the shelf above her head and pulled down on one of the pumps. "There you go." She put the drink down on a towelling bar mat. "Is that your friend?" she said. The doors swung inwards and a middle-aged man in a gabardine raincoat with short, neatly clipped grey hair, pushed into the pub.

Fuller glanced around and threw a salute at the man. "Yes, that's him. You'd better pour a pint of Guinness. I'm sure his tastes haven't changed. Grab a table, Charlie," he called. "I'll bring the drinks over."

Somers took off his raincoat, hung it on a stand in the corner and sat at a table by the window. Fuller took the drinks over and settled himself opposite, pushing the Guinness across to the older man. "Thanks for coming," he said.

"Free beer. How could I resist?" Somers picked up the pint and downed half of it in one long gulp. He wiped the creamy froth from his top lip and sat forward. "Now, what did you want to say that you couldn't talk about over the phone?"

Fuller sipped at his pint. "Thomas Usher."

Somers glared at him and pushed his glass away angrily. "Is that what you dragged me up here for? I thought more of you than that, Eddie." He started to get to his feet.

Fuller laid his hand on the older man's arm. "Simmer down, Charlie. Sit down. Just hear me out."

"About Usher? You have to be kidding me. That bastard put the kybosh on my career. He certainly made sure I'd never climb higher in the force than DI, and I was already that when I joined the Met."

"They say that if you lie down with rats you never get the stink of the sewer off you."

"The inquiry cleared me of any wrongdoing." Somers' glare intensified. For a moment Fuller thought his old boss might thump him.

"But both you and I know that they didn't have all the facts," Fuller said.

"Are you saying I'm dirty, Eddie? Because if that's what you're implying, I'll take your sodding head off."

Fuller held up his hands. "Christ, Charlie, calm down. That's not what I'm saying at all. I know you were never in Usher's pocket, but your connection to him did rub a lot of people up the wrong way."

"Does your current guvnor know that you're talking to me about this?" said Somers.

Fuller shook his head. "I told him I'd never heard of Usher."

"Do you think that was wise? I know Jack Callum's reputation. Nothing much gets past him. He made Barry Fisher look bloody stupid last year when the superintendent was up here on a case. And Fisher's no fool, believe me. Jack Callum doesn't sound like the type of man you want to cross." Somers leaned back and picked up his glass again.

"Look, Charlie, Jack's a great boss and I think of him as a friend. He told me to get onto Division and find out all I can about Usher. But you're my friend as well and I wanted to speak to you before I did."

"Well, you don't have to bother Division. I have everything you need to know, up here." He tapped the side of his head. "I suppose you know that Usher's out of the picture now."

Fuller nodded. "So I hear."

"Yeah. A stroke. From what I've heard, they've got him stashed away in a nursing home somewhere in Kent. He's little more than a vegetable these days. Serves the bastard right." He finished his pint. "I'll have another of those."

Fuller picked up the glass and took it across to Judy for a refill.

By the time he took it back to Somers, his old boss had lit a briar pipe. He was watching two of the locals playing a game of darts.

"Those two couldn't hit a cow's arse with a banjo," he said. "I hope they're not in your pub's darts team."

"They're not. I remember you used to be quite handy with the arrows yourself."

"I gave it up when my eyesight started failing. I need glasses just to drive the sodding car these days." He took a long pull of the Guinness. "So why the sudden interest in Usher? He was never really in your bailiwick."

"No, but his business partner was."

"Usher had lots of business partners. Anyone I know?"

"The actor, Tony Tanner. We found him yesterday evening. He was nailed to a tree, tortured, with his throat cut."

Somers blew out through his lips. "Nasty. I see now why you're asking about Usher. That kind of thing was his stock in trade. Did Tanner still have his conkers?"

"Conkers?" Fuller said.

"Conkers, testicles, gonads . . . his *balls*."

"Yes, I think so."

"It wasn't Usher then. Castration was Tommy's trademark, his calling card."

"I think you'd better tell me everything you know about him."

"Do you have your notebook?"

Fuller nodded.

"Let's just hope you have enough pages."

CHAPTER 6

THURSDAY MARCH 19th, 1959

Jack sat at his desk reading through Tony Tanner's post mortem report.

"Any surprises?" Fuller said. He took a seat at a desk alongside Jack's. Office sharing was Chief Superintendent Henry Lane's latest cost-cutting measure as he struggled with county council cuts to the police budget.

"I don't like it any more than you do, Jack. But needs must . . ." Lane had said.

Well, Lane wouldn't be sharing *his* office with anyone, that was for sure. Jack had no real problem sharing his space with Eddie Fuller. They worked so closely together that Annie had once joked they were practically joined at the hip.

He looked up at his sergeant. "Pretty much as we expected. Cause of death was massive blood loss from a severed carotid artery. The wounds to the body were mostly superficial, as Barry Fenwick said. Designed to cause maximum pain without being life-threatening."

"So, you think that whoever did this knew what they were doing?"

"I would think so."

"Was Tanner castrated?"

Jack flicked over a page. "It doesn't say so here."

"It can't be Usher then."

"What makes you say that? Oh, yes, you spoke to Division, didn't you?"

"Yes . . . I er, yes I did." A slight flush came to Fuller's cheeks. "Castration of his victims was Thomas Usher's signature, apparently." He avoided Jack's gaze.

"Well, don't keep me in suspense. What else did you find out?"

"Usher was a thoroughly nasty piece of work in his day. He built himself a criminal empire from south of the river right up to the West End. He had his fingers in many pies, all of them illegal. From prostitution to gambling dens, illegal drinking clubs, large scale smuggling of cigarettes and booze, protection racket . . . You name it, if it was against the law and brought in the cash then Usher was involved. He was linked to several bank robberies, but never got arrested. There was always a lack of evidence. It was the same story with the murders. Potential witnesses ended up disappearing in suspicious circumstances, but there was nothing to link Usher directly to any of them.

"He had his legitimate interests as well. He owned a nightclub in Bloomsbury, the 'Purple Flamingo,' and the escort agency he ran with Tony Tanner. The Met were about to look into it when Tanner shut it down."

"And you still don't think he's our man?"

"He had a stroke, guv. From what they say, he's not compos mentis these days. He's certainly not in any condition to kill anyone, or even to order someone else to do it for him."

"Which more or less confirms what Laurence Tanner told me. I just wanted to check to see if the old man was flannelling me. It seems not. Thanks, Eddie. Good work. I didn't think it was going to be that easy."

There was a knock at the door and a uniformed WPC entered the room. It took Jack a few seconds to recognise Myra Banks.

"Myra! Back in uniform?"

Myra smiled tightly. "My secondment to CID ended yesterday. Back in the blues. Orders from Chief Superintendent Lane."

There was a tremor in her voice.

"Doctor Francombe confirmed Lois Tanner's story, and I've got some new images of Tony Tanner and his wife." She laid two black and white photographs on his desk.

"Much better. Are you still in charge of the incident board?" said Jack.

"Until I'm told otherwise."

He frowned. "Well, that's not going to happen. You'd better take the photos downstairs and pin them up on the board."

"Yes, sir."

"One more thing. What did the chief superintendent say about your application to join CID?"

"He turned it down flat." She was unable to keep the bitterness from her voice.

"Did he give you a reason?"

She shook her head. "He just said not at this time."

"You leave it to me. I make no promises, but I'll see what I can do."

"Yes, sir. Thank you, sir."

"Well, that'll be all for the moment."

Myra stiffened to attention. "Yes, sir." Her hand moved slightly at her side.

"Myra, if you salute me I'll have you thrown into one of the cells," Jack said gently.

Myra left the office with a smile playing on her lips.

* * *

"Why the make-up and the false nose?" Fuller said. He was reading through the post mortem result.

"That's what's been bothering me. He'd just finished a run at the Lyric theatre and the next thing he had lined up was a film in two weeks' time. So he wasn't working on another play. Yet there he was, wearing make-up to darken his skin, a false moustache and that bloody wax nose."

"So it was a disguise of some sort."

"Yes, but not much of one. It might have convinced the front row of the stalls, but close to it would have been fairly obvious." Jack thought for a moment. "But maybe that was the point. It only had to be convincing to someone twenty feet away."

"For what reason?"

Jack scratched his head. "I don't know, Eddie. Maybe we're coming at this the wrong way. Maybe it has nothing to do with his association with criminals like Thomas Usher."

"The acting world?"

Jack reached into his pocket and took out Lois Tanner's list and handed it to Fuller. "You and Frank start checking out these names. Look into their backgrounds. See if any of them strike you as likely candidates. There are a couple of fairly well-known actors there. But apart from professional jealousy I can't see any motive for murder. I didn't like Tanner when I met him, and I can see how he could easily get people's backs up. But it's a huge leap from being annoyed with someone to nailing them to a tree and slitting their throat. I spoke with him at about noon on Tuesday and by five o' clock he'd been murdered. We need to find out what he was doing in the hours preceding his death. I think I'm going to talk to the wife again. See if she can shed any light."

"Do you want me to come along?"

Jack shook his head. "No, I'll take Myra with me. She didn't buy any of that loving spouse stuff. In fact she was quite unsympathetic to the woman. We men are soft touches, we're easily taken in by a few tears. Women are made of tougher stuff."

"You really like her, don't you?"

"She reminds me of my Joanie. She's a marshmallow exterior with a steel core at her centre. She'll make a fine detective one day. I just don't know why Lane can't see that." He shook his head. "I'm going to have a word with him. I'll see if I can't get him to change his mind."

"Good luck with that," Fuller said. "When Frank Lesser complained to him about having to share an office with Trevor Walsh and Harry Grant, he threatened to sack him."

"He's under a lot of pressure at the moment what with the cuts in the police budget. I doubt that Chief Constable Rix is making life easy for him either, setting impossible targets just to appease the county council. But I have to try. Myra deserves it. She's worked hard these past six months."

* * *

Jack walked into Lane's office. "You turned down Myra Banks's application to join CID."

Lane looked up from his work. "Has knocking gone out of fashion?"

Jack glanced back at the door. "It was open."

"My door is always open," Lane said blithely, "to people with a genuine grievance."

"But I've worked with Myra Banks day in, day out, for six months now, and I know she's got what it takes to make a damned fine addition to my team."

"Actually, you've had her for a little over eight months. I added another two months to her secondment while I monitored her progress. So you should be counting your blessings. I could have had her back in uniform in January."

"So why now? And why block her application to join CID?"

Lane regarded him steadily for a moment. "Take a seat, Jack."

"It's okay, I'll stand."

"Sit down, Chief Inspector!"

Jack pulled up a hard chair and sat.

"Right." Lane cleared his throat. "Firstly let me say that I don't have to justify my decisions to you, or anyone else in this station." He took off his glasses and cleaned them with a handkerchief. "Secondly." He placed the glasses back on the bridge of his nose. "I think Myra Banks is a very fine police constable, but at the moment that's her level. CID? I think not."

Jack opened his mouth to speak. Lane raised a finger.

"I haven't finished. Please do me the courtesy of listening without interrupting."

Jack nodded.

"Very well." Lane leaned forward in his seat. "Do you know how many female CID officers there are in the country, Jack?"

Jack shook his head.

"Less than fifty. Do you know the reason for that?"

"I'd imagine it's not their lack of intelligence or commitment."

"No, it's not. As I said, I've seen Banks's work and she's very good at what she does . . ."

"But?"

"But the truth is, Jack, in a few years' time she will have married and left the force." Lane smiled as if he were lecturing a child. "She'll be domiciled in some two up, two down, popping out babies with monotonous regularity, and . . ." He paused. "And my budget won't stretch to training someone who'll be gone in the blink of an eye."

"And does the chief constable agree with that view?"

Lane snorted derisively. "Most senior police officers do, including the chief constable."

"So you're telling me that you're willing to sacrifice a valuable member of my team to budgetary restrictions? I see that the budget allowed you to redecorate this office last year."

Lane's eyes narrowed. "Careful, Jack."

"I'm sorry, sir, but I just don't understand your priorities."

Lane held up his hand to stop him. "You don't have to understand them, Jack. That's why *I'm* the chief superintendent and you're not. I'm paid to make the difficult decisions. You're paid to follow my orders, and I'm ordering you to drop this right now."

Jack was silent.

"For your information, the only reason I had my office decorated was because I have a friend in the Rotary Club. He runs a painting and decorating business and he had some paint left over from a hotel contract his firm had just completed. He offered to do the work for the cost of the labour. Take a look around you, Jack. This building is old and will soon need a complete overhaul. Either that or it will be pulled down to make way for one of those concrete and glass monstrosities that seem to be popping up all over the country. The decoration of my office was a small step towards getting this building up to standard, and it was well within the maintenance budget. In fact the chief constable congratulated me personally about it."

"I'm very pleased for you, sir," Jack said heavily.

Lane got up from his chair, walked around the desk and perched on the edge of it. "Look, Jack, I know you had high hopes for Myra Banks, and I can see why. As I said to you the other day, she's a bright girl. But face the facts. The police force is a man's world. It always has been, and I can't see it changing, not in my lifetime anyway. Accept my decision for the good of your team. It doesn't need a disgruntled boss just now, not with the workload and all the other changes we've had to accept recently. I need you to rise above the mundane politicking that is going on at the moment. At least until the county council sees sense, anyway. Her day will come, one way or another." He went back to his seat and sat down. "How are you getting on with the murder of that actor chap?"

Jack brought him up to date. He could barely restrain himself from storming out of the room.

* * *

"Bloody dinosaur!" he said as he walked back into his office.

Fuller looked up. "It went well with the chief super, then."

Jack glowered at him. He sat down at his desk, pulled a file from the mounting pile in his in-tray and flipped it open.

He stared at it blankly for a moment. Then he closed it and slammed it down on the desk. He went across to the coat rack. "I'm going out. To interview Lois Tanner again." He snatched his coat and stormed out.

CHAPTER 7

THURSDAY

"Myra, get your coat. You're coming with me," Jack called as he walked into the squad room.

Myra looked up from her desk and hesitated.

"We haven't got all day." Without waiting for her to follow, he headed out to the car park.

Myra sat at her desk, her mouth slightly agape. She had never seen him look so angry.

"I think you'd better get your skates on, love," Andy Brewer, the desk sergeant said. "Don't keep him waiting."

Myra grabbed her coat and hurried after her boss as if she'd been stung.

She caught up with him in the car park. "Where are we going?" she gasped as she tried to catch her breath.

"To talk to the Tanner woman again," Jack said. He unlocked the car door.

"And you want me along?"

He looked at her sharply. "Why shouldn't I? You know the turf. Get in the car."

"Right, sir. Yes, sir." She climbed into the passenger seat.

Myra watched him as he drove. His face was set in a frown and his mouth was a thin, grim line. This wasn't the Jack Callum she was used to seeing and it unnerved her.

"Is everything all right, sir? Only you seem a little put out."

He glanced round at her. "I'm not a *little put out*, Myra. I'm bloody furious. Here we are investigating a savage murder, and the chief superintendent deprives me of one of my best officers."

"He wouldn't budge on my application rejection then."

"No, Myra, he would not, and I'm sorry. It was wrong of me to raise your hopes."

"I didn't want you to stick your neck out, sir. Not on my behalf."

"Well, who the hell's going to, Myra? Tell me that. Did you know that there are less than fifty women in the CID in the entire country? It's a bloody disgrace and men like Chief Superintendent Lane are largely responsible for that situation."

"Why do you think that is, sir?"

"Backward thinking. It's a hangover from the time just after the war when the men of this country returned home and women were expected to go back to being housewives. Some were happy to do so, to go back to what it was like before the conflict, but others were used to having something more to do with their lives than cleaning the house, looking after the kids, and making sure there was a hot meal on the table when their husbands got in from work. During the war women kept this country going. Some worked in factories, others drove lorries or toiled on the land. Without their contribution this country would have ground to a halt. My Annie was one of them. She worked in a munitions factory, as well as running a house and bringing up three small children."

"She doesn't work now though?"

"That's entirely her choice. If she wanted to get a job I certainly wouldn't stand in her way. We're entering a new era, Myra, and I think it's going to be a time of change. The police force is just one institution that is going to have to rethink the role of women within its workforce."

"You seem very passionate about it."

"I live in a house with three very strong women," Jack said. "They keep me in my place." He flashed Myra a smile. "Lecture over."

"Don't mind me. It's good to know there's men like you on our side. It gives me hope."

"There's always hope, Myra, if nothing else."

Myra was silent for a while. "How do you intend to deal with Lois Tanner this time?"

"I don't intend to deal with her." He gave her a knowing smile. "You will. You seem to have her measure. I'll give you an idea of what we need to find out, and this time I want to speak to the daughter as well. You didn't see her last time, but she was there."

"Oh, I saw her, sir. Pretty little thing. Blonde hair."

"That's Geraldine. You saw her?"

Myra nodded. "She was on the stairs when we arrived, but she ducked out of sight when she realised I'd clocked her."

"Yes, I saw her as well. She's pretty highly strung, apparently."

"You've met her before then?"

Jack told her about meeting Geraldine Tanner at the school.

"Why would she say such a thing?" Myra said. "Killing her brother. That's pretty macabre, even for a teenage girl."

"That's what I thought. Her father's murder puts it in a new light, though. That family just aren't right."

"And you're going to try to find out what makes them tick?"

Jack nodded. "And open their closets to see if I can't shake out a few skeletons."

Myra smiled. "I almost pity Lois Tanner. *Almost.*"

For the rest of the drive to Elsinore, Jack primed Myra for the interview. Lane mightn't see how valuable she was, but he certainly could.

* * *

"Chief Inspector Callum to see Mrs Tanner," Jack said to Hester.

"Yes, of course. I'll fetch her for you. Come in."

They stood in the hallway, listening to someone playing a piano inside the house. A Chopin étude, Jack thought. A pretty decent attempt.

It was a few minutes before Lois Tanner finally made an appearance. The Chopin continued as Lois sashayed down the hall towards them. She stumbled in her high heels. When she reached them it was obvious from her glazed eyes and the smell of whisky on her breath that she'd been drinking.

"Hello, Chief Inspector. What can I do for you this time?" Her words were slurred.

"A few more questions," Jack said.

She led them towards Tanner's office. She glanced back over her shoulder, blinked, refocused, and made a beckoning motion with her arm. "Come through."

"Actually, Constable Banks has the questions. I'd like a word with your stepdaughter."

Lois gazed at him as if he were speaking a foreign language. She blinked again. "Geraldine? What do . . . Oh, never mind. Hester, show the chief inspector through to the conservatory."

Hester stepped forward. "This way, sir."

Jack turned to Myra. "You go with Mrs Tanner."

Myra grimaced. "Certainly, sir."

Jack followed Hester through to the back of the house.

* * *

The conservatory was no mere sun lounge. It was four times the size of Tanner's office and took up the entire back of the house. The bamboo furniture was upholstered in chintz. Ferns in large terracotta pots were spaced out underneath wide picture windows. A full-sized concert grand piano occupied the centre of the room.

The slight figure of Geraldine Tanner sat with her head bowed. Her fingers moved effortlessly over the keys.

"Geraldine!" Hester said loudly over the Chopin. "There's someone here to see you."

Gerry's fingers stopped in mid-arpeggio and she glanced round at Jack.

"Oh, hello."

"Hello, Gerry." Hester was moving towards the door. Jack turned to her.

"If you could stay."

"What? Oh, yes, all right." She sat in one of the bamboo chairs and folded her arms.

Jack sat next to Geraldine on the piano stool. "You play very well."

"I know," Geraldine Tanner said. There was no hint of conceit in her voice. "I want to go to the Royal College of Music to study composition. I suppose that will all change now."

"Yes, yes, of course. Look, shall we sit in comfort?" He indicated the bamboo sofa.

Geraldine shrugged. "Okay."

Jack went across to the sofa and sat down. Geraldine joined him, curling her legs underneath her.

He caught the disapproving look on Hester's face, but the woman said nothing. She edged forward in her seat.

"I'm sorry about your father, Gerry," Jack said.

Geraldine gave a non-committal shrug.

"After he brought you home on Tuesday, he went out again in the afternoon."

She nodded.

"Do you have any idea where he was going?"

"He was meeting someone in town." Geraldine's bright, open face showed no trace of guile.

"Do you know who?"

"He didn't say. When we got back on Tuesday I came straight in here to practice and he went upstairs. I didn't see him again." She bit her lip. Jack realised she wanted to cry, but was forcing herself not to.

"Not at all? Not even as he left the house?"

"She told you," Hester said. "She didn't see him again after she came in here."

"Thank you, Mrs . . ."

"Gough. Hester Gough."

"Well, thank you, Mrs Gough. I'd like Gerry to answer for herself if you don't mind."

"Her name is Geraldine," Hester said tartly.

"I like Gerry better," Geraldine said. She glared at Hester.

Jack tried again. "So you didn't see him again. Did he tell you who he was going to meet?"

"We weren't talking by the time we got home. We had an argument in the car. That was why I came straight in here. I had to get out of his way."

"Did you argue often?"

Hester Gough cleared her throat. Loudly.

Jack asked the question again.

"We never used to argue at all when mum was alive. It's only since *she* came to live with us."

"You mean your stepmother?"

Geraldine gave him a scornful look. "Who do you think I meant?"

"I take it you and she don't always see eye to eye."

"Try never. You've seen what she's like. If she isn't drunk, she's drugged up to the eyeballs."

"Geraldine! That's enough!" Hester Gough was on her feet. "I'll not sit here and listen to you say such horrible things about your mother."

"She's *not* my mother!" Geraldine's voice rose to a shout. "She's just dad's wife. *My* mother died."

Jack took her hand and squeezed it. "Okay, Gerry, calm down. I'm sure Mrs Gough didn't . . ."

"It's not *Mrs* Gough. It's *Miss*," Geraldine said. "Ask her about *her* relationship with my stepmother. Her *darling Lois*."

Hester moved towards her. "Not another word, you ungrateful child. If it wasn't for you, your brother would still be alive."

"Now that's enough!" Jack sprang to his feet, placing himself between them. Geraldine was cowering slightly on the sofa, her eyes brimming with tears.

Jack put his arm around Hester's shoulders and with some effort guided her towards the door and out of the room.

"Would you mind explaining that last comment you made?" he said.

Hester was red in the face and breathing loudly. "It was that little bitch and her constant demands and temper tantrums that brought about Lois's miscarriage."

"You can't blame a thirteen-year-old girl for that." Jack was fighting down his own temper now.

"That's what her father said. Always giving in to her. Letting her have everything she wanted. He was a weak, weak man. I just don't know what Lois saw in him."

Jack looked up to see Myra walking towards them.

"Is the interview over?" said Jack.

"You could say that." Myra smiled. "She passed out on the settee."

"Is Lois all right?" said Hester, her voice rising in panic.

"She will be once she's slept it off," Myra said.

Hester glared and pushed past her. "I think you'd better leave." She hurried away to tend to her mistress.

"What now?" said Myra.

"Come through to the conservatory and meet Gerry. I think you'll like her. She's got spark. She's a bit like you really."

CHAPTER 8

THURSDAY

Jack led Myra through to the conservatory. Geraldine had returned to the piano and was idly playing scales. "Gerry, I'd like you to meet Myra Banks. Myra, Miss Geraldine Tanner. Known to her friends as Gerry."

"Hello, Gerry," Myra said. She stepped forward and stuck out her hand.

Geraldine shook it enthusiastically. "Are you police too, like Mr. Callum?"

"Yes," Myra said. "But I'm only a lowly constable — a WPC they call it."

"I saw you," Geraldine said. "The other night."

"Yes, and I saw you too. You should have come and said hello."

"I was trying to hide." Geraldine said.

"Yes, I thought you were."

"I was trying to hear what was going on. Did she really pass out on you?"

Myra smiled. "Sparko. Out like a light."

Geraldine giggled. "Serves her right. She's been drinking all morning."

"Are you going to be all right?" Jack said. "Only Miss Gough made it quite clear she wants us to leave."

"I'll be fine. Hester will be busy with Lois. She won't even notice what I'm doing."

"And what *will* you do?" Myra said.

"What I always do. I'll amuse myself."

"If you're sure . . ." Jack frowned.

Geraldine gave him an old-fashioned look. "I'm not a child, Mr Callum."

"Well, take care," he said. He took a card from his pocket, scribbled down two telephone numbers and handed the card to her. "If you need me during the day, call the top number. The bottom number is my home. I'm available night or day."

Geraldine took the card and stared at it. "Thank you. You know, you're not so bad — for a copper."

"I try," Jack said. "I try."

* * *

DS Frank Lesser was sitting in the office he shared with two detective constables, Trevor Walsh and Harry Grant. He looked round as Eddie Fuller walked in. A T-shaped dressing covered Lesser's nose and there was bruising around his eyes. "Christ, Frank, what happened to you? You look like you've just gone fifteen rounds with Rocky Marciano," said Fuller.

"Bad night at the Seymour Hall," Lesser said. "Lincoln put me in with a kid from Stepney whose only wrestling experience was in a booth at Southend. The bloody fool tried a dropkick. He'd never done one before and thought it was easy, but he missed my chest completely and the heel of his boot broke my nose. Blood everywhere. The referee had no choice but to stop the match and award it to the kid on a technical knockout. Technical knockout, my arse! Technical cock-up, more like. You wait till I see Paul bloody Lincoln again. Putting me in with amateurs!"

"At least you kept your mask on," Grant said. "He didn't blow your cover."

Lesser had been moonlighting as a professional wrestler for the last five years. He fought under a mask and a *nom de guerre*, as the 'Black Phantom.' So far most of his superior officers appeared to be unaware of his extra-curricular activities. This situation could be about to change, thanks to a spotty teenager from Stepney. If he ever had the misfortune to fight him again, Lesser would show the boy the error of his ways.

"Wasn't Lincoln watching last night?" Grant said.

Lesser shook his head. "No, he was probably at his coffee bar. It seems to take up all his time these days. That, and bloody rock and roll. Wrestling is taking a back seat with him at the moment. I can't remember when Dr Death last fought." Dr Death was wrestling promoter Paul Lincoln's alter ego. It was much more successful than Black Phantom.

"Can you still work?" Fuller said.

"I'll be out of the ring for the next three weeks, until this nose mends."

"I was talking about police work."

"Oh yes. I can still do that."

"Well, cast your eyes over this." Fuller handed Lesser the list Jack had given him. "The guv wants us to check out these names in connection with the Tony Tanner murder."

"Where did he get this from? There are some names on here I recognise."

"From Tanner's old lady. It's a list of people who might have had it in for him."

"Look, Fred Tozer's name is on here. He's a bloody dancer, isn't he?"

"Not in the same league as Fred Astaire, though," Fuller said.

"And Betsy Maclaren? I've seen her in a film, a musical I think it was."

Grant and Walsh gave a hoot of laughter. Even Fuller was smiling.

"What?" Lesser sounded slightly hurt. "I *like* musicals."

"And is the Black Phantom planning a song and dance routine during his next bout?" Walsh said.

Lesser glared at him. "Shut up and get on with your work."

"Seriously," Fuller said. "We should divide this list up and work out who is going to check out who."

Lesser sat forward in his seat. "Bloody hell! Thomas Usher's name is here. I heard about him when I was working at Camden. I don't fancy going anywhere near him. He's a mean bastard."

"Not anymore," Fuller said. "He had a stroke. I doubt he could even tie his own shoelaces these days, so don't worry about him. The guv has already discounted him. I meant to cross him off the list."

"That will make our lives a lot easier — and a lot safer."

"Yes, it will." Fuller took the list and laid it flat on the desk. "Right, let's start breaking this down."

"Wasn't there an inquiry about Usher's relationship with some Met officers a couple of years ago?" Lesser said. "Your old guvnor Charlie Somers was involved, wasn't he?"

Lesser could have sworn that Eddie Fuller looked frightened. "You know about that?" he said.

"I remember reading something about it in the *Police Gazette*. Jack Callum will know. He always reads it," said Lesser.

* * *

"Was that wise?" Myra said as they drove away. "Giving her your home number?"

"She needs someone, Myra."

"I agree. But why you?"

"Because I owe her. Did you get any information out of Lois before she passed out?"

"Not much. She was pretty incoherent. She confirmed that her husband went out in the afternoon, but she couldn't say where he went. Apparently she was in bed with a headache. I suspect she was nursing a hangover."

"Gerry confirms that. According to her he was going out to meet someone, but she didn't know who it was. Did Lois say what car he was driving?"

"A maroon Singer Gazelle Coupe de Ville."

"A convertible shouldn't be too hard to find in Letchworth. Get on to the registration office at the council and see if you can't get a licence plate number. I'll put a call out when I get back to the station and get the beat bobbies onto it. I wouldn't have thought it would be too far away from Norton Common."

* * *

"They've found the car," Eddie Fuller said.

Jack looked up. "That was quick. Where?"

"Letchworth train station."

"Right. Let's get over there."

Thirty minutes later they were driving into the car park of Letchworth station. A lone police constable was standing guard over the maroon convertible. He saluted as Jack approached.

"Have you touched it at all?" said Jack.

"No, sir," the PC replied. "I was just passing when it caught my eye, sitting over here in the corner. Couldn't believe my luck really. I'd only just been told to keep an eye out for it as I was setting off on my beat."

"Well, good work." The PC gave another salute. Jack turned to Fuller. "Right, let's take a look at this. Can we get the boot open?"

"We have the keys we found in Tanner's pocket."

"Well, what are you waiting for? Get the bloody thing open."

Fuller put the key in the lock and twisted. There was a satisfying click and the boot lid sprang open.

Jack looked inside. He took out a wooden box about twelve inches square, with a hinged lid. "Now what do we have here?" He put the box down and lifted the lid.

"What is it?" Fuller looked over Jack's shoulder. The box held rows of bottles and tubes, all arranged neatly in compartments. Jack removed one of the tubes and unscrewed the cap. He squeezed the tube slightly and watched a pinkish cream ease out from the end. "Make-up. The theatrical kind. This is Tanner's kit."

He lifted out an inner tray. Beneath it were skeins of crepe hair and a tin of mortician's wax.

"So he comes to the station, parks his car here and while he waits for the person he's meeting, he disguises himself with a false nose and moustache and darkens his skin with greasepaint."

Fuller shook his head. "It seems a bit elaborate to me, especially as the disguise wasn't that convincing."

Jack nodded. "The question is, who was he here to meet? Check the inside of the car for fingerprints and get them to the lab as quickly as possible. We may just get lucky."

"Not if it's anything like the crime scene on the common. Not a fingerprint or a footprint. Nothing."

"Then it's time for our luck to turn."

"I wish I had your confidence, sir," said Fuller.

"Call it blind faith." Jack smiled and walked back to his car.

CHAPTER 9

THURSDAY

When Jack walked into the bedroom that night, Annie was sitting up in bed reading a magazine. Jack took off his dressing gown and climbed in beside her with a yawn.

"Long day?" she said.

He glanced round at the alarm clock on the bedside table. The luminous hands were pointing to eleven o'clock. He yawned again. "I'm bushed."

Annie put down her magazine. "I was talking to Rosie earlier."

Jack adjusted his reading glasses and turned his newspaper to the sports pages. "And?"

"Mrs Painter is looking for someone to work in the baker's a couple of mornings a week."

"As well as Rosie?"

Rosie had been working at Painter's, the bakers, for just over a year now. It was undemanding work but she seemed happy enough.

"Yes. Gladys Newton, who's been with them for years, has handed in her notice. Apparently her husband has just retired and she wants them to spend more time together."

"How does this affect Rosie?"

"It doesn't. Not directly."

"I see," Jack said. He didn't. He went back to his newspaper.

Annie took a sip from her cocoa. "I was thinking of popping along to see Mrs Painter tomorrow and putting my name down."

Jack glanced round at her. "For what?"

Annie raised her eyes skywards. "Jack, are you being deliberately obtuse? For the job. What else?"

Jack lowered his newspaper. "A *job*? I thought you were happy at home."

"I am, Jack . . . at least I was."

"What's changed?"

She let out a long sigh. "I'm starting to feel redundant."

Jack stared at her in silence. After a while he took her hand and said, "Elaborate."

"Well, for years now I've kept house and raised our children. I've looked after my gorgeous husband, and I've been happy to do so. It's been a labour of love and I've enjoyed every minute of it . . . well, mostly."

"So what's changed?"

"Nothing." She shook her head. "No, that's not true. Everything. Eric's getting older and if he's not rehearsing with his friends then he's down at the youth club. Rosie is at work all day. I thought that when Joanie came back to us, I would at least have something to occupy myself with, but now she's got this job with Avril. It means I'm going to be kicking around the house all day on my own. There's only so much housework a girl can do, you know."

"Phew! It seems like you've given this some thought."

"You wouldn't mind, would you, Jack? It's only four mornings a week."

"You said it was a *couple*."

"Well, it's four . . . but I wouldn't be working Saturdays."

"I should hope not."

"So may I go along there and put my name down?"

"I'm not happy about it. I think you should say no, for now." Jack opened his mouth to say more when the telephone started to ring in the hall. "Damn! Who's calling at this time of night?" Cursing, he threw back the bedclothes. "I'd better get that before it wakes the whole house." His feet found his slippers and he padded out of the room.

Annie sighed and muttered, "Saved by the bell, Jack."

* * *

"Chief Inspector Callum?" The voice on the other end of the line was shaky.

"Yes?"

"It's Hester Gough . . . from Elsinore."

Hester Gough was the last person Jack expected to be calling him. "What can I do for you, Miss Gough?"

It sounded as if she was crying. "I'm sorry to call you so late, but I'm at my wits end." She drew in a ragged breath. "It's Geraldine. She's gone."

"Calm yourself, Miss Gough. What do you mean, she's gone?"

"Just that. I took her cocoa up to her about half an hour ago, but she wasn't in her room. I spent the next twenty minutes searching the house, but there was no sign of her. When I went back to her room I realised that the window was wide open and the bed was still made. I fear something terrible has happened to her."

"How did you get this number, Miss Gough?" Jack said.

"I found it. There was a card on her dressing table and it had your name and number on it."

"Right. Don't touch anything else. Go and make yourself a cup of strong, sweet tea. I'll be with you shortly."

Jack rushed into the bedroom, tore off his dressing gown and started pulling on his trousers.

"Where are you going?" Annie said.

As he dressed he told her briefly what Hester Gough had said.

"That's awful. Of course you must go round there."

"You try to get to sleep." He pecked her on the cheek. "I'll be back just as soon as I can. I'll try not to wake you when I come in." He rushed to the door, stopped and put his head back into the room. "We'll continue our conversation in the morning." And then he was gone.

* * *

Hester was waiting just outside Elsinore's front door as Jack pulled up. She came down the steps to greet him as he stepped out of the car. "Thank you so much for coming. I really didn't know what else to do."

"You did the right thing by calling me. Has Mrs Tanner been informed?"

Hester shook her head. "Lois took some sleeping tablets at about nine. She's still fast asleep."

"Very well. Can you take me up and show me Gerry's room?"

Hester led him into the house.

Geraldine's room was huge. It had a large oak wardrobe, a glass-topped dressing table and a king-sized bed. Floral curtains billowed fitfully in the breeze that blew in from an open sash window. The other window was shut. On the walls were framed pictures of Geraldine's heroes. Mozart, Chopin, and Arthur Rubenstein shared wall space with French jazz pianist, Jacques Loussier. Geraldine evidently had eclectic tastes.

"How did she seem this evening?" Jack said.

"Fine. I really didn't see much of her, to be honest. She was practising in the conservatory until dinner, and then she went up to her room. I didn't see her again."

"She didn't seem upset or distressed? She has, after all, just lost her father."

"As I say, she seemed fine, but Geraldine's a very secretive child. She keeps herself very much to herself."

Apart from when she's telling a perfect stranger that she'd killed her brother, Jack thought. "May I use the phone?" he said. "I should call this through to the station."

* * *

"And now we wait," Jack said. "They're sending a team along. Did you make that tea?"

"Yes." Hester was dabbing at her eyes with an embroidered handkerchief. "Come through to the kitchen." She led him through to the back of the house.

A large pine refectory table dominated the room. Against one wall was a huge American-style refrigerator, and a cream Aga was set into the chimney wall. Hester moved a kettle onto the top. "It just has to boil again."

Jack sat down at the kitchen table. "I gave a talk at Geraldine's school and she came to speak to me afterwards. She told me that she'd killed her brother."

Hester tutted. "Foolish girl," she said dismissively.

"Only I noticed that you said a similar thing to her yourself when we were here, in reference to Mrs Tanner's miscarriage."

Hester turned away and made a great play of pouring boiling water into a large brown teapot.

"Miss Gough?" Jack said, determined not to let the woman off the hook. "You do realise the damaging effect a comment like the one you made can have on a young mind?"

"Nonsense. That girl's quite clever enough to know I didn't mean anything by it."

Jack glared at her. "I think it was a completely irresponsible thing for you to say."

"When I want advice on how to talk to children, Chief Inspector, I ask for it. Until I do I'll thank you to keep your opinions to yourself." The frail, tearful Hester Gough had suddenly become a hard, no-nonsense woman who was not at all intimidated by his presence. "All I want you to do is to find the girl before her mother wakes up and realises she's not here."

So that's it, Jack thought. She's more worried about Lois Tanner's disapproval than Gerry's safety.

"We'll do all we can to find her."

"Good."

Hester poured the tea.

* * *

Twenty minutes later two police cars pulled up on the drive. Two uniformed and four plain clothed officers got out and approached the house. Jack met them at the door.

"Hello, sir. We got here as soon as we could," DI Alan Healy said. "What's the story? We were told it's a missing girl."

"Geraldine Tanner. Thirteen. Went missing from her home some time this evening."

"Abduction or runaway?"

"That's what you're here to find out," Jack said. "I'm hoping it's the latter. The former doesn't bear thinking about."

"Then best we get started straight away. Do you want me to take point on this?"

Jack rubbed his eyes. "I'd rather you did. Your mind will be sharper than mine. I've been up since six o'clock this morning. Come inside and I'll give you what I know."

* * *

It didn't take long to bring the team up to date. When the rest of them had dispersed to various parts of the house and garden to begin their search, Healy stayed behind in the kitchen. "If I were you, sir," he said to Jack. "I'd get off home and let us take it from here."

Jack liked Alan Healy. He was only in his mid-thirties but had already proved himself to be a fine detective. He had solved some very high profile cases by means of thoroughness and dogged attention to detail. "If anything turns up, call me straight away. If you don't find anything, then call me before you clock off in the morning."

"Hopefully I'll have some good news before then."

"Fingers crossed."

"Before you go, sir, what's the story with the old girl?"

"Her name's Hester Gough. She's a kind of housekeeper-cum-nursemaid to Geraldine *and* her mother Lois."

"Is the mother around?"

"In bed asleep, apparently. Knocked out on sleeping pills, so she won't be much help to you. And watch out for Hester Gough," he added quietly. "She's not really worried about Geraldine. She's more concerned about Lois getting upset. She couldn't really give two hoots about the girl. So take anything she may tell you with a very large pinch of salt." He looked up at the night sky. A thin drizzle had just started to fall, dampening the earth outside and beading on the bonnet of his car. "Sometimes God doesn't make our job any easier."

"He likes us to work for our money," Healy said. He pulled up the collar of his raincoat.

CHAPTER 10

FRIDAY MARCH 20th, 1959

"What time did you get back last night?" Annie said as Jack walked into the kitchen.

"This morning. It was one o'clock and you were sound asleep."

She poured his tea. "Did she turn up?"

Jack shook his head. "I left Alan Healy in charge. He was going to phone if she did."

"Try not to worry."

"She's thirteen, Annie. A child. Younger than Eric."

She sat down at the table next to him, took his hand in hers and squeezed it. "There's nothing you could have done, Jack."

"Knowing that doesn't make it any easier."

"I know, pet. I know. Let me make you some breakfast. Toast?"

He returned her squeeze and nodded. Annie went to the larder and took out half a loaf. She cut off a doorstep and slipped it under the grill.

The smell of toasting bread reminded Jack of last night's conversation. "I think you should go and see Barbara Painter."

Annie glanced round at him. "Are you sure?"

"I'm sure. It'll do you good to get out of the house for a few mornings a week."

"And the extra money will come in handy."

"I'm sure it will. But it's *your* money. You do whatever you like with it."

"I'll save it. For a holiday perhaps, or maybe I'll renew my wardrobe. Having Joanie here has made me realise how drab I've got. I feel like I've been letting myself go."

"You still look beautiful to me."

"Take off those rose-tinted glasses and put on your real ones." She smiled at him as she buttered his toast. "Maybe I'll ask Joanie to do my hair for me . . . Then again I could always use the money to rent a television."

He looked round at her sharply. "We don't need a television."

"That's not what Rosie and Eric say. They're starting to feel deprived."

"Deprived?"

"Yes, *deprived*. Eric feels like he's being left out. All the boys talk about at school is what they watched on television the night before. Rosie tells me that the people who come into the bakers' are always asking her if she saw this or that, and she can't answer them."

"We have the wireless. What do we need a television for?"

"I've just told you."

"And you're willing to spend your hard-earned money so our children can talk to their friends?"

"If necessary."

"My wife getting a job. Us with a television. Ye Gods! It will be the end of family life as we know it."

"Don't exaggerate."

"You'll see. But as I said, it's *your* money." As Jack bit into his toast the telephone started to ring. "That will be Healy." He dropped the toast onto his plate and went to answer it.

Annie followed him out of the kitchen and stood in the doorway.

"Any news?" she said.

He blew through his teeth. "No sign of her."

Annie's face fell.

"But there's no sign that there was anyone else in her room either. So it doesn't look like she was taken."

"That's good, isn't it?" she said.

"In one way, yes. But it still means there's a teenage girl out there somewhere, and we don't know where to start looking for her."

* * *

"DI Healy left this for you this morning, sir." Desk Sergeant Andy Brewer said as Jack walked into the police station. He passed across a colour photograph of Geraldine Tanner.

"Thanks, Andy."

"And this arrived for you this morning." He handed Jack a large, white envelope.

Jack stared at it, turning it over in his hand. Printed across the front was DCI CALLUM in bold capitals. There was no stamp so it must have been delivered by hand.

"It was in the box with all the other post, so whoever dropped it in must have got here early. The postman usually comes at about eight, and it was there at the bottom of the pile," said Brewer.

Jack tore open the flap and looked inside. The envelope contained another photograph and a folded piece of paper. He rolled the envelope into a tube and slipped it into his pocket. He took the photograph of Geraldine Tanner through to the squad room and pinned it to the board next to that of her father.

"Right. Gather round." The officers collected around the board. "This is Geraldine Tanner," Jack said. "Some time during yesterday evening she disappeared from her house on the Broadway."

"Was she taken?" Frank Lesser said.

"I don't know. DI Healy was leading the investigation last night. His team found no indication that anyone broke into the house. But her bedroom window was wide open."

"Do you think she might have run away?" Lesser said.

"It's a possibility. Her home life isn't what you could call harmonious."

"But her bedroom is on the first floor," Myra said.

"I know. Underneath her window is a trellis that supports a wisteria. She could have climbed down that."

"She didn't strike me as the tomboy type."

"Nor me, but she could have done it if she was desperate enough."

"Surely, if she climbed down to the ground she would have left her footprints at the base of the wisteria," Lesser said.

"Maybe she did, but when I left there last night it had started to rain. Healy's men couldn't find any trace of footprints."

"Of course, she could have just walked out through the front door," Myra said. "I doubt Miss Gough would have noticed."

"And Lois Tanner was out cold, drugged up to her eyeballs on sleeping pills. Either way she's gone, and it's down to us to find her. Frank, she has grandparents who live in Shillington. Get over there and have a chat with them. Before you go, I'll see you in my office. Myra, get down to Dispatch and see if anyone's called in to say they've seen a young girl walking the streets in the middle of the night."

"That's a bit of a long shot," Fuller said.

"Yes, Eddie, it is, but it's worth trying. You never know, some public-spirited resident might have seen her and reported it. The rest of you get out there with your ears to the ground. Use your contacts, your snouts, your friends if necessary. I want her found." He sighed. "I mean now. Not next week."

Suddenly they all rushed to the door.

Jack turned back to the incident board and stared at the photograph of the smiling girl with the blonde corkscrew hair. When he spoke it was almost a whisper. "Where are you, Gerry? Where the hell are you?"

* * *

"Nothing's been reported," Myra said.

"Well, Sergeant Fuller said it would be a long shot. Myra, if you were a young girl running away from home, where would you go?"

"If I had no family nearby, then probably to a friend's house. Somewhere I felt safe, I suppose."

"Then go along to the school. Have a word with Geraldine's friends, if she has any, and see if any of them have heard from her."

"Yes, sir. What school does she go to?"

"Hatfield County. You can walk it from here."

"I know, sir. I went there myself. Is Mrs Arnold still the head?"

"Yes, she's still there."

"The old trout. I couldn't stand her, and she didn't like me much either."

"Use your charm, Myra. You know how to do that, don't you?"

Myra smiled. "I'll do my best."

"Oh, I'm sure you will."

* * *

Lesser was standing outside Jack's office.

"Come in, Frank," he said.

Lesser followed him in. Eddie Fuller was seated at a desk in the corner.

"Eddie, go and get yourself a cup of tea."

"Pardon?" Fuller glanced round, saw Lesser, and got to his feet. "Yes, right," he said, and went out.

"Take a seat, Frank."

Lesser dropped into the seat vacated by Fuller.

Jack sat down at his desk. "Right. Tell me how you got the broken nose."

"I walked into a door, sir."

"Really? A door? Or an opponent's foot?"

Lesser flushed and stared down at his shoes. "The latter," he mumbled.

Jack nodded. "I thought so."

"He was green, sir. Just a kid—"

Jack raised his hand. "Spare me the details, Frank."

"How did you know I was wrestling, sir?"

"Frank, I'm a detective. I've been aware of it from the beginning, as you damn well know. You didn't honestly think you could keep it a secret from me, did you? Besides, I've *seen* you wrestle. I took my son Eric to one of your shows. He thought you were pretty good."

"Don't you mind?"

"As long as it doesn't interfere with your job, why should I? I dare say you're one of the fittest officers in the Hertfordshire Constabulary, and it's nice to know you can handle yourself should the need ever arise. I know and I don't mind, but I don't think Chief Superintendent Lane would view it the same way. And with this injury you're on perilously thin ice. He's bound to ask me how you picked up the broken nose, and he's canny enough to see through your excuse that you walked into a door."

Colour spread across Lesser's cheeks.

"So, if he asks, I'll tell him that you picked it up in the line of duty. An altercation with a drunk, or something like that."

"That's good of you, sir. But why would you go out on a limb for me?"

"Because I'm a bloody fool, Frank. No, actually I think you're a very good DS and I don't want to lose you from the team. WPC Banks has been sent back to uniform and she won't be replaced. We've got a murder and a missing girl on the books, as well as all our other cases. Cases that are going to have to take a back seat for now. I can't be another man down."

"Yes, sir. Thank you, sir."

"Just try to be a little more careful in future." He scribbled down Laurence Tanner's address on a piece of paper and handed it across to Lesser. "And just remember, this man has just lost his son. You're going to tell him his granddaughter is missing as well, so tread lightly."

Lesser took the note and nodded. He paused at the office door and looked back. "Who was I fighting, sir, when you brought your son?"

"A rather large chap. Hunter was it? It was at the Granada, Edmonton. Spring last year."

"Rebel Ray. Yeah, he's good. Took him down in the fifth round. It was meant to be the fourth, but I messed up the suplex and nearly brained myself in the process. He carried me for another round until he could make the pin fall look convincing."

Jack smiled. "Now, get yourself over to Shillington."

It was only after Lesser had gone that Jack remembered the envelope in his pocket. He opened it and tipped it up. A photograph and a folded piece of paper slipped out onto the desk blotter. He unfolded the paper. It was a note that said simply, *I hope this is useful.* It wasn't signed.

He picked up the black and white print. It showed the audience at a boxing match. Taken from the other side of the ring and shot through the boxers' legs, it focused on the men sitting in the front row. One of them was Tony Tanner.

Tanner was leaning back in his seat, a fat cigar clamped between his teeth. Jack scanned the faces of his neighbours but failed to recognise any of them. Yet bells began to ring at the back of his mind.

He flipped the photograph over. The names were neatly printed on the back. *From L to R. Simon Docherty, Thomas Usher, Tony Tanner, Det. Insp. Charles Somers.*

In the right-hand corner was a small blue printed stamp: *Property of J Talbot & Son, Photographers.*

Jack turned the photograph over and studied the faces again.

Simon Docherty was in his late thirties, conventionally handsome, with fair hair styled in a crew cut. Charles Somers was older, with a rugged face and short grey hair. But Jack's eyes were drawn to Thomas Usher. With his swarthy skin, slightly hooked nose and moustache, he looked continental. Jack stared. Then he made the connection. He reached for Tanner's file.

He opened it and flicked through until he came to the crime scene photos.

Tony Tanner in full theatrical make-up, hanging from a tree, his throat a red slash. He placed it on the desk next to the boxing photo. The likeness between Thomas Usher and the deceased Tony Tanner was unmistakable.

Now he knew who Tanner had been impersonating.

CHAPTER 11

FRIDAY

As Jack stared at the photo, Fuller came back into the office.

"Take a look at this," Jack said.

Fuller peered over his boss's shoulder. "What am I meant to be looking at?"

Jack jabbed his finger at Thomas Usher's face. "The resemblance between him and this." He moved his finger to Tony Tanner's made up face.

Fuller looked closer. "Could be twins. Who's the one at ringside?"

Jack jabbed at the photograph with his index finger. "Thomas Usher. That's Tony Tanner just two seats away from him. And isn't that your old boss, Charlie Somers?"

Fuller's gaze followed Jack's finger as it moved across to hover underneath Charlie Somers' face. He took a breath. "Yes, that's Charlie all right."

"When were you going to tell me that he knew both Thomas Usher and Tony Tanner, Eddie?"

"I didn't know, Jack," Fuller lied. "I've never seen this photo before."

Jack stared at him for a long moment. After a while he slipped the photograph and note back into the envelope, left the office and went downstairs to the front desk.

* * *

"Andy, are you sure you didn't see who dropped this off? You normally get here before the post arrives." Jack handed the envelope to the desk sergeant.

Brewer shook his head. "I heard the postman deliver the letters. I'd checked the box when I first got in and it was empty.'

"So, sometime between you checking the letter box and the postman coming, someone hand-delivered this. You say you didn't see who that person was?"

Brewer shook his head.

"And yet you were at the desk all the time, with a clear view of the front door."

"I saw nothing." Brewer said defensively. "I swear."

Jack frowned. "I don't like mysteries. Someone stuck this through the door, Andy. Did you leave the desk at any time, to answer a call of nature perhaps?" He looked down at the enamel mug on the desk.

"Well, I did leave the desk for a second, to make myself a cup of tea."

"Then that was probably when he came and dropped it off," said Jack.

"I'm sorry, sir." Brewer avoided Jack's eyes.

"Don't trouble yourself, Sergeant."

"Yes, sir, but even so . . ."

"I said, don't trouble yourself. It's not the end of the world. Might be lucky, in fact."

"Yes, sir. Very good, sir."

Jack went back to his office.

"Did Andy see who left the envelope?" Fuller said.

Jack shook his head. "He was out the back making tea." He took the note from the envelope and handed it across the desk to Fuller.

"Look carefully," Jack said. "Do you recognise the writing?"

Fuller recognised Charlie Somers' neat and precise printing immediately. He shook his head. "No. It means nothing to me."

"Well, someone's trying to help us, Eddie. Whoever it is thinks there's a link between Tony Tanner's death and Thomas Usher. Perhaps I was too hasty in dismissing Usher. I think we need to look into him a little more deeply."

"If you say so, sir. Where do we start?"

* * *

The bell jangled and Annie walked into Painter's. Rosie stepped out from behind the counter and hugged her mother. "You came then," she said. "I wasn't sure dad would let you."

"He was fine about it . . . in his usual grumpy old bear kind of way. Is Mrs Painter in?"

"Out the back." Rosie jerked her thumb in the direction of the door behind the counter. "I said you were coming in, so she's expecting you."

Annie gripped her daughter's hand. "Why do I feel so nervous? It's a part-time job at the local bakers. It's not as if I'm running for government or something . . . but I've got butterflies."

"Just go in and see her, Mum. She doesn't bite."

Annie patted down a flyaway strand of hair and took a deep breath. "Right." She walked towards the door. "Here goes nothing. Wish me luck."

* * *

"Do you still see Charlie Somers?" Jack said.

Fuller took a breath. Now he was wishing he had come clean with Jack at the start. It was all becoming awkward and he hated the deceit. "Occasionally."

"Well, make a point of catching up with him. Find out what he knows about Tanner and Usher."

"Yes, guv. Will do."

"And do it sooner rather than later."

"I'll see if he's free tonight. I can pop over and see him."

"I thought you told me he'd moved to London."

"He joined the Met, but he still lives in Stevenage. It won't take long to drive out to see him."

"Well, do that if he's free to see you." Jack slipped the photo out again. "Simon Docherty. Do we know anything about him?"

"I don't recognise him, and the name means nothing," Fuller said, truthfully this time.

"I'll pop down and check with Bob Lock, see if he has anything on him. While I'm doing that, track down the photographer, Talbot. Find out where and when this photograph was taken."

* * *

Sergeant Bob Lock had been running the Welwyn and Hatfield collator's office since before Jack transferred to Hertfordshire. Lock was the best collator he had ever worked with. His office was lined almost from floor to ceiling with wooden filing cabinets crammed with files. These contained records of crimes committed in the area over four decades. Lock had an almost photographic memory and an uncanny ability to recall case details. He was sitting at his desk in the cramped office, eating a cheese and pickle sandwich. He put down the sandwich and dabbed his lips with a handkerchief.

"Chief Inspector. What brings you down to my dungeon?"

Lock was approaching retirement age, but with his pale skin, almost white hair and rheumy eyes he looked a lot older. But as Jack knew only too well, looks could be deceptive. Bob Lock's mind remained as sharp and as incisive as a surgeon's scalpel.

"Simon Docherty, Bob. Does the name mean anything to you?"

Lock closed his eyes and leaned back in his chair. "Simon Docherty. American lawyer. Harvard educated and as crooked as they come."

"You know him, just like that?"

"Know thine enemy, Chief Inspector."

"You've come across him before, then."

Lock sat forward in his seat. "His name has floated across my desk from time to time. The Met have a file on him that makes for some interesting reading."

Jack sat down at the desk. "Anything you'd like to share?"

"Nothing specific. I could go through the files, but that would take some time. From what I remember, he first appeared on our shores just after the war. He got his qualifications to practice law in this country a few years later, and started to work as brief to some of the underworld's biggest names."

"Was Thomas Usher on his client list?"

Lock's eyes narrowed. "Usher? You're taking me on a trip down memory lane, sir. Only Thomas Usher has been off the scene for a while."

"I heard he'd had a stroke."

Lock chuckled. "Yes, I heard that one too."

"So it's not true?"

Lock shrugged. "It could be for all I know. There were so many stories circulating back then that it's hard to tell fact from fiction."

"You have your doubts about the stroke then?"

"All I know for sure is that Usher disappeared from public life a while back and hasn't resurfaced. It was around the time Scotland Yard were turning their attention to Soho's gangland, so I don't think it was a coincidence."

"Do you know if Usher was one of Docherty's clients?"

"That's one I can't answer with any degree of certainty, but I wouldn't be at all surprised."

"I have a photograph of the two of them together at a boxing match. Look." Jack handed him the photo.

Lock stared at it for a moment and then flipped it over to read the names on the back. "Well, it speaks volumes, but proves nothing, I'm afraid."

* * *

"Well? How did you get on?" Rosie said.

"She said I'd been out of circulation and stuck at home for too long to be of use."

Rosie grabbed her mother's arm. "Mum, you're kidding. That's outrageous. The old . . ."

Annie laughed. "No, I *am* kidding. I start Monday."

"Seriously?"

"Yes, seriously. Barbara's lovely. We were chatting for ages, and not just about the job. Did you know she was a fan of Frank Sinatra?"

"No, but I knew *you* were."

"Well, so is she. She went to see him at the London Palladium when he came over here in 1950. And he sang 'Nancy.' That's always been one of my favourites. Dad was going to take me to that one, but something came up at work so we never made it. I was *so* disappointed."

"Ancient history."

"Don't. Imagine it was one of the boys you like to listen to, that Cliff Richards for instance."

"His name's Cliff *Richard* and it's totally different. Cliff's *dreamy*."

"And so is Frank. In my eyes anyway. So it's just the same for me as it is for you."

"I suppose," Rosie said. "I don't think dad would agree though."

"Your dad's taste in music is different. It wouldn't do if we all liked the same thing."

Rosie quickly grew bored with these musical comparisons. She and her mother would never agree. Sometimes her mother could be so *square*. "So, are you going to walk to work with me on Monday?"

"If you don't mind. I'm sure Joanie can get Eric his breakfast," Annie said.

"Eric can get his own breakfast, the lazy little bugger."

"Rosie! Language!"

"Get used to it, Mum. We're work colleagues now."

Annie rolled her eyes. "Perhaps this wasn't such a good idea after all."

Rosie grinned at her. "Don't be daft. We'll have fun. Besides, you ought to hear Mrs Painter if her sausage rolls don't turn out just so. She could make a navvy blush."

"Are you telling tales, Rosie Callum?" Barbara Painter emerged from the back room. "See you Monday, Annie. Bright and early."

Annie smiled at her. "See you then, Barbara." The butterflies had gone now, to be replaced by a different flutter — excitement. New beginnings, she thought.

CHAPTER 12

FRIDAY

Frank Lesser knocked at the Tanners' bungalow. A frail, grey-haired woman answered the door.

"Is your husband in?" he said.

She peered up at him through a pair of rimless spectacles, taking in Lesser's battered face and not liking what she saw. She took a step back, her hand on the door, ready to pull it shut. "Who wants to know?" she said.

Lesser produced his warrant card and held it out to her.

"Detective Sergeant Lesser, Welwyn and Hatfield CID," he said.

"Oh, you're a policeman." The woman stared at his bandaged broken nose. "You don't look much like one."

"Your husband?" Lesser said.

"My husband is out. I'm Jean Tanner. How may I help you?"

"May I come in?"

"I suppose so."

Inside, Lesser sat down on a threadbare armchair. "You have a granddaughter — Geraldine?"

"Yes, I do."

"Have you had any contact with her in the last twenty-four hours?"

"I haven't had any contact with her in the last twenty-four *months*, Sergeant," Jean Tanner said. "Not since my son . . ." Her voice trailed off and tears filled her eyes. She took a handkerchief from the pocket of her housecoat and wiped them away, "I'm sorry." She blew her nose. "It's been so difficult since I learned of Anthony's . . ." The tears spilled.

An elderly man walked into the room. "What's the meaning of this? Who are you, coming in here and upsetting my wife?"

Lesser got to his feet. "I'm sorry, sir. I take it you're Laurence Tanner. Only your wife said you were out."

Tanner glared at him. "And so I was. Out in the garden."

"DS Lesser." Frank Lesser held out his hand. "I actually came to see you, sir. It's about your granddaughter."

Tanner ignored the proffered hand. "What about my granddaughter?"

"She's missing, sir. Disappeared from her home last night. We have teams out searching for her."

"Geraldine? Missing?"

"I was wondering if she'd contacted you recently."

Laurence Tanner sat down on the settee next to his wife, and rested a hand on her knee. "Go and lie down, Jean. I'll take it from here."

Jean Tanner stood up and smiled at her husband tearfully. She gripped his hand in both of hers. "Would you, dear? I don't think I can cope with any more bad news." She left the room, still dabbing at her eyes.

Lesser listened to her heavy tread go up the stairs. "I'm sorry, sir. I didn't mean to upset her."

Tanner wheeled on him.

"Understand this, Sergeant. The last few days have been very difficult for us. Difficult and deeply upsetting, especially for my wife. She's not a strong woman. You march in here in your size twelves, looking like something out of an Edward G Robinson gangster film. You scared her half to death. Of course she's upset."

"I'm sorry, sir. I had to come. I need to ask if you've seen or heard from your granddaughter."

Tanner glared at him. "Well, the answer to your question, Sergeant, is no. Geraldine hasn't been in touch with us for months."

"Aren't you concerned, sir, that something might have happened to her?"

"Damn your impertinence, man!" Tanner said. "Of course I'm concerned about my granddaughter. But if she's gone missing then surely it's up to you and your men to find her. You should be out there now, looking for her, not harassing an elderly couple in their own home."

Lesser looked down at his feet. "Yes, sir. I'm sorry. Perhaps I'd better leave."

"Perhaps you had. And be good enough to contact me as soon as you find her."

"Yes, of course." Lesser headed to the door.

Once back in his car Lesser sat back in his seat and whistled through his teeth. For an old man, Laurence Tanner was a formidable opponent. He'd rather face six rounds with Dr Death any day.

* * *

Waiting outside the headmistress's door brought back uncomfortable memories for Myra Banks. She had managed to clash with Cynthia Arnold on her very first day at Hatfield County, and things had not improved in the years that followed. Myra was given detentions almost weekly, and the headmistress had made it very clear that she could see no future for her. It would be odd to go back as an adult to interview her old nemesis, knowing that despite the woman's gloomy predictions, she had managed to make something of herself.

Cynthia Arnold sat up straight in her chair as Myra entered the office. "Ah, it *is* you. I wondered if WPC Banks was the same Myra Banks who led me such a merry dance when she was here. I heard you'd joined the police force and I must say I was sceptical, but now I see I was mistaken. How is that line of work progressing for you?"

Myra bridled at the woman's sneering tone. She sat with her fist clenched. Her fingernails dug into the fleshy part of her hand.

"It's progressing well, Mrs Arnold," Myra said tightly. "It's been suggested that I join the CID."

"Yes. I could always see you being connected to the criminal world in some way or another."

You bitch! Myra thought. She smiled.

"I'm here to ask for your help, Mrs Arnold. My boss, DCI Callum—"

"Charming man," Cynthia interrupted. "And so helpful."

"Yes, well. DCI Callum suggested I come to speak with you about Geraldine Tanner."

"Her again." Cynthia rubbed her forehead wearily. "You realise she hasn't come in to school today?"

"No. Ma'am, Geraldine is missing. We think she might have run away from home."

"But that's terrible. Her poor father."

"Her father was killed on Tuesday evening." Myra watched with guilty satisfaction as shock bleached the older woman's face.

"Killed?" Cynthia laid her palm across her eyes. "That's awful. Positively dreadful."

"Which is why DCI Callum wanted me to come and see you. To see if you could help us in our inquiries."

Cynthia glared at her. "I really don't see how *I* can help you. You'd be as well to go back to the chief inspector and tell him that I—"

Myra held up a hand. "You're her headmistress. You may be able to tell me the names of Geraldine's school friends."

Cynthia Arnold sagged slightly in her seat as if the fight had suddenly gone out of her. "I know she's very tight with Sally Wilson," she said. "They take music together. I think Geraldine's helping her with her piano studies. There's Sally, and Phyllis Mayhew. Thick as thieves those three are. I don't think they have a lot of time for anyone else in the school."

"And are Sally and Phyllis in school today?"

"I believe I saw them in assembly this morning, but you'll have to check with their form mistress, Mrs Rosser, to be certain."

"I remember Mrs Rosser," Myra said. *Another bitch.*

"Then you'll remember where her form room is."

Myra got to her feet. "Yes, I do. Thank you for your help."

"She'll either be there or . . ." She glanced at her wristwatch. "Or you'll find her in the domestic science block.

Do you know where that is? From what I remember, you were never a regular attendee at cookery classes."

Myra summoned up her most charming smile. "No. I always hated cookery, and I still do. But I do remember where the block is though."

Without another word Myra walked out of the office.

* * *

The sign above the shop read *J Talbot and Son, Photographers.* In the window several easels held framed wedding photographs. In others, contented-looking families dressed in their Sunday best wore tight smiles as they posed for posterity.

As he drew closer to the window Fuller realised the photographs were faded and dust had gathered around the easels. The dust extended to the floor of the window display where it formed a grey carpet, dotted with the bodies of dead flies and wasps.

He pushed open the door and the dusty brass bell clanged.

A glass-topped counter, also dusty, stood along one wall. A metal magazine rack held ancient, dog-eared copies of amateur photography magazines, their pages now sepia with age.

An old man shuffled out from behind a bead curtain at the back of the shop. He was dressed in stained khaki trousers with threadbare knees, and a dark green cardigan that hung on his thin frame like a mouldy sack. His tan carpet slippers had holes in the toes. He peered at Fuller through a pair of pebble glasses.

"Can I help you?" he said in a voice that sounded out of practice.

"Mr Talbot?"

"Eh? You'll have to speak up. The battery in my hearing aid has gone."

"Mr Talbot," Fuller said loudly. "I was wondering if you could take a look at this photo and tell me when it was taken." He took out the boxing photograph and laid it on the counter.

The old man leaned forward and adjusted his glasses. He stared at the photograph for a few seconds and then shook his head. "Not one of mine."

"But it has your stamp on the back."

The old man picked up the photograph with fingers that shook and turned it over. He held it close to his eyes to read the blue lettering. "It says J Talbot and Son."

"Yes," Fuller said patiently. "That's why I'm here."

"Well, I didn't take it," the old man said. "This is my son's work."

"Ah, I see. Would it be possible to have a word with your son then?"

"Yes, you can speak to him. Just get along to Highgate cemetery and take a medium with you."

"Your son's dead?"

The old man nodded sharply. "Eighteen months ago. Walked out in front of a bus. Bloody fool. They had to scrape his body off the road."

Fuller saw tears misting the old man's eyes. He softened his voice. "I see. So you've no idea when he took this."

"Before he died."

"I gathered as much. Have you any idea when and where it was taken?"

"Looks like a boxing match."

"Have you any idea where the venue might be?"

"York Hall, Bethnal Green, I should imagine. Benny used to photograph all the fights there."

"Benny being your son?"

The old man nodded. "It was his passion, had been since I first got him into photography. As I said, he was a bloody fool. Weddings and portraiture, that's where the money is in this game, bread and butter shots. Not taking snaps at sporting events on the off chance of selling them to the newspapers. That's a mug's game. Mind you, he did manage to get rid of this one."

"Really? He sold it? Where?"

"The *Police Gazette* of all places. The bloody *Police Gazette*! I remember when he sold it — two weeks before he died. He was crowing so loudly about it. Mind you, they only paid him pennies for it. 'That's not going to make your fortune,' I told him, but did he listen? Did he hell. He wouldn't listen to his old man. He was always on the lookout for what he called the 'money shot.' The one photograph that the newspapers would pay him a fortune for. That's how he got himself killed, trying to snap someone as they came out of the Purple Flamingo in Tottenham Court Road. Stepped into the road to get a better angle and a bus hit him. Bloody fool!" The old man slapped his palm down on the counter. "You don't get hit by buses at weddings."

"No. I should imagine not."

"I lost heart in the business when Benny passed." He rubbed his palm across his face and squeezed the bridge of his nose with his thumb and forefinger. "I don't know. You spend your life building something up. Something to pass on to your nearest and dearest, and then in a split second it all goes to hell under the wheels of a number twenty-nine bus."

Fuller left the old man to his bitter memories and headed back to the station.

CHAPTER 13

FRIDAY

Myra guessed it was the girls' first time in the staffroom. They entered their teachers' inner sanctum with wide eyes. Myra smiled to herself.

"Okay, girls. Take a seat and make yourselves comfortable."

There were a dozen matching leatherette armchairs in the room, and several low coffee tables, complete with used coffee cups and overflowing ashtrays. It stank of old coffee and stale cigarette smoke.

Sally Wilson wrinkled her nose and took a seat by an open window. Phyllis Mayhew hesitated for a moment and then chose an armchair beside her friend. She sat down, hugging her satchel to her chest. Her rather plain, moon face looked apprehensive.

"It's okay, girls. You're not in any trouble," Myra said.

Phyllis exhaled noisily. Sally, a more attractive girl with curly red hair and freckles, stared out of the window, a *couldn't-give-a-damn* look in her green eyes.

Myra stood at the front of the room and cleared her throat. "Geraldine Tanner. She's not in school today. Have either of you any idea where she might be?"

Phyllis was quick to shake her head. Sally continued to stare out of the window.

"Sally?" Myra said.

"I haven't seen her since afternoon break yesterday." The girl responded in a bored voice.

"And you, Phyllis? Have you seen Geraldine since yesterday?"

The girl looked close to tears. She screwed up her eyes and shook her head vehemently.

"So neither of you have any idea at all where Geraldine might be today?"

"Erm . . ." Phyllis started, but Sally rounded on her.

"Sshh, Phyll! We promised!"

"Okay." Myra clapped her hands together. "*Pax, fainites*. I don't want you two to fall out over this . . . and I'm sure Geraldine wouldn't want that either."

"Her name's *Gerry*, and she swore us to secrecy," Sally said.

"I wasn't going to say anything, Sal." A tear ran down Phyllis's cheek.

Sally glared at her.

"All right, Phyllis," Myra said gently. "You can go back to your class."

Phyllis got to her feet and, still hugging her school bag, hurried to the door.

Sally stood.

"Not you, Sally," Myra said in a stern voice. "Please sit down."

Sally glared at Myra, but she sat back in the chair and again directed her gaze out through the window.

Myra sat in the seat that Phyllis had just vacated. "Gerry's not in any trouble, Sally. I want you to understand that. It's just that we're all worried about her."

Sally blinked hard, twice.

"If you tell me what you know, you won't get into any trouble either."

"But Gerry will know I told you," Sally said. "And she made me promise."

"You care about Gerry, don't you?"

Sally nodded.

"Then you'll be helping her. Really you will."

Sally continued to stare out through the window but tears were welling in her eyes. The room was silent.

You're nowhere near as tough as you think you are, Myra thought.

"They beat her, you know," Sally said suddenly.

"Who beats her? Her parents?"

"Her stepmother and the old bag that lives with them during the week."

"Hester Gough?"

Sally nodded. "She's the worst. She hates Gerry, and Gerry hates her."

Myra took a breath. "I see."

Sally shook her head. "No, you don't. You have no idea how awful it is for Gerry, living in that house."

"Then tell me, and tell me where she's gone. Will you do that?"

"She threatened to break Gerry's fingers!" Tears were running freely down Sally Wilson's cheeks now. She nodded her head slowly. "All right. I'll tell."

* * *

"Threatened to break her fingers? What kind of people are we dealing with here?"

"I wouldn't want them on my Christmas card list," Myra said.

"Nor me. Break her fingers! Music — the piano — is everything to that child," said Jack.

"So you can see why she ran away."

"Oh, yes, I see. Only too well. Did this Sally Wilson have any idea where Gerry might have gone?"

Myra shook her head. "Gerry wouldn't tell her. Only that it was somewhere safe."

Jack sat back in his chair and rubbed his chin. "The poor girl was probably scared out of her wits."

"They used to beat her regularly."

Myra had a violent, drunken father and a weak and ineffectual mother. Throughout her teenage years she never knew where the next blow or slap would come from. It was what had made her want to become a policewoman. She was determined to bring to book those who preyed on others weaker than themselves.

"Is DS Lesser back from seeing the grandparents?" Jack said.

"He'd just got in when I came up."

"Then send him up to see me. Let's see if he's had any luck. Hopefully Gerry won't be missing for much longer."

"What are you going to do about Hester Gough and Lois Tanner, sir?"

Jack looked at her grimly. "Oh, I'll deal with those two. In my own time and in my own way."

* * *

"How did you get on, Frank?"

Lesser grinned. "Old man Tanner's a bit fierce, isn't he? Sent me away with a flea in my ear."

"Did he indeed? Sit down and tell me what he said."

Lesser pulled up a chair.

"Did he seem upset that his granddaughter was missing?"

"Not especially," Lesser said. "He seemed more concerned with getting me out of the house and back on the streets to look for her."

"What about Mrs Tanner? Did you get to see her?"

"Bit of a wet weekend that one."

"But you saw her, which is more than I managed. Did *she* seem upset? If it were my granddaughter and someone told me she was missing, just days after my son had been murdered, I think I'd be frantic with worry."

"You, guv?"

"Think, Lesser. Your only granddaughter has gone. For all you know she's been taken by the same person who killed your son. You'd be hysterical."

"Well, she was crying, but it was more like I'd told her that her dog had run away."

Jack scratched the back of his neck. "I'm going to go and see them myself."

"You think they might be lying about it?"

"Through their teeth, Sergeant. In fact I wouldn't be at all surprised if Gerry Tanner was with them in the house all the time you were there. She might well have been sitting in one of the other rooms."

"I should have checked."

"My fault. I told you to tread lightly. Gerry told her school friend that she was going to go somewhere safe. Where safer than with her grandparents?"

"Then why didn't the Tanners say something? They must know that we're wasting our man hours looking for their granddaughter."

"They probably think we'd just ship Gerry back to her stepmother and Miss Gough. If they knew what her life was like with those two bitches they'd go out on a limb to protect her from it. Leave it with me, Frank. I'll drive over there again once I've spoken to Eddie. He's up in Islington checking out a lead for me. He should be back any time."

* * *

"Stepped under a bus?" Jack said.

"Apparently. He was snapping someone either going into or coming out of the Purple Flamingo nightclub on the Tottenham Court Road. Stepped into the road to get a better angle and wham!" He clapped his hands. "Goodnight, Vienna."

"So let me get this straight. Benny Talbot sells a picture of Thomas Usher and his cronies at a boxing match to the *Police Gazette*. Two weeks later he falls under a bus outside Usher's nightclub. Is it just me, or does that sound like an unlikely coincidence?"

"When you put it like that."

"How else would you put it, Eddie? Those are the facts." Jack got up and took his raincoat from the stand. "Have you contacted your old guvnor?"

"Yes, I'm going to drive over to see him this evening."

"Well, there's another thing you can ask him now. Did the Met look into the circumstances surrounding Benny Talbot's *accident*? Because, to my mind, this stinks like a haddock left out too long in the sun."

"I'll check with him." Fuller watched his boss walk out of the office. He leaned back in his seat and closed his eyes, wondering what the hell Charlie was up to.

* * *

Jack almost made it out of the front door. He had his hand on the door handle when Andy Brewer called him back.

"What is it, Sergeant?"

"Gentleman to see you, sir." Brewer nodded towards a youngish man sitting on a bench under the public information notice board.

The man got to his feet. He was pencil-thin, with stringy black hair and a protruding Adam's apple. A pair of thick, rimless glasses sat on the bridge of his hooked nose. As he spoke his Adam's apple bobbed up and down. "Chief Inspector Callum? Neil Clarke. *News of the World*."

A reporter. All I need, thought Jack.

"It's about the Tony Tanner murder."

"Then I'm afraid you're going to have to make an appointment to see Chief Superintendent Lane. He deals with all the press reports issued from this station. Sergeant Brewer here should have told you that." Andy Brewer, meanwhile, had just developed an acute interest in a pile of missing pet forms on his desk.

"Ah." Clarke pushed back his glasses and peered at Jack. "I've just seen your chief superintendent, sir. He told me to wait here and have a word with you. Since you are, 'in charge of the investigation'. His words, not mine."

Thank you, Henry. Chief Superintendent Henry Lane rarely missed an opportunity to get his name in the papers, so why was he passing the buck now? Perhaps if it was the *Sunday Times* and not this scandal sheet, he'd have been keener to give a quote.

"Perhaps you can answer a few of my questions? Superintendent Lane gave me the outline of the case, the bread and butter so to speak, but I need you to supply the meat for the sandwich."

Meat? Sandwiches? Jack thought. What the hell is he talking about?

"I'm sorry, Mr Clarke. I really haven't got time for this. You need to make an appointment to see me. There's somewhere I need to be. Urgently." He looked pointedly at his watch and moved towards the door. Clarke moved with him.

"Yes," he said. "I'll make an appointment. Just one thing before you dash off though. Bearing in mind Mr Tanner's past relationship with Thomas Usher, would you say there is a connection between his murder and the long-standing gang rivalry between Usher and Albert Klein?"

Jack looked at the reporter blankly, and then shook his head. "I'm not at liberty to discuss the details of our investigation."

"Would that be a 'No comment' then?"

Jack glared at him. "Yes, Mr Clarke, it would."

Clarke gave him an obsequious smile. "Thank you, Chief Inspector. That will be all for now. I'll call and make that appointment." He pushed past Jack out of the station, letting the doors swing shut behind him.

"Why have I got the feeling I've just been stitched up?" Jack said to Brewer.

Brewer smiled. "Because you just gave him the golden answer: 'no comment.' For a reporter that's like being handed the keys to the kingdom. He's free now to write any kind of speculative nonsense he likes. Do you read the *News of the World*, sir?"

"I wouldn't let that rag through my letter box."

"Speculation and innuendo are their stock in trade. I think they invented the motto, 'never let the facts get in the way of a good story.'"

Jack shook his head. "Marvellous. Absolutely bloody marvellous."

CHAPTER 14

FRIDAY

"Chief Inspector. Twice in one day? To what do I owe this dubious honour?" Bob Lock said.

"Was Thomas Usher involved in some kind of turf war with a chap called Albert Klein?"

Lock thought for a moment. "You might call it that. In his heyday Usher had the south pretty much sewn up, from the Thames down to the coast. Albert Klein has north of the river, almost as far up as Watford."

"Why haven't I heard about Klein before? Why does it take some hack from the gutter press to tell me something I should already know?"

Lock smiled. "I call it the 'Hertfordshire effect.' Once you come to live out here, London's grimy criminal world just passes you by."

Jack shook his head. "I'm slipping, Bob. I should know what's going on, especially in London."

Lock shook his head. "No, sir, not really. There's more than enough crime up here to deal with, without importing more from the smoke."

"But *you've* heard of this Klein chap?"

"My job is a blessing and a curse. I get the chance to read everything that lands on my desk. Ninety per cent of it doesn't concern Hertfordshire Constabulary at all. What does goes on file but, because I've read it, the rest lodges in here." He tapped the side of his head. "And I have the devil's own job getting rid of it."

"Well, dig out everything you have about Usher and Albert Klein. I'll be out for a couple of hours, so have it ready on my desk when I return."

"Your wish is my command."

"Do genies live in dungeons?"

"Apparently this one does," Lock said.

* * *

Jack pulled up outside the Tanners' bungalow, switched his engine off and sat watching the windows. The bungalow had heavy net curtains, but after a few minutes he saw what he was expecting to see. He got out of the car and walked up the path. He pressed the doorbell and rapped on the door with his fist for good measure.

Laurence Tanner opened the door. When he saw it was Jack, his face contorted in an angry frown. "You again."

"I just want to talk to her, Mr Tanner."

"I don't know what you're talking about." Tanner flushed.

"I think you do. Now, we could stand out here in the street and have a slanging match, or you can invite me inside so that I can talk to Geraldine."

Tanner's shoulders sagged. Suddenly he looked a good ten years older. He opened the door and stood aside for Jack to enter.

"Who is it, pet?" Jean Tanner called from the living room. Her face fell when Jack walked in. Geraldine was sitting on the settee, leafing through a magazine. She too looked up at Jack. She froze like a startled deer.

"I'm not going back," she said.

Jack smiled at her kindly. "And no one's suggesting that you should. I just had to satisfy myself that you're all right."

"She's better off here," said Jean Tanner.

"We can't send her back to that house," Laurence Tanner said. He sounded perfectly reasonable now.

"May I sit down?" said Jack.

"As you wish." Tanner planted his bony frame on a hard chair by the dining table.

Jack settled himself opposite the girl. "You gave us quite a scare, Gerry."

"I just couldn't stay there. Hester said she would break my fingers."

"Yes. I'll be having words with Miss Gough." He turned to Tanner. "May I use your phone? I need to let my people know that Geraldine is safe."

Geraldine grasped her grandmother's hand.

"Gerry, it's okay. No one's going to take you away from here. I can see you're in a much better place."

"Thank you," Jean Tanner said.

"But I must call this in. My chief superintendent will have my guts if I don't."

"The telephone is out in the hall. This way." Tanner led Jack out of the room and closed the door behind them. He turned to Jack, his voice low. "You can't guarantee that Geraldine won't be taken away from us."

"No, I can't. But I'll do my level best to see that Geraldine is settled with you. I can't see her stepmother putting up too much of a fight, can you?"

Laurence Tanner smiled tightly. "I think not."

* * *

"Well. You look like the cat that got all the cream," Annie said as Jack walked in that evening.

Jack told her what had happened at the Tanners' bungalow.

"Jack, that's wonderful news."

"All we have to do now is find out who killed Gerry's father."

Annie pointed at his overstuffed leather briefcase. "What's in there?"

"Homework. I asked Bob Lock to give me all he had on two villains I'm investigating. I wasn't expecting this much."

"It looks like they've been busy."

"And then some. I think I'd best take this through to the back room, so I can spread it out on the table."

"Don't you want to know how I got on today — with Barbara Painter?"

Jack looked puzzled for a moment. "Yes, sorry, the job at the bakers."

"I got it!" Annie grinned. "I start on Monday."

"That's wonderful. Congratulations. Well done!"

"Okay, okay. Don't overdo it."

"But I'm pleased for you."

"Are you, Jack? Really?"

He dropped the briefcase onto the floor, wrapped his arms around Annie and pulled her close. "Really," he said into her ear. "Mind you, there are plenty of men who would have put their foot down. Told you where a woman's place was, and it wouldn't be out earning a living. That's a man's role."

"That doesn't sound like you, Jack Callum," Annie said. "Though you do have your stubborn moments."

"I can't pretend I like the way everything is going these days, but it strikes me some change is good. I can see no reason why a woman shouldn't be treated — in some circumstances — the same as a man." He kissed her cheek. "Just don't you go broadcasting it."

Annie kissed him back, passionately, on the lips. When she finally broke away, he said, "Hey, you should get a job every day."

"Thank you." She snuggled into his chest. "I love you, Jack Callum."

"Never mind that, woman. There are some changes I don't approve of. I said *some* circumstances. Where's my dinner?" He pulled her closer.

"In the oven." She pushed him away and gave him a playful slap.

"Ouch! I am famished by the way. I haven't eaten since breakfast."

"Patience, darling. All things come, etcetera, etcetera. By the way, on the way back from Painter's, I called in at Howard's, the electrical store in town. You know, the one on the corner of Station Road."

"I know it."

"They'll let us have a set for eight shillings a week. Both channels — BBC and ITV, and a fifteen-inch screen."

"Is that good?"

"It's wonderful. If you go in there in the morning and countersign the rental agreement, they'll deliver it on Monday."

"That quickly, eh?"

Annie nodded excitedly.

"Hold on a moment. Before you get carried away, we'll both be at work on Monday. There'll be nobody here to let them in."

"Joanie will be here. Avril doesn't need her until later in the week."

Jack shook his head. "Well, that's that then. The end of civilisation as we know it."

"Oh, shut up, you old bear. Come here and kiss me again."

* * *

"'Allo, Eddie," Françoise Somers kissed the air either side of Fuller's cheeks. He wasn't used to these French ways and didn't know how to respond. "Charles is in the games room. Come through."

Charlie Somers' wife was a slender beauty who wore her straight brown hair cut into a blunt fringe that just touched her eyebrows. She had large brown eyes and a retroussé nose. Her lips were full and, Fuller thought, very kissable.

How a grizzled old reprobate like Somers had ended up married to such a beauty was one of life's enduring mysteries.

Fuller went through to the back of the house, where he heard the clacking of snooker balls. Somers was leaning over the baize. His hand formed a bridge on which he rested his cue. He was attempting a difficult cut into the centre pocket, and Fuller could see beads of perspiration on his brow as he strained to make the shot.

"A dollar a frame," Somers said. "Fancy it?"

Fuller laid two half-crowns on the edge of the table. "Why not?"

"Go and grab yourself a cue while I frame up."

The snooker cues were kept in a rack in a corner of the large games room. Fuller took one out and peered down its length, checking to see if it was true. Satisfied, he walked back to the table and picked up a piece of chalk hanging from a length of string tied to the top corner pocket.

"You can break," Charlie said.

Fuller positioned the cue ball and took the shot.

"Hmmm," Somers said. "Not bad. Have you been practising?"

"The result of a misspent youth."

"Well, let's see what I can do with this." Somers bent to take the shot.

"Why did you send the photo to my guvnor, Charlie?" Fuller said as Somers drew back his cue. Somers glanced up at him and struck the cue ball down the table.

"I thought it might help him." Somers glared at the balls. Several had landed in vulnerable positions.

"Well, it's certainly got him thinking." Fuller bent to pot his first of four red balls. "Did the Met investigate the death of Benny Talbot — the bloke who took the photograph?"

"From what I remember, he fell under a bus on the Tottenham Court Road," Charlie said.

"Yes, a number twenty-nine. But did he have any help?"

"You mean, was he pushed?"

"Yes."

"There were several witnesses who saw him fall."

"Credible ones?"

"I wasn't personally involved in the investigation, but I believe so. It was deemed an accident, and that was that."

Fuller missed an easy black into the corner pocket, and Somers came back to the table.

"You know, Jack Callum's not going to let that photograph go," Fuller said.

Somers glanced round at him. "Are you deliberately trying to put me off my stroke?"

"My five bob looks safe from where I'm standing."

CHAPTER 15

FRIDAY

The door to the games room opened. Françoise walked in carrying a tray with a coffee jug and cups.

Eddie Fuller found it hard not to stare as she moved around the room and deposited the tray on a corner table. "Who's winning?" she asked.

"He is," Somers said sourly.

Françoise produced a smile that lit up the room. "Well done, Eddie. Charles hates to lose. He doesn't very often."

She pronounced her husband's name the French way. It sounded endearing and incredibly sexy. The door closed behind her.

"You're a lucky so and so," Fuller said.

"And don't think I'm not aware of it. I count my blessings every day."

"How did you two get together?"

Somers smiled. "It was all thanks to Tommy Usher. Françoise used to work for him."

"As what?"

"As a whore, Eddie. She was nothing more than a common prostitute. Of course Usher always described his girls as *escorts.*"

"A rose by any other name . . ."

Somers smiled. "We'd been seeing each other in a professional capacity and, believe it or not, we fell in love. She was afraid Tommy would be furious, that he might even stripe her, but he was as nice as pie. I suppose he figured that now he had a detective inspector in his pocket it was worth losing her services. I told the inquiry about it. So that's not one of the skeletons rattling around in my closet."

"You mean there are others?"

"Oh, plenty. But none that I lose any sleep over. So let Chief Inspector Callum do his worst — or his best. As I said before, the inquiry cleared me of any wrongdoing."

"And as *I* said before, they weren't in possession of all the facts."

Somers potted an easy black and rested his fists on the table. "Listen, Eddie, I like you, so I won't take what you say as personal. Whatever you think you saw when you worked for me, I was trying to get Tommy Usher off the streets. I would have succeeded if fate hadn't intervened before I could make an arrest."

"The stroke, you mean."

"Yes, the bloody stroke. His people spirited him away to a private sanatorium, first in Switzerland and then from there to Brussels. We lost track of him when they moved him to Germany."

"And you believe that he's back in the country, living in a nursing home in the South of England?"

"Yes. Kent, like I said."

"But it's just an assumption. You don't know that for certain," Fuller said.

Somers shook his head. "No, but it would make sense. He always had strong family ties to that part of the word."

"Did you pursue it further?"

"I did. But by the time I heard he was back in the country, the investigation had gone cold. The chief constable said the Met had wasted enough money trying to bring Usher down. The general thinking was that the good Lord had done their work for them. A private nursing home was as good as prison in their opinion. Usher was out of their hair. And it hadn't cost the taxpayer a penny."

"So everybody wins," Fuller said.

Somers glared at him. "No, Eddie. Nobody wins. What about justice? Where is the justice for the poor bastards Usher maimed? The ordinary people whose livelihoods were ruined and the families destroyed by his crimes? What about them? I joined the force to fight for people like them, the little people. To make sure thugs like Usher got what was coming to them." There was passion in his voice.

"So that's why you sent my guvnor the photograph. You're hoping Jack Callum will reopen the case and get the result you wanted but could never have."

Somers nodded. He cracked the pink ball into the centre pocket. "That's a dollar you owe me." He grinned in triumph.

Fuller slid the two half-crowns across the table. "Why involve Jack?"

"Because he's not part of the Met and their hidebound ways. If he's half the copper I've heard he is, he should have no trouble getting Tommy Usher put away."

"You hate Usher *that* much?"

Somers poured coffee into a tiny cup. "Listen, Eddie, the only good thing to come from my association with Usher was Françoise. The rest sits on my conscience like a stain that no amount of scrubbing will remove. Another frame?"

Fuller sighed. "Might as well. I'd forgotten how good you are."

"Southern area police snooker champion — or had you forgotten that too?"

"Go on then, you old rogue, frame them up." Fuller sipped his coffee. "Has anyone seen Usher since he had the stroke?"

"Nobody from my team."

"Did he really have one, a stroke I mean?"

"There were witnesses."

"Credible ones? Like those who witnessed Benny Talbot falling under a bus?" Fuller said.

"What are you implying, Eddie?"

"Could Usher have faked it, just to get the Met off his back?"

Somers watched the cue ball roll back into baulk and gave a satisfied nod. "That's what I thought initially. It was all too bloody convenient, but reliable sources told us that the stroke was genuine. A doctor from Barts' hospital, where the bastard was treated, spoke to my Sergeant. The doctor told him that it was touch and go at first for Usher, and he had no reason to lie. And his firm suddenly dropped off our radar, almost as if they had stopped trading."

"Has another firm stepped in to fill the vacuum? Blast!" The cue ball cannoned off the black and dropped into a corner pocket.

"Careless. Seven points to me. You need to concentrate, Eddie."

"I know. I would have thought all the others would've been queuing up to fill Usher's shoes."

Somers shook his head. "The Richardson gang were sniffing around about a month after it happened. We had them in the frame for a couple of post office jobs but we never made anything stick. Then they dropped out of the picture."

"So, since Usher's stroke, the South's been crime free?"

Somers laughed. He potted a red, followed by a blue, and then another red. "Don't be so bloody naïve. There're still as many incidents, thieving, assaults, and the brothels are still making money. If anything, business has increased since Usher left the scene, but there hasn't been any significant gang-related crime."

"Don't you find that odd?"

Somers rested the end of his cue on the floor. "Frankly, Eddie, yes I do. But my superiors take a different view. They don't believe in looking a gift horse in the proverbial. Overall, the crime figures have fallen, so my bosses are toasting their success — the bloody fools."

Fuller drained his coffee cup and poured himself another. He watched Somers build a break of thirty-five. "Bob Lock, our collator, says Jack is looking into Albert Klein. Do you know anything about him?"

"Mr Callum is a busy boy, isn't he? First Usher, now Klein. What's he trying to do, wipe out all the crime in the whole country?"

"I haven't spoken to him about Klein. I wanted to have your thoughts first."

Somers finished the break with a missed black. "Damn! Eddie, are you sure you want to do this?"

"Do what?"

"Do you want to keep going behind your boss's back? If I found out my sergeant had been consulting his old DI, I'd string him up by his nuts."

"I'm just trying to be a good detective."

"I realise that. But, there are ways and means. If Jack Callum wants my help, he can come straight to me." He leaned over the table and attempted a difficult cannon, missed it and swore again. "Divided loyalties, Eddie. Never a good thing in our line of work."

"I never thought of it like that."

"Bollocks you didn't. I know you, Eddie. You're a bloody good copper. And you're bloody ambitious. How old were you when you made detective sergeant? The youngest DS in the South, weren't you?"

"Maybe."

"You know damned well you were. So don't be bloody coy about it."

Fuller looked down. "This isn't about me."

"Isn't it?"

Eddie Fuller shook his head.

"Well, try telling that to Jack Callum when he hears we've been talking."

"Jack *told* me to come and see you, he said to find out what you knew about Usher and Tony Tanner."

"You haven't mentioned Tanner once since you got here."

"I was working my way round to it."

"A long way round." Somers rested his cue against the table and put his hands on his hips. "Let's stop pissing around, shall we? Just tell me what you and your guvnor want, and let's see where that gets us." He walked to the door. "Françoise? More coffee please, angel. And can you bring that bottle of brandy and two glasses from the lounge."

Fuller leaned over the snooker table and sank a red into the centre pocket.

* * *

After another five shillings had found their way into Charlie Somers' pocket, the two men sat together on a comfortable old sofa in the corner of the room.

"Tony Tanner was nothing more than a thrill-seeker and a hanger-on. He liked to associate himself with criminals. You see that a lot with theatricals. Personally I've always found it rather pathetic. Tommy Usher was always looking for an angle and, with Tony Tanner's show business connections, he struck gold. So he kept the poor sod around, stroking his ego and mining his contacts for new business opportunities. He got a certain respectability from being seen with a famous actor. Then it all turned to shit when Tanner met that awful Franklin woman and married her."

"You knew Tanner's wife, Lois?"

Somers grimaced. "I met her a few times. She's a lush, and a few saucers short of a tea service, if you want my opinion. Tanner was besotted by her. He thought the sun shone out of her *derrière*. He was carrying on with her while his poor wife lay dying of cancer in hospital. Bastard!"

"And Albert Klein?"

"A different proposition altogether. He's a villain of the old school. He's Jewish and devout too. He attends the synagogue every Sabbath, takes time off from his criminal activities for the Jewish festivals. But he's a nasty piece of work, vicious and as crooked as they come."

"Worse than Usher?"

"In some ways, yes. He runs North London like his own private fiefdom. Woe betide any who challenge his position. Those twins from Bethnal Green found that out when they tried to muscle in on his protection rackets. Klein sent them packing."

Somers swallowed a mouthful of brandy with a contented sigh. "They'll have him in the end though. Reggie and Ronnie are mad and dangerous, real psychopaths. At one time there was talk of Klein and Usher joining forces, but Tommy Usher wasn't about to take time off for religious holidays. They had other differences as well."

"Such as?"

"Well, drugs were the main one. Klein gets most of his income from trafficking and dealing in drugs. Dope and amphetamines mainly, and cocaine and heroin for those who can afford it. Tommy Usher kept right away from drugs. He had an almost pathological hatred of them. He lost his younger brother, Cyril, to a heroin overdose just after the war. Klein wasn't about to sacrifice any of his income just to climb into bed with Usher, so the unholy union never happened."

"Do you think Klein could be involved in Tony Tanner's death?"

"As far as I know, they never actually met. Why would you think that?"

"Because when Tanner was found dead, he was made up to look like Tommy Usher, complete with false moustache and fake nose."

Somers eyes widened. "Really? Well, I'm blowed." He drained his glass. "But I can't see Klein's fingerprints on it. He and Usher didn't get on, sure, but they respected each other, as well as the North/South divide. If Callum's going down that route, I think he'll hit a brick wall. Honour amongst thieves and all that crap. Another frame before you go?"

"To give me a chance to win my money back?"

"You'll be lucky."

CHAPTER 16

SATURDAY MARCH 21st, 1959

Jack was carrying the stepladder along the landing when he heard the alarm clock sound in Rosie's room. She had an early start at the bakers this morning. He set the ladder under the loft hatch and started to climb.

"Couldn't you sleep, Dad?" Rosie yawned, rubbing the sleep from her eyes as she came out of her bedroom.

"Just looking for something." Jack released the catch and let the hatch swing down.

"Is Mum awake?"

Jack put his finger to his lips. "It's only you and me so far. Let's try to keep it that way for another hour at least."

"Quiet as a mouse," she whispered, and tiptoed into the bathroom.

Jack hoisted himself into the loft and found the light switch. The loft was as well ordered as his garden shed. He had no trouble locating the large suitcase containing copies of the *Police Gazette* that went as far back as 1950.

He unfolded a dusty card table and a small canvas camping chair. He opened the case, set it down on the table and started going through the old periodicals.

About half an hour later he found the edition he'd been searching for. There, taking up a third of a page was the boxing photograph. The caption read: 'Senior Officer cleared of Corruption Charges.' The three-column story went on to report how Detective Inspector Charles Somers had been absolved of misconduct. The article described his relationship with certain gangland figures, one of whom was Thomas Usher. The piece ended with the police commissioner praising Inspector Somers for his diligent work in gathering intelligence on organised crime in the capital.

Jack stared at the photograph. Who had sent it to him? Why? One of the other characters, Simon Docherty, looked vaguely familiar. He stared hard at Docherty's face. He was sure he had never seen him before, but the man's face reminded him of something and he couldn't think what.

From down below he could hear stirrings. Annie was awake and moving about the bedroom.

Rolling up the Gazette, he stuffed it into his cardigan pocket and put the suitcase away. He was lowering himself out of the loft as his wife came out of the bedroom.

Annie looked up at him and yawned. "I thought I heard someone moving about up there. I guessed it'd be you."

"Sorry. I didn't mean to wake you."

"Don't worry. The milkman already did that with his bloody whistling. What have you been doing?"

"Looking for something." He brandished the *Police Gazette.* "I found it."

"Good. What time did you turn in last night? I didn't hear you come up."

"After one." Jack closed the loft hatch and shut up the stepladder.

Annie shook her head. "I'm thinking candles. Burning? Both ends?"

"You worry too much." He pecked her on the cheek.

"Well, someone's got to. Eggs for breakfast?"

He glanced at his watch and shook his head. "Just tea and toast for me. I'll have to get a move on if you want me to drop in at Howard's about that television on my way to the station."

***

"How did your meeting with Charlie Somers go?" Jack asked Eddie Fuller.

"Cost me fifteen bob it did."

"How come?"

"Snooker. The old bugger took me to the cleaners."

"Serves you right. Did he shed any light on Usher's relationship with Tony Tanner?"

"Oh yes," Fuller said. It took him thirty minutes to recap the conversation with his old guvnor.

"What did he have to say about Benny Talbot and his argument with the number twenty-nine bus?"

"The Met treated it as an accident."

Jack was silent for a moment. Then he said, "What happened to the camera?"

Fuller looked puzzled.

"Benny Talbot's camera. Who was he trying to photograph when he met with his *accident*?"

"I didn't ask, and I doubt that Charlie would know. It wasn't his case."

"Shame. I'd like to see that roll of film."

"Why?"

"I'm not really sure. There's something buzzing around my brain at the moment." He picked up his mug of station tea, took a swig and shuddered. "Bloody awful. Who makes this stuff? What about Albert Klein? Did Charlie have anything to say about him?"

"He's a North London villain, a devout Jew who respects the Sabbath and observes all the religious holidays—"

"And is good to his mother, no doubt. Any history between him and Usher that Tanner might have fallen foul of?"

"Charlie can't recall Klein and Tanner ever meeting."

Jack sighed. "Round and round in circles. Well, let's see what Frank comes up with. He's working his way through his half of the list Lois Tanner gave us. I believe he's up in the West End today, trying to speak to that dancer chappie."

"Fred Tozer?"

"Yes, him. It'll probably be another dead end, but who knows?"

* * *

Frank Lesser stood in the wings of the Carlton theatre. There were twenty dancers on the stage and something about Fred Tozer set him apart from all the others. *Charisma.* Lesser had seen it in the wrestling ring. Some performers had it and could have the crowd eating out of their hand, others didn't and would remain lower to middle card throughout their careers.

Tozer had it in spades, which was probably why his name was up in lights.

The tap routine ended and an assistant threw Tozer a towel. Then he spoke into the dancer's ear and pointed towards Lesser.

Wiping the perspiration from his face, Tozer walked towards him. He called back over his shoulder, "Take five! And then we go again, from the top."

The groans rippled across the stage.

"Are you Lester?" said Tozer.

"*Lesser*, sir. Detective Sergeant. Welwyn and Hatfield Police."

"Bit out of your jurisdiction, aren't you, Sergeant?"

"It concerns an incident that happened in our area a few days ago. Can we go somewhere and talk? I have a few questions."

"Very well. We can talk in my dressing room. This way."

Lesser followed him through a maze of narrow walkways until they came to a door at the end of a long corridor. It had a star affixed to it. Tozer held the door open for Lesser to enter.

Tozer sat down at a dressing table in front of a large mirror. Small light bulbs showed up the age-lines wrinkling Tozer's face. He was still good-looking, though, with almost symmetrical features, a finely chiselled nose and full lips. His body was lean and toned and the muscles of his legs were clearly defined under his black nylon tights. He wouldn't have looked out of place in a wrestling ring, Lesser thought.

"Grab a seat." Tozer pointed to a wooden chair standing in the corner.

Lesser grabbed it and set it down facing Tozer.

"So, what do you want to ask me about?"

"Tony Tanner," Lesser said.

Tozer frowned. "He's dead. There were a couple of paragraphs in *The Stage*. It said his death was being treated as suspicious and the police . . . That's why you're here, isn't it?"

Lesser nodded.

"Well, I didn't kill him, if that's what you think."

"Why should I think that, sir?"

"I have enough reason to, God knows. But no, Sergeant, I'm not your man."

"Glad to hear it." Lesser took out his notebook. "Can you tell me where you were last Tuesday afternoon, the seventeenth?"

"Yes. Here."

"And do you have any witnesses who can corroborate that?"

Tozer smiled. "Yes. About five hundred of them. We give a matinee performance on Tuesdays."

Lesser wrote in his notebook. "What time did the show end?"

"It runs from two-thirty till five, with a fifteen minute intermission."

"And you were on stage all that time — apart from the intermission of course?"

"Come to the show, Sergeant. You'll see for yourself what a demanding performance it is."

"Perhaps I will," Lesser said. He had no intention of doing so.

Then the dressing room door swung open and crashed against the wall. A short, bald man stormed into the room.

"There you are, you bastard!" he yelled at Tozer. He ran across the room and yanked the dancer out of his seat. "I ought to smash your bleedin' face in."

Lesser sprang to his feet and pinned the fat man against the wall, forcing his arm up behind his back. "Here, what's your game?" Lesser applied pressure to his arm and the man yelped.

Fred Tozer smiled. "It's all right, Sergeant. You can let him go."

Lesser looked at him uncertainly.

"Really. Julian's bark is far worse than his bite."

"You know this man, sir?"

Tozer chuckled. "Yes, more's the pity. I've known him all my life. Detective Sergeant Lesser, may I introduce you to Mr Julian Tozer, my brother."

"Your brother?" Lesser released the fat man. He stared at him, searching for a hint of resemblance, and finding none.

"Yes," Tozer said, ironically. "The likeness is astonishing, isn't it?" He turned to his brother. "Calm down, Julian. You'll give yourself another coronary."

Julian Tozer was breathing heavily and his face was red. Lesser pulled up the chair and placed it behind Julian's knees. "I'd sit down, sir, if I were you."

Julian Tozer gave Lesser a filthy look and flopped onto the chair. "Are you here to arrest him?"

"Not today," Lesser said.

"Well, you should. He's a bloody thief."

Lesser turned towards Fred Tozer. "Something I should know about, sir?"

"Ignore him, Sergeant. Julian's just upset because our recently departed mother favoured me in her will and left the rest of her money to a donkey sanctuary in Dorset."

Lesser shook his head. "None of my concern, sir. But if you don't mind me asking, what did you have against Tony Tanner?"

"The man was a welsher, Sergeant. He owed me several hundred pounds. I helped him out when his career was on the skids, more fool me."

"And he never paid you back?"

"Not a brass farthing, the bastard. And it's not as if he didn't have it."

"Serves you bloody well right," said Julian Tozer.

"Be quiet, Julian! Will there be anything else, Sergeant?"

"No. I've taken up enough of your time," said Lesser.

"Are you a boxer, Sergeant? You certainly seem to know how to handle yourself, and judging from your face . . ."

"A wrestler, sir."

"Ah, so that's why you seemed so at ease. Most people who come backstage are somewhat . . . awestruck for want of a better word."

Lesser nodded. "Yes, you could say that." Theatres' nether regions held no mystery for him. Many of his bouts were held in run-down provincial venues not so different from this one.

Lesser excused himself and headed off to Shaftesbury Avenue. In another theatre Betsy Maclaren was appearing in a Noël Coward play.

CHAPTER 17

SATURDAY

An hour later he was sitting in another dressing room. This one was cramped and cluttered and had no star on the door. Betsy Maclaren's star had been fading of late, along with her ingénue status and her girl-next-door looks.

She sat opposite Lesser, drawing occasionally on a pink Sobranie cocktail cigarette clutched between nicotine-stained fingers. "Polly Tanner was my best friend," she said. "We trained at Webber Douglas and graduated together. I was bridesmaid at her wedding, for Christ's sake."

"So you must have taken her death very badly."

"I cried for weeks." Betsy inhaled. "But I'd been crying for Polly a long time before her death, ever since I learned what that piece of scum Tanner was doing. Polly was a lovely girl, one of life's little gems. We shared a flat in Ladbroke Grove when we were first starting out. She was twice the actress I am, but so modest and self-effacing. When that bastard betrayed their marriage vows and started sleeping with that . . . that bitch, Lois Franklin. . . It was one of the cruellest things I have ever witnessed."

Tears were welling in Betsy Maclaren's eyes. She was torturing a silk handkerchief, twisting it tightly around her fingers.

"I had no idea that Polly Tanner was an actress too," said Lesser.

"That was how they met. She was Eliza to his Professor Higgins in Bristol rep. He was far too young for the part, of course, but Polly's Eliza was praised by the critics and the play was a success. It was the worst part she could have chosen."

"Oh?"

"She fell in love with her leading man." She sighed and ran a hand through her hair. "After that, convinced *he* was going to be the major star, she put her own career on the back burner. After Geraldine was born she put all her effort into his career." She took a savage draw on the Sobranie and ground it out in an overflowing ashtray.

"You seem very bitter about it."

"You could say that. When I think what Polly sacrificed for that pig . . ." She shuddered. "I hope one day fate catches up with him and he goes to the hell he so richly deserves."

"You haven't heard?" Lesser said.

"Heard what?"

"Tony Tanner was murdered last Tuesday evening."

"Murdered? Tony?"

Lesser nodded.

Betsy reached for another Sobranie. "Good. Murdered you say? I hope the little worm suffered."

"Where were you on Tuesday afternoon?"

Betsy Maclaren's mouth dropped open and the cigarette fell from her lips. "You don't think I killed him, surely?"

"You seem to have had a lot of animosity towards him."

"I did. I'm delighted, absolutely delighted, that he's dead. Last Tuesday I was here all afternoon, rehearsing. Twenty or so people saw me and will back me up." Her chin tilted up. "Do I look like a murderer to you?"

"Crippen didn't look much like a murderer either."

Betsy glared at him. "No offence, Sergeant, but I'm going to tell you to piss off now."

Lesser stared at the diminutive Betsy Maclaren. Her blonde curls and blue, doe eyes were at odds with her language. He got to his feet. "I'll check your alibi before I go."

"Yes, do that," she said coldly. She turned her back on him, drawing furiously on her Sobranie.

***

"Bloody theatricals!" Frank Lesser said as he walked into Jack's office later that afternoon.

"What are you moaning about, Frank? You're almost one of them yourself," Fuller said from his desk.

"Watch it, son. I'm a sportsman and an athlete."

Fuller gave a fake yawn. "If you say so, Frank."

"I bloody well do." Lesser moved towards Fuller.

"That's enough, you two!" Jack said loudly. "Save your squabbles for the bloody playground. Sergeant Lesser, would you mind sitting down and telling me what you found out today?"

Looking daggers at Eddie Fuller, Lesser pulled a chair up to Jack's desk.

"Two suspects questioned, both with alibis for Tuesday afternoon."

"So, a trip to London's West End wasted?"

"Not really, sir. I found out that Tony Tanner was a bit of a shit."

"We knew that already," Fuller said.

"Be quiet, Eddie. Let Frank continue," said Jack.

"Thank you, sir. As I was saying, Tony Tanner was a—"

Jack cut him off. "Yes. I think that's well established by now. You don't think either Fred Tozer or Betsy Maclaren could be responsible for the murder?"

"Only Tozer has the strength to have pulled it off. He's a trained dancer, athletic and well-muscled. But his alibi is rock solid. Betsy Maclaren is about five foot four and probably weighs seven stone soaking wet. Again, a strong alibi, and she didn't even know Tanner was dead. It came as quite a shock to her."

"She's a bloody actress, Frank," Fuller said. "She could have been putting on a performance for your benefit."

"Sir?" Lesser turned to Jack.

Jack glared at Fuller again. "Button it, Eddie. I think Frank's more than capable of recognising when someone is telling the truth."

"Thank you, sir." Lesser directed a sly smile at Fuller.

"Type out your report and have it on my desk by three o'clock," Jack said to him. Lesser left the room.

"Eddie, how are you getting on tracking the names on your list?"

"I've got an appointment with Michael Lewin later this afternoon."

"Who's Lewin?"

"He's the last name on the list. An architect. I've yet to find out how he connects to Tanner."

"Well, let me know as soon as you do. Are you coming round to give Eric his guitar lesson later?"

"No. He got Bert Weedon's *Play in a Day* book from the library last week."

"Bert Weedon's written a book?" said Jack.

"Have you heard of him?"

Jack chuckled. "I remember him when he used to play with Ted Heath and Mantovani. Well, I suppose Eric can't go far wrong if he's learning that kind of music."

"Well, just to warn you, he's discovering rock and roll as well. He'll be asking for an electric guitar and an amplifier soon."

"Good God. He's only just got your old one."

Fuller shrugged. "That's how these things go. My first instrument was a banjo. I graduated to the guitar within six months, and got a better one two weeks later. Anyway, Eric reckons he doesn't need me anymore. It will save you five bob a week, anyway."

"More for you to lose on your snooker matches with Charlie Somers."

"You have to be kidding. That old devil is good."

"Southern area champion three years running, from what I hear."

"You knew that?" Fuller said.

"I knew it. I also knew it was Somers you went to for information, when I specifically told you to contact Division." Jack gave a wry smile.

Fuller blushed. "You knew that too?"

"Oh, yes."

"And you don't mind?"

"I only mind that you didn't tell me. I need to be able to trust my sergeants, Eddie."

"You *can* trust me, Jack."

"Actually, I applaud your initiative. I would have done the same thing."

"So you're not annoyed?" Fuller said.

"Bloody furious, but only because I didn't think of it first. Just keep me in the picture in future, yes?"

"Yes," Fuller said.

"You found Talbot, the photographer, in Islington, right?"

"On the Holloway Road."

"Then that's where I'll be this afternoon. I'm going to pay him a visit."

"Is there any point?"

"You used your initiative, Eddie. Now I'm using mine."

* * *

It wasn't easy to park on the Holloway Road. Saturday shoppers were out in force, and had taken all the spaces close to the shops. Jack finally managed to squeeze his Morris Oxford in between a blue Hillman Minx and a Bedford van.

The old man behind the counter glanced up briefly as Jack entered the shop. Then he went back to polishing a camera lens.

"Mr Talbot?"

"Jacob Talbot, yes," said the man.

Jack introduced himself. "You spoke with my sergeant yesterday. I was sorry to learn about your son."

Talbot put down the camera on the glass-topped counter.

"I was wondering about his camera," Jack said.

"What about it?"

"What happened to it, after the accident?"

"The bus ran over that too. Shame. It was a *Leica M3*. It cost him an arm and a leg — and a whole lot more than that in the end."

Jack shook his head in sympathy. "Was the film recovered?"

"The camera was crushed, the film ruined. I've got the bits if you want to see them. The police gave me a brown paper bag with Benny's effects in it. Want to see?"

"That won't be necessary," said Jack.

"Then why are you asking?"

"I was just wondering who he was taking photos of when he died. You told my sergeant the accident happened outside the Purple Flamingo nightclub."

"That's right, on the Tottenham Court Road. Benny was always hanging around there in the evenings when he wasn't at the boxing. What he was trying to achieve I can't imagine. Getting snaps of people coming and going. I suppose there's a market for that sort of thing, but I don't think Benny ever made much out of it."

Jack looked through the grubby glass counter at the cameras and lenses steadily gathering dust on the shelves. "I don't suppose Benny kept hold of the photos he took?"

"Are you kidding me? Benny never threw anything away. He called them his legacy, though who he was preserving them for I'll never know. Certainly not for me."

"You still have them?"

The old man nodded. "Didn't seem right, somehow, to just throw them away. I suppose I'll have to one day. I'm selling the shop and whoever buys it isn't going to want them."

"Could I see them?"

"All of them? There're hundreds," said the old man.

"Well, maybe the ones taken in his last six months or so. I take it he had some kind of filing system?"

"Oh yes, he had that all right." Talbot came around the counter and walked to the front door. He locked it and flipped the sign from *open* to *closed.*

"I don't want to interfere with your business."

Talbot gave a bitter laugh. "What bloody business? You're the first person to come in here today." He shuffled back behind the counter and pushed aside a curtain, revealing a wooden staircase. He beckoned to Jack. "Come through. He kept them up here."

Jack followed him up a flight of stairs. Talbot opened a door off the landing. "In here." He pressed the Bakelite light switch.

"My son's legacy." The light from a single bulb hanging from a twisted flex cast a milky glow over the boxes. They were arranged on shelves that covered three of the walls from floor to ceiling. "He spent a lot of his time up here. He was either in here or the darkroom next door when he should have been downstairs helping me in the shop."

Jack stared at the stacks of boxes. Neatly printed on each box was the year in which they had been taken.

"The last year is on the shelf to your right."

Jack located a box labelled 1958 and took it back to the table.

"Switch on the lamp. You'll strain your eyes otherwise."

"Yes, of course." Jack switched on the lamp and groaned inwardly when he saw the hundreds of photographs inside the box. He began to take them out, spreading them on the table.

"I'll leave you to it then. You seem to know what you're looking for."

Jack glanced around at him. "Yes, fine. I'll come down when I've finished."

Jack listened to Talbot's heavy tread on the stairs as he went back downstairs. This could take hours, he thought. He picked up a magnifying glass that was lying beside the lamp and began to search for familiar faces among the many hundreds Benny Talbot had snapped.

CHAPTER 18

SATURDAY

Lewin and Stern, Architects, occupied a modern office in the centre of Welwyn Garden City. Eddie Fuller stood in a spacious foyer dominated by a large model of a modern town centre rendered in white cardboard. Fuller stared at it and decided it was not a place he'd like to live. "Bloody rabbit warren," he muttered under his breath.

"May I help you?" a female voice sounded at his elbow. He turned and found himself face to face with a young and very attractive blonde woman. She looked as if she had just stepped from the pages of Vogue magazine. She wore an elegant navy-blue suit over a crisp white blouse, secured at the collar by a cameo brooch. Her hair was cut in a pageboy style, finished with a blunt fringe above clear blue, smiling eyes.

Fuller returned her smile. "Detective Sergeant Fuller. I telephoned and made an appointment to see Mr Lewin."

The young woman checked her wristwatch. "You're very prompt, Sergeant Fuller."

"I try to be."

She pointed to a pair of leather and chrome easy chairs set either side of a large potted plant. "Take a seat. I'll tell Michael you're here." She flashed him another smile and disappeared through an oak-panelled door.

She returned almost immediately.

"He'll see you now." The smile had gone from her eyes and her demeanour had chilled slightly.

Michael Lewin was in his mid-thirties. He was seated on a high stool before a large drawing board. His face was thin and pointed, and a couple of days' stubble darkened his chin. His hair was curly and flopped over one eye, giving him a rakish look. He brushed it back impatiently and stared at Fuller. "You're not what I was expecting."

"Really?" Fuller said.

"I thought you'd be older, dressed in tweeds with size twelve brogues. You look more like a Teddy boy, not like a policeman at all."

Lewin spoke in an arrogant, slightly sarcastic tone.

Fuller smiled at him blandly. "We come in all shapes and sizes."

Lewin slid off the high stool and sat down behind his desk. "Pull up a chair, and then you can tell me why you want to see me. I hope it won't take long. I'm rather busy."

Fuller sat facing Lewin across the desk. "Anthony Tanner. I believe you were acquainted with him."

"*Were*? Has something happened to him?"

"He was killed on Tuesday evening, sir." Fuller watched Lewin closely. The shock on Michael Lewin's face seemed genuine enough. "Tony's dead?"

Fuller nodded.

"Good God! How?"

"He was murdered."

"Oh, my Christ!"

"Did you know him well, sir?"

Lewin averted his eyes, swallowed loudly and nodded.

"How well?"

"We shared digs when we were at Birmingham rep in our late teens." Lewin swallowed again.

"So you two were friends."

"Very good friends." Lewin opened the desk drawer and took out a packet of cigarettes. He lit one with a red-tipped Swan Vesta match that he struck on the side of the desk. His hand shook as he raised the match.

"And you had no reason to kill him?"

"How dare you! I could never hurt Tony. How dare you even suggest such a thing!"

Fuller held up his hands. "Then perhaps I've been misinformed."

"Yes, you bloody have. Tony Tanner was like a brother to me. We started out in rep together."

"You were an actor then?"

Lewin nodded. "Not much of one, I'll grant you. I didn't have a tenth of Tony's talent. I had the basics, but he carried me. He was always supportive. He encouraged me right up until the time I realised I was never going to make it as an actor. When he got the call from Rank it was a turning point, not only in his career but also in our relationship. He nearly didn't take up their offer. I had to force his hand." He was gazing into the distance, lost in the past.

"And how did you do that?"

He shook his head as if to clear his thoughts. "By quitting the business and moving out of our digs, coming here and retraining. I'd always had an aptitude for design at school. I was pretty good at technical drawing, so it was an obvious choice."

"So there was no ill feeling when you made the decision to quit acting?"

"No. None at all. I came back here to Welwyn and Tony went on to be groomed by Rank and the rest, as they say, is history. Why on earth would someone kill him?"

"That's what we're trying to find out. Did you stay in touch with him when you left the acting profession?"

"Oh . . . birthdays, Christmas, that sort of thing. But we moved in different circles. Our paths rarely crossed, despite both of us living in Hertfordshire, a stone's throw from each other."

"When did you last see him?"

Lewin winced, as if stung by the memory. "At Christmas, actually. Last Christmas. He invited me to spend a few days with him at Elsinore."

"And you haven't seen him since December?"

"No." Lewin ground out his cigarette and lit another. "It wasn't an altogether successful reunion and I was in no rush to repeat it."

"Why was that?"

“I hadn’t seen him for a few years. I’m afraid I’d let things drift somewhat. When we last met he was married to Polly. I knew her from our days at Birmingham and we used to get along famously. She was a lovely girl. Lois, his new wife, was quite a different kettle of fish. She was brash, loud — and a bloody Yank. I clashed with her throughout the holiday. I didn’t like her and she certainly didn’t like me. I think she saw me as some kind of threat. A ghost from Tony’s past, if you like. She made it very plain that I wasn’t welcome.”

“How did he seem to you when you last saw him?”

“What do you mean?”

“Did he seem troubled? Bothered about anything?”

Lewin leaned back in his chair. “He seemed different,” he said after a pause. “But it had been a few years since I’d last seen him and people do change. He’d been through a lot, dealing with Polly’s illness and then her death. Of course he had Geraldine to bring up too. That couldn’t have been easy.” Lewin took a long pull on his cigarette. “But there was something else about him that I’d never seen before. I suppose you could call it melancholia.”

“And how did this *melancholia* show itself?”

“It was Boxing Day morning. He suggested we go for a walk, get some country air. I was happy to get out of the house and away from Lois and her blasted brother. He was also spending the holiday with them, and was just as obnoxious as his sister. Tony asked Geraldine to come along, but she had a piano exam coming up and wanted to practice, so it was just him and me.”

Fuller nodded.

“I had visited Elsinore a number of times in the past when he’d first bought the place with Polly. We set off on a familiar route across the fields, mostly keeping to the paths along the edge. There had been a frost that morning, so the mud had frozen. The path took us through a farm. Tony had christened it ‘Squashed Rat Farm’. They farmed cereal crops, so vermin were a problem.

“We were walking past the grain silos when Tony pointed down at a frozen puddle. Caught in the ice was the flattened body of a rat, preserved like a fly in amber. ‘See that, Mikey,’ he said. He always called me Mikey. ‘See that, Mikey. That’s a pretty good approximation of how I feel at the moment.’ I tried to joke him out of it. I knew Tony could lean towards the melodramatic sometimes — he was an actor after all. But no amount of bantering from me could lift his mood. In the end I gave up and we walked home pretty much in silence.

"I didn't hang around when we got back. Lois and her brother had started on the eggnog and cherry brandy at breakfast. They were both three sheets to the wind and I could tell Lois was spoiling for a fight. I invented a maiden aunt I'd promised to visit, made my excuses and left. And that was the last time I saw him."

Lewin lapsed into silence. There were tears in his eyes.

Fuller stood up. "Just one more thing before I go. Can you account for your whereabouts on Tuesday afternoon?"

Lewin looked at him. "Eh? What?"

"Tuesday afternoon?"

"I was here. Sally will confirm that. Have a word with her on your way out."

"Yes. I'll do that."

Michael Lewin did not kill Tony Tanner. Fuller was absolutely sure of it.

CHAPTER 19

SATURDAY

Jack clasped his fingers behind his neck and stretched. He had just finished going through his third box of photographs and so far they had yielded nothing useful. Jack yawned, took his fourth box and opened it. He sat up straighter. His luck had suddenly got better.

The shots in this box were all taken at night on the Tottenham Court Road. They showed the people going in and out of the Purple Flamingo nightclub. Familiar faces started to appear. Jack knew a couple of them from his rare jaunts to the cinema — Douglas Fairbanks and Judy Garland. There were faces from the world of politics and sport. He was pretty sure one of them was the boxer Freddie Mills.

Jack recognised one face immediately. Hooked nose over a pencil-thin moustache, and dark eyes set in a rugged, swarthy face. Thomas Usher. Well, he did own the club after all. But the blonde woman hanging onto Usher's arm took Jack by surprise.

He put the picture to one side and continued to rifle through the others. Within twenty minutes he had amassed a large pile of ten by eight inch black and white photographs. These would need closer scrutiny under brighter lights than the one in Talbot's room. He ran downstairs.

"I'd like to take these with me, if I may," Jack said to Talbot.

"You can take the bloody lot. They're no damned use to me. I told you, I'm selling up."

"I wouldn't want to deprive you of your son's legacy. Just these will be fine for now. They'll help with a case I'm investigating."

* * *

Jack dropped the photographs onto Fuller's desk. "What do you make of these?"

Fuller leaned back in his chair and started leafing through them. He held up the one showing Thomas Usher leaving the club with a pretty blonde. "That's Lois Tanner."

"Yes, that's what I thought. Obviously taken before her agoraphobia came on."

"Do you know when, exactly?"

"It came from a box of photos marked 1957. I can't be more precise than that, but it must have been before Usher had his stroke."

"She was married to Tony Tanner then. Do you think she was carrying on with Usher?"

"A picture paints a thousand words, as they say. But we can't be sure. All I know is we'll have to dig a little deeper into Lois Tanner's background. See what other skeletons we can unearth."

"When do you want me to start?"

Jack shook his head. "Not you this time, Eddie. I'm putting Myra onto it. She seems to have a nose for this kind of thing."

"But she's not a detective."

"She is in all but name, and more's the pity. But just because she's in uniform it doesn't mean I can't make use of her services."

"The chief super will have kittens when he finds out you're going against his orders."

"Which is why I won't be telling him. Will you?"

Fuller covered his lips with his hand. "Speak no evil, hear no evil, see no evil, that's me."

"Have a word with the others. Make sure they know, but tell them to keep it to themselves. Take a look at the rest of the photos and tell me what you see."

"There are a lot of famous people here," said Fuller.

"Ignore them and look at some of the other faces." He took the boxing photograph from the file and dropped it onto Fuller's desk. "See if you can spot any of these."

After a while Fuller said, "Well, Tony Tanner seems to be a frequent visitor, as does this bloke." He pointed to a man pictured coming out of the club.

"Simon Docherty. Keep looking, there's an interesting one of him with Lois Tanner coming up."

Fuller continued. "This one? It looks like he's holding hands with her. Quite a girl, our Lois, isn't she? Who is Simon Docherty?"

"According to Bob Lock, Mr Docherty is an American lawyer. He retrained to practice law over here and it seems he's represented most of the top criminals, Usher included."

"American, you say? Lois Tanner is a Yank. Perhaps he was her lawyer back in the United States."

"It's a possibility. I'd like you to look into it. In fact, I want to know everything there is to know about our Mr Docherty."

Fuller laid three prints on the desk. "These ones speak volumes."

It was a sequence of shots featuring Thomas Usher. The first had Usher leaving the club with Lois Tanner. The second had two heavy-set men in suits moving across in front of them. In the third photo one of the men was walking across the road towards the camera, his face contorted with aggression. One of his hands was balled into a fist, the other reached out, fingers splayed, to block the shot.

"Looks like Benny Talbot got under someone's skin, doesn't it?" Jack said.

"This bloke looks intent on shutting Benny down. I wonder if that includes throwing him under a bus."

"These photos were some of the last he took. Not long after he took and developed these shots he went under the wheels of the number twenty-nine."

"Is the Purple Flamingo club still there?"

"Yes, it's still there, but I don't know who owns it now."

"But it has no connection to Thomas Usher?"

"Not according to Bob Lock. As far as he knows the place changed hands a year or so back."

"After Usher's stroke."

Jack nodded. "So it would seem. We need to find out who's been looking after Thomas Usher's business interests since he had the stroke. Who, for instance, was behind moving him abroad, and who is paying for the nursing home."

"You think it might be Simon Docherty?"

"I wouldn't be a bit surprised," Jack said. "Not surprised in the least."

* * *

"I'm going to have to start charging you rent, sir," Bob Lock said.

"I have some photos I'd like you to take a look at."

Lock took the sheaf of photographs and looked through them.

"Do you see anyone you recognise?"

"Well, that there is Douglas Fairbanks Junior."

"Ignore the film stars. Focus on the other faces."

Lock smiled and carried on flicking through. "Well, there's Tommy Usher. Hardly surprising seeing as it's *his* club."

He reached the shot of the thug with the fist and the hand out to stop the photographer. "And that's Jimmy Dymond. I'd know his ugly mug anywhere."

"Who's Jimmy Dymond?" Jack said.

"Tommy Usher's muscle. His enforcer. Nasty piece of work. The Met's been after him for years."

"And they haven't been successful?"

"No. He's a slippery one, our Jimmy. He's been arrested more times than I've had cups of tea, but he always seems to wriggle out of the charges. Witnesses either change their stories completely or vanish off the face of the earth. He must either scare them into silence or persuade them to take a holiday — or worse."

"And I should imagine that if Usher's paying, Dymond has a very good lawyer."

"Speaking of whom." Lock took a photo from the pile and laid it down on the desk. "Simon Docherty, Usher's brief."

"Yes, I recognised him from the boxing photograph."

"I'm sure you did . . . but look who he's talking to."

Jack took the picture across to the light bulb hanging from the ceiling and peered at it. He shook his head. "Means nothing to me."

"I suppose it wouldn't really. But that is Isaac Gold, Albert Klein's right-hand man."

"So why would Usher's brief be deep in conversation with one of the head men of a rival firm?"

Lock shrugged. "Search me. But you must admit it's a bit rum. The way they are standing, in the shadows, off the main thoroughfare, hunched in that doorway. It's almost as if they're trying not to be seen together, to hide."

"And then along comes Benny Talbot and takes their photo. 'Say cheese, boys.' It's hardly going to make him popular is it? Klein's right-hand man, Gold, talking with Usher's lawyer."

"You're thinking that Talbot may have had some help falling under the bus. But the witnesses . . ."

"As you said earlier, witnesses can be coerced or threatened into changing their stories."

"So . . . what? Are you delving into Benny Talbot's death now?"

Jack shook his head. "No, I have enough on my plate with Tanner's murder. The Talbot case is closed and besides, it's outside my jurisdiction. The boys down in Met-land won't thank me for raking over their closed cases. I didn't exactly earn many bouquets the last time I had contact with the Met."

"So why the interest?"

"Because the more I dive into the murky waters of London's underworld, the more secrets or unlikely coincidences float to the surface. There's some connection between Tony Tanner's murder and the human flotsam in these photographs. I just haven't found it yet."

"Well, good luck with that. Many before you have tried and failed to get to the bottom of that particular pool."

Jack looked at the old collator bleakly. "It never gets any easier, does it, Bob?"

"You wouldn't want it any other way, sir, would you?"

Jack smiled. "I suppose not. But it would be nice to catch a break once in a while."

"So would having Christmas once a week, but it's not likely to happen, is it?"

"Wise words indeed," said Jack. "This one is a real mystery, Bob. I'll deny saying this, but I'm starting to think I'm barking up the wrong tree."

"Look, leave these with me. Give me a day or so and I'll go through them and compare the faces with those I have on file. I might get a match."

"That would be good."

"I'm not promising anything mind, but you never know. I might get lucky."

Jack selected a few, rolled them up and slipped them into his pocket. "I'll take the ones of the people we've already identified, and leave you the rest to go through at your leisure. Work your magic, Bob."

"Who do you think I am, David bloody Nixon?"

Jack looked at him blankly.

"He's a conjurer, on the telly. Oh, I forgot, you still live in the dark ages. Still listening to the wireless for your evening's entertainment?"

"Not for much longer, apparently. There's been a coup."

* * *

Annie was sitting at the kitchen table with Joan, Rosie and Eric. All of them looked up with expectant faces as Jack walked in. "Did you manage to call in at Howard's this morning, about the television?" Annie said.

"Do you mind if I take my coat off first before subjecting me to the third degree?"

"I'll pour you a cuppa," Joan said.

"I'll fetch your slippers," said Eric, and raced out of the kitchen.

"Do you want your pipe, Dad?" Rosie asked.

"Ye Gods!" Jack shrugged himself out of his overcoat and sat down at the table. He took a mouthful of tea. Eric dropped his slippers at his feet and Rosie handed him his pipe.

Jack took off his shoes, flexing his toes before sliding them into the soft leather of the slippers.

"Pipe, Dad?" Rosie handed him the briar.

"What about you, Annie? What can I expect? A massage, perhaps? Or maybe some grapes peeled for me?"

"I'll scrub your back when you next take a bath if you like." She smiled. "Well? Did you call in at Howard's?"

Jack chuckled. "Yes, I called in there. The television will be here first thing Monday morning. Can you be here to let it in, Joanie?"

"She'll be here, Dad," Eric said.

"I was asking your sister."

"Of course I'll let them in," Joan said. "I've already cleared a space for it in the sitting room."

"Well, you didn't waste any time, did you? What would you have done if I hadn't gone in there this morning?"

"I knew you wouldn't let us down," Joanie said.

"You never let us down, Dad," Rosie echoed.

Jack shook his head. "You all think I'm a pushover, don't you?"

Annie got to her feet, wrapped her arms around his neck and kissed the top of his head. "We *know* you're a pushover, darling, but you're *our* pushover and we love you dearly."

"Food, woman." Jack leaned back into her embrace. "I need my dinner."

"Coming right up, oh lord and master." Annie skipped away to the cooker.

CHAPTER 20

SUNDAY MARCH 22nd, 1959

Rosie poked her head into the greenhouse. "There's someone here to see you, Dad."

Jack was cutting a begonia leaf ready for propagation. He glanced around and nicked his finger with the blade. "Damn!" He stuck the finger into his mouth. "Who is it?"

"He didn't say. He just asked me to give you this." She handed him a folded page from a newspaper.

Jack took it from her and spread it out on the potting table. It was a page from today's *News of the World.*

The headline read, "Tony Tanner and his Scandalous Underworld Links."

Jack scanned the half-page article that followed. There was mention of Thomas Usher and Lois Tanner, along with an inset photograph of Lois as the Cadence Girl, and a head shot of Tanner taken from a theatre programme. As he read down he saw his own name. "Chief Inspector Callum, of Welwyn and Hatfield CID said: 'We have no comment to make regarding these allegations.'"

"This man at the door, is he about thirty, thin-faced, with thick glasses and a protruding Adam's apple?" said Jack, thinking of the reporter who had ambushed him at the station.

"No. He's much older, about your age. He's got red cheeks and his breath smells of drink."

"Okay, I'll come in." Jack followed Rosie into the house, still sucking his finger.

The man standing on the doorstep looked vaguely familiar. "Can I help you?" Jack said.

Charles Somers smiled. He stuck out his hand. "DI Charles Somers. Eddie Fuller's old boss. You can call me Charlie."

Jack took the proffered hand and shook it once. "Well, that was a dramatic way of introducing yourself. You could have just given Rosie your name. It would have worked just as well. Better, in fact. I thought you might have been that reporter chap again. I almost wasn't at home."

"But I wasn't sure it *would* get your attention. I don't know what Eddie has told you about me — and my input into your case. So I thought it was time we met face to face."

"He's told me enough. You could have gone through official channels and come to the station, *during working hours*. I would have seen you."

"You and everyone else, including the cleaner. I wanted our meeting to be a little more discreet. It isn't official."

"Yes, I'm beginning to realise that. I suppose you won't want to be seen hanging around on my doorstep then. You'd better come in. Come through to the front room. We won't be disturbed." Jack ushered Somers inside.

In the front room, Eric was sitting with his head bowed over his guitar, chord charts open on the arm of the chair.

"Can you take your practice upstairs to your room, son?"

"I *was* up there. Joanie told me to come downstairs. She's lying down, *says* she has a headache. It's amazing how many headaches people in this house seem to get since I bought this guitar."

"Well, that must tell you something." Jack smiled indulgently. "Now hop it." He jerked his thumb at the door.

Grumbling, Eric grabbed his guitar and left the room.

"Bright lad," Somers said. "How old?"

"Fourteen. Sees himself as the next Tommy Steele."

"And why not? If it can happen for a cockney sailor like Steele, it can happen for your lad. It didn't sound too bad from where I was standing."

"It seems like any kid with a penny-worth of musical talent can make a record these days."

"You're not a fan of skiffle and rock and roll, then?" Somers said.

"You didn't come here on a Sunday morning to discuss my tastes in music."

Somers smiled. "I can see why you're a detective."

"Take a seat." Jack pointed at the armchair recently vacated by his son. "And then you can tell me the real reason for your visit. Tea?"

Somers' smile widened. "Unless you have something stronger?"

"Tea it is then. Sugar and milk?"

"Milk, no sugar."

"Right. I'll be back in a moment. There're magazines in the rack. Help yourself."

* * *

"Who's your guest, Jack?" Annie sat at the kitchen table peeling potatoes for dinner.

"Eddie's old governor. Charlie Somers."

"What's he doing here on a Sunday?"

Jack poured boiling water into the brown earthenware teapot. "I'll know that once I've made the tea and gone back to the front room. Tell the kids that we're not to be disturbed."

"No worries there. Rosie's just gone out for a walk. Eric's gone upstairs in a huff, and Joanie's lying down with . . ."

"With a headache. Yes, I know. Is she all right?"

"One too many Babychams last night."

"Serves her right then." Jack put cups, saucers, the teapot and a milk jug on a tray and carried it through to the front room.

Somers was sitting in an armchair, legs crossed, reading the article about himself in the *Police Gazette*. "If you'd known I was coming to see you, I'd have said you left this here deliberately."

"I'm not that devious. I was looking at it last night before I went to bed."

"So what do you think?"

"About the article or the facts?"

"Both."

Jack sat down on the sofa and poured the tea. "It read like a fair account. Whether it's true or not, I can't say. I wasn't involved. Met business. I left that behind me a long time ago."

"Do you miss it?"

"Not at all. There's enough crime up here in Hertfordshire to keep me busy."

"Is there anything about London you *do* miss?"

"Tottenham Hotspur. I used to go to every home match, work permitting. When they weren't playing at home, I used to go and watch the reserves. The 'up and comers.'"

"And the 'over the hillers.'"

"Them too, but whoever was playing you usually saw a good game." He handed Somers his tea. "Why have you come to see me, Charlie?"

"Tommy Usher. The photo I sent obviously prompted you to dig a little deeper. Hence . . ." He raised the *Police Gazette.*

"Why did you drop it off anonymously?"

"I wasn't sure how much Eddie had told you about my involvement. I didn't want to get the lad into trouble with you. He's a good'un, is Eddie. He'll go far."

"I agree. But not when he goes behind my back. Then I could happily throttle him."

"Don't be too hard on the lad. He was using his initiative. He knew about my relationship with Usher and exploited it."

"Agreed. Do you think Usher could have been involved with Tanner's murder?"

"No." Somers shook his head. "In his heyday, yes, most definitely, but not now, not since . . ."

"The stroke. The convenient stroke."

"You seem sceptical."

"I am."

"There's no need to be. I have it on good authority that the stroke was real enough."

"So why do you want to talk to me about him?"

Somers uncrossed his legs and sat forward in the armchair. "Usher's firm was large, packed with South London's lowlifes. Has it occurred to you that another member of the firm could be behind Tanner's death?" He paused and swallowed his tea. "When Usher was rendered incapable and couldn't continue, there was a brief period of jockeying for position. Ultimately it came to nothing, and the whole thing imploded. All the members scattered like fleas sprayed with DDT. Good news for us, of course, but over the last few months we've seen factions starting to emerge. Members of the old firm are coming together again. The only thing they lack is a figurehead, a leader to draw all the disparate parties under one banner again."

Jack frowned. "So what has that got to do with Tony Tanner?"

"I understand that Tanner was made up to bear a striking resemblance to Tommy Usher. Perhaps he was being used as a kind of totem, designed to unite the troops."

Jack shook his head. "It's a novel theory, Charlie, but I saw Tanner after his death. His disguise might have been effective on stage, but it wouldn't pass muster close to."

"I'm sure there's a connection to Usher somewhere along the line. It has his mucky fingerprints all over it." Somers sounded bitter.

"Only it hasn't. Not literally anyway. The murder scene was remarkably clean, even down to the nail used to pin him to the tree. Not a print, not even a smudged one. You *want* Usher to be involved, don't you? Because you hate him."

"With a passion."

"And you want me to start investigating Usher because your superiors won't. Am I right?"

"I heard from Brian Fisher that you were good at your job. A pain in the backside, insubordinate, but bloody good at what you do."

"Generous of him." Jack still had a nasty taste in his mouth following his last encounter with Chief Superintendent Brian Fisher.

"I want you to dig deep into Usher's organisation. Expose it for the serpents' nest it is. I'm taking retirement at the end of this year. It would be nice to see the thing finished with before I go."

Jack felt rather sorry for Somers. His theory about Usher's firm might have some validity, but he had enough battles of his own to fight, without taking on somebody else's.

He stood abruptly. He got his briefcase from the hall and took out the sheaf of Benny Talbot's photographs. He handed one to Somers. "Taken outside the Purple Flamingo. Recognise them?"

Somers peered at the photo. "That's Simon Docherty."

"And the other chap?"

Somers angled the photograph into the light coming from the window. "Unless I'm mistaken, that's Isaac Gold. What the hell's Docherty doing with Gold? They're the last people you'd expect to see passing the time of day outside a nightclub owned by one of their bosses."

"From their attitude, they seem to be doing a bit more than passing the time of day."

"I knew Simon Docherty quite well. He used to dance around Tommy Usher like a trained monkey. I thought he was an irritating little sod, but I never said anything. I knew that Usher liked him and I didn't want to upset the apple cart."

"And Isaac Gold?"

"I met him a couple of times but didn't know him well. He has a reputation for cleverness and for being just about as ruthless as Albert Klein when he needs to be." Somers eyed the photographs in Jack's hand. "Have you got any more gems like that?"

Jack handed him the photos. "Take a look. More tea?"

"If I'm not outstaying my welcome."

"I'll put the kettle on."

CHAPTER 21

MONDAY MARCH 23rd, 1959

Jack slid into the car beside Eddie Fuller. "Your old governor came to see me yesterday."

"Charlie Somers came to your house?" Fuller froze for an instant, then started the engine and eased into the traffic. "Why?"

"Don't look so nervous, Eddie. He had nothing but good things to say about you."

Fuller gave an audible sigh of relief.

"Apart from the fact that you're a lousy snooker player. It seems you start well but can't keep it up."

"Cheek! But I know what he means. I'm impatient to get to the end of the frame so I take risks."

"Sometimes it's a good thing. I've been accused of that myself."

"So what did he want?"

"Resolution. The Thomas Usher business isn't over for Charlie Somers. He took the whole internal inquiry thing very badly. He feels his superiors hung him out to dry."

"I tend to agree with him." Fuller turned left into a street lined with trees. "They tasked him to do a job. They told him to get close to Usher and monitor his criminal activities. Then, when he started getting results, those same superiors decided he was too close to the action and branded him a dirty copper." Fuller scowled angrily. "Charlie Somers has more integrity in his little finger than the lot of them between them. Granted, he sometimes skated close to the edge but he never once crossed the line into illegality. Quite a number of Usher's gang went down for long stretches thanks to his willingness to put himself in the firing line." Fuller was now gripping the wheel tightly, his knuckles white.

"Okay, Eddie, simmer down. If it means anything, I liked him. He reminded me of myself."

"You remind me of him too."

"But, I'm not convinced there's a direct link between Thomas Usher and Tony Tanner's murder. We shouldn't blinker ourselves. We still have a number of other avenues we need to check out first. When we get in, tell Myra to come up to my office."

They swung into the police station car park. "You can tell her yourself. There she is." Fuller nodded towards the far side of the car park. "Just getting out of that car."

The dark green Morris Minor appeared to have limped into work. Rust peppered the bodywork in between grey patches of body filler. The offside wing was dented.

"Is that car roadworthy, Officer?" Jack said.

Myra Banks sighed. "Please don't say anything. It was my dad's. He gave it to me when I passed my test last November. It's taken me until now to get it on the road — and to pluck up the courage to drive it. I only picked it up from the garage on Saturday. They did something to the timing. It wouldn't be *my* choice for a first car, but you know what they say about gift horses."

"I also know the one that goes, 'Beware of Greeks bearing gifts.' He's not Greek, is he, your dad?"

"Welsh actually." Myra grinned. "Was there something you wanted, sir?"

"Yes, Myra, there is. Come up to my office. I have a job for you."

* * *

"I want you to find out everything you can about Lois Tanner *née* Franklin." Jack said to Myra when they were seated in his office.

"Everything?"

"Everything. There's more to that woman than meets the eye. See if you can find out from her doctor when this condition of hers, the agoraphobia, started." He handed Myra the photograph of Lois leaving the Purple Flamingo on the arm of Thomas Usher. "That was taken nearly eighteen months ago, and obviously being out and about didn't bother her too much then."

Myra stared at the picture. "But at that time she was married to Tony Tanner, and she and Usher look like they are more than just friends."

"Exactly, and that's another thing I want you to find out. How solid was their marriage? Go and have a chat with Hester Gough at Elsinore. Have a quiet word with the neighbours. Anybody at all, for that matter, who might have known them."

"Will do. But I wouldn't bank on me getting anything out of Lois's doctor. When I spoke to Francombe on Wednesday he was reluctant to tell me anything at all, claiming confidentiality."

"Well, do what you can. You have a way of winkling things out of people."

Myra tilted her head. "Should I take that as a compliment?"

"I should. They don't come along very often. When they do, you have to grab them with both hands."

* * *

Jack stepped into Bob Lock's grotto.

"I need to interview Albert Klein."

"Why don't you send for him?"

Jack shook his head. "I want it to be a less formal meeting."

"Visit him at home then. He has a house in Hampstead. Bishops Avenue. Quite a pile, I believe."

Jack held out his hand. Lock would have the address. Of course he would.

Lock scribbled down the address. "Do you know it?"

"I know Hampstead. I shouldn't have too much trouble tracking it down."

Back in his office Jack told Fuller that he would be out for the rest of the morning.

"Do you need me?"

Jack automatically shook his head and then stopped. "On second thoughts, yes. Come along. I don't know what kind of reception I'll get, so it won't do any harm if two of us turn up on his doorstep."

* * *

The drive to Hampstead in the Monday morning traffic was incident-free and, fifty minutes later Fuller swung the Wolseley in through the gates of the Bishops Avenue house. "And they say crime doesn't pay," he said. They drove past verdant lawns and stately poplar trees up to a huge detached house built from yellow brick. "There's probably a swimming pool in the back garden."

"I wouldn't be at all surprised. Ah, it looks like we've got a welcoming committee."

The front door of the house was open. Three men stood in the doorway, one slightly in front. Fuller recognised Isaac Gold. The other two were both heavy-set and had hard, brutal faces. Sensing potential trouble Fuller took out his warrant card and brandished it as he took a step towards them. "Detective Sergeant Fuller. This is Chief Inspector Callum. We'd like to see Albert Klein."

Gold stepped down and studied Fuller's warrant card intently. "Hampstead is a little outside your jurisdiction, isn't it?" The mellifluous, almost singsong voice contrasted sharply with his narrow eyes and menacing gaze.

Jack stepped forward and showed the man his warrant card. "We'd like to speak with Mr Klein regarding one of our cases." He smiled benignly. "For background information only."

Gold studied Jack's card and stared at him. He didn't seem very impressed with what he saw. Finally he bowed his head slightly. "I'll ascertain whether Mr Klein will be able to see you." He went back inside, leaving Jack, Fuller and the two thugs to their staring contest. Gold came back a few moments later.

"Mr Klein has agreed to see you." Gold appeared to be disappointed at this. "You have ten minutes. Follow me."

Inside, Albert Klein's house was every bit as impressive as the exterior suggested. The entrance hall was decorated in a deep red, embossed wall-covering hung with framed watercolours of hunting scenes. The doors leading off from it were oak, polished to a rich lustre. I'll bet the carpet's Persian, thought Jack.

Gold led them into a vast room with a high glass roof. The walls were given over to expansive picture windows that maximised the light from outside. "There's your pool," Jack said quietly to Fuller.

Their footsteps echoed on white ceramic tiles that surrounded a large swimming pool. A heat haze shimmered above the blue water, and they stood watching as the sole occupant swam with easy, effortless strokes towards the stainless steel ladder closest to them.

The man who emerged from the water had a well-muscled body, tanned and gleaming. He was completely bald. Albert Klein was a good-looking man in his forties with bright blue eyes. "Don't fuss, Isaac. I can dry myself," he snapped as Gold draped a white towelling robe around his shoulders and patted his bald pate with a hand towel. Gold stepped back deferentially and handed Klein the towel.

Glancing at Jack and Fuller, Klein made his way to a small marble-topped table in the corner of the poolroom.

"Won't you join me, gentlemen?" Klein sat down at the table and pulled a cigar from a brown leather case. Gold was immediately ready with a cigar lighter. "Isaac tells me you're investigating a crime in your area. Hertfordshire?"

"Letchworth Garden City." Fuller took the lead.

"Don't know it. Is it nice in that neck of the woods?"

"Green. Very green."

Klein puffed at the cigar. "So, what's the crime?"

"Murder. An actor was murdered. Tony Tanner. You might know him."

"No. Never heard of him." He turned to Isaac Gold, who was hovering in the background. "Have you heard of him, Isaac, this actor Tony Tanner? Does the name mean anything to you?"

"Means nothing to me," said Gold.

Klein gave an exaggerated shrug. "Well, there you are, gentlemen. It seems you've had a wasted trip.

Jack said, "One of our lines of inquiry has taken us in the direction of Thomas Usher. I'm sure you're familiar with that name."

A slight smile hovered about Klein's lips. "You seriously have old Tommy in the frame for this? You know he had a stroke a while back, don't you?"

"We were aware of that."

"Then forgive me for saying so, gentlemen, but you seem to barking up the wrong tree." Klein got to his feet. "Now, if you'll excuse me I have to go and put some clothes on. I have a business meeting in a little while. We'll continue this shortly."

Before they could respond, Klein disappeared into a small dressing room, followed closely by Gold who turned and closed the door behind them.

Fuller gave a low whistle. "Well, he's a cool customer. Do you think he's right? About barking up the wrong tree?"

Jack was staring into the depths of the swimming pool.

"Sir?" Fuller said.

Jack seemed to shake himself. "Yes. Probably. I don't know."

"Is something wrong?"

"Something's nagging away at the back of my mind. I know him from somewhere. I'm sure I've met Klein before but I just can't place where."

"Hardly a surprise. You've crossed swords with lots of villains in your time."

"But none as wealthy as this."

They lapsed into silence, the only noise the steady hum of the swimming pool pump and the occasional gushing sound as the inlet valves opened and allowed warm water in from the heater.

Eventually the changing room door opened and Gold stepped out, the robe and towel draped over his arm, wet trunks clasped in his fist. He walked past them and disappeared into the house.

Finally Klein emerged. He was dressed casually in a pink jumper over grey slacks and white canvas deck shoes. He had covered his bald head with a blond wig that transformed his face, softening the hard features.

Jack stared at him as he approached and let out a breath. "Albie Small!" he said almost to himself as recognition finally dawned.

CHAPTER 22

MONDAY

"I wondered when the penny would finally drop." Klein smiled.

"You two know each other?" Fuller said.

"They say in the nick that you never forget the first copper to feel your collar. Your chief inspector here was the first rozzer to arrest me. That's right, isn't it, Mr Callum?" Klein said.

Jack nodded. "You've done all right for yourself since those days, Albie."

"Albert now, Mr Callum. Albie Small was a skinny little runt from Ponders End. A world away from all this."

"You changed your surname too," Fuller said.

"Not legally. Klein was always my family name, but in the England of the twenties and thirties, it was not a good thing to be seen as Jewish. Those were the days of Oswald Mosley and his fascist blackshirts, Sergeant. My father owned a tailor's shop in Palmers Green, and the blackshirts would come around regularly and smash it up — and him. When they firebombed it my mum decided enough was enough and persuaded the old man to sell up and move. That's how we ended up in Ponders End. Not the most salubrious area of North London, but a damned sight safer for us than Palmers Green. We changed our name from Klein to Small and dad started a business working from home. The blackshirts didn't bother us again."

"So why didn't you follow your father into the trade? Instead of becoming a hoodlum?" Jack said.

"Because I saw what tailoring did to him. He had a curved spine from hours spent hunched over some garment he was stitching. His hands were crippled with arthritis and his eyesight was pretty much shot by the time he was forty. No." He shook his head. "Not for me. I wanted better out of life."

"And so you became a petty thief."

Klein smiled at Jack. "Fair play. That's what I was when you first collared me. But I seem to remember you used to wear blue serge with three stripes on your arm, and look at you now. We move on. Adolf Hitler changed my life."

Jack's eyes narrowed. "He changed a lot of peoples' lives. For the worse."

"Mine changed all right when a Nazi stick grenade landed in my Jeep and blew it to hell. I was invalided out of the army and sent home. For me the war was over. I was in hospital for the best part of six months while they patched me up, and they did a bloody good job of it. Most of the scars have disappeared now, but my insides were a mess and I'm still on daily medication. The hair never grew back. Alopecia they said, brought on by the stress of the explosion and the resulting injuries. But wartime Britain was a land of endless opportunity for those with an eye for an easy profit."

"You became a black marketeer," said Jack.

"An entrepreneur."

"*Entrepreneur*?" Jack said.

"Sour grapes, Chief Inspector? Surely not. But Judaism changed me and helped me get my life back on track." He paused. "Ah, I can see you are sceptical. Shame. Let me try to convince you."

"In a moment, perhaps." Jack took out the photograph of Isaac Gold and Simon Docherty taken outside the Purple Flamingo and laid it down on the table.

Klein picked it up. "Why are you showing me this?"

Jack pointed to one of the figures in the photograph. "That's your man, Isaac Gold?"

"Yes, that's Isaac. I don't know who the other fellow is though."

"His name is Simon Docherty, legal advisor to Thomas Usher. The picture was taken outside Usher's nightclub on the Tottenham Court Road. I was just wondering why your man was having what appears to be a deep conversation with the brief of one of your business rivals."

Klein dropped the photograph back on the table. "Isaac's not *my* man. I'm sure he had his reasons. Whoever he decides to converse with is entirely his own business. It has nothing to do with me, and certainly has nothing to do with the police."

"I was given that photograph by the father of the young man who took it. He's a Jewish businessman like yourself, who is mourning the death of his photographer son. That son died under the wheels of a bus right where the photograph was taken."

"Fate can be a swine sometimes. I hope you're not suggesting that this has anything to do with me."

Jack smiled at him easily. "Not at all. His death was deemed an unfortunate accident. It's just me, the way I work. I'm trying to tie all the strands of this case together. You said that we appear to be barking up the wrong tree, but trees have branches, and I'm following them all. Strangely enough, they all appear to lead to Usher's business, or yours."

"A conundrum indeed," Klein said. Isaac Gold walked into the poolroom. "Ah, here's Isaac now. Show him your photograph. Perhaps he can shed some light on it. Isaac, if you could spare a minute?" Klein said.

Gold came over to the table.

"The chief inspector here has a photograph he'd like you to take a look at."

Gold looked at the photograph. "That's me. When was it taken? Some time ago, I'd guess. I haven't worn that suit in over a year. I ripped the pocket and never got it repaired."

"You should let me take a look at it, Isaac. I could probably fix it for you. Invisible mending was one of my father's specialities," Klein said.

"It was taken about eighteen months ago, outside the Purple Flamingo on the Tottenham Court Road," said Jack.

"It's that nightclub Tommy Usher used to own," Klein said. "And apparently that's Usher's brief you're talking with."

Gold shrugged. "Well, I'd hardly call it talking. He was just asking me the time. I thought he was one of the club's customers, so I obliged."

"And there was nothing more to it than that?" Klein said.

"No."

"Well, that clears that up then. Happenstance, Mr Callum. It has brought you all the way over to Hampstead from the *very* green environs of Hertfordshire on a wild goose chase. I wouldn't want your job, Chief Inspector. It seems a very frustrating, unrewarding occupation to me."

"Someone has to do it. Thank you for your time, Albie." Jack walked to the door. "Just out of interest, where were you last Tuesday afternoon?"

"Oh, that's easy. I was at my uncle's house in Highgate, sitting Shiva for his wife, aunt Miriam, who died on Monday."

"My condolences."

"If you need that corroborated, Jacob Bloom, *Rabbi* Bloom, was also there. He works out of the Golders Green synagogue. Or I can give you the names of the other mourners if you need more."

"That won't be necessary. Goodbye."

"But don't you want the grand tour of the house and grounds? It's not often I get the chance to show off."

"Maybe next time I come to see you."

Klein smiled and shook his head. "Oh, I doubt there will be a next time, Mr Callum. I doubt that very much. Good day."

Jack and Fuller made their way out to the Wolseley.

"Would you mind telling me what that achieved?" Fuller said.

"It was an itch that needed scratching."

"And that's all?"

"For the time being, Sergeant."

Fuller shook his head and started the car.

* * *

Myra Banks picked up the phone and called down to Elaine Simmons on the switchboard. "Elaine, could you get me Northrop Chemicals?"

"Give me one moment," Elaine was a forty-eight-year-old spinster with a motherly bosom. Her naturally happy disposition was infectious and the sound of her voice made everyone smile.

She was a surrogate mother to all the younger officers at the station, Myra included. She was totally reliable, and provided a discreet shoulder to cry on. "I have the number, Myra love. Would you like me to me to put you through?"

"If you would, Elaine, thanks."

"Do you want to go to the Two Brewers for a drink on Thursday? There's a few of us going. It's my birthday."

"I wouldn't miss it."

"Lovely. Connecting you now."

The switchboard operator at Northrop Chemicals was polite but had none of Elaine's warmth.

"I'd like to speak to the person in charge of advertising," Myra said. "Whoever was responsible for the Cadence campaign a few years ago."

"I'll put you through to our marketing director. Who shall I say is calling?"

Myra introduced herself and the operator put her through.

"Stephen Sullivan, Marketing."

"Hello, Mr Sullivan. This is WPC Banks of the Welwyn and Hatfield police. I'm trying to get some information regarding Lois Franklin, your Cadence Girl."

"Ah yes, a very successful advertising campaign. I think I can take much of the credit for making Miss Franklin such a success. Lois had the perfect face, you see. It called out from the adverts. Beautiful, beguiling and yet no threat to the women our products were aimed at. I like to think that they could see themselves in Lois."

Well, I didn't, Myra thought, and I used Cadence.

"What can you tell me about Lois Franklin?" she said.

There was a pause.

"Mr Sullivan?"

"Sorry. I was just trying to remember. You see I didn't really get to know her that well. We had dinner a couple of times after the photo shoots, but they were very much group affairs. All I really know about Lois is that she was an American and very beautiful. Of course, like everyone else, I read in the papers about her sordid little affair with that actor chappie. We changed our marketing strategy as soon as the story hit the dailies." He laughed softly. "Not good for business, as you can imagine."

"I can indeed. So you can't tell me much about her?"

"Sorry. We engaged her through an agency. They would be the people to ask."

"And can you tell me which agency that would be?"

"Zoom."

"Pardon?"

"Sorry. The 'Zoom' Modelling Agency. It's based in London and pretty exclusive. I think all the girls we've used in our campaigns have come through them."

"Could you give me their address and telephone number?"

"Of course." There was another slight pause accompanied by the sound of shuffling paper. "Do you have a pen?"

* * *

Myra dialled the number Sullivan had given her.

"Hullo?" The woman who answered had a voice like cut glass.

"Hello," Myra said cheerily. "Is that the Zoom Modelling Agency?"

"It is. How may I help you?" Myra imagined a glacial blonde with a condescending manner.

"I need some information about one of your models. Lois Tanner, though you probably have her on your books as Lois Franklin, the 'Cadence Girl.'"

The voice's temperature dropped further. "I'm afraid Miss Franklin is no longer on our books."

"No, I didn't think she would be. I need any information you can give me about her."

"Who is this?" The voice was now sub-zero.

"WPC Myra Banks. I'm with the Welwyn and Hatfield Police."

Myra heard the mouthpiece being covered and the muted murmur of voices. Suddenly a man's voice rang out like a pistol shot.

"Who is this again?" Educated, perfect enunciation.

Myra repeated her name.

"How do I know you are who you say you are?"

"I assure you—"

"Assurances mean nothing. Where is the proof? I know the way Fleet Street works. For all I know, you could be a reporter, trawling for a juicy bit of scandal."

"I can you give you the station's number. Then you can ring me back here."

"Again it proves nothing. You could give me any old number, with another hack on the end of the line. No. As you were informed, Miss Franklin is no longer with us, but I still have a duty to respect her privacy."

"Who am *I* talking to?" Myra said.

"Cedric Bannister. I own the Zoom Agency."

"Mr Bannister, I really need the information. It's regarding an investigation I'm working on. A *murder* investigation."

There was a slight pause and then Bannister said, "If you are who you say you are, then you need to prove it. In person."

"You want me to come up to London?"

"Precisely. And bring identification with you. Do that and I'll see what I can do to help you."

Myra sighed inwardly. "I'll be with you first thing tomorrow."

"Very well. You know where we are? Holborn Viaduct?"

"I have your address."

"Then I'll expect to see you in the morning. Good day."

Myra shook her head in disbelief and replaced the receiver.

CHAPTER 23

MONDAY

"Have you been in touch with Simon Docherty yet, Frank?"

Lesser spun round in his seat as Jack came into the squad room. "Not yet, guv."

Jack frowned. "How hard can it be to track down a solicitor? Criminals manage it, why can't you?"

"It's been nigh on impossible. Brick walls at every turn. I phoned his office in Belgravia and they say they haven't seen him since the middle of last week. They wouldn't give me his home address. They got very snooty about it, even when I told them I was police and I needed his help in a murder investigation."

"He must be in the telephone directory."

"You would think. But other than his office number I can't find him. It's the same story with the Law Society. They'll let me have the Belgravia address, but won't divulge any personal details."

Jack sat down at his desk and opened the case file. "Have you tried Bob Lock? He might have Docherty's home address on file somewhere."

"I did and he hasn't."

"Give me the number for the Belgravia office. *I'll* call them and give them a rocket. Their reluctance to give us what we need is interfering with an ongoing police investigation. We can't have that."

Jack dialled the number.

"Good day, this is Chief Inspector Callum of the Welwyn and Hatfield Police. I need to speak with Simon Docherty. It's a matter of great urgency."

"I'm afraid Mr Docherty is not in the office at the moment." The woman had a soft Belgravia drawl. "If you leave me your telephone number, I will make sure Mr Docherty calls you as soon as he comes in."

"Can you tell me when that's likely to be?"

"I'm afraid I can't."

"Who am I speaking to?" Jack's voice took on a harder edge.

"This is Sara Gibson, Mr Docherty's secretary."

"Well, Miss Gibson. When Detective Sergeant Lesser called you earlier today, he made it quite clear that this concerns a murder investigation. Not being able to speak with Mr Docherty is seriously hampering our inquiries. So please be good enough to give me his home address."

"I really am not at liberty to disclose that."

"Miss Gibson, what part of 'murder investigation' did you fail to comprehend? I must inform you that the *modus operandi* of the killer in this case is particularly brutal. We have reason to believe that he has targeted Mr Docherty. We are gravely concerned by the fact that he hasn't been in the office since the middle of last week. So, his home address if you please."

"Simon could be a target? His life could be in danger?"

"It's a chance I'm not willing to take. Nor, I imagine, are you."

There was a pause, and then she said, "Do you have a pen?"

* * *

"Docherty lives in St Albans. Number thirteen, Devon Street."

"I didn't realise Docherty's life was in danger." Lesser said.

Jack smiled. "As far as I'm aware, it's not, but his secretary doesn't know that, does she?"

"Very cunning, sir."

"It's called good police work, Frank, or bending the truth to achieve the result you want. They don't teach it at Hendon, but I've found it works quite well. Sergeant Fuller and I will now go and pay Mr Simon Docherty a visit."

Fuller came into the office carrying an enamel mug.

"No time for tea, Eddie. We're going to St Albans to speak to Simon Docherty."

Fuller muttered an oath under his breath. He put the mug down on Frank Lesser's desk. "A cuppa for you, Frank."

"You're too kind." Lesser picked it up and took a swig, then spat the tea back into the mug. "Hey! There's sugar in this."

"Beggars can't be choosers, Frank." Fuller whistled cheerfully as he walked out.

* * *

"Sir. Excuse me, sir." Myra ran across the station foyer.

Jack paused as he was about to push through the doors and follow Fuller out into the car park. "What is it, WPC Banks?"

"Nearly missed you, sir. I've managed to locate the modelling agency that Lois Tanner worked through."

"Splendid. What information did you glean from them?"

"That's just it, sir." Myra shifted her weight from foot to foot.

"Go on, girl, spit it out. What have you found out?"

"Nothing. They won't speak to me unless I can prove I am who I say I am. They want me to go there in person. They won't talk to me until they see I'm not a reporter trying to rake up some muck on their ex-client."

Jack took off his hat and ran a hand through his hair. "Where is this agency?"

"London, sir. It's called the Zoom Modelling Agency. They're based in Holborn Viaduct."

"So you have to trek all the way to Holborn, just so they can see you're a policewoman asking genuine questions?"

"That's about the long and the short of it, sir. The man who runs the agency, a Mr Cedric Bannister, is the suspicious type. I wouldn't be surprised if he's been *had* before."

"There's no trust in this world anymore, Myra."

"Yes, sir. I said I'd go up there tomorrow."

His eyes narrowed. "Did you indeed?"

"I thought you'd want to know whatever they can tell me."

He suppressed a smile. "Yes, I do. Fair enough. Go up there by train in the morning. Get a receipt for the fare and let me have it. I'll see that you're reimbursed. Come and see me when you get back and tell me everything they said."

"Very good, sir."

Jack pushed open the doors. "Oh, and Myra?"

"Yes, sir?"

"Good work."

"Yes, sir. Thank you, sir."

* * *

"You did yourself no harm there," Andy Brewer said from the desk as the doors closed behind Jack.

"I wasn't sure he'd allow me to go."

Brewer laughed. "Are you pulling my leg? Everyone knows you're Jack Callum's favourite. He was never going to say no."

"Now you're pulling *my* leg. I'm nothing special. Just an ordinary WPC doing my job, that's me."

"That's not what they're saying in the canteen," Brewer muttered. Myra heard him.

"Just what are they saying in the canteen, Sergeant Brewer?"

"Come on, Myra love, don't play the innocent. You've got our chief inspector wrapped around your little finger, or as my old dad used to say, you've got him on a piece of string. You tug it and he jumps. I should remind you, Constable, that he's a married man."

"What are you implying, Sergeant?"

"I'm only repeating what I've heard. You can play coy all you like, but you work in a police station, for heaven's sake. Everyone around here is well used to uncovering dirty little secrets. You can't pull the wool over their eyes."

Myra felt the implication like a kick in the stomach. It took her breath away and hot tears sprang to her eyes. She clenched her fists, digging her fingernails into the heels of her hands, trying to keep the tears from running down her cheeks.

"I don't know what gossip you've heard, Sergeant Brewer," she said, fighting to keep her voice even. "But, I assure you, you are wrong. You are all wrong. DCI Callum treats me the same as any other police constable."

"If you believe that, girl, you'll believe anything."

Myra flushed and walked quickly from the foyer.

But I do believe that, she thought. Really I do. Andy Brewer's comments, and the knowing wink he gave her, had upset her more than she would have imagined possible. Worse, they had unearthed thoughts that she had been trying to bury for months.

* * *

"Hello, Myra. What brings you to my humble abode?" Elaine Simmons said. Elaine was alone in the Dispatch room, apart from an older woman called Esther who had headphones covering her ears as she spoke softly into a microphone mounted in front of her.

"Are you all right, love?" Elaine said.

Myra glanced at Esther.

"Pay her no mind. She's calling her husband. She thinks I don't know. She'll be another half an hour yet."

"Can we go somewhere to talk? I need to ask you something. In private."

Elaine smiled at Myra indulgently. "Of course. It can't wait until we go for our drink tomorrow? I suppose that won't be very private though, will it?"

Myra could not keep the desperation out of her voice when she spoke. "Please?"

"Okay, love. Let's go to the Ladies. We should be private enough in there."

The small lavatory smelt of disinfectant. There were just three stalls and Elaine pushed open all three doors to make sure they were empty and then she turned to Myra. "Okay, pet. What's the problem?"

Now she was here, Myra felt tongue-tied and foolish. She cleared her throat. "I . . . I don't know where to start," she began. Then her tears began to flow. "I'm sorry."

"Hey now." Elaine wrapped a motherly arm around Myra's shoulders and hugged her. "Whatever's wrong?"

Myra sniffed. "I'm just being stupid."

"Let me be the judge of that."

"All right. You take your lunch in the canteen, don't you?"

"Most days. It gets me away from the phones and the radio for an hour."

"Have you heard any gossip? About me?"

Elaine pulled away slightly.

"You have, haven't you?"

Elaine sighed. "You know what men are like when they all get together. You just have to take no notice of them."

"But none of it's true, Elaine! DCI Callum is just my boss. I can't help it if he gives me interesting stuff to do."

"Stuff the other PCs would give their eye teeth for. I'm afraid that Jack Callum's preferential treatment of you has put a few people's noses out of joint. I'm sure that wasn't his intention, but it has ruffled a few feathers."

"But that's not my fault. I never asked to be treated any differently to anyone else."

"But it doesn't alter the fact that he does treat you differently. People are beginning to resent it, and when the resentment sets in, those same people start to ask why."

"There's nothing like that going on between us, Elaine. You must believe that."

Elaine chuckled. "Oh, I do, love. I've known Jack Callum for years and he's a straight arrow. He's a loving husband and a committed family man. He wouldn't be interested in a slip of a girl like you, no matter how pretty you are. Lord knows, you're not that much older than Joan, his eldest daughter."

"So how do I convince the others and stop the gossip?"

"Ah, there you have me. I really can't say. Once rumours start circulating, it's hard to know how to stop them without fanning the fires that give them life. Best just to let them smoulder for a while. Deprive them of oxygen and eventually they'll burn themselves out."

"And until they do?"

"Keep your head down and work diligently. Show the gossips in the canteen that you've earned the special treatment you're shown with hard work and nothing more. Show them that you are simply good at your job. Once they realise that, the rumours will stop."

"I hope you're right."

"And if they come to me with their rubbish, I'll tell them straight out what I think of their tall tales."

"You'd do that, Elaine?"

"As long as I'm sure there's no truth to them. But I have seen the way you look at him sometimes, when you think he isn't looking. Not that I blame you. Jack Callum's a very attractive, *older* man."

"Oh, hell! Am I that obvious?" Myra said.

Elaine smiled. "I'm afraid so."

"Damn!"

"Well, I'd better get back to the phones. Esther's probably still on with her hubby and something important might come up."

"Thank you, Elaine."

"Any time, dear. And don't forget about drinks tomorrow."

Myra washed her face and then stared at herself in the mirror above the sink. "Get a grip, Myra," she said.

CHAPTER 24

MONDAY

They parked beside a row of well-kept Edwardian cottages. Devon Street was half a mile from St Albans city centre.

"There's money here," Eddie Fuller said. "I couldn't afford anything like this on my wages."

"You want to think about promotion, Eddie. I'm sure you could make inspector easily." Jack climbed out of the car.

"I'm taking the exams this October."

Jack turned to look at him sharply. "You kept that bloody quiet."

"I've been swotting up for weeks now."

"Why haven't you mentioned it before? I could have given you a few pointers."

"I didn't want to get anyone's expectations up."

"Meaning mine?"

"Yours, and the rest of the station. I already get enough stick from Frank Lesser without giving him more ammunition."

"It will be a different story if you make inspector." Jack walked across the street and stood outside number thirteen. "If you get the promotion do you think you'll stay at Welwyn, or will you be looking to move further afield?"

"I haven't decided yet. It depends on whether there's a place for me at the nick. I quite fancy the Met. Life in the big city has a certain appeal."

"And some very large drawbacks. I'd be sorry to see you go, Eddie."

Fuller stared up at the cottage. All the windows were closed, the curtains pulled tightly shut. "It doesn't look like there's anyone in." He pressed the brass bell. A ringing sounded deep within the cottage.

They waited. Fuller pressed the doorbell again.

Jack put his ear to the door. "We're wasting our time. Docherty's not here."

"Either that, or he's seen who it is and he's not answering."

Further along the street an elderly road sweeper had parked his cart and was pushing his broom along the gutter, whistling tunelessly to himself. Jack went across to him. "Is this street part of your regular route?"

The road sweeper looked at him with rheumy eyes and rubbed at the stubble on his chin. "Depends who's asking." His voice rasped like two sheets of sandpaper being rubbed together. He hawked and spat a gob of phlegm onto the street at Jack's feet.

"Police," he said. "Now please could you answer the question."

Fear and cunning jostled for position in the old man's eyes. "It might be."

"Well, is it or isn't it, man? The question is simple enough." Jack was more impatient than he normally would be. He wasn't sure if this was irritation at the road sweeper's contrariness, or the fact that he'd been blindsided by his sergeant's bombshell.

"Come on, soldier." Fuller added. "Just give the man a straight answer."

"I was at El Alamein, you know. Eighth Army. Served under Monty himself. Took a bullet that shattered my leg bone. Shovelling up other people's rubbish is all I'm good for now."

Jack noticed the two medals hanging from the old man's coat. The metal was tarnished and the ribbons threadbare. He softened. "That's the Africa Star, isn't it?"

The old man straightened up. "It is."

"I got my star in Burma."

"What rank were you?"

"Captain."

The road sweeper saluted. "Lance corporal, sir."

"So, is this your regular route, Lance Corporal?"

"Yes, sir."

"And number thirteen over there. Have you seen the man who lives there?"

"Yes, sir. I've seen him. Saw him last Wednesday morning, getting into a taxi with a suitcase. Haven't seen him since. He looked shifty to me. Kept looking up and down the street. He paid no mind to me though. I doubt he even saw me. Invisible I am, these days."

"You're sure it was last Wednesday?"

"I always do Devon Street Mondays and Wednesdays. It wasn't Monday, so I'm sure."

"Well, thank you, Lance Corporal . . ."

"Rogers, sir. Lance Corporal Ernie Rogers."

"I don't suppose you heard the address he gave the driver?"

"He was a bit too far away. My ears aren't what they were when I was in service, sir."

"Never mind. It was very observant of you anyway. You've been a great help." Jack proffered his hand and when the old man took it he pressed a folded ten-shilling note into Rogers's palm.

The old man raised himself to his full height and saluted smartly. "Happy to oblige, sir!"

Jack returned the salute. They went back to the car. Fuller started the engine.

"Tony Tanner is killed on Tuesday afternoon. On the Wednesday morning Simon Docherty takes a taxi to an unknown destination and hasn't been seen since. Coincidence? I think not." Jack drummed his fingers on the dashboard. "What are we missing, Eddie?"

"Do you think you could have been right when you told Docherty's secretary that he might be the killer's next target?"

"Or was Docherty himself the killer?"

"Shall I take you home? It's after five," said Fuller.

"Drop me at the station and then get off yourself. We'll start again tomorrow. I can't shake the feeling that this one is getting away from us."

* * *

When Jack got back to the station, Henry Lane was waiting for him. "It's been a week now, Jack. Tell me you're making some serious progress on the Tanner case. Are you expecting to make an arrest soon?"

"We're making progress, sir. I've just come back from trying to interview Simon Docherty, Thomas Usher's brief."

"You say 'trying' to interview Docherty. I take it things didn't go so well."

"He's done a flit, sir. Moved out of his place in St Albans last Wednesday morning, heading for destinations unknown."

"That's not so clever, Jack. It can't be a coincidence that Docherty disappears the day after Tanner's murdered."

"My thoughts exactly."

Lane glanced at his watch. "Ah well, I just needed to be brought up to date. I'm having dinner with the assistant chief constable tonight. He's bound to ask how the investigation is progressing."

"Tell him that we're following significant leads then, sir. That would be a good bone to throw him."

"ACC Hazelhurst is not a dog, Chief Inspector."

"No, sir."

"But it's a good enough line to keep him off my back for a day or so. Oh, and next time you decide to give an interview to the press, don't. Leave that to me. Some of us have a knack for that kind of thing and some of us don't. I'd put you very much in the latter category."

"Yes, sir. Not my forte I'm afraid."

"Quite."

Immediately after Lane left the office someone rapped on the door. "What now?" Jack grumbled.

Bob Lock came into the office.

"Yes, Bob?"

"Just call me David Nixon." The collator smiled and laid a photograph on the blotter in front of him.

The photograph showed two men stepping out from the Purple Flamingo. Both men wore their black hair in crew cuts and were dressed in almost identical expensive-looking black suits and smart white shirts with dark ties.

"Who am I looking at here, Bob?"

"Those two are the O'Brien brothers, Fergus and Connor."

Jack stared at the photograph. "Sorry, the names mean nothing to me. What are they? Irish?"

"Irish American, from the Bronx in New York. They're the sons of Padraig, head of the O'Brien family, one of most notorious crime families on the East Coast of America."

"How did you recognise them?"

"I looked at the photo again and their faces set bells ringing in the back of my mind. I knew I'd seen them before, but just couldn't place them. It's taken me until today to finally solve it." He pointed to a chair by the desk. "May I?"

"Please do."

Lock sat down. "Every month or so Scotland Yard send out notifications to regional stations if there's a person or persons of interest they want us to be on the lookout for. Normally I give them a quick once over and file them away for future reference." He laid out a sheet of paper on the desk. "I had this filed under the wrong heading. I had it under 'undesirable aliens', instead of 'foreign villains we'd very much like to get our hands on.'"

Jack picked up the sheet of paper and stared at it. There were two separate mug shots. Official photos taken of the two men at the time of their arrest by the New York police department. Both men were photographed holding cards with their names printed on them. Neither looked happy.

Lock produced another piece of paper and glanced at it. "Those snaps were taken at the time of the brothers' arrest for a punch up at an Irish bar in Brooklyn. They were arrested but never charged. Insufficient evidence, apparently. New York's finest provided Scotland Yard with a comprehensive record of the O'Briens' suspected crimes. It makes for interesting reading. The family has its fingers in every type of illegal activity — murder, racketeering, bootlegging, prostitution, narcotics. You'd be hard pressed to find something dodgy they're not involved in."

"So why did the New York police tell the Met about them? Surely the O'Briens are very much their problem."

"They were tipping Scotland Yard the wink. Apparently rumours had been circulating for some time that the family were looking to expand their criminal empire. Specifically, they were looking to expand it over here. This photograph shows that the intelligence they provided was pretty spot on. Have another look at it. Use your glass."

Jack picked up his magnifying glass and scrutinised the photograph.

"Do you see? Who's that coming out of the club behind the brothers?"

"That's Isaac Gold. Klein's man."

"And if you look closer, who's just behind him? You have to look closely as his face is mostly in shadow."

Jack peered through the magnifying glass. "Albert Klein."

Lock clapped his hands. "Give that man a coconut. So tell me, why are Klein and Gold coming out of Tommy Usher's nightclub, hot on the heels of two of New York's most wanted?"

"You tell me, Bob."

Lock sat back in the seat. "The way I see it, the O'Briens were meeting with North London's most notorious gang leader with a view of striking up some kind of deal or arrangement. Personally, I reckon it's drugs. The brothers are trying to open up an untapped market for their wares. By doing a deal with Klein they get North London and beyond, possibly as far up as Manchester. That's a huge market for them. Then if they get Usher on board they get the South of England as well, all the way down to the ports, thus guaranteeing their supply line. Klein and Usher would stand to make millions out of the deal."

"I like your thinking, Bob. It certainly seems plausible, apart from the fly in the ointment."

"What fly?" Lock said.

"Thomas Usher."

"But they're coming out of Usher's club, so he's got to be involved."

"Usher is the fly in the ointment. He won't have anything to do with drugs. He's hated them with a passion since he lost his brother Cyril to heroin. It's the main reason why he never formed any kind of business relationship with Albert Klein. He could never square Klein's involvement with drugs with his own hatred of them. So I can't see him having any truck with the O'Brien family if that's their business. There must be another scenario playing out here."

Lock looked crestfallen.

"Never mind, Bob. It was a good theory."

"But one that won't float." He got to his feet. "Well, I've taken up enough of your time. I'll let you get off home. Goodnight, sir."

"Night, Bob."

Jack took his coat from the rack. Time to call it a day.

CHAPTER 25

MONDAY

The atmosphere in the house that evening was strangely muted. He had expected to find his family gathered together on the settee, their attention fixed on the box in the corner. Instead the family room was in darkness and the only sign of life was the sound of Annie's light soprano as she sang a fairly tuneful rendition of 'Happy Talk' from Rogers and Hammerstein's musical, *South Pacific.*

The kitchen was the only lighted room in the house. Stony faces greeted his cheerful, "Good evening, one and all." His children sat around the kitchen table. Joan was reading a magazine, Rosie, a paperback Agatha Christie novel, while Eric had his nose buried in Bert Weedon's Play in a Day book, his guitar resting across his knee.

Annie flitted across from the cooker, still singing 'Happy Talk.' It was beginning to sound distinctly ironic.

"What on earth has happened here? Has somebody died?" he said.

"They'll tell you," Annie said.

He turned to his children. "Well? Would someone mind explaining to me why my kitchen resembles a dentist's waiting room? And why your mother here has for some reason turned into Bloody Mary for the evening?"

"Language, Dad!" Rosie said.

"I'm not swearing. That was the name of the woman in *South Pacific*. Bloody Mary. Though I will start swearing if someone doesn't tell me what's going on. Did the television arrive?"

"Oh, it arrived," Joan said.

"It's just a shame the aerial didn't," Eric said.

"So we can't actually watch it." Annie prodded the sausages in the frying pan with a fork, pricking their skins so they didn't burst. Jack felt for them.

"I didn't think . . ." he said.

"Evidently." Annie put the fork down on the counter. "Didn't Mr Howard say anything to you about it when you went in on Saturday? Something along the lines of, 'I trust you have an aerial on your roof, Mr Callum?' or, 'Do you need an indoor aerial for that, Jack?'"

"I didn't see Mr Howard. It was that Saturday boy of his. He seemed most intent on making sure I signed the rental agreement in the right place. Sorry. I've had a lot on my mind lately."

"No matter." Annie relented and smiled at him. "I called them. They're coming to fit an aerial to the chimney on Wednesday, and they'll lend me an indoor one for tomorrow evening so we can test the set. I'll pick it up on my way home from work."

It took a moment for his weary mind to register her words. "Work! Yes, of course. How did your first day go?"

"Not too bad," said Annie.

"Not too bad?" Rosie said. "The customers loved her, Dad, especially the lunchtime crowd. Our iced buns flew off the shelves and our muffins sold . . ."

". . . like hot cakes," Eric said. "That joke was old when you told it the first time, Rosie."

"Suffice it to say that mum was a hit." Joan finally looked up from her magazine. "A hundred per cent success. You should be very proud of her."

"I am."

"Don't make such a fuss." Annie dabbed perspiration from her forehead with the hem of her apron. "It's not as if I've never worked before."

"But not for years," Eric said. "Years and years."

"Careful, son," Jack shot Eric a warning look. "It's not been that long."

"But it is, Jack," Annie said. "Not since the war. I was as nervous as a kitten when I went into Painter's this morning. Luckily the customers seemed to like me, and I didn't make any mistakes on the till."

"So, Mrs Painter wants you back then? That's lucky."

She screwed up her face. He'd always found that expression adorable. "Go and wash your hands, Jack Callum. Dinner will be ready in five minutes."

* * *

"I'm home!" Myra let herself into the terraced house she shared with her parents.

"We're in here." Her mother's voice floated out from the front room. Myra pushed the door and peeked around it. Her parents were sitting in front of their small television. Her mother was knitting, the clacking of the needles drowning out the sound from the television. Myra's father leaned forward in his wheelchair, trying to hear.

"Why don't you turn it up, Mum? Dad can't hear it."

"He doesn't deserve to hear it. Not after the way he's behaved today."

Myra rested her head tiredly on the doorframe. Another day, another argument. She sometimes wondered how her parents had stayed married for so long, especially since her father's accident. He'd worked at the non-ferrous metal factory since he was fourteen. An accident there had left him paralysed from the waist down and confined to a wheelchair.

"What's he done today?"

"That nice Nurse Meadows came to apply the embrocation to his legs. He spent the entire time speaking at her in Welsh. The poor girl didn't have a clue what he was waffling on about. I wouldn't mind, but he's lived in Hitchin since he was ten years old and hasn't been back to the Valleys since the day he left."

"Do you think he's all right? You don't think he's going . . . you know?"

"Senile? What him? No. He was just being a cantankerous old goat. As usual." Her mother put her knitting down.

"Thank God for that," Mr Banks muttered.

On the television a couple in scuba gear were examining the marine life inhabiting an under-sea wreck.

"Are you really interested in that, Dad? Isn't there anything on the other side that mum might like?" Myra had been playing the role of peacekeeper ever since the accident had thrown her parents together twenty-four hours a day.

"She's all right. She's got her programme on later. That'll do her."

"It's the Ann Shelton Show tonight," Mrs Banks said. "I love her voice. Oh, and your dinner's on the stove keeping warm. I didn't know when you'd be in, so we've had ours. It's herrings. I hope that's all right for you."

"Thanks, Mum." Myra pulled the door shut, leaving them to their rancorous evening.

Judging from the condensation streaming down the windows and the reek of boiled fish that filled the room she guessed that her parents had eaten some time ago. Myra gagged at the sight of an anaemic herring swimming in a cloudy sea of liquefied mashed potato. Grey peas added a few dots of contrast.

I can't eat this, she thought. She washed the liquid potato and peas down the drain, lifted out the drowned herring and threw it out into the back garden for next door's cat. Then she went up to her room.

Since the accident her parents had lived downstairs, so Myra had the entire top floor of the house to herself. She had converted the old master bedroom into a sitting room, with a second-hand sofa, a small drop-leaf table and dining chair, and a Utility style sideboard. On top of the sideboard rested her one luxury item, a Dansette record player with an autochanger. A small pile of records was positioned on the autochanger's post. She switched it on and waited for the first disc to drop onto the turntable. As the mellow voice of Pat Boone filled the room with 'April Love,' she flopped down onto the sofa and took out a packet of crisps from her handbag. She opened the blue waxed-paper twist and sprinkled salt over the crisps. These and a chocolate bar would be her dinner tonight. Well, at least hunger would take her mind off Jack Callum and the unfortunate rumours circulating at work.

* * *

Jack sat at the dining table, with half a dozen photographs laid out before him. He stared at each of the prints in turn, looking for connections between them, and anything that struck him as odd.

In the centre was the boxing photograph Charlie Somers had sent him. He picked up each of the others in turn, looking to see if any of the other patrons of the Purple Flamingo had attended the fight, apart from the three he had already identified. He was reminded of the card game Pelmanism he used to play as a child, where he would spread the cards face down on the floor and pick two at random, trying to match a pair. It took all his concentration to remember where he had replaced the cards on the floor. The card game was different, but the level of concentration was pretty much the same.

His neck ached from being hunched over the table, and he was developing a headache.

Joan came in to fetch another magazine. "Do we have any aspirin in the house?" he said.

"I think so. There's probably a bottle in the bathroom cabinet. Do you want me to look?"

"Would you?"

"I'll be back in a tick."

She returned a few moments later with a small brown bottle and a tumbler of water.

"Thanks." He unscrewed the cap on the bottle, pulled out the cotton wool wadding and shook three white tablets into his palm. He tossed three pills into his mouth and took a gulp of water.

Joan peered over his shoulder. "Are you doing anything interesting?"

"Just work. Quite boring, really."

"Hey, that's Tony Tanner. Have you got any more like these? I bet the *News of the World* would pay for them."

"They're not for sale."

She reached across him and picked up the photo from the table. "Who's in the rest of the row?"

Jack pointed to each face in turn. "That's Charlie Somers, Eddie's old boss, and that," he jabbed at Thomas Usher, "is one of the most vicious criminals south of the river."

"Imagine, policemen and criminals enjoying a night at the fights together. Oh, I know it goes on. Fraternisation, isn't that what they call it? I used to see policemen mixing with all types of dodgy characters when I worked at the pub. I used to call them Heroes and Villains nights. Have you got any more shots of the criminal? Oh, wait, there he is!"

She picked up the photograph of Lois Tanner holding onto Usher's arm. She stared at it for a few seconds. "False alarm. I thought it was the bloke in the boxing photo, but it's not."

Jack turned and stared at her. "But it is. That's Tommy Usher, leaving his club with Tony Tanner's wife, Lois, and that's him at the boxing, chomping on a cigar."

"Sorry, Dad. You're wrong. I mean they look very similar, and they could be mistaken for twins, in a darkened room, but they're definitely two different men."

He took the photograph and peered at it through the magnifying glass. "It beats me how you can say that. It's obviously the same man. Thomas Usher."

Joan shrugged. "Have it your way, Dad." She moved as if to go back to her room.

"Wait. Pull up a chair and tell me how you reached your decision."

"When I was a kid, my favourite thing in my comic was 'spot the difference.' You know the one, where they print two pictures side by side that look identical, but actually have ten or twelve subtle differences. Do you want to play?"

"I'm game."

"Right. Put the photographs down side by side on the table."

He laid them down next to each other and offered her the magnifying glass.

"That's okay. I don't need it. Just look at the pictures closely."

Jack stared at them, not sure what he was supposed to be seeing.

Joan tapped the nightclub photograph three times. "There, there and there. Look at the ears. He's got longer earlobes. If you look closely you can see that the one in the boxing photo has the tip of his little finger missing. You have to look hard because it's almost hidden by the fold in his jacket. The chap leaving the nightclub has all his fingers intact, but the main difference is the nose. The man leaving the club has a slightly different shape of bridge to his nose than the man at the boxing match. Again it's subtle, but once you spot one difference you start seeing the others." Joan sat back in her seat, a satisfied smile on her face.

Jack continued to stare at the photographs. The differences between the two men were now so obvious he was stunned that he hadn't seen them before. "We could use you on the force."

"Why? Could your chief superintendent do with a shampoo and set?"

"Ha!" He spun in his seat and hugged her. "Thank you, Joanie. You might just have cracked this case."

"How's the headache?"

"What headache?" He kissed her cheek. "Would you like a cup of tea to celebrate?"

"I'd prefer champagne."

"I'm sure you would. I'll put the kettle on. I'll go and see if your mother wants one."

"She'll be easy to find. She's in the kitchen, doing the ironing."

CHAPTER 26

TUESDAY MARCH 24th, 1959

The moment Eddie Fuller walked into the office, Jack said, "I want another meeting with Charlie Somers." He had spent a largely sleepless night turning over the implications of Joan's discovery the previous evening. "What station does he work out of these days?"

"Kings Cross."

"Make arrangements for us to go and pay him a visit."

"I don't think he'll be very happy about us turning up at Kings Cross nick for a chat."

"I couldn't give a tinker's cuss whether he's happy with it or not. He involved himself in our investigation. It's on his head if our lines of inquiry don't sit conveniently with him."

Fuller had seen his boss in this kind of mood before. Like a terrier with a ferret, he'd shake the idea to death before releasing it. "I'll call him."

"Good."

Ten minutes and a fractious telephone call later, Fuller came over to Jack's desk. "He's agreed to see us but he wants us to meet him at a local pub, the Carpenters, in the Kings Cross Road at midday."

"That suits me. We'll take a car. While we're up in London I want to go on somewhere else afterwards."

* * *

With her uniform freshly pressed and her wavy hair lacquered, Myra stepped out of the Holborn underground station and made her way smartly to the Zoom offices.

The Zoom Advertising Agency offices were on the first floor of an undistinguished redbrick building above a cobbler's shop. Myra tapped on a glass door and pushed it open, and her earlier confidence about her appearance evaporated like dew in the morning sunshine. She found herself in a small wood-panelled room, its walls adorned with framed colour photographs of some of the most beautiful women she had ever seen. A door opened and another glamorous young woman walked in. She was about thirty, with short dark hair and an hourglass figure encased in a crisp beige silk suit. She smiled and held out her hand. Her lips were red and her perfect teeth gleamed. "Hello. I'm Marion, Cedric's secretary."

"WPC Banks."

"Of course you are. I mean, who else could you be?" The secretary gave a girlish giggle.

"Mr Bannister is expecting me?"

"Indeed he is. Please take a seat." Marion pointed to a small hard chair in the corner of the room. "Cedric's in a meeting with a client, so Larry has agreed to see you."

"Larry?"

"Larry Barker. He and Wendy Worthing are Cedric's business partners. He'll be with you presently."

Myra sat, drumming her fingers on her knee. The beauties adorning the wall seemed to be mocking her. A few minutes later the door opened again. A short man with hair slick with brilliantine and a pencil-thin moustache hurried through the room. He gave her a furtive glance as he passed.

Seconds later, another man entered the room. He was young, tall and good-looking in an Errol Flynn type of way, with thick wavy hair and a wolfish grin. Larry Barker stood just inside the doorway, watching Myra as she got to her feet.

"WPC Myra Banks," Myra said.

Barker looked her up and down. "Good figure. Nice pins. Pretty face though the eyebrows could use some work. Lovely eyes. It's just a shame about the constipated hair. Is it straight or wavy? I can't tell with that style."

"Mr Barker . . ."

He put his fingers to his lips. "Never refuse a compliment. It's one of the first things I tell the girls. Compliments build confidence. Never forget that."

"I really feel we should get to the matter in hand," Myra said stiffly. She'd met types like Larry Barker in all the dancehalls from Hertford to Hackney. They did not impress her, let alone turn her head.

Barker inclined his head. "As you wish. Come through to the office."

As they passed, Myra noticed the secretary smile adoringly at Bannister. Another notch on the bedpost, thought Myra.

The office was large and expensively furnished. Myra was surprised to see three desks. Two of them were occupied, one by a woman. She might have been in her forties, though it was hard to tell through the make-up. The man was talking on the telephone and Myra recognised Cedric Bannister's voice. He didn't look up as they entered.

"Must you bring that in here, Larry? Can't you see that we're working?" the woman said.

"Now, now, Wendy," Barker said. "Be polite. WPC Banks here has some questions for us." He turned to Myra. "Please excuse Wendy."

"I'll be as brief as possible," Myra said. Wendy Worthing gave her a cool stare.

"Here's my desk," Barker said. "Please take a seat and make yourself comfortable."

Myra sat and took her notebook from her pocket.

"Shall we begin then?" Barker settled in a plush office chair across the desk from her.

Myra crossed her legs and rested the notebook on her knee. "Lois Franklin. What can you tell me about her?"

"We made her into a star," Barker said.

Myra wondered how many other people were going to take the credit for Lois's success. First Stephen Sullivan at Northrop Chemicals and now Larry Barker.

"At Zoom we pride ourselves on being able to see the potential in apparently unpromising material." Larry Barker lit a cigarette and leaned back. "Rather like I did to you outside.

When I first saw you, WPC Banks, I saw a young woman confined by her uniform, destined to play an unglamorous role in life. One of the grey people who slip through the decades unnoticed, anonymous. Instead you should think of yourself as a lump of clay, raw material waiting to be sculpted and moulded into someone special, unique. A sow's ear transformed into a silk purse. It's why we called the agency Zoom. With our help you can go zoom! High as you like. We can give you a face and body that will sell anything from plum puddings to platinum jewellery, dumplings to diamonds. Zoom!" He raised his hand, his index finger pointing at the ceiling.

Give me strength, Myra thought. "Lois Franklin?" she said.

"A case in point." Barker went across to a filing cabinet in the corner of the room. He pulled open a drawer and flicked through the files. He found the one he wanted and came back to the desk. He took out a colour photograph and laid it down for Myra to see.

It was a head and shoulders shot of a rather plain girl, with uneven, slightly discoloured teeth, bad skin and lank, mousy hair.

"From that . . ." Barker produced another photograph. The Cadence Girl, with her shimmering golden hair, perfect features and flawless complexion. ". . . to this." Barker beamed at her. "You see what I mean. The magic of Zoom."

Myra picked up the photographs. "They're the same girl?"

"It's hard to credit, isn't it? I must admit that even I was sceptical when she first walked in here. But Wendy saw something in that girl, something most people had failed to see."

Wendy looked across at them.

"That's right, Wendy, isn't it? You spotted the potential in Lois Franklin from the off."

Wendy scowled. "That's right. I spotted her, the ungrateful little hussy."

"I'm afraid Wendy's still bitter because Lois left us," said Barker.

Wendy stood over them, glaring down at the photographs. "When I think of the time I wasted on that girl, it makes my blood boil. I gave her new hair, new teeth, contact lenses. I reshaped her eyebrows, showed her how to apply her make-up. I taught her how to stand, sit and pose for photographs. I even gave her a new name. Whoever heard of an international model called Bláthnaid?"

"Bláthnaid? How do you spell that?"

"Horrendous, isn't it?" Wendy seemed quite animated now. "It conjures up peat bogs and potatoes, and that awful fiddle music. The name had to go. Lois is much more sophisticated."

"But Bláthnaid is an Irish name. I thought Lois Franklin was American."

Barker read from a piece of paper out of the file. "Born into an Irish family and grew up in Brooklyn, New York. She came to us a month after she arrived in this country, looking for modelling work. Though why she thought she had any chance at all is anyone's guess. But you saw the potential in her, didn't you, Wendy?"

"I saw the unformed lump of clay," Wendy said. "I've spent more than twenty years transforming clay into fine porcelain. It was a challenge."

Myra mentioned Lois's agoraphobia.

"She's not still using that old chestnut, is she? Larry Barker said.

"Do you mean she doesn't have it?" Myra said.

Wendy smirked. "Like I've got two heads and the bubonic plague. That woman collects spurious ailments the way other people collect stamps or cigarette cards."

"She used it with us, when she was trying to get out of her contract," Barker said.

Phone call over, Cedric Bannister came and stood with his partners.

"But her doctor . . ." Myra flipped back the pages of her notebook. "Mark Francombe, confirmed it."

Wendy sighed. "I do hope that the rest of our brave police force aren't as naïve as you."

"What do you mean?"

"The agoraphobia was a godsend for her. Actually I was rather surprised she had the intelligence to think it up. Obviously, due to the condition, she couldn't go to the surgery, so her Dr Francombe would come to visit. Usually when that drip of a husband of hers was away touring or shooting a film."

"I'm sorry, I'm still not sure I follow your drift." Myra scratched an itch behind her ear with the end of her pen. I used too much hair lacquer, she thought.

Wendy Worthing shook her head. "You must have had a very sheltered upbringing, Constable Banks. She was sleeping with him."

"Lois uses her sex appeal as a bargaining tool," Barker added. "I've seen her turn the most ruthless marketing director into a drooling mess with the bat of an eyelash."

"But surely it didn't do her any good when she had the affair with Tony Tanner? The newspapers crucified them."

"It all but destroyed his career," Bannister said.

"And sent hers skyrocketing," Wendy added.

"Zoom." Larry Barker pointed to the ceiling.

"There was a mad rush to book her." By now Bannister had warmed to the subject. "There's nothing like a sex scandal to add value to a model's worth."

"But Lois wasn't willing to play the game with us," Wendy said. "After all the money we'd invested in her, and all the hours I put into grooming her, she decided she could go her own way and make more money freelancing."

"That was when the agoraphobia reared its ugly, and entirely fictitious, head again," Bannister said. "Only this time she used it to obstruct the contract negotiations. Missing meetings, that sort of thing. Not that her solicitor needed any help. He was running rings around my man. Sometimes it helps when your lawyer is also your brother."

"Her brother?"

"Yes, and very good he was too. In fact, if he hadn't had a vested interest in his sister's career, I would have sacked my man and hired him myself."

Myra was scribbling rapidly. I really need to take a Pitman's course, she thought. "And you think her marriage to Tony Tanner was a sham?"

"I think it was about as genuine as everything else to do with Lois Tanner," Wendy said. "I was there when they first met at a dinner party at the Savoy, hosted by Noël Coward. She had Tanner eating out of her hand by the end of the *aperitifs*. It was pitiful to see him."

"Like a lamb to the slaughter," Barker said.

"Can you give me the name of her solicitor?" Myra said.

"Docherty," Bannister said. "Simon Docherty."

"I thought you said he was her brother."

"And so he is. I changed her name to Lois Franklin from *Bláthnaid Docherty*. As I said, peat bogs and fiddle music," Wendy said.

CHAPTER 27

TUESDAY

The public bar of the Carpenters was heaving. All the tables were occupied and there was queue at the bar. Three barmen were rushing backwards and forwards behind the long oak counter, dispensing trays of drinks, taking pound notes from customers and stowing them away in a cash register that was constantly ringing up sales. The air was heavy with cigarette smoke and the malty aroma of beer. The general hubbub of conversation was punctuated with the occasional eruption of cheers.

Jack looked about him critically. The chance of having any kind of conversation in here was slim. "Are you sure he said to meet in here?"

"That's what he said," Fuller answered.

And there was Charlie Somers, tugging at Fuller's elbow. "Sorry. Darts match. I forgot. Come through to the saloon bar."

They moved through a frosted-glass door to an oasis of quiet.

"Find a table and I'll get them in." Somers walked up to the bar. "Half of bitter, Eddie? And you, Jack?"

"Orange squash. I'm driving." They found a seat in a booth.

"So why the urgent visit to my home turf? Has something come up?" Somers said when he had returned with the drinks.

"A couple of things." Jack laid out the photographs. "I'd like you to take a look at these."

Somers glanced at them. "Why are you showing me these?" He pointed to the boxing photograph. "That's the one I gave you."

"Bear with me." Jack took out the photograph of the O'Brien brothers and laid it down with the others. "Recognise them?"

A slow smile spread over Somers face. "Fergus and Connor O'Brien. You don't think those two are caught up in all this, do you?"

"Very much so, Charlie. In fact I believe they're a large part of the reason for *all this*. Tell me what you know about them."

"Probably about as much as you do, if you saw the memo Scotland Yard sent round. Irish Americans. The O'Brien family hail from County Cork. In the days when they were scrabbling around Ireland's illicit underbelly, they sent the crime rates soaring. The old man, Padraig, packed up the entire family and emigrated to the United States before the *Garda* could pull them in. If this photo was taken in London it looks like the Yard were right. They did come over here." Somers leaned back in his chair. "You're awfully quiet, Eddie. Cat got your tongue?"

"I'm just wondering where all this is leading." Fuller turned to Jack. "Guv?"

"All in good time, Eddie," Jack said. Then, to Somers, Tell me, when did Thomas Usher have his stroke?"

"About six months after that boxing match at the York Hall. Fifth of December, 1956."

"Interesting," Jack said. "According to Benny Talbot's filing system, this photograph . . ." He pointed to the shot of Lois Tanner leaving the Purple Flamingo on Usher's arm. "This photograph was taken in 1957."

"Usher looks remarkably healthy for a man who's just had a stroke," Fuller said.

"I'd agree with you, Eddie. But that's not Thomas Usher."

Fuller picked up the photo and stared at it. "Then if it's not Usher, it must be . . ."

"Tony Tanner," Somers said. "Well, I'll be . . . Here, let me look at that."

Fuller slid the photograph across the table.

"Stone me," said Somers. "Do you think you could be right? It certainly looks like Usher to me."

"I am right." Jack pointed out the differences his daughter had spotted the previous day.

"It still doesn't make a lot of sense, Jack. It's common knowledge that Usher had a stroke and is pretty much gaga these days. What would be the point of impersonating him when everyone knows the truth?"

"Usher's stroke must have been very inconvenient for the higher ups running the firm. There was a power vacuum, and yet nobody stepped up to take his place. Did you ever ask yourself why?"

"I wondered but, as I told Eddie, my bosses were just relieved that Usher was out of their hair."

"Only he wasn't. See, there he is leaving the night club." Jack pointed to the photo.

"But it's not him," Fuller said.

"Yes, but the photo had us fooled. Tanner's impersonation may have hoodwinked others into believing that Usher was still active. Usher's stroke was always regarded as a convenience. You thought so yourself, Charlie. A way to stop the investigation into his criminal activities and, let's be honest, it worked. The Met effectively wrote him off as a threat."

"Only after the stroke was confirmed."

"But what if word was spread among the criminal fraternity that it had been a ruse all along? Usher was well and still running things in the South, and to confirm it Tommy Usher would be seen at his night club, fit and healthy. On the strength of his reputation alone, no one with any regard for their safety was going to question it. Quite the reverse in fact. He would be seen as a criminal mastermind, putting one over on Scotland Yard. He'd be hailed as a hero."

"Word would have reached the Yard if that were the case," Somers said.

"You mean Scotland Yard had a string of informers ready to risk life and limb by telling you that Thomas Usher was still in charge? That the stroke was just one huge deception?"

"Fair point, I suppose." Somers sipped at his Guinness. "So who do you think is running the show now?"

"I have my suspicions," Jack said.

"Do you want to share them?"

Jack laid down the photograph of Simon Docherty in conversation with Isaac Gold.

Somers stared at it.

"Gold told Eddie and me that Docherty was just asking him for the time. I didn't believe it then and I don't believe now. I think they're working together."

"Which means Albert Klein would be running London, north and south."

"Yes, but covertly, along with Simon Docherty, who has been Usher's right-hand man for a few years now. There are factions in South London who would never take orders from an American lawyer and a North London Jew. It would go too much against the grain. But if those instructions were thought to be coming from Usher himself, no one is going to complain."

"So Tony Tanner, dressed and made up to look like Tommy Usher, appears every so often, just to make it seem that the boss still around?" Somers scratched his head. "It's a bit of a stretch, Jack."

"Not when you consider how high the stakes are, especially when you bring the O'Brien family into the equation."

Fuller drained his glass. "Now you've lost me."

"Usher's main objection to joining forces with Albert Klein was Klein's drug business. It was the one criminal activity he would have no truck with after his brother died. Suddenly the O'Brien family arrive on the scene, offering untold riches if London will come into their drug market. Klein can't capitalise on the opportunity because he'd never get Usher to guarantee the supply line from the coast into London and the rest of the UK. The O'Briens would never risk going into a venture that was only fifty per cent certain. So for Klein, Usher's stroke was both a godsend and a curse. On one hand Usher — the fly in the ointment — has been removed. On the other, the O'Briens would never be persuaded to commit to anything without dealing directly with both Klein *and* Usher. So they meet at Usher's nightclub, with Tanner playing the role of *mein host*, the deal is done and all parties get what they want." Jack sat back in his seat, waiting for a reaction. "Well? What do you think?"

Somers and Fuller exchanged looks. Somers shook his head. "Sorry, Jack. I'm not buying it. Obviously you've put a lot of thought into your theory, but it's too far-fetched. This is the

London underworld we're dealing with here. You're presenting us with a scenario of Machiavellian proportions. I doubt that any of the participants in your story have the intelligence to come up with such a scheme."

"And it still doesn't explain why Tony Tanner ended up tortured and nailed to a tree in the middle of Letchworth," Fuller said.

"Agreed, Eddie, it doesn't explain that. But I must disagree with you, Charlie. If, as we suspect, it *is* Simon Docherty running the show in the South, just remember he's a trained lawyer. His devious legal mind would be more than capable of thinking this whole thing up. Albert Klein is no slouch in the intelligence department either. You don't go from being a snotty kid from Ponders End to being the head of North London's top criminal firm without having something special about you."

Somers drained his glass. "If you can find some evidence to support your crazy idea I'll be willing to suspend my disbelief, take it to my superiors and get them to restart the investigations. But all this Shakespearian drama stuff will get me laughed out of the chief constable's office and wreck what little reputation and credibility I have left. Sorry, Jack, but I can't help you on this."

"Ah, well," Jack said, draining the last of his orange squash. "It was worth a try."

"Shall I get them in again?"

Jack shook his head. "Not now, Charlie. We have to be going. Places to go, people to see."

"Fair enough." Somers got to his feet. "I'll leave you with one thought, though. You mentioned the O'Brien brothers. The most infamous incident involving them was that of Joey the Fish, one of the bookies on the O'Briens' payroll. Joey swindled the brothers out of thousands of dollars and met an untimely end under the wheels of a Greyhound bus. The NYPD could never prove that it was anything other than an accident, but everyone knew that the O'Briens were just exacting their revenge. I might get in touch with Roy Armitage who led the investigation into Benny Talbot's death. He might be interested to know that not only were the brothers in the Tottenham Court Road area around that time, but Benny Talbot snapped them coming out of Tommy Usher's club, and I doubt they were much pleased by that. Who knows, it might lead somewhere."

CHAPTER 28

TUESDAY

"Is DI Callum in his office, Sergeant?"

Andy Brewer looked at Myra coldly. "He's out."

"Sergeant Fuller?"

"He's out too."

"Well, when they return, I'll be in the canteen."

"Don't expect them to come looking for you, girl. They have enough on their plates."

"I didn't mean they should . . . Never mind. I'll find them when they get back."

"Yeah, you do that."

"Sergeant Brewer, have you got a problem with me?"

She knew she couldn't let this situation continue. After a mostly sleepless night, tossing around thoughts of Jack Callum and their supposed flirtation, she had reached the conclusion that she could not let the rumours fester any longer. She had to act.

"A problem? Whatever gave you that idea?"

"You're not exactly being very helpful."

Brewer looked blankly at her.

"Oh, never mind." She turned and started to walk towards the canteen.

"You're being paranoid, girl," Brewer said, as she walked away from him. "My wife gets like it, once a month without fail."

She hesitated for a second, and then carried on walking.

She reached the canteen and her stomach growled. You can't live on crisps and chocolate, Myra, she chided herself.

"Shepherds pie, love?" said Yvonne, the cook.

"Yes. Great."

A few seconds later she was carrying a plate piled high with mashed potato, minced lamb and onions, drenched in Yvonne the cook's famous gravy.

As she laid her plate down on the blue Formica-topped table, it struck Myra that she always ate alone these days. When she had first come to the station, there had been a strong feeling of camaraderie and Myra was often invited to eat with her fellow officers. She was certain that they had begun to ostracise her when she was seconded to CID. Suddenly she was excluded from the general mealtime banter. She ate her meal without really tasting it, aware of the occasional furtive glance and whispered aside. She put down her knife and fork, picked up her plate and took it back to the hatch.

"Steamed syrup sponge with custard for afters," Yvonne said brightly. "Can I tempt you?"

Myra looked back at the canteen. Only a few of her colleagues were still eating. One of them was DC Trevor Walsh, Frank Lesser's number two.

"Just a small portion, Yvonne. That dinner filled me up."

The cook handed her a bowl of steaming dessert. "Enjoy it. It will put meat on your bones."

Myra smiled at her. "As if I need it."

She carried the bowl across to Walsh, who was sitting alone.

"Do you mind if I join you?"

Walsh shrugged and nodded to an empty seat across from him.

He was twenty-eight, a year older than her. He had come through Hendon at more or less the same time as Myra. She had always had a kind of sisterly relationship with him, despite one alcoholic fumble at a staff party. But they had quickly recovered themselves, apologised and the incident was never mentioned again. Now Trevor Walsh was looking more than a little uncomfortable. He had a newspaper propped up against a tomato ketchup bottle and appeared to be engrossed in the racing results.

"There's nothing going on you know. Between Jack Callum and me. Nothing at all."

Walsh looked over the top of the newspaper at her.

"Okay."

"Honestly, Trev. I wouldn't lie to you. We've known each other too long."

"Okay."

Myra stood up, knocking her chair over. "Christ! What do I have to do to convince you all?"

Everyone looked up. Even Yvonne was staring at her from the serving hatch.

"It might help if the chief inspector stopped giving you all the plum jobs and shared them out among the rest of us," Chris Tate said. He was a uniformed PC like Myra. "It's bloody obvious you're his favourite. It's not our fault that we draw the obvious conclusion."

Myra looked at Walsh, beseeching him to say something.

"He's got a point, Myra."

"You too, Trev?"

Walsh shrugged. "Listen all of you! There is *nothing going on* between me and DCI Callum. Has it ever occurred to any of you that I get given the plum jobs because I just happen to be a good police officer? Or can't you accept that a woman can do this job just as well as you can?"

She glared around the room. No one spoke.

"Well, Jack Callum believes in me, and I don't need to open my legs to convince him." With tears of anger and frustration stinging her eyes, Myra stormed from the canteen.

She ran to the Ladies toilet and locked herself into a stall, taking deep gulps of air as she fought to get herself under control. After a minute or so, she gave up and her shoulders heaved with sobs.

"It's not fair," she said to herself. "It's not bloody fair."

* * *

A mop and bucket propped the doors open. Jack and Fuller walked around them and entered the dimly lit foyer of the Purple Flamingo.

"Anyone around?" Fuller called out.

"Sorry, we're not open yet." An elderly man dressed in shirtsleeves and stained dungarees emerged from a toilet to the left of a smart reception desk. A semi-circle of fuzzy white hair sat on his head like a fallen halo.

"It's all right, George. I'll handle this." A younger man emerged. He was young, fit, with a thick neck and a boxer's features. He regarded Jack and his sergeant with hostility. "We're closed. Anyway, it's members only. Are you two members? Do you have your cards?"

Jack took out his warrant card and waved it under the man's nose. "This is my card."

The man glanced at it and snorted. "Plods. I might have known. I didn't think you looked like our regular punters."

"What gave us away?" Fuller smiled at the man.

"Your feet are too fucking big for one thing. Fucking flatfoots."

"And what charm school did you go to . .?" Jack peered at the brass name badge on the man's lapel. "Irving?"

"Didn't go to no fucking charm school."

"I didn't think so," said Jack.

"What do you want?"

"We'd like to have a look around your club," said Jack.

"Got a warrant?"

"We don't need a warrant. We don't want to search the place, just have a general look around."

"Well, you can't, so you can just sling your hook," said Irving.

"Irving! Irving, that's no way to treat our guests." A third man appeared out of the gloom. He was slightly built, wore a purple silk suit and too much cologne.

"Are you the Purple Flamingo?" Fuller said.

"Miles Clarke. I'm the manager here." He stuck out a hand.

"They're old bill." Irving said morosely.

Clarke smiled benignly but dropped his hand. "Ah. Gentlemen from London's finest. What can I do for you?"

"We'd like to take a look around your club," Jack said.

The smile widened but the eyes were watchful. "And why would that be?"

"Let's pretend we're looking for a venue for the next policeman's ball, shall we?"

"Is that so? I must say it would be an honour for us to host such an event."

"Thanks. Good of you to play along. Word has it that you can organise a good 'do'. I'd just like to check the place out first."

Clarke pushed the doors open. "Why don't you come through to the club itself."

They found themselves in a large room with a small stage at one end. Tables and chairs surrounded a rectangular, highly polished dance floor. There was a balcony on one wall and opposite the stage was a raised area with three booths, each furnished with opulent sofas and more tables. The colour purple dominated, from the silk drapes on the walls to the flamingo motif picked out in fluorescent tubes above the stage. Even the grand piano that occupied one side of the stage had been painted purple and speckled with glitter.

"And where does Mr Usher sit when he comes in?" Jack said.

"That's his private booth in the centre," Clarke said, pointing up at the raised area.

"I suppose he doesn't get in much these days, since his illness."

"On the contrary, he was in only last wee . . . Oh, Mr *Usher*. The one who used to own the club. No, he hasn't been in here since his stroke."

Jack smiled at him. "Yes, that's what I thought." He walked out to the centre of the dance floor and stared up at Usher's booth. He called Fuller over. "Pretty gloomy," he said quietly, pointing at the subdued lighting. "Anyone could be sitting up there, and unless you were told who it was, you wouldn't have a clue."

"There might be a small presentation at our . . . er, 'do,' and we'd like to make it somewhere where everyone can see. Can anything be done about the lighting up there?"

Clarke shook his head. "No. All the bulbs are low wattage, I'm afraid. We like to keep the lighting discreet so our patrons have some privacy."

"Well, I think we've seen enough. We still have a couple of venues we need to check out while we're in the area. Thank you for your time."

"My pleasure. And *do* keep us in mind," said Clarke.

Jack shook his rather clammy hand. "I'm moving you up to the top of the list."

Then they were out on the Tottenham Court Road and walking back to where they'd left the car.

"Do you still think my theory was off-kilter, Eddie?"

"I don't know, Jack."

"But you heard him yourself. Usher was in the night club last week. Last *week*, Eddie."

They reached the car. "I suppose you could be right," Fuller said. "Let's get back to the station. I hate London. It gives me the itch."

"I thought you were considering the Met as your next possible port of call?"

"Just an idea. Not a good one after all."

"As I said, London has its drawbacks."

CHAPTER 29

TUESDAY

"Please give this to DCI Callum when he gets in," Myra said. She handed Brewer a sealed brown envelope.

Brewer took it and turned it over in his hands.

"What's this? Your resignation?"

Myra had washed her face and her eyes were only a little red. She regarded him coolly. "Please just see that he gets it as soon as he comes in." She turned on her heel and walked through the doors. They swung shut behind her.

"Hey! Where are you off to?" Brewer called. But Myra was already crossing the car park towards her Morris Minor. She climbed inside, slammed the door behind her and drove quickly out into the street.

Andy Brewer slipped the envelope into one of the pigeonholes on the wall behind the desk and went back to tidying the forms in the wall racks.

* * *

Leaving her car parked in the road, Myra walked in through Elsinore's gates and approached the front of the house. The door was ajar but she pressed the doorbell and waited. When no one came she nudged the door open with her toe and looked inside. Then she stepped to the side. Her heart thudded. Hester Gough was lying face upwards in the centre of the hall. Myra took a few deep breaths and pushed the door open.

Had she been driving a pool car with a radio she would have called in to the station to ask for back-up. She was driving her own, battered Morris Minor, with no way of contacting the station and help. Angry at her stupidity and lack of foresight, she entered the house cautiously.

* * *

Jack and Fuller walked into the station and went straight to the canteen for a cup of tea. They took their drinks to a table in the corner.

"All right," Fuller said. "Supposing your theory is right. It's like I said before, it still doesn't explain why Tanner was killed. Even if the rest of it makes some kind of sense, that part doesn't. If someone's using Tony Tanner as some kind of puppet to put one over on the O'Briens or whoever, why kill him? It's like cutting your nose off to spite your face. I can't see that Docherty or Klein would have anything to gain from it."

"Excuse me, sir. I thought I saw you come in." Andy Brewer came into the canteen and stood by their table.

"What can I do for you, Sergeant?"

"WPC Banks asked me to give you this, sir."

> *Sir,*
> *This is the information obtained from the Zoom Modelling Agency:*
>
> *Lois Tanner does not have agoraphobia. She uses it as a ruse so she can carry on an affair with her doctor, Mark Francombe. Whether or not her husband was complicit in this charade is not clear, though I suspect not. Why should he be as it was him she was cheating on?*
>
> *Lois is not her birth name, which was Bláthnaid. Her surname is Docherty. Thomas Usher's solicitor, Simon Docherty, is her brother*

In the light of this information I think another interview is in order. You are out at the moment and Sergeant Brewer can't give me any idea when you might return. As time is of the essence I am going along to Elsinore to confront her with these newly acquired facts. I will report to you on my return.
WPC Banks.

Jack folded the letter in half and slipped it into his pocket.

"Has she come up with anything useful?" Fuller said.

"You could say that. She's gone out to Elsinore to have another chat with Lois Tanner." He turned back to Brewer. "How long ago did she leave this?"

Brewer shrugged. "An hour ago? Ninety minutes?"

Jack glared at him. "Well, which is it?"

Brewer looked up at the clock on the wall. "Ninety minutes, sir."

"I should be there," Jack said to Fuller. "Coming?"

They walked towards the door.

"Sergeant Fuller!" Henry Lane appeared at the top of the stairs.

"Yes, sir?"

"If I could see you in my office?"

Fuller and Jack exchanged looks.

"When you're ready, Sergeant," Lane said.

"You'd better not keep the chief super waiting, Eddie," Jack said quietly.

"Looks like I'll have to catch you up."

"Okay. You know where it is." Jack went out to the car park and signed out a pool car.

* * *

Hester Gough was very dead. There was a neat bullet hole in the centre of her forehead, almost free of blood. That had pooled at the back of her head and soaked into the carpet. Myra reached out and closed the staring eyes with her fingertips. Then she looked round. She listened. All she could hear was the sound of her own breathing and the rhythmic thud of her heartbeat. She pushed herself to her feet, still looking about her.

All the doors leading off from the hall were closed except the one to the conservatory. Moving around Hester's body, Myra crept on tiptoe towards the open door. She approached the doorway, looked into the room and pulled back when she saw what was inside.

Lois Tanner was slumped face down on the bamboo couch. Blood and brains from a wound in her head dripped onto the tiles below. Beside the piano was a wheelchair. Thomas Usher had his legs covered with a plaid blanket, and his greying head was slumped to one side. His eyes were open but unfocused. Spittle dribbled down one side of his chin from an open, lopsided mouth.

He didn't move. He appeared not to see Myra as she crossed to Lois Tanner to check her pulse. Myra let the wrist drop and got to her feet. Then she froze as a voice rang out.

"At least you're prettier than the other plods I've had on my tail over the years."

Myra spun round and stared into Thomas Usher's very alert and smiling face.

CHAPTER 30

TUESDAY

Usher was sitting upright in the wheelchair, his eyes bright and clear. He'd wiped the drool from his chin.

"I . . . I thought . . ."

"So did everyone. I think I played the role of the pathetic invalid quite well, don't you? Better than Tony Tanner could have done anyway. Driving is still a problem for me, but one of my lads brought me over here. He's waiting in the van, just up the road by the phone box. I'll call for him to pick me up when I finish here."

Myra stared at him.

"What's your name by the way?"

"Banks. WPC Banks."

"Well, WPC Banks, do you have your handcuffs on you?"

Myra nodded.

"Good. Go over to the wall, sit down on the floor and cuff yourself to the radiator."

As she opened her mouth to protest, Usher took his hand out from under the blanket. His fingers were curled around the stock of a black revolver. He jerked it. "I won't tell you twice," he said. He was still smiling benignly.

When she didn't move, he fired. The bullet kicked up dust and chips of ceramic and buried itself in the tiles at her feet.

Myra threw herself back against the wall. Winded, she slid down until she was sitting on the floor. She took out her handcuffs and threaded one cuff through the pipes of the cast iron radiator, and closed it around her wrist.

"And the other wrist." The revolver twitched again. He watched her closely as she attached the other cuff. The radiator was on and the metal burned her skin.

"That's better." Usher lowered the gun. "I hate using these things. I always feel it makes me less of a man. But as you see, I'm hardly in a position to use my strength to persuade you."

"I thought you said you were acting."

"Ah, you misunderstand me, WPC Banks. My stroke was real. It has left me with certain disabilities, but I've let people think it was a lot worse." He gave a short bark of laughter. "At least it got you lot off my tail for a while. 'Poor old Tommy Usher. He's a cabbage now, I hear'. You wouldn't believe some of the tales."

"I've heard some of those tales myself," said Myra.

"Plods like you have never been the sharpest chisels in the toolbox. Your governors use you like blunt instruments. You do all the donkey work while they stand around and wait to collect the glory."

Myra shifted on the floor. The pain in her wrists from the hot radiator was becoming unbearable. She bit the inside of her cheek to stop herself crying out.

"What about *your* governor, Miss Banks? Is he a uniformed glory-seeker?"

"Jack Callum's a damned fine policeman!" Now why did she say that?

"Chief Inspector Callum . . . So *he's* your boss? I know the name but not the man. So it's him you have to thank for your current predicament."

Myra tilted her chin and glared at him. "He's got your number."

"Really?" Usher smiled. He cupped a hand to his ear. "I can't hear any bells of approaching salvation. Perhaps your faith in him is misplaced."

"Why did you kill Tony Tanner?" Myra said.

"Because he was becoming a bloody nuisance." The smile disappeared.

Now Myra saw what was behind the urbane mask. It scared her.

"His impersonations of me were fun at first and they could be very useful, but he took it too far. It started out as a skit, a fortieth birthday party spoof, and it proved to be a great boon in the years that followed. He and a couple of his actor cronies dreamed up a comedy sketch with Tony portraying me as some kind of Al Capone figure. His impersonation was spot on, and I saw its potential. He'd just provided me with the perfect alibi. Christ, the fun I had then. I pulled job after job all over the South. Every time there were twenty or thirty witnesses to tell your lot that I was at my club all evening and never left my private booth, not for a second. Tony didn't complain. His career had hit the skids anyway and was sliding all the way down the toilet. Plus he owed me for pulling out of the escort business.

"Then it all came to an end when that bastard stroke got me. At least I thought it had. Simon bloody Docherty had other ideas. When they brought me back from Switzerland, he staged a welcome home party for me at the Flamingo. The guest list had some of the nastiest bastards in the South London underworld. There was I, sitting in my private booth, the picture of health after my miraculous recovery in foreign parts. In actual fact I was in a nursing home by the coast. Tony Tanner took my place that night and for many more nights afterwards. All the guests were sworn to secrecy. They knew that if word leaked out that I was back in the game, the police investigation would start again, and no one wanted that.

"You have to hand it to Simon. It was something of a masterstroke. He could carry on with business, with my supposed approval, without having to involve me at all. I was out of the way at the seaside, so he had free rein to do as he liked.

"It all worked out fine for a while. I played the role of pathetic invalid. Docherty and his bitch of a sister would come to visit and speak to each other in front of me. They thought I couldn't understand what they were saying, and even if I did I couldn't do anything about it. But they were wrong. I understood every single word. Especially the deals they were making with that piece of slime, Albert Klein. That maggot with his drug dealing, killing kids like my brother Cyril."

Usher lapsed into silence.

Myra began to feel the pain of her scorched wrist. Maybe she should just keep him talking. "So what did you do? There was Simon Docherty and his sister effectively taking over your business, and there's you in a Dimchurch nursing home, unable to do a thing about it."

Usher suddenly snapped back to the present. "Ah, but that's where they were wrong. I still had people who were loyal to me. Jimmy Dymond, for one. Jimmy and I went to school together in Peckham. He didn't have much in the way of brains, but he was a big kid for his age, and tough. He was my protector when we were growing up. In return, I did his schoolwork for him. The school never caught on. When we left and I started my own business, money lending, I took Jimmy on as my debt collector. He's been at my side ever since, loyal to a fault.

"It was Jimmy who came to tell me that Docherty, Klein, Gold and Tanner had restarted negotiations with those Americans, the O'Briens. I wasn't happy. I needed to know what they were planning. The meeting last Tuesday was a strictly private affair, then Jimmy and a couple of his lads followed Tanner back here to Letchworth. They took him over to the common to find out what had been discussed. As I said, Jimmy's not intellectually blessed, but he does have a talent for extracting information."

"So he nailed Tanner to a tree and tortured him," Myra said.

"Did I mention that Jimmy has got an awful temper? I don't think he intended to kill Tony at first. But he had watched them playing this bloody game for a long time. He figured they were just taking the piss out of me, and his protective instinct got the better of him."

"So Jimmy Dymond killed Tony Tanner. Not you."

Usher nodded his head. "I have my reputation to think of. Anyway, if I'd done it myself, I would have cut off his balls and sent them to that bitch of a wife of his."

"I heard she spoke highly of you too." Myra moved her arms to keep her wrists from the heat.

Usher laughed. "My word, I like you, WPC Banks. You've got spunk. I'll give you that. Not a lot of sense, but spunk. I admire that in a woman."

Usher wheeled himself across the floor until he was beside her. He reached down and lifted one of her wrists, pulling it as far away from the radiator as her other cuffed hand would allow. She winced as he ran a finger over the scorched skin.

"Nasty. I think that's going to blister," he said. He let her arm drop.

"Are you going to kill me?"

He looked at her steadily and raised an eyebrow. He rolled the wheelchair back to the centre of the room.

"There's no rush, is there? I don't get much chance to talk these days, what with keeping up this bloody charade. You don't mind me bending your ear, do you?"

"I'm happy to listen." If she could just keep him talking, Myra thought, she might be able to find a way out.

"Good."

"I'd be happier if I could move away from the radiator though. The burning is distracting me."

Usher thought for a moment. "All right," he said. He rolled back to her and held out his hand. "I never enjoyed hurting women, even coppers. Key?"

"It's in my tunic." She nodded at her left breast pocket.

He reached into the pocket, took out the key and slipped it into the cuff securing her right wrist. He held the gun in his other hand.

"When I unlock it, very carefully take the cuff from behind the radiator and secure yourself again. If you try anything stupid or reckless I'll put a bullet between your eyes. I may not like these bloody things but I do know how to use one." He twisted the key in the lock and the cuff fell free.

All thoughts of making a dash for it evaporated when he tapped her on the forehead with the barrel of the revolver. With a sigh, she hooked the cuff over her wrist and closed it again.

"Now, what shall we talk about?" said Usher. "As you can see, I've killed Lois and the old biddy that lives with her. Perhaps I'll tell you what I'm planning to do to her brother. If he thinks he can bring the O'Briens and their filthy drugs onto my manor, he has another think coming."

"Yes, Tommy, tell us how you plan to kill Simon Docherty," Jack said from the doorway. "I've heard enough already to guarantee you finish your life at the end of a rope."

CHAPTER 31

TUESDAY

Usher raised the gun, while his other hand pushed down on a wheel to turn himself around. As he turned, Myra kicked out with both feet and sent the wheelchair spinning. The impact caused Usher's finger to jerk on the trigger, and a shot rang out. Myra grunted as the bullet slammed into her and she fell backwards onto the floor.

Jack launched himself across the room, landing on top of Usher and knocking the gun from his hand. The momentum carried both men to the floor, where they landed in a tangle of arms, legs and wheelchair. Usher was on top and he put his hands round Jack's neck. He pressed his thumbs into Jack's windpipe.

"Fucking rozzer!" Usher gritted his teeth as he tightened his grip. Jack's vision began to darken. Then, all at once, as if someone had thrown a switch, Usher's fingers loosened. One side of his face sagged. He gave a strangled cry and pitched forward, his face smacking into the tiled floor.

Both lay still for a moment, and then Jack rolled Usher's body aside and got to his feet. He crouched down beside Myra and searched his pocket for a handkerchief. He folded it into a pad and pressed it against the hole in her shoulder. It quickly became soaked with blood.

Fuller walked into the room. "Bloody hell! What happened here?"

"Call for an ambulance, Eddie!" Jack shouted.

"I think Usher is beyond their help."

"It's not for him. It's for Myra!"

Fuller stared for a moment and then turned and dashed out to the car to use the radio.

"Myra?" Jack said softly. Her eyes fluttered open.

"Hello, sir," she croaked.

"That was quick thinking, kicking the chair like that. You saved my life."

Myra's voice was weak. "It's the same chair as my dad has," she said. "They turn on a sixpence if you give them a shove. Wasn't counting on getting shot though." She glanced down at the bloody handkerchief, gave a soft sigh and passed out.

Somewhere in the house a telephone began to ring. After a few seconds a disembodied voice sounded.

"This is a recording. Lois Tanner is not here at the moment to take your call. If you would like to leave a message, you can do so after the tone."

There followed a short beeping sound.

"Lois, it's Simon again. Lois? Lois? Damn it, Bláthnaid! Pick up the bloody phone! Bloody answering machines. Okay, perhaps you're not there. I'm at the hotel now, but I have to leave to get to the airport. Our flight leaves in just over an hour. I'll leave your ticket at the check-in counter."

The line went dead.

"Looks like you'll be travelling alone," Jack said quietly. The bell of an approaching ambulance cut through the afternoon silence.

* * *

Jack and Fuller sat in the car and watched the ambulance pull out of the gates.

"Is she going to be all right?" Fuller said.

"It was a clean shot to the shoulder. The bullet went straight through, missing her collarbone. According to the ambulance-man she should make a full recovery. It means she'll be out of commission for a few weeks, but it could have been a lot worse. She was lucky."

"You must be relieved."

"I am. It doesn't say a lot for me as a boss when one of my officers makes a rash decision and puts her life at risk."

"I think Myra had something to prove," said Fuller.

"What do you mean?"

Fuller leaned against the car. "It doesn't matter."

"On the contrary, Sergeant. I think it matters a lot. We're not going anywhere. There's plenty of time before the crime scene laddies arrive."

"Just let it lie, Jack."

"Sorry. Not good enough, Eddie. You're keeping something from me. What did I say to you the other day about being able to trust my sergeants? Spit it out, man."

Fuller pulled out his cigarettes. "Er . . . I suppose you're aware of the gossip going around the station about you and Myra?"

"Yes, Eddie, I'm aware of it."

"And it doesn't bother you?"

"If I bothered about all the old toffee that's said about me, I wouldn't be able to do my job."

"Nevertheless, you can't just let the rumours carry on."

"Trust me, Eddie, I won't. But I'll deal with them in my own way and in my own time. They're just stories. The people who made them up possibly feel their careers aren't going as they'd hoped. They're full of resentment. Myra's an easy target because she's a woman and is doing well. A lot of men can't stand that — some women too. The stories don't bother me, and they certainly don't bother Mrs Callum."

"You've told her about them?"

"She's my wife. Of course I've told her about them."

"What was her reaction?"

"She laughed. She was tickled to think I could be involved with a girl young enough to be my daughter."

Fuller gave a low whistle. "She's quite a woman."

"That's why I married her. I'm fortunate enough to have some remarkable women in my life, and I include Myra Banks among them. I told you the other day that she reminds me of my Joanie. I can imagine Joanie being just as reckless as Myra."

"I don't know how you do it," said Fuller.

"How I do what?"

"Get that kind of loyalty from your wife. Judy doesn't trust me at all."

Jack smiled. "It's easy. I just remember my old man's answer on the day of his golden wedding anniversary. Someone asked him how he had managed to stay married to the same woman for fifty years. Do you know what he said?"

Fuller shook his head.

"'Whatever you do, never take them for granted.' And you'd do well to remember that, Eddie, if your relationship with Judy Taylor ever makes it off the starting blocks. Never take her for granted. I use that in my work as much as I do in my personal life. At the end of the day, it's all about respect. If we don't respect the people around us, then there's no hope for us."

"You're a lucky man, Jack."

"And don't I know it."

Fuller hesitated. "I wonder if that was partly why Myra didn't get kept on."

"What? Because people are making up stories about her?"

"It's just a thought."

"Not one I'd had, I must say. I'll have to think on that. By the way, what did the chief super want?"

"He'd just seen that I'm going for promotion. He seemed rather pleased. He wanted to reassure me that I have his backing. He said he'll put all the resources of his office at my disposal."

"Generous of him."

"He also wanted to make it clear that if I do make inspector, there will be a job for me at Welwyn."

"Despite all the budget cuts?"

"Apparently."

"Well. Good for you. I'm pleased."

"Really?"

"Yes, really. Good number twos are hard to come by."

"You mean that?"

"You know me, Eddie. I wouldn't have said it if I didn't mean it. Just remember, though. He blocked Myra but he's backing you. Man's world, Eddie."

"She'll be okay though, won't she? The shooting I mean."

"She'll be fine. But it puts paid to any thoughts of promotion for the time being, doesn't it."

* * *

Simon Docherty slammed down the telephone. It was time to get out. Going back to the United States was no longer an option for him or his sister. The O'Briens had pulled out of the deal that he and Albert Klein had worked so hard to put together, and were now after his blood. The people who killed Tony Tanner no doubt had him marked as their next target. He just couldn't see how things could have gone so wrong. But now their flight to Canada was booked. In a few hours' time he'd be jetting off across the Atlantic.

There was a knock at the hotel door.

"Who's there?"

"Room service."

"I haven't ordered anything."

There was another knock.

Furious, Docherty walked to the door and yanked it open. "I told you, I haven't—"

A fist smashed into his mouth, splitting his lips and knocking two of his front teeth down his throat. He didn't recognise the two men who barrelled in through the door. He did know the man who followed them. Docherty's bladder emptied.

The two thugs knocked him to the floor and pinned him there.

Jimmy Dymond said, "Oh, look, lads. He's wet himself. Pissed his pants like a little baby."

Docherty moaned. His head moved from side to side.

"I think baby needs changing," Dymond said. "Would you do the honours, boys? Relieve him of his trousers."

They pulled the sodden trousers down over his thighs.

Docherty struggled briefly, but was slapped into submission.

Dymond leaned over him. "I expect you're wondering how we found you."

Docherty was unable to speak.

"You seem to forget, Simon. This is my home turf. I have hundreds of eyes out there, all waiting to tell me what I need to know."

Docherty whimpered.

"Well, good news, mate. It happens to be your lucky day. I have a present from a mutual friend. Want to see?"

Docherty shook his head frantically.

"No?" Dymond said. "Well, I'll show you anyway." He took a step back and opened the heavy coat he was wearing. "Surprise! Tommy Usher sends his regards."

Docherty's eyes were wide with terror. Dymond took the newly-sharpened garden shears from his belt and opened them out. He snapped them in the air above Docherty. "Playtime," he said. Docherty gave a howl of anguish. It rose to a shrill scream that echoed off the walls and then went silent.

CHAPTER 32

SATURDAY MARCH 28th, 1959

"Almost there," Jack said.

Eric peered out through the window of the Morris Oxford. "Shillington? What's at Shillington?"

"Just some people I have to see."

"Do they know we're coming, Jack?" Annie said. She checked her lipstick in the mirror of her powder compact.

"I telephoned first thing this morning."

Laurence Tanner opened the door to the bungalow almost before the doorbell stopped ringing. "Jack!" he said. "So good of you to come. And you've brought your lovely family. Splendid."

This was not the Laurence Tanner Jack had met just over a week ago. His demeanour had changed completely and he looked a good ten years younger.

"You're looking well, Mr Tanner."

"Now, Jack, please. Call me Laurence. And thank you. I feel much better. Especially now this ghastly business with my son and his wife is over."

"He's a changed man since Gerry came to live with us, Chief Inspector." Jean Tanner appeared at her husband's side.

"We're done with formalities, Jean. It's Jack, and his lovely wife. I'm sorry I didn't catch your name, my dear."

"Annie," she said. "And this is our son, Eric."

"Well, what are we doing standing out here? Come in, come in."

They followed the elderly couple into the sitting room. Gerry Tanner was on the sofa, her legs curled underneath her. She was adding crochets and quavers to a sheet of manuscript paper.

"Look, Gerry. Chief Inspector Callum has come to see us, and he's brought his family," Jean Tanner said.

Gerry Tanner laid down the manuscript paper and stood up, smiling. She was wearing jeans and a T-shirt and had tied her hair in a ponytail. She too looked different, Jack thought. The tension had gone, and her cheeks had the ruddy glow of a child who played outside in the sunshine.

Jack said hello and introduced her to Annie and Eric. "Eric's a musician too," he added.

"Dad!" Eric muttered.

"That's all right, son. Gerry's a fine pianist, and I'm sure her grandparents are always singing her praises."

Laurence and Jean Tanner nodded.

"What instrument do you play?" Gerry said to Eric.

"Guitar," Eric said. "I've not been playing that long. I'm not very good."

"From what I've heard, you don't seem too bad."

"Dad!"

"Would you like to hear me play?" Gerry said. "I don't get much of a chance to even *talk* to other musicians, let alone show off to them." Eric nodded. "Come on. We'll go in the back room where the piano is, and leave the grown-ups to their chattering." She grabbed a rather bemused Eric by the hand and led him from the room.

"Well, they seemed to hit it off," Tanner said.

Annie laughed. "Judging from the expression on his face I don't think he knew what hit him. She's very confident, your Gerry."

"She is now," Jean agreed. "You wouldn't think she was the same girl. It was only last week that she ran away from that hell hole Elsinore. Shall I put the kettle on?"

"That would be lovely," Annie said. "I'll give you a hand."

Tanner took Jack's arm and led him to the French doors. They looked out onto a beautifully tended garden. "Talking of hell holes, I'd like your advice."

"I'm listening."

Tanner opened one of the doors and they stepped out into the garden. "Are you a gardener, Jack?"

"I potter." He paused. "Actually, no I don't. Gardening is something of a passion with me. It's the perfect antidote for the type of work I do."

"Yes, I can see that. I had thirty-odd years in the Civil Service before I retired and if I hadn't had the garden, I swear I would have cracked up. Planting and growing my flowers kept me sane."

"You said you wanted some advice?" Jack said.

"It's Gerry. It looks like Jean and I will be made her legal guardians."

"That seems the most likely outcome."

"We're thinking of taking her back to Elsinore. Bloody stupid name for a house, pardon my French. Her music room is there, and I know she's missing her piano."

"But surely you have a piano here?"

"Yes, we do, but it's a rather ancient overstrung jobbie. It's more suitable for playing 'Roll Out The Barrel' than a Rachmaninoff concerto. Seedlings need nurturing. Give them the best in the early days and they'll reward you with succulent blooms year after year. I want Gerry to have every opportunity to succeed in her ambition to become a top class pianist. So taking her back to her piano and her music room seems about the best we can do for her. But Jean is worried that all the horror that's happened in that house might have some adverse effect on her. What do you think?"

The delicate sounds of 'Clair de Lune' floated through the warm spring air, though the tone was closer to Winifred Atwell. "See what I mean?" Tanner said.

"I take your point." Jack said. "If you want my advice, I'd get the whole house professionally cleaned from top to bottom. Move back in and start a new life as a proper family. It's something Gerry's missed since her mother died. Then, sit back and watch her bloom."

Laurence Tanner slapped Jack on the back. "Thank you," he said. "That's what I hoped you'd say."

"Tea's up!" Annie called.

* * *

"What did you think of Gerry?" Jack asked his son as they drove away.

"She's very talented. She puts me to shame."

"Oh, Eric," Annie said. "Don't be so hard on yourself. You've only been playing a few months. Gerry's been doing it for years."

"I suppose so."

"Of course so," Jack said. "Listen to your mother. She's quite right . . . as always."

"Just you watch it, Jack Callum. You're not too big for a smack."

"Anyway," Eric said. "She said that when she's moved back to Letchworth, I can go around to her house and practice my guitar there. She's got a big music room."

"That's right, she has. I've seen it," Jack said, trying to blot out the memory of Lois Tanner lying dead on the bamboo couch, and Thomas Usher on the floor. He hoped he had given Laurence Tanner the right advice.

"A penny for them," said Annie.

"Eh?"

"A penny? For your thoughts?"

"You wouldn't want them, Annie. Really you wouldn't."

CHAPTER 33

EPILOGUE

SATURDAY JUNE 14th, 1959

"You don't need a tie, dad." Rosie said. "It's St Mary's Youth Club, not the Royal Albert Hall. Wear that pullover mum got you for Christmas. That's plenty smart enough."

"Talking of your mother, where is she?" Jack removed the tie.

"Downstairs in the back room. Joanie's doing her hair."

"*Joanie* is doing her hair?" Jack said. "I thought I heard Avril arrive earlier."

"You did. It's a team effort."

Jack knew he should be used to female beauty regimens by now, but there always seemed to be something new to surprise him. "Shouldn't you be getting down to the club to rehearse? Eric will be wondering where you are."

"There's no rush. I've only got two songs this evening and I know them backwards. Besides they're debuting a new member of the group this evening. They want to run through a few things before I get down there cluttering up the stage. I might even cadge a lift from you."

"What's wrong with your bike?"

"Nothing. I just thought it might be nice to arrive in style for a change." Rosie grinned at him.

"I'm not your chauffer, you know."

"Ah well. It was worth a try."

* * *

Jack sat in his armchair, listening to the radio. The new television glowered at him from the corner of the room as if challenging him to switch it on. Moments like this, sitting in his favourite armchair listening to a classical concert on the BBC's Third Programme, were precious and would soon be part of history. The thought made him slightly melancholy.

The door opened. Joan stood in the entrance and cleared her throat. "Tonight, John '*Jack*' Callum, father, policeman, catcher of criminals, scourge of the Hertfordshire underworld — and husband . . . tonight *This Is Your Wife!*" She stood to one side, glanced back over her shoulder, gave a low bow, and made a beckoning gesture with her arm. "Now, Mum," she hissed.

Jack got to his feet and stood as Annie, his wife of twenty years, walked shyly into the room. Jack's mouth began to drop open. He snapped it shut.

Annie patted her newly cut and permed hair. "Do you like it, Jack?" Her look begged him to say yes.

Jack swallowed and crossed to the doorway. He pulled at the hair at the nape of Annie's neck. It straightened and then sprang back into a curl.

"Hey, you," Joan protested. "Don't you go spoiling the style with your great banana fingers."

"Jack. Do you like it?" Annie said again. "Avril cut it for me and Joanie permed it. What do you think?"

Jack took a breath. "I think you look beautiful."

"Yes, but do you like the hairstyle, Dad?" Joan said.

"Yes." Jack nodded his head slowly. "I love it."

"You see, Mum," Joan crowed. "I told you he would."

"I wasn't sure you would."

"It makes you look younger. Like a new woman."

"I'll settle for younger. I don't want to be a new woman, Jack. I want to be the same old Annie Callum, wife and mother."

"And sexpot," Jack said.

"Jack!"

"Dad!"

"A man's entitled to his opinion." Jack glanced at his watch. "Anyway, we have to get going. Eric will kill us if we miss the beginning of the show. It's his big night." He turned off the radiogram.

"I'll get my coat." Joan called back over her shoulder. "Can I get yours, Mum?"

"If you would, love. I'm wearing my navy duster coat tonight." Annie put her arms round Jack's waist. "Do you *really* like it, Jack? I was so scared when Joanie suggested it. I know you always preferred my hair long."

He returned her embrace. "Times are changing, pet." He kissed her on the forehead. "It wouldn't do if we didn't change with them. My first instinct was to say no when you wanted to take that job at the bakers. I didn't want that confounded television either. But yes, I meant it. I think your hair looks lovely. Come on, let's go."

She moved towards the door.

"And I meant what I said when I called you a sexpot too."

She glanced back at him with what his mother would have called an old-fashioned look. "Jack Callum, you're incorrigible."

"I know. And I also know which battles I'll never win."

* * *

By the time they got to St Mary's church hall there was already quite a crowd inside. Thirty or forty people milled about the dusty, cavernous room. Most of them were trying to get near the stage, a small platform at one end of the hall. Most of them were Eric's school friends, but there were a handful of adults, standing at the back of the hall.

"You see," Annie said. "We're not the oldest ones here. Phillip Langton's parents are here, and they're older than us."

They looked towards the stage as Reverend Williams, a short, rotund man with ruddy skin and thinning hair, climbed onto it. He clapped his hands. "Ladies and gentlemen, boys and girls." The chatter in the hall quietened and the vicar continued. "Thank you all for coming to this . . . this . . . concert, which will help us raise funds for St Mary's Youth Club."

A smattering of applause rippled through the audience.

Reverend Williams bowed his head slightly and continued. "When Eric Callum came to me with the proposal that his skiffle group put on a show, I must admit that at first I was sceptical."

A few of the adults in the hall smiled and nodded.

"But since then I have heard them play, and I'm sure you're in for a treat this evening. So, if you'll put your hands together and welcome to the stage, Eric and the Vikings."

"*Eric and the Vikings?* When did he dream that one up?" Joan said.

Annie shushed her.

Jack smiled.

The crowd parted and Eric Callum led his group onto the stage.

Joan raised her eyes to the ceiling. "This will go straight to his head. He's going to be impossible from now on. At least Rosie's there to keep his feet on the ground."

The group started their first number. It was an up-tempo song Jack hadn't heard before and his foot began tapping. Rosie came to the front of the stage and started to sing, slapping her thigh in time to the music. But Jack was not watching his daughter. Instead his gaze was fixed on the pianist who sat at the side of the stage, hunched over the keys. The piano filled out the sound of the group and, in Jack's opinion, was a one hundred per cent improvement from the last time he heard them.

Annie followed his gaze. "Isn't that . . ?"

"Yes, it is." Jack was smiling. The pianist turned from the keyboard and stared into the audience, finding his smile and returning it. "Well done," he mouthed.

Gerry Tanner winked at him and turned her attention back to the keys.

"When I introduced her to Eric, I thought her classical training would rub off on him. Seems I got it the wrong way round," Jack said quietly to his wife.

Annie squeezed her husband's hand. "He's his father's son. Ploughing his own furrow. Would you have it any other way?"

Jack smiled broadly. "Not for the world."

THE END

CHARACTER LIST (contains spoilers)

THE FAMILY

Jack Callum: Detective Chief Inspector. He has a keen mind and is passionate about his job. Doesn't believe in capital punishment but has caught a few villains whose life has come to an end on the gallows. Believes the attitudes of the day need changing — such as a woman's place in society. Loves his children and has a firm but fair style of parenting.

Anne Callum (nee Bailey): Jack's wife. A bright vivacious brunette. Loves her husband deeply and acts as his confidante. her role as a housekeeper and home-maker. Once had aspirations of a stage career, but is now beginning to spread her wings with a new part-time job and new clothes.

Joan Callum: 19 years old. Estranged daughter. Eloped with Ivan, a Czech émigré, at sixteen. Very pretty. Recently returned to the family home and is beginning a career as a hairdresser.

Rose Callum: 16, Jack's daughter. A sweet girl who is always falling in love. She has her mother's hair and eyes. Has no shortage of potential suitors, but is holding out for Mr Right. Attended the local high school and got good grades. Harbours ambitions to be a vet. The apple of Jack's eye.

Eric Callum: 14, Jack's son and a chip off the old block. Has inherited his father's love of football, but recently persuaded his parents to buy him a guitar so he can pursue his love of skiffle music. His idol is Lonnie Donegan.

THE POLICE

Chief Superintendent Henry Lane: A self-made man. Has hauled himself through the ranks by his bootstraps and expects excellence from his junior officers, but is not a martinet and gets results with a friendly word or kind gesture. Very supportive of the men under him and has special regard for **Jack Callum**, who he thinks, despite being a year younger, is twice the copper he is himself.

DS Eddie Fuller: A prominent member of CID, effectively Callum's number two. A bit of a ladies' man and has some unorthodox ways of getting results.

DC Harry Grant: Fuller's number two.

WPC Myra Brent: The only woman officer at the station and resents the fact, while at the same time never missing an opportunity to use it to her advantage. A bright young woman who **Jack** has tipped for a CID job.

DS Frank Lesser: Moonlights as a part-time wrestler, who wrestles under a mask as Black Phantom and is as tough as nails. Married with a young family.

DC Trevor Walsh: Lesser's number two.

Sergeant Andy Brewer: Desk sergeant at the station. The hub of the station. Knows everybody and tends to be the gossip filter.

PC Alistair Kirby: A beat policeman. Ex-military. Does his beat around town with his Alsatian, Satan. Local tearaways are scared of him.

Barry Fenwick: the police doctor. Views the body at the crime scene, pronounces death and conducts the post mortem.

Bob Lock: keeper of the records and files.

Charlie Somers: Eddie Fuller's old boss from his previous police posting.

THE VILLAINS AND VICTIMS

Anthony Tanner: an actor, and once in a shady business deal with Thomas Usher.

Geraldine Tanner: Tony's daughter.

Lois Tanner: nee Bláthnaid Docherty — second wife of Tony and also sister of Simon.

Hester Gough: housekeeper to Lois.

Laurence Tanner: father of Tony.

Jean Tanner: mother of Tony.

Thomas Usher: underworld villain who was once in business with Tony.

Jimmy Dymond: right-hand man and muscle for Usher.

Albert Klein: another London villain and rival to Usher.

Isaac Gold: right-hand man and muscle for Klein.

Simon Docherty: crooked lawyer and brother to Lois as well as being involved with both Usher and Klein.

Fergus and Connor O'Brien: two American brothers trying to do business in London with or without Usher and/or Klein.

GLOSSARY OF BRITISH AND PERIOD SLANG

a cabbage: brain dead
a set of pipes on her: a good singer
addles your brain: messes with your head
all hands to the pumps: lots of help needed
a welsher: reneges on deals, doesn't pay their debts
Babycham: cheap alternative to champagne – made from pears
balloon's gone up: an emergency situation
balls-up: an error, a mistake
banana boat: derogatory term for immigrants transport to UK
barrel of laughs: sarcastic term for a serious character
beat bobby: uniformed police officer who patrols the streets
bee's knees: something special
be sick: vomit
bells ringing: equivalent of police sirens today
belter: It was a fantastic goal
better step on it: hurry up
Biscuits: cookies
Black Maria: a police van
bod: derogatory term – anonymous person
bonnet of his car: the hood & (UK boot = US trunk)
boozy: A bit drunk
bread-and-butter work: Routine work
brief: lawyer
Brylcreem: hair cream/gel to give men's hair shine and smoothness
calling in the cavalry: asking for reinforcements
Cambridge University: prestigious British university
car park: parking lot
cat that got all the cream: satisfied
CID: Criminal investigation division
clobbered: hit hard
cobbler's shop: shoe menders
copper: slang for policeman
couldn't hit a cow's arse with a banjo: not very good at aiming a dart or arrow
council estate: social housing

crazy-paving: patio, concrete slabs in random pattern
cuppa: A cup of tea
cut along to: go along to
David Nixon: UK TV magician
dessert: pudding
digs: lodgings, boarding house
dollar a frame: two half crowns in old UK money = five shillings - called a dollar and five bob
doormat: meek
dressing down: telling off
emergency police box: telephone box for police use
en-print: an 8 x 10 photograph
excuse my French: sorry I swore
fellow: boyfriend
flatfoots: derogatory name for police
fly in the ointment: problem
get you a brew: a cup of tea
get your skates on: Hurry up
glasshouse: greenhouse
go to the dogs: go to rack and ruin, be destroyed
good collars: good arrests
guv'nor: the boss (& guv)
gymkhana: horse-riding event
gymslips: school uniform of bib and skirt design
had it in spades: has a lot of it
half of bitter: beer.
Harold MacMillan: British Prime minister 1957-63
haversack: backpack, rucksack
Hendon: police training school
Herbert Beerbohm-Tree and Mrs Patrick Campbell: actors
his beat: the area he patrols
hit a brick wall: come up against an obstacle
huge chip on her shoulder: resentful
I'm blowed: I am surprised
I'm spitting nails: very angry
keep it under your hat: keep it a secret
keep mum about it: keep it a secret
Keep your hair on: don't get so excited
knighted: given a British honour
knock his block off: punch him hard, block = head
late birds: go to bed at a late hour

lavatory: restroom
load of tripe: lot of nonsense
little hussy: girl of loose morals
Lonnnie Donegan: father of British skiffle music
loo: toilet (also bog, khasi)
LSE: London School of Economics
mantelpiece: shelf above a fireplace
Marmite or Bovril: meat-based sandwich spreads
Mickey Finn: a drugged drink which makes the drinker unconscious
milkman: person who delivers milk to the house
Mosquito: British airplane used in Second World War
mooning over a boy: teenage girl infatuated with a boy
News of the World: British tabloid newspaper
North London / South London: separated by the River Thames
off his chump: slang for being mad, crazy
old chestnut: weak excuse
off-licence: shop selling alcohol
old toffee: lies
on my tail: after me, chasing me
on the game: prostitute
Ovaltine: malted milk beverage – served hot
Pax, fainites: children's terms for a truce in hostilities
Palais: dance hall
Pathé News and Pearl and Dean: adverts before the movie starts
pin money: small amount of earnings
pissing around: messing about, not telling the whole truth
playing cards close to her chest: being coy with the truth
plods: derogatory name for police
Police Gazette: newspaper produced to publish notices of wanted criminals
pounding the beat: working as a uniformed officer on the streets
pretty good going-over : a thorough investigation (can also mean beating up)
prick: slang for penis
pull the wool over their eyes: fool people
pulling *my* leg: having a joke at my expense, teasing
pushover: soft touch, easily manipulated
quite sweet on you: likes you romantically
Reggie and Ronnie: the Kray twins, criminals
restroom: place where staff can relax or recover in

rozzers: policemen
ructions: disagreements
S.P.: starting price = the truth about what is being said
School Friend: comic aimed at teenage girls
settee: sofa
sick: vomit
skiffle: 1950s style of popular music
slacks: UK trousers/ US pants
sling your hook: go away
snapshot: photograph (also snap, shot, print, photo)
spewed: vomited
stick of rock: a cylinder of candy often sold at the seaside
sticking plaster: Band-Aid
stinks like a haddock left out too long in the sun: doesn't sound correct
stitching me up: framing me
swot: a nerd, a geek, someone keen on their studies
tabard: apron worn for some work
tart: woman with loose morals
tart's boudoir: a hooker's bedroom
Teddy boys: Thugs and young tearaways
Ten bob: ten shillings: pre-decimal money — half of £1 = ten-shilling note
This Is Your Wife: parody of TV show This Is Your Life
tightly permed hair: hair artificially curled
Tizer: fizzy pop/soda
Tommy Steele: 1950s-60s pop star
Trousers: pants
tugging my forelock: acting in a subservient manner
tuppenny tart: a cheap hooker
two hoots: couldn't care less
two peas in a pod.: two people similar to one another
ugly mug: ugly face
up and comers: young and rising sports people (over the hillers = past their best sports people)
very snarled up: gridlocked traffic
Victor Sylvester: popular ballroom dancer and band-leader in the 1950s
whistles and bells: top specifications
winkle-picker shoe: long narrow male shoe
Wolseley: model of saloon car used by the police

yobs: thugs and young tearaways
your lazy arse: ass
your racket: your loud noise

ABOUT THE AUTHOR

Len Maynard & Mick Sims (Maynard Sims) are the authors of several novels with more coming soon. They have written stories, novellas, essays, award winning screenplays, and have worked as editors. www.maynard-sims.com

Jack has his own website too! http://www.jackcallum.co.uk/

Thank you for reading this book. If you enjoyed it please leave feedback on Amazon, and if there is anything we missed or you have a question about then please get in touch. The author and publishing team appreciate your feedback and time reading this book.

Our email is jasper@joffebooks.com

http://joffebooks.com

Follow us on facebook www.facebook.com/joffebooks for news on Maynard Sims' next book arriving soon

FOR HER SINS

(Jack Callum Book 3)

MAYNARD SIMS

First published 2016
Joffe Books, London
www.joffebooks.com

THERE IS A GLOSSARY OF ENGLISH SLANG IN THE BACK OF THIS BOOK FOR US READERS.

DEDICATION

To Lyn Clarke for her unceasing support and enthusiasm.

AUTHOR'S NOTE

Certain liberties have been taken with the geography of Hertfordshire for the benefit of the story. Hopefully the residents of that beautiful county, which has been my home for many years, will be forgiving. MS

CHAPTER 1

MONDAY 7 DECEMBER 1959

The rubber soles of Sister Marguerite's sandals squeaked on the highly polished linoleum as she hurried along the corridor to the chapel. Behind her she could hear the laughter of the audience in the orphanage refectory as the tedious black and white comedy film neared its end. Even when she was younger she had never found George Formby funny and as an adult, she found the toothy comic from Lancashire puerile and slightly offensive.

Film nights had become a monthly routine at St Joseph's Home for Boys and Girls since the local 'men's committee' had taken it upon themselves to provide celluloid entertainment for the seventy or so resident children. She supposed they meant well, especially Leslie Parsons, who approached the charity work with a zealot's gleam in his eye. She wasn't so sure about the other men in his 'committee.' Why a group of young, fairly presentable bachelors should want to devote so much of their free time to helping a motley collection of waifs and strays was anyone's guess. She chided herself for her cynicism. Had she become so distrustful of people's motives? In a word, yes. Post war Britain was no longer the country she had grown up in. It was a harder, more ruthless place now, where greed seemed to be the norm, and charitable acts were viewed with suspicion.

Not that Leslie Parsons was a young bachelor. He was in his early thirties, had a wife, and at least three children to the best of her knowledge, but he was a recent convert to the Catholic faith. Like many who had heard God's word relatively late in life, he seemed determined to prove to all, but mostly to himself, that he merited his "calling."

She pushed open the chapel door and entered the darkened sanctuary. She genuflected automatically in front of the large wooden crucifix that hung on the wall above a modest altar, sidled into a pew at the back, bowed her head and began to pray.

It was only when she lifted her head from her devotions and her eyes had become accustomed to the gloom that Sister Marguerite saw that she was not alone in the chapel.

Prostrated in the aisle in front of the altar was a nun dressed in the white habit of the novitiate. There was only one novice at St Joseph's — Sister Bernadette, sent here by the Mother Superior at St Luke's monastery in Hitchin to learn humility and strengthen her faith before taking her final vows.

Sister Marguerite watched the girl for another ten minutes. Bernadette continued to lie there, face down, arms outstretched, motionless. Sister Marguerite edged her way to the end of her pew. "Bernadette?" she called softly. "Bernadette!"

Getting no response, she finally pushed herself to her feet and approached slowly. She was reluctant to disturb the girl's devotions but also did not want to nurse her in the infirmary should she catch a chill from lying on the chapel's freezing flagstones. She trod softly, not wishing to alarm the girl. Then, from the back of the chapel, came an ungodly crash, as a pile of hymnals clattered to the floor.

She gasped and spun around in time to see a boy break from the cover of a heavy brocade curtain and run to the door.

She recognised him at once. "Raymond Oliver? Is that you? What mischief have you been making?"

The boy yanked the door open and ran out into the corridor. The curtain rippled again, and another boy broke cover and dashed towards the door.

"And if that was Raymond Oliver, then that must be Terry Lloyd. Terry! Stop this instant." But she was too late. The door opened again and Terry Lloyd beat a hasty retreat from the chapel. Marguerite listened to the footfalls and their braying laughter as they ran away.

She turned back to the girl, certain that the sudden noise ripping through the stillness of the chapel would have alerted her, but Sister Bernadette continued to lay prone on the floor, unmoving.

In an effort to steady her beating heart, Marguerite walked across to the light switch and snapped it down. As the bulbs in the chapel ceiling bled out their meagre light, she walked briskly up the aisle. "Enough is enough, Bernadette. You'll catch your death lying there like that."

Then she froze, her mouth still open to speak.

Now she was closer she could see that Bernadette was not face down at all. Instead the girl's pretty face was turned to one side. Her eyes were open and she was staring blankly at the wall. Marguerite saw the blood that had trickled from her nose and the corner of her mouth. She ran to the girl and gazed down at the pool of blood spread out beneath her. Marguerite clamped her hand over her lips as her gorge began to rise. She spun on her heel and bolted from the chapel, back to the refectory, her feet slapping on the linoleum giving her a solo round of applause.

Heads turned as she burst into the crowded dining hall. She dropped her hands from her mouth and a fountain of vomit exploded from her lips.

"Eeee, it's turned out nice again, hasn't it?" George Formby said as the credits began to roll.

CHAPTER 2

MONDAY

There were already three police cars parked outside the gates of the orphanage when Jack Callum arrived. He pulled in behind one of the black Wolseleys, got out, and was immediately buffeted by a blast of icy December wind swooping down the quiet residential street.

He had driven past St Joseph's on countless occasions and had barely taken any notice of it. All he had seen was a sprawling grey brick building. Erected in Victorian times as a workhouse, it had lost nothing of its forbidding presence. Even this evening, with many of the windows ablaze with electric light, the building still exuded a feeling of melancholy and quiet desperation, as if those traits had somehow been woven into its very fabric.

Jack pushed through iron gates and walked up the gravel path to a large black front door. The thud of the brass knocker echoed within. A young constable with bright eyes and bad skin opened the door and pulled it wide, saluting Jack as he walked into a brightly lit vestibule. The hall was dominated by a floor-to-ceiling painting of the Virgin Mary, her hands spread out in a gesture of welcome. Jack stared up at the beatific expression on Mary's angelic face and couldn't suppress a shudder. The painting brought back memories of the childhood horrors of Sunday school, and the vicar's ranting fire and brimstone sermons that had literally put the fear of God into him.

"Sorry to drag you out this evening, sir." Nigel Barrett emerged from a room to Jack's left. Barrett was an experienced detective sergeant who usually worked the night shift with Alan Healy. Inspector Healy's absence from tonight's proceedings was the reason Jack had been called away from his cosy evening. He had been ensconced in front of a roaring log fire, enjoying a relaxing time listening to records with his wife, Annie, and two of their three children.

"It doesn't matter, Sergeant. Have you heard from DI Healy?"

"Still at the hospital, sir. Mrs Healy went into labour about six this evening and is still there."

Jack glanced at his watch. It read 9.30. *Early days yet*, he thought, remembering the three times he had been in Healy's situation. It seemed like only yesterday.

"What have you got for me?"

"A young woman, dead in the chapel. Multiple stab wounds by the look of it. Doctor Fenwick's with her now."

"You'd better take me to her."

Barrett led him through a series of corridors painted light green. The shiny lino floors smelt of lavender polish and wintergreen.

"The forensic team from Stevenage is on its way," said Barrett.

"Good."

As they passed along the corridor leading down to the chapel, Jack saw a crowd of people — adults, children and nuns, just inside the refectory doorway. They were being held back by a uniformed PC.

"What's going on down there?"

"The Home was having one of its monthly film nights when the body was discovered. I think most of them want to know what's happened, although there's one chap in there who seems very eager to get off home."

"Does he indeed. Who's the officer on the door?"

"White, sir. Dickie White."

"Well, point me in the direction of the chapel and go and give White a hand. Nobody leaves, absolutely no one, until we've had a chance to talk to them."

Barrett pointed to the end of the corridor. "Just down there, sir, and turn right. You can't miss it."

Jack continued along the corridor, turned right and came to the chapel doors. He stood for a moment, took a breath and pushed his way inside.

The lighting in the chapel left a lot to be desired. Three CID officers were using their torches to scour the chapel for clues. In the aisle Barry Fenwick, the police doctor, was crouched over the body of a young woman dressed in a white habit.

"They didn't tell me it was a nun," Jack muttered under his breath. He swore silently.

Fenwick looked up as Jack appeared behind him. "Young woman, about nineteen or twenty. She was found lying face down. I turned her over onto her back and found the stab wounds to her body. Ten to the upper torso, three to the abdomen area, all non-fatal I would say. The one that killed her was the one to her throat. The knife entered here." He pointed to the wound. "It punctured her windpipe, and then the knife was yanked sideways to slice through the muscles. I think he was going for the carotid but he barely nicked it. There would be a lot more blood if he'd done a better job, but it was enough. It's too early to say for sure until they get her back to the morgue and the post mortem is done, but my guess would be that she drowned in her own blood." Fenwick got to his feet and nodded at an object lying on the flagstones a couple of feet away from the body. "Did you see that?"

Jack stared down at a brass cross, about twelve inches long, the lower half of the vertical member caked with blood. "Surely that's not the murder weapon?"

Fenwick regarded him bleakly. "I wish it were. Look." He lifted the hem of the girl's habit and raised the skirt for Jack to see beneath it.

Jack stared down at the girl's lower body. "Oh, good grief! Who the devil could do such a thing?"

"The devil indeed, Chief Inspector," Fenwick said, and let the skirt fall.

"The forensic team should be here shortly. Best we leave everything just as it is. How long ago do you think she was killed?" Jack asked.

"My best guess would be within the last two hours."

"So while everyone was in the refectory enjoying a film show, she was in here being sexually violated and murdered. The chapel walls are thick and the dining room is some way away, so it's doubtful that anyone would have heard her screams."

Fenwick shrugged. "Who can say? Her God certainly deserted her tonight. I've seen some terrible things in my time, but nothing like the savagery exhibited here. Whoever did this was either driven by crazed bloodlust, or they had some kind of personal grudge against the girl. Not that it's for me to say, of course. But whoever did this, I hope you catch him soon."

"Are you sure a man did this?"

Fenwick shrugged again. "That's where my job ends and yours begins."

"When can I expect the post mortem results?"

"I've already called it in and there's a home office pathologist arriving first thing in the morning. I don't expect you'll have anything concrete to go on until Wednesday morning at the earliest."

"Well, thanks for all your efforts tonight, Barry."

"Has anyone heard how Jenny Healy's doing? I understand she went into labour earlier this evening."

Jack shook his head. "The last I heard she's still there."

Fenwick stared down at the body and shuddered. "What a bloody awful world to bring a child into."

* * *

Nigel Barrett had his hands full. He stood blocking the refectory doors, but inside the mood had changed from stunned silence to murmured resentment. The man who was so anxious to leave was doing a fine job of stirring up the others with a campaign of sarcastic whispers and acidic asides.

"I'm sure it won't be long now," Barrett said to him.

The man had a thin, sour face, too much oil in his hair and bad breath. "You said that twenty minutes ago," he called out.

Jack stepped in. "Is everything all right here, Sergeant?"

Barrett lowered his voice to a whisper. "The natives are getting restless, sir. Especially *Halitosis Harry* there, who's geeing everybody up."

The man spotted Jack and pushed his way to the front of the throng milling around the door. "Are you in charge here?" he asked.

Jack glanced up at a picture of Christ hanging above the doorway. "Hardly," he said. "I'm Chief Inspector Callum. I'll be heading things from now on."

"Well, Chief Inspector, I insist that you let us leave. We all have homes to go to, and some of us have work tomorrow. You can't keep us cooped up in here."

"May I have your name, sir?"

The man glared at him. "Why would you want my name?"

Jack regarded him patiently. "If you please, sir."

The man bridled. "Pennington. Marcus Pennington."

Jack wrote it down in his notebook. "Right, Mr Pennington. For your benefit, and for any of you others who are listening, let me tell you what we're dealing with here. A young woman has been killed, brutally murdered, while you were in here enjoying your film." He gazed at the shocked faces that stared back at him.

"Now, I am here to get to the bottom of all this and find her killer. So you might as well make yourselves as comfortable as possible, because none of you are leaving until I or my men have had a chance to talk with each and every one of you."

"But that's outrageous," Pennington said. He tried to push his way through the door.

Jack laid a hand on Pennington's shoulder and guided him back into the room. "As I said, Mr Pennington, nobody leaves until you have been cleared to do so by either me or one of my officers."

"But it's gone ten o'clock," Pennington said petulantly.

"And it might be three in the morning before we're finished here. I'm missing my cocoa as much as the next man, believe me, but I trust I can count on your patience. Do we understand each other?" He turned to Barrett. "Who discovered the body?"

"Sister Marguerite, sir. She's in Sister Rosalie's office. Rosalie's the head nun."

"Don't you mean Mother Superior, Sergeant?"

"She just told me she was the 'head nun.'"

"Right, get onto the station. We need more men down here immediately if we intend getting everyone out of here tonight. I know I told Pennington that I'd keep them all until three, but I wasn't lying when I said I was missing my cocoa. I'd like to get home tonight if possible. Now, where is Sister Rosalie's office?"

"Down there, sir." Barrett pointed back down the corridor. "Second door on the right."

Jack walked briskly down the corridor and rapped sharply on the door.

"Enter."

He walked into a spartan office. There was a desk, two chairs, a bookcase, a small wooden filing cabinet, and very little else.

Sister Rosalie was dressed in a blue-grey habit overlaid with a grey apron and wearing a starched white cornette on her head. She looked out at the world through round, rimless glasses. Probably in her late fifties or early sixties, Sister Rosalie gave a very good impression of a wise old owl.

"Sister Rosalie?" Jack took off his hat. "I'm Chief Inspector Callum, Welwyn and Hatfield Police."

"Sister Rosalie of the Daughters of Charity," the nun replied. "Now the introductions are out of the way, shall we get down to business?" There was a no-nonsense gruffness about her manner that was belied by the warmth and kindness of the eyes behind her spectacles.

"You described yourself to my sergeant as the 'head nun'. Not Mother Superior?"

"You can see for yourself, Mr Callum, there's nothing very superior about me."

"Yes, but . . ."

"Yes but nothing. The Daughters of Charity, or to give us our full title, the Daughters of Charity of Saint Vincent de Paul, are working nuns. We are here only to serve the poor and the needy. We are not a cloistered order, shut away from life to spend our days in quiet contemplation and endless devotion. We get out to where we are needed and get our hands dirty, working to help others. We are all Sisters and have no regard or need for hierarchy. I call myself the 'head' because it puts casual outsiders at their ease. They know they have someone to blame if things don't go according to plan. I run the business side of things because that was what I trained for in civilian life, but I'm no more important in the general scheme of things than Sister Marguerite here."

Jack saw another nun, sitting on a hard wooden chair in the corner of the room. She wore the same grey/blue habit as Sister Rosalie but her apron was stained with what looked like vomit.

She had taken off her cornette and wore a simple white linen cap that covered her hair.

Jack looked across at her, and she lowered her eyes and bowed her head slightly.

"Actually it was Sister Marguerite I came to see." He turned and spoke to her. "I understand it was you who made the discovery in the chapel."

The woman kept her gaze averted, crossed herself and started to weep silently.

Rosalie came out from behind the desk and crouched down beside Marguerite, putting her arm around her shoulders.

"As you can see, Mr Callum, the discovery of Sister Bernadette's body has shocked the Sister deeply. I don't think putting her through the ordeal of answering questions is going to help either you or her. In fact I think Sister Marguerite should retire to bed now. She, like us all, has a very early start in the morning. Four a.m."

"But—"

Sister Rosalie raised her hand. "Sister Marguerite has given me a full account of what transpired in the chapel. I should be able to answer any questions you have." She turned to Marguerite. "Run along to your room now, Sister. Good night, and may God go with you."

Marguerite got to her feet and hurried from the office.

"I really wanted to talk to her directly," Jack said.

Sister Rosalie returned to her seat behind the desk. "Mr Callum, one of life's great disappointments is that we can't always have what we want."

Jack suppressed a smile. Sister Rosalie of the Daughters of Charity of Saint Vincent de Paul was evidently a most formidable woman.

CHAPTER 3

MONDAY

"What can you tell me about Sister Bernadette?"

Sister Rosalie's face took on a troubled expression. "A lost sheep trying to find her way back to her flock would probably be the best way of putting it."

I doubt that, Jack thought. He waited for Sister Rosalie to expand on the comment. Nothing was forthcoming.

"Was she a troublemaker?"

"That's a very harsh way of looking at it. Bernadette had only been with us for six months. Before that she was at St Luke's monastery in Hitchin. The Mother Superior there is one of my oldest friends and she had spoken to me about Bernadette on several occasions. St Luke's is a Carmelite order. While neither of us doubted the sincerity of Sister Bernadette's beliefs, we both agreed that a life of contemplation and prayer in an enclosed order might not be the best way for her to follow her vocation. I suggested she come to St Joseph's and spend some time living with the Sisters here in a more relaxed environment."

"But what can you tell me about Bernadette the person? I'll take it as read that you and the Mother Superior at St Luke's had her spiritual wellbeing covered."

"Her full name was Bernadette O'Farrell and she had just turned twenty-one. She came from a devout family in Liverpool, the youngest of three sisters. The elder two had also taken the veil in their late teens."

"So she was following in the family business, so to speak."

Sister Rosalie's eyes twinkled behind her glasses. "So to speak. My friend and I both identified that as her main problem. We could never be sure if the girl had come to God's family of her own volition or whether she had been pressed-ganged into it by her family." She took off her glasses and wiped the lenses with a handkerchief taken from the sleeve of her habit. "We never really got to the bottom of it and now, sadly, we never will." Tears welled in her eyes and she used the handkerchief to dab them away. "Excuse me. I'm no stranger to death in all its forms, many of them brutal and violent. I was a missionary in Singapore when the Japanese occupied it during the war, so I know what kind of atrocities man can inflict upon his fellow man. But Bernadette . . . she was just a child. I went down to the chapel but they wouldn't let me see her. I understand it wasn't a peaceful passing."

"No," Jack said, picturing what was beneath Bernadette's habit. "It wasn't peaceful."

"Then all I can do is pray that her soul finds the peace in heaven that eluded her in life."

"You said that you went down to the chapel but they wouldn't let you see her. Who were 'they?'"

"Your sergeant Barrett, another young policeman, and someone, a detective I think he was, who had a camera and was taking photographs."

"You didn't think to go down to the chapel before, when Sister Marguerite announced what she'd found there?"

Sister Rosalie shook her head. "I suppose I should have, but Sister Marguerite was in a terrible state. I brought her here to the office and tried to comfort her. She told me everything, about finding Sister Bernadette lying there, prostrated on the floor and about Raymond Oliver and Terry Lloyd running out of the chapel."

"Who are they?"

"Two of our boys. Sister Marguerite disturbed them. They were obviously up to some mischief or other while everyone else was watching the film."

Jack rubbed at his head. "And you didn't think it was important enough to mention them before now?"

"Well, they can't be involved in this, Mr Callum. They're just little boys."

"How little?"

"They're both fifteen."

"My son is fifteen and he's almost as big as me."

There was a short silence. Sister Rosalie closed her eyes. Jack waited for her to open them again before continuing. "Raymond Oliver and Terry Lloyd. What can you tell me about them?"

"Raymond is the dominant one. Wherever Raymond leads, Terry's sure to follow."

"Are they violent?"

"They're teenage boys, Mr Callum. Tearaways yes, but no more violent than any other boys of their age."

"I'm going to have to interview them. Do you know where they might be now?"

Sister Rosalie stood up, opened her desk drawer and took out a large bunch of keys. "They're locked in the room next door. I thought you might want to talk to them so I had them found. They were both in the boys' dormitory, smoking cigarettes out of the window."

"And they didn't object to being dragged to a room and locked in?"

Sister Rosalie regarded him with a steely gaze. "They know better than that. Come along. You can see them now."

She walked out into the corridor. As she went to open one of the doors, Jack moved forward and reached for the keys. "Shouldn't you let me do that?"

Sister Rosalie batted his hand away. "I'm perfectly capable of handling two of my boys." She unlocked the door and pushed it open, then turned back to Jack. "I'll leave you to your questions. Would you mind if I send the younger children to bed now? It's hard enough getting them up for school in the mornings, without them having the excuse of a really late night."

"That should be fine."

"Please come and see me before you leave. I'll be in my office."

Jack promised he would, walked into the room, and closed the door behind him.

The air in the room was thick with cigarette smoke. In the centre of the room was a plain plywood-topped table. A large round plate placed in the centre was being used as an ashtray by the three figures sitting around the table on wooden seats. There were two boys and one man.

One of the boys had a gaunt face pocked with acne, and some wispy hair on his chin. He was chewing gum and kept smacking it in his mouth, making wet, popping sounds. He regarded Jack with arrogant hostility. This was obviously Raymond Oliver.

The second boy had a cherub's face with scrubbed and blotchy pink skin. His mousy hair styled in a crew cut looked at odds with his angelic features. A smattering of freckles coated the middle part of his face and covered his nose and cheeks. Terry Lloyd looked out at the world through watery blue eyes that showed fear every time he lifted his gaze from the table top. Both boys smoked furiously, although it seemed it was only Oliver who was inhaling. He was taking long draws and exhaling smoke through his nostrils and pursed lips. Lloyd sucked smoke into his mouth and expelled it again, blowing grey clouds in the direction of the man sitting opposite him.

The man seemed to be in his early-to-mid thirties with a shiny bald head, fringed with a semi-circle of dark ginger hair. He was slim and athletic looking and had a pleasant, if bland, face. He had only one eye. That eye glittered with intelligence, while the glass orb stared straight ahead. He got to his feet as Jack entered the room and adjusted his bottle-green woollen waistcoat.

"Hello," he said. His voice was mellow and confident. "Leslie Parsons." He stuck out a hand. "I thought I ought to sit in with Ray and Terry while you question them, as they're still juveniles."

Jack shook Parsons' hand, which was dry and had a firm grip. "It's okay, Mr Parsons. We stopped using rubber truncheons to beat the answers out of people some years ago. Chief Inspector Jack Callum."

"I wasn't suggesting . . ." Parsons began and then realised that Jack wasn't being serious. "Oh, yes, I see. Sorry. I *was* being a trifle pompous." He smiled and sat back down.

Jack dragged a chair from the side of the room and sat down at the head of the table. He reached out and picked up the packet of Senior Service cigarettes sitting open in front of Oliver. He slid one out. "May I?"

The boy shrugged. "Help yourself."

Jack took a Swan Vesta from a box, struck the red tip on the sandpaper strip at the side and dipped the end of the cigarette into the flame. It tasted foul. He hadn't smoked a fag in years, but the gesture of doing so might help to establish some common ground with the boys.

He blew smoke into the fuggy atmosphere. "Right, boys. Would you mind telling me what you were doing in the chapel earlier this evening?"

"Trying to get away from George bloody Formby," Oliver shot back. "Bloody kids' film."

"He's a very funny man," Parsons said.

"Belongs in the ark with Noah, only then there'd be bloody two of them," Oliver said with a sneer.

"I suppose you'd prefer John Wayne," Parsons said. "But the younger children were watching the film as well, and they don't all want to see cowboys shooting Indians."

"They might do. You haven't asked them. 'When I'm cleaning windows,'" he sang in a passable impression of the Lancashire comedy legend. "Bloody rubbish!"

Jack watched the exchange with wry amusement, then brought them back to the here and now. "Did you see Sister Bernadette when you were in the chapel?"

"I saw her," Oliver said, jutting out his chin. "So?"

"Didn't you think it strange that she was lying on the floor?"

"We thought she was praying, didn't we, Ray? Some of them pray like that, lying face down on the floor, arms spread out."

Jack turned to Raymond Oliver. "Is that what you thought, Ray?"

"No. I thought she was dead," he said flatly.

"And you did nothing?"

"We were going to, then Sister Marguerite came in and I thought she'd blame us, so we legged it."

"Did you see anyone else in the chapel that evening?"

The two boys exchanged looks. "Only the Sisters," Oliver said.

"And you, Terry?"

"Like what Ray said."

Jack stood up and stubbed out the cigarette in the ashtray. "Okay, boys. I think we're finished here for tonight."

"Is that it?" Oliver looked affronted, as if his time had been wasted.

"Well, I could ask you what mischief you were getting up to in the chapel, and I could sit here until you tell me, but I have a home to go to. Mr Parsons, can you see that the boys get off to bed?"

"Aren't you going to ask *me* if I saw anything?"

"Were you in the chapel as well?"

Parsons shook his head. "No, I was in the refectory tending to the projector. I got it second-hand and it's a bit temperamental."

"Then I'm not going to bother. I'll have enough witness statements to go through in the morning without adding yours to the pile." Jack walked to the door and opened it. "If you do remember anything, boys, perhaps you'll tell Mr Parsons here."

The boys stared at him blankly and Jack went back to Sister Rosalie's office.

CHAPTER 4

MONDAY

There was another person in conversation with Sister Rosalie.

"Mr Callum, you haven't met Father Harvey, have you? He looks after our spiritual needs here at St Joseph's."

The priest rose and extended his hand. "Martin Harvey." He was in his thirties with handsome, chiselled features, as tall as Jack but more lithe. As he smiled his dark brown eyes came alive.

Jack shook his hand.

"Father Harvey got here as soon as he could," Sister Rosalie said.

"I was rehearsing the choir at St Augustine's for this year's carol concert," the priest explained. "Otherwise I would have been here sooner. Sister Bernadette's death is an awful tragedy. She was such a sweet girl."

"You knew her then, Father?"

"Yes. She and I had many conversations."

"Would you describe her as the outgoing type, easy in other peoples' company, quick to make friends?"

The smile in his eyes went out. "None of those things, I'm afraid. Bernadette was troubled."

"Troubled in what way?"

"Conflicted. In her heart and mind she knew that she was walking the correct path, but I think her body was telling her something else."

"Where did your conversations with her take place?"

"Here mostly."

"Father Harvey comes to see us at least once a week," Sister Rosalie said. "He has his hands full with his work at St Augustine's, but he always finds time for us."

"You said 'here *mostly*'. Did you meet with her outside of St Joseph's?"

"Ah, yes, I see what you're driving at."

"So can I," Sister Rosalie said. She gave Jack a withering look. "And I can assure you, Chief Inspector, that everything was above board."

"I wasn't suggesting otherwise."

Harvey had a look of mild confusion in his eyes. "She had been here about two months when I mentioned to her that she might like to come down to help out at the youth club. It's at St Augustine's on a Wednesday evening. I thought it might be good for her to meet some people closer to her own age."

"But surely she had that here? I imagine the home has a number of older teenagers living here."

"Yes, they do, of course they do, but I wanted Bernadette to meet some children from regular families. With the best will in the world, life at St Joseph's can seem a little . . ." He paused and glanced uncertainly at Sister Rosalie, who was sitting slightly forward in her seat.

"Artificial," Father Harvey continued. "I'm sure Sister Rosalie will agree. Life here has to be more ordered than in a regular family."

Sister Rosalie continued. "Which is why we are in the process of building what we like to call our family homes. They are two three-bedroom houses where groups of children can live together in an environment close to that of a normal family."

Father Harvey smiled at her. "A noble enterprise indeed, and Sister Rosalie is to be applauded for her forward-thinking attitude."

"So you asked Sister Bernadette to come and help out at the youth club?" Jack said, forestalling further outbursts of self-congratulation. "How did that work out?"

Father Harvey sighed. "Not as well as I would have liked."

"And why was that?"

The priest sat back in his chair and crossed his long legs, exposing a black and grey striped sock. "I've thought long and hard about the reason it was such a failure. Bernadette was an exceptionally pretty girl, and I think she was given a bit of a rough ride by a number of the boys, and a few of the girls. The boys obviously found her attractive, and the girls, well, quite frankly, they were jealous of her."

"But she was a nun."

"I really don't think that matters at that age," Father Harvey said.

"Did any of the boys try to touch her inappropriately?"

The priest's eyes widened. "Good Heavens, nothing like that went on. I'm rather appalled you could suggest such a thing."

"I should tell you," Jack said, "that Sister Bernadette was not only killed, but she had been sexually violated with a large brass cross."

Father Harvey's face drained of colour and Sister Rosalie gasped. Fingering the rosary beads that hung from her neck, she began to pray.

"So, you see, my question was pertinent and not disrespectful."

Father Harvey shook his head. "As I said, there was no touching. Any abuse Sister Bernadette received was strictly verbal, and in that respect the girls were worse than the boys. With the boys it was restricted to a few lewd comments, but the girls could be more spiteful. As it was, Bernadette stopped coming after a few weeks. But, going back to your original question, we used to talk sometimes, after the youth club had turned out for the evening. And before you ask, what we said is subject to the constraints of the confessional. I am bound by God to keep to its strictures."

"I understand, and I would never expect you to betray the girl's secrets."

"Trust, Mr Callum. It's about betraying her trust, and that holds good despite the fact that Sister Bernadette is no longer with us."

"I'll need to talk with you both again," Jack said. An ambulance bell echoed in the night air.

"You can find me at St Augustine's presbytery," Father Harvey said.

"And you know where to find me." Sister Rosalie stood up. "I'll see you out, Chief Inspector."

"Thank you, but that won't be necessary. I want to check on my men before I leave. I'm afraid I've left them with a lot of the donkeywork to do. I'll be back in the morning."

"The morning?" Sister Rosalie looked surprised.

"Yes. I'll be here as soon as I can."

"But why?"

"I'm sorry if I gave the impression that our investigations were at an end. In fact they're only just beginning. But, given the lateness of the hour, I'm not sure much more can be achieved tonight. So tomorrow, a fresh day and a fresh start." He smiled at them. "And I *will* want to speak to Sister Marguerite. I prefer my witness statements to come from the actual witness and are not, with respect, second-hand accounts. Good night to you."

Two ambulance men were sliding Sister Bernadette's body into the back of their vehicle, supervised by Nigel Barrett.

"How's it coming, Sergeant?"

"We're nearly done, sir. The forensic boys have finished. They've taken the cross away for a once-over, but an initial inspection revealed no usable prints. My boys have searched the chapel from top to bottom, but there's no sign of the murder weapon. We'd like to check outside, but given the dark and the weather, I think launching any kind of search would be counter-productive. There are a couple of outbuildings, the kitchens I think, that could do with going over, but again we could do with daylight. I'm leaving two men here overnight to see that things aren't disturbed."

"Then I'll arrange for a few of my team to search tomorrow. How are you getting on with processing the witnesses?"

Barrett raised his eyebrows. "Most of them are pretty useless. They can give a good account of the film, and a few can describe George Formby's antics in detail, but none of them are of much use to us."

"Which is pretty much what I expected. What about Halitosis Harry, Marcus Pennington?"

"I was leaving him until last. He was such a pain in the neck earlier. Apart from him, there are just a couple of people to talk to. The rest have either been sent home or, in the case of the children, sent to bed."

"I think I'll come in and speak to Pennington myself. I want to know why he was in such a tearing hurry to leave tonight, and why he was here in the first place. Is he one of Parsons' 'men's committee'?"

"If he is, Parsons didn't mention him. There were only three members of the committee here this evening. John Holmes, Tony Smythe and Parsons himself. There are only six members of the committee in all, and Parsons uses a rota system so the workload is shared between them."

The back doors of the orphanage opened with a creak and Leslie Parsons stepped out into the cold December night. He was pushing a trolley on which a film projector was precariously perched.

"You get back into the warm, Sergeant. I'll just have a word with Parsons and then I'll join you."

Parsons pushed the trolley towards an Austin A35 van that sat a few yards away from the building, its back doors open wide. Parsons manoeuvred the trolley across the ground and stopped it a few feet away from the van. He lifted the projector and tried to get it inside the van, but as soon as he had the cumbersome machine in his arms, a strong gust of wind blew one of the van doors shut.

Jack heard the muttered curse from several yards away. "Can I give you a hand with that?" he called. Parsons looked across at him with relief on his face.

"Would you?"

"My pleasure." Jack pulled open the back door of the van and propped it there with his body. "Can you manage on your own?"

"I think so. That's why I told Tony and John to go home." Parsons lifted the projector again and swung round, deftly sliding it into the back of the van next to a brown Rexine-clad loudspeaker and three metal film cans.

Parsons closed the back of the van, leaned against the doors, looked at his watch and groaned. "I could have done with an early night tonight. My shift at work changes tomorrow and I'll be fit for nothing in the morning."

"Where do you work?"

"I'm a toolmaker at Grants over at Stevenage."

"Really? Have you been there long?"

"Since I was fifteen. Started as an apprentice and worked my way up. I'm foreman there now. Mind you, it cost me."

Parsons tapped his glass eye with his fingernail. "A splinter of metal. I should have been wearing my goggles but I left them off for a moment and the lathe I was working on spat a shard up into my eye. The doctor who operated tried to reach it but it had gone in too deep, so he ended up taking my eye out before it could work its way through to my brain."

"That sounds horrific."

"It was, but it taught me a couple of valuable lessons. Firstly, always protect your eyes, and secondly, never underestimate God's teachings. Everything happens for a reason. I lost an eye, but I learned an awful lot about myself, and what I am capable of achieving. It was a test, you see? God was testing me."

"Yes, I can see that." Jack coughed. "I will need to speak to you about the 'men's committee' among other things, but not tonight. I'll let you get off home. Did you give my sergeant your address?"

"Address and telephone number and, as I told him, you can contact me any time. I'll be only too glad to help in whatever way I can."

CHAPTER 5

MONDAY

The refectory had almost emptied. The green tubular steel and canvas seats stood in high stacks around the walls, and several of the dining tables had been brought into the centre of the room. Each was manned by a police officer taking statements. On the far side of the refectory Marcus Pennington sat alone, slouched on a chair, legs crossed, glancing at his watch every few seconds and tutting.

Jack pulled up a chair opposite him and sat down. He took a pen from his pocket and wrote 'Marcus Pennington' on his notepad. "Sorry to keep you."

"No you're not," Pennington said. "I know what your game is, 'make him suffer,' just because I was the only one to stand up and express my dissatisfaction."

"I can assure you—"

"You can assure all you like, but it won't make a ha'porth of difference. As I said, I know your game."

"As you wish. Tell me why you're here tonight."

Pennington stared at him with contempt, as if he had just asked the most asinine question in the world. He answered as if he were addressing a two year old. "I came to watch a film."

Jack nodded slowly. "I see. What is your relationship with St Joseph's?"

"My relationship, as you put it, goes back years."

"How so?"

"I was dumped here by my mother when I was two years old, before she cleared off to Australia."

"So you were once a resident here?"

"Yes. I was one of the *raggedy* kids, an orphan in all but name."

Jack apologised. "I didn't realise."

"Not many people do, but then it's not something you advertise, is it? Not very good for business."

"And what is your business, Mr Pennington?"

"You would have seen it if you drove in from the south on the A1. Pennington's Paper Mill."

Jack hadn't seen it, but he was aware of the factory. "So that's you?"

"That's me. I started as a kid with a barrow, collecting waste newspapers the day after the war ended, and I built it up from there."

"You're to be congratulated. So now, perhaps, you'll tell me the real reason you're here tonight. I can't see a businessman like you, with all the responsibilities of running a successful company, choosing to waste an evening watching George Formby."

Pennington allowed himself a smile. His aggression seemed to drain away and he relaxed in his seat. "I came for a business meeting with Sister Rosalie."

"May I ask the purpose of the meeting?"

"You obviously saw the building work going on across the way?"

"Sister Rosalie mentioned it earlier. A pair of family homes, to help the orphans here experience a more normal life."

"Well, who do you think is paying for them? It's certainly not the Catholic Church. Sister Rosalie faces an almost daily battle to get funding from them. When she told me what she wanted to do with that strip of land, I rallied a few business contacts and put together a plan to raise the money to pay for it. I came here tonight for a progress report."

Jack was impressed. He would have to re-evaluate the man. "And you did all this out of the goodness of your heart?"

Pennington laughed. "Of course not. I'm doing it for self-aggrandizement. Sister Rosalie has promised to name one of the houses *St Marcus's*. Let's face it, Chief Inspector, it's the only way a chancer like me will ever achieve sainthood."

Jack smiled wryly. "Yes, I can see that." He changed tack. "Did you know the nun who was killed here tonight, Sister Bernadette?"

Pennington shook his head. "I saw her in the corridor when I came here a couple of months ago, but the only reason I noticed her was because she was a new face. I couldn't recall ever seeing her before."

"And you haven't seen her since that first time?"

"Only in passing. In all honesty I don't have any reason to come back here that often. When I do, it stirs up memories that are best left buried. When I walked out of the front doors at the age of twenty-one, I thought I was done with the place. My years here were never that edifying, but a few years after I left, when I was building my business, I felt a void in my life that I suppose most *normal* people fill with family. When I first came back for a visit, Sister Rosalie had taken over the helm and I found that the whole atmosphere of the place had changed for the better. The more I visited, the more I got to know her and the more I wanted to help her achieve the vision she had for St Joe's. I felt I owed the old place something, I suppose. After all, it took me in when no other sod in the world wanted me. I was in its debt."

"I suppose you've seen some changes since your time here."

Pennington considered the question for a moment. "Sister Rosalie?"

"Her certainly, but I was thinking more of the 'men's committee'."

Pennington laughed. "*Parsons' boys* you mean?"

Jack nodded.

"Bunch of bloody mugs."

"That's a rather harsh judgement."

"But true nonetheless. Oh, I'm sure Parsons' heart is in the right place. The others too for that matter, but they have no idea of the reality of living in a place like this. It can be described in three simple words: dog eat dog. It's the survival of the fittest, and anyone who tells you differently is lying through their teeth. As I said, Parsons' heart is in the right place, but most of the kids here just see him as an easy mark, someone to be manipulated to get exactly what they want. I mean, film shows?

Come on. When I was here there wasn't even a wireless to help you pass the long, boring evenings before turning in for bed. And then there's all the other stuff he does. Do you know he has groups of the boys to his house some evenings to teach them cross-stitch and rug-making? He pays for all the materials himself. No wonder Father Harvey and his boss, Canon Flood, encourage it. It's money that doesn't have to come out of the church coffers. The kids just take advantage of Parsons' good nature. They know they're onto a good thing and they milk it for all they're worth."

"That's a very cynical view."

"Cynical but true. It's his wife I feel sorry for, Estelle. She's going to inherit the earth one day. She's so meek she wouldn't say boo to a gosling, let alone a full-grown goose. She's stuck at home raising three little'uns, and once a week she has her home invaded by a bunch of yobs. She probably has locks on her cupboards and drawers just to keep their thieving mitts off her valuables. And not so valuables. With the Joeys, if it's not nailed down it's a fair target."

"You're not painting a very pretty picture of the place."

"I'm not going to dress it up for you, Chief Inspector. That would be like putting a tiara on a turd and calling it a princess. I'm just telling you the way it is. Sister Rosalie and the other nuns do their best, but they know they're fighting a losing battle. If you're a kid, stuck here because your folks have either snuffed it, or worse, don't want you, you learn to become self-sufficient very quickly. As I said, dog eat dog. Do unto others before the buggers can do it unto you. As for the other men in Parsons' committee, well, most of them are misfits. They're unable to fit in with normal society so they've built themselves a little kingdom here. It gives them a sense of worth that is sorely lacking in their everyday lives. The exception might be Tony Smythe, who was here earlier. He's an ex-Joey like me. He was here about the same time, but our paths never crossed that often. He was one of the older kids, but he wasn't like the others. He used to read a lot. Not just the religious stuff, but philosophy, psychology, that kind of thing. Always had his head buried in a book that one, and it was always the heavy stuff, not the westerns and science fiction that I used to enjoy. Tony's very quiet, but very smart. What his motive is for joining Parsons' happy band is anybody's guess, but he'll have one, believe you me."

"Well, thank you for your time," Jack said. "It's been illuminating."

"My pleasure." Pennington smiled. "I'm sorry I was a pain in the rear earlier. It was just the inner 'Joey' in me coming to the surface I suppose. Always give the rozzers a hard time. It's second nature."

* * *

Jack drove home feeling that tonight he had witnessed every facet of humanity, good and bad, but mostly good. He thought he should feel uplifted in some way. Instead he felt bone-achingly tired and emotionally drained.

As he slipped into bed beside Annie he looked across at the alarm clock on the bedside cabinet. The luminous hands were pointing to two o'clock. He yawned and Annie stirred. "Your feet are like blocks of ice," she mumbled drowsily.

"Sorry, love. Go back to sleep."

"Eddie called. He said he's got an errand to run on the way to you in the morning, so he won't be able to pick you up until half past eight. You can have a lie-in tomorrow."

"And don't I need it." He kissed the nape of her neck, wrapped an arm across her waist and, keeping his feet far away from her, he closed his eyes.

I never got my cocoa. Damn! Seconds later he was asleep.

CHAPTER 6

TUESDAY 8 DECEMBER 1959

"Hello, Mrs C," Eddie Fuller said when Annie answered his knock at the back door.

Annie pulled the door open. "Come inside out of the wind. Jack shouldn't be long. He's just shaving. He had a very late night. And you can wipe that silly smirk off your face, Eddie Fuller. He was out on a case."

Fuller wiped the smirk and replaced it with a smile.

"Aren't you working today, Mrs C?"

Annie seemed flustered, unlike her usual calm self. "Yes, I am, and I'm late. I woke up when Jack came in and couldn't get back to sleep again. Unlike him, who was snoring as soon as his head touched the pillow." She hurried out into the hall and called up the stairs. "Jack! Eddie's here!"

Jack stuck his head over the banister rail, his chin half-covered in shaving soap. "Can you get a cup of tea down him? Only we're not going in to the station until later."

"There's one in the pot. He can pour it himself. I've got to dash. I'm late enough as it is. Bye, love."

"Bye." Jack made his way back to the bathroom.

Annie came back to the kitchen. "Did you hear all that?"

Fuller was still smiling. "Is the milk in the fridge?"

"And the cups are in the usual place. Anyway, I've got to get my skates on. Rosie left half an hour ago. She'll give me a rocket when I get in."

"But she's your daughter."

"Try telling her that. She started working for Barbara Painter a full year before I did, so in theory that makes her my superior. Anyway, bye."

She went out of the back door and Fuller listened to her heels clacking on the concrete path.

Shaking his head wryly, he took a cup from a hook on the dresser and poured himself some tea.

"Morning, Eddie. Had your exam results yet?" Jack and Annie's eldest daughter, Joan, hurried into the kitchen, a cup of tea in her hand.

"I'm still waiting. They should come through any day now, and then I'll know if I've made Inspector or not."

"Well, dad thinks you're going to do all right. I'll keep my fingers crossed for you." Joan poured tea from her cup into the saucer and blew across it. "I'm all at sixes and sevens today. Dad's alarm didn't go off, and I rely on that. I hear it through the wall and it wakes me up."

A car horn sounded. "That will be Avril." Joan poured the lukewarm tea back into the cup and downed it. Wiping her mouth with the back of her hand, she said, "Bye, Eddie. Wish me luck."

"Do you need it?"

"Do I? Avril's letting me do my first haircut today, and I'm as nervous as a kitten."

"Good luck then."

"Thanks." Joan ran along the hall to the front door. A car door slammed and she was gone. Fuller sat down at the table and sipped his tea. He was still drinking it when Jack came into the kitchen, pulling on his overcoat.

Fuller looked up at him. "What's going on, Jack? It's been like Piccadilly Circus in here this morning."

"Eh?" Jack seemed distracted. He scooped up a handful of change from a china dish on the dresser and dropped the coins into his pocket.

"I said . . ." Fuller shook his head. "It doesn't matter. Mrs C said you had a late one last night."

"I did. Finish that and we'll get going. I'll tell you about it in the car."

* * *

"A nun?" Fuller said.

"I know. It beggars belief, doesn't it?"

"How did she die?"

"Multiple stab wounds to her body, but it was the one to her throat that killed her."

Fuller blew through his teeth and shook his head.

"There's more." Jack told him about what had been done to the body.

Fuller closed his eyes for a moment. "Any leads?"

"There's been nothing to write home about so far. Two boys were seen running from the chapel, but I'd put money on them not being the killers. They're a couple of tearaways, but I don't see them as psychopathic murderers. Whoever killed Sister Bernadette wasn't right, up here." He tapped his temple.

* * *

Jack didn't recognise the nun who opened the door to them that morning. "I'm Sister Theresa," she said, holding the door open for them to enter. "You must be the policemen Sister Rosalie told me to expect."

Jack showed her his warrant card. "And this is Sergeant Fuller."

"Come up to Sister Rosalie's office. She apologises that she can't be here this morning but she has some pressing private matters to attend to today." She followed them into the office. She was a slight woman with pinched features. Her watery blue eyes were magnified by horn-rimmed glasses with thick lenses that perched on the bridge of her thin and slightly pointed nose. She sat in Sister Rosalie's office chair as if she was used to doing so, and folded her hands before her on the desk. "Now, how may I help you?" Her voice suited her perfectly. It was thin and reedy with a soft Irish lilt.

"We would like to see Sister Bernadette's bedroom, and after that we'd like to speak to Sister Marguerite."

Sister Theresa clucked her tongue. "I'm not sure it would be appropriate to take you up to our sleeping quarters. I don't think Sister Rosalie would approve."

Jack smiled benignly. "That may be, Sister, but I'm afraid I'm going to have to insist. It's vital to our investigation."

"Vital," Fuller echoed.

Sister Theresa shifted uncomfortably in her seat.

"Is there anyone occupying the sleeping quarters at the moment?" Jack said. "Because I assure you we will be discreet."

"We won't look, if that's what you're afraid of," Fuller added.

"Yes, thank you, Sergeant." Jack frowned at him. "I'm sure Sister Theresa understands that."

Fuller shrugged.

After a few more seconds, Sister Theresa took a bunch of keys from the desk drawer and stood. "Very well. I'll show you the way."

She led them out of the office to a flight of stone stairs. "Our quarters are up here."

They followed her up the staircase to a corridor with a series of plain wooden doors running along each side. Sister Theresa stopped about halfway along, found a key and unlocked a door. "It has been locked since Sister Marguerite found poor Sister Bernadette yesterday."

"So no one has been in here since then?"

The nun shook her head. "Nobody. Sister Rosalie insisted that no one should disturb anything." Sister Theresa pushed the door open and stood to one side. "I shall wait here."

Jack nodded his thanks and entered the room.

The room was no more than ten feet square, painted off-white, with a cot bed, a wooden chair and a small plywood chest of drawers. Two cups sat on the chest. He glanced back at the nun. She was standing to one side of the doorway, her eyes averted, as if reluctant to look into the room.

Fuller followed Jack inside and pushed the door shut behind him.

"Have you got a problem, Sergeant? Your attitude towards Sister Theresa left a lot to be desired."

"Nuns, sir. They give me the willies."

Jack raised his eyebrows and shaking his head slightly, went across to the chest. With a handkerchief he picked up one of the cups and sniffed. "Tea, same as in the other one. It looks like Sister Bernadette was entertaining in here sometime yesterday."

Fuller was staring at the wall. "Did you notice that?"

There was a nail sticking out of the wall and beneath it, slightly lighter than the rest of the wall, the unmistakable outline of a cross.

"Yes, I saw it when I first walked in here. It's about the same size as the cross the killer used to . . ." He let the sentence tail off, shuddering slightly as he remembered the scene in the chapel. He put the cup back down on the chest. "I take it you brought some evidence bags with you?"

Fuller took a couple of polythene bags from his pocket.

"Bag the cups separately, and try not to spill any of the tea left in them." Jack pulled open the top drawer of the chest. Apart from a few items of white cotton underwear and a white towel there was nothing there. The second drawer down yielded even less. There was a spare habit and, incongruously, a pair of black woollen gloves. The bottom drawer contained a Catholic bible, a hymnal, two prayer books, a rosary made from white plastic beads with a wooden crucifix attached to it, and three small aluminium medallions depicting saints.

Jack shut the drawers. "Anything under the bed?"

Fuller was on his knees, reaching under the cot. "Only this." He dragged out a small leather suitcase and lifted it onto the bed.

"Open it up," Jack said. "Let's see if there's anything in there that will tell us a little bit more about Sister Bernadette."

"It's locked."

"Have you got a penknife?"

Fuller nodded.

"Get on with it then. I don't think Sister Bernadette's going to mind somehow."

Fuller jimmied the two latches on the case with the penknife and lifted the lid. "Well! What do you make of this?" he said, and lifted out a small vest-like garment. He laid it on the bed next to the case.

Jack picked it up. The material was light brown and coarse, rough to the touch. "My guess would be some kind of hair shirt. It would be very uncomfortable to wear next to the skin. What else is in there?"

The next item looked like a small whip, with a handle and four knotted cords hanging from it.

In the bottom of the case was a canvas bag about twelve inches square, secured with a metal zip along the top. Fuller took it out and unzipped it, shaking the contents out onto the bed. Both men watched open-mouthed as an array of flimsy, red and black silk underwear dropped onto the grey blanket, along with a cardboard container about three inches long.

Taking a pen from his pocket Fuller threaded it through the strap of the brassiere and lifted it up. "I was not expecting this."

"Or this." Jack had opened the container. The gold tube that slid out into his palm had a gold sticker with writing on it. It read 'Summer Blush' in blue script. He took the cap from the tube and twisted. The rounded tip of a bright red lipstick emerged from the tube.

Jack shook his head. "It seems there was a lot more to Sister Bernadette than I first thought." He put the cap back on the lipstick and dropped it on top of the underwear. "Put it all back in the case. We'll take it with us and pass it on to the forensic team. I need to have another word with Father Harvey."

"Why?" said Fuller.

"Something he said last night that I didn't pick up on at the time. Now, seeing all this, it makes a lot more sense."

"What did he say?"

"I was asking about Sister Bernadette and he told me that in his opinion she was 'conflicted'. He said something like, 'she knew that she was walking the correct path, but *her body* was telling her something else.'"

CHAPTER 7

TUESDAY

"We'll see Sister Marguerite now," Jack said to Sister Theresa as he closed the boot. The officious little nun had been hovering just behind them since they emerged from Sister Bernadette's room with the evidence bags and suitcase. She clucked her tongue in disapproval as they loaded the spoils into the boot of the car.

"I'll have her called to Sister Rosalie's office. Please go and wait there for her. I don't want the children to see policemen trampling through the home." She went back inside.

A grey Morris A30 pulled in through the gates and Sister Rosalie stepped out.

"Ah, Mr Callum," she said as she joined them on the steps.

She was holding her starched cornette in one hand and a shopping bag in the other. Her head was covered by a white cap similar to the one Sister Marguerite had been wearing the previous evening. Without the white wings sprouting from her headdress the woman looked less imposing. "I'm sorry I wasn't here to greet you when you arrived but I had to go and see Canon Flood. I telephoned him last night to tell him of the terrible news, but I wanted to see him in person today."

"Does he live far?" Jack said, nodding at the Morris.

"St Albans. Far enough away to make catching a bus impractical." She smiled. "The car belongs to St Joseph's. We make use of it when the need arises."

"I didn't know nuns were allowed to drive," Fuller said.

"I think you'd be surprised by what we're *allowed* to do . . . sorry, I don't know your name."

"Fuller . . . er . . . Miss," Fuller said awkwardly. "Detective Sergeant Fuller."

Sister Rosalie extended her hand. "Very pleased to meet you, Sergeant Fuller. For your information, I drove an ambulance during the war, so pootling around the leafy streets of Hertfordshire is no great stretch . . . even for a nun. Anyway, I hope you will do your best to help Mr Callum find out who was responsible for this unholy matter."

Jack stepped in to save Fuller's blushes. "My officers will all be working flat out to solve this case."

Sister Rosalie clapped her hands. "Good. I've very pleased to hear that, and I'm sure that Father Harvey and Canon Flood will be too. Let's go to my office. I'm sure you will want to speak to Sister Marguerite now. That's if you haven't done so already."

"Sister Theresa was going to bring her to your office."

Sister Rosalie shook her head. "What was she thinking? Today is Tuesday. Sister Marguerite will be on duty in the nursery. We have three under twos and a new-born here at the moment. She'll be ministering to their needs. If you wait in my office, I'll fetch her."

* * *

Fuller and Jack sat down to wait. "It's another world, isn't it?" said Fuller.

Jack crossed his legs. "It's certainly opened my eyes. I've seen the sisters going about their business in town, but I had no idea what they did here."

The door opened and Sister Rosalie entered, with Sister Marguerite following close behind. "You may sit in my chair, Sister." To Jack she said, "I shall in be in the nursery when you have finished. Please come and see me before you leave. The sister here will show you the way."

Sister Marguerite took her place and sat, glancing up at a painting of the Virgin Mary on the wall.

"Sister Rosalie gave me her account of what happened yesterday evening, but I'd like to hear it in your own words."

"I don't like George Formby," she said. "I started watching because I thought it was my duty to do so, but I thought the film was vulgar, so I slipped out and went to the chapel, for some peace and quiet as much as anything."

"What time did you leave the refectory and go to the chapel?"

"It had just turned eight o'clock."

"Did you see anybody on your way there?" Fuller asked. His pencil was poised over a notebook open on his knee.

The sister shook her head. "Everyone was in the refectory, apart from Sister Cassidy, who was upstairs keeping an eye on the little ones who were in bed asleep."

"And while you were in the refectory, did you see anyone else slip out like you did?" Jack said.

"No, the refectory was full. Mr Parsons only brings the films once a month, so there's a bit of a crush when he does. All of the seats were taken. Myself and three other Sisters were standing at the back of the room, close to the doors, so if anyone had left they would have walked straight past us."

"Did you see Sister Bernadette earlier that evening?"

The sister shook her head again. "Not that evening, although I did see her earlier in the day."

"Oh? When was that?"

"At morning prayers."

"What time was that?"

"Five in the morning. We have to have them then so we can get the children up and ready for school."

"Don't you have evening prayers as well?" Jack said.

"Yes, at five thirty in the evening."

"And didn't you see Sister Bernadette then?"

Sister Marguerite flushed slightly. "I'm sorry, but I didn't. The children come for evening prayers and so it's always something of a squeeze in the chapel then."

"So you were in the chapel at five thirty," Fuller said, making a note. "How long do the evening prayers last?"

"We like to have the younger children in bed by seven thirty, so we have to get them out of the chapel by six forty-five."

Jack leaned forward in his seat. "So everyone has left the chapel by a quarter to seven. You go back there at eight o'clock and find Sister Bernadette lying face down in the aisle. Didn't you think to raise the alarm straight away?"

Sister Marguerite flinched. "I'm sorry," she said. "I didn't see her at first. It's awfully dark in the chapel at night. I just slipped into a pew at the back and started to pray. It was only when I opened my eyes again that I saw her on the floor. At first I thought she was prostrating herself before the cross. She had come to us from St Luke's and it's not an unusual attitude of worship for our Carmelite Sisters. But the floor in the chapel is cold, freezing in this weather, and I was worried she'd get a chill. I approached her, and that's when I saw that she wasn't praying at all."

"She was dead," Fuller said bluntly.

Sister Marguerite closed her eyes briefly and then snapped them open. "But before I realised there was something badly wrong, Raymond and Terry knocked over a pile of books at the back of the chapel."

"Raymond Oliver and Terry Lloyd?"

"Yes, the rascals. I called out to them. I would have chased them but my leg tends to play up after I've been kneeling for a while. Yesterday, with the cold, it was very painful, so I went back to Sister Bernadette. That's when I realised she wasn't breathing, and then I saw the blood." Sister Marguerite crossed herself and gripped her rosary beads. "I ran back to the refectory to raise the alarm. Then, I'm afraid, I was very sick. It was the shock, I suppose."

"Who went to the chapel to see what was wrong?"

She shook her head. "I can't say for sure. I think it was one of Mr Parsons' men. Mr Smythe, I think. He was the one nearest the doors."

"Apart from Sister Bernadette, Raymond Oliver and Terry Lloyd, you saw nobody else in the chapel?"

"No one."

Jack got to his feet. "Well, I think we've kept you from the nursery for long enough. Thank you for your help, Sister."

Sister Marguerite stood. "Bernadette was a good child," she said. "Whoever took her life slaughtered an innocent."

Images of flimsy red and black underwear and scarlet lipstick entered his mind. Jack pushed them away. "I'm sure you're right."

* * *

"We don't encourage visitors in our private quarters, Mr Callum." Sister Rosalie walked with them down the stone staircase from the nursery. "I won't say we frown upon it, because some of the Sisters have family members who come to visit from time to time but, as I say, it's not actively encouraged. Sister Bernadette had tea with someone, you say?"

"There were two tea cups in her room," Jack said. "So that would be the most likely explanation."

"Well, I can't imagine who she was entertaining. I've known her for six months now and I wasn't aware that she had any friends. Her parents are both deceased and her two sisters belong to closed orders in Ireland. She never requested to accommodate visitors."

"What about Father Harvey?"

"What about him?"

"He and Sister Bernadette have had conversations."

Sister Rosalie paused at the bottom of the stairs. "I'm not sure where this line of questioning is leading, Mr Callum. Are you suggesting that there is anything improper in a priest giving counsel to a member of his congregation? I've pulled you up on your salacious line of questioning before, haven't I?"

Jack shook his head. "I'm not suggesting anything of the sort, Sister. I'm just trying to make sense of Sister Bernadette's murder. So far, the only thing out of the ordinary that happened yesterday was that she entertained someone in her room which, according to what you've just told me, is an uncommon event."

"When I handed nursery duties back to Sister Theresa just now, she told me you were taking things away from Sister Bernadette's room. May I ask what they were?"

"The tea cups. I intend to have them tested for fingerprints," Jack said.

"And a suitcase," Fuller added, earning himself a disapproving look from his boss.

"A suitcase? May I see what is in this suitcase? The Daughters of Charity have no need of personal possessions. Our everyday clothes are kept in a repository at the back of the chapel for the rare occasion when we might need them. Otherwise we lead a frugal and simple life here. Sister Theresa saw you put the case in the boot of your car, am I right?"

Jack nodded.

"Very well then. You can show it to me as you leave. This way."

As they walked to the car Jack said, "Since Sister Bernadette had no available next of kin, I'm going to have to ask you to come to the mortuary to identify the body."

"Is that absolutely necessary?"

"I'm afraid it is. Shall we say some time this afternoon? I'll send a car, and an officer will bring you back here in time for evening prayers."

Sister Rosalie slapped a hand to her mouth when Jack opened the case and showed her the contents of the canvas bag.

Fuller looked over his shoulder. "The lipstick's called 'Summer Blush', in case you were wondering," he said.

Sister Rosalie shook her head. "I'm sorry," she said. "I have no explanation for this. I had no idea . . . I need to seek guidance. I'm sorry, there's nothing more I can tell you."

Without waiting for them to drive away, Sister Rosalie hurried back inside and closed the door behind her.

"Well, that wiped the smile off of her pious face," Fuller said, as he climbed in behind the wheel.

Jack shook his head. "Sometimes, Eddie, you can be a bloody arse."

"What did I say?" Fuller said disingenuously.

"Just drive."

CHAPTER 8

TUESDAY

"Is Alistair Kirby out on his beat yet?"

Desk Sergeant Andy Brewer looked at his watch. "Not yet, sir. I believe he's in the canteen on his break."

"Well, don't interrupt him, Andy, but before he goes out, tell him I'd like to see him in my office." Jack trotted up the stairs, Fuller following close behind.

Chief Superintendent Henry Lane stepped into the stairwell. "Ah, Sergeant Fuller. I'd like to see you in my office." He turned to Jack. "You can come along too, Jack. This concerns you as well."

Jack and Fuller exchanged glances as Lane led them along the corridor.

"Come in, both of you, and take a seat." Lane went around to the other side of the desk and sat down in a plush leather office chair. He opened a file lying on the desk before him and started to scan through it. After a few seconds he looked up and stared at Fuller.

Fuller stared back, trying to guess what was behind Lane's inscrutable expression.

"The results of your inspector's exams have come through, Sergeant, and I thought it only fair I give them to you personally."

I've failed, Fuller thought. *Well, that's it, for this year at least.* "Yes, sir. Thank you, sir," Fuller said gloomily. He started to get up.

"I haven't told you what they are yet, man. Sit back down."

"Yes, sir." Fuller's heart was thumping. *Just get it over with. Put me out of my misery.*

"Ninety-three per cent," Lane said. "You've passed, Sergeant Fuller or I should say, Detective Inspector Fuller."

Fuller let out a breath he hadn't been aware he was holding. "Thank you, sir."

"A remarkably high percentage. I know for a fact that they were tough this year, so you are to be congratulated. It shows that you have worked hard and diligently," Lane said.

Jack shook Fuller's hand. "Well done, Eddie. I knew you had it in you."

"Thanks, guv."

"Have you had any more thoughts on what I said to you about staying on here at Welwyn?" Fuller tried to focus his thoughts and concentrate on what the chief superintendent was saying.

"Yes, sir. I'd like to stay," he finally managed.

"I was hoping you were going to say that. We can't afford to lose officers of your calibre. We'll have to move you to another office, of course. I think it's high time that DCI Callum had his office to himself again. Sharing with him was only meant to be a temporary budgetary measure, but it has dragged on a bit."

"I didn't mind, sir," Fuller said.

"I'm sure you didn't. You can learn a lot working cheek by jowl with someone like DCI Callum, but I'm not sure he's been so sanguine."

Jack smiled.

"So I'm moving you to the office next door to his." This brought a smile to Fuller's lips and widened Jack's.

"That's fine, sir." Fuller could scarcely believe his luck.

"And have you given any thought to who you'd like as your bagman?"

"Not really, sir. To be quite honest with you, I wasn't expecting to pass."

"Nonsense. You sailed through, man."

"Well, on my more optimistic days I did think Trevor Welsh could be a good match."

"Ah. Well, that's not going to happen, I'm afraid. He's already in a team with DS Lesser. I know Frank Lesser can be a difficult cove, but Welsh has worked with him long enough now to get his measure. Besides, I had somebody else in mind."

"Do you mind me asking who that might be, sir?"

"Not at all." Lane looked past them towards the doorway and made a beckoning motion.

Myra Banks walked into the room.

"You both remember WPC Banks, or should I say Detective Constable Banks as she is now."

Jack stared at Lane, a question in his eyes.

Myra Banks was hiding a smile. Dressed in a smart grey suit over a black roll-neck sweater with her hair pulled back in a neat bun, she looked more mature than when they had last seen her. Then she had been propped up in a hospital bed recovering from a gunshot wound in her shoulder.

"How are you feeling now, Myra?" Jack said, getting to his feet.

"I'm delighted to say DC Banks has made a full recovery, Jack," Lane said, coming around the desk.

"So *you* want to be my bagman?" Fuller said.

"If you'll let me, sir," Myra said.

"Of course he will, won't you, Serg . . . sorry, Inspector? Besides, the experience will be good for both of you." Lane walked to the door. "Well, cut along to your new office. Jack, if you will stay for a moment." Lane beamed a smile at Fuller and Myra as they left the room.

* * *

Jack settled back in his seat and crossed his legs. "I suppose you could call that bowling me a googly."

Lane frowned until the cricket analogy finally filtered through. "Ah yes, a googly. I see what you mean. Yes, sorry about that. I did spring it on you somewhat. It was never my intention of course, but you must admit it's good to have Myra Banks back at the station, and looking so well too. An added bonus, I think."

"Tommy Usher could have killed her. She was a very lucky girl."

"And when the Chief Constable read your report on the Tony Tanner case, he agreed with you."

The case was still fresh in Jack's mind. Thomas Usher, the boss of a North London criminal gang had arranged the killing of an actor, Tony Tanner. He had him nailed to a tree on Letchworth's Norton Common and his throat was cut.

"Without her quick thinking we'd probably not be sitting here having this conversation. She damned near saved my life."

"A fact the Chief Constable acknowledges."

"She deserves a medal. A QPM at least."

"And don't think I didn't push for it," Lane said. "Can you imagine? One of my officers awarded the Queen's Police Medal? Think what a morale booster it would have been for everyone here at Welwyn."

"So why didn't he recommend her for it?"

Lane frowned and sat down heavily at his desk. "He gave the go ahead for her move to CID. Believe you me, that was a hard enough pill for the CC to swallow but, in light of her performance on the case, he couldn't really deny my request. A medal would have been a step too far."

"So *you* actually asked for Myra's appointment?" Jack said incredulously. "You turned down her first request to join CID."

"Yes, I did. The time wasn't right then. Now it is. And you really shouldn't be surprised, Jack. I knew it was what you wanted, and I always thought that Myra Banks was a very bright girl and a more than capable officer. Plus, the fact that it's *me* moving her to CID and not you should put the tin hat on those ugly rumours about you and her that were buzzing about the station earlier in the year."

"I'd already dealt with them."

"After a fashion, I suppose you did. I just needed to draw a line under them once and for all, and I think I've achieved that. I want the ship that I captain to be a happy vessel."

"Okay," Jack said after a pause. "I'll buy that. What I'm not so sure about is my position here at Welwyn. You've taken Eddie Fuller on as DI and appointed Myra Banks as his bagman. Where does that leave me exactly?"

"In the same place as before. You're the Chief Inspector here, Jack. That hasn't changed. You're still in overall charge of your teams. Having DI Fuller here should lighten your load somewhat. You don't need to be out chasing after villains now you've got Fuller here to do it."

"I happen to like chasing after villains," Jack said. "And I don't want to stop doing it."

"Jack, I know better than to think I could stop you, even if I wanted to. All I'm saying is you don't *have* to do it, when you have younger and fitter legs to do it for you."

"When should I book my place in the old peoples' home?"

"Don't be difficult, Jack. None of us care much for change, but you can't halt progress by stamping your feet and throwing tantrums. All I ask is that you give it some time. See how the new system pans out. If, say, after six months, you find it's not working out for you, then come and see me again and we can discuss your options."

"Which sounds to me like either shape up or ship out."

Lane sucked his tongue. "I never had you pegged as melodramatic, Jack. Let's not fall out over this, eh?"

Jack smiled. He got to his feet. "No dramas, Henry. Eddie Fuller will make a bloody good DI, and having Myra Banks in CID will be a real blessing. Was there anything else?"

Lane sat back in his chair and smiled. "No," he said. "Nothing else."

"I'll get on then. I've got the murder of a nun to solve."

* * *

When he got back to his office, he found PC Alistair Kirby sitting outside.

"You wanted to see me, sir?"

"Yes, come in, Constable. Take a seat."

Kirby perched on the edge of a chair at the desk.

"And relax, man," Jack said. "I just want a chat. I need to pick your brains."

Kirby frowned and sat back a little. Smiling didn't come easily to him when he was wearing his uniform. When he was on duty his bristly ginger moustache rarely moved from the horizontal. His ramrod straight posture had been drilled into him in the army, where he had been a regimental sergeant major. It now served him equally as well when he patrolled the Hertfordshire streets with his black Alsatian police dog, Satan. The name 'Copper Kirby' was enough to make some of the hardest criminals tremble.

"What dealings have you had with the kids from St Joseph's?" Jack asked.

Kirby adjusted the knees of his tunic trousers and crossed his legs. "I've had endless dealings with them, sir, probably once or twice a week. You could say that the Joeys used to be the bane of my life. While I admire what Sister Rosalie and the other Sisters are trying to achieve there, it has to be said that St Joseph's Home for Boys and Girls is a source of much of the petty crime in Hatfield."

"I can't say it's ever registered with me."

"Well, it wouldn't, sir. The crimes are so minor they wouldn't appear on your radar. There's shoplifting and thievery in general, affray, car theft, and general punch-ups with some of the local gangs. Those who come from settled, so-called *normal*, backgrounds."

"It sounds like a hopeless case."

"And so it was, sir. It used to be really bad until a couple of years ago when Les Parsons and his 'men's committee' started taking an interest in the place. Since then there has been a significant improvement. It's still bad, but nowhere near what it once was."

"Tell me about Parsons."

"Les is a truly good man. One of the few I've ever met. Selfless and very wise for his years — he's only in his early thirties. He really cares for the kids in the home. He and I meet up about once a week. He either comes up to my stables or I go to see him at his home, and we discuss the children and how we can best keep them out of High Mount Approved School. That's where a lot of them would end up if Les didn't intervene, there or borstal."

"Is their behaviour really that bad?"

"Oh, some of them certainly. There are two boys that I know of currently serving fifteen months at the borstal in Leicester. The Flack twins, Alan and Alfie."

"Why were they sent down?"

"Affray and GBH. The two of them took on a local gang, the Hatfield Town Boys, all twelve or thirteen of them. They carved new smiles on four of their faces with their cut-throats before we could get in there and break up the fight."

"You're making it sound pretty grim, Constable."

"It was. But, as I say, since Parsons appeared on the scene, things have started to improve."

Jack sat thinking for a moment. "I think I'll call him in for a chat."

"If you'll take advice from an old campaigner, sir, go to his home to see him. It's here in Hatfield, in Lockley Crescent. You'll get a better understanding of what the man is about."

"Right, I'll do that."

"And while you're there, get him to show you his *Black Museum*," Kirby said. "It will give you a clearer idea of what we're up against with the Joeys."

CHAPTER 9

TUESDAY

As Kirby left the office the telephone on Jack's desk rang. He picked it up. "Callum."

"Hello, sir. It's Elaine, on the switchboard. A call came in earlier for you, from North Herts Hospital. The home office pathologist wants to see you. He said he knows you're waiting for his report, and he thinks he's got something that you'll want to see."

"He didn't give you any clue as to what it was, did he?"

"I just work the switchboard, sir. He wasn't going to tell me anything."

Jack sighed. "Okay, Elaine. I'll get over there."

He pulled on his coat and hat, and then went back to the phone. "Elaine. Can you put me through to a Leslie Parsons? I believe he lives in Lockley Crescent."

A minute or so later he heard a phone ringing on the other end of the line.

After a dozen rings a female voice came on. She sounded harassed. "Hello?" In the background a baby was crying. "Phillip, give Annabel her dummy. I'm on the phone and I can't hear a thing." There was a brief pause as the crying ceased. "Sorry. Who is this?"

Jack introduced himself. "Mrs Parsons, I was hoping to speak to your husband."

"Sorry, he's still at work. He won't be in until six."

"I'd like to come and see him."

"Well, you'll have to be quick. He has a Toc H meeting at half past seven, and I have to get his dinner down him before he goes."

"I'll try to get to you just after six. I won't keep him long. Would that be all right?" The baby started wailing again.

"Phillip? Phillip! Oh, never mind." She said, "Yes, fine. Six o'clock," and put down the receiver.

Jack took a breath and called down to Elaine again. "Did the pathologist leave a name?"

"Strong, sir. Professor Strong."

"Okay. Can you give him a call back and tell him I'll be there in thirty minutes?"

He checked his watch and left the station.

* * *

In the mortuary it was cold enough to make his breath mist. Jack entered the small office.

"Professor Strong?"

A man looked up from the papers he was perusing. "You must be DCI Callum. Thirty minutes on the dot. You're very punctual. I can't tell you how refreshing that is."

Strong was in his late forties with longish salt and pepper hair and a small goatee beard. "Good of you to come at such short notice. I really thought you ought to see a couple of things before I start cutting her up. Follow me."

He led Jack to the main part of the mortuary, where Sister Bernadette's body lay on a stainless steel table, covered by a sheet.

An elderly lab technician was standing at a sink on the other side of the room. He turned as the two men entered. "Are you ready to begin, sir?" he said to Strong. He grabbed a wheeled trolley containing an assortment of operating tools and started to push it in their direction.

"In just a few moments, Henning. Right now I'll need your assistance to turn the body over onto her stomach, so don't go anywhere."

Henning let go of the trolley and, grumbling, went back to the items he was washing in the sink.

"Sorry about Henning," Strong whispered to Jack. "But I've kept him hanging about most of the day. I think he's missed his lunch, so he's a bit tetchy."

He reached out for the sheet covering the body. "Before I do this, I want you to prepare yourself. She isn't a pretty sight."

"I know. I saw her in the chapel."

Strong smiled grimly. "She looks worse without her clothes on."

With a sharp tug, Strong pulled the sheet back from the girl's body.

Jack winced. He had seen some pretty nasty sights during the war but this was worse somehow. This was not some war-hardened soldier, cut down in the heat of battle, but a girl, young enough to be his daughter, who had been attacked brutally and savagely.

"Good grief! I knew it wasn't going to be pleasant, but I had no idea just how bad it would be. How many times was she stabbed?"

"Four wounds to her abdomen and three to her breasts. Three more penetrated her rib cage under her breasts but missed the heart and, of course, the knife wound to the throat. I think that was the one that killed her. Then there's the mess he made of her genital area with the cross. I've never seen anything quite so horrendous, not with injuries deliberately inflicted anyway."

"Is this what you wanted to show me?"

Strong gave a curt shake of his head and a lock of hair dropped over one eye. Impatiently he swept it back. "Take a good look at her breasts. Ignore the stab wounds, if you can, and concentrate on the nipples and the aureoles. Use this." He handed Jack a large magnifying glass.

Jack peered through the glass. "They seem unnaturally pink."

"That's what I thought, so I used this." He handed Jack a piece of white muslin. It was streaked with what looked like a child's crayon.

"'Summer Blush'. It's lipstick," Jack said.

"Yes, that was my conclusion. I'll send this over to the forensic lab at Stevenage to verify of course, but I'm pretty sure that's what it is. There's more." He called to Henning. "If I could have your assistance in turning the body?"

Together Henning and Strong lifted Sister Bernadette and rolled her over onto her stomach.

"What do you make of these, Chief Inspector?"

Jack didn't need the magnifying glass to see the latticework of scars marking the girl's back and buttocks.

Jack peered at the girl's back. "These look like old scars."

"And they are, mostly. I should think some of them go back to childhood, at least to puberty. But these are recent." He pulled an overhead lamp across and switched it on. "Can you see?" Strong pointed to a series of fine pink lines that travelled down Sister Bernadette's back in diagonal stripes. "These are much more recent. Obviously they're nowhere near as severe as the other marks, but I would say they were inflicted within the last few days."

Strong bent over the body and traced one of the lines with his fingertip. "If you look closely, you'll observe that the lines aren't even. Every few inches there's a deeper bruise. See?"

Jack used the glass again and nodded slowly. "They're whip marks. The whip was made with strands of knotted cord."

Strong stood upright and took a step back. "Very good, Mr Callum. My thoughts exactly. Have you had any formal training in these matters?"

Jack shook his head. "No. I found such a whip among Sister Bernadette's possessions. You say these were inflicted recently?"

"As I said, almost certainly within the last few days."

"Anything else you think I should see?"

"Nothing else obvious. Of course I'll let you have my complete findings once I've done the post mortem, but I'd say that the old marks on her back are consistent with years of flagellation. Given that she was a Catholic nun, I would say the scars bear all the hallmarks of the mortification of the flesh. Of course, that's just speculation on my part and I must admit I've never come across it in one so young. How old was she exactly? Eighteen? Nineteen?"

"Sister Bernadette had just turned twenty-one."

"She looks younger," Strong said. "Little more than a child."

"Yes," Jack said. "Little more than a child."

* * *

"These places were originally built as railway workers' cottages," Leslie Parsons said. "Of course, I've made some improvements over the years."

"Very nice."

"Well, it suits us. Both the boys have their own bedroom, and the box room will do as a nursery for Annabel for another couple of years yet." Parsons led Jack through a small hallway and the adjoining dining room, to a lounge that ran the entire width of the house.

In the corner a television was blaring out a weather forecast. Sitting opposite in a low armchair was a young woman with careworn features and tired eyes. She was nursing a baby in her lap. On the floor lay two small boys on their stomachs, their noses buried in the pages of their comics.

"Chief Inspector. May I introduce my wife, Estelle? And this is my daughter, Annabel, our latest arrival. The two little monsters lying down there are our twins, Phillip and Peter. Boys, we have a visitor."

The twins, who looked to be about six or seven, both turned their heads to look up at Jack. Finding nothing to interest them, they went back to their comics. The baby stirred on Estelle Parsons' lap. She made a shushing noise and hugged the baby tightly.

Parsons looked at his family's apparent indifference to Jack's presence. "I'll tell you what, come back out to the dining room. We can talk there."

Jack followed Parsons back the way they had come.

"It's quite a sizable place for a cottage," Jack said. He was staring at a rectangular dining table big enough to seat six comfortably, though it seemed it wasn't used much for dining. The surface was covered with small stacks of typing paper, an open box of carbon paper, a couple of foolscap notepads, pens and a small portable typewriter. To one side of the typewriter sat an ashtray, a briar pipe and an open tin of Gallaher's Rich Dark Honeydew pipe tobacco.

On the far side of the dining table was an oak sideboard that was just about coping with the overspill from the table. A duplicating machine occupied the entire cloth-covered top and on the floor next to the sideboard sat a pile of stencils and two large bottles of purple liquid.

Parsons noticed Jack's interest. "Yes," he said. "It's a Ditto machine, a spirit duplicator. I use it to run off copies of our monthly newsletter. Sorry if the spirit pongs a bit. You get used to it by the time you're halfway through a run. I can't smell it anymore, but my wife tells me it stinks, so I take her word for it."

"Don't trouble yourself," Jack said. "I think the smell's quite pleasant actually. When I was a kid, my elder brother ran a small football league and used to write and copy out match reports. Our dad worked at the Gestetner factory in Tottenham Hale and he acquired an old reconditioned duplicating machine from them. A similar principle to yours, I think, but the Gestetner used ink."

"A Gestetner. Very nice. I'm afraid committee funds couldn't run to one of those."

Common ground established, Jack sat on the dining chair Parsons pulled out for him.

As he sat down at the table, Parsons seated himself in front of the typewriter. "Right," he said. "What do you want to ask me?"

CHAPTER 10

TUESDAY

Andy Brewer looked up as Chief Superintendent Lane approached the desk. "Sergeant Brewer, can you get everyone assembled in the canteen? I have a couple of announcements to make before people start drifting off for the evening."

"It won't be everyone, sir. PC Kirby's still out on the beat and DCI Callum is questioning people regarding the St Joseph's murder. He'll be going on home afterwards."

"Mr Callum already knows the main thrust of my announcement, and you can bring Kirby up to date in the morning. But I'll expect to see everyone else assembled in the canteen within twenty minutes."

"Very good, sir."

Ten minutes later Henry Lane, flanked by Eddie Fuller and Myra Banks, walked into a canteen filled with curious police officers.

Lane took a position at the front of the room and cleared his throat. "Thank you for getting down here so quickly. I'm sorry to disrupt your day, but I have some announcements to make. Some good news for a change." He smiled as a murmur of anticipation rippled around the room. "Firstly, I'm delighted to say that the Welwyn and Hatfield family is growing. At 16.30 hours today, after an epic twenty hours in labour, Jenny Healy gave birth to a baby girl."

A few cheers broke out.

"What did she weigh?" Yvonne Morrison called from the serving hatch. Yvonne had been preparing meals for the station for nearly fifteen years and took a motherly interest in the people she cooked for.

Lane consulted his notebook. "She weighed in at seven pounds six ounces, and the Healys are calling her Gwendoline, after Jenny's mother apparently." He snapped the book shut. "I think a round of applause for DI Healy and his family is in order, don't you?"

With Yvonne Morrison taking the lead, the whole canteen burst into a furious round of clapping, cheering and whooping whistles.

After a few seconds Lane held up his hand. "Thank you for that. Sergeant Brewer will be bringing round his helmet at the end of my announcements. I know you'll all be generous."

Lane looked at his staff. "Now to my second item of news. Over the past few months, some of you will have noticed DS Fuller here with his face buried in numerous textbooks. Well, he was studying for his exams and I'm delighted to tell you all that he passed said exams with flying colours. He achieved a creditable ninety-three per cent, and so, from tomorrow, he should be addressed as Detective Inspector Fuller."

More applause and cheering swept around the room.

Lane waited for it to abate and began again. "For my final announcement I want you to cast your minds back to March of this year and the awful murder of the actor, Tony Tanner. You might recall that in the apprehension of the perpetrator, one of our colleagues, WPC Myra Banks, suffered a gunshot wound and was seriously injured. Well, as you can see, after a period of convalescence, she has made a full recovery and is here today beside me." Another round of applause threatened to break out but Lane held up his hand. "I haven't quite finished. Owing to Myra's outstanding bravery, the Chief Constable himself has agreed to my request that she join CID as this station's first female detective. So step forward Detective Constable Banks, and accept the applause you so richly deserve."

Myra blushed. At this moment all she wanted was for the floor to open up and swallow her. She'd had no idea that Lane was going to make a great song and dance over her transfer to

CID. She would have preferred a more subtle way of informing her colleagues about this controversial piece of news.

Hesitantly she stepped forward to absolute silence in the room. She gazed at the faces staring back at her and saw expressions of disbelief, amazement, outrage and anger. She took a step back.

"Good for you, girl!"

Oh, bless you, Yvonne Morrison, Myra thought, as Yvonne's solo round of applause was picked up by Lane and Fuller, and gradually spread to a few others.

Lane turned to her and said quietly, "Well, I think that went rather well, don't you?" He smiled.

"Yes, sir. Thank you, sir," Myra said. "May I go now? I'd like to get home to tell Mum and Dad."

"Oh, yes. Yes, of course. You must tell them the good news." He turned back to the room and held up his hand again. "Thank you for your indulgence, everyone. There's nothing more, so you can get on with what you were doing." Without a backward glance, Chief Superintendent Henry Lane walked smartly from the canteen and back to his office.

* * *

"Did you know Sister Bernadette?" Jack asked Parsons.

"Only by sight. She hadn't been at St Joseph's very long, since the summer I think and to be quite honest she didn't involve herself much in our activities."

"Would that be the 'men's committee' activities?"

"Yes. The football and table tennis teams, the chess society and the philately club. But then they are very much boys' activities. The girls have their own interests, cooking and sewing and suchlike, and the Sisters look after those. The only times the girls and boys come together are the film nights, and every couple of months or so we hold a dance in the main hall. The younger boys only attend under sufferance — I think they view such things as rather sissy. The older ones don't of course, but then we're talking about something completely different, if you get my drift."

Jack smiled. "I think I do. Tell me, who pays for all these activities? Do you have financial help from the church or the county council?"

Parsons laughed. "If only we did. No. We, that is, the committee, pay for them out of our own pockets. We each donate a small percentage of our weekly wages to keep it all afloat, and we have the occasional fundraising events throughout the year — the dances for instance. We charge a small admission fee and advertise them locally. The tickets usually sell quite well, so that helps to keep us going. We hold a summer fete in May and a sports day in July. Again, any money we make goes to pay for sports equipment and materials for things like the rug-making and cross-stitch lessons."

"For the boys?"

"Oh yes. All of us on the committee host evenings for the half dozen or so boys who show an interest or aptitude. I've got one here tomorrow, as a matter of fact."

"And the boys don't find cross-stitch and rug-making, er, *sissy*?"

"Oh, I'm sure some of them do, but it gets them out of St Joseph's. They get to go to places where they can sit in comfort for an evening and have drinkable tea, so they don't complain."

"Don't your wives object to having their houses invaded by a bunch of teenage boys?"

"I'm the only one of us who's married," Parsons said. "And Estelle is something of a saint when it comes to St Joseph's. I've been involved there for nearly three years now, so I think she's become used to sharing me with them."

A saint indeed. Jack couldn't imagine Annie having the forbearance to deal with a husband whose family played second fiddle to his charitable sensibilities.

So far, everything Parsons had told him corresponded with what Marcus Pennington had said the night before. "I'll need the names and addresses of the other members of your committee."

Parsons picked up a foolscap pad and flipped it open. "Yes, I thought you might. I wrote them all down when I got home last night." He peeled off a sheet of lined paper from the pad and slid it across the table. Jack picked it up and slipped it into his pocket.

"I was talking to Alistair Kirby earlier today."

"Ah, Copper Kirby. What a great chap. Al's been a terrific help to me over the past few years."

"He said I should ask you to show me your, as he put it, 'Black Museum.'"

"Oh, did he indeed?" Parsons said with a smile. He stood up and walked to the sideboard, produced a small bunch of keys from his trouser pocket, crouched down and slid a key into the small keyhole in the bottom drawer. "I keep this one locked. I shudder to think of the twins getting their hands on some of the stuff in here." He pulled open a drawer. "Take a look."

Jack went across to the sideboard and stared down into the drawer. He wasn't sure what he was expecting to see, but it certainly wasn't this miniature arsenal.

There were knuckledusters, catapults, a couple of sheath knives, three cutthroat razors, something that looked suspiciously like an illegal flick knife and, most disturbingly, two Webley air pistols. Jack blew through his teeth. "Where on earth did all these come from?"

Parsons looked up at him. "From the boys. Confiscated over the past couple of years."

"Great Heavens!" Jack said. "You certainly have your work cut out for you if you're having to deal with all this."

"I'm lucky to have grown the 'men's committee' over the same period. When I first started there was only John Holmes, but we've managed to rope in a few more over the years. Two of the chaps on the list are St Joseph old boys. Actually it was one of them, Bernard Gallagher, who alerted me to the fact that some of the boys were collecting and dealing in weapons."

"Where did the boys get the money to pay all for them all? Airguns aren't particularly all that cheap."

Parsons gave Jack an almost pitying look. "They didn't *pay* for any of them, Mr Callum. Some of our boys are light-fingered, and a few of the shops have these things on open display. I think the razors, for instance, came from visits to the barbers."

The smell of frying sausages drifted into the room.

Estelle Parsons stuck her head around the door. "Dinner in ten minutes, Les. Can you clear a space on the table?"

"Okay, love," Parsons said. He looked at Jack, shrugged, and picked up the typewriter. "I'm sorry. Was there anything else you wanted to ask me, only I'm due at a Toc H meeting in an hour?"

Jack shook his head. "No. I think I've taken up enough of your time. You carry on with your tidying. I'll see myself out."

Back in the squad car, Jack took out the list of names, switched on the overhead light and read through it. Then he checked his watch.

Tomorrow, Jack. They can all wait until tomorrow, he thought. He started the car and headed home.

CHAPTER 11

TUESDAY

When he let himself in through the back door Jack found Annie and Joan sitting at the kitchen table, deep in conversation. The atmosphere seemed rather strained.

"Is it just us three for dinner tonight?" he inquired lightly.

Annie looked up. "Eric's over at Gerry's house practising some new songs and Rosie's in the other room watching television."

"That girl will get square eyes. So what the devil's up with you two? You look like you've lost ten bob and found sixpence."

"Joanie thinks Avril's husband is beating her."

"What? Are you sure, Joanie? That's quite an accusation."

Joan looked at him bleakly. "She came to work today with a black eye and told me she'd walked into a door. I know that excuse well. I often used it myself, when I was with Ivan."

Annie looked at her daughter and winced. "Can the police do anything about it, Jack?"

Jack sat down at the table. "Not really, Annie, to be honest. Unless Avril comes into the station and makes an official complaint our hands are tied, and even if she does, there's no guarantee any action will be taken. Very few officers are willing to come between a husband and wife."

"So it has to reach a point where Alf Kendall kills Avril before the police will take any action?" Joan said.

"I'm not saying that, Joanie. Now you're being melodramatic."

"Am I, Dad? Avril's terrified of him. That's why she won't make it official."

"I'm sorry, love. That's just the way it is."

Joan slammed her palms down on the table and pushed herself up. "Well, if you won't do anything about it, I will."

"Joanie," Annie said, covering Joan's hand with her own. "Just calm down and stay out of it. If Avril wanted your help, I'm sure she would have asked for it. She's covering it up because she probably wants to deal with it in her own way."

"Christ! Why is everyone so spineless?" Joan said and stormed from the kitchen.

Jack rose to follow her but Annie grabbed his arm. "Leave her, Jack. She's been like this ever since she got in this evening. She's fired up and angry. Seeing what's happening to Avril has probably opened up some old wounds of her own."

Jack sat back down. "The older I get, Annie, the more people disappoint me. I met Alf Kendall once, just after they married. He seemed like a nice enough chap, quiet and thoughtful, placid even."

"They say still waters run deep," Annie said.

"As I'm finding out the more I dig into the murder at the orphanage."

"Is it bad?"

"They're all bad, pet. But some are worse than others."

Annie went to fill the kettle. "There must be something we can do to help Avril. She's a sweet girl. She deserves better."

"Until she admits that she has a problem and is ready to deal with it, or will let someone deal with it for her, there's nothing I, or anyone else, can do."

Annie shook her head. "Yes, I know. Sometimes I wonder how you do your job. It must be so frustrating."

"That's an understatement," Jack said.

* * *

Jack was sleeping soundly. Annie slipped out of bed and threw on a woollen dressing gown. It was dark out on the landing but a strip of light was showing under Joan's door. Annie tapped lightly and stepped inside. Joan was in bed, propped up on her pillows, the blankets pulled up to her chin.

Her knees were raised and a magazine rested against the slope of her thighs.

Annie padded over and sat on the end of the bed. "Have you calmed down a bit now?" She kept her voice low, so as not to wake anyone else.

"A bit, I suppose. I'm still seething though."

"Don't blame your dad, love. He has to work within the confines of the law."

Joan sighed. "I know, Mum. I'm not blaming him personally. It's the system that's stupid. How men like Alf Kendall can get away with beating up their wives . . . it's just wrong."

Annie looked at her daughter steadily. "Just how violent was Ivan when you were with him?"

Joan gave a small shake of her head. "When we first got together he wasn't at all violent. We'd argue and usually agree to disagree. But as time went on he found it harder and harder to control his temper. English was his second language and that became a problem. He couldn't express himself. I spoke no Czech so we used English all the time. I could tie him up in knots, verbally. It came to a head one afternoon when we were going shopping in Wood Green. We were the only ones up on the top deck of the bus and we were arguing. I can't remember now what it was about, but I was winning. I was being a bit of a cow really, poking fun at his poor English. He lashed out with his hand and caught me square in the mouth, splitting my lip. When he saw the blood, he was mortified. He kept saying he was sorry and promised he would never do it again."

"A promise he broke?"

Joan gave a bitter laugh. "Oh yes. He broke his promise during our very next argument. He broke his promise and broke my heart, but I toughed it out for months. I think, deep down, I was waiting for the Ivan I fell in love with to come back to me."

"But he never did?"

Joan shook her head and sniffed. Her eyes were brimming with tears. "No, he never did. It was easier for him to shut me up with a smack, rather than try to express himself in words."

Annie reached out and gripped her daughter's hand. "It must have been awful."

Joan squeezed back. "The awful part was that I blamed myself. Every time he hit me I'd find an excuse for him, telling myself that I'd pushed him too far. I was taking advantage of his poor English, or he was tired after a hard day's work. Any excuse, rather than face the fact that he was just vicious and bad tempered. So I understand Avril not wanting to tell me about Alf's violence. You see, if you tell someone about it that makes it real somehow. And once you accept it's real, you have to do something about it. So instead, you find yourself making up ridiculous explanations for the latest black eye or swollen lip."

Annie moved up and sat next to her daughter, wrapping an arm around her shoulder. Joan lifted the covers to let Annie slip her feet into the bed.

"We let you down," Annie said. "We had no idea you were going through such a nightmare. You should have left him and come home the first time he hit you."

"I would have done if I thought dad would take me back. Besides, I wanted to make the marriage work. I'd chosen to elope with him. I'd made my bed and I felt obliged to lie in it, however uncomfortable it was." Joan barked a laugh. "The irony of it was, *he* ended up leaving me."

"So now you're trying to make up for your mistake by standing in Avril's corner."

"Something like that. Is it so very wrong?"

Annie hugged her. "No. In fact I'm rather proud of you. Believe it or not, you and your dad are very much alike. You both rail against injustice and both of you are willing to fight for the underdog."

"And we're both stubborn."

"Like a couple of mules." Annie ruffled Joan's hair. "Listen, I'm seeing Avril on Thursday for a trim. Would you like me to broach the subject?"

"If you can do it subtly. I don't want her to think I've been gossiping about her."

"I can be subtle."

"I'd appreciate it."

Annie kissed Joan on the cheek and stood up. "Try to get some sleep. And don't worry. Together we'll get this sorted out."

* * *

"Has she calmed down?" Jack said, as Annie slid into the bed beside him.

"I thought you were asleep."

"Just resting my eyes."

"Do you usually snore when you're resting your eyes?"

"Well? How is she?"

Annie reached across and switched on the bedside light. "You knew that Ivan used to beat her, didn't you?"

"She told me the day after she came back to us."

"And you said nothing to me."

He shifted uncomfortably in the bed. "I didn't want to upset you. It was emotional enough just having her back under our roof, after we'd almost accepted that we'd never see her again."

"I still think you should have told me, if not then but maybe later. We've always shared things like that."

"Annie, I don't want us to fall out over this."

Annie sat up abruptly. Her voice was tight. "Jack, we're discussing our daughter. *Our* daughter. It's a pretty poor show if I can't talk about Joanie without the risk of falling out with you."

Jack sank down into the pillow and closed his eyes. When Ivan had left Joan and she had no option but to swallow her pride and come home to them, he had talked to his daughter at length. She'd told him secrets then, secrets like the illegal abortion she'd had and Ivan's marital brutality. He'd decided to keep these things from Annie out of fear of upsetting her. Now he was starting to doubt the wisdom of that decision. He and Annie had never kept secrets from each other. Honouring Joan's confidences had put him in an awkward position, and placed an unwanted strain on his relationship with Annie. "I'm sorry. I should have told you sooner."

"Yes," she said frostily. "You should."

"Turn out the light and let's get some sleep."

Annie didn't move to switch off the light. "You asked if Joanie had calmed down."

"Has she?"

"She has, but that's no thanks to you and your precious police force." Angrily she threw back the covers, slipped her dressing gown on again and walked to the door. "I'm going to make a cup of tea," she said and walked from the room.

Jack watched her go and rolled over onto his back. "Oh, damn it to hell," he said to the ceiling.

When Annie came back to bed an hour later he was feigning sleep but was very much awake. He felt her arm slide over his chest and she whispered in his ear, "I'm a big girl now, Jack. I don't always need you to fight my battles for me. I don't need protecting, but bless you for thinking of me."

He took her hand and lightly squeezed her fingers. He said nothing more. No further words were needed.

CHAPTER 12

WEDNESDAY 9 DECEMBER 1959

"Andy, I'm going to need a driver now that Eddie Fuller has been promoted. Who can you recommend?"

Andy Brewer glanced around to the small office behind the station's front desk. "The chap there, filling in his football pools." He took a step towards the office. "Constable Meadows, put away your dreams of untold riches and come out here. DCI Callum has need of your services."

Robert Meadows jumped out of his seat, dropped the pen on the floor, grabbed the pools coupon and stuffed it into his tunic pocket. He straightened his jacket, ran a hand over his thick, wavy hair, trying in vain to sweep it out of his eyes, and came out to stand to attention behind the desk.

"Sergeant Brewer here tells me you can drive," Jack said. "How well?"

"I passed the Advanced Driving exam at Hendon. I'm qualified to drive for the flying squad and Q cars, as well as regular patrol vehicles, sir."

Jack stroked his chin thoughtfully. "A tad over-qualified to be ferrying me around. You'll do."

"I'll be happy to do it, sir," Meadows said eagerly. "It would be better than being tied to this office day after day . . . no offence, Sarge."

"None taken, lad," Brewer said. "Being stuck behind a desk isn't the most exciting thing in the world for a young chap like you."

"Well, that's settled then," Jack said. "Constable Meadows, bring my car around to the front of the building in ten minutes." He turned to Brewer. "Thanks, Andy."

"My pleasure, sir. To be honest, it will be good to get him out from under my feet. It only needs one of us on the desk most of the time anyway."

Upstairs, Eddie Fuller and Myra Banks were busy shifting a couple of wooden filing cabinets around the room, trying to get them positioned behind Myra's desk.

"Busy, Inspector Fuller?" Jack said as he entered the tiny office.

Fuller grinned. "Just trying to make efficient use of the space, sir."

With two desks, two filing cabinets, four chairs and a hat stand, the room looked full to bursting. "I don't envy you that job."

"It's not as cramped as it looks, sir," Myra said. "We'll soon have it sorted."

"I wish I shared her optimism," Fuller said, flopping down into the chair behind his desk. "What can I do for you, sir?"

"Leslie Parsons' 'men's committee'. I want you to check out the other names on this list." He handed Fuller a sheet of foolscap paper. "Take no notice of the first three names. I'm going to see them myself, but I'll leave the other two to you. I want them to account for their movements on Monday — all day, not just the evening. I want to know how well they knew Sister Bernadette and how much, if any, contact they've had with her since her arrival at St Joseph's. Before you do that, call into the Home, pick up Sister Rosalie and take her to North Herts Hospital. She's going to make the formal identification. Once she's made it, take her back to St Joseph's and then you can start interviewing people."

"You want me to take her?" Fuller said, slightly incredulously.

"Yes, Eddie, I do. Besides, it will be good experience for DC Banks. I don't think she's ever been exposed to the dubious pleasures of a hospital mortuary."

Myra looked startled.

"Get your coat, DC Banks. We have work to do." Fuller walked from the room.

Myra got to her feet and made to follow him.

"Keep an eye on him, Myra," Jack said quietly. "Inspector Fuller seems to have a prejudice against the Sisters — or it might just be nuns in general. The last thing we want to do is upset the Catholic Church."

Myra raised her eyebrows.

"Don't keep him waiting, Constable."

"Yes, sir," she said, and hurried from the room.

Jack went back downstairs and out of the station. Meadows was sitting behind the wheel of one of the newer Wolseleys, its engine idling. Jack climbed into the back. "Beaconsfield Road, Constable. Don't break any speed limits. There's no rush."

Meadows nodded at the rear-view mirror, let out the clutch and eased the car into the street.

* * *

Beaconsfield Road was just three streets away from Lockley Crescent and Lesley Parsons. Giovanni Fabrizi was the first name on Parsons' list. Jack knew nothing about the man other than that he worked most evenings and was at home during the day.

"Do you want me to come with you, sir, or shall I wait here?"

"What, with the engine running in case we need a quick getaway?" Jack smiled. "No, Constable. Come along. You can take notes."

As they approached the semi-detached house, Jack could hear a trumpet being played. Someone was playing a hit from a few years ago, 'Oh Mein Papa.' Jack decided that whatever My Papa had done in the past, he certainly didn't deserve to be tortured so badly. Whatever else Fabrizi was, he was certainly no musician.

Meadows knocked loudly on the door and they waited. The trumpet music died for a moment and then began again. Meadows' hand reached for the knocker as the door was pulled open.

"Yes? Can I help you?" A slightly built man with thin features peered out into the bright winter sunshine.

"I'd like to speak to Giovanni Fabrizi," Jack said.

"Now? It's not really a good time."

"I'm afraid it will have to be. We're the police. So, if you would be so kind as to interrupt Mr Fabrizi's trumpet practice I would be very grateful."

The man stared at him for a moment. "You mean . . . you think that's . . ." He laughed. "Blimey! What a hoot." This was said in a broad cockney accent. "You'd better come in."

He led them into the house, along a narrow hallway and into a large lounge. A heavy-set man with a light beard stood at a music stand in the centre of the room, cheeks inflated like hamster pouches as he squeezed more tortured notes out of a silver trumpet.

"Mr Fabrizi?" Jack said, approaching the music stand. "If I could have a few moments of your time."

The portly man stopped playing and took the instrument away from his lips. "Eh?"

"It's all right, Dennis. A case of mistaken identity." He looked at a clock on the mantelpiece. "You're over your time anyway, so we'll call it a day. You're doing well. Keep practising that until I see you next week." He turned back to Jack. "I'm Giovanni Fabrizi."

"Ah."

Jack watched Dennis shake the spittle from the trumpet and place it lovingly in its padded case.

Fabrizi led the would-be trumpeter to the door and saw him out with another exhortation to "keep practising."

"God knows, he needs it," Fabrizi said as he came back to the lounge. He was cramming a ten shilling note into the pocket of his grey slacks.

"I'm sorry for the misunderstanding. It was the accent. I was expecting you to be Italian."

"And so I am. Born in Napoli and proud of it. My parents brought me to England in twenty-eight when I was four. Dad could see the direction Mussolini and his fascist thugs were heading and he wanted no part of it, so he brought us over here. My mother, my two sisters and me. We settled in Clerkenwell and they still live there. Dad drives a taxi and Mum, Louisa and Alba run a café in St John Street."

"Are you getting this, Constable Meadows?"

A look of alarm crossed the young constable's face. He rummaged in his pockets for notebook and pen and started writing. "Clerkenwell. That's in London, isn't it?"

"EC1," Fabrizi said, with the trace of a smile.

"So, how come you ended up in Hatfield?" Jack said.

"I didn't fancy driving a black cab or making sandwiches all my life so I studied music. I learned to play the violin and the trumpet. I moved out to Hertfordshire after my grandmother left me some money in her will. I started passing on my skills, so to speak. There isn't much call for a violin tutor in Clerkenwell, and even less for a trumpet teacher, but here's pretty good. Out here there're quite a few people with money who want some kind of challenge in their lives."

"Are you any good?"

Fabrizi laughed. "Yes. Despite what you just heard, I think I am. I have more luck with my violin students though. Trouble with the trumpet is that every idiot who once played bugle for the Boys Brigade thinks they're going to be the next Eddie Calvert. I do what I can for them, and I never shatter their dreams. I never tell them they've got lips like bicycle inner tubes and don't have a hope of mastering the instrument, like old Dennis for instance. Fifty quid he spent on that trumpet and he'd have been better off paying a tanner for a kazoo. But a man's got to eat, so I'm happy to take his ten bob just for an hour of listening to him commit musical homicide." He winked. He lifted a pile of sheet music from a battered-looking sofa and dropped it onto the floor. "Take a seat. You too, Constable. I saw Les at Toc H last night, so I know why you're here."

Jack sat and Meadows perched on the arm. He appeared to be unsure whether he should sit next to Jack or not.

"Sister Bernadette," Jack began. "How well did you know her?"

Fabrizi pulled up a dining chair, turned it around and sat astride it. "Hardly at all. Our paths never really crossed."

"She was never at the film shows?"

"That's hard to say. I never go to them. I work most evenings."

"And what do you do?"

Fabrizi smiled. "You'll laugh." He reached behind him to a drawer in the sideboard and passed them a colourful handbill. It advertised a restaurant in Cambridge that offered all manner of Cordon Bleu meals. "I'm at the bottom."

"'Featuring Giovanni, the gypsy violinist'. Is that you?" Jack said.

"Yes. For my crimes. I'm the gypsy violinist, serenading the diners as they tuck into meals I could never afford. They do let me have some of the leftovers, which is quite a useful perk, and the tips of course."

"And this accounts for most of your evenings?"

"Six nights a week. Toc H takes care of the other one."

"So you don't spend much time at St Josephs."

"My evenings are crammed, but my days are mostly free. I only have six regulars coming here for lessons, so I get to the Home when I can. I take the boys for five-a-side football and at the moment I'm organising the Christmas show for both the boys and girls. Three days from the 19th to the 21st of December. You should come along. Bring the family. There're songs and sketches. I've even persuaded three of the Sisters to do a skit on the Beverley Sisters and that'll be fun. I did approach Sister Bernadette about it. I heard her singing in the chapel once and she had a wonderful soprano. But she ran away from me like a scalded cat as soon as I mentioned it to her."

"So she didn't like to draw attention to herself."

"Not in that way," Fabrizi said, staring uncomfortably at the floor.

"But she did in other ways?"

Fabrizi shook his head. "No, it's nothing. I shouldn't speak ill of the dead."

Jack leaned forward in his seat. "I'm not asking you to, Mr Fabrizi."

"Giovanni, please. 'Mr Fabrizi' makes it sound like you're talking to my father."

"Ok, Giovanni. I'm trying discover a motive for Sister Bernadette's murder. I can only do that if the people who knew her can shed some light on the less obvious areas of her life. So, if you know something about her that might help me, I must insist that you tell me."

Fabrizi shifted in his seat. "Okay . . . Let me put it this way. Bernadette was a flirt. She flirted with several members of the committee, as well as some of the older boys at the home."

“Mr Fabrizi, she was a nun. Are you sure you’re right about that? Couldn’t her manner have been misinterpreted, perhaps?”

“Perhaps,” Fabrizi said. “If you’d spent your life as a monk and never had any contact with women. But for someone like me, who’d been raised with two older sisters, I was onto her game like a shot. She could twist men around her little finger with a single bat of her eyelashes.”

“It could have been innocent. She might not have been aware of her, what can I call it? Her allure.”

“Yeah, that’s what I thought at first. But then I saw how she worked on Danny Gallagher and how he used to respond to her. He was like a lovesick puppy around Bernadette. In fact I was surprised he never rolled onto his back for her to tickle his belly. Then again, for all I know, he might have done. Danny’s younger than the rest of us and was brought up at St Joseph’s, so he’s a bit more gullible than we are. No, Sister Bernadette knew exactly what she was doing.”

“Mr Gallagher’s next on the list of people I need to talk to.”

“Well, you won’t find him at home. He’s an apprentice mechanic at Welland’s Garage, in town. Has been since before he left St Joe’s.”

CHAPTER 13

WEDNESDAY

"Yes, that's her." Sister Rosalie's voice reverberated from the bare walls of the mortuary anteroom.

A young technician drew the sheet over the body's cold, white face and Myra took the nun's arm. She led her from the claustrophobic room, back out into the hallway.

Once there, Rosalie reached for a steel and canvas chair and lowered herself into it. "She looks like she's sleeping," she said. "I was expecting . . ."

"I'll take you back to St Joseph's," Myra said.

Sister Rosalie looked up at her with eyes full of tears. "I just need a moment." She lowered her head and her mouth worked, silently forming words of prayer.

Fuller stepped away from the wall where he'd been leaning. "The hospital has a chapel, if you'd prefer to do your praying there."

Myra glared at him.

"Only trying to be helpful."

Myra opened her mouth to reply when a middle-aged man with salt and pepper hair stepped into the hallway. "Where is Chief Inspector Callum?"

"Pursuing his inquiries," Fuller said.

"And you are . . ?"

"Detective Serg . . . Inspector Fuller."

The man stuck out his hand. "Professor Strong, Home Office pathologist. Could we have a chat?" He glanced at Myra and Sister Rosalie, who was still running the rosary through her fingers and praying. "In private."

"Yes," Fuller said. "Yes, of course."

Strong led him through the mortuary to an office at the back and sat down at a desk. Fuller pulled up a chair.

Strong had a file on the desk in front of him. He tapped it with elegant fingers. "In here are my findings. You're welcome to take them with you to give to Mr Callum, but there are a few things I want to draw your attention to." He handed the file across to Fuller who opened it and scanned the pages.

"If you turn to page three. Stomach contents." Strong waited while Fuller found the page. "As you can see, she'd had hardly anything to eat that day, so it was mostly liquid. Tea mainly, but there was the undigested remains of a biscuit — digestive probably. All quite unremarkable. I've found that few young women partake of large meals these days. They all seem preoccupied with watching their waistlines. But I digress. There were also traces of a barbiturate. I sent a sample off to the lab for analysis and they rushed it through, as they did with the blood sample I sent them. The barbiturate had already entered her bloodstream."

"What effect would that have?"

"There wasn't enough recorded to knock her out. Barbiturates are in a group we call hypnotics. They make very effective sleeping pills, and the levels were high enough to make her quite drowsy. The urge to sleep would be there but she would remain conscious. Do you know if she was on any sleep medication?"

"We found nothing in her room to suggest that, no."

"Then it seems quite likely that someone else administered it."

"You think she may have been drugged?"

"That's not for me to comment, but a sleeping tablet dissolved in, say, a cup of tea, would quickly induce a state of lethargy."

"So, if she were drugged in her room, how easy would it be to get her downstairs to the chapel?"

"Very easy I should think. The barbiturate would depress her willpower, making her vulnerable to suggestion. If someone had a mind to, they could drug her and get her down the stairs with little trouble. There wouldn't be much resistance on her part."

"Interesting." Fuller rubbed his chin. "That gives me a lot to think about." He closed the file and started to rise from his seat. Strong raised a finger to stop him.

"There's something else," he said. "Something I didn't want to discuss in front of the ladies."

"Oh?"

"Obviously in an autopsy we have to cover pretty much everything. I've never before had occasion to perform one on a nun, so you can imagine my shock . . . read page five."

Fuller flicked through and read. After a few seconds he lowered the pages and stared across the desk. "You're sure about this?"

"Without a shadow of a doubt."

"Pregnant?"

"About eight or nine weeks."

"Good God!"

"I don't think so, Inspector. This was no immaculate conception. Sister Bernadette showed all the signs of being a sexually active young woman."

"Then who was the father?"

"Find him and you might find who killed her," Strong said.

* * *

They pulled up outside the orphanage. Myra got out of the car and went around to open the back door. "Are you going to be all right?" she said as she helped Sister Rosalie out.

The woman seemed to have aged ten years during the trip to the hospital. Her face was grey and her eyes had lost their lustre. "I'll be fine. My Sisters will look after me. What I really need is a strong cup of tea."

"Well, thank you for your help," Myra said. "If there's anything you need . . ."

"You've been very kind, but God will help me from now on. Will you thank Inspector Fuller for me? I imagine he'll be glad to see the back of me."

"He's not that bad really."

Sister Rosalie gave her a wan smile. "If you say so." She walked up the steps to the front doors.

Myra got back behind the wheel, slammed the door behind her and started the engine. "Back to the station, sir?"

Fuller sat staring out through the windscreen. He'd said nothing since leaving the hospital. He said nothing now.

"Sir?"

Fuller looked round at her. "No. We'll go straight on to Warrington Street and speak to Tony Smythe. He's the first name on the list. Do you know where it is?"

"I think so," Myra said. "It runs under the railway bridge." She eased the car out onto the road. "By the way, Sister Rosalie said thanks."

Fuller grunted.

"If you don't mind me saying, sir, you were bloody rude to her."

"Don't take that tone with me, Constable."

"Well, what's she done to get under your skin? She seemed perfectly pleasant."

"Don't talk to me about things you can't possibly understand."

"Then help me understand, Eddie. I've worked with you long enough to know you weren't yourself today."

Fuller leaned back in his seat and closed his eyes. "I don't want to talk about it."

Myra glanced around at him. "So there *is* something. I knew there was."

"Christ, you don't let up, do you? I see why Jack wants you on the team. You're like a dog with a bone."

"The months I spent with CID, and with you and DCI Callum in particular, taught me a lot. Persistence is everything. When something's bothering you, don't let up until you have the answer."

"Concentrate on the road ahead."

"So, are you going to tell me what's bothering you about Sister Rosalie? Or is it nuns and Catholics in general?"

"I was born and raised a Catholic."

Myra looked at him sharply.

"I lapsed a long time ago, after the accident in fact."

"What accident?"

Fuller looked at her steadily. "It's not something I like to talk about."

"I'm listening."

Fuller took a breath. "When I was seven we were coming back from a trip to Whipsnade Park Zoo. A proper family outing it was — Mum, Dad, my nan and granddad and Beth, my younger sister. I didn't see the lorry. I was busy in the back seat, playing a game of 'I-spy' with Beth. I just remember the sounds. A huge bang, and the crunch of metal as the lorry ploughed into us and knocked us into a ditch. I must have hit my head, because the next thing I knew I was waking up in hospital. My arm was in plaster and I was bruised all over. But I was lucky. I was the only one who was pulled out of the wreckage alive. Everyone else died, even Beth, and we'd been sitting next to each other."

Fuller glanced around at Myra. Her hands were gripping the steering wheel, her knuckles white, and tears were trickling down her cheeks.

"I'm so sorry, Eddie," she whispered.

"When they let me out of the hospital I went straight into council care. Our local priest, Father Patrick, pulled a few strings and I was transferred to an orphanage in Muswell Hill. That's where I first encountered Sister Beatrice. Remember, I was seven years old and had just been through a life-changing tragedy. You'd expect kindness and understanding, wouldn't you? Well, Sister Beatrice was a tyrant. She ran the orphanage like a wartime prison camp. Everything was regimented, with strict discipline and regular beatings for the smallest misdemeanours. The other nuns were just as bad. There wasn't an ounce of compassion or kindness between them. That's when I began to see my faith for the sham it was. Suffer the children, the Bible says. And by Christ, were we made to suffer."

"How long were you there?"

"About six months. Then the couple I came to know, and still do to this day, as Mum and dad, rescued me. They fostered me and then adopted me. They took me away from that hellhole for good and gave me a home with them. Every day I count my blessings that Arthur and Gwen Fuller came to visit the orphanage and saw something in me that appealed to them."

Fuller took another breath. There were tears pricking at *his* eyes now. "Anyway, that's why I find it hard to be around nuns of any kind. Maybe Sister Rosalie and the others at St Joseph's are all good Christians with hearts of gold, but the nuns at Muswell Hill left their mark. To this day, I can't forgive or forget."

"I don't blame you. I understand now."

Fuller let out a low whistle. "Phew! I've never told anyone the whole story before."

"You probably feel better for getting it off your chest."

Fuller shook his head. "Not really. You pick at unhealed scabs and they just bleed some more. That's why I've never told Jack. He doesn't even know I'm adopted. I want to keep it like that. Understand?"

Myra nodded. "I won't mention it, Eddie."

"Good, and when we're back at the station you call me Inspector Fuller or sir. I don't want the likes of Frank Lesser thinking I'm a soft touch, right?"

Myra smiled and nodded.

"So long as you know. Warrington Street is just up here on the right."

"Yes, sir. I know."

CHAPTER 14

WEDNESDAY

"Did what Fabrizi said shock you, Constable?" Jack said as they pulled away from the house.

Meadows glanced at him in the rear-view mirror. "Just a bit, sir. I mean, she was a nun, and I thought they were above that sort of thing, using feminine wiles and such like."

"I'm discovering that Sister Bernadette wasn't your average nun. Forget the whole religious aspect for a moment and we'll see that Bernadette O'Farrell was a very mixed-up young woman."

Meadows said nothing. All this was way outside his experience. He was more comfortable just concentrating on his driving.

"Do you know Welland's?" Jack's voice broke into Meadow's thoughts.

"It's where I get my car serviced, sir."

"Yes, me too. I probably met Gallagher when I last took my car there. There was certainly a young man there — a big lad, tough-looking."

"I know who you mean, but I never caught his name. He did my last oil change."

Jack opened his briefcase, took out a file and started leafing through it. "Give me a shout when we're almost there."

* * *

Welland's Garage was a large affair, with three petrol pumps, a used-car showroom, and workshops at the back. The forecourt contained more second-hand cars, less expensive than the ones in the showroom.

Meadows drove slowly to the back of the lot, parking just outside the workshop's large double doors. One of the doors was open and they could see a maroon Daimler, its bonnet raised and two of the mechanics working on the engine.

Jack called out, "Shop!" and walked in. The air was heavy with the smells of engine oil, grease and rubber. A transistor radio was playing Ted Heath and his Orchestra.

One of the mechanics lifted his head from under the bonnet and looked up. His elderly face was smeared with grease and his grizzled hair was partly hidden under a bottle-green cap streaked with engine oil. "Can I help you?"

Jack produced his warrant card. "We're looking for Bernard Gallagher. We've been told he works here."

The mechanic squinted at the identification. "Yeah, that he does. What's he done?"

Jack smiled. "He hasn't done anything. We just need to ask him a few questions."

The mechanic pointed towards twin doors at the rear of the workshop. "He's out back cleaning a car we've just serviced. Don't keep him gassing, the owner's coming back for it in half an hour."

"We won't keep him too long," Jack said. On the radio, the band launched into a Glenn Miller classic.

"Bernard Gallagher?"

The young man was waxing the bodywork of a red Hillman Minx. "That's me," he said.

"Police," Jack said. "Have you heard what happened at St Joseph's on Monday?"

Gallagher nodded. "Les Parsons called to tell me."

"Did you know Sister Bernadette?"

Gallagher glanced back at the workshop. The old mechanic was standing in the doorway, obviously straining to hear what was being said. Gallagher opened the Hillman's door. "Get in the car," he said. "We can talk in there. I don't want that old bugger hearing my business."

"Sorry about that," said Gallagher when they were all inside the car. Mac's a great bloke but he'll be down the pub tonight telling anyone who'll buy him a pint about the excitement at Welland's today. And he'll get it all arse about face. Best we don't add fuel to his fire."

"So, did you know Sister Bernadette?" Jack asked.

"Yes. I got to see her quite a lot in the short time she was there."

Jack leaned forward. "Really. Why was that?"

"Have you seen that heap of a car St Joe's owns?"

"The Morris?"

Gallagher made a face. "I swear it's only divine intervention that keeps it on the road, helped by my skills as a mechanic. Sister Bernadette was on the phone practically every week, asking me to fix this, that or the other."

"She used to drive the car?"

"Usually. Sister Rosalie was always asking her to run errands for her because she had a licence. I suppose Sister Rosalie thought that giving Bernadette something to do might keep her out of trouble."

"Why did she call you and not go directly to Welland's?"

"Because if she went through the office, St Joe's would be charged. She knew I'd do the repairs for nothing. The orphanage has always been run on a shoestring so I never objected. Besides, Sister Rosalie has known me for years and trusts me."

"As a mechanic, or as a man?"

Gallagher's eyes narrowed. "What do you mean?"

"Sister Bernadette was a very pretty young woman."

A shadow passed over Gallagher's face. "And a nun. I don't know about you, but I was raised a Catholic. I still am, so I find what you're implying offensive. Extremely offensive." The young man reached for the door handle and yanked it down.

"Okay, okay. Simmer down. These questions have to be asked. So you're telling me you saw Sister Bernadette regularly about work on the car."

Gallagher let go of the door handle and sank back in his seat. "That's about the long and the short of it, yes."

"When did you last see her?"

"Saturday afternoon. She was supposed to drive to St Albans and she was worried about an oil leak. That bloody Morris leaked oil like a punctured sardine can. So I went to the

Home and topped it up for her, enough to get her to St Albans and back anyway. I told her she'd have to have a word with Sister Rosalie about the car because it's really on its last legs."

"And that was the last time you saw her?"

"Pretty much."

"What do you mean by that?"

"I saw her again that day, in the afternoon."

"Did you speak?"

Gallagher shook his head. "She drove past me, heading back to St Joe's. I waved but I don't think she saw me. I don't think she saw anyone. She was hunched over the wheel, staring straight ahead and she looked . . ." His words tailed away and he gazed out of the car window.

Jack gave him a moment. "How did she look, Bernard?"

"Like she was crying."

"Did you get that down, Constable?"

Meadows was sitting in the passenger seat, staring intently at the young man's troubled face. He shook himself. "Crying. Yes, sir." He scribbled it down in his notebook.

Jack addressed Gallagher again. "I don't suppose you have any idea what she was upset about?"

Gallagher shrugged. "Search me."

"Only I thought you knew her quite well."

"I think I said that I'd seen her a number of times in the past six months, but it was only when she wanted my help with the Morris."

"But surely you must have spoken with her, just chatted maybe, when you were fixing the car?"

Gallagher laughed.

"What's so funny?"

"You didn't know her, but Sister Bernadette wasn't the type of girl you 'chatted' with. I mean you wouldn't seek her out if you wanted a good old natter."

"She wasn't the gregarious type?"

"She was a Carmelite nun, for Pete's sake. The Carmelites are hardly the most talkative of orders. Didn't anyone tell you about Sister Bernadette's history?"

"They did, but I understood she'd left the monastery at Hitchin to come to work at St Joseph's."

"Well, she didn't automatically become 'chatty.' Far from it. Getting her to talk at all was like squeezing blood out of a stone, and even then you'd only get a drip at a time. Hard work, it was. Are we finished here? Only, the owner of this car will be along in a tick to pick it up."

"Yes, I think we're done. All I need to know now is whether you can account for your time on Monday afternoon through to the evening."

"Easy," Gallagher said. "I was here all day up until about half past seven. Check with Mac. He'll back me up on that."

* * *

Jack slid into the passenger seat next to Meadows and picked up the radio. "Put me through me to Inspector Fuller."

There was a brief pause and Fuller came on the line. "Yes, sir?"

"Did Sister Rosalie make the formal identification?"

"She did and she's now safely back at St Joseph's."

"Good. Anything else to report?"

"We're on our way to see Tony Smythe now."

"Okay."

"Sir, one more thing. I was going to wait until I got back to the station to tell you but, as you're on the radio . . ." Fuller paused.

Jack heard an uncharacteristic reticence in Fuller's voice. "Fire away."

"I saw the pathologist at the mortuary and he gave me his report to pass on to you. It seems that Sister Bernadette had been drugged with a sleeping pill."

"That would explain why there was no sign of a struggle. Was there anything else?"

"Yes, there is." There was another pause.

"Go on, Eddie. Spit it out."

"She was pregnant, sir. Seven or eight weeks or thereabouts."

Fuller's voice filled the car and Jack saw Meadows' eyes widen. "Right. I'm heading back now. I'll meet you there. Forget Smythe. He'll keep until later. I want to read that report for myself." He handed the radio back to Meadows. "Back to the station, Constable."

CHAPTER 15

WEDNESDAY

Jack sat at his desk reading through Professor Strong's pathology report. The sounds of moving furniture came from the office next door, as Eddie Fuller and Myra Banks tried to shift chairs, desks and filing cabinets into a workable configuration.

He lifted his gaze from the closely typed report and let it settle on the photographs lying across his desk. They were the latest images of the enigma he had come to know as Bernadette O'Farrell, the *conflicted* Sister Bernadette.

The photographs followed a chronological sequence. The first showed how the Sister had been found — lying prone, arms stretched out in supplication, but with her head turned to one side. The sightless eyes stared at nothing, and the mild surprise on her face was registered by the small O of her slightly open lips.

Her killer had turned her over onto her stomach, to hide the carnage he had wrought there, and posed her deliberately, making her look as if she were in a state of prayer. Was that some kind of sick joke, or maybe it was an attempt to show her asking the Lord for some kind of redemption? He was in no doubt that the Sister's death was related to her fall from grace.

He needed to dig a lot deeper into Sister Bernadette's past to better understand her recent behaviour.

The old scars that Strong had pointed out to him spoke of savage beatings inflicted on her as a child. But the whip marks streaking her back suggested the self-flagellation of a devout woman seeking to atone for her misdeeds.

He needed to speak to Sister Rosalie again.

The noises in the other room fell silent.

Fuller stuck his head around the door. "We're off to see Tony Smythe now. Lucky we didn't call in earlier. Myra phoned him five minutes ago and he's only just got home."

Jack grabbed his coat from the hat stand. "I'm off to St Joseph's again. We'll compare notes in the morning."

"Isn't it something you can send Frank or one of the others to do?"

Jack's eyes narrowed. "Christ! You're starting to sound like Lane. 'You sit in your office, Jack, and shuffle papers. Let others do the legwork for you.' No thanks. I want us three to handle the preliminary interviews. If we start sharing them out it's likely that we'll miss something, so we'll keep it contained for now."

Fuller smiled. "You're the boss."

"Yes, Eddie, I am. And the day I stop doing my own legwork will be the day I put in my papers."

"Understood." Eddie Fuller was still smiling.

***

"Mr Callum, I wasn't expecting to see the police again today," Sister Rosalie said.

Jack took a seat at her desk. "I wasn't planning on bothering you again, but a few things have come up that I'm hoping you'll be able to shed some light on."

"I'll do what I can to help."

"Sister Bernadette drove to St Albans on Saturday. Was she on St Joseph's business?"

"St Albans, you say?" The nun stared at him in surprise.

"That's what I've been led to believe."

"Well, I certainly sent her out on some errands on Saturday, but visiting St Albans wasn't on the list. They were all local calls. Why would she drive out to St Albans, unless it was to call on Canon Flood?"

"Did she often visit Canon Flood?"

Sister Rosalie shook her head. "Not that I'm aware of. The Canon is a very busy man. I wouldn't have approved if I thought Sister Bernadette was bothering him unnecessarily."

"Maybe it *was* necessary. Look, Sister, the pathologist discovered something during the autopsy that I think might shock you."

"Please don't spare my feelings, Mr Callum. After going through a world war and having the running of St Joseph's to contend with, very little shocks me these days."

Jack looked across the desk into those wise old eyes. "Sister Bernadette was pregnant," he said flatly.

The eyes widened almost imperceptibly, but the calm façade remained unchanged. "How many weeks?" she said. Her voice had all the emotion of someone asking the date of the next church fete.

"The pathologist estimates that she was about seven or eight weeks along."

Sister Rosalie shook her head sadly. "The poor child. To think she had to bear that knowledge alone for all that time. She must have been terrified."

"That's if she knew at all."

"Oh, I think she must have done. She went to see Dr Molly Williams last week, and I should think Molly would have told her."

"So you were aware she went to see her doctor?"

"Yes, I knew, but I thought it was for something else entirely. She told me she was suffering from severe headaches. I was the one who suggested she should go and see Molly."

"So, she comes back from the doctor knowing she is going to have a baby. I would have thought her first course of action would be to seek advice from someone she trusted. You, perhaps, or one of the other Sisters."

"She certainly didn't confide in me, and she wasn't really close to anyone here at the Home but, I agree, she would have felt the need to confess. Her soul must have been in torment."

"Perhaps that's why she went to St Alban's, to confess her sins to Canon Flood."

Sister Rosalie shook her head. "She barely knew him. If she confided in anyone, it would have been Father Harvey. He was very good with her." She thought for a moment. "You're sure she went to St Albans?"

"That's what she told Bernard Gallagher. She asked him to fix an oil leak so the car wouldn't break down on the way."

"Only I'm wondering now if she could have gone to Hitchin, back to St Luke's."

"From whence she came, so to speak."

"I would think that would be a more likely destination than Canon Flood in St Albans. I can call the Reverend Mother there and ask her if that was the case."

"Your friend, the Mother Superior?"

Sister Rosalie nodded. "Sister Concepta and I have known each other for many years."

"I will need to speak with her myself."

"I really don't think that's necessary," said Sister Rosalie.

"Unfortunately, I think it is. I need to get a clearer picture of Sister Bernadette's past life, before she came here to St Joseph's."

"Very well. I'll mention it when I speak to her. Was there anything else, only you said the autopsy uncovered a few things?"

"Do you know if the Sister was taking pills to help her sleep?"

"Absolutely not."

"You seem very sure."

"Oh, I am Mr Callum. On the rare occasion that one of the Sisters is unwell enough to need drugs, they give their prescriptions to me and I take them to the chemist to get them filled. I hold onto the tablets or the medicines and see that they are administered correctly."

"That seems a little . . ."

"Draconian? Well, yes, I suppose it does, but experience has taught me that people cannot always be relied upon to take the correct dosage. I regulate it myself so that there are no mistakes. I can tell you quite categorically that Sister Bernadette was on no medication of any kind."

"How much do you know about her childhood in Liverpool?"

Sister Rosalie gave a small shake of her head. "I only know what Sister Concepta told me. Her family was very religious. I think I mentioned that her elder sisters had taken their vows."

"Yes, you did. You also told me that her parents were dead. Do you know how they died?"

"I believe they died in a fire at their home. At the time it was thought it had been started deliberately."

"Was Sister Bernadette in the house at the time?"

"Yes. It was a miracle that she survived. I think that event inspired her to become a nun. She felt that she'd been spared for a purpose, and that purpose was to serve Our Father."

Jack leaned forward in his seat. "That's not what you told me when we first spoke about Sister Bernadette. You were speculating that perhaps she was under pressure from her family to enter the church."

"And I think I was speaking out of turn. If you knew the girl, you wouldn't have doubted her sincerity. She was very devout."

"Yet the pathologist's opinion was that she enjoyed a healthy sex life, which surely goes against the church's moral teachings."

Sister Rosalie lapsed into silence. Her fingers reached for her rosary.

"Forgive me, Sister, but I don't think you're being straight with me."

Blood rushed to Sister Rosalie's cheeks. "I don't know what you mean."

"Oh, I think you do. Look. Sister Bernadette died a horrible death and I'm going to catch whoever was responsible. When I do and they are convicted I will do my best to see that they face the full penalty of the law. But in order to do my job, to bring her killer to justice, I need to know everything there is to know about her. Were you aware, for instance, that she was beaten as a child, thrashed so savagely that she carried the scars on her back and buttocks until the day she died?"

Jack sat back in his seat and watched his words hit home. He hated himself for being so brutal with the woman, but he was growing impatient. Sister Bernadette's history and character were being concealed from him. He was sure that those shielding the real Bernadette O'Farrell were well-meaning, but they were hampering his investigation.

The old nun's eyes were moist. She took off her glasses and wiped the tears away impatiently. She nodded slowly.

"I knew," she said softly. "I noticed them when she first arrived. I asked Sister Concepta about them."

Jack lowered his voice to match hers. "How did she get them?"

Sister Rosalie sniffed away the tears. "Apparently Bernadette was a difficult child. You saw how pretty she was. Well, it seems she was turning heads from a very early age, about eleven or twelve. By the age of thirteen she had a swarm of boys buzzing around her like bees around a honey pot."

Sister Rosalie stood suddenly and went across to a filing cabinet in the corner of the room. She pulled open a drawer and took from it a small bottle of brandy and two tumblers. "I keep this for medicinal purposes," she said. Her gaze travelled up to a picture of the Virgin Mary that hung on the wall. "I'm sure Our Lady will allow me this small transgression. Will you join me?"

Jack allowed a smile. "A small one. If you're sure."

"Bernadette enjoyed the power she exerted over the boys. It made her feel special. Loved perhaps."

"Didn't she feel love at home?"

"Her father worked at Albert dock in Liverpool. From what I can gather, whenever he wasn't working he drank away his time at one of the many pubs in the area, so it was left to the mother to bring up the three girls. Of necessity she became the family disciplinarian. It was she who administered the beatings. She was the devout one, not her husband, and I think she felt that she could beat the sin out of her daughter. Whether Bernadette's sisters were treated the same way I have no way of knowing, but it wouldn't surprise me.

"After the house fire Bernadette was taken into care by the nuns at St Francis Priory in Speke, but her behaviour didn't change. Eventually it was decided that she would only prosper if she moved away from the area, so the Abbess at St Francis contacted Sister Concepta at St Luke's monastery and arranged for her to come down to Hertfordshire."

"It sounds like Bernadette was shoved from pillar to post."

"It was all meant for her own good. It was felt that Bernadette's soul was in danger of being lost and that she needed saving from herself. When she arrived at St Luke's it became obvious that the secluded life of a Carmelite was not right for her. For her own protection, Sister Concepta thought that Bernadette should remain part of the holy family. Which is why I agreed that she should come here. I genuinely believed we could help her." Sister Rosalie lowered her gaze and sipped her brandy, shuddering slightly as the raw spirit trickled down her throat. "It seems I was mistaken."

"You mentioned her doctor. Williams, wasn't it? Do you have her address?"

"Yes, Molly Williams. She has a practice in Cross Street, on the other side of the park. Number fifteen, I think."

"Then I'll pay her a visit."

CHAPTER 16

WEDNESDAY

"I think it's just up here under the bridge." Myra touched the brake with the toe of her shoe and changed gear, slowing down to a crawl.

She steered the squad car under a railway bridge and looked to her left. "It's a bookshop," she said, as the first building came into view.

Fuller frowned and checked the address written on the paper in front of him. "It says number eighty-three. That's number eighty-three."

The bookshop was first in a terraced row of residential houses, but its façade had been remodelled as a shop front. A sign attached to the wall above the picture window read, 'Charles Moon. Antiquarian and Second-hand Books.'

There was a half-glazed door set to one side of the window with an Open sign hanging in it, and a banner was fixed to the wall beside it. "Maps and Prints a Speciality," proclaimed the gold script.

Myra drew up at the kerb and switched off the engine. "Are we going to try anyway?"

"Might as well. Nothing ventured . . ."

They got out of the Wolseley and walked up to the window, peering through cupped hands into the gloomy interior.

"There's someone in there," Fuller said. "It looks like an old woman."

The building shook as a train thundered over the bridge above them, spewing out steam and soot.

"The Kings Cross express," Myra said. She twisted the door handle and stepped into the shop.

Fuller glanced up apprehensively at the behemoth barrelling along above him. "I'm surprised this place is still standing."

The interior of the shop was as gloomy as it had looked from the outside. From floor to ceiling stood bookcases, full to overflowing, some with fine bindings and gold lettering, some with tired, cloth-bound covers and others with bare spines. A passage between the shelves led to an antique table with Queen Anne legs, piled high with more books and a wooden cash register. An elderly woman sat there, adding numbers to a column in a spidery script.

The air was heavy with dust and the smell of old mildewed paper. Fuller wrinkled his nose and grimaced at Myra.

"It's the smell of culture," she hissed. "My granddad's house smelt the same. The smell of old books is like nothing else on earth."

Fuller stopped to crouch down in front of a well-stocked bookcase. He peered at the titles on one of the lower shelves. "There's a set of Biggles books here! I used to love them when I was a kid. Up until the age of fourteen, I was convinced I wanted to be a pilot, just like him."

"What changed your mind?"

"Arthur Conan Doyle. I discovered Sherlock Holmes and being a detective seemed a much more interesting career than being a fighter pilot, so when I left school I joined the police. The rest, as they say, is history."

"Shame," Myra said. "I think you'd cut a rather dashing figure in a flying helmet and goggles. Somehow I can't quite see you in a deerstalker. Doesn't fit."

"May I help you?" The voice was querulous, a little shaky.

Myra threaded between the books towards the table. "Detective Constable Banks, Welwyn and Hatfield Police. This is Inspector Fuller."

The old lady peered up at them over half-rimmed glasses. Her skin looked desiccated and her white hair was piled on top of her head, secured with three tortoiseshell combs. "My word. The police? Are you here to arrest me?"

"Why? What have you done?" Myra said with a smile.

"Oh, lots . . . when I was your age. Not a lot in the past thirty years mind, but I was quite a girl back in the twenties. A real flapper."

"I bet you dance a mean Charleston."

The old woman smiled at her. "Bless you. I'm afraid my dancing days are behind me, and have been for quite a while now."

Fuller was smiling too. "We have this address for Tony Smythe."

"Yes, that's right."

"Mr Smythe lives here?"

"He has rooms in the attic."

"We'd like to speak with him if we can," Myra said.

The old lady turned to her. "Did you call earlier? He told me a young lady had rung him. Quite excited, he was." She lowered her voice to a conspiratorial whisper. "It doesn't happen very often, bless him. He's out the back, in the workshop." She pointed to a door behind her. "Go on through."

Myra pushed it open and looked inside.

More books. Racks of them. Some looked brand new, others were showing signs of distress, with ripped and stained covers. Some had no covers at all. A workbench occupied a space in the centre of the room and a young man sat, head bowed, working a soft cloth over a water stain on the green leather binding of a large folio. There was a dish of fluid at his side and an acrid chemical odour hung in the air. Myra's eyes began to water and she dabbed at them with a handkerchief.

"Mr Smythe?"

The young man looked up. "Sorry about the smell. Occupational hazard, I'm afraid."

"I called earlier. Detective Constable Banks?"

"Ah, yes." Smythe dropped the cloth and wiped his hands on a grubby towel. "Come in. Bring your friend."

"This is Inspector Fuller. As I said on the phone, we'd like to ask you some questions."

Smythe stood. He was wearing a brown canvas apron over a grubby-looking white shirt and loose-fitting fawn slacks. "Yes, you did, but you didn't say what about."

Myra stepped into the room. "It's about what happened at St Joseph's on Monday evening. I understand you were there."

Smythe stared down at the desk. "I found her, in the chapel." He looked up and beyond them towards the shop. The old woman was looking at them, obviously trying to listen.

"I'd rather not talk about it down here," he said. "Come up to the flat."

He called out, "The police are here to ask me some questions, Dorothy. I'll take them upstairs, if that's all right with you." He turned back to Myra and Fuller. "I'm sorry. This is Dorothy Moon. She owns the shop."

Myra smiled at the old woman. "We've met."

"Oh, right. Follow me then." Smythe led them through the maze of bookcases to a door that gave onto a flight of uncarpeted stairs. "Up here."

He walked with a limp, favouring his right leg. As they climbed, he hung on tightly to a wooden handrail, hauling himself up, step by step. He glanced back at them. "Bear with me. I'm a bit slow. I contracted poliomyelitis as a child and it left me with this gammy leg."

"There's no rush," Myra said. "Is it much further?"

"My rooms are at the top of the house, I'm afraid."

"That must be very inconvenient for you," Fuller added.

"It's not ideal. But beggars can't be choosers and the flat comes free with the job."

Myra resisted the urge to push Smythe up the stairs in front of her. "What is your job exactly?"

"I help Dorothy run the shop. I have done since her husband died. When Charles went she was all for giving it up, but I persuaded her to carry on, offering to give her any assistance I could for a small financial consideration."

"And a roof over your head," Fuller said.

Myra shot him a look. "I think what the inspector means, is that it was very generous of you, offering to help like that."

"Yes, very generous," Fuller said. The sarcasm appeared to pass unnoticed.

"It's a mutually beneficial arrangement. Here we are."

Smythe unlocked a door and ushered them into a sparsely furnished sitting room.

"Right. Take a seat." He indicated a small sofa with stained upholstery. He sat down on a wooden dining chair, stretching out his bad leg in front of him.

Fuller squeezed onto the sofa next to Myra. "How well did you know Sister Bernadette?"

"Quite well. She knew I worked in a bookshop so she often asked me to find books for her."

"What kind of books?" Myra sat forward.

"Oh, religious works mostly, although she asked for a copy of *Ben Hur* once. *Moby Dick* was another one. She was quite a reader, but then I suppose there's not a lot to do at St Joseph's once the children are in bed."

"Was it you who called the police?" Fuller said.

Smythe nodded. "It was the first thing I did when I left the chapel."

"But you didn't wait for them to arrive."

"No. Les sent me home. He saw how shaken up I was, finding her like that."

"Didn't it occur to you that they might want to speak to you, seeing that you were the one to find the body?"

"I didn't . . . couldn't think about anything. Seeing Sister Bernadette like that . . . the blood . . . her awful dead eyes . . ."

Myra struggled to her feet. "I'm sorry, Mr Smythe, but is there a bathroom I can use?"

"Eh? Oh, yes. Just through there." He pointed to a door on the far side of the room.

"Thank you."

Myra found herself in a small bathroom with a toilet. Above the washbasin was a wooden cabinet with a mirrored door. Along with the usual men's toiletries and shaving gear were a few small brown bottles of tablets. There was nothing on the labels apart from the directions for use: 'one to be taken, with food, every morning . . . Two to be taken when necessary. No more than four tablets per day. One tablet, four times a day.'

Myra took a clean handkerchief from her coat pocket, and opened a bottle, removing the cotton wool wadding and shaking out a pill into the palm of her hand. She unfolded the handkerchief and laid it in the washbasin and laid the pill on the crisp white linen. She repeated the process with each bottle, screwed the caps back on and replaced them in the cabinet where she'd found them, and then she folded the handkerchief over the pills and slipped it back into her pocket. She gave the chain on the cistern a good tug, waited for the flush to engage and went back out to the sitting room.

Fuller was asking Smythe for the details of his whereabouts on Monday afternoon. Myra stood listening rather than squeezing herself back on the sofa next to Fuller.

"I was here until about five when Les picked me up in the van. We drove to St Joseph's and I was there until Les sent me home."

"How did you get back?" Fuller said.

"I took one of the bikes and cycled home."

"Bikes?" Myra said.

"Yes. The home has about half a dozen of them for the children to use. They keep them in a shed at the back. All donated, of course. People can be very generous with the things they no longer need."

Fuller got to his feet. "Well, I think that will be all for now. If you think of anything else you can call me or DC Banks at the station." He stuck out his hand. Smythe's clasp was limp and clammy. He gave a sickly smile as he said goodbye.

CHAPTER 17

WEDNESDAY

Jack headed to his office and picked up the telephone. He dialed a number from his address book and waited.

On the seventh ring a gruff voice with a heavy Liverpool accent said, "Reynolds."

"Hello, Bill. It's Jack Callum."

There was a long pause. "Good God! You were the last person I expected to hear from. How long has it been?"

"About twenty years, give or take."

"Twenty-three actually, since I won the fight."

Jack laughed. "July the 18th, 1936. That date is etched on my memory and I still think I was robbed. You never knocked me out."

"A points win is still a win," Reynolds said. "You're not still bitter about it, are you?"

Jack laughed again. "No, Bill. I was bitter up to 1939 and then war broke out. After that I had tougher enemies to fight."

"Ah, it was a good scrap though, wasn't it? We were very evenly matched."

"Yes, it was a good fight, but you were the one who walked away with the Inter-division heavyweight belt around your waist."

"So what are you calling me for? Do you want a rematch?" Reynolds laughed.

"I'd love one, but I don't think many people would pay to see a couple of dinosaurs like us lumbering about in a boxing ring."

"You speak for yourself. I keep in shape. I'm still a regular at the gym, but these days I help to train the younger fighters. Kids mostly. Some of them can pack a hell of a punch."

"You're still with the force then? I wondered if the number I had would find you after so long."

"I'm still catching the villains. I'm Chief Superintendent Reynolds now. What about you?"

"Yes, still serving. I made it to DCI and then stopped going for promotion. I didn't fancy being shackled to a desk for the rest of my time. And I'm no longer with the Met. I transferred out to the North Hertfordshire constabulary."

"You've gone soft," Reynolds teased.

"Don't you believe it. Crime outside the smoke can be just as brutal and twice as nasty. Like the current case I'm working on."

"Oh yes?"

Jack told him about the killing of Sister Bernadette.

"Good grief," Reynolds said. "I see what you mean. In all my years I've never had the murder of a nun to deal with. How does this relate to us up here? I figure it must in some way or else you wouldn't have called."

"I'm looking into her past and she was from Liverpool. Her family were killed in an unexplained house fire on your patch. Arson was suspected, so I figure there must have been a police investigation. I was wondering if you knew anything."

"When was this fire?"

"About seven or eight years ago."

"It didn't happen yesterday then."

"No, and I don't have any details, apart from the family's name. O'Farrell. Does it ring any bells?"

Reynolds sighed. "You don't expect much, do you, Jack? Mind you, you always were an optimist — like expecting to outbox a three times champion like me."

Jack chuckled. "I did give you a run for your money though."

"Aye, you did that. Listen, it's not ringing any bells in *my* head, but give me a while. I'll ask around. I'm sure someone will remember something. Where can I reach you?"

Jack gave him his work and home phone numbers. "Any time, day or night."

"I'll be in touch. It's been good to hear from you again, Jack. It's nice to relive one's glory days once in a while."

Jack rang off and called down to the desk sergeant. "Has the report come back from the lab yet, Andy?"

"It has and I passed it onto Sergeant Lesser," Andy Brewer said. "I tried to call you but you were engaged and I thought the report might be important, so I gave it to him."

"You did the right thing, Andy. It is."

Jack went down to the squad room.

Frank Lesser sat at his desk, the forensic report spread out in front of him. Jack pulled up a chair and sat down. He picked up a page and scanned through it.

Lesser glanced at him. "There's an interesting bit in there about the contents of the tea cups you sent them. There were no tea leaves of any kind in either cup, which suggests the tea was made somewhere else and taken there in a vacuum flask. One lot was just tea, plain and simple, but the other was drugged with barbiturate. So whoever poured Sister Bernadette her drink must have added the sleeping pill to her cup. A vacuum flask makes sense because none of the kitchen staff saw anyone making a pot of tea on Monday afternoon. Whoever visited her came prepared, with the tea and the sleeping pills. So I figure that this murder was premeditated."

Jack nodded. "I never thought it was anything else. The killer went to St Joseph's with the sole intention of murdering Sister Bernadette."

Lesser shuddered. "The killer had the presence of mind to take the vacuum flask away with them, but not enough to remember the cups."

"It's mistakes like that that make our job a little easier," Jack said. "Still, the killer wasn't stupid. They must have gained her trust in order to be invited up to her room to take tea with her." He picked up another page. "Sister Bernadette's fingerprints on one cup, not a single print on the other."

"Do you think he wiped them?"

"Either that, or he wore gloves. It was bitterly cold on Monday, and I was in Bernadette's room on Tuesday morning. It wasn't a lot warmer in there than outside — the Sisters don't go in much for creature comforts. So I doubt Bernadette thought her guest's decision to keep their gloves on was unusual."

Fuller came into the squad room, followed closely by Myra.

Jack glanced around at them. "Any joy with Smythe?"

"I found these, sir." Myra reached into her pocket and took out a neatly folded handkerchief. She opened it out on Lesser's desk to reveal three tablets, two white and one blue. "There were three bottles in Smythe's bathroom cabinet, so I took a pill from each one."

"Other than that, his alibi checks out," Fuller said. "Mind you, he's a bit of a strange one."

"In what way?"

"Well, he's in his mid-thirties but I wouldn't mind betting that he's still a virgin."

"There's no crime in that," Jack said. "I'm sure there are lots of men out there who don't have your libido."

Fuller blushed. He cast a surreptitious glance at Myra, who was grinning. "You make me sound like a wolf."

"If the cap fits, Eddie . . ." Jack turned to Myra. "Don't stand there smirking, Constable. Get those pills over to Stevenage for analysis. They might be totally unrelated but we need to be sure. Wait there until you get the results."

Myra glanced at her watch. "But that could take hours, sir, and I have to drive Inspector Fuller home."

"Welcome to the CID, Myra, and don't worry about Inspector Fuller. He'll get home, one way or another. Now, get your skates on and get those pills tested."

"Yes, sir," Myra said. She rushed from the room.

"Eddie, you come with me. John Holmes is the last name on Parsons' list. We'll go together and I'll get my new driver to run you home afterwards."

* * *

John Holmes lived in the basement flat of a large Victorian house close to the town centre. A heavy iron fence bordered the stone steps leading down to the front door. Light had drained from the late afternoon sky and the climb down the steps was hazardous. When they were halfway down the dim light trickling out from behind a pair of grubby net curtains revealed the various obstacles placed on the steps as if to trip would-be callers. Terracotta plant pots appeared to be the first line of defence, followed by a pile of roofing tiles, old tins of paint and a plastic bucket containing muddy water with a few twigs sprouting from it.

"Salubrious," Fuller said.

"At least he has a roof over his head."

"A leaky one, if those tiles are anything to go by."

Jack knocked on the door.

"Just a minute," called a voice from inside.

"John Holmes?" Fuller said, as the door was pulled open.

"You must be the police," Holmes said. "I got a phone call."

"Indeed." Jack flashed his warrant card. Les Parsons' jungle drums were obviously very efficient. "Then you know why we're here."

"Yes, I do. I was at the Home on Monday night, helping Les out."

"And yet you disappeared before we could ask you any questions."

"Yes, I did. Look, let's not stand here. We're letting all the heat out. Come in and I'll put the kettle on."

Holmes lived in a bedsitter which had a small kitchenette hidden from the room by a plastic curtain. He pulled the curtain aside to reveal a small earthenware sink fed by a single brass tap with an ancient water heater fixed to the wall above it. There was a tatty kitchen cupboard with no doors, on which stood a two-ringed electric hob. A couple of wall cupboards with glass doors housed an unedifying selection of canned goods. Holmes' staple diet appeared to consist of tinned spaghetti and baked beans.

"No tea for me, thanks," Fuller said, having seen a cockroach scuttle across the formica worktop, and a couple of silverfish wriggling their way back into the shadows under the hob.

Holmes paused, his hand on the kettle. "And you, Chief Inspector?"

"No, I'm fine. We just need to ask you a few questions and then we'll be out of your hair."

"Very well." Holmes dropped his hand. "Well, sit where you can. I'm afraid I've not much in the way of furniture. I don't have that many people around, apart from the boys for their cross-stitch lessons. Then we tend to sit on the floor or the bed and just muck in together."

Holmes seemed affable enough. He dressed older than his years. The turn-ups of his black slacks looked ragged, and the slacks themselves had seen better days. They were baggy at the knees and so threadbare in the rear that Jack could see the clear outline of the man's Y fronts. Holmes sat on the bed and curled his legs beneath him. Jack and Fuller remained standing.

"Perhaps you can tell us why you left the film show early?" Jack said.

"I always do. I'm not a big film fan actually. I just go to help Les out, wiring the speakers and that kind of thing. I trained as an electrician when I left school, so I know what wire goes where. It saves him electrocuting himself. After I'm sure it's all running safely I usually come back here to listen to the wireless. That's what I did on Monday. There was a play on the Third Programme that I was keen to listen to."

"So you missed all the excitement?" Fuller said, shifting from foot to foot.

"Yes, I did, but Les told me about it. Poor Sister Bernadette. She hadn't been at the home that long."

Fuller shuffled again. "Sorry to be a pain, but do you have a bathroom?"

"Eh?" Holmes stared at Fuller for a moment. "Oh, I see. Yes, I do. But you need to go upstairs. I share the amenities, I'm afraid. Go through that door there and up the stairs. Second left on the first floor."

Fuller nodded and left the room.

"We'll carry on," Jack said. "Did you know Sister Bernadette well?"

Holmes shook his head. "I hardly knew her at all. Our paths rarely crossed. She asked me to change a fuse at St Joe's once and accompanied me to the fuse box, which was a bit of a waste of time because I know very well where it is. I'm an old boy and know just about every square inch of the place."

"It seems that a number of you 'old boys' have formed quite an attachment to St Joseph's. You, Bernard Gallagher, Tony Smythe, and I met Marcus Pennington there on Monday as well. What keeps you going back?"

Holmes chuckled. "I could give you the names of a dozen more who keep going back too. What can I say? It gets into your blood. Once a Joey always . . ." Fuller came back into the room. "Did you find it okay?"

"Yes, thank you." Fuller was wiping his damp hands on the legs of his trousers. "There wasn't a towel."

"Ah, I should have warned you about that. I usually take my own up when I go." Holmes turned back to Jack. "Any more questions?"

"Yes. Do you take tablets to help you sleep?"

Fuller look at Jack sharply.

"Sleeping pills? Good heavens, no. I never have any problem in the sleep department. I work so damned hard that sometimes it's as much as I can do to get through an evening with my eyes open."

"So you're an electrician."

"I *was* an electrician," Holmes corrected him. "I'm not now."

"What do you do now?"

Holmes chuckled. "You mentioned him just now. Marcus Pennington. I work for him."

"In what capacity?"

"Nothing very glamorous, I'm afraid. I drive a forklift truck in the paper mill. A bit of a comedown really. I used to have my own electrical business, but while I'm good with my hands and can rewire a house with my eyes closed, I could never get to grips with the pricing and estimating for jobs, so I was constantly losing money. In the end I was doing a spot of off-the-books work for Marcus and he offered me the job of driving the forklift. Saved my bacon, I can tell you. I was well behind with the rent and thought I was going to get turned out on my ear. But that's the best thing about being an ex-Joey. We look out for each other."

Jack nodded. "Yes, I can see that. Can anyone verify that you were here on Monday evening?"

"Mrs Barlow, the old biddy who lives in the flat above this one. She thinks I have the wireless on too loud so she bangs on the floor with her stick, and she was in fine form on Monday evening. Every bloody five minutes she was hammering. In the end I had to move the wireless onto the bed, just so I could hear it."

"Well, you've been very helpful, Mr Holmes." Jack handed him a card. "If you can think of anything else that might help us with our inquiries, you can reach me at the station. We'll see ourselves out."

Once they were back on the street, Fuller said, "I think I could use a hot bath. Did you see the bugs in the kitchen?"

"And the mouse droppings on the lino. What about the bathroom?"

"I was trying to be subtle, trying to sneak a look in his bathroom cabinet without him knowing, like Myra did at Tony Smythe's."

"Eddie, it's a shared house with a common bathroom. Any pills you found there could have belonged to any of the residents. Did you find any?"

Fuller shook his head. "As well as there being no towel to dry your hands, there was no bathroom cabinet, and as for the state of the bath . . ." He shuddered again. "How do people live like that?"

"It takes all sorts, Eddie. Come on. Let's get you home. You'll be wanting to spend some time with Judy."

"Ah, about that . . ." Fuller said as they reached the car. "Judy and I are no longer an item."

"I thought you two were living together."

"Yeah, well. It seemed like a good idea when she asked me to move into her flat above the Dog and Duck. Living in sin, no matter what people thought. It almost felt exciting, but actually it was a real pain. I'm just not cut out for domesticity, not with Judy anyway. They change, you know, women, when they get you where they think they want you. Suddenly you start arguing over stupid things like whose turn it is to make the bed or do the washing up. I really couldn't be doing with it. That's why I was late getting to you on Tuesday morning. I moved all my clothes back to my old flat. Luckily it was still vacant and old Mr Drysdale welcomed me back with open arms. Saved him the bother of trying to rent it out again, he said. For a moment on Monday I thought I was going have to get digs in the Section House."

"Thank Heavens for old Mr Drysdale then." Jack smiled. "Sorry about you and Judy though."

"Some things are just not meant to be."

CHAPTER 18

WEDNESDAY

Jack arrived home to the all-too familiar sound of Bert Weedon playing 'Guitar Boogie Shuffle,' a tune that had formed the background to his home life ever since the summer. He walked into the sitting room. His fifteen-year old son, Eric, was standing next to the radiogram, his guitar slung from a cord around his neck as he played along, producing an accurate, if tinny, facsimile of the record.

"Have you done your homework?" Jack asked him.

Eric nodded without looking up from the fret board.

Jack's daughter, Rosie, stood in front of the mirror above the mantelpiece, applying lipstick.

"You should be doing that in the bathroom."

Her reflection smiled at him. "Do you know how cold it is up there?"

"Are you going out?"

"Brian's picking me up at half past. We're going to the pictures."

"Brian? Is that the boy with the motorbike?" Jack said, slightly alarmed.

"Oh, keep up, Dad. That was Roger. I finished with him last month. This is Brian, Brian Smedley. His parents own the greengrocer's in Leys Avenue."

"Well, I want you home by eleven."

Rosie pursed her lips and kissed a sheet of tissue. "That won't be a problem. Brian has a car."

"What film are you going to see?"

"It's the new Laurence Harvey film, *Room at the Top*."

"What's it about?"

"Life in the North of England."

"Sounds interesting," Jack said sardonically. "Would I like it?"

Rosie smiled. "I doubt it, Dad. It might be a bit racy for you."

Bert Weedon finished playing and Eric moved the arm of the record player back to the start of the record.

"Not again, Eric!" Rosie called. "You promised I could have Craig Douglas next. Put 'Only Sixteen' on."

"I have to practise 'Guitar Boogie,' Sis. The Vikings want to do it at the dance next Saturday." The Vikings was Eric's group and they were making quite a name for themselves in the youth clubs of Letchworth and Baldock.

Jack looked from his daughter to his son and shook his head. "Sometimes I wonder about my children."

"Mum's in the kitchen," Rosie said helpfully. She went across to the radiogram to change the record.

As the dulcet tones of teen heart-throb Craig Douglas, filled the room, Jack went out to the kitchen.

Annie was standing at the cooker, stirring a pot of delicious-smelling stew. "Dinner in ten minutes," she said, as Jack came up behind her and nuzzled her neck.

"Is Joanie home from work yet?"

"She's not coming home tonight," Annie said. "She's staying over with Avril."

"And what does Avril's husband think of that?"

"He won't be there. He's driving a cargo of machine parts up to Newcastle, staying overnight in digs and then heading off to Sunderland to pick up a lorry-load of tyres to bring back down here. And that's all I've been told, so don't ask me for any more details."

"I wasn't going to. So what are Joanie and Avril going to do while he's away? Go through his wardrobe and cut up his clothes?"

"Not that he doesn't deserve it the way he treats Avril, but no, they're having an Amami night."

"A what?"

Annie rolled her eyes. "An Amami night. 'Amami' is a setting lotion. They're curling each other's hair."

For the second time that evening Jack shook his head in despair. "You know, sometimes when I get home it feels like I've strayed onto an alien planet."

"Oh, don't exaggerate," Annie teased. "You love us really, despite our foibles."

He kissed her lightly on the lips. "True. Did you have a word with Mrs Painter about her son's guitar?"

Annie glanced at the doorway, checking to see that Eric was out of earshot. "I did, and we can have it. Geoffrey goes down to Portsmouth to join his ship the day after Boxing Day and he's told Barbara he wants the guitar and amplifier gone before he comes home on leave in March. So when I told her I wanted to buy them for Eric's Christmas present, she was delighted. She said it would save her the job of advertising them in the 'Comet' and all the bother that can bring. People coming to the house, not sure whether they want to buy or not. She had enough of those problems when she sold her three piece suite way back in June."

"Do you think we're doing the right thing by him? If he cared as much about his schoolwork as he does about music, he could do really well. He's a bright kid. He could even go on to university."

"You didn't go to university and it never did you any harm."

"Yes, I know, but this is our son we're talking about. I don't want to see him ending up in a dead-end job, and I hardly think he's police material — not that I'd choose that for him anyway. One plod in the family is enough in my book."

"He's bright, but not academically. Don't worry about him. He might surprise you one day and make a career for himself in music. It's been done before."

"As a hip-swivelling lip curler like Elvis Presley or Cliff Richard. I can't see any mileage in that somehow. Give it a year and the kids will have moved on to something new. They always do."

"You said that about skiffle music."

"I rest my case. A nine day wonder."

"Did you know that Gerry's teaching him to read music?"

Jack raised his eyebrows. "No. I wasn't aware of that."

"Introducing Eric to Geraldine Tanner was one of your better ideas, dear husband," Annie said. "I remember you saying at the time that you hoped her classical training would rub off on him and, from what I've seen — and heard — it certainly seems to be working."

"I must admit, I heard him playing when I got in and it sounded pretty good to me."

"Well, there's the answer to your question. Yes, we're doing the right thing by getting him an electric guitar. You never know, he might make a fortune as a rock-and-roller and be able to keep us in luxury in our old age."

Jack hugged her. "I love your optimism."

"Stranger things have happened."

* * *

Jack was starting to enjoy a quiet evening, puffing on one of his irregular pipes and listening to Mantovani playing on the radiogram when Myra Banks telephoned. Annie was watching some inane drivel on the television and Eric was up in his room, practising his guitar. With Joan staying over at Avril's and Rosie still at the cinema, the house was pleasantly peaceful.

"Sorry to disturb you at home, sir, but I've just got back from the lab and I thought you'd want to know the results of the tests."

Jack glanced at his watch. "Sorry, Myra, I didn't mean for you to be so late back."

"Actually, sir, you did me a favour. Mum's a terrible cook and tonight she did rissoles. When I didn't come in at my usual time she left them in the oven to keep warm. I've just tried them and they've dried out. They're now the size of walnuts and twice as hard, so it's fish and chips for me this evening."

Jack smiled to himself. "The results, Myra?"

"Oh yes, of course. One was an anti-histamine, one was for constipation and the last one was plain old aspirin."

"So no sleeping pills?"

"Well, the anti-histamine can make you drowsy and they recommend you don't operate heavy machinery when taking them, but there was nothing there that could be used as a Mickey Finn."

"Well, thanks for letting me know, Myra. Enjoy your cod and chips."

"Not me, sir. I'm a rock eel type of girl."

"Good night, Myra. See you in the morning."

"Night, sir."

"Who was that?" Annie said when he came back to the sitting room.

"Work. Nothing to worry about."

"They never let you rest, do they?"

"Such is life," he said. He settled headphones over his ears to drown out the annoying voice of the quizmaster on the television programme Annie was watching.

A few moments later, Annie slipped out of her chair, switched the television off and went across to him, lifting the headphones from his head.

"How about cocoa and an early night."

"I'm not tired."

She smiled at him. "Strangely enough, neither am I."

"Has anyone ever told you you're a wicked temptress?"

"I think you've mentioned it once or twice." She took his hands and hauled him out of his easy chair.

"Forget the cocoa," he said. He switched off the radiogram and let her lead him out of the room and up the stairs.

CHAPTER 19

WEDNESDAY

Father Martin Harvey sat in his darkened study, sipping Scotch from a tumbler and staring blankly into space. Since hearing the news of Sister Bernadette's death he had been going about his business and performing his parish duties like an automaton. A light had gone out from his world and he could not summon the strength to drag himself out of the self-pitying funk that was eating away at him.

In the grate the coals were dying, and a chill crept through the room, seeping through his clothes and making him shiver. He took another mouthful of Scotch, swilling it around his mouth before swallowing and letting the neat spirit warm him from within.

Out in the hallway the doorbell chimed. With a sigh he pushed himself out of his armchair and went to see who was calling on him this late in the evening. At the door he switched on the porch light and peered through the stained glass to see if he could identify his visitor, but he could see no one. Irritably he pulled open the front door but the doorstep was empty.

An icy winter wind swept into the house, displacing what little warmth there was left inside and he swore softly. He wasn't in the mood for games. His watch read 9.30. Surely it wouldn't be children playing 'knock down ginger' at this time of night.

From the presbytery he had a clear view across the street to the church. The yew trees that stood between the headstones in St Augustine's churchyard rose up like monstrous shrouds, their tops bathed by the silver light of the moon. For some reason, tonight he found their black bulk forbidding and slightly sinister. He shivered again, but it had nothing to do with the chill December air. Shaking his head he grabbed hold of the door and was about to push it shut when he caught sight of something out of the corner of his eye.

A light was flickering behind the windows of the church, as if someone holding a candle or a small lamp was moving about inside. The thought of thieves attempting to steal the church's silver and gold plate made him reach for his coat and head out into the night. In his five years as incumbent at St Augustine's he had steadfastly ignored the advice of his predecessor and left the doors to the church unlocked. He firmly believed that God's house should never be shut to those souls that were in need of succour, day or night. Despite the lurid tales of theft and vandalism from other parish priests, his belief in the goodness of his fellow man had yet to be shaken.

Tonight, though, whether it was the whisky he had drunk, or just a symptom of his dark mood, he felt apprehensive as he crossed the street to the church.

He gripped the large wrought iron ring, turned it to lift the latch, and pushed the huge oak door open. As he stepped into the small vestibule, he reached for a light switch on the wall.

Listening closely, he heard no sounds coming from inside the church. He opened the inner door of the vestibule and stepped through. "Hello? Is there anyone here?" His breath steamed in the cold air. "Hello?" he called again, but apart from the faint echo of his own voice there was only silence.

The electric light in the main body of the church was weak and offered scant illumination. He strode into the centre of the nave and called again. Ahead of him was the altar and cross. He genuflected and was about to turn to leave when he saw something move in one of the confessionals. Drawing in a breath he walked slowly towards the wooden booths. The centre booth was where he sat to hear the confessions. The left hand booth was in darkness, but through the mesh in the door of the booth to the right a light was flickering.

He approached cautiously. A yard away from the door he called, "Who's in there?"

Silence. He stretched out his hand, gripped the small brass knob and tugged the door open.

In the centre of the wooden bench seat was a fat church candle, its flickering flame illuminating a ragged piece of cardboard propped up against the wall. One word was scrawled on the card in heavy black ink.

'REPENT!'

"What the—"

He heard a noise behind him and turned in time to catch a glimpse of something metal arcing through the air towards him. He didn't have time to duck as the heavy object cracked against the side of his head, stunning him and sending him reeling into the booth. His falling body knocked the candle to the floor where it sputtered and went out. As he fell, his fingers clutched the cardboard sign, dragging it from the bench.

He landed awkwardly, his back slamming against the bench, knocking the breath from his lungs. A weight settled on his legs and he felt a series of dull blows to his chest. His last sensations were of someone's fingers fumbling with the belt of his trousers and an insistent tugging as the trousers themselves were pulled down over his knees. Then darkness claimed him.

CHAPTER 20

THURSDAY 10th DECEMBER 1959

Doctor Barry Fenwick looked up at Jack bleakly. "Judging by the pattern of the stab wounds and the mess down below, I'd guess that you're looking for the same person who killed Sister Bernadette."

Jack stared down at Martin Harvey's mutilated body and shook his head sadly. "Was he castrated?"

"More than that. They took the lot. No surgical skill involved. It was more like butchering a piece of meat, probably with the same knife they used to stab him. Oh, and one gruesome fact — the butchery took place ante-mortem."

"He was still alive."

"Very much so. He was probably dazed or knocked unconscious by the blow to the head from that thing there." He pointed to a bloodstained brass candlestick lying on the floor a few feet away. "Then the killer got to work. Judging from the amount of blood, and you can see that a lot of it soaked into his clothes, I'd say that the victim bled to death."

"And he took the genitals as some kind of trophy?"

"That's what I thought at first. Then DC Banks made a rather macabre — and frankly disgusting — discovery."

Jack glanced back along the aisle. Myra Banks was sitting in the front pew, bent over, her forehead almost touching her knees. Eddie Fuller sat beside her, his hand resting on her back. Jack went to join them. "What is it, Eddie?"

Fuller didn't look up. "Myra found it in there," he said flatly, gesturing to a Romanesque stone baptismal font ten feet away. "She's pretty shaken up."

Jack crossed to the font and stared down into the water, once holy and now defiled and stained crimson.

Fuller came up behind him but kept his eyes averted. "Do you think he was desecrating the church by doing this?"

"Either that or he was sanctifying Father Harvey's genitals in holy water. You saw the cardboard sign?"

"*Repent*. Yes, I saw it. It was laid across his chest. Dr Fenwick had to move it to get a closer look at the stab wounds."

"Did the doc give you any idea of the time of death?"

"He thinks about nine to ten p.m. yesterday."

"I think this has all the signs of a punishment killing, Eddie. In the killer's mind, Father Harvey had done something that warranted this kind of retribution."

"Like fathering the child Sister Bernadette was carrying?"

Jack rubbed his chin. "That was the thought running through my mind." He switched tack. "Was there any sign of the murder weapon?"

Fuller shook his head. "He must have taken it with him. The doc thinks it was a fairly small blade, single-sided. Razor sharp though. It cut through Harvey's overcoat, jumper and shirt easily enough, as well as doing the . . . other thing."

A flash of light lit the church. Jack turned and glared at the constable wielding a camera, taking photos of the crime scene. "Haven't you finished yet, Constable?"

"Nearly done, sir," the officer called back, and lined up another shot.

"Well, make it quick. Just remember where you are." He turned to Fuller. "Who found the body?"

"A woman who comes in a couple of days a week to do the flowers."

Jack stared at the wilted blooms scattered randomly across the stone floor. "Not much of a display, is it?"

"She was hysterical. WPC Taylor took her across to the presbytery. I told Taylor to make the old girl a cup of tea and sit with her until you got here."

"Ok. I'll pop in and see her before I head off to St Albans to give Canon Flood the news. He was Father Harvey's boss. He deserves to be told in person, rather than finding out some other way." He glanced back at Father Harvey's body sprawled in the confessional. "Sometimes, Eddie, when you think you've seen every depravity the human race is capable of, this job lets you know that you're just kidding yourself. Get uniform to canvass door to door along the street. Someone might have seen something last night. And get that candlestick checked for fingerprints. We might just get lucky."

* * *

A woman opened the door of a large detached house set in a leafy St Albans lane. "I'd like to see Canon Flood," Jack said

The woman was in her thirties and had a stern, unsmiling face. Her dark hair was pulled severely back in a tight bun, and her clothes were plain, no-nonsense grey tweed. The only colour was provided by a floral-patterned apron that covered her skirt. "Do you have an appointment?"

Jack presented his warrant card. "I don't need one, but I'd appreciate it if you could tell him I'd like to speak with him."

The woman's expression softened slightly. "I'm sorry, Chief Inspector. My name is Ruth Beech. I'm the Canon's housekeeper. Come in and wait in the hall. I'll find him and tell him you're here."

Jack stepped inside and Ruth Beech closed the door behind him before scurrying back into the house in search of her employer.

A few minutes later an elderly man, short and stout with a shock of curly white hair surrounding a shiny bald head, emerged from a room at the back of the house. As he approached, he dabbed at his lips with a napkin. Judging from the streak of egg yolk on the Canon's black woollen cardigan, Jack guessed he had interrupted the man's breakfast.

"Chief Inspector Callum, is it?" He held out his hand. "Gerald Flood. To what do I owe the pleasure of a visit from the police?"

Jack shook his hand. "I'm afraid I come bearing bad news."

The smile slipped from Canon Flood's avuncular face. "That's rather depressing to hear, but then, when a policeman comes calling at this time of the morning he's hardly going to be the bearer of glad tidings. Come through to the study. We can talk in there." Flood opened a heavy door and ushered Jack inside.

Flood closed the door behind them, pulled up a chair for Jack, then went around to the rear of a large mahogany desk and lowered his bulk into a studded green leather captain's chair.

Flood moved deliberately and cautiously, as if he were in great pain.

"Right," the Canon said once he was seated at his desk. "What is this bad news you wish to impart?"

* * *

"This seems to be turning into 'Kill a Catholic' week," Flood said. He took a handkerchief from his pocket and mopped perspiration from his brow. His face had turned a sickly grey and his breathing was ragged.

Jack leaned forward in his seat, concerned the man was about to have a seizure.

Flood held out a restraining hand. "Give me a moment. I need some time to digest this." His breathing gradually settled. "Forgive me. I wasn't being glib or irreverent before, but first Sister Bernadette at St Joseph's and now this." He shook his head. "It does seem that my faith is somehow under attack."

"From our preliminary inquiries it would seem that the killings are connected."

Flood's hand came up again. "Please, if you could keep your voice down. I don't want Miss Beech to hear us. I'll tell her quietly when we're on our own. She thought the world of Father Harvey. This news is going to devastate her."

"Did she know him well?"

"She was *his* housekeeper before coming to work for me."

"I didn't realise. Had I known, I wouldn't have come in here like a bull in a china shop."

"It was Martin's idea that she come and help me out. When my own housekeeper passed away in August, Martin saw that I was going to struggle to keep this place going by myself. I'm not in the best of health these days, you see. I have a weak heart, rarely sleep, and this damned arthritic hip gives me hell. So Martin, bless his kind heart, suggested that she come here to take care of me until I can find a suitable replacement. But that was

Martin Harvey, always putting the needs of others before his own. Oh, I will miss him so."

"Would you say he was a man to make enemies?"

"Martin? Great Heavens no! I can't imagine a kinder, sweeter man. Everybody loved him."

"Well, obviously not everybody."

Flood sank back into his seat and mopped his forehead again. "Quite," he said. "But I can't think who would do such an awful thing."

"Had he fallen out with anyone in recent weeks? One of his parishioners perhaps?"

Flood shook his head. "You obviously didn't know Martin very well. The word 'appeasement' could have been coined specifically for him. He had a way of diffusing trouble — nipping it in the bud before it could ever escalate into unpleasantness."

There was a tap at the door and Miss Beech looked into the room. "I was wondering if you gentlemen would care for some tea. I've just put the kettle on."

Flood composed himself, letting the genial mask settle back on his face. "Bless you, Ruth. That's very thoughtful of you, but I think we're just about finished here. The Chief Inspector is just about to leave. That's right, isn't it, Mr Callum?"

Jack stood. "Yes. I think we're almost done." He turned and smiled at Ruth Beech, who bowed her head slightly and closed the door.

"A diamond," Flood said. "An absolute gem, that woman."

"Before I go," Jack said, "what were your thoughts about Sister Bernadette?"

"Well, to be frank with you I hardly knew the girl. But I do know she strained Sister Rosalie's patience, and that woman is rarely vexed. She couldn't run a place like St Joseph's if she was. Some of the children there are rather a handful. She meets the challenges they throw at her with good grace, and those challenges come at her on an almost daily basis."

"What did Sister Bernadette do to make herself such a problem to Sister Rosalie?

"Well, I won't speak ill of the dead — may Our Father bless her soul — but Bernadette was what you would call 'a difficult child.'"

"Father Harvey called her 'conflicted.'"

"Ah, that's Martin. Hitting the nail bang on the head as usual. I'm going to miss his wisdom. He used to counsel me, would you believe? You'd think it would be the other way around. No, 'conflicted' is a very accurate way of describing her. Despite her apparent desire to take holy orders, I can't think of a person less suited to take on the rigours of the veil. Serving our Lord can take its toll on the strongest of us, and Sister Bernadette could best be described as 'fragile'. I understand she had a very difficult childhood."

"Were you told how it was difficult?"

Flood shook his head. "No. Nobody betrayed her confidence but, reading between the lines, I got the impression that she was badly mistreated as a child. I think that, for her, the church was an escape, a place of safety, a sanctuary if you like. Tragic really. I mean, God is always there, ready to help the weak and those who are less able to cope with life but He shouldn't be used to hide behind."

"And you think that's what Sister Bernadette was doing? Hiding from something in her past?"

"Or her present. Maybe she was just hiding from herself. Her *real* self."

"Just one more thing," Jack said. "I understand that Sister Bernadette drove over to St Albans last Saturday. I wondered if she came to see you."

Flood shook his head. "No. Sister Bernadette never came here. Never, in all the time I knew her. Besides, I wasn't here on Saturday. I was over in Ware, giving a talk to the boys of Junior House at St Edmond's College. St Edmond's is a seminary and I make it a point to call in three times a year to give the students an insight into life in the priesthood. I studied there myself and I see my talks as a way of giving something back to an institution that gave me so much."

"Well, thank you for your time, Canon. I'm sorry that we should meet under such tragic circumstances."

"God tests us all in so many different ways," Flood said, getting to his feet and showing Jack to the door. "I trust you'll keep me abreast of any developments. I'll now have to go and explain this latest ungodly event to the Bishop."

Well, good luck with that, Jack thought. He trudged back to the car.

CHAPTER 21

THURSDAY

"Jack, I need a word with you."

Jack followed Chief Superintendent Henry Lane into his office.

"Come in, shut the door and take a seat," Lane said gruffly.

Jack pulled up a chair and Lane went round to the other side of the desk.

"I've just had Bishop Rawlings on the phone," Lane said without preamble. "To say he's agitated would be an understatement."

"Flood works fast," Jack said under his breath.

"What's that? Speak up, man."

"I was saying that I only informed Canon Flood of Father Harvey's murder half an hour ago. He said he was going to have to inform the Bishop, but I wasn't expecting the fall-out so soon."

"Well, what *did* you expect? A nun *and* a priest murdered since Monday, and today's only Thursday. God knows how many we'll have lost by the weekend. All the good Catholics will be going to church on Sunday and no one left alive to take the mass."

"A bit of an exaggeration, sir, if you don't mind me saying so."

"I *do* mind, Jack. I'm not having this kind of killing spree on my patch. What are you doing about it?"

"Look, Henry, you know how these things work. We're making inquiries, but it takes time."

"Which is exactly what I said to Bishop Rawlings. But he wants the culprit brought to justice, and he wants it handled discreetly and as quickly as possible."

"But—"

"Never mind 'but.' Just tell me what progress you've made so far. How do you see this case shaping up?"

"Well, it would be a help if I didn't keep getting half-truths and evasions from all the people I interview. The criminal underworld could learn a great deal from the Church when it comes to keeping your mouth shut. I'm having to piece things together from hints, whispers, and what I can deduce from the little evidence I have managed to uncover. It would have taken half the time if people were just straight with me."

"For example?"

Jack sighed. "Sister Bernadette has been described to me as 'conflicted,' 'difficult,' 'fragile' and 'a troubled child.' All I can see is a young woman, who had possible nymphomaniac tendencies and a degree of masochism thrown in for good measure, shoehorned into a life for which she was totally unsuited. And then there's Father Harvey. If Canon Flood is to be taken at his word, he was half an inch away from sainthood, but I'm starting to believe that he abused Bernadette O'Malley's trust and got her pregnant."

Lane bristled. "That's a wicked accusation to make."

"I agree it's unsavoury, but it certainly explains the scenario that's been played out over the past few days. I think Sister Bernadette confided in someone about her relationship with Father Harvey and possibly mentioned the fact that she was expecting his child. That person, driven by some kind of moral outrage, decided to punish them both in the most horrendous way possible."

"And what evidence do you have to support such a wild theory?"

"The facts are that Bernadette was a sexually active young woman, and we know she was certainly pregnant. We found lipstick and scanty underwear in her room. The whip and the recent lash marks on her back indicate that Father Harvey was right about her. She was 'conflicted,' and unable to accept her desires. She set herself on a course of self-flagellation to drive the badness from her soul."

Lane was shaking his head. "I think what you have so far, Jack, is all bull. Nothing but wild speculation. I think you're twisting the evidence, shaping it to suit your own anti-religious bigotry. I expected more from you, Chief Inspector, I really did. Do you really expect me to go to the Bishop with this obscene farrago, this hogwash of yours?"

Jack stared open-mouthed at Lane. "You know me better than that, Henry. I'm not a bigot, anti-religious or otherwise, and never have been. I'm simply calling the case as I see it. Of course there are other possible scenarios, but the one I've outlined makes the most sense to me."

"Which leads me to wonder if you're the right person to be heading up this case. Perhaps I should get someone else to take the reins."

"With respect, sir, the only person qualified to take over from me is Eddie Fuller. Despite his many qualities — ones I heartily endorse — I don't think he's ready yet to take this on as his first case in charge."

Lane sat back in his chair, took off his glasses and squeezed the bridge of his nose. Eventually he replaced them and shook his head again. "Reluctantly I have to agree. No, Jack, you'll have to carry on with it, but for pity's sake, temper your more outré imaginings and tread lightly. Report to me as soon as you have something to go on that's more substantial — and more believable."

"Yes, sir," Jack said tightly. He left the office.

* * *

"Would you say I was a bigot, Frank?" Jack asked DS Lesser as he walked into the squad room.

"If you are, you've certainly kept it well hidden in the years I've known you. Why do you ask?"

"It's this case. The nun and the priest. Lane just accused me of being an anti-religious bigot."

Lesser gave a hoot of laughter. "Oh, that's classic. You *do* know that the chief super's a Roman, don't you? He plays golf with Bishop Rawlings twice a month. They're like that." He crossed his fingers.

"I had no idea."

"If you don't mind me saying so, sir, you're a thief-taker. Politics isn't really your strong point."

"I agree with you there, Frank, it isn't," Jack said. "I'm just surprised it's yours."

Lesser shook his head. "It isn't really, but I'm a wrestler, a grunter and groaner, and there isn't a more political sport out there. Fighters sucking up to promoters, keeping the fight bookers sweet, jockeying for position and not minding who they stab in the back on their way up the card. I recognise the signs when I see them."

"I despair," Jack said. He went up to his office, where the telephone was ringing.

"Yes?"

"I have a Chief Superintendent Reynolds of the Merseyside constabulary on the phone for you, sir."

"Put him through, Elaine."

"Yes, sir."

"Jack?"

"Hello, Bill. I wasn't expecting you to get back to me so soon."

"I thought you might want to hear what I've found out sooner rather than later."

"Go on."

"Well, there *was* a fire and we did investigate. DI Salmon led the investigation. Unfortunately he's since retired, but I spoke to the sergeant who was on the case. He maintains that Salmon was convinced the fire was started deliberately, but he couldn't prove it."

"Did he have someone in the frame?"

"He did. Of all the people living in the house, only one survived the blaze. The O'Malley's youngest daughter, Bernadette."

"What did he base his suspicions on?"

"On speaking to neighbours who knew the family. The street where they lived is in a poorer part of town, but the O'Malleys, particularly the mother, Bridget, liked to put on airs, mainly because her two elder daughters had been accepted into a Dominican Priory in Speke. She often spoke of her youngest, Bernadette, following her sisters on their devotional path." Reynolds paused. Jack heard the unmistakable strike of a match and a long draw on a cigarette. In his mind's eye he could see Bill Reynolds sitting in his Liverpool office, feet on the desk, a mug of coffee growing cold in one hand, a Capstan Navy Cut cigarette clenched between the nicotine-stained fingers of the other, the telephone handset wedged between his chin and his shoulder.

"But I'm guessing Mrs O'Malley's ambitions for her daughter didn't come to anything?"

Reynolds chuckled. "I'll say. It seems that our Bernadette was not exactly the pious type. One neighbour described her as 'the town bike,' and bear in mind, the girl was only twelve or thirteen at the time. To say that Bridget O'Malley was disappointed in her daughter would be the understatement to end all understatements. So, if the neighbours are to be believed, Bridget took on the task of banishing the devil from her daughter with regular beatings, using a thin, whippy cane."

"Didn't anyone come to the child's aid?"

"Yes. The local priest, but he was only a young man, straight out of the seminary. He was still wet behind the ears, and he didn't have the wherewithal to put a stop to Bridget O'Malley's cruelty. He was soon sent packing with a firm order from Bernadette's mother to, I quote, 'keep his nose out of God's business.' Well, Salmon saw the arson as Bernadette's revenge on her parents, but he could never make it stick. Pressure was brought to bear on him to wind down his investigation and write the whole sorry mess off as misadventure."

"Pressure from whom?"

"Three guesses. The Church took Bernadette into their care, saw to it that she was protected from any criminal charges and never had to suffer any consequences for her actions."

"Can they do that sort of thing up there?" Jack said.

"Oh, wake up, Jack. They do that sort of thing all the time, not just up here, but all over the world. And don't think I'm singling out the Catholic Church. Any powerful organisation, be it religious, political or even big business, that has limitless funds and resources at its disposal will do whatever it takes to see that its image remains untarnished. And the Vatican is just such an organisation. Pat Salmon was only forty-two when he was offered early retirement, with a very strong recommendation that he spend the rest of his life doing something like gardening or keeping bees."

"And he took it?"

"What do you think? If he hadn't, I dread to think what the consequences would have been."

"That's quite a sobering thought."

"Well, think on that, Jack, before you go any further with this. I'm putting my pension on the line simply by having this conversation with you. The only reason I'm doing so is because you earned my respect thirty odd years ago, and I liked you . . . still do as it happens."

"I won't be bothering you again, Bill."

"No, *do* bother me, but next time let's limit our conversation to boxing and how we could both have been 'contenders,' to paraphrase Marlon Brando."

Jack hung up and sat for a moment staring at the phone. He looked up as Eddie Fuller came into the room.

"I've contacted Father Harvey's parents about the identification and they're catching a train up from Gloucester. They should be arriving mid-afternoon."

Jack rose from the desk and followed Fuller back to his office.

Myra was seated at a typewriter, transcribing the notes she had scribbled down at St Augustine's.

"Feeling better now, Myra?"

Her two fingers paused on the keys but she didn't look up. "I'm okay. It was just a bit of a shock, seeing it floating there like that."

"Take the rest of the day off if you like. You were late home last night. Go Christmas shopping, do something to take your mind off it."

"No, I'll carry on here, if it's all right with you," she said. "I'm sure Inspector Fuller has lots for me to do."

"That's it, Constable," Fuller said. "Nose to the grindstone, shoulder to the wheel. That's the best cure for trauma."

Jack caught Fuller's eye. "You're all heart, Eddie. Go and meet the Harveys at Paddington and take them straight to the mortuary. Let's make it as easy as possible for them. Take Myra along with you. It will be good experience for her."

CHAPTER 22

THURSDAY

"Bring the car around to the front, Meadows. We're going out."

Meadows saluted briefly and hurried out to the car pool at the rear of the station.

"Shall I tell the chief super where you've gone?" Andy Brewer said.

"Tell him I have a date with the Reverend Mother at St Luke's monastery, but only if he asks. If he doesn't, don't volunteer the information."

"Very good, sir."

Jack climbed into the back of the squad car and handed Meadows a map. "I've marked where we're going."

The constable studied the map briefly. "It's okay, sir. I know the place. It's not that far from where I was born."

"Good. It will save us getting lost. When we get there, you wait in the car. If I go in alone it will be less intimidating for the nuns."

"That's if they let you in at all, sir. My grandma always said they were a funny lot up at the monastery. She wouldn't have any truck with them. If they came into her shop, gran would always disappear out the back and let one of the junior assistants deal with them."

"What kind of shop did your grandmother have, Constable?"

"Ladies underwear, that kind of thing, and before you ask, no, the nuns never came in to buy anything. They were looking for donations for whatever charitable cause they were sponsoring that week. The assistant would give them a bob or two just to get rid of them."

"You paint quite a picture."

"My gran used to call them the bane of her life. But then she said that about anyone who came into the shop with no intention of buying anything."

Jack smiled. He closed his eyes as the squad car ate up the miles to Hitchin.

St Luke's monastery sat on the outskirts of Hitchin. It was surrounded by a high brick wall. As they approached the iron gates, the white buildings with their red-tiled roofs surrounding a central bell tower looked surprisingly grand and not a little intimidating.

It had started to snow and Jack turned up the collar of his overcoat. He got out of the car and approached the gate. He jabbed a brass bell push with his thumb and waited. After a couple of minutes one of the large doors in the main building opened and a nun holding an umbrella walked slowly down the paved path towards him, hunched against the weather. She stopped a yard from the gate and looked at him, a question in her eyes.

Jack produced his warrant card. "Chief Inspector Callum, Welwyn and Hatfield CID. I called earlier. I have an appointment with the Reverend Mother."

The nun smiled and nodded, reaching under the folds of her habit to produce a heavy bunch of keys secured with a large metal ring. She selected an iron key from the bunch and slotted it into the lock on the gate. Without a word she twisted the key and pulled the gate open for him to enter, closing and locking it behind them. Beckoning, she led him back along the path to the main doors.

As he entered the building he was struck by the silence that seemed to hang in the air like a physical presence. Then he noticed the number of Sisters moving about the large building, almost gliding from room to room with an absolute economy of movement. Jack was used to the hustle and bustle of life in a police station and the constant noise at home, especially since the advent of the television. The tranquillity of this place was almost overpowering. It used to be that his small oases of calm were the times spent in his sitting room, listening to records or something of interest on the wireless, but since the arrival of television in his life, he had lost those all-too-brief moments.

Such is the price we pay for progress, he thought.

The nun tapped on a door, opened it and ushered Jack through to an office furnished with a large, plain desk, several filing cabinets and three large bookcases filled with books.

A large crucifix hung from the wall, dwarfing the elderly woman sitting at the desk in front of it.

"Reverend Mother, I'm sorry for this intrusion." Jack doffed his hat.

"Take a seat, Chief Inspector. You may call me Sister Concepta."

Jack nodded. "Thank you. Jack Callum."

"I take it that your visit concerns the deaths of Father Harvey and Sister Bernadette."

"You are well-informed."

Sister Concepta smiled. "I've been told our intelligence network is almost as efficient as the British Army's."

Jack returned the smile. "I'm impressed. Father Harvey and Bernadette O'Malley were both killed by person or persons unknown. I'm investigating their murder."

"And your investigations have brought you to our door."

"Yes, they have."

Sister Concepta folded her hands on the desk in front of her. "In the case of Sister Bernadette, I can understand why you think we may be able to help you. I'm sure you're aware that she was with us for several years. But Father Harvey rarely visited us. I think he had his hands rather full at St Augustine's."

"Well, what can you tell me about Sister Bernadette?"

Sister Concepta looked at him and spread her hands. "Where to start?"

"I'll make it easier for you," Jack said. He told her everything he'd learned about Bernadette O'Malley.

When he finished, Sister Concepta leaned forward in her seat. "Well, you certainly seem to have done your homework, Mr Callum."

"That's my job. But now I have hit something of a dead end. I know she went out on Saturday afternoon in the car belonging to the orphanage. The initial information I received seemed to suggest that she was heading to St Albans. I thought she might have driven over to see Canon Flood, but he was at the seminary in Ware, giving a talk to the junior boys, so I was wondering if she came here. Someone saw her late Saturday afternoon, driving back towards St Joseph's. Apparently she was distressed. She was crying as she drove."

Sister Concepta shook her head slowly. "I'm afraid you've had a wasted trip, Chief Inspector. The last time I saw Sister Bernadette was in late May. Father Harvey was driving her out through our gates on her way to St Joseph's."

"But Sister Bernadette could drive."

"Yes, I know. We taught her. But as she was leaving our monastery on a permanent basis, we couldn't let her take our car. Luckily for us, Father Harvey volunteered his services."

She got to her feet. "Come, let me show you out."

* * *

"Back to Hatfield, Constable."

"No joy, sir?"

"Back to bloody square one," Jack said wearily. He slid onto the back seat of the squad car and slammed the door shut. "Take us to Cross Street. Number fifteen. We're going to the doctor's."

Cross Street was a quiet residential street consisting of medium-sized detached houses. Number fifteen was easy to spot.

A white glass globe with 'SURGERY' written on it in black, hung from the roof of the porch. A brass plate affixed to the wall announced that the surgery belonged to Dr Molly Williams.

The front door was half-glazed with stained glass in an orange and white sunburst pattern. Jack opened it and stepped into a small hallway with a door leading off. Ahead of him was a white-painted wooden wall. A window was set about two thirds of the way up, and below the window was a sign that said 'RECEPTION,' and a black bell push. He pressed it and the window slid open. A middle-aged woman with frizzy ginger hair and a freckled face smiled at him from the desk. "Are you here to see the doctor?"

"Yes, I am."

"Name, please."

"Chief Inspector Callum, Welwyn and Hatfield Police."

"Do you have an appointment, Mr Callum?"

"No, but I was hoping Dr Williams could fit me in. It's rather urgent."

"Is it an emergency?"

"No. But it is quite urgent."

The receptionist frowned. "Let me check the book . . . I can fit you in if you'd care to wait. The waiting room's just through there."

"Thank you. Will Dr Williams be long?"

"Just through that door there."

The waiting room was empty but Jack could hear voices and a baby's cry coming from behind a door to the left. A few minutes later the door opened and a young woman came out into the waiting room carrying a small child on her hip – a little girl with tear-streaked cheeks and wearing a pink bonnet. The woman glanced back through the open door. "Thank you, Doctor. I'll make another appointment before I leave." She smiled at Jack.

"Vaccinations," she said. "Her second diphtheria injection." She nodded towards the child. "I hate putting her through it, but you can't be too careful, can you?"

"Indeed not." Jack smiled at the little girl who managed a toothless grin, her recent trauma already forgotten. "Is Doctor Williams free now?"

The young woman looked at him uncertainly. "I'm sure she'll call you when she's ready," she said, and hurried from the room.

Jack rapped sharply on the door.

"Come in," a voice called.

Jack stepped inside. "Doctor Williams?"

The woman behind the desk got to her feet.

Dependable, Jack decided. From her tightly set mousy hair, all the way down past her olive green woollen suit and thick brown stockings, to the sensible and sturdy black brogues, the middle-aged woman exuded an aura of reliability. She glanced down at her notes on the desk. "You must be Mr Callum: 'urgent, but not an emergency'. Am I right?"

"Mostly, but it's Chief Inspector Callum. I'm with the police and I'd like to ask you some questions about one of your patients."

Molly Williams looked at him. "Before you start, I have to tell you that I'm forbidden to talk about my patients. Doctor/patient confidentiality you understand."

"Of course. But I thought that only applied to patients who were still living."

"That's right."

"Then it shouldn't be a problem for you. The patient I want to ask you about died last Monday."

"Oh? Who might that be? I've heard nothing about any patients of mine dying."

"I'm referring to Bernadette O'Malley. Sister Bernadette of the St Joseph's orphanage."

Molly Williams sat down heavily in her desk chair. "Monday? But I only saw her last week and she was as fit as a flea."

"I'm afraid, Doctor, that Sister Bernadette was murdered."

CHAPTER 23

THURSDAY

"I see. Do you have any idea who killed her?" Molly Williams' voice was flat and unemotional. She might have been asking him about the price of lamb's liver at the butchers.

"We're following a couple of lines of inquiry. If you don't mind me saying, you don't seem very shocked, or even surprised by the news."

"I never saw Bernadette making old bones. The only thing that surprises me is that someone killed her before she could take her own life."

Jack sat back in his seat. Reliable Molly Williams was turning out to be something of a cold fish. "Would you like to elaborate on that statement?"

"Certainly, Mr Callum. All of the Sisters and most of the children at St Joseph's are patients of mine, and have been for years. Bernadette O'Malley had only recently started coming to this surgery. I could see when she first came that she wasn't really settling in at St Joseph's."

"What do you mean by that exactly?"

"She was a square peg, a misfit if you like."

"You didn't like her?"

"I didn't say that. It was hard not to warm to her. She was very charismatic. Bright and lively, with an easy manner and a wicked, almost irreverent sense of humour. But she seemed no more suited to holy orders than I am. I'm something of a cynic myself and I can't be doing with superstitious mumbo jumbo."

"Do you think her supposed desire to be a nun was an act?"

"No, that's not what I'm saying. I think that there was a side of her that embraced her faith as passionately as any of the Sisters at St Joseph's, even more so in some ways, but there was another part that railed against the Church. She almost seemed to resent the constraints her chosen vocation placed upon her."

"Why do you think that was?"

"That's a question I'm not qualified to answer. I only saw her a handful of times, but she was always very open and talked frankly about her life. She told me some quite horrific things about her violent upbringing in Liverpool. She had a fractured relationship with her mother, who abused her."

"She bore the scars from beatings inflicted by her mother. I saw them on her back and legs in the mortuary."

Molly Williams shook her head sadly. "She told me about the beatings. She never showed me the scars, but I can't say I'm surprised. Her mother sounded to me like a psychopath. I wanted Bernadette to see someone. She needed to talk about the things that were troubling her to someone who was a lot better qualified than I to deal with them."

"Who for instance? A psychiatrist?"

"That would have been a good place to start. I did recommend someone to her, a very good man up in London. I even went so far as to write a referral letter for her, but it didn't get any further than that, which puts me to shame. In my defence I would say that I have a great number of patients on my books and if I gave every one of them the time that I gave Bernadette, I would be working round the clock."

"Didn't you express your concerns to anyone else? Sister Rosalie, for instance?"

The doctor shook her head again. "Bernadette expressly forbade me to tell anyone about her problems and, of course, I was bound by my professional ethics. Doctor/patient confidentiality exists for a reason. Things my patients tell me are as sacrosanct as matters divulged to a priest in the confessional. More's the pity in Bernadette's case, but there it is."

"When did she find out she was pregnant?"

Molly Williams looked uncomfortable. "So you know about that? But of course, it would have come up during the post mortem. I assume there *was* a post mortem."

"Yes."

"Last week," Molly said. "She came to me about something else entirely, but pregnancy was always a possibility."

"Even though she was . . ."

"Please don't say it, Mr Callum. Whatever Bernadette was, she was a woman first. I wasn't concerned about the moral issues. To me she was a young woman, no more than a girl emotionally, who needed my help. I sent her blood test away and the results came back positive. I gave her the news last Saturday morning."

"Saturday morning?"

"Yes, I called her in especially."

Jack sat back in his seat, his mind racing. "How did she take the news?"

"How do you think? She was distraught. I begged her again to go and talk to Sister Rosalie. I know the woman quite well and I've always found her to be non-judgemental, a pragmatist like myself."

"And how did Bernadette respond to that?"

"She wouldn't hear of it and she begged me to say nothing to anyone. I'm not even comfortable telling you now, but as she's no longer with us . . ."

"If you want to see justice for the poor girl, you're doing the right thing. The more I know about every aspect of her life, the easier it will be for me to find her killer. Did she tell you what her next step might be?"

"She said she knew someone who might be able to help her."

"Physically or spiritually?"

"I assumed the latter . . . The other thing didn't enter my mind."

"Did she tell you who the father was?"

"No, and I didn't ask. But, from what she said, I gathered that he would suffer as much as her. 'It will ruin his life,' she said."

"What do you think she meant by that?"

She shrugged. "Your guess is as good as mine. Think about it, Mr Callum. She was a very striking young woman and there are at least a dozen young men at St Joseph's alone who could have fathered a child. That's as well as all the other men she came into contact with. The Daughters of Charity are actively encouraged to get out into the community to perform their charitable works. Someone like Bernadette, young, naïve and, perhaps I shouldn't say this, highly sexed, would be an easy target for a certain type of man."

Jack got to his feet. "Well, thank you for being so open with me. Candour has been in short supply in this investigation."

"Did you expect anything else? Your enquiries are bound to ruffle feathers that are best left untouched. I don't envy you."

* * *

Jack got back in the car. The engine was running and the heater was pumping out warmth.

"Where to, sir?" Meadows asked.

"Back to Canon Flood's house, and pass me the radio."

Jack called the station. "Put me through to Inspector Fuller."

Eddie Fuller's voice crackled over the speaker. "What can I do for you, guv?"

"Get on to St Edmund's College in Ware. I want to know what time Canon Flood arrived there on Saturday and what time he left, if he was ever there at all."

"Righto. Oh, and the results on the candlestick came back from the lab. The only prints were Father Harvey's but they'd been smudged, so I suspect the killer wore gloves."

"Why doesn't that surprise me? Get back to me as soon as you know about Flood."

Fuller was back on the radio less than ten minutes later. "He *was* there, guv. Arrived at ten, gave his talk and was out of there by twelve thirty."

"That's all I needed to know. Thanks, Eddie."

Jack relaxed back in his seat and let the air blowing from the heater warm his ankles. Canon Flood had some explaining to do.

* * *

Ruth Beech opened the door at his first ring. She had obviously been crying — her eyes were red-rimmed. "I'll tell Canon Flood you're here. If you'll wait in the study."

"I don't think you were being completely straight with me this morning," Jack said when Flood appeared. "You told me you were at St Edmund's College on Saturday."

Flood's smooth brow crinkled into a frown. "And so I was. You can check with the college."

"I did. They told me you left there at lunchtime. Twelve thirty, to be exact. What time did you get back here?"

"I think it was about one, but you'll have to check with Miss Beech to be certain. Ruth drove me on Saturday. I can't drive." Never had the inclination so I never bothered to learn."

"So if Sister Bernadette did come here, you would have seen her."

The colour left his face. He went to sit down behind the desk. He seemed to want to put a barrier between himself and Jack.

"I'll prevaricate no longer. Sister Bernadette did indeed come here on Saturday. But I didn't see her."

"Please explain."

Flood sighed, the sound of defeat.

"I was feeling quite ill on Saturday. I hadn't slept at all well on Friday night, and when we left here Saturday morning I was pretty wretched. I'd promised St Edmund's that I'd give my talk, so I couldn't let them down. Anyway, as I said, Ruth drove me over to Ware, waited for me to finish and drove me straight back. When we arrived home she saw to it that I had my medication and sent me straight to bed. I vaguely remember hearing the doorbell ring at some point during the afternoon, but by the time I woke up, I'd forgotten all about it. It came back to me during dinner and I asked Ruth who had called. She said it was Sister Bernadette from St Joseph's and she'd told her I wasn't in, so as not to disturb me. She knew I needed my sleep."

"Do you take sleep medication, Canon? Pills?"

"For all the good they do me, yes I do."

"I'll need to speak with Miss Beech to corroborate your story."

Flood nodded. "I understand. But please, I beseech you, be gentle with her. I broke the news about Martin Harvey just after you left this morning, and it shattered her. She's in a very fragile state at the moment."

"I'll tread carefully. Can you call her?"

"She'll be in the kitchen preparing my tea. Speak to her there. Home turf, that sort of thing. Better than me summoning her here to answer your questions. Less intimidating for her."

"And the kitchen is . . ?"

"The passageway at the side of the stairs. It will lead you straight there."

* * *

Ruth Beech stood at a wooden table sawing slices of bread from a crusty loaf and spreading them thickly with butter.

"Sorry to disturb you, Miss Beech, but I need to ask you a few questions about Saturday."

The woman continued sawing. "What do you want to know?" Her voice was flat and expressionless. Jack got the impression that she was fighting to keep her emotions in check. At any moment something might cause the dam to burst and send tears flooding down her cheeks.

"Canon Flood tells me you drove him to St Edmund's in Ware on Saturday, brought him back afterwards and sent him to bed."

"He wasn't well on Saturday so I made sure he went back to bed to recover. These speaking engagements of his drain him terribly."

"What time did you get back here?"

"Ten past one."

"That's very precise."

"I turned on the radio when I got back. I like to have some music on while I work, and the announcer gave the time just as I switched it on."

There was no radio playing in the kitchen while she made the Canon's tea. Perhaps she deemed it disrespectful in light of what had happened to Father Harvey.

"Did you have a visitor on Saturday afternoon? Canon Flood said he remembers hearing the doorbell."

"That's right. One of the nuns from St Joseph's home called. Sister Bernadette. She wanted to see the Canon but I'm afraid I had to send her away. Not a very Christian thing to do, but Gerald's health has got to be my main concern. Martin sent me here to look after him and I would be failing in my duty if I let anything disturb him."

"I can understand that. Did you get a chance to speak with Sister Bernadette? Only I was wondering what her state of mind might have been."

"Lost," Ruth Beech said.

"In what way?"

"I could see she had been crying. Something had upset her."

"But you didn't feel it was important enough to disturb the Canon's afternoon nap?"

Ruth Beech started to spread the butter again.

"Frankly, no, I didn't. I felt for the girl, of course, but, as I said, Gerald's wellbeing is my prime concern. The girl had all the other Sisters at St Joseph's to turn to if she was troubled. So I sent her away. God will judge my actions, as only He has a right to."

"You obviously hold Canon Flood in high regard."

Ruth Beech put the butter knife down on the table, took a kettle from the stove and went to the tap to fill it. "You've met him. Gerald is a truly good human being."

"As was Father Harvey."

Water spilled over the top of the kettle. "Quite." Ruth Beech turned and put it back on the stove. "Will there be anything else, Chief Inspector? Because I need to get on." There were tears pressing at the corners of her eyes, waiting to spill. Jack regretted mentioning the priest. She should not have sent Bernadette away, but she had done so out of concern for her employer.

"No," he said. "I have no more questions. I'll leave you in peace."

"Good day."

On his way back through the house he poked his head around the door of the study. Canon Flood was still behind the desk, his head buried in a book.

"I'm finished here. I'll be off."

Flood looked up and smiled. "I hope you've satisfied your curiosity about Saturday's events."

"Yes. All cleared up now." Jack stepped into the room. "Just one more thing before I go. Could you let me have one of your sleeping tablets?"

Flood looked at him sharply. "Why on earth would you want one of those?"

"Insomnia," Jack lied. "I've had it for weeks now and I was wondering if some kind of medication might work for me."

Flood pulled open his desk drawer and took out a small brown glass bottle. He unscrewed the cap, shook out a tablet and handed it to Jack. "I'm not sure you should be taking these without a prescription, but they're not that strong. At least I don't find they're much use, but you're welcome to try one. Insomnia is one of the many trials Satan visits upon us."

Jack wrapped the small white pill in his handkerchief. "Thank you for this. And for your time."

"Only too happy to help," Canon Flood said and went back to his book.

CHAPTER 24

THURSDAY

Annie Callum breathed a huge sigh of relief as she stepped out of the driving sleet into the interior of Brown's the butcher's shop. Avril Kendall lived above the shop with her husband, Alf.

A small corridor ran along the inside of the shop, towards another door that led up to the flat. A pall of raw meat hung heavy in the air, and Annie gagged slightly as she hurried along the corridor. She pressed the doorbell and heard the sound of footsteps descending the stairs. Avril opened the door. She was an attractive thirty-two-year-old but she was not looking her best this morning. She was dressed in a pink quilted housecoat, and her face was bare of make-up. Her blonde hair was released from its overnight curlers but was yet to be brushed through. Avril looked as if she had just climbed out of bed. Without the make-up, the yellowish purple bruise high on her cheek, inflicted earlier that week by her husband, looked painful. Avril raised her hand to hide it and squinted at Annie out of one eye.

"Hello."

"I'm sorry, Avril," Annie said. "I'm not too early, am I? Only you said to come round at ten."

Avril tried for a smile but it turned into a yawn. "No, *I'm* sorry, Mrs C. I'm all over the place today. Blame your daughter. Joanie and I sat up into the wee small hours polishing off a bottle of sherry and we're not long out of bed. Come up.

Joanie's in the kitchen and she'll make you a cup of tea if you ask her nicely. I need to go and finish my hair, and put my face on. I'll join you in about ten minutes." She turned and trotted back up the stairs. Annie followed.

She came up behind Joan, who was standing in her bra and knickers, washing schooner glasses in the kitchen's small enamel sink. "Did you have a nice evening?" Annie asked brightly.

Joan yawned and looked round at her mother, bleary-eyed. "Keep your voice down. Someone's using a pneumatic drill in my head. You're far too bright and breezy, and *much* too loud."

"Cup of tea?"

Joan nodded, wincing slightly. "There's milk on the cold shelf in the pantry. Avril doesn't have a fridge."

The pantry was a small curtained-off area by the back window. A half-full bottle of milk stood on a sheet of white marble on the windowsill. Annie picked it up and sniffed. "It's off," she said.

"Sweet black coffee then," Joan said, drying her hands on a tea towel. "Avril will have the same. I'm going to get some clothes on."

"So you should, before you catch your death. It's like an ice well in here."

"Is it? I can't feel it. All the alcohol I drank last night must be keeping me warm. Back in a mo."

Annie found three mugs in a kitchen cupboard. By the time Avril and Joan returned, three steaming cups of strong black coffee were waiting for them on a drop-leaf table in the sitting room.

"You're a life saver, Mrs C." Avril picked up a mug, inhaled the steam, went to a transistor radio hanging from a hook on the door and switched it on. The radio crackled into life and the tinny sound of Michael Holliday singing 'The Story of my Life' filled the tiny flat.

Joan found a packet of Osborne biscuits in the cupboard, and the three women sat sipping coffee.

Avril hummed along with Michael Holliday. She had managed to disguise most of the black eye with make-up and looked less wretched.

"Sshh," Joan said. "You're hurting my head."

Avril smiled. "You shouldn't have had that last glass of sherry. I *did* warn you."

Joan glowered at her.

"You could have come to mine today," Annie said. "After all, it's my hair you're cutting. It would have made more sense."

"It made sense to me when I suggested you come here," Avril said, "but I hadn't counted on Joanie leading me astray."

"You didn't take much leading," Joan said.

Avril took a final mouthful of coffee. "Shall we get started then?"

Annie stood up. "Ready when you are."

"Come through to the bathroom then, and I'll wash your hair."

"I'll make us another coffee," Joan said.

* * *

Annie knelt on a fluffy pink mat to protect her knees from the cold lino floor and leaned her head over the bath. Mixing hot water from a large Ascot heater, and cold from the mains, Avril filled a glass jug and doused Annie's hair. She poured shampoo into her palm and massaged it into Annie's scalp.

After another application of shampoo and two rinses, she wrapped Annie's head in a towel and led her through to the sitting room.

Joan had placed a dining chair in the centre of the room and Annie sat as Avril towel-dried her hair. "I want Joanie to watch this. It's all part of her training. Are you okay with that, Mrs C?"

"I don't mind at all, Avril, but please stop calling me 'Mrs C.' We've known each other long enough by now for you to call me Annie."

"I don't know . . . It doesn't seem right somehow."

"Tell her not to be so silly, Joanie," Annie said.

"I'll just sit here, keep my mouth shut and watch," Joan said.

"Coward."

"She's my boss. You still call Barbara Painter 'Mrs Painter,' and you've known her for years."

"When we're at work I do. Anyway, it's different with Avril. She's more like a friend. I tell her all my secrets."

"*All* your secrets, Mum?"

"Well, perhaps not all, but she knows enough about me to make formality a bit of a nonsense."

Avril held up her hands. "Okay. I don't want to come between mother and daughter. Annie it is from now on."

She ran a comb through Annie's wet hair and then froze. A key was turning in the front door lock. "It's Alf," she said, sounding frightened. "I didn't think he was due back until this evening."

"Is that a problem?"

Annie saw the colour drain from Avril's face as the door opened and Alf Kendall walked into the flat, shaking water from his umbrella.

A wave of alcohol fumes entered with him. He stood there, swaying slightly and staring at them with unfocussed eyes, as if he wasn't sure where he was.

"I wasn't expecting you home this early," Avril said to him brightly.

Alf said nothing.

There were remnants of a good-looking man beneath his scowling façade, but years of heavy drinking had taken their toll. He gripped the doorframe and then launched himself forward, across the room. He staggered into the bedroom and kicked the door closed behind him.

There was a silence. Avril put her comb and scissors down on the table next to the coffee cups. "I'd better go and see if he's all right," she said.

"Call if you need us," Joan said. She gave Avril's hand a reassuring squeeze.

"I'll be fine." Avril went into the bedroom.

Joan turned to Annie. "Did you get the chance to talk to her when she was washing your hair?"

Annie shook her wet head. "No. I was trying to find a way to broach the subject, but I couldn't find the right words."

"I know what you mean. We danced around the subject all evening. I thought that if she had enough to drink she might open up, but I made the mistake of matching her glass for glass and her resistance to alcohol is much stronger than mine. I ended up passed out on the bed without mentioning it once."

Annie stared at the bedroom door. "It's awfully quiet in there. Do you think she's okay?"

"Sshh. Listen."

There were murmurings coming from behind the door. They could hear Avril's light tones but not what she was saying. Alf was responding in a low rumble.

Joan shrugged at Annie. "I can't hear what they're say—"

A loud bass yell exploded through the flat, followed by a squeal from Avril and the sound of glass breaking.

Joan's eyes widened and another crash came from the bedroom. "He's killing her in there," she said, and rushed to the door.

"Joanie, wait!"

Joan pulled open the door.

Avril was lying on the floor between the bed and the wardrobe. The mirror on the wardrobe door had smashed and long shards of glass were scattered on the floor. Avril was struggling to get to her feet. Her husband was standing over her, still swaying but with his fists clenched menacingly.

"Avril! Are you all right?" Joan said. It was a stupid question. Her friend was bleeding profusely from a gash on her forehead. Blood had matted her blonde hair and ran down into her eyes.

"Leave her alone, you pig!" Joan yelled at Alf and ran across the room to help her friend. Alf lashed out and caught her a glancing blow on the shoulder that sent her sprawling onto the bed.

Through the open door, Annie saw what had happened. She grabbed Avril's scissors from the table and ran towards the bedroom.

At the bedroom door she stood a yard away from Alf and held the scissors out in front of her. For what seemed an age they stood face to face. Alf seemed to be trying to focus his eyes. He shifted his gaze from Annie's blanched face to the wickedly pointed scissors held like a dagger in her trembling hand.

Joan scrambled from the bed and helped Avril to her feet. "We need to get you to a hospital," she whispered.

Brandishing the scissors, Annie took a step forward, positioning herself between the two women and Alf. He stood there, slack-jawed.

"Get Avril downstairs," she hissed at Joan.

Joan led her friend from the room. Annie's hand was shaking so much she had to hold it steady with her other one. Slowly she started to back out of the room.

The moment she moved, Alf seemed to shake himself. He lunged forward but his feet tangled in the bedspread lying on the floor and he fell to his knees. He glared up at Annie and mouthed, "bitch!" and pitched forward onto the glass-strewn floor.

Annie turned and rushed from the flat, almost running into Avril and Joan, standing in the downstairs corridor. "How are we going to get to the hospital?"

"We'll take my car," Avril said. She was holding a piece of butcher's muslin to her head wound to stem the blood. She was shaking.

"You're in no condition to drive," Annie said. "And I've never driven in my life."

"I can drive," Joan said. "Ivan taught me, but I never took my test."

Inside the shop, the butcher and two of his female customers were watching them with shocked curiosity.

Annie ignored them. "Okay. You drive. If we get stopped by the police, then so much the better."

Sleeting rain cut into their faces as they left the shelter of the corridor. They hurried along the street to where Avril's car, a grey forties Humber Hawk, was parked. Avril fumbled in the pocket of her slacks and handed her car keys to Joan. Joan opened up, slid behind the wheel of the Humber and started the engine.

Joan glanced in the rear-view mirror and saw Alf Kendall emerging from the doorway. Panicking, she let in the clutch and the car shot forward, kangarooing up the road.

Behind them Alf broke into a stumbling run, shouting and waving his arms.

Joan finally got control of the car and pressed her foot down on the accelerator. When she looked in the mirror again, Alf had stopped running and was standing bent over in the middle of the road.

Soon he was just a dot in the distance.

CHAPTER 25

THURSDAY

It was unusually busy in the casualty department of the North Herts Hospital. An early morning frost had turned the roads and pavements into skating rinks. The doctors and nurses were dealing with sprained ankles from minor falls, as well as the aftermath of a car skidding into a tree on the St Albans road.

Joan and Avril sat patiently in the waiting area watching the clock on the wall eating up the day. Out in the hospital entrance, Annie tried again to get through to Jack on the public telephone. She had borrowed a few pennies from a nurse who'd taken pity on their plight. They had left Avril's flat without their coats and the same nurse had also furnished them with thick blue hospital blankets.

"Welwyn and Hatfield Police."

"At last. Andy? Is that you?"

Andy Brewer took the telephone away from his ear and stared at it. "It is," he said cautiously.

"It's Annie Callum. I'm trying to get hold of Jack, but there's no answer on his private line."

"He's out interviewing witnesses, Mrs Callum."

"Have you any idea when he might be back?"

"I'm afraid not. Can I put you through to anyone else?"

Annie closed her eyes. *Blast!*

"No. That's all right. I'll try again later. Thanks, Andy." She replaced the handset and went back to join the others.

Joan was sitting by herself on one of the hard plastic chairs. "They've taken Avril though to get her stitched up. She shouldn't be long. Any luck getting through to dad?"

Annie shook her head.

"Then we'll go to the station when we leave here," Joan said.

"Will Avril agree to that?"

"Yes. I think getting her head smashed into a mirror made her realise that this can't go on. She's ready to make an official complaint."

"Then let's hope someone will take her seriously when we get there."

"She's got the wounds to prove it this time," Joan said.

"We'll see. Dad didn't sound very optimistic when we spoke about it the other night. That was why I wanted to talk to him first, rather than just turning up at the station on the off-chance."

They drifted into silence, watching the comings and goings of the department.

It was four o'clock before Avril emerged from a side room. The wound on her brow had been dressed with heavy gauze and three strips of sticking plaster. She managed a wan smile as she approached them and pointed to the dressing. "Pretty, eh?"

"At least you're not bleeding over everything," Joan said. She hugged her.

"Come on, let's get out of here," Avril said. "Hospitals make me ill."

* * *

"Do you feel up to driving?" Annie said to Avril. "I'm worried that if Joanie drives us to the police station she might get arrested for not having a licence."

Avril looked doubtful. Annie wasn't sure whether it was about her ability to drive or their intended destination.

Joan gripped Avril's hand. "You agreed, Av. You can't let him get away with it any more. You've had four years of marriage and three years of hell. It can't go on."

Avril got in, gripped the steering wheel and took a deep breath. "Right," she said, sticking her chin out determinedly. "Let's get this over with."

* * *

"I'd like to report an assault."

The desk sergeant looked across at the young woman's battered face.

One eye was blackened and a large medical dressing was taped above the other.

Andy Brewer pulled out a slightly creased form from a cubbyhole under the desk and smoothed it out. "Name?"

"Avril Kendall."

Avril glanced round at Annie and Joan. They were smiling and nodding.

"And who perpetrated the assault?"

"My husband, Alfred Kendall."

The desk sergeant's pen hovered over the form. "Are you sure about that?"

"She's sure," Joan said.

"And who might you be?"

Annie stepped forward. "We're her witnesses."

Brewer turned to Annie. "But you're . . ."

"Anne Callum. Chief Inspector Callum's wife. This is my daughter, Joan."

"I'm sorry," he stammered. "I didn't . . . I mean . . . the hair and . . ."

"You must be Sergeant Brewer," Annie said. "We've spoken on the phone."

"Yes . . . right . . . of course."

"Is my husband back yet? You told me earlier that he was out questioning witnesses?"

"It's all right, Andy. I'll take it from here." Frank Lesser strolled out of the squad room and approached Annie, hand outstretched.

Annie smiled at him. "Detective Sergeant Lesser. Frank. We shared a waltz at last year's dinner and dance."

Lesser beamed at her. "You remembered."

Annie smiled. "My feet do. You stepped on them, more than once I seem to recall."

Lesser's smile faded.

"It's okay, Frank. I have remarkable powers of recovery. Three day's bed rest and I was back to normal."

Now he looked positively alarmed.

Annie was grinning. "It's all right. I'm teasing you."

Lesser looked relieved. "I'm afraid your husband isn't back yet. What can I do to help?"

"This is a very good friend of mine and she wants to report a serious assault."

Avril stepped forward. "Avril Kendall."

"Well," Lesser said. "Come through to the interview room and we'll take down some details." He turned to Brewer. "Is interview room one free?"

Brewer nodded.

Lesser called back into the squad room, "Constable Taylor, if I could borrow you? Bring your notepad."

Lesser led them along a corridor. Helen Taylor, a WPC with a pleasant face, opened a door to a plain room with a wooden table and four tubular-steel-framed chairs. She stood aside to let them enter.

Lesser turned to Annie. "If you and your daughter could wait in the foyer? If you have a word with the desk sergeant I'm sure he can rustle up a pot of tea. Tell him we'll have some in here as well — and biscuits." He closed the door behind them.

They had hardly started on their tea when the door of the interview room opened and Avril came back out into the corridor. Behind her they could see Lesser and WPC Taylor sitting at the table. Lesser tore a sheet of paper from Taylor's notepad, screwed it into a ball and tossed it into a wastepaper bin. Helen Taylor laughed, crossed to the door and shut it.

"How did it go?" Joan said, taking Avril's arm.

Avril shook her head. "Can we go now?"

"Is that it? Aren't they going to investigate?"

"I would have got more action from them if I'd told them my pet budgerigar had gone missing," Avril said tightly, tears in her eyes. "Let's just go home."

Joan rose to her feet. "You're not going back to the flat."

"What choice do I have?"

"You can come and stay with us," Annie said. "You're certainly not going back to that man. It will mean you and Joanie sharing a bed for the time being, but maybe we can sort out another bed at the weekend. We can fit the two of you into Joanie's room."

Avril looked doubtful. "Are you all right with that, Joanie?"

"It's fine by me."

"Well, that's settled then. You're staying with us until we can resolve this."

Avril shook her head. "No, Mrs . . . Annie, I couldn't impose, really."

Annie tutted. "Nonsense. It's not an imposition. I wouldn't be able to sleep at night if I knew you were alone with . . . that man."

"But you've got Rosie and Eric to think about, never mind your husband. What's he going to say? And how could I possibly repay you?"

"You'd be surprised what the Callum family will do for free haircuts," Joan said. She took Avril by the arm and led her towards the station doors.

Just as they got there, Jack pushed them open.

"Annie! What on earth are you doing here? Joanie, you too?" His eyes settled on Avril's face. "And what happened to you?"

"Alf Kendall happened. He smashed Avril's head into the wardrobe mirror and knocked me sideways onto the bed," Joan said. "I told you this would happen."

"We brought Avril along to make a formal complaint," Annie said. "But I'm afraid it fell on deaf ears."

Jack frowned. "Let me handle this. Who did you see?"

"Frank Lesser."

"And WPC Taylor," Avril said. "But she was no help. No help at all. In fact she looked like she was enjoying my story. It seemed to amuse her."

"Right," Jack said. "Take Avril and get home quickly. Carry on walking around like that and you'll all go down with pneumonia." He took off his overcoat and draped it around Annie's shoulders.

"I've told Avril she can stay with us for a while, until things are settled."

Jack smiled at Avril. "Fine." Then he noticed Joan, whose lips had turned blue. She was starting to shiver.

Jack called back over his shoulder. "Andy, I need two blankets here. There are some in the emergency supply cupboard. Bring two of those and, Meadows, run these young ladies home in the squad car."

"We came in Avril's car," Annie said. "It's in the car park."

"Don't worry about that. I'll drive it back to our house after my shift."

"Thanks Mr C," Avril said.

"It's not a problem, Avril. Just leave everything to me."

* * *

"Sergeant Lesser, a word in my office. You too, WPC Taylor." Jack led them up the stairs. "Come in and shut the door behind you." Jack sat down, folded his arms and looked at the two officers. "The young lady you just interviewed. Tell me about it."

Lesser pulled up a chair.

"I asked you to tell me about the interview, not to make yourself comfortable."

Frank Lesser stiffened and remained standing. The smile fell from Taylor's lips.

"You don't expect us to take that seriously, sir, do you?" Lesser said.

"So you feel you can pick and choose which assaults we take seriously?"

Helen Taylor stepped forward. "I think what Sergeant Lesser means, sir, is that—"

"Sergeant Lesser is perfectly capable of speaking for himself, Constable."

"It was just a domestic dust-up, sir. Hardly a matter for the police," Lesser said.

"You really think that, do you, Sergeant?"

"Sir, if we acted on every domestic, we'd be spending Friday nights after the pubs close running from pillar to post. The 'Friday Night Fights,' sir. It's almost a tradition."

Jack pushed himself angrily to his feet. "Well, it's not a tradition in *my* world, and it may have escaped your attention that it's not Friday night but Thursday bloody afternoon. That assault was a criminal offence and, as such, I expect my officers to deal with it. Do I make myself clear?"

Helen Taylor swallowed loudly. Her cheeks were flushed and her eyes had grown moist. "Yes, sir."

"Crystal clear, sir," Lesser said.

"Good. So now I want you to go and bring Alf Kendall in for a chat. If he doesn't want to come, arrest him. Use handcuffs if necessary."

Lesser glanced at Taylor. "You took Mrs Kendall's address, Constable."

"And you tore it out of my book and threw it away."

"Might I suggest that you get yourselves organised?" Jack said. "In other words, bugger off and find it. I want Kendall back here within the hour. Understood?"

"Yes, sir."

CHAPTER 26

THURSDAY

Jack walked into Fuller's office. "How did the identification go?"

"Smoothly enough, though the Harveys weren't how I'd imagined them. He was ex-army, officer class, and she told me she was a local magistrate in Gloucester. They were both very stiff upper lip. Neither of them showed much emotion at all."

"I think it might have been their way of coping, sir," Myra said from her desk. "Everyone has their own way of dealing with grief. Perhaps that was *their* way."

"You could be right. Did they say anything about their son?"

"Not a lot. Mr Harvey seemed a touch disappointed with his son's chosen vocation." Myra adopted a posh voice. "'Of course, in my day it was always the idiot son who entered the Church — the family's way of getting rid of him and out of harm's way. Martin actually *chose* that life for himself and look where it got him.'"

"He actually said that?"

Fuller was smiling. "Yes, he actually said that. I'm not really sure he knows what century this is."

"And her?"

"As the inspector said, sir, stiff upper lip all the way," Myra said. "Not a single tear."

Jack shook his head. "Sad. Myra, I have another job for you." He fished in his pocket, took out his handkerchief and opened it out on Myra's desk, revealing the tablet Canon Flood had given him.

"The lab again, sir?"

"Yes, I'm afraid so, but take it in on your way home and get them to analyse it overnight. Tell them you'll pick up the results on your way in tomorrow."

"Where did that come from?" Fuller said.

"Canon Flood. It seems he has difficulty sleeping. I want to see if it's the same barbiturate the killer used on Sister Bernadette."

"And if it is?"

"Then hopefully we're a step closer to solving this case."

"You surely don't suspect Canon Flood?"

"Myra, at the moment I suspect everyone apart from those who have a cast iron alibi for Monday. If this case has taught me anything it's that we must put aside our preconceptions. That's why I was keen to hear what Martin Harvey was really like from his parents. I think I've got Bernadette O'Malley pretty much figured out, but the rest are just shadowy figures. Any one of them could be our killer. I also want a 'murder board' put up in the squad room. We're not getting the whole picture. Perhaps if we have everything laid out in front of us we'll be able to see what we're missing."

"I'll get right on it, sir," Myra said. "Can I raid the file for photographs?"

"Where we have them, yes. Where we don't, just print the names. Then you can play join the dots. You never know, something might reveal itself."

"Does that mean you want to bring everyone in now?"

"Loosely, yes. We'll take the main thrust of the investigation, but it will do no harm to see if anyone else has a theory that stands up."

Andy Brewer stuck his head around the door. "DS Lesser's back, sir. He's got Alf Kendall in tow."

A shadow crossed Jack's face. "Good. Tell Frank to take him to the interview room. I'll be down in a moment."

"Is this about the case?" Fuller said.

"No," Jack said. "I'll handle it on my own. It's a personal matter."

"Are you sure?"
"Just leave it be, Eddie."

* * *

Jack smelt the alcohol as soon as he entered the interview room. Alf Kendall was sitting at the table with Frank Lesser across from him.

"Thank you, Sergeant Lesser. I'll take it from here," Jack said. He took off his jacket and draped it over the back of a chair.

Lesser, still seated at the table, watched his boss roll up his shirt-sleeves. Jack's presence brought a tension to the room. Alf Kendall looked alarmed. "Hey, what have you dragged me in here for?" he said.

"Like I told you, Mr Kendall. We just want a friendly chat," Lesser said.

"*You* might, but what about *him*?" Alf nodded at Jack.

"My guvnor? He just wants to see that I do it right. That's right, sir, isn't it?"

"Go and get yourself a cup of tea, Sergeant," Jack said. His voice was low and heavy with menace.

"You're not leaving me alone with him, are you?" Alf looked from Lesser to Jack.

Jack sat down at the table and folded his arms. "What's the matter, Mr Kendall? Do I alarm you in some way?"

"I know who you are," Alf said. He swallowed several times.

Jack allowed himself a flicker of a smile. "I wondered if you'd remember me." He turned to Lesser. "Frank. I told you to get yourself a cup of tea." Jack nodded at the door.

Lesser started to rise. Alf's hand shot out and grasped his sleeve.

"I didn't touch her!" he said, his voice rising in pitch. "She came at me with the scissors."

"Who did?" Jack reached across and pried Kendall's fingers away from Lesser's sleeve, one by one.

"Your wife. But I never touched her."

Lesser looked at Jack and raised his eyebrows.

"It's okay, Sergeant. He's quite right. He didn't hurt Mrs Callum . . . which is more than can be said for his wife. And my daughter for that matter." Jack had hold of Kendall's index finger, and he bent it back sharply

Kendall squealed.

"Sir!" Lesser said.

The door of the interview room burst open. "That's quite enough of that, Chief Inspector."

Chief Superintendent Henry Lane stepped into the room.

Lane glared at Jack and Lesser and jerked his head in the direction of the door. "Outside. Both of you. Now."

Jack let go of Kendall's finger, dragged his jacket from the back of the chair and brushed past Lane on his way out. Lesser followed.

"Here! What about me?" Kendall said in a plaintive wail.

Lane ignored him and followed Lesser out of the room. In the corridor he rounded on Jack. "Do you think I'm running some sort of cowboy operation here? Well, let me tell you, this is not the Wild West."

"I'm well aware of that," Jack said. He heard a slight sniffing sound. Further along the corridor, dabbing at her eyes with a handkerchief, stood Helen Taylor.

"What did WPC Taylor tell you?"

Lane glanced along at the weeping policewoman. "She came to me because she thought you might do something foolish. From what I saw when I walked into the interview room, she wasn't far wrong." He turned to Lesser. "Get back in there, Sergeant. Thank Mr Kendall for his time and tell him he's free to go."

"Henry—" Jack began.

Lane cut him off. "I'll see you in my office, Chief Inspector. Now." He spun on his heel and stalked away.

Jack followed the chief superintendent along the corridor. As he passed Helen Taylor, she ducked her head and pressed herself against the wall. Jack ignored her.

"I'm starting to lose patience with you, Chief Inspector," Lane said as they reached his office. "Sit down."

Jack sat like a scolded schoolboy. "I can explain, Henry."

"Oh, I'm sure you can." Lane lowered himself into his office chair. "Alf Kendall has a habit of beating up his wife and today he also threatened your wife and your daughter with violence. Am I getting the gist of this so far?"

"More or less."

"So you had him dragged in here. For what purpose? To tell him not to be such a naughty boy in future?"

"More or less," Jack said again.

"And breaking his fingers was an incentive for him to follow your advice?"

"I wouldn't have gone that far."

"Wouldn't you, Jack? I seem to recall that the last time someone threatened one of your family you were ready to shoot them."

Jack shifted in his seat. "That's not fair, Henry."

"Isn't it? I think it's a perfectly fair observation." He crossed his hands on the desk and his tone softened. "Listen, Jack, I'm not going to pretend that I don't sympathise with you. I do. Brutes like Kendall deserve everything they get. But I can't sit back and simply watch as one of my best officers flushes his career down the toilet."

"You're exaggerating."

"No, Jack, I'm not. That's exactly what would have happened if you'd damaged Kendall and he then sought legal advice. I can name about half a dozen solicitors in the Hertfordshire area alone who'd have slapped a writ on us for police brutality before they'd had their supper, and smiled as they did so. I'm not prepared to give them that kind of satisfaction." Lane shook his head. "It's not going to happen, Jack. Not on my watch."

"Half a dozen?"

"At least. Like I said, Jack, I sympathise with you. Men who beat their wives are the scum of the earth. I've been married to Mrs Lane for nearly thirty years and in all that time I've never raised my voice to her, let alone my fist. Oh, I know it happens, but, at the end of the day, it's a private, domestic matter and not one that concerns the police."

"And that's just plain wrong. You didn't see the state of Avril Kendall. He smashed her head into a wardrobe mirror."

"Mrs Kendall didn't lodge a formal complaint against her husband."

"She tried to. But she wasn't taken seriously when she came here to do so. I've had a word with the officers involved but I doubt that I changed their minds, because the attitude you've just described is so widespread in the force."

"There you go again, Jack, tilting at windmills. You've really got to learn how to choose your battles."

"I think I'm a bit long in the tooth for that, Henry."

"Pity," Lane said. "Because one day you'll try something stupid and I won't be there to stop you. Now, leave the Kendall affair to your junior officers and get your mind back on the double murder case. Solve that, instead of running around playing the white knight."

* * *

Downstairs in the foyer, Alf Kendall stumbled to the front doors, pressing a bloodstained handkerchief to his face. With a fearful glance back at the station, he tugged the doors open and propelled himself out into the freezing December night.

"What happened to him?" Jack said.

Lesser walked casually into the foyer and watched the doors swing shut. "Clumsy family, that one. She goes about walking into doors, hitting her head on the wardrobe mirror, cutting her face up. Then there's him falling over in the interview room, smashing his face on the table and breaking his nose. Just unlucky, I guess."

Jack tried hard to suppress a smile. "Yes, Frank, you're probably right. Some people just seem to have all the bad luck."

CHAPTER 27

THURSDAY

"You don't need to run me home this evening, Meadows."

"Very good, sir. Eight o'clock tomorrow morning?"

"As always." Jack walked out into the night. The sleet of earlier in the day had turned to snow. Flurries of penny-sized flakes floated down from the night sky and Avril's Humber Hawk already had a half-inch coating. With his leather-gloved hand Jack cleared a gap in the snow on the windscreen, got in behind the wheel and adjusted the seat to give himself some legroom. The engine stuttered to a start and he drove from the station car park and out onto a fairly deserted road. Most people had had the good sense to stay indoors tonight, out of the blizzard.

The air inside the car was stale, heavy with the acrid smell of perming lotion, overlaid with hair lacquer. He wound the window down an inch to allow some fresh air into the car, but quickly closed it again as an icy blast swept in. The Humber's heater was broken and he had to keep clearing condensation from the windscreen with a rag he found in the glove compartment. He now regretted his offer to drive the Humber home. He could be sitting in the comparative luxury and warmth of a squad car being driven back to Letchworth by Constable Meadows. Instead he was hunched forward in his seat, nose almost pressed to the glass. The wipers struggled to disperse the snow pelting against the windscreen. Jack squinted out at the road ahead of him.

Finally he left the lighted streets of Hatfield behind him and eased the car onto the dual carriageway leading to Letchworth and home.

He pressed down on the accelerator and the Humber's ancient engine let out a groan of protest before finally picking up some speed. After about five miles he was able to sit back in his seat. He was on the outskirts of Stevenage and the blizzard had eased. The windscreen wipers were picking up some kind of speed now they were freed from their burden of pushing cold, wet snow to one side with every pass.

He was almost starting to enjoy the drive when the rear-view mirror reflected a blinding light into his eyes. He adjusted it but the vehicle behind was advancing on him. The headlights were fierce and drawing closer.

Braving the freezing wind he wound down the window and stuck out his right arm, indicating that the vehicle should overtake him. Soon the cold had numbed his hand and he pulled his arm back inside, winding the window back up. Whoever was behind him was obviously in no hurry to get anywhere. Despite the almost empty road, the other driver seemed to want to keep behind him and dazzle him with his headlights on full beam.

"Moron," Jack muttered. He pressed down harder on the accelerator, trying to put some distance between them.

The Humber reluctantly picked up speed but whoever was behind kept pace with him. If anything, he was closing the space between them. The lights of a car coming in the opposite direction lit up the road and Jack glanced behind him. The vehicle following was the size of a large van or a lorry. Jack began to feel uneasy. Something wasn't right here . . .

When it came the impact shook him, and his frozen fingers lost their grip on the steering wheel. He looked in the mirror to see the lights behind him recede for a moment before coming at him again. He clamped his hands on the steering wheel, regaining control of the car, and braced himself for another hit. Again he was struck from behind, but he was ready for it this time and managed to steer in a straight line.

All he could see in his mirror was the vehicle's radiator grill and the glare of the headlights. It was too big to be a van. The lorry seemed to be attached to the Humber's rear, pushing him along and picking up speed. The Humber could go no faster and all Jack could do was grip the steering wheel tightly and hope for the best.

The lorry pulled back and Jack prepared to be shunted again. Instead the lights came up on his right-hand side as the lorry started to overtake him. The driver pulled down hard on the wheel and the lorry swerved towards him. There was a scream as metal struck metal and it smashed into the side of the Humber. Jack fought the wheel and veered to the left. He glanced out of the side window in time to see the lorry coming for him again. As the lorry closed the gap between them, Jack stomped down hard on the brake and the Humber's wheels locked, throwing him forward in the seat. The lorry driver twisted his own steering wheel sharply, trying to correct his line, but the momentum was too great and the lorry went into a skid.

As the Humber slowed to a stop Jack watched the lorry, a flatbed truck, skid out of control and sweep across the tarmac, heading for the side of the road.

Running along the side of the dual carriageway was a line of trees and a deep drainage ditch. As the lorry skidded over the side of the road one of its front wheels dropped into the ditch while the rear of the vehicle continued to skid. It dropped for a second into the ditch before being catapulted out of it again to smash against a line of stout elm trees.

Jack sat at the wheel of the Humber, breathing hard, his hands shaking. Nothing moved in the snow, which was still falling in a hazy white cloud.

The lorry's headlights had been smashed but the red taillights glowed, pointing up at a crazy angle.

As he tried to get to grips with what had just happened, another light lit up the car, this time smaller and coming in through the side window. Almost immediately it was extinguished to be replaced by an insistent knocking on the glass.

Wearily, Jack wound down the side window.

"Are you all right, sir? I saw everything. That maniac tried to force you off the road."

Jack blinked. He made out a concerned middle-aged face under a brown peaked cap.

"What?"

"The AA, sir. Patrolman Dennis Bartholomew at your service."

Jack looked at the man blankly. All he could think of to say was, "But I'm not a member of the AA."

"Well, we won't stand on ceremony this time," Bartholomew said, and smiled. "Are you okay?"

"I think so."

"Can't say the same for him." He swung the beam of his torch at the wreckage of the lorry in the ditch.

Jack shook himself. "We'd better go and see if we can do anything."

"Yes. Yes, of course," Bartholomew said. His eyes shone with excitement. This was clearly more interesting than changing flat tyres on the side of the road for stranded motorists, or sticking his head under someone's bonnet.

"If you could just stand back so I can get out."

"Yes, sir, of course . . . He nearly did for you there," he said as Jack climbed out into the snowy night.

"You might be asked to give evidence to that effect," Jack said. "I'm with the police."

Patrolman Dennis Bartholomew took another step back, pulled himself to attention and saluted. "Only too willing to help another member of the Emergency Services."

Jack looked back at the patrolman's yellow motorcycle combination parked at the side of the road a few yards away. "Use the radio on that thing and call this in. We need more police and an ambulance here as soon as possible."

"Yes, sir." Bartholomew saluted again and rushed back to his machine.

"Have you got another torch?" Jack called after him. "We need lights over there."

"I'll go one better, sir." The sound of a motorbike being kick started broke through the snowy silence. A second later the motorbike and sidecar swept past him, heading for the wrecked lorry.

Bartholomew parked his bike on the side of the dual carriageway and, with the engine purring smoothly, he directed the beam of the headlamp at the drainage ditch.

Jack pulled his overcoat tightly around him and made his way towards the carnage.

Bartholomew stood by his bike. "I've called it in, sir. They'll be with us shortly."

"Good man."

The lorry was on its side in the ditch, one back wheel still spinning.

"We need to get the engine turned off," Jack said.

"I think I can reach the driver's door. If you can just hold onto the belt of my tunic as I climb over."

Jack grabbed the brown leather belt and the patrolman started to climb.

Despite his age, the man made the climb effortlessly. He yanked down on the door handle and lifted the door clear, letting it topple backwards. Then he ducked into the cab, hauling himself out a moment later, the lorry's ignition key clutched in his hand.

"Well done," Jack said, letting go of his belt.

Bartholomew jumped down to the ground. "I got the key but I don't hold out much hope for the driver. He's smashed himself up against the steering wheel. Head's a bit of a mess."

"Let me have your torch."

The patrolman handed it over and Jack climbed onto the cab, shining the beam down inside.

Alf Kendall stared sightlessly back at him.

Jack pushed himself away from the cab and jumped back down to the ground.

"I said he was a bit of a mess, sir. You've gone very white."

Jack stood on the cold, wet tarmac and fought down the desire to vomit. For all the contempt he had for Kendall, the man had not deserved to die. Not like this.

Jack felt a comforting hand on his shoulder. "Are you all right, sir? You're not going to puke, are you? Not that I'd blame you. Nasty business."

In the distance they could hear the emergency bells growing nearer.

"Ah, the welcome sounds of the cavalry," Bartholomew said.

"You've done a good job here tonight, officer," Jack said. "I'll see that your superiors are made aware of that."

"Thank you, sir." Bartholomew drew himself up and saluted again.

Moments later they were surrounded by half a dozen emergency vehicles. Jack climbed back into the Humber Hawk and waited while dozens of figures rushed towards the scene.

CHAPTER 28

THURSDAY

Wearily, Jack let himself in through the back door. He had just crossed the threshold when Joan launched herself across the kitchen and threw her arms around him. "Dad! I'm so, so sorry. I had no idea that Alf would try to kill you. I just wanted you to help Avril."

Jack took her in his arms and stroked her hair. "Whoa, slow down. He didn't try to kill me," he said, trying to calm her.

"That's not what we heard," Joan said, her face buried in his overcoat. "Eddie's here. He came to tell us what happened."

Jack gently disengaged himself from her embrace. "Where's Avril?"

Joan looked up at him, her cheeks streaked with tears. "In bed. She took herself off upstairs. I don't think she could face you."

"And the others?"

"Mum's in the front room talking to Eddie. I was just making them a pot of tea."

"Don't let me stop you. I could use one myself."

Joan went back to the stove and waited for the kettle to boil. "Eddie said that Alf tried to run you off the road."

Jack took off his coat. "He tried to run the Humber off the road," he said gently. "But he couldn't have had any idea it was me behind the wheel."

Joan looked at him steadily for a moment until his words sunk in. Then her eyes widened and she threw a hand across her mouth. "So Alf thought it was Avril driving? He was trying to kill her!"

"Sshh, keep your voice down," Jack said. "You don't want her to hear. That poor girl's been through enough today. I'm going in to see your mum. Bring the tea through when it's ready."

"Is that you, Jack?" Annie's voice floated out from the front room.

Annie was sitting on the settee, her legs drawn up under her chin and her arms around them. Her eyes were red. Eddie Fuller was sitting in an armchair across from her. His face was serious, and a cigarette smouldered in an overflowing ashtray beside him. He got up with a start as Jack walked into the room. "Christ! We were worried about you."

Annie looked up at her husband. "Oh, Jack," she said, and began to cry.

"Hey, hey." He sat down beside her on the settee and put his arm around her shoulder. "I'm okay, really."

"But you could have been killed. I couldn't stand it if anything happened to you."

"Well, it didn't happen," Jack said. "I'm here, aren't I?"

"I'd best make a move," Fuller said. "Leave you both to it."

"Stay, Eddie, and have a cuppa before you head off," Jack said. "It's a filthy night out there."

"Yes, please stay," Annie said. "I don't know what I would have done if you hadn't been here."

Joan came into the room carrying a tray. She looked at Fuller. "Where do you think you're going? I've just made tea."

Fuller looked helplessly at Jack.

Jack chuckled. "You might as well sit down again, Eddie. You're up against two of the Callum women. There's no contest."

Fuller smiled and shrugged. He reclaimed his seat and picked up his cigarette from the ashtray, took one final pull and stubbed it out among the pile of dog-ends. "I was trying to quit these filthy things. Then you go and pull a stunt like tonight and I'm puffing away like a trooper again."

"It's nice to see that everyone was so concerned about me."

Annie gave his knee a playful slap. "What did you expect, Jack Callum? We were worried sick."

Jack turned to Joan. "Tell Avril she's going to need a new car. The Humber is a write-off."

"That old heap? It's no great loss. She was always moaning about it. This will give her an excuse to get a newer one."

"One with a heater would be a good idea. I swear my hands turned blue tonight as I was driving."

"I heard voices."

They all turned as Avril walked into the room. Her blonde hair was awry, mascara streaked her cheeks, and the surgical dressing on her forehead was stained with blood.

"I thought you were asleep," Joan said.

"Come and sit by the fire, pet, and get warm." Annie shifted along on the settee, making a space for her.

Avril squeezed herself between Annie and the arm of the settee and pulled her candlewick dressing gown around her. "Mr Callum, I'm sorry for everything I've put you through."

"There's no apology necessary, Avril. You had no control over your husband's actions. I just regret the tragic way things have worked out."

"Do you think Alf suffered?"

Jack shook his head. "I doubt that he knew very much about it. It all happened so quickly. If there's anything we can do to help, you know you only have to ask."

Avril turned to Annie. "I was going to ask you if you'll come to the hospital with me tomorrow. Eddie was saying that I'm going to have to identify Alf's body."

"I didn't mean straight away," Fuller said, flushing slightly.

"It's okay, Eddie. I want to get it over and done with as soon as possible. Then there's the funeral to arrange. It's funny. It seems like only yesterday I was organising things for our wedding. I don't know who I'm going to invite."

"I'll help," Joan said. "We'll put our heads together. Make a list."

"At least I won't have to do a seating plan," Avril said, and gave a little laugh.

"Shock," Annie mouthed at Jack.

Avril saw. "No, Annie. I'm pleased he's gone, even though it's wicked of me to say it. My life has been hell for the past three years."

"I had no idea Alf was such a violent man," Jack said. "I was saying to Annie only the other night that when I met him he seemed quiet, placid almost."

"And so he was, when he wasn't drinking. But he was just like his father, a mean and spiteful drunk. As soon as he'd had a couple of whiskies he became a different person. I grew to hate that side of him."

There was silence.

Fuller broke the spell by swallowing the last of his tea and putting the cup back in its saucer. "Well, that's me done. I'm off. Got an early start in the morning. Good night all."

Jack got to his feet. "I'll see you out, Eddie."

Out in the hall, Jack helped Fuller on with his coat and pulled the sitting room door closed. "Thanks for everything tonight, Eddie."

Fuller shrugged. "My pleasure . . . if that's the right word."

Jack smiled. "Probably not. You know, I thought I was a goner tonight. When Alf Kendall was smashing his lorry into me, for a moment there I wondered if I would ever see my family again. It scared me silly. Stupid, eh?"

"Not at all, Jack. You've got a lot to live for. More than most of us."

"I was thinking on the way home . . . perhaps it's time to put in my papers."

Fuller looked at him, open-mouthed. "Retire? You? How are you going to spend your time? Raising begonias, or whatever it is you do with them?"

"I could think of worse ways to pass the time."

"You'd be pulling your hair out within a week. I guarantee it."

"I don't know. I spoke to an old friend the other day, another policeman I'd boxed with, back in the thirties. I described us as a couple of dinosaurs. Sometimes that's just how I feel — old and out of touch. Avril came to me and asked for my help and there was precious little I could do for her. Now she's a widow, at thirty-two, because I sat back and did nothing."

"Oh no you don't. I'm not having you blaming yourself for that. It's the system and police attitudes that are wrong, not you."

Jack shrugged. "I must admit, I smiled when Frank Lesser gave Kendall a pasting. I would have done it myself if Lane hadn't stopped me. I shouldn't be taking the law into my own hands. It goes against all my training, everything I've learned over the years. I should be able to accomplish what I need to using the rule of law, not stepping outside it. That leads to anarchy."

"Then it's the law that needs to change, not you, Jack. Men like you make it easier for the rest of us. We look up to you. We see what you can achieve playing by the rules. You manage to do that without compromising your integrity, and it gives us hope that we can work within the system, despite our frustration with it."

"Thanks, Eddie. You've got quite a brain in that noggin of yours, haven't you?"

"Don't let on. I have a reputation to keep up. Good night, Jack. Sleep well. Things will seem a little brighter in the morning."

"Yeah, you're probably right. Good night, Eddie. Drive safely. I think it's starting to freeze out there."

Back in the front room, the women were on their feet. "We're going up," Joan announced, taking Avril by the hand.

Annie picked up the tray. "I'm just going to wash these up, then I'm turning in myself. Are you coming?"

Jack smiled. "I'll give you a hand. You wash, I'll dry." He kissed Joan goodnight, gave Avril a brief hug and followed Annie out to the kitchen.

She was standing at the sink, filling the washing-up bowl with hot water. She turned as he entered and put her arms around him. "It really scared me tonight, just how quickly all this could be snatched away from me."

"It scared me a bit as well."

She brushed her lips against his and turned back to the sink, squirting detergent into the bowl. "I'm not going to say something stupid like 'try to be more careful in future,' because life doesn't work like that. We don't choose when our number's up. It just is."

"Hey, that's enough of that kind of talk." He wrapped his arms around her waist. "I'm not planning on checking out any time soon."

She twisted in his embrace until their faces were inches away from each other. "Promise me?"

"I promise," he said.

"I'm holding you to that."

"I'm banking on it." He kissed her deeply.

"I overheard what you were saying to Eddie in the hall. You're not so bad for an old dinosaur."

"Not so much of the 'old' if you don't mind."

"Let's go to bed."

"What about the washing up?"

"It can wait until tomorrow."

"You're the boss."

She smiled. "That's right."

CHAPTER 29

FRIDAY 11 DECEMBER 1959

Jack walked into the station, brushing snow from his overcoat. "Has Frank Lesser come in yet?"

Andy Brewer shook his head. "He's up in town today, sir. Giving evidence at the Old Bailey."

"The Wilson fraud case," Jack said. "Damn! It slipped my mind. Not to worry. It can wait."

"He should be in tomorrow, sir."

Jack climbed the stairs, noting how much his back ached. A night's sleep had done little to iron out the kinks from the buffeting his muscles had taken yesterday evening.

He paused at Fuller's office. "Any joy with the lab, Myra?"

She glanced up from the typewriter and shook her head. "I pushed my luck with them the last time I went there and just hung around. I think they're sick of the sight of me now."

"You told them it was urgent?"

"Of course. Had it come from you or the inspector it might have meant something, but I don't think they take me seriously."

"We'll see about that. I'll call them and give them a rocket."

"I'd rather you didn't do that, sir. If I'm ever going to have a chance of earning their respect, I have to do it myself. They said I would have the results later today. Leave it with me. I'll call them and keep pestering until I get them . . . The inspector told me what happened yesterday evening. Are you okay now?"

"I feel like I've gone fifteen rounds with Henry Cooper, but apart from that I'm fine. Where *is* Inspector Fuller?"

"Down in the cells. The custody sergeant had trouble with one of the drunks overnight. The inspector's down there now reading him the riot act."

"Tell him to pop in and see me when he gets back."

"Yes, sir, will do."

Fifteen minutes later Eddie Fuller came into his office.

"Trouble with one of our guests, Eddie?"

"Old man Huntley, one of our regulars. Spent the wee small hours singing an obscene version of 'Rudolf the Red Nosed Reindeer.' He kept the other prisoners awake most of the night. You wanted to see me?"

"Did you see the board Myra's put up in the squad room?"

"It's very good, very comprehensive. She has a knack for that kind of thing."

"Any other observations?"

"Only that we seem a little short on suspects."

"Yes, that fact hadn't escaped me. It's a shame Father Harvey was killed. I had him in the frame for Sister Bernadette."

"You didn't say anything."

"Walking on eggshells, Eddie. We can't upset the Bishop."

"Bollocks to that," Fuller said. "A killer's a killer, whatever god he chooses to worship."

"My thoughts exactly. Unfortunately the chief super has other ideas."

"Frightened it might ruin his reputation at the golf club if we start making waves in that area?"

"I'll pretend I didn't hear that," Jack said. "You have a point, though. That's half the trouble with this case. We're having to work with one arm tied behind our backs for fear of offending the great and the good."

The telephone rang.

"It's Les. Les Parsons."

"And what can I do for you today, Les?"

Fuller turned to go back to his office. Jack signalled for him to stay.

"I have some information about Monday that you might find . . . significant," Parsons said. He spoke the last word in a low tone as if to emphasise its importance.

"Interesting. Would you like to come in to see me?"

"I would rather you came to me . . . but not here. Can we meet at St Joseph's?"

"Aren't you working today?"

"As I said the other night, my firm have been messing around with my shifts. I've got today off."

"Then what time would suit you?"

"Shall we say midday? He'll be back from school then."

"Who will?"

"Does midday suit you?" Parsons said again.

"Why don't you tell me over the phone, Les?"

There was a pause, and then Parsons said, "No, you need to hear this yourself, and in private."

"Very well. I'll be with you at noon." Jack rang off.

"What was all that about?" Fuller said.

"Parsons isn't saying. He'll only discuss it face to face and in private."

"Mysterious."

"I think it concerns one of the boys. He said something to the effect that if I met him at lunchtime 'he' would be 'back from school then.'"

"Who was he talking about?"

"I haven't the foggiest, but I think Myra might soon have another name to add to her board."

* * *

"Mr Callum, I wasn't expecting to see you again so soon," Sister Rosalie said.

"My apologies, Sister. Les Parsons asked me to meet him here at midday."

"Well, he's said nothing to me about it."

There was a knock on her office door.

"Come!"

The door opened and Les Parsons stepped into the room. "Ah," he said, looking at Jack. "You beat me to it. Sorry, Sister. I arranged for the chief inspector to meet me here."

"I can see that, Les. Would you mind telling me why?"

"We're here to see Terry Lloyd. Is he back from school yet?"

Sister Rosalie studied her wristwatch. "It's only twelve o'clock, Les. He doesn't get back from school until four."

"He's making an exception today. He said he'd be here during the dinner break. I think he wanted to avoid Ray Oliver, and was going to slip away without him knowing."

"Really, Les, is all this subterfuge necessary?"

"I think so, Sister. I don't think Terry would be so ready to talk to Mr Callum if Ray was around."

"Anyone would think that Terry is scared of Raymond."

"You don't know the half of it, Sister."

Jack watched this exchange with interest. "Has Terry come forward with something he omitted to tell me on Monday?"

"Yes. But I want him to tell you in his own words. He should be here by now. It's only a five minute walk from the school."

There was another, more hesitant knock on the door.

"That'll be him now," Parsons said. He opened the door. "Terry, good lad. I knew you wouldn't let me down. Chief Inspector Callum's here. You can tell him what you told me."

Jack looked at the boy standing in the doorway and felt for him. Terry Lloyd's expression was fearful.

"It's all right, son. I don't bite," he said.

"You're still a rozzer," Terry said. He looked close to tears.

"How old are you, Terry?"

"Fifteen."

"My son's your age. He doesn't like talking to me much either."

Terry looked at him uncertainly.

"He's quite musical — plays the guitar. Do you play any instruments, Terry?"

Terry shook his head. "I can sing though."

"Well, there you go then. You *are* musical."

"Terry's the leading light in St Augustine's choir," Les Parsons said. "Father Harvey says he's . . ."

Jack stared at him.

Jack turned to Sister Rosalie. "Is there somewhere we can talk in private? Perhaps that room you let us have on Monday?"

Sister Rosalie took the bunch of keys from her desk drawer. "Of course."

A few minutes later they were sitting around the table in the small room.

"Now, Terry. Tell Mr Callum exactly what you told me about Monday afternoon."

All the bravado Terry Lloyd had shown on Monday evening had melted away. He looked every inch the frightened schoolboy. Jack waited patiently for him to begin. He was reluctant to prompt him in case it sent the boy scurrying back into his protective shell of surly insolence.

Terry's gaze flicked around the room, looking everywhere rather than at Jack. "I was here Monday afternoon."

Parsons leaned forward in his seat. "And why weren't you at school, Terry?"

"Ray and me, we hopped off. We had double games and it was bloody freezing."

"What he means is that he was playing truant," Parsons said to Jack.

"I know what hopping off means, Les. I used to do it a lot when I was his age. Let Terry tell me his story his own way."

Parsons sat back in his seat and stared at the floor.

"So you hopped off on Monday, Terry."

"Like I said. Double games. Ugh! Anyway, we spent an hour over the park, but that was no better than being out on the playing field, just as cold, so we came back here. There's a back way into St Joe's. The Sisters don't know it so they never catch you."

"What time did you get back here, son?"

"About half past one. I mean, it's not that warm here, but it's a darned sight warmer than being outside. Ray and I decided to sneak up to the dorm for a fag. That's when we saw Sister Bernadette, heading towards the chapel."

Jack tried to sound casual. "And that was at one thirty?"

"More like two o'clock. We were messing around downstairs first. Ray thought he knew where Sister Rosalie keeps the communion wine, but he didn't find it, so we decided to go upstairs for a smoke instead."

"And that's when you ran into Sister Bernadette?"

"Yeah. It threw us, I can tell you. She was heading towards the back stairs and hardly anyone uses them — apart from Ray and me of course." Terry allowed himself a grin. "Anyway, we heard her coming along the corridor. We knew it was her because she's the only one of the Sisters who has Blakeys on her shoes and she was clip-clopping down the passage towards us."

"Blakeys are metal caps you nail to the heels of your shoes to protect them and stop the leather wearing down," Parsons said.

Jack crossed his legs, showing the metal segments attached to the heel of his shoe.

"Ah," Parsons said. "I see you're acquainted with them."

Jack stared at Parsons. The man fell silent. "You were saying, Terry?" he said.

"Like I said, she was clacking towards us, so we hid behind the door till she went past and started going down to the chapel. You can go the other way but it's busier — more likely to run into one of the Sisters."

"And was Sister Bernadette going down to the chapel on her own?"

Terry shook his head. He glanced at Parsons.

"Go on, Terry. You can tell Mr Callum. You won't get into any trouble."

"All right. She wasn't on her own. Canon Flood was with her."

"Canon Flood," Jack said. "Are you sure?"

"See?" Terry said to Parsons. "I told you he wouldn't believe me."

Jack reached out and covered Terry's hand with his own. "It's all right, son. I *do* believe you. And you say it was about two o'clock when you saw the two of them going down to the chapel together?"

Terry Lloyd nodded.

"You've done well, lad. Good observational skills," Jack said. "Do you mind telling me why you didn't mention this before?"

"Because Ray would do his nut if he knew I was talking to you. Hates the police, Ray does."

"And he has good reason to," Parsons said. "Raymond Oliver's a little thug, and you'd do well to steer clear of him, Terry."

"He's my mate," Terry said.

"Why are you telling us this, Terry? Why now?"

Terry blushed. "I liked Sister Bernadette. She was always very kind to me . . . and I want you to catch the sod who killed her." The last part of his statement was delivered with such vehemence that the words put to rest any doubts Jack might have had about Terry's honesty. "Thank you, Terry. I *am* going to catch the sod. Believe you me."

CHAPTER 30

FRIDAY

"Eddie, are you busy?"

"Nothing that won't wait."

"Good," Jack said. "Come with me to St Albans. We're going to see Canon Flood."

"Can't you handle him on your own?"

"Don't be bloody silly, of course I can. But I need a senior officer with me to attest that I didn't step on his toes."

"You're taking no chances."

"Too bloody right I'm not, not with Bishop Rawlings on the warpath. Come on. I'll drive."

Thirty minutes later they were pulling up outside Canon Flood's house in St Albans.

Jack rang the doorbell.

"Chief Inspector Callum," Ruth Beech said. "You'll be wanting to see Gerald."

"I do indeed. This is my colleague, Inspector Fuller."

"Do come in. I'll tell him you're here."

Moments later she was back. "He says he'll see you in his study. Do you know where that is?"

"Yes, I remember."

Jack led the way through the house.

Canon Flood rose from his desk as Jack and Fuller walked into his study. "Don't get up, Canon. I know it pains you."

Flood collapsed back into his seat. "Thank you. The leg's no better, and the cold does it no favours. Now, what can I do for you, gentlemen?"

Jack and Fuller sat down opposite Flood. "You weren't exactly straight with me the other day," Jack began.

Flood frowned. "Oh? In what way?"

"You intimated that you hadn't seen Sister Bernadette recently, and that you had her turned away from the house on Saturday."

"That's right."

"But you failed to mention that you went to see her at St Joseph's on Monday."

"But—"

"Before you deny it, sir, you were seen, accompanying her down the stairs to St Joseph's chapel. Where, and I'm sure I don't need to remind you, she met her end."

Gerald Flood's face turned grey. He took out a handkerchief and mopped his brow. "Oh dear," he said. "Oh dear. I can see how bad this looks."

"Perhaps you'd care to explain."

Fuller took out his notebook and sat, pen poised.

Flood patted his brow again. "I assure you that my motives for seeing Sister Bernadette on Monday were honourable and Christian. I felt guilty that I'd sent the poor girl away on Saturday and I spent most of the following day asking the Lord for guidance. By Monday morning I had decided what I should do and I asked Ruth to drive me over to St Joseph's. I wanted to beg Sister Bernadette's forgiveness and persuade her to tell me why she had come to see me on Saturday."

"And did she?" Fuller asked.

"Yes. She told me she came to see me because she had encountered a serious problem of a personal nature. She wanted me to take her confession. I did mention to you that she was a troubled child?"

Jack sighed. "To be frank with you, Canon, I'm getting a bit tired of hearing that one wheeled out. Bernadette was a very unhappy and confused young woman. She was pregnant. Was that the sin she wanted to confess?"

Flood spread his hands helplessly. "I can't say. I took her down to St Joseph's chapel so she could unburden herself within the sanctity of the confessional."

Jack leaned forward. "And then?"

Flood sighed. "Then I gave her my blessing and left."

"Just like that. You left this 'troubled child,' this frightened young woman who had just bared her soul to you, to just sit there alone and stew?"

"It wasn't like that," Flood said hotly. "I believe I really did help her. Our faith teaches us that confession is good for the soul, and I could tell from her demeanour that many of her troubles had gone. When I left her in the chapel she looked content, almost serene."

"And a short while later she was lying there, abused and dead."

Flood winced.

"I assure you—"

"Save your assurances, Canon. Just describe your movements for the rest of the day."

"I'm not sure that I like your tone."

"I don't give a tuppenny damn whether you like my tone or not," Jack said. "Your movements. What did you do after your marvellous act of Christian charity?"

Fuller glanced nervously at Jack.

"Ruth drove me over to St Augustine's. I'd promised Father Harvey that I'd sit in on his choir practice and offer any advice I could."

"And you stayed there until?"

"Until the practice finished. About seven, I suppose."

"And now Father Harvey is no longer around to verify it. Are there any other witnesses who can corroborate your story?"

Flood shook his head. "I kept out of sight, I'm afraid. I didn't want to put the choir off. Some of them can get very nervous if they feel they're being observed. I stayed up at the back of the organ loft . . . Wait a minute . . . Jenkins! Of course!"

"Pardon?"

"Harold Jenkins, the organist at St Augustine's. He can verify my story . . . and Ruth, of course. She drove me there and drove me home afterwards."

Jack got to his feet. "Right, Canon, I'll certainly be checking your story. I'll be back if I find you've been anything less than frank with me."

On the way out Jack found Ruth Beech in the kitchen and asked her about Monday.

"Yes, that's right. I took the Canon to St Augustine's and drove him home afterwards."

"And you're sure he was there all evening?"

"Well, hand on heart I can't really say. I wasn't going to freeze in a draughty church for several hours, much as I adore choral music and the choir at St Augustine's in particular, so I drove to my sister's. She only lives a mile away from the church and has a television, so I spent the evening there, until it was time to take him home."

Jack and Fuller left the house.

"Well, bang goes that part of his alibi," Fuller said as they reached the car.

"Come on," Jack said. "Let's pay a visit to St Augustine's. We'll try to track down Harold Jenkins and see if he's singing from the same hymn sheet as Canon Flood."

* * *

Strains of 'Jesu, Joy of Man's Desiring' met them at the entrance to St Augustine's.

"Well, he didn't take much tracking down," Fuller said.

"It must be our lucky day."

They could see Jenkins in the distance, sitting at the organ in an alcove raised a good six feet off the floor.

"Harold Jenkins?" Jack called. As they drew closer, Jack saw the mirror fixed to the wall above Jenkins' head. The organist had been watching them.

The music stopped. "Wait a minute. I'll come down."

A few seconds later, Jenkins came out through a door to the right of the organ loft. "How can I help?" His voice had a distinct Welsh lilt.

He was much older than Jack had expected — probably in his mid-seventies. He was elegant, with white hair swept back from a craggy, leathery face. His blue eyes sparkled with warmth and good humour.

"Practising?" Jack said.

"Indulging myself. Since retiring from the bank, I grab every opportunity I can to get behind the manuals."

"Manuals?"

"Keyboards. Forgive me, I expect everyone to know the lingo. I'm afraid I'm a bit of a sad case when it comes to organs. I love them so much. I've even driven the keys at St Albans

Cathedral, thanks to an old friend of mine who was dean there. Four manuals! Over sixty stops and a full-sized pedalboard! It makes the organ here seem like a child's toy. I had the time of my life . . . sorry, I'm prattling on."

Jack smiled indulgently. "I understand there was a choir practice on Monday night."

Jenkins nodded enthusiastically. "Yes, that's right."

"So the carol concert is still going ahead then," Fuller said. "Despite what happened to Father Harvey?"

"But of course. I think Martin would be most put out if we cancelled this late in the day. He worked so hard on it."

"Yes, of course. I understand Canon Flood was here on Monday."

"Yes, that's right. He sat up there at the back. I must admit I found it a bit off-putting at first, but once the choir was in full voice I forgot about everything but the music. I think Martin would have appreciated Canon Flood being here. The man knows nothing about organs, but he knows his way around a choral chart all right."

"And he was here all evening, you say?"

Jenkins looked away. "I didn't say that exactly. Where he sat was just out of my line of vision. I had my hands full just reading the score and looking to see what stops I was pulling out. For the rest of the time I was looking in the mirror at Martin conducting the choir."

"So, you can't actually confirm that he was here for the entire duration of the practice?" Jack said.

Jenkins shook his head. "Sorry. Is it important?"

"Is it possible that he could have slipped out while you weren't looking?" Fuller said.

Jenkins frowned. "It's feasible, I suppose. The only thing I can swear to was that he was with me at the beginning of the practice, and sitting there at the end."

"Thank you, Mr Jenkins. You've been most helpful."

"Oh? I'm not quite sure how."

Jack tapped the side of his nose and winked. "From little acorns mighty oaks, and all that."

Jenkins looked confused. "I really have no idea what you're talking about. And who are you anyway, coming here and asking all these questions about Canon Flood?"

"We're the police, sir," Fuller said. "And you've been helping us with our inquiries."

Jenkins eyes widened. "Have I really? Well, I never. And here I was, wittering on about organs when you could have been out there finding Martin Harvey's killer. I think it was a tramp myself. You get them dossing down in here sometimes. I told Martin more times than I can remember to keep the doors locked at night. But did he listen? No, he did not and look where it got him."

* * *

"Bang goes another alibi," Fuller said. "Shall we go back and arrest Flood?"

Jack shook his head. "We need a bit more than a couple of dodgy alibis that may or may not be true."

"What else do we need?"

"For one thing we need something that puts him at the chapel at the time Bernadette was killed. For another, I'm struggling to see a motive. Without that we don't have a case, just a lot of hearsay and some circumstantial evidence. It's not enough, Eddie. Not nearly enough."

Jack climbed in behind the wheel. "And have you asked yourself how he got from here to St Joseph's and back again. He doesn't drive and you saw the state of him. He's crippled with arthritis. He can barely walk."

"Unless he's faking it?"

"And in his secret life he's as nimble as Fred Astaire? No, Eddie, I don't think so."

"Then what?"

"Back to the drawing board, I'd say — Myra's board. We go through everything again, establish a time-line and fit everybody around it. We've missed something important here and we've just got to establish what it is."

"A walk in the park," Fuller said.

"If only it was," Jack said grimly.

CHAPTER 31

FRIDAY

Back at the station they spent ninety minutes reviewing Myra's board. Jack encouraged everyone in the squad room to come up with their theories and suggestions, however outlandish they might sound.

When the clock struck six, Jack said, "That's it. I've had enough for one day. Myra? The lab?"

"Still nothing, sir. I'm waiting for them to call me back."

"I've had enough of them messing us around." He picked up the telephone. "Elaine, get me the Stevenage forensic lab."

"Hello?"

"Who am I speaking to?"

"Mark. Mark Brady. I'm the junior technician here."

"This is DCI Callum, Welwyn and Hatfield CID. Put me through to your supervisor."

"Sorry, no can do."

"What do you mean 'no can do?' There must be someone in charge there."

"There is, sir. Professor Gideon, but he's up to his eyeballs and can't be disturbed."

"That's preposterous. There must be somebody there I can talk to."

"Only me, sir, sorry. We've got a bit of a flap on here at the moment. There was a pile up in the snow on the AI earlier today. Six dead and thirteen injured. There's so much to process it's hard to know where to start. Do we test for alcohol in the victims' blood, or check the stomach contents, or . . ."

"All right, you've made your point. One of my officers brought a pill in to you yesterday to be analysed and compared to the traces of the drug found in a murder victim's stomach. I need those results now."

"Case 47B. I know the one. A girl brought it in, Detective Constable Banks. A bit of a looker."

"Rein in your hormones, Brady. When can I have the results?"

"Tomorrow. First thing. I'll work through the night if necessary. I'm probably going to be stuck here anyway. Tell Miss Banks she can pick the results up in the morning on her way in to work. I'll still be here. Tell her to ask for me."

Jack thanked him and rang off. "You've got a fan, Myra. A lad called Brady?"

Myra grimaced. "Oh yes. Him. All Brylcreem and acne. He's got a dozen cheesy chat-up lines and likes to try them all out — often."

"Well, he's taken quite a shine to you. He'll have the results for you tomorrow. Call in to the lab on your way to the station. Ask for him."

"And wear something revealing," Fuller said, grinning.

Myra mouthed an obscenity. ". . . *sir.*"

"Temper, temper, Detective Constable."

Jack smiled. "Go on, get off home, the lot of you. I heard the night shift arriving."

* * *

The all-too familiar strains of 'Guitar Boogie Shuffle' greeted Jack as he entered the house. "Give me strength," he muttered, and went into the living room.

Eric was in his usual pose, standing next to the radiogram, head bowed over his guitar.

"Bert Weedon again, Eric? Must you?"

"He's almost got it nailed, Mr Callum."

At the sound of the voice, Jack turned. Gerry Tanner uncurled herself from an armchair and went to stand next to Eric. She tugged at his sleeve. "Eric? Eric! Your dad's home."

"Sorry, Dad. I didn't hear you come in." Eric lifted the arm of the record player.

"I'm not surprised, with that racket going on." Jack shrugged off his overcoat. "What are you practising in the living room for? And why is Gerry here, on a Friday evening?"

"I'm staying the night." Gerry had changed a great deal in the past few months. Gone was the shy, hesitant child who had once approached him at her school. Gerry was now a bright, attractive teenager. She still had that smattering of freckles across her nose, but her wayward, curly blonde hair had been tamed. It was pulled away from her face, held in a ponytail with a white ribbon.

"Staying the night, eh?"

"Nan and Granddad are going up to town."

"Jack?" Annie called from the kitchen.

"Excuse me, Gerry," Jack said, and went to find her.

"I thought I heard your voice," Annie said.

"What's going on? Gerry's staying the night? Where's she going to sleep? We've already got Avril here."

Annie skipped across the floor and pecked him on the lips. "Joanie and Avril have gone back to the flat for the night, now that Alf's off the scene. We left it in a bit of a mess yesterday and Avril wants to get it tidied. Now her car's out of action, she's going to have to work from home."

"And Gerry?"

"Ah, that was short notice. Laurence called round and asked if we could babysit tonight. Friends have invited him and Jean to a new jazz club that opened last month in Gerard Street, in Soho. Owned by a trumpeter, Ronnie somebody-or-other."

"Ronnie Scott, and he's a saxophonist."

"That's him. Anyway, Laurence was very excited at the prospect of going there so I couldn't refuse. After all, Eric's spending so much time at their house these days, practising his guitar and learning to read music with Gerry. I felt I owed them."

Jack smiled. "It's fine. She can sleep in Joanie's bed. If Avril's planning on moving back to the flat, I suppose we won't have to find another bed for Joanie's room."

"No, we won't. I don't think Joanie's going to be living here for much longer, either."

"What? Why? I've just got used to having her back."

"I overheard her and Avril talking. Obviously, with Alf gone, Avril is going to find it tough keeping the flat on. It would make sense if she shared with someone, to help out with the rent and bills and Joanie's the obvious candidate. They get on so well, and they'll be working together from home."

"And the world rolls on without me," Jack said wistfully.

"Oh, don't look so sad. You've still got Rosie and Eric . . . and me."

"I'll settle for that. What's for dinner?"

"Lamb hotpot. Your favourite."

"Is that intended to butter me up?"

"Sweetening the pill."

"You're a devious little minx."

"The way to a man's heart et cetera, et cetera."

Annie kissed him and went back to the cooker.

* * *

Jack was standing at the draining board drying plates. "Did it arrive?"

"It's upstairs, in the wardrobe. Geoffrey brought it round after lunch."

"Let's take a look at it then."

He tossed the tea towel onto the kitchen table and trotted up the stairs.

"Well? What do you think?" Annie came into the bedroom, still drying her hands on a towel.

Jack was standing beside the bed, holding a semi-acoustic guitar. He turned it over and over, admiringly. "It's certainly a handsome beast."

"Geoffrey told me that it's a Hofner 125. Blonde, single cutaway, with one pick-up and . . . er . . ." She pulled a scrap of paper from her apron pocket. ". . . a tortoiseshell scratch and a Bigsby tremolo arm."

"You might as well be talking another language," Jack said.

"That's why I wrote it down. Geoffrey seemed to think that Eric would find the information interesting."

"It's not as heavy as I expected." He laid the guitar down on the bed, reached into the wardrobe and took out something that looked like a small suitcase. It was covered in grey Rexine and had a circular grille in the centre of it with 'Truvoice' emblazoned across it. "This is the amplifier, I suppose."

Annie read from the paper again. "It's a Truvoice amplifier, made by Selmer in 1955. Fifteen watts, whatever that means. There's a lead and a strap in that carrier bag."

"Let's hope he's happy with it. Are you sure you want to give it to him tonight? You don't want to wait until Christmas Day?"

Annie shook her head. "He's playing at that dance at the youth club on the 19th. If we give it to him now, he'll have time to practise with it."

"You spoil that boy."

"Well, you spoil the girls, so we're even on that score."

"Come on then. Let's see what he thinks of his Christmas present."

* * *

"A Hofner 125!" Eric yelled.

Jack nodded.

"Happy Christmas," Annie said. "I know we're early, but we thought you'd prefer to have it sooner rather than later."

"Do I!" Eric said, grinning.

"Just don't expect to have anything to open on Christmas morning."

"I won't. A Hofner 125!" Eric turned it over and over in his hands, examining it from every angle. "You two are the best parents anyone could ask for."

"I'm so glad you like it," Annie said.

"Plug it in," Jack said. "Play us that guitar boogie thing."

"You really want to hear me play it? I thought you were sick of Bert Weedon."

"I am sick of Bert Weedon, but I like hearing you play."

Eric looked at Jack and tears welled in his eyes. "Thanks, Dad."

* * *

An hour and four renditions of 'Guitar Boogie Shuffle' later, Jack called a halt. "Right, that's the last one. Time for bed."

Eric switched off the amplifier. "Okay."

Annie's eyes widened. "Are you all right? No protests? No pleading for another ten minutes? What have you done with the real Eric?"

"I think he's just happy, Mrs Callum," Gerry Tanner said.

Annie smiled at her. "I've put clean sheets on Joanie's bed, so you can just do your teeth and slip straight in there.

"Thanks, Mrs Callum. Hey, Eric, now you've got two guitars, you can teach me to play."

Eric smiled at her. "Yeah, why not?"

Once Eric and Gerry had gone upstairs, Annie and Jack sat on, holding hands.

"You do realise we're raising our own Les Paul and Mary Ford here, don't you?" Annie said.

"Could be worse. I think I've still got one of their records in the loft. 'How High the Moon,' that's the one. I'll dig it out for them."

"I wouldn't bother. It's hardly rock and roll, is it?" Annie said.

"Eric will probably hate it, but I think Gerry might appreciate their harmonies. She's very musical, and seems to have quite an open mind." He glanced up at the clock on the mantle. "Is Rosie out with Brian again tonight?"

"The pictures," Annie said.

"What have they gone to see?"

"The new Audrey Hepburn film: *The Nun's Story*."

Jack flinched. "A little too close to home."

"Oh, Jack, I'm sorry. I wasn't thinking."

"It's all right," he said. "Did you really threaten Alf Kendall with the scissors?"

Annie nodded.

"Would you have stabbed him?"

"Well, I wasn't going to give him a short back and sides."

"Am I seeing another Annie Callum here?"

"He knocked Joanie over, and hit Avril. I wasn't going to let that pig hurt them again."

"Protecting your cubs."

"Pardon?"

"You. You're like a lioness, protecting her cubs."

Annie growled at him playfully. "Come on, let's go up. Rosie can let herself in tonight."

"I'll make the cocoa," Jack said. He leaned forward and kissed the top of her head.

"You're such a romantic."

"Eat your heart out, Valentino."

CHAPTER 32

SATURDAY 12 DECEMBER 1959.

"Frank, have you got a moment?"

Frank Lesser sat down at Jack's desk. "I know what you're going to say, guv. I shouldn't have hit Kendall."

"No, you shouldn't. Why did you?"

Lesser shrugged. "I don't know really. When I'm in the ring, I'm often pushed and it's a struggle to keep my temper. Some of the younger wrestlers — and some of the older mid-carders as well, who think they have something to prove — will sometimes try to needle you, get under your skin. Most of the time I can rise above it, but once in a while something hits my buttons and I just see red."

"And that happened with Kendall?"

Lesser nodded. "Two things I really hate. Envy, because you know that if envious people pushed themselves, they could get what they envy others for having. They're just too bloody lazy to try. I mean, when I first heard that Eddie Fuller had been promoted to inspector, I felt a pang. I had to have a word with myself. If I wanted it, I could work as hard as he's done over the past year, but the truth is, what with the wrestling and my home life, I really don't have that kind of dedication. That's not to say I don't have ambition, I do, but I'll get there in my own time, and my own way, so there's no point envying Eddie his promotion." He paused for a moment, then went on.

"Jealousy is the other one. That's a really ugly emotion, and that's what I found so hard to take with Alf Kendall. He told me about his life and how he worried that when he was away on a driving job, his wife would start seeing other men. The worry started early on in their marriage. He would get himself tanked up just to get those kinds of thoughts out of his head. Then she started working for herself and going into people's homes and his fantasies of her having illicit affairs grew until he was obsessed with the idea. He'd accuse her, she'd deny it, they'd argue and he'd finish the row with a backhander, or a punch. But what really triggered it for me was when he said that he'd rather kill her than see her with another man. He crossed a line with that one, crossed *my* line, so I clouted him. I wanted to let him know what it feels like when someone bigger and stronger than you are lets you have it with all their strength. I thought it might teach him a lesson. We'll never know now if it had any effect on him."

"He actually said that he'd kill Avril rather than see her with someone else?"

"Oh, yes. He meant it too. I could tell from the way he said it —cold and unemotional. I figure it was lucky for Avril Kendall that he had the accident."

"Can somebody really be that jealous? That they'd kill someone they loved rather than see them with somebody else?"

"I'm sure there are cases on file where that's happened."

Jack nodded. "Yes, you're probably right. Thanks, Frank, you've given me something to think about. Now, don't let me keep you from your work."

"I can go?"

"Yes, run along."

Lesser got to his feet. "I thought you'd called me in here to chew my ears off."

"I'll leave that dubious pleasure to your opponents in the wrestling ring. Go on, get out of here."

Jack sat back in his chair and took his pipe from the desk drawer. Minutes later, Myra Banks tapped on the door and walked into his office.

She handed him a slim manila envelope. "I got the results from the lab at last."

He took out the sheet of paper and read.

"Phenobarbital. The drug they found in Bernadette's stomach."

"And you took the pill from Canon Flood?"

"No. He gave it to me, to help with my insomnia."

"I didn't know you had insomnia," Myra said.

Jack smiled. "I don't. Subterfuge, Myra, like asking Tony Smythe to use his facilities and then raiding his bathroom cabinet."

"They didn't teach me it at Hendon. I guess it must be second nature, sir."

"Yes, I thought that might be the case. Whether you were taught or not, you're very good at it."

He sat back, put his feet up on the desk and drew on his pipe.

* * *

"Does anyone have a pen for this board?"

"What's going on?" Eddie Fuller said, entering the squad room with Myra Banks.

"It looks like the guvnor's adding another name to the list."

"Who is it, sir?" Myra said. A small crowd had gathered around the board.

Fuller read. "Ruth Beech. Canon Flood's housekeeper, who also worked for Father Harvey."

"A link," Myra said.

"And a strong one, but I didn't consider her because I didn't have a motive," said Jack.

"What changed?" Frank Lesser said.

"Something you said to me. You spoke about someone being jealous enough to kill the person they loved rather than see them with somebody else."

"That's a bit abstract, sir," Grant said. "We went through it all yesterday evening. Why didn't we stumble across it then?"

"Because we weren't looking for it. Ever since Monday we've been blinded by the obvious. Because a nun was murdered, and then a priest, we assumed there was some kind of religious motivation behind the killings."

"A reasonable assumption," Lesser said.

"Maybe so, but all it did was to keep us looking in the wrong direction. We should have been looking for the most common motive for murder. Unrequited or spurned love."

His audience looked doubtful.

"You don't believe me? Fine. Look at what we have here. Ruth Beech was Harvey's housekeeper for about five years. He was a good-looking young man. She was a spinster of the parish. What if she was carrying a torch for him all that time? Canon Flood's housekeeper dies and Harvey unloads Beech onto the old man and starts having a relationship with Sister Bernadette. Once she found out about it, Ruth Beech would be pretty miffed, wouldn't she?"

"Come on, sir," Harry Grant said. "We're talking about nuns and priests here."

"No, Harry, *you're* talking about nuns and priests. I'm talking about men and women — people with the same feelings and passions as the rest of us. We know that Bernadette O'Malley was a nymphomaniac, and very pretty. If she set her sights on Harvey, his vow of celibacy would have to be more unbreachable than a chastity belt. I, for one, don't believe it was."

Jack looked from face to face. "Okay. I can see you have doubts, but indulge me for a moment. Let's go back to Saturday afternoon. Bernadette visits Canon Flood and Ruth Beech tells her to go away. How do we know that Beech sent her away? We only have Flood's word for it and he was upstairs in bed trying to sleep. We don't know that there wasn't a longer conversation between the two women. Maybe Bernadette told a sympathetic Beech about her love affair with Harvey and that she was carrying his child. Jump forward to Monday. Beech drives Flood to St Joseph's to meet with Bernadette, and then on to St Augustine's to help Father Harvey with his choir practice. By her own admission she didn't stay at the church. What if she went back to St Joseph's armed with a vacuum flask of tea and some of Flood's sleeping pills, and killed Bernadette in a fit of jealous rage?"

"But she didn't. She went to her sister's to watch television," Eddie Fuller said.

"And we know that for a fact, do we, Eddie? I haven't checked her alibi. Have you?"

Fuller shook his head. "I believed her," he said.

"Don't feel bad about it. I did too. I had no reason not to. But now we have to check her story out and see if it holds up.

Myra, she said her sister lives a mile away from St Augustine's. Check to see if there's anyone named Beech in that area."

"What if the sister is married?" Grant said.

"And what if she isn't? Positive thinking, Grant."

"There's an Agnes Beech," Myra said, looking up from the telephone directory. "She lives at 46 Raglan Way. It's the other side of the railway line. Not the most salubrious of neighbourhoods."

"I don't care about that. It has to be her. I'll go and interview her. Meadows!" he called. "Bring the car round."

"Do you want Myra or me to come with you?"

Jack shook his head. "Not this time, Eddie. Just get on with your duties. This is my wild goose, so I'll chase it."

CHAPTER 33

SATURDAY

They pulled up outside a small semi-detached house.

Jack got out of the car, turned up his collar and put on his hat to ward off the snow.

"Wait here, Constable. I shouldn't be long."

The house looked run down. It was bordered by a threadbare privet hedge, with a muddy path leading through a scrubby front garden to the door. There was a handwritten 'No Hawkers' sign pinned above the letterbox.

Jack raised the doorknocker and let it fall. Seconds later the door was opened by a blowsy woman with hair the colour and texture of straw. She wore too much make-up and kept her ample charms barely concealed under a pink nylon housecoat. A cigarette dangled from her painted lips.

"Yes?" she said.

"Agnes Beech?"

"Yes, that's me. Who wants to know?"

"Jack Callum. Welwyn and Hatfield police."

"All right," she said. "What do you want?"

He proffered his warrant card but she waved it away.

"Don't you want to see some identification?"

"Why should I? What can you do anyway? Rape and pillage me? It would make a change from doing the bloody laundry. Besides, you've got an honest face, so I figure I'm safe enough."

"Do you have a sister? Ruth Beech?"

The woman's face broke into a smile. "Little Ruth. Yes, she's my sister. What's she done?"

"Did you happen to see her last Monday? Only she said she paid you a visit, late afternoon."

The woman took a long pull on the cigarette, dropped it onto the doorstep and ground it out.

"Mister . . . Callum is it? My sister hasn't been here to visit for over five years. Not since she caught religion and moved away."

"There seems to be a discrepancy between her story and yours."

Agnes Beech snorted. "Well, there would be. Ruth wouldn't know the truth if it came up behind her and bit her on the arse. You'd better come in and I'll put the kettle on. Excuse the place, won't you? I'm not a great one for housework."

Inside the front door was a passageway, wallpapered up to the dado rail in Lincrusta, its bubbled surface painted glossy brown. Above the dado rail the walls were a smoky tobacco colour. The ceiling was whitewashed, and patchy.

"The place needs decorating," she said. "This was my mum and dad's house, and it hasn't been touched since they died."

"When was that?"

"Just after the war, the influenza outbreak of forty-six. The flu carried them both off. Come through to the scullery." She led him through to a bleak, grey-walled room with a rusty red quarry-tiled floor. The windows ran with condensation caused by steam belching from an antique copper in the corner. A clothes airer hung from the ceiling, its wooden slats draped with washing, and in the corners of the room flypapers hung in twisted ringlets, specked with the desiccated carcasses of summer visitors who had flown in but never left.

Agnes lifted two white enamel mugs from hooks under a dusty shelf and poured a tablespoon of Camp liquid coffee and chicory essence into each one. The kettle on the old blue enamelled stove started a mournful whistle.

"You don't mind having a bit of music while we have this, do you? It helps pass the time."

"Not at all." Jack sat down at a small wooden table. Its top was covered in red and white spotted sticky-backed plastic.

Agnes twisted a knob on a Bakelite radio sitting on the shelf, and 'Workers' Playtime' filled the scullery with lively big band music.

"Now," Agnes Beech said, setting the mugs down on the table. "Tell me what that cow of a sister of mine has been up to."

Jack sipped at his coffee and winced. There was a glass sugar bowl in the centre of the table. He scooped two heaped teaspoons into his cup and stirred them into the muddy liquid. "I don't know that she's been up to anything. It just seems odd to me that she said she'd come to visit you on Monday when she'd plainly done no such thing."

Agnes Beech shrugged. "What do you want me to say? I'm not going to lie for her."

Jack tried the coffee again. At least it was sweet now. "What can you tell me about her?"

"What do you want to know?"

"I take it you grew up together?"

Agnes nodded. "Here in this very house."

"Would you say you got on well?"

"Not really. She didn't like me much, and I always thought she had ideas above her station. I mean, come on, Mr Callum. Take a good look around at this place. It's hardly Hatfield House, is it? But to hear her speak, you'd think she was high-born, not dragged up by a common factory worker and his dowdy little wife in a house at the fag-end of town."

"Apart from putting on airs, how was she? Did she have boyfriends?"

"Yes, but they never stayed around very long . . . apart from George. He and Ruth ended up living together in a small flat above the funeral parlour in town. If you think this place is bad, you should have seen that flat. It was the kind of place where you'd wipe your feet on the way *out*." She laughed again. It had echoes of a death rattle.

"She's not with George now?"

Agnes shook her bleached hair. "Nah. It lasted three years before he'd had enough of her. Oh, it was all right when they first got together. Love's young dream, you might say, but he soon learned what she was really like."

"Which was?"

"A slovenly bitch, as well as being cruel and heartless. She had a streak of jealousy in her that would have had me calling the men in white coats if I were her boyfriend."

"You say they lived together."

"In sin, yes. She used to call herself 'Mrs,' so the neighbours wouldn't talk."

"But she and George never married?"

"The only sensible thing that man did . . . apart from leaving her."

"How did she react when he went?"

"She was livid. She went absolutely crazy. She couldn't afford to keep the flat on so she came back to live here. Lucky me, eh?"

"Did you see George again?"

She nodded. "He was in a right state by then, poor devil. She'd scared him out of his wits. Do you know, during one of their many rows, she actually attacked him with a knife! He showed me the scar, and bloody unpleasant it was too. He didn't deserve any of it. He was a kind, sweet man who deserved better in life. He's in Canada now. He emigrated just to get away from her. I think he wanted to put as much water between them as possible. The last time I saw him he warned me about her. He said she had — quote: 'an insatiable appetite for evil.' I asked him what he meant, but he wouldn't go into detail. He just hopped on a plane and fled the country, poor sod."

"But did *you* ever find out what he meant?"

"Well, I soon found out once she moved back in with me."

"How did it manifest itself?"

"It was as if she wanted to control everything I did — when I went out, who I went out with, when I would be coming back. It was suffocating, a bloody nightmare. Woe betide you if you crossed her. She could make you pay in ways you wouldn't believe possible."

"Pay? In what way?"

Agnes took a mouthful of coffee and swallowed loudly. "I'll give you an example. It was the final straw really." She pulled an unfiltered Players cigarette from a packet in her housecoat and lit it from the stove. Jack noticed that her hand was visibly shaking.

She sat down and took another swig of coffee.

"I bought her a kitten, something for her to love, to take her mind off George leaving her. And boy, did she love it. It was an adorable bundle of fluff, pure black with the prettiest face. It lasted three months."

"What happened to it?"

"Ruth happened to it. You know what kittens are like. They pounce on everything, just playing. This one made the mistake of pouncing on Ruth and left a trail of scratches down her arm."

"That must have made her angry. Did she hit the kitten?"

Agnes shook her head. "No, not at all. She just lifted it off of her — she was lying on the bed at the time — and put it down gently on the floor."

"That doesn't seem so bad."

"I never saw the kitten again . . . not alive anyway. I found bits of it in the garden, a paw here, a leg there. The tail was floating in the fishpond. I never found the rest of it. I figured she'd buried it somewhere but, knowing her, she probably just put it in the dustbin." Agnes exhaled. "She used a bread knife to kill it and cut it up. I know that for a fact because she boasted about it, describing how she . . ." Agnes stopped talking and shuddered. "I couldn't live with her after that. I was scared to open my mouth in case I met the same fate as the kitten."

"But surely she wouldn't have attacked you, her sister?"

"Have you ever met her? Look at her eyes. There's nothing there. They are empty. When he said 'an insatiable appetite for evil,' I think George got it spot on."

"How did you end it? You say you couldn't live with her after that."

"I didn't have to. As I say, she caught religion. We were born and raised as Catholics, not that we took it seriously. St Michael's Church on Sunday, when Mum could be bothered to take us. Dad was usually nursing a hangover from Saturday night, so he didn't come very often, but Ruth always loved it. She liked the chanting and incense, but really it was the attention she got. You may not think it to look at us now, but we were pretty girls. Dressed in our Sunday best, with our hair brushed and shining, we stood out. Ruth's hair was glorious, all wavy and brown with chestnut highlights. Mine wasn't bad, but nowhere near as pretty as hers. I bleach it now, of course. But I remember our local priest, Father Thomas, used to make a great fuss of Ruth. He used to lay his hand on her hair when we took communion and always let it linger there a little bit too long, almost stroking it. It made my skin crawl but Ruth lapped it up.

"When she got older and was on her own she started going to St Augustine's. They had a handsome young priest there, Father Harvey, and somehow she landed a job as his housekeeper. I was relieved. It got her out of my life."

She stubbed out the cigarette and swallowed the last of her coffee.

"I've only seen her once since she moved out. I bumped into her in town, and she was like a stranger. We went to the ABC café for a cup of tea, but all she could talk about was her new life and how religion had given it purpose. It was Father Harvey this and Father Harvey that. Sounded like the Second Coming personified. We had our tea, said goodbye and I haven't seen her since that day."

"Where to, Guv?" Meadows said as Jack got into the car.

"Back to St Albans and Canon Flood's."

CHAPTER 34

SATURDAY

Jack pressed the doorbell for the third time. "There doesn't seem to be anybody in, sir," Meadows said.

"The car's still here," he said, pointing to Canon Flood's light green Singer Gazelle parked on the drive. He pressed the bell for the fourth time and shook his head. "No. We're wasting our time here. Let's try round the back."

They walked past the parked Singer, down a paved path, through a high wooden gate and found themselves in a large, neatly kept garden. An ornamental fishpond, complete with lichen-covered statuary, sat in the middle of the lawn. Curved stone benches were set at intervals around the circumference. Beyond a small vegetable patch was a large wooden greenhouse, its green panes covered with algae.

At the back of the house a wheelbarrow leaned against the outside wall of a tool shed, alongside a wooden stepladder with paint-stained treads. A small set of freestanding shelves leaned precariously against the back wall of the house, with a dented, galvanised steel watering can beside them.

Curtains were drawn across the French doors, and the back door had no window. Meadows stood with his hand on the Bakelite doorknob. "Shall I try it, sir?"

"Go ahead."

He twisted the knob, and the door swung inwards.

They walked into a large kitchen, dominated by an oak refectory table. Cake tins, wooden spoons, sieves and bowls, bags of flour and a half-full carton of eggs were strewn across it.

The Aga's fire had long been extinguished and the cast iron was cold to the touch.

"Hello?" Jack called. "Is anyone here?" All he heard was the ticking of a clock pendulum.

The kitchen door opened onto the passageway he'd come down before. There were a couple of doors along it, and a carpeted staircase leading to the upper floor.

Jack called up the stairs. "Hello?" He turned to Meadows. "Wait here in case Miss Beech shows herself. I'm going to check upstairs."

He took the stairs two at a time until he reached the landing. He called again. Silence.

The first door he tried was the bathroom. It was a man's bathroom, containing little but shaving equipment. There was nothing there to suggest that a woman lived in the house with Canon Flood. Perhaps Ruth Beech kept a wash bag in her bedroom. The second door along opened into an unused bedroom with a single steel-framed bed, its sprung base covered with a lumpy feather mattress.

The next room he tried belonged to Ruth Beech.

The furniture was dark and heavy. Spread out across the surface of the dressing table were all manner of cosmetics. Amongst them sat a silver-backed hairbrush and hand mirror, and a manicure set in a tortoiseshell case. There was no sign of Ruth Beech. A silver photo frame occupied pride of place on the bedside cabinet.

Jack picked it up and stared at it.

It was a photograph of a young, fresh-faced Martin Harvey, clean-shaven and scrubbed. He looked as if he'd stepped straight from the seminary, proud of his starched white dog collar.

Jack replaced the photograph on the cabinet and went to a room on the other side of the landing.

It was dark in here. Heavy brocade curtains had been drawn across the windows, shutting out the daylight. Once his eyes had adjusted to the gloom, Jack saw a figure lying on the bed.

"Canon Flood?"

The figure didn't stir.

Jack drew closer and looked down at Flood. He was lying in the middle of the bed, under the covers. His hands lay on top, crossed over his chest.

"Sir?"

The room was silent. There was no sound of breathing. Jack went back to the doorway and snapped on the overhead light. He returned to the bed, grabbed a corner of the bedclothes and pulled them back sharply.

Flood lay there, naked, his ankles tied with twine. His chest was punctured by stab wounds. His eyes, milky and unseeing, stared straight ahead. What had he seen in his final moments?

Jack cursed and reeled away from the bed. He ran from the room and back along the landing to the stairs. "Meadows? Meadows!"

Getting no answer, he ran down the stairs and along the passageway to the kitchen.

Robert Meadows was lying on his back on the floor, his eyes closed, with his head resting in Ruth Beech's lap. She was kneeling, bending over Meadows. There was a heavy china rolling pin at her side. She was pressing a short, lethal-looking knife against Meadows' neck. Its sharp point had drawn a bead of blood from the skin above his carotid artery. There was more blood, on the white china rolling pin and on the gash it had made when Ruth Beech smashed it into Meadows' skull.

"Meadows?" Jack said quietly.

Ruth Beech swayed slightly and looked up at the sound of Jack's voice. Her eyes widened.

"I *will* kill him," she said.

Ruth Beech's brown hair was freed from its tight bun and hung, wild and loose, to her shoulders. Her face was made up with rouge and mascara, her eyelids dusted with blue eye shadow, her lips a vibrant red. "I said, I *will* kill him."

"I'm sure you will," Jack said steadily. "After all, isn't that what you do to people who don't do what you say? People who hurt you in some way?"

"I don't know what you're talking about."

"Oh, I think you do, Ruth Beech. What did Bernadette O'Malley do to you? Steal the man you loved? Is that why you killed her?"

A sly smile spread over her lips. "Silly little slut. I gave her tea and sympathy, and a shoulder to cry on. Gerald had gone earlier to take her confession, but that wasn't enough for her. She wanted to talk, woman to woman, like she had at the weekend. And where was Gerald then? In bed, that's where, lying there like a fat white slug and telling me to send her away, when all she wanted to do was talk. About her precious Martin, and his bastard growing in her womb." A shadow passed across her face. "It should have been mine," she hissed. "He should have planted his seed in *me*, not her!"

And then she giggled, like a little girl.

"But I showed her. I showed her she couldn't take him from me. After I gave her the pill, she was like putty. So easy to bend and shape. 'Come down to the chapel with me, dear. Pray with me, dear . . .' and she came, like a lamb. She took that cross from the wall and hugged it to her all the way down the stairs. Her God, the healer. Her protector. Precious little good He did her. I showed her the error of her ways. The little slut!"

She jerked the knife against Meadows' throat.

"You showed her, Ruth, like you showed Martin. Like you showed Canon Flood." Jack's only hope was to distract her.

". . . Gerald refused me! He didn't want to touch me, and I'd made myself so pretty for him. How could he say no, just like that? Like I was rubbish. Like her. Like that fucking nun!"

"They all hurt you in the end, don't they, Ruth? Agnes, George, Gerald, Martin . . . even the little kitten you loved so much?"

She shook her head. "No. No! They loved me. They all loved me."

"No, they didn't, Ruth. They hurt you. The kitten scratched you and George left you. Martin rejected you and passed you onto Gerald Flood like an old coat he no longer wanted." Jack was baiting her, waiting for the moment when she was distracted enough for him to disarm her.

She was twisting the point of the knife in Meadows' neck and stroking his hair with her other hand, cooing softly. "You loved me, Martin, didn't you?"

Jack pressed on harshly. "Only he didn't, Ruth, did he? He never loved you and that's why you killed him, because he passed you over for somebody else — Bernadette. He threw you away!"

"No!" she said vehemently. "You don't know anything."

"He threw you away, because you were broken, Ruth. Broken."

She was shaking her head and rocking back and forth. "No, no, no!" she screamed at him and moved her hand, too fast for Jack to see.

A red gash opened up under Ruth Beech's chin and started gushing blood.

She looked down at the blood soaking into the front of her dress and splashing onto Meadows' upturned face. The knife slipped from her fingers. She opened her mouth and made a small noise, a liquid whisper, and then she toppled backwards onto the floor. Her head cracked against the quarry-tiled floor with a sickening crunch.

Robert Meadows opened his eyes and jerked upright.

"Call for an ambulance, man!" Jack shouted at him.

While Meadows got to his feet, Jack rushed across the room and grabbed a tea towel hanging from the back of a chair. He pressed it hard against Ruth's throat, trying to stem the flow of blood.

For a moment her eyelids fluttered and she opened her eyes. She looked up at him and Jack saw that Agnes Beech had been right. There was nothing in Ruth's deep brown eyes. Nothing at all.

Her lips were moving. She was trying to speak. Jack lowered his face and listened.

"Broken," she managed. Then her body convulsed, and a fountain of blood poured from her mouth, covering the lower part of her face.

Ruth Beech was dead.

Jack let go of the tea towel and pushed himself to his feet. In the distance he could hear the bell of the approaching ambulance.

"Too late," he said. "For everything."

CHAPTER 35

SATURDAY 19 DECEMBER 1959

Jack sat in front of the dressing table, staring at himself in the mirror.

"Aren't you ready yet?" Annie came into the bedroom, wrapped in a towel, her hair damp and her face flushed from her bath. "Squeeze up," she said, and sat beside him on the bench

"I'm just sitting here," he said. "Pondering."

She picked up a lipstick and unscrewed the cap. "Well, ponder yourself off to the bathroom and have a shave. I told Joanie we'd pick her and Avril up at seven, and it's six o'clock now."

Jack didn't move.

"What's wrong?" she said. "I was watching you earlier, when you were listening to the football results. Spurs beat Newcastle United four nil and you didn't even crack a smile. Normally a result like that would have you dancing around the room."

"The other week I told Eddie that I was thinking of putting in my papers."

"Retiring? You? I don't want you here all day, getting under my feet."

"That shouldn't be a problem. You're at Painter's five days a week now."

She paused, lipstick poised, and looked at him in the mirror. "Is that what this moody's all about? Because I'm working full time?"

Jack held up his hands. "No. Not at all. Without you doing the extra hours we couldn't have afforded Eric's guitar. No, I have no problem with you working. It's *my* job I'm having difficulties with."

"It's that last case, isn't it? You haven't been right for a week now."

"It's not just that case. It's all of them."

Annie put the lipstick down. "Do you want to talk about it?"

"Not really."

"Okay." She picked up the lipstick again.

Jack took a breath. "I've been thinking about life lately. It's like a game of snooker."

She painted her top lip. "Go on," she said to his reflection.

"In snooker, when you break initially, you send the cue ball down the table to glance off a red in the pack, that triangle of balls at the top of the table, hitting them but not disturbing them. That's the object and it's what careful players do. But there are some, the more reckless ones, who slam the ball down the table as hard as they can and smash into the pack, sending the reds spinning off, cannoning into each other, without a thought of where anything's going to end up and what kind of mess they're going to be in the next time they go to the table."

Annie set the lipstick down again and reached for her eye shadow, "Carry on. I'm listening."

"The point is, with one reckless action, those players can cause havoc in the game. They effectively throw a brick into the pond and the ripples spread out and keep on spreading. When Alf Kendall first hit Avril, he changed not only his life but the life of others around him. It's certainly changed Avril's, and it changed ours. Joanie's moved out and is now living at Avril's. I hear that the AA patrolman who helped me at the scene of the crash got promoted to a desk job and is no longer out on the road. Do you see what I mean?"

"I think so," Annie said uncertainly.

"Take Bernadette O'Malley. When she fell in love with Martin Harvey, it led to four deaths, including her own."

"Wasn't Ruth Beech more to blame?"

Jack stared at the floor.

Annie's eyes narrowed. "That's what all this soul searching is about," she said. "You're still blaming yourself because she killed herself in front of you, and you couldn't do a damned thing about it."

"Rubbish," Jack said.

Annie shook her head. "Oh, no, Jack Callum. I'm not swallowing that one. I've known you too long and have been through too much with you not to recognise when you're feeling guilty about something."

He sighed wearily. "I practically goaded her into taking her own life."

"What you did was heroic. You were trying to save Robert Meadows' life. If you hadn't done what you did she would have cut his throat, just like the nun and the priest. I was talking to him the other morning when he came to pick you up. Did you know he only got married last year, and he and Lisa, his wife, have a baby on the way? You saved a young woman from becoming a widow and a child from growing up without a father. You may not have been able to save Ruth Beech, but I know one family who are bloody glad you didn't. You're a hero, Jack. Accept it and embrace it."

Jack stared at Annie in the mirror.

"What?" she said.

"You're a remarkable woman, Annie. Where would I be without you?"

She smiled at him and squeezed his hand. "I dread to think."

"How's Rosie getting there tonight?" Jack said.

"Brian's borrowed his dad's van. He's taking Rosie, Eric, the Vikings and all their gear to the youth club."

"I haven't really met Brian yet. What's he like?"

"You'll meet him tonight. You can make up your mind about him then. I think he's a nice lad."

"A bit gullible if Eric's got him ferrying the group and their gear around."

"I think you'll like him. Now go and have a shave."

* * *

The youth club Christmas dance was in full swing.

At the piano Gerry Tanner led the Vikings through a variety of waltzes, quicksteps and foxtrots. She was remarkably adept at all styles of music and the dancers who packed the floor of the church hall were quick to show their appreciation, applauding her after every number. She turned from the piano and treated them to one of her dazzling smiles.

Jack came up to Laurence and Jean Tanner. "Gerry's very good. She's certainly knocked Eric and the boys into shape. I never thought I'd hear them playing waltzes, of all things."

Jean Tanner smiled. "Your son's getting proficient on that guitar, and the others have improved as well. Not so percussive."

She had a point. Tea chest, broomstick and string had been replaced by a proper double bass, and the washboard had given way to a rudimentary drum kit — three drums and a cymbal. The overall effect was altogether more musical and as she said, less 'percussive'.

The music stopped and they looked towards the small stage as Eric strode to the centre, strapping on his new electric guitar as he approached the microphone. He tapped it with his finger and heard the hollow boom from the speaker, and then he spoke. "Now we're going to up the tempo for all you jivers out there."

As he started to play the opening bars of 'Guitar Boogie Shuffle,' Annie came up behind Jack. "You could have gone to the carol concert at St Augustine's tonight, or the Christmas show that they're putting on at St Joseph's, and yet you wanted to come here. Why?"

Jack looked towards the stage, tapping his foot in time to the music. "That's our son up there, Annie, entertaining people as if he was born to it. That's why I wanted to come here tonight. I'm enjoying being here with my wonderful family and I can't think of a single other place I'd rather be."

THE END

CHARACTER LIST

THE FAMILY

Jack Callum: 49. Detective Chief Inspector. He has a keen mind and is passionate about his job. Doesn't believe in capital punishment but has caught a few villains whose life has come to an end on the gallows. Believes the attitudes of the day need changing - such as women's place in society. Loves his children equally and has a firm but fair style of parenting.

Anne Callum: 45. Jack's wife. A bright, vivacious brunette. Loves her husband deeply and acts as his confidante. A housewife. See her role as a housekeeper and home-maker. Once had aspirations of a stage career, but is now beginning to spread her wings with a new part time job and new clothes and hairstyle.

Joan Callum: 20. Estranged daughter. Eloped with Ivan, a Czech émigré, at sixteen. Very pretty. Recently returned to the family home and is beginning a career as a hairdresser.

Rose Callum: 17. Jack's daughter. A sweet girl who is always falling in love. A pretty girl who has her mother's hair and eyes. Has no shortage of potential suitors, but is holding out for Mr. Right. Attended the local high school and achieved good grades. Works in the local baker's. The apple of Jack Callum's eye.

Eric Callum: 15. Jack's son and to all intents and purposes a chip off the old block. Has inherited his father's love of football, but persuaded his parents to buy him a guitar so he can further his love of music. Now plays in a group, Eric and the Vikings, with some friends. Started as a skiffle group but is gradually moving towards rock and roll

Geraldine(Gerry)Tanner:14. Daughter of the actor Tony Tanner who was murdered in Prime Evil. Plays piano in Eric

Callum's pop group as well as teaching him to read music, and is now his girlfriend.

THE POLICE

Chief Superintendent Henry Lane: 48. A self-made man. Has hauled himself through the ranks by his bootstraps and expects excellence from his junior officers, but is not a martinet and gets results with a friendly word or kind gesture. Very supportive of the men under him and has special regard for Jack Callum, who he thinks, despite being a year younger, is twice the copper he is himself.

DI Eddie Fuller: 36. A prominent member of CID. Recently promoted to DI and is effectively Callum's number two. A bit of a ladies' man and has some unorthodox methods of getting results.

DC Harry Grant: 27. Was Fuller's number two, but has moved on since Fuller's promotion.

DC Myra Banks: 29. The only woman CID officer at the station, a job she has aspired to for some time, but has had to fight the institutional sexism to achieve it. A bright young woman who Jack backed for the CID job.

DS Frank Lesser: 33. Moonlights as a part-time wrestler, who wrestles under a mask as Black Phantom and is as hard as nails. Married with a young family.

ST JOSEPH'S HOME FOR BOYS AND GIRLS

THE NUNS:

Sister Bernadette: 21. Novice and the first victim.
Sister Rosalie: 65. The head nun/Mother Superior at St Joseph's Home for Boys and Girls. A kind and compassionate

woman. Was a missionary in Singapore during the war and has a pragmatic worldview.
Sister Marguerite: 52. Timid and prissy woman. Easily shocked.
Sister Theresa: 45. Second in command at St Joseph's.
Sister Concepta: 64. Mother Superior at St Luke's Carmelite monastery. Sister Rosalie's oldest friend.

THE MEN'S COMMITTEE:

A group of men brought together to help out at St Joseph's: taking the boys for football, other sporting activities as well as organising monthly film shows and supervising an annual seaside holiday for the children.

Leslie Parsons: 35. Instigator of the committee. A fairly recent convert to Catholicism but deeply committed to the faith. Has a wife (Estelle) and three children. Works as a toolmaker at Grant's a local factory, where he lost an eye in a workshop accident.
Giovanni Fabrizi: 29. Son of and Italian émigré but raised in London's East End. A music teacher who works for the society when he's not performing at Giovanni, the Gypsy Violinist at a local restaurant
Tony Smythe: 34. A St Joseph's old boy. Helps run a bookshop but helps out with the committee in whatever free time he has.
Bernard Gallagher: 24. A mechanic at the local garage. Services and maintains the St Joseph's car. Another St Joseph's old boy.
John Holmes: 30. Helped Leslie Parsons form 'men's committee'. Works at Pennington's Paper Mill.

THE CHILDREN:

Raymond Oliver: 16. A tearaway. Always in trouble.
Terry Lloyd: 15. A bright freckled faced child with cherubic features. Very much in the thrall of Oliver and often led into trouble by him.

THE CLERGY:

Father Martin Harvey: 34. Priest at St Augustine's Church. Looks after the spiritual needs of the sisters and children of St Joseph's

Canon Gerald Flood: 70. From his base in St Albans shares parochial duties with Father Harvey and is his immediate superior.
Bishop Rawlings: 60. Oversees the North Hertfordshire diocese. Golfing partner of Chief Superintendent Lane.

OTHER CHARACTERS:

Avril Kendall: 32. Hairdresser. Employs Joan Callum and is Annie's hairdresser.
Alf Kendall: 36. Avril's husband and a long distance lorry driver.
Marcus Pennington: 40. Local businessman and a St Joseph's old boy.
Ruth Beech: 28. Spinster. Once Father Harvey's housekeeper, now keeps house for Canon Flood.
Agnes Beech: 35. Ruth's older sister.

GLOSSARY OF BRITISH AND PERIOD SLANG

a cabbage: brain dead
a set of pipes on her: a good singer
addles your brain: messes with your head
all hands to the pumps: lots of help needed
a welsher: reneges on deals, doesn't pay their debts
Babycham: cheap alternative to champagne – made from pears
balloon's gone up: an emergency situation
balls-up: an error, a mistake
banana boat: derogatory term for immigrants transport to UK
barrel of laughs: sarcastic term for a serious character
beat bobby: uniformed police officer who patrols the streets
bee's knees: something special
be sick: vomit
bells ringing: equivalent of police sirens today
belter: It was a fantastic goal
better step on it: hurry up
Biscuits: cookies
Black Maria: a police van
bod: derogatory term – anonymous person
bonnet of his car: the hood & (UK boot = US trunk)
boozy: A bit drunk
Bowling me a googly: Cricketing term. To take by surprise
bread-and-butter work: Routine work
brief: lawyer
Brylcreem: hair cream/gel to give men's hair shine and smoothness
calling in the cavalry: asking for reinforcements
Cambridge University: prestigious British university
Canon: a rank of clergymen
car park: parking lot
cat that got all the cream: satisfied
CID: Criminal investigation division
clobbered: hit hard
cobbler's shop: shoe menders
copper: slang for policeman

couldn't hit a cow's arse with a banjo: not very good at aiming a dart or arrow
council estate: social housing
crazy-paving: patio, concrete slabs in random pattern
cuppa: A cup of tea
cut along to: go along to
David Nixon: UK TV magician
dessert: pudding
digs: lodgings, boarding house
dollar a frame: two half crowns in old UK money = five shillings - called a dollar and five bob
doormat: meek
dressing down: telling off
emergency police box: telephone box for police use
en-print: an 8 x 10 photograph
excuse my French: sorry I swore
fellow: boyfriend
flatfoots: derogatory name for police
fly in the ointment: problem
George Formby: musical comedian
get you a brew: a cup of tea
get your skates on: Hurry up
glasshouse: greenhouse
go to the dogs: go to rack and ruin, be destroyed
good collars: good arrests
guv'nor: the boss (& guv)
gymkhana: horse-riding event
gymslips: school uniform of bib and skirt design
had it in spades: has a lot of it
half of bitter: beer.
Harold MacMillan: British Prime minister 1957-63
haversack: backpack, rucksack
Hendon: police training school
Herbert Beerbohm-Tree and Mrs Patrick Campbell: actors
his beat: the area he patrols
hit a brick wall: come up against an obstacle
huge chip on her shoulder: resentful
I'm blowed: I am surprised
I'm spitting nails: very angry
keep it under your hat: keep it a secret
keep mum about it: keep it a secret

Keep your hair on: don't get so excited
knighted: given a British honour
knock his block off: punch him hard, block = head
late birds: go to bed at a late hour
lavatory: restroom
load of tripe: lot of nonsense
little hussy: girl of loose morals
Lonnnie Donegan: father of British skiffle music
loo: toilet (also bog, khasi)
LSE: London School of Economics
mantelpiece: shelf above a fireplace
Marmite or Bovril: meat-based sandwich spreads
Mickey Finn: a drugged drink which makes the drinker unconscious
milkman: person who delivers milk to the house
Mosquito: British airplane used in Second World War
mooning over a boy: teenage girl infatuated with a boy
News of the World: British tabloid newspaper
North London / South London: separated by the River Thames
off his chump: slang for being mad, crazy
old chestnut: weak excuse
off-licence: shop selling alcohol
old toffee: lies
on my tail: after me, chasing me
on the game: prostitute
Ovaltine: malted milk beverage – served hot
Pax, fainites: children's terms for a truce in hostilities
Palais: dance hall
Pathé News and Pearl and Dean: adverts before the movie starts
pin money: small amount of earnings
pissing around: messing about, not telling the whole truth
playing cards close to her chest: being coy with the truth
plods: derogatory name for police
Police Gazette: newspaper produced to publish notices of wanted criminals
pounding the beat: working as a uniformed officer on the streets
pretty good going-over : a thorough investigation (can also mean beating up)
prick: slang for penis
pull the wool over their eyes: fool people
pulling *my* leg: having a joke at my expense, teasing

pushover: soft touch, easily manipulated
Q cars: A car that has a high performance engine and an unassuming exterior
quite sweet on you: likes you romantically
Reggie and Ronnie: the Kray twins, criminals
restroom: place where staff can relax or recover in
rozzers: policemen
ructions: disagreements
S.P.: starting price = the truth about what is being said
School Friend: comic aimed at teenage girls
settee: sofa
sick: vomit
skiffle: 1950s style of popular music
slacks: UK trousers/ US pants
sling your hook: go away
snapshot: photograph (also snap, shot, print, photo)
spewed: vomited
stick of rock: a cylinder of candy often sold at the seaside
sticking plaster: Band-Aid
stinks like a haddock left out too long in the sun: doesn't sound correct
stitching me up: framing me
swot: a nerd, a geek, someone keen on their studies
tabard: apron worn for some work
tart: woman with loose morals
tart's boudoir: a hooker's bedroom
Teddy boys: Thugs and young tearaways
Ten bob: ten shillings: pre-decimal money — half of £1 = ten-shilling note
This Is Your Wife: parody of TV show This Is Your Life
tightly permed hair: hair artificially curled
Tizer: fizzy pop/soda
Tommy Steele: 1950s-60s pop star
Trousers: pants
tugging my forelock: acting in a subservient manner
tuppenny tart: a cheap hooker
two hoots: couldn't care less
two peas in a pod.: two people similar to one another
ugly mug: ugly face
up and comers: young and rising sports people (over the hillers = past their best sports people)

very snarled up: gridlocked traffic
Victor Sylvester: popular ballroom dancer and band-leader in the 1950s
whistles and bells: top specifications
winkle-picker shoe: long narrow male shoe
Wolseley: model of saloon car used by the police
yobs: thugs and young tearaways
your lazy arse: ass
your racket: your loud noise

MUSIC LINKS

It's Turned Out Nice Again – George Formby
https://www.youtube.com/watch?v=P0qyrnGLnsw

Guitar Boogie Shuffle – Bert Weedon
https://www.youtube.com/watch?v=E0F42lasles

Only Sixteen – Craig Douglas
https://www.youtube.com/watch?v=uxXJ1OebPaI

The Story of my Life – Michael Holliday
https://www.youtube.com/watch?v=Gzk0bdlDr3Y

How High the Moon – Les Paul and Mary Ford
https://www.youtube.com/watch?v=NkGf1GHAxhE

ABOUT THE AUTHOR

Len Maynard & Mick Sims (Maynard Sims) are the authors of several novels with more coming soon. They have written stories, novellas, essays, award winning screenplays, and have worked as editors. www.maynard-sims.com

Jack has his own website too! http://www.jackcallum.co.uk/

Thank you for reading this book. If you enjoyed it please leave feedback on Amazon, and if there is anything we missed or you have a question about then please get in touch. The author and publishing team appreciate your feedback and time reading this book.

Our email is office@joffebooks.com

http://joffebooks.com

Thank you for reading this book. If you enjoyed it please leave feedback on Amazon, and if there is anything we missed or you have a question about then please get in touch. The author and publishing team appreciate your feedback and time reading this book.

Our email is office@joffebooks.com

www.joffebooks.com

19324152R00414

Printed in Great Britain
by Amazon